Praise for Pauline Gedge

PENGUIN CANADA

THE TWICE BORN

PAULINE GEDGE is the award-winning and best-selling author of eleven previous novels, eight of which are inspired by Egyptian history. Her first, *Child of the Morning*, won the Alberta Search-for-a-New Novelist Competition. In France, her second novel, *The Eagle and the Raven*, received the Jean Boujassy award from the Société des Gens des Lettres, and *The Twelfth Transforming*, the second of her Egyptian novels, won the Writers Guild of Alberta Best Novel of the Year Award. Her books have sold more than 250,000 copies in Canada alone; worldwide, they have sold more than six million copies and have been translated into eighteen languages. Pauline Gedge lives in Alberta.

Also by Pauline Gedge

Child of the Morning

The Eagle and the Raven

Stargate

The Twelfth Transforming

Scroll of Saqqara

The Covenant

House of Dreams

House of Illusions

The Hippopotamus Marsh:
Lords of the Two Lands, Volume One

The Oasis: Lords of the Two Lands, Volume Two

The Horus Road: Lords of the Two Lands,
Volume Three

THE
TWICE
BORN

PAULINE
GEDGE

PENGUIN
CANADA

PENGUIN CANADA

Published by the Penguin Group

Penguin Group (Canada), 90 Eglinton Avenue East, Suite 700, Toronto,
Ontario, Canada M4P 2Y3 (a division of Pearson Canada Inc.)

Penguin Group (USA) Inc., 375 Hudson Street, New York,
New York 10014, U.S.A.
Penguin Books Ltd, 80 Strand, London WC2R 0RL, England
Penguin Ireland, 25 St Stephen's Green, Dublin 2, Ireland (a division of
Penguin Books Ltd)
Penguin Group (Australia), 250 Camberwell Road, Camberwell, Victoria
3124, Australia (a division of Pearson Australia Group Pty Ltd)
Penguin Books India Pvt Ltd, 11 Community Centre, Panchsheel Park,
New Delhi – 110 017, India
Penguin Group (NZ), 67 Apollo Drive, Rosedale, North Shore 0632,
New Zealand (a division of Pearson New Zealand Ltd)
Penguin Books (South Africa) (Pty) Ltd, 24 Sturdee Avenue, Rosebank,
Johannesburg 2196, South Africa

Penguin Books Ltd, Registered Offices: 80 Strand, London WC2R 0RL,
England

First published in a Penguin Canada hardcover by Penguin Group (Canada),
a division of Pearson Canada Inc., 2007
Published in this edition, 2008

1 2 3 4 5 6 7 8 9 10 (OPM)

Copyright © Pauline Gedge, 2007

Excerpt from *Egyptian Mysteries: New Light on Ancient Spiritual Knowledge* by
Lucie Lamy, translated from the French by Deborah Lawlor, © 1981 Lucie
Lamy. Reprinted by kind permission of Thames and Hudson Ltd, London.

Manufactured in the U.S.A.

LIBRARY AND ARCHIVES CANADA CATALOGUING IN PUBLICATION

Gedge, Pauline, 1945–
The twice born/Pauline Gedge.

ISBN 978-0-14-305292-0

I. Title.

PS8563.E33T94 2008   C813'.54   C2008-902654-3

Visit the Penguin Group (Canada) website at **www.penguin.ca**

Special and corporate bulk purchase rates available; please see
www.penguin.ca/corporatesales or call 1-800-810-3104, ext. 477 or 474

AUTHOR'S NOTE

The Book of Thoth was purported to contain all knowledge regarding the creation of the cosmos, gods, and men as well as the laws relating to magic, nature, and the afterlife. It was dictated by Atum, the creator-god, to Thoth, god of writing, the sciences, and time, who set down the information on forty-two scrolls, which were divided between the temples of Ra at Iunu and Thoth at Khmun.

It survives in fragmented form as the so-called Pyramid Texts, found on the walls of the burial chambers of pyramids of the Fifth and Sixth Dynasties, at the temples of Esna and Edfu, and in certain coffins, where it is called, of course, the Coffin Texts. Pieces of it also appear in "The Book of Knowing the Modes of Existence of Ra and of Overthrowing the Serpent Apophis" and "The Book of Coming Forth by Day," commonly known as the Book of the Dead.

According to Egyptian legend, before the reign of King Menes of the Protodynastic Period, the country was ruled for 13,420 years by the Servitors of Horus, the Shemsu-Hor. The Book of Thoth was said to predate the Shemsu-Hor by over 20,000 years.

The Greeks identified Thoth with their god Hermes. Hence the Hermetica, a collection of modernized writings attributed to Thoth.

Huy son of Hapu, later known as Amunhotep son of Hapu, was born of a peasant family in the modest Delta town of Hut-herib, yet became a very significant figure in Egyptian history. Although much is known of his great achievements, everything inscribed refers to his public accomplishments. His private existence remains blank. In *The Twice Born,* I have attempted to solve the puzzle of his early years.

THE TWICE BORN

1

Huy stood in his bedroom, his mother Itu beside him, looking with dismay at the toys laid out so carefully on his cot. Although the day was bright with heat, the breeze wafting through the window and lifting a corner of Huy's linen sheet still held a little of the previous night's coolness. Huy did not notice. Hands behind his back, he stared mutinously at his treasures. His mother sighed.

"It must be something you value, Huy," she prompted him gently. "Something the god will know you did not really want to give up."

"Why?" Huy burst out. "Why must I give him anything? I haven't given him anything before! We haven't ever gone to his home before!"

"Because tomorrow is the anniversary of your Naming Day. I've already told you that. Tomorrow you will be four years old, and you and I and your father will go to Khenti-kheti's shrine to thank him for your health and safety. Make a choice, Huy. What about your paints?"

"No. Uncle Ker and Aunt Heruben gave them to me. They would be upset if I gave them away. Unless they brought me some more?" He turned an anxious face up to Itu. "You love to see me paint, Mother. You would be upset as well if I couldn't paint anymore."

The whitewashed walls of his house offered a dazzling surface on which to create fat brown hippopotami, yellow boats sailing on a hectically blue Nile, portraits of himself as a warrior with spear in hand, and he had no intention of relinquishing that heady pleasure. No, the palette must go back into his sycamore chest.

"Very well." Itu's tone was faintly disapproving. "Something else, then."

Huy considered. Well, what of his wooden dog on wheels? He had towed it about the garden many times, its jaws opening and closing rythmically while he barked for it, because it was dumb. But Hapu, his father, had spent hours carving it, and would be even more upset than Uncle Ker if he gave it away. Did gods play with toys, anyway?

That left the skittles, the leather ball, and the spinning top. Definitely not the spinning top. Chasing it through the house as it teetered this way and that and then whipping it into a fresh whirl of speed when it began to falter was the very best way to spend the boring summer afternoons that never seemed to end. The skittles, then. They were fun to play with, but the game soon became boring and the wooden ball never would roll quite straight to the pins. His big leather ball, however, needed someone to catch it and throw it back to him. It made Mother or Hapzefa give him all their attention. Not the leather ball either. Khenti-kheti would understand. Being a god, he might even decide to make the wooden ball perfectly smooth and then invite the other gods to play with him.

"Seeing that you are making me do this, the god can have the skittles," Huy said. "I really do love my skittles, Mother." He tugged at the linen bag in Itu's hand. She relinquished it without another word and left the room. Satisfied but guilty, Huy returned everything else to the chest and thrust the six skittles and the offending ball into the bag, dropping it by the door on his way out.

In the passage his best papyrus sandals sat neatly waiting for tomorrow morning and out by the kitchen Hapzefa was washing and starching the little kilt he would wear. Huy grimaced as he ran towards the dappled sunlight of the garden. Sandals and an itchy kilt. But he knew that when he returned from the temple his favourite food would be waiting for him and his aunt and uncle would offer him new and exciting gifts to mark the solemn occasion.

He was a spoilt child, the only darling of a doting family. His aunt was barren in spite of repeated pilgrimages to the temple of Tauret, goddess of child-bearing, and to the tomb of the mighty Imhotep, who could heal any infirmity if he so wished, and all her needy affection was poured out upon her brother-in-law's little boy. Huy divided his time between his own home and the comfortable estate owned by his uncle, a place he much preferred, for his uncle was rich, being a famous maker of perfumes worn by the King himself, while Hapu, his father, simply tended the plants that Huy's uncle and his staff turned miraculously into the oils adorning the most powerful people in the world.

Not that Huy disdained his own modest home. He adored his parents with all the selfish unreflectiveness of the young child, but there was always something new to do and see on his uncle's estate, and he was never bored there as he often was in the quiet of Hapu's domain. Intelligent, curious, and sure of himself as the centre of the universe, having suffered no hurts other than the inevitable tumbles and mild indispositions inherent in his natural development, with the stamp of a future handsomeness already on his face and emerging with the harmony of his healthy body, he was suffused with the unconscious certainty of his own immortality.

The garden was empty and quiet in the heat of the afternoon. Huy trotted past the fishpond with no more than a glance at its border of untidy sedge and its tiered terraces for lettuce, onions, garlic, and other vegetables. He knew that until sunset the fish would be lurking deep down in the water where it was cool and dark, and even the frogs would have taken refuge beneath the spreading green pads of the water lilies whose waxy blue blooms had closed until the following morning. His mother had added white lilies to the pool so that there would be flowers floating on its placid surface at every hour of the day, for the white lilies opened their petals just as the blue ones folded in upon themselves, and would remain so until the following noon.

Such aesthetic niceties were of no concern to Huy. All he knew was that the frogs seemed to prefer to squat beside the blue flowers, where they could be easily caught and held, spreading a delectable coolness over his palms before he placed them gently back on their lily pads and watched them spring offendedly into the depths. His mother had warned him to treat them with respect. They were symbols of resurrection, she had said, and as such were regarded as holy. Because he could not imagine death, the concept of resurrection meant nothing to Huy, although Itu had done her best to explain it to him; but he handled the frogs with care anyway. He loved them, loved to lie on his stomach over the silent protests of crushed lettuce and cabbage nubs and slender shoots of leek, with the wet earth slick against his skin and his face inches above the mysterious, silent life of the green water, watching unnameable things flow and flicker below him.

More than once Hapzefa had lifted him onto the warm grass and scolded him mildly. "You're hurting the vegetables, Master Huy," she had said. "If you keep lying on them, they'll die. Besides, what if you fell into the pond and drowned? I can't watch you all the time. I've too many other things to do." It seemed that being drowned was a way to be dead, and as being dead, according to his mother, seemed to involve lying still with your eyes shut and not being able to move anymore, Huy had pulled up the vegetable seedlings in his way and had continued to wriggle into the soil and gaze into the pool. He had understood no more than the connection between lying on the vegetables and falling into the water; therefore, removing the plants would ensure that no matter what he did he could not possibly end up headfirst in the pond. It must have been the right thing to do, because he was not reprimanded for it.

But today he sought the shade cast by the high wall
that separated the grounds of the house from the vast
orchards and gardens where his father and the gardeners tended the crops that his uncle used to make the
perfumes. Huy had been enveloped in the aroma of
the countless blossoms wafting over the wall ever since
he was born. He only became aware of it by a lessening
of its intensity when he was taken into the town, and
even there the mingled flower odours continued to
hang over the streets and mud-brick buildings of
Hut-herib. It was thick today with the increased humidity the rising Inundation always caused, but Huy,
oblivious, sat down with his back to the sheltering wall
and picked his clay soldiers out of the grass where he
had left them yesterday. His uncle's chief gardener had
made them for him, a small battalion of brown men
with white-painted kilts and corrugated heads to represent the short black wigs worn by military men. Some
held pieces of whittled twig in their stiff hands for spears
and some clutched clay swords. All had tiny pieces of
leather moulded into their arms for shields. One, the
most prized, had a yellow kilt and a blue helmet with a
snake rearing above his forehead. That was the King
himself, the mighty Men-kheper-Ra Thothmes, the
third of that illustrious name, who had marched his
army into Rethennu as soon as he gained the Holy
Throne and had not stopped until he had forged an
empire for his beloved Egypt. For seventeen years he
had battled his way through the petty kingdoms of the
East, conquering and forcing treaty on lesser states, so
that tribute of every kind had begun to flow steadily
into the royal coffers from obedient vassals, and Egypt

herself was slowly becoming rich. That was twenty-six years ago. The Son of the Sun was now in his forty-third year of godhood and his seventieth year of life, closeted in his palace far away to the south at Weset, where the air was dry and scentless and the desert rolled in great yellow dunes to the very edge of the fields beside the river. So Huy had been told. Reverently he set up his model of the Good God and ranked his guard behind him. The enemy was hiding in the bushes not far away, but with his all-powerful ears the King could hear them rustling and whispering, and soon he would charge them and put them to rout.

The rustling grew louder and Huy, lying on his stomach in the grass, his nose level with the army, began to be annoyed. "I know it's you, Ishat," he shouted. "Go away. I don't want to play with you today." The command was ignored. Ishat emerged from the shrubbery and squatted beside Huy. A grubby little hand reached out to pick up one of Huy's men. Huy smacked at it and sat up.

"You can still have the King," Ishat said. "Come on, Huy. I'll be a general again. You can give me the battle orders."

"No." Huy began to gather up the toy soldiers. "You'll make them dirty if you touch them. I have to go in now."

"No you don't. You only just got here. I was waiting for you. Why won't you play with me?"

"Because you're a girl and girls can't be soldiers," Huy said nastily. "I let you be a general before and you didn't do the right things." He stood and she rose with him. They glared at one another, the scrawny girl with her mud-caked knees and matted black hair and a considerably cleaner Huy, who was trying to keep his army from falling out of his grasp.

Ishat took one step towards him. "I know something you don't know," she half sang in the mocking voice that always infuriated him.

Huy shrugged. The King toppled onto the ground and he bent to retrieve him. "I don't care. You're only just three and I'll be four tomorrow. You know one thing, but I know lots and lots." She was smiling at him in the superior way that always made him lose his temper, but having been forced earlier into parting with even one of his toys, and his mother's unspoken but obvious disappointment with his choice, made him feel suddenly lonely. "Tell me, then," he finished lamely. "But I bet it's nothing much."

"Yes it is. It's about you. If I tell you, will you let me play armies?"

"About me?" Huy tried to hide his sudden interest. Dropping his men, he sat back down nonchalantly. Ishat, wriggling with pleasure, settled herself beside him. "If it's good, I suppose you can be a general."

"Promise?" He nodded. She began to pick the pieces of grass out of the dried mud between her toes, making him wait, her eyes on the toy soldiers scattered about. Then she relented. "I heard my mother tell my father after I was in bed. They thought I was asleep. You're going away to school, Huy. That's really why you have to take a present to the god tomorrow. It's so that he'll look after you while you're gone." She glanced at him to see his reaction, but he just seemed puzzled.

"School? You're lying so that I'll let you play with me, Ishat! Only rich boys go to school."

"It's true. My mother said your uncle Ker is going to pay."

"Hapzefa is a servant and my mother says that she gossips."

"Gossip isn't like lying!" Ishat responded hotly. "My mother doesn't lie! Go and ask your father if you don't believe me." Deliberately she picked up a soldier. "Now you have to let me play. You promised."

Furious at being tricked, Huy could only nod dumbly. Not for the first time, he wished Ishat were a boy. Surely boys didn't have to think up silly lies to get their own way. Snatching the toy out of her hand, he pinched her hard before throwing it back to her. "You can play, but only because I promised. Hapzefa loves me and you heard it wrong."

Ishat rubbed her arm. "No I didn't. Now give me a general."

They played more or less amicably until Hapzefa called Huy to come in for the afternoon nap. At once Ishat disappeared in the direction of the orchard and Huy gathered up his men. He was tired but refused to admit it, and once washed and laid on his cot he only had time to consider calling out for a cup of water before he succumbed to the soporific quiet of the house.

In the evening, while Huy played with his lentil stew, his mother told his father Hapu what gift he had decided to give to Khenti-kheti. The three of them were sitting on cushions around the low central table of sycamore wood Huy's father had made. Mosquitoes had drifted in through the open door of the one room where the little family both ate and received their guests, and were whining above their heads. A long shaft of late sunlight lay across the beaten earth of the floor, its warm length reaching for Huy's toes. He took a clove of roasted garlic, dropped it into his stew, and mashed it down with one finger, glancing sideways to see just how close the sun's ray was. If he let it touch his skin, then that would mean he would be burned by his mother's anger. Or his father's. He eyed Hapu briefly. Hapu was watching him over the rim of his wine cup, both eyebrows raised.

Huy bit into a piece of melon. "With my set of skittles he can play with the other gods if he gets lonely," he announced.

"Indeed," his father said dryly. "I had no idea that the skittles held such a place of importance in your heart, Huy. The god will doubtless be impressed by your selflessness." He swallowed and set his cup back on the table. Huy could smell the shedeh-wine, heavy and sweet, that his father made from his own pomegranates.

"I expect he will," Huy responded promptly. "Can I have some wine please, Father?"

"Pass me your water and I'll add a little," Itu said, lifting the jug. "And wipe your mouth, Huy. You have melon juice all over your chin. Don't you like the stew? If you finish it, you may have some fresh figs."

The sunlight had begun to fade only inches from Huy's foot. Pushing away the dish of lentils, he emptied his cup, loving the sweet-tart tang of the wine. He rubbed his face with the square of linen by his hand and smiled at his mother. "Hapzefa has put a lot of coriander in the stew," he remarked. "It makes my nose run. Figs will take the taste away."

His father sighed. "Itu, you indulge him too much," he said as his wife pushed the figs across the table towards Huy. "And this matter of the gift is certainly the last straw. Huy, we have decided to send you to school."

"This is no way to tell him, Hapu!" Itu said hotly. "We were going to wait until after tomorrow, let him enjoy his Naming Day!"

Hapu leaned forward. "I would have waited, but Huy does not deserve such consideration. What gift has our son chosen to lay before the god of our city as a thanksgiving for his life?" He sat back. "And for health, a quick intelligence, people who love him, an existence untainted by any want. What gift? A thing he does not care to keep, that will cause him no pain when he bends his head. Everyone loves him," he went on gently, seeing his wife grow pale. "Ptah created a miracle in your womb, Itu, and there he sits, with his huge dark eyes like yours, and his black hair and the sheen of perfection on his skin. Tomorrow my brother Ker will come, and Heruben, bringing a small mountain of gifts for him, not just because he is four but also because their affection for him has no bounds. And is he grateful? Not any longer. He is becoming selfish and greedy. He begins to accept everything as his right. That evil seed must not be allowed to grow."

"You and your plants!" Itu choked. "Surely you exaggerate! It is natural for a baby to want to hold on to the things that make him happy. We have not explained to him the importance of the sacrifice he is expected to make, that's all. Explain it and he will run to his room and prepare to give the god his paints or his big ball instead. He has a generous heart, my husband! He does!"

"No, I don't think so," Hapu said slowly. "How has it been possible for him to express this generosity? He is our only child. His world is made up of adoring adults and the creatures of the garden and the orchards. It is too late to change the gift. The choice has been made, and made from a self-centredness that bodes ill for his future. We have not raised him sensibly," he finished, shaking his head. "However Khenti-kheti receives the skittles, whether to reward the outward act or punish the inward holding-back, the die is cast."

Huy had been listening to this interchange with increasing dread. His glance flicked between his parents. His father had bitten into the fleshy fruit of a fig and was placing the stem on his plate. His mother's hands had disappeared under the edge of the table. She looked mutinous.

"Am I really going to school, Father?" Huy demanded. "Ishat told me so, but I didn't believe her." Suddenly the wine was making his throat sting. "Father? I don't want to go to school! The chief gardener's little boys go to school and they get beaten all the time! School is for stupid children! I'm not stupid!" He had not understood most of the words his father had used, but his mother's last outburst seemed clear enough. He had better exchange the skittles for something else. "If you think that the god won't want my skittles, then he can have my toy dog," he put in hopefully. "I don't care." His parents ignored him. Neither of them even looked his way.

He began to cry, crawling across the floor and clambering onto Itu's lap. His arms went around her neck. "Mother, don't make me go!" he sobbed. "Please don't! I'll be good, I promise! I won't tease Hapzefa anymore and I won't run away when you call me and I won't keep asking for water at night when I don't want to go to sleep!" Her arms tightened protectively around him.

"See what you've done, Hapu?" she said. "Surely there could have been a better way!"

Her husband got up and, coming around the table, squatted beside them. His hand went to his son's head and he kissed the hot little cheek. "Many boys from poor families cannot go to school, Huy, and so they remain poor all their lives, hefting stone and making bricks. Their lives are shortened. Their bodies break. All because they cannot read and write. I am not sending you to the school in town. Your uncle Ker recognizes your aptitude and has offered to meet all your expenses at the temple school in Iunu. It is a great opportunity for you. The priests there are famous for their learning. There are many boys your own age who live together. You will make friends. You will do well."

"But I don't want to make friends!" Huy sobbed. "I don't like other boys! Anyway, I have a friend already! I don't need any more friends!" His father held a cup to his mouth and he drank in great gulps in spite of the ache in his throat, tasting a grain of the bitter lees before Hapu set the vessel back on the table. The shedeh-wine had been undiluted.

"You call Ishat your friend, but you are not kind to her," Hapu went on. "You tease her. You hide from her when she comes to play with you. You throw spiders at her."

"She tries to be my Overseer," Huy protested. The strong wine had instantly begun to calm him. He felt a pleasant and wholly unique sensation of numbness stealing over his limbs. "She always wants her own way, but that is not fair because she is only the daughter of a servant. She should do what I say." His words were interspersed with hiccups as the storm of crying receded.

Hapu rocked back on his heels. He regarded his son gravely. "I love you, Huy. But there are lessons about being a man that you must learn early, for if you do not, then no one will want to play with you at all, ever. You do not deserve Ishat." He stood. "Itu, put him to bed. And Huy, I do not want to see the skittles exchanged for something else when you open that bag at the temple tomorrow."

Huy let out a howl. "But I want my figs!"

For answer his father walked around the table, folded himself once more onto his cushion, and poured himself more wine. After a moment Itu also rose, Huy still in her arms. "I know you are right, my husband," she said hoarsely. "But like every mother I wish that he could remain a little boy forever."

When he was an old man, feared and worshipped by the whole of Egypt, wealthy beyond the dreams of any save the King himself, Huy would find himself pondering those words. But now he stood rebelliously while his mother washed and dried him. Then she laid him on his cot and drew the sheet up over him. "Little brother," she said softly, using the greatest term of endearment possible, "you will learn to read and write at school. Think of it! I can do neither. You will be more clever than I! Won't that be fun?" For answer he turned on his side and showed her his back. He heard her sigh then walk across the room and pull the wooden shutters closed. At once the dusky light of sunset dimmed. Coming back, she kissed his hair. "There is fresh water beside you," she told him. "You may be thirsty in the night. Your father should not have given you strong wine, but it made you feel better, didn't it? He always knows what is best for us, Huy. Sleep now. Tomorrow is your Naming Day. Think about that."

He wanted her to go away. With one petulant gesture he deliberately brushed the kiss away, and at that she said no more. Hapzefa came in, picked up the basin of dirty water, bade him a good night, and presently he sensed that he was alone at last. Wriggling onto his back, he lay gazing up at the ceiling. The whitewashed mud bricks had several interesting cracks in them that snaked over his head. On most nights he imagined that one was the river and he was sailing north on it, through the Delta and out into the Great Green to have adventures with the Lycian pirates who often attacked the island of Alashia and were even impudent enough to make light-ning raids on the coast of Egypt itself. He was the King's Destroyer of Pirates, and with his crew of warriors he chased the Lycians, sinking their ships and dragging them back to Weset to be rewarded by a grateful monarch. "Huy, you are a good boy and have served me well," the King would say. "This toy boat has a steering oar and ramming prow and you can really float it. It is my gift to you. Also some gold."

Another crack could sometimes be sinister. It zigzagged from the door towards him and had a rough triangle at the end of it, like a snake, like Apep the evil one, so Huy preferred to pretend that it was a path leading to a swamp where there might be hippopotami, or pretty bird's eggs to gather, pierce, empty, and sit on the shelf above his sycamore chest.

Tonight, in the gathering gloom, the cracks all looked like routes to Iunu, a city Huy knew of vaguely because the great god Ra had a temple there. He did not want to think of that. *Perhaps I should run away,* he mused. *Then Father would be frightened and sorry and let me stay home forever. But where would I go? To Uncle Ker's house? But Uncle Ker is the one who is paying to send me to school. Maybe Ishat knows somewhere I could hide. She lives in the hut behind the garden with her parents, but she often goes out into Uncle's fields with her father and she goes into the markets with Hapzefa to buy our fish and meat.* However, he remembered what his father had said about the way he treated Ishat. It was true that he could be kinder to her. Probably she would not help him out of spite because he enjoyed teasing her and hearing her shriek when he made her close her eyes, expecting some treat or other, and he put a lizard or a beetle in her hand.

The effects of the shedeh-wine were wearing off, and all of a sudden Huy felt miserable. He wanted his mother's kiss replaced. He wanted her to lie beside him, the way she did when he had a bad dream, and say the prayer that kept the night demons away while she cuddled him against her warm body. "I don't want to grow up," he said aloud. "Not ever. And no one can make me."

At dawn Hapzefa woke him with his breakfast of fruit, milk, and bread. He thanked her dutifully, and when she had gone he stared at it disconsolately, not cheered by the sight of the figs someone, his mother probably, had added to the dark grapes and little yellow persea hearts that always ripened when the river rose. The bread was still warm, studded with sesame seeds and dripping with butter. He was not hungry, but he knew that if he did not eat there would be a fuss, so he drank the milk and crunched up the grapes, but he pushed the figs to the side of the plate and laid the piece of bread over them.

He remained mute while once more he was washed, and dressed in his best stiff white kilt. His mother was wearing white linen that wrapped around her body and fell in many small pleats to her ankles, and she had braided her dark hair and wound it around her head. A Nefer amulet encircled her neck, and when she had finished fastening Huy's sandals she shook a smaller one from her wrist and put it over his head so that it hung against his breastbone. "The clay has been baked and painted red in the correct manner," she said. "May it bring you happiness on your Naming Day and continued good luck throughout your life. I love you."

Huy fingered the representation of an animal's windpipe wound around its heart and managed a smile. "Thank you, my mother," he replied. "I suppose we have to go to the temple now, before it gets too hot."

She looked at him anxiously. "Are you still upset? You can't go to school until the flood has gone down in another two months, you know. Not until sometime in Tybi. You have plenty of time left to play with the frogs, so please do your best to enjoy yourself today. Now we must go. Your father will be waiting."

Huy felt better. A lot could happen in two months. Isis might simply keep crying and the flood never shrink so that Hut-herib remained a series of islands. Father's tiny fishing skiff could never brave the current out of the south, not all the way to Iunu, and Uncle Ker's barge might hit a rock and be holed. The teachers at the temple school might fall ill of some horrible disease. Perhaps the temple itself might just fall down. But that blasphemous thought frightened him so that he slid his hand into his mother's and trotted beside her into the passage.

The town of Hut-herib in the Delta had been built between two tributaries on a series of wide, flat mounds that became islands during the Inundation, and to the east lay one of the largest agricultural areas in the country. Although on higher ground that required irrigation with innumerable intersecting canals, it was lush with grazing land, shaded by cultivated date and doum palms and by the spreading evergreen sycamore fig, rich in crops of wheat, barley, and flax, its humid air fragrant with the scent of many blossoms, its trees and waterways alive with birds and creatures of every description. Hapu and his family lived on the western edge of this luxuriant profusion, with the bulk of the town between his house and the eastern tributary.

Huy had seldom seen the river traffic that flowed past, carrying goods and tribute south to the heart of power in Mennofer. Until now his father had considered him too young to go to the docks with his uncle's retainers. There they oversaw the embarkation of the perfumes destined not only for the King's court but also for nations far across the Great Green, or waited to unload the precious cinnamon and cassia, perfume ingredients that must come by sea. The docks were rough and noisy, and Huy might have enjoyed the constant bustle, but as yet he had no interest in Ker's lucrative business other than, like Ker himself, as a source of rich gifts.

He and his parents walked slowly towards Khenti-kheti's shrine, sometimes abreast, sometimes in single file as they crossed the flood on top of the dikes flung up every year to keep in the life-giving water and its equally vital silt. The day promised to be hot but as yet was merely pleasant. A breeze wafted out of the north. Huy, wanting to slip off the sandals whose thongs were already rubbing him between his toes, stared enviously at the naked children jumping in and out of the swollen canals while their mothers, coarse linen skirts bunched up around their knees, beat at their laundry with rocks and gossiped.

The homes of the wealthy lined the tributary, surrounded by high mud-brick walls and sheltered by thick groves of trees whose branches drooped above the beaten paths behind their dwellings. Ker and Heruben could have afforded a place beside the mayor, but Ker preferred to live close to the acres of blooms from which his income was derived. Farther back, the town became a maze of narrow, wandering streets choked with donkey carts, vending stalls, and slow-moving crowds dispersing only to trickle across the hard mud of the dike crests to reach another haphazard sprawl of buildings and alleys on one of the other mounds. The coherence of the settlement was lost at this time of the year, divided into broad atolls rising from a vast lake that would continue to rise for some weeks to come.

Khenti-kheti's shrine, not far from the main western tributary, was a haven of peace amid the babble of an early spring morning. Walled and gated, it contained a small area of grass in the midst of which grew a tall sycamore, and a stone-flagged path leading to the modest domain of the god with his priest's hut adjoining it. No pylon led the way to the single court, where worshippers stood talking quietly or moved close to the inner room to prostrate themselves before the god's door, but the whole precinct was harmonious in its design.

One guard watched the ebb and flow of the sparse gathering, and Huy looked about with interest as he and his parents took off their sandals and proceeded barefoot to present themselves to the priest. Huy had not been here before. His home held a modest household shrine containing the images of Khenti-kheti, Amun, and Osiris that his father would open most evenings for brief prayers, but this was different. Here the stone god carved in the likeness of a crocodile held the soul of the god himself. This sanctuary was his actual residence. Huy was filled with awe.

The priest who opened to Hapu's knock, seeing the trio in their best clothes and Huy clutching the linen bag, gave them a smile. "So this is a special occasion?" he asked Huy. "Is it the remembrance of your Naming Day?" Huy nodded. "Then you are one of the fortunates destined to die of nothing more terrible than old age," the man continued. "This is your gift for Khenti-kheti? Good. Wait a moment and we will go into the holy place together." He withdrew, reappearing some minutes later arrayed in a long white sheath and carrying a white rod topped with a tiny crocodile head. "Give me your hand," he ordered, and Huy did so.

The two of them crossed the court, passing through the double doors of cedar that stood open to allow worshippers a view of the closed sanctuary. The priest turned and pulled them shut and at once a dim coolness surrounded Huy, broken only by shafts of morning light angling down from the slitted clerestory windows high under the roof. Smaller double doors now faced him, and before the priest opened them he took an incense holder that lay at the foot of the wall, lit the charcoal in its cup, and shook a few grains of incense into it. He asked Huy his name. "Do you know any of the thanksgiving prayers, Huy?" he wanted to know, then answered himself. "No, I suppose not. I have never seen your family here before. Well, I will say them and you will repeat them after me. Can you do that?"

Huy nodded. Thin wisps of grey smoke were beginning to curl up into the motionless air and Huy sniffed at them appreciatively. The odour was not sweet. Neither was it bitter. It reminded Huy of the sticky sap that sometimes oozed from the sycamore fig growing in the garden, but that was not right either, for this was richer and gentler and other strange smells were combined in it. The priest saw him craning to inhale it with eyes half closed. "You have not smelt frankincense before?" he inquired. "Your parents do not bring you to the shrine on Khenti-kheti's feast days." He sighed. "This incense is only used on very special occasions, Huy. It is expensive because it comes from far away behind the mountains where there is never any rain. In the mighty temples of Iunu and Abtu and Mennofer the gods may delight in its fragrance every day."

"I am to go to school at Iunu after the flood," Huy blurted. He liked this man's gentle manner. "I don't want to go. I'm scared."

The priest set the incense carefully on the stone floor and bent close to Huy, laying a hand on the boy's thin shoulder. "Of course you don't," he agreed. "You are safe at home. Everything is known to you. Every person, every room in your house, every corner of your garden. And what is Iunu? It is the name of a place you cannot imagine, full of people you have never seen, where strangers will tell you to do things you think will be beyond your power. Is it not so?" Miserably Huy nodded. The hand moved to his chin. "But you will go, little Huy, because you are not a coward, and because although you do not yet know it, Iunu is full of interesting things to see and do. You need not fear anything but the pictures you make in your head, the ones that try to tell you how unhappy you will be. They do that, don't they?"

Huy looked up into the friendly face. "Yes," he whispered. "They do."

"Well, they are partly right." The man straightened. "You will be very homesick for a while, and everything will seem too big and too confusing, and you will feel very small and unimportant, but that will not last long. Then something wonderful will happen. You will begin

to learn the secrets of the great god Thoth, and everything else will fall into place."

Huy's eyes grew round. "What secrets?" he
demanded.

The priest retrieved the incense. "Set your bag on the
floor," he said, and taking Huy's fingers he closed them
around the long holder. "Keep it level," he warned.
"Because this is your Naming Day you are privileged to
be an acolyte. The secrets of Thoth begin with a mastery
over the sacred hieroglyphs he gave to Egypt so that we
would not be crude and ignorant like the animals but
would learn the graces of dignity and nobility and thus
be fitted to sit under the Ished Tree in Paradise."

The holder was not heavy, but it was long and
required careful balancing if you were only four years
old. Huy held it out in front of him with both hands.
"Master, I don't know those words," he protested.

"I speak of the knowledge of reading and writing,"
the man explained. "You will learn these marvellous
skills at Iunu, and you are most fortunate to be able to
do so. Knowledge is power, Huy. Don't ever forget
what I tell you. I want you to make me a promise."

Breathless with this exciting interpretation of
something both his parents had described as not only
commonplace but also alarming, Huy stuttered,
"A . . . a . . . all right."

"I want you to write me a letter as soon as you are
able. My name is Methen. Will you do that?"

The prospect of being able to write his own name,
let alone a whole letter, seemed as improbable to Huy
as waking up one day to find himself sprouting wings,
but he nodded vigorously. "I promise."

"Very good. And what is my name?"

"You are Methen, priest of Khenti-kheti at Hut-herib."

Methen laughed. "Excellent. Now we will pray."

Opening the door to the shrine, he prostrated himself before the figure that had been revealed, came to his feet, and began the prayers of thanksgiving. Huy repeated the words automatically as he scanned Khenti-kheti's image with fascination. It was not very big, no bigger in fact than Methen if it had not been standing on a pedestal. Its tiny black eyes regarded him thoughtfully. Its long jaw was slightly open, revealing a red tongue and white-painted, rather vicious-looking pointed teeth. Huy would have liked to feel one with a finger, just to see how sharp it was.

By the time the priest had finished the prayers, Huy realized guiltily that he had been saying the words without trying to understand their meaning. Methen took back the holder. Hastily Huy stepped forward, laid the bag containing the offending skittles at the foot of the pedestal, executed a clumsy kiss in the direction of the painted feet, and withdrew. Methen carefully tapped the remains of the incense and charcoal into a nearby urn, stood the holder against the wall, bowed to the god, and taking Huy's hand he backed out, closing the sanctuary doors behind them.

The sunlight in the outer court was dazzling. Solemnly Huy came up to his waiting parents. "I have decided to go to school after all," he told them haughtily. "I am going to learn the secrets of Thoth." Their gaze fled to Methen, who appeared to be leaning on his staff of office. Hapu raised his eyebrows.

"We have had an absorbing conversation, Huy and I," the priest said. "All about the marvels of Iunu and Thoth's gifts to our forebears." There was a subtle warning in his tone. "Your son seems eager to explore both. You must be very proud of his enthusiasm."

Hapu moved forward and placed a small coil of copper on the man's palm. "For the indulgence of the god," he murmured. "I don't know how you did it, Master, but we are very grateful." With a short bow he turned away, Itu and Huy behind.

"How is it," Itu remarked in aggrieved tones, "that a stranger can accomplish what we could not? Do you think he cast a spell on Huy?"

"Don't be ridiculous, Itu!" her husband snapped. "Why would he bother to do such a thing? He does not know us at all."

"Well, he did something," she muttered under her breath. Hapu heard her but chose not to reply, and they went on their way in silence.

Hapzefa had set out a feast composed of Huy's favourite foods in the shade of the garden. Bowls of chickpeas, slices of watermelon, salads of lettuce and cucumber, and cold fried inet-fish lay invitingly beside fresh dates and figs, newly picked grapes, and succulent sweet doum fruit. Huy pounced on a dish of ribbed pods. "Bak seeds! Is Uncle Ker here?"

Hapzefa tapped his hand away. "Of course, or how would the seeds get here? What a strange child you are, mad to crunch up those pungent things! He and your aunt are in the orchard. Did you make a proper obeisance to the god, or did you squirm and grumble under your breath? Your father has included Ishat in your celebration meal. Be nice to her, Master Huy. Here—keep the flies away from the food while you wait. I must unseal the wine." She thrust a fly whisk at him and hurried away.

For a while Huy amused himself in trying to accurately knock the insects out of the air just as they were about to settle on some chosen morsel, but the lure of the bak seeds proved too strong. His mouth was still full of the sweetly bitter radish taste of both pod and seeds when his uncle and aunt came through the gate leading from the orchard. He rose to greet them as his aunt flung herself upon him.

"Huy! Darling Huy! So you are four today! The gods have answered our prayers and kept you safe for another year! Give your Aunt Heruben a big kiss!" Obediently, Huy allowed himself to be crushed to her fashionably bejewelled bosom, kissing her cheek while inhaling her perfume, which he liked. His mother had told him that it was the most rare and expensive perfume his uncle made, a blend of imported cinnamon, myrrh, and cassia in a base of balan oil, unlike the simple aura of lilies Itu carried around with her. Ker provided Itu with that popular perfume also, and Huy loved it because when it drifted into his nostrils it meant that she was near. But Aunt Heruben smelled of faraway places, and that was almost as good.

Hapzefa reappeared carrying a tray, and behind her came Itu and Hapu, who presented Huy with the traditional bouquet of flowers. "We give you life, dear Huy," Hapu said.

Huy buried his face in the cool blooms. Everyone loved him, and somehow the priest Methen had taken away his fears. Contentment filled him, and he beamed at them all as they sought the cushions scattered about. "I'm a lucky boy, aren't I, Mother? Can I have wine today?"

Everyone laughed. Hapu nodded and Hapzefa bent almost double to offer him the tray. "Date wine, grape wine, or shedeh?" she asked. Beside the cups a square of spotless linen was folded. Hapzefa indicated it with a jerk of her head. "And that is my gift to you," she went on. "I sewed it myself."

Huy pulled it off the tray and it shook out to reveal a little shirt with yellow ankhs embroidered around the scooped neck and down the front. "Like gold," Huy said, standing so that he could wriggle into it. It felt soft against his skin. He shrugged his shoulders experimentally. "I really like it, Hapzefa. Thank you very much."

Seeing his genuine pleasure, the servant grunted. "Well, try not to get it dirty, and don't wear it if you're going to lie in the soil by the pond. What wine do you want? Are you ready to eat?"

He chose grape wine although he liked the pomegranate better. Adults drank a lot of grape wine and today he felt as though, with the anniversary of his Naming Day, he was much closer to being grown up himself.

He was allowed to fill his plate first, which he did with a child's omnivorous appetite, chewing and sipping with serious concentration, taking care not to spill anything on his new shirt, and he had almost reached the point of satiation before he realized that he had not once thought about the gifts he knew his relatives would have brought for him. They were talking quietly with his parents about amounts of seed to sow, and the plague of dock leaves and wild oats that had infested the flower beds last season from a careless local farmer's neglected fields, and the reasons for the poor crop of mandrakes. Huy lay back in the grass and dreamily watched the play of light and shadow in the leaves above.

Someone landed beside him. He could sense who it was before he turned his head to find Ishat rapidly filling her plate. Hapzefa had tied back her long black hair with a red ribbon. Her bony shoulders were hunched as she bent forward over her short kilt and bare, scratched toes to snatch pieces of fish and slices of cucumber. Huy sat up. "Ishat, you are late and I can't hear Hapzefa objecting."

Her strong white teeth bit a half moon from a sliver of melon. She glanced at him out of the corner of her eye. "I know," she replied. "I was wading out in the flower fields with Father while he checked the dikes, and I tripped and fell. I muddied my kilt." She lifted it away from her knees. "I had to wash it and it's still wet. My other one was too stained to put on. I found a present for you, though."

"You did?"

She shook the melon juice from her fingers and attacked a fig. "I wanted to keep it for myself, but I'm a nicer person than you, Huy, so I decided to let you have it." At three years old Ishat was already no stranger to the instinctive combination of goading and enticement that constituted coquetry. "But I won't give it to you if you're going to try and drag me around by my hair when the others have gone inside for the afternoon sleep."

Rapidly Huy looked her over. Nothing could possibly be hiding on that wiry little body. "I hate you, Ishat," he hissed. "You are mocking me again."

"No I'm not, but you can wait until I've finished eating," she retorted. "Did Mother set out any date juice? She won't let me drink wine."

Huy grudgingly responded to the hint, passing her his cup. She drank greedily, wrinkled her nose, licked the purple rim from her lips, and pulling a lettuce leaf from under the remains of the chickpeas, set it on the grass by her hip and continued her meal.

Huy did his best to appear uninterested, but his curiosity was aroused, and by the time Ishat finally dabbled her fingers in the bowl of warm water already clouded from the hands of the adults and dried them on her kilt, he was preparing to be nasty. She seemed to sense that she had pushed him as far as she dared. Reaching beside her, she set something on the lettuce leaf and, balancing it carefully on her hand, held it out to him, eyes fixed steadily on his face. "I wish you happiness on your Naming Day," she said solemnly.

Huy saw the gleam of it first, a sheen of bright colour that coalesced as it came closer into a golden scarab beetle, its smooth carapace as richly hued as the sunlight glancing off Aunt Heruben's thick gold bracelet. With a gasp of wonder he took the leaf and stared down at the dead creature's tiny golden head, its golden legs almost as thin as the whiskers on an ear of barley, the way in which other colours seemed to glint deep within it as he turned it to and fro.

"I found it floating on the flood," Ishat said with a studied casualness. "My father told me that scarabs are very rare here in the Delta. They like to live in the desert. He said it would bring me good luck, but I said Huy needs it more than I do, seeing that he has to go away to school. I was right about that, wasn't I?"

Huy looked across at her. "Thank you, Ishat," he said thickly. "It is the most perfect present. I promise not to be mean to you ever again. Mother, look! See what Ishat has given me!" He held out the lettuce leaf for the admiration of the gathering.

Ker leaned close. "It is a great omen for both of you. Ishat for finding it and you, Huy, for receiving it on this special day. Keep it safe."

"Be careful with it," Hapu added. "It will dry out quickly and become brittle. Do not handle it too much." Huy could not resist touching its warm silkiness, broken almost imperceptibly by the division down its back under which its wings lay invisibly folded.

"I did a very unselfish thing," Ishat pointed out complacently. "The gods will reward me." At any other time such a statement would have earned her a repri-mand from whichever adult heard it, together with a vicious pinch from Huy, but today no one disagreed.

Huy nodded. "You can have the last bak seed pod," he offered, and Ishat took it with all the lofty entitlement of a queen.

The gift-giving that followed was something of an anticlimax and Ishat knew it, watching smugly as one after another of Huy's family produced the proofs of their homage. Hapu had made his son a sennet game, painting the squares on the board himself, gilding the cones and making the spools look as though they had been fashioned out of ebony. "This is an absorbing and magical game," he told Huy, "and you are old enough to learn how to play it. There's a drawer under the board itself where you can keep the pieces, together with the sticks that are tossed to determine each move. They resemble fingers. That was your mother's idea."

Huy thanked them dutifully. Indeed, his eye was caught by the vivid colours his father had painstakingly used, but all the time he was opening and closing the drawer experimentally and rolling the cones around on his palm he was aware of the scarab resting in the grass by his knee.

His aunt and uncle gave him an ivory monkey with a thin copper wire protruding from the top of its head. When it was pulled, the monkey clapped its paws together with a clinking sound over its smooth, rotund belly. Ishat exclaimed at it in awe, but Huy, although he expressed his gratitude, found it a little frightening. He did not think that he wanted it sitting beside his cot in the darkness, and the stuff from which it was carved felt cold as he held it. "Ivory comes from the land of Kush, far to the south," Heruben offered. "It is taken from an enormous animal called an elephant."

"Is it the bones?" Huy wanted to know. The idea was both distasteful and exciting.

"In a way," Ker answered for his wife. "Ivory grows out of the animal's head, to either side of its mouth. It has a long, long nose that reaches to the ground."

Huy tried to imagine such a thing, and shuddered at the grotesque picture his mind had conjured. For politeness he tugged on the wire a few times and the monkey tinkled its response.

Itu sensed his distaste. "It is one of Thoth's baboons, clapping to help the sun to rise," she said. Huy set it down. Beside the scarab's iridescence it looked sickly and dull.

Ker presented him with a small cedar box. On its lid, delicately inlaid in silver, was an image of the god of eternity, Heh, kneeling and holding in each hand the notched palm ribs that denoted millions of years. The subtle aroma of the wood filled Huy's nostrils so that he put his face closer to it. His uncle's ringed forefinger interposed. "See, just above the god's head, the hieroglyphs strung between the palm ribs? That is your name, Huy. I and your aunt wish you many years of health and prosperity. If you lift the lid, you will see several small compartments. They are for the things you most want to keep safe and perhaps draw out in times to come to remind yourself of a person or an event in your past. As yet you have very little past," he finished gently, "but when you are an old man like me, such objects will be precious to you."

"Thank you, Uncle Ker," Huy said fervently. "The first thing I will put in it will be my golden scarab. Hapzefa will give me a piece of linen to rest it on." Ishat squirmed approvingly. The other adults laughed with indulgence. Huy stared down at the three symbols that meant his name and decided to get out his paintbox in the morning and practise writing them on the door of his room. *Then I will already be ahead of the other boys at school,* he thought happily, *and my teacher will be pleased with me.*

His aunt was yawning and his mother had sunk onto her elbow. Hapzefa hovered just out of earshot, vainly signalling at Ishat, who had rolled onto her stomach and was deliberately gazing into the shrubbery. "I am not supposed to 'outstay my welcome' as my mother says," she muttered. "But seeing that no one has told me to go away, I will stay here."

In truth Huy wanted all of them to go away so that he could examine the scarab again at his leisure. "She will want to put me to bed for the afternoon sleep and then clear the mess," he responded hopefully. "But if you like, you can come back later and play with me, Ishat."

She shot him a dark look. "I will if you don't forget your promise never to be mean to me again."

The party was breaking up. Ker and Heruben said their effusive goodbyes. Huy suffered himself to be kissed repeatedly before they made their way to where their litter-bearers drowsed just beyond Hapu's main gate. Ishat rose reluctantly, waved dismissively at her mother, and disappeared in the direction of her hut.

"You look tired, Huy," Itu said. "You will sleep well this afternoon. Have you enjoyed your celebration?" She scooped him up and hugged him, but he protested, getting down to retrieve his gifts, balancing the monkey on top of the sennet in one hand and the scarab on the box in the other as he walked carefully towards the house.

Hapzefa undressed him, grunted approvingly at the pristine state of his new shirt, stood the monkey on the table by his cot, slid the sennet game under it, and produced a square of soft folded linen. "It was left over from the shirt, Master Huy. It will make a good bed for your scarab. Perhaps you should place it upside down in the box so that its legs do not break off." But

Huy wanted to see the bright curve of its back whenever he lifted the lid, and once she had freshened the
water in his cup and had closed his door behind her,
he patted down the linen and reverently set the beetle
on it. He fell asleep with the box clutched tightly
against his chest.

He did not forget his promise to Ishat, and in the
following days they spent much time together. As usual
they had many fights, but Huy, mindful of the golden
treasure that she had bestowed on him, was learning to
control his urge to respond to her baiting with a slap
or a pinch, and he missed her when she did not come
prancing into the garden to while away the dead hours
between the afternoon rest and the evening meal. She
usually had good suggestions about what to play,
although when he wanted her to be a Vizier and he the
King, she seldom agreed. "Viziers are men," she would
say. "Anyway, being one is boring. I want to be Queen
Meryet-Hatshepset. You can be Pharaoh Men-kheper-
Ra Thothmes." Eventually they took turns conceding
to one another.

In a burst of affection he gave her his dog. He
would have liked to make her a present of the ivory
monkey, but his father indignantly refused to counte-
nance the idea. "Your uncle gave gold for that toy," he
told Huy. "It was very expensive. What would he say if
he came to visit and saw Ishat playing with it? Why
don't you like it, you foolish boy?" Huy could not say
why. All he knew was that it frightened him more as
time went by. At first he had simply turned away
from its idiotic grin when he wanted to sleep, but the
atmosphere of blind malevolence around it seemed to

spread farther into his room each day, until he could no longer banish an awareness of its presence by showing it his back. He put it under his cot, not even liking the cool feel of it when he picked it up, but that was somehow worse than not being able to see it. What if it began to clap its paws together all by itself, there beneath him? He knew that he was being silly, that it was really only a lump of inanimate matter (although he was unable to use those words), yet he remembered being told that the kas of the gods lived in their likenesses, making the stone come alive, and his dread grew. What if one of Thoth's holy baboons was bad-tempered and restless and did not like children? What if its ka had left its home and found this ivory toy in some craftsman's workshop, and had sunk into it so that it could torment whatever little boy came to own it?

"Carry it around with you as if you love it," Ishat advised him matter-of-factly when he told her of his fear. "Then, when no one is looking, find a big rock to drop on it. If you are lucky, its limbs will shatter instead of snapping off so it can't be fixed and you can tell a lie and say it was an accident." But Huy, although he had no scruples about lying occasionally, could not bear the thought of having it against his skin for any length of time. In the end he dropped it at the bottom of his clothes chest under his kilts and shirts. Of course, Hapzefa found it there, but she said nothing. *Perhaps,* Huy reasoned, *she did not like it either*.

So the weeks passed. The third week of Huy's birth month, Paophi, was taken up with the universal celebration of the Amun-feast of Hapi, god of the river, whose banks had overflowed into a satisfying flood that promised another year of good harvests. The heat began to moderate as the river, together with the population of mosquitoes and flies, continued to rise. Paophi became Athyr, and still the water slowly lifted, lapping over the sunken fields and giving back to those who watched it the distorted reflections of the trees that stood isolated amid its calm expanse.

On the first of Khoiak the feast of Hathor, goddess of love and beauty, was observed by the whole country. It signalled a month of many religious observances, a flurry of activity within and without the temples that included three solemn and important rites of Osiris, but Hapu's favourite, indeed the only one he cared to participate in actively, was the Feast of the Hoeing of the Earth, for it meant that the water was at last receding, the flower fields would be calf-deep in life-giving silt, and in a very short time he and the other peasants could begin the sowing.

Huy had pushed the knowledge of his impending departure to the back of his mind, content to catch frogs and play with Ishat, or sit with his father, the sennet board between them, and play the game that he had found easy to learn but difficult to master. Hapu made no concessions to his age. On many occasions Huy, reduced to tears of sheer rage, would see his spools ruthlessly tumbled onto the water square one by one and, losing, would sweep them onto the floor. Hapu remained indifferent, ordering his son to pick them up and replace them on the board, but on the day when Huy beat him for the first time he roared with laughter, pulled him from his cushion, swung him over his head, and hugged him fiercely. From then on Huy looked forward to their contests and behaved with a great deal more equanimity when he lost.

But the end of Khoiak saw Hapu out in the fields, breaking the dikes that had held in the precious water so that it could now flow away and leave the soil exposed, and miserably Huy remembered that Tybi was almost upon him and, with it, the time to leave his home for the first time. "How horrible!" Ishat had said when he told her how few days he had left. "I don't ever want to go farther than the markets, and I certainly don't want to learn to read or write. Why should I? I am perfectly content." But seeing his expression, she relented. "Poor Huy!" she exclaimed. "I will pray every day that you finish school quickly and get sent home so that I won't be lonely." Huy did not think that learning to read and write was something you managed to do quickly. Suddenly jealous of her continued freedom, he refused to tell her how much he would miss her.

He saw little of his father in the days leading up to his departure. Hapu rose early, ate sparingly, and was gone to the fields before Hapzefa opened the shutters on Huy's window. The mornings were chilly. Often Huy would run into his parents' room, climbing onto their bed and snuggling up to Itu as she drowsed, herself unwilling to get up. Sometimes Huy went back to sleep curled into the crook of her arm and he did not know that she lay crying quietly, inhaling his warm child smell, aware that no matter how often she was privileged to hold him in the future it would never be the same. His childhood was almost over.

His father gave him a large leather bag for his clothes and sandals and a smaller one for whatever personal items he did not need but wanted to take. Huy received them in silence. Hapzefa and his mother took charge of the larger one, filling it with loincloths and new kilts and shirts, a comb and a plain copper mirror, natron and linen cloths for washing himself, his drinking cup, a knife and a dish. Itu fretted continuously. Would there be someone to help him dress, wash his clothes, tie his sandals if he knotted the thongs—and what if he became ill? Would anyone notice or care? Surely the local school could give him an adequate education! Wisely Hapzefa did not respond to Itu's panicked questions that had no answers, and Hapu, tired and filthy when he returned late from the fields, could only keep reassuring her that many boys had begun their careers at Iunu and had come to no harm, that Huy was healthy and resilient, and that Ker had promised not only to deliver Huy to the temple and see that he was safe but also to visit Iunu as often as possible during Huy's first six months at the school. Itu was not mollified, but having voiced every worry several times she found their stings less painful and lapsed into a precarious quiet.

Huy put the sennet game and his paints into the bottom of his bag. He wondered if he would be allowed to paint on the temple walls. He had already mastered the writing of his name and had daubed it not only on his door but on every outside wall of the house. Into his cedar box went the scarab and his Nefer amulet. The other compartments remained empty and he wondered what precious trophies might fill them in the years to come. He left the hated monkey on the table by his cot. "It will be there to welcome me when I come home," he told Itu mendaciously. "It might be stolen if I take it with me." Hapzefa coughed discreetly and turned back to the packing.

His mother smiled. "How very thoughtful of you, Huy." The smile broadened. "I will make sure that it comes to no harm." Huy, catching her eye, wondered for the first time whether she had ever believed any of his lies.

Then, suddenly, too suddenly, Hapzefa was washing him for the last time, his mother had come into his room to kiss him good night for the last time, and he laid his head on his pillow for what he believed, with a cold shiver, to be his final sleep on his cot. "Ker will come for you in the morning," Itu told him, "and he will take you right to the temple and talk to the priest in charge of your class. You are expected, Huy. Shall I leave a lamp with you?"

He nodded, numb with a dread he had not felt since the evening his father had broken the news to him that he really would be going away. He tried to remember the kind priest's words but could not as he watched Itu's dark hair fall over her brown shoulder, and inhaled the lilies of her perfume. *Save me, Mother!* he wanted to scream. *Tell me it was all a joke!*

Itu went to his empty clothes chest, knelt, and, lifting the lid, brought up the monkey. "I think I had better start looking after this right away, don't you, Huy?" she said gravely. "I will move it to my own chest, where it will be undisturbed. Until the morning, little one." She left quietly and Huy was alone.

It was a great relief to know that the monkey was not lying in the chest, eyes open in the darkness, peering about for him. For a long time Huy lay gazing up at the sweet familiarity of the cracks across the ceiling, trying to stay awake, to make every remaining moment count, but before long his eyelids grew heavy and he slept.

2

Huy had imagined that the journey to Iunu would take many weeks. It had seemed to him that the walk to Khenti-kheti's shrine from his home had gone on forever, and having been no farther afield than that, he could not envisage a greater distance. But Ker had told him that Iunu was a mere forty miles upstream, reachable in one day if necessary, although he would not tire his rowers by forcing them to fight the northward current when speed was not essential. "We will make a leisurely trip, Huy," Ker had said as his barge pulled away from the dock at Hut-herib and the steersman fought to avoid the other craft jockeying for position in the crowded tributary. "Very soon we will strike the river itself. Later, towards evening, we will pull into some little bay and build a fire, fry some fish, and you can sleep in my cabin. That will be fun, won't it?"

Huy, clinging tightly to the guardrail while the steersman shouted curses at his compatriots on all sides, could only nod. The noise was alarming. So was the rocking of the deck under his feet. His mind filled with the last sight of his parents, standing forlornly at the gate, his father holding a sack of seeds ready to go out to the fields, his mother swathed in her woollen cloak, for the pre-dawn air was cold. Their goodbyes had been quietly perfunctory. Ker had brought a litter so that Huy might ride to the water, but Huy, crawling up into it, was oblivious to his uncle's kindly gesture. Craning his neck for a last look at all that was dearly familiar as the bearers began to move off, he spotted Ishat hovering by the orchard wall, arms folded, grinding one bare foot on top of the other. He did not wave. Neither did she. Waving was a cheerful gesture and, besides, it meant a parting, and he stubbornly refused to consider what was to come. Ishat continued to stand there awkwardly until he was out of sight.

Ker's barge smelled of dressed wood mingled with the rather sour odour of the water lapping against its sides. At any other time Huy would have excitedly filled his nostrils with the novelty of it as his uncle took his hand and led him up the ramp and onto the cool planking of the deck, but today he was insensible to anything new. He followed Ker to the cabin, where his uncle's belongings were already stowed neatly in one corner. Ker set Huy's two leather bags beside his own. "When you are tired, you can come and sleep in here," he told the boy. "It will be cool and quiet for you. But now, let's stand by the rail and watch the town slide away behind us. Then we will eat. Yes?"

Huy could hardly breathe for the lump in his throat. Ker shouted a command to the rowers and the boat began to move. He talked gently to Huy, pointing out the various sorts of craft around them, what cargo they might be carrying, where they had come from, the meaning of the flags most of them were flying. "You see that one there?" He pointed to a sleek, gilded skiff with pennants of blue and white fixed fore and aft. "Blue and white are the imperial colours. Whoever is on that boat is here on the business of our King. Probably a herald. The craft is too small for goods." He smiled down at Huy. "When I deliver perfumes to Weset I am allowed to display the blue and white." He chatted on, trying to put Huy at ease, but Huy was not comforted. Full of that childish desperation which is always mingled with helplessness, he felt the dawn breeze lift his hair and the first rays of the rising sun strike his skin, and he began to cry.

Nevertheless a sort of security quickly grew up around him as hour by hour the rowers beat their way upstream. For the time being he was safe with a man who loved him, and isolated on a river whose banks still showed him the familiar lush vegetation he might find on his father's acres. Between the palm trees to either side he could see sowers strewing seed onto the rich black soil as his father was doubtless doing, sacks slung around their necks, brown arms moving to and fro, followed by the inevitable flock of greedy gulls and pigeons wheeling in a graceful white rhythm behind them. Cows stood in the shallows, water dripping from their muzzles as they lifted their heads, curious as always to see what was going by. Yellow-crested ibises stalked through the papyrus swamps, and now and then in an iridescent blue flash a kingfisher dove between the feathery fronds of the sedge. In the heat of the afternoon Huy slept on the cushions of the cabin, lulled by the motion of the vessel he had at first found distressing, and Ker lay propped against the cabin wall under a canopy, drowsily sipping beer.

Although the river had retreated to the level it held for most of the year, the current was still running strongly, and before the sun lipped the western horizon Ker directed the helmsman to a tiny cove ringed with the tangled trunks and bright yellow button flowers of acacia trees. He sent Huy to gather wood for a fire while the helmsman set out his fishing line and the rowers waded into the water to wash off their sweat. Briefly Huy forgot the fate awaiting him at Iunu. Proudly he piled twigs and a few dry branches near the hollow in the sand Ker had made, and as his uncle laid and lit the fire he went and stood ankle-deep in the shallows, watching the rowers laugh and splash away their fatigue.

They all dined on perch fried in olive oil, sitting in the sand as the light turned red and gradually faded and the shadows under the jumbled acacia grew dense. Huy, full and content, pressed close to his uncle as night deepened, his eyes on the leap and crackle of the fire, his ears full of the rough accents of the sailors as they made jokes about things he did not understand and spoke to him teasingly but kindly. At last, worn out and yawning, he was carried back on board the boat, laid in the cabin, and bade to sleep well. Ker assured him that he himself would be just outside the door if he needed anything, but before his uncle had finished speaking Huy was asleep.

In the morning there was bread, goat's cheese, and grapes that were beginning to wrinkle into sweet raisins, and once Huy had finished eating Ker told him to take some natron down to the water and give himself a good scrubbing. Huy was horrified. He had never washed himself, and as he stood naked and shivering on the deck, a bag of natron in one hand and a square of coarse linen in the other, the bleakness of his situation came rushing back. "I can't!" he wailed. "Hapzefa always does it! I want Hapzefa! I'm cold and I want to go home!"

Ker scooped him up and hugged him. "I know, little one, I know," he said soothingly. "One day you will thank me for putting you through this nasty ordeal, but now you must be clean and put on fresh linen so that you need not be ashamed when I present you to the Overseer of the temple school. You have been very brave so far," he continued, moving towards the ramp. "Try to hold on to that courage. I and your aunt love you very much. We would never do anything to hurt you. This distress is temporary." He had reached the edge of the water. Setting the boy down, he began to instruct him. "The other pupils will all be able to wash themselves," he encouraged Huy. "First you must wet yourself all over, even your hair. Then take a little natron out of the bag, and cupping it in your hand, you must rub it all over you, your face, even on top of your head. Look, I will show you." He pulled off his kilt, unwound his loincloth, and ran into the water. "See!" he called. "Wet all over!"

He held out his arms and unwillingly Huy waded after him. The water seemed warmer than the air. Huy could not swim and did not want to immerse himself completely, but under his uncle's urging he took a deep breath and plunged beneath the surface, coming up to Ker's clapping. "Now we go back to the shore and get

PAULINE GEDGE

the natron," he ordered, and together they regained the sand. Huy found that he rather enjoyed the rough feel of the natron against his skin, and besides, the rubbing was heating him. He returned to the river with a new confidence to rinse off the salt, dried himself competently, and managed to tie his kilt around his waist without any assistance. Suddenly the boat erupted in a chorus of cheers and, startled, Huy realized that the sailors had been watching his efforts. He grinned, embarrassed but pleased. Ker produced a short stick of dried rush, peeled it, and crushed the end so it was splayed. Huy knew what it was for. Taking it, he brushed his teeth vigorously.

Ker handed him a tiny green faience bottle. "Civilized people perfume the mouth every morning. This is lemongrass in a base of ben oil. When you have cleaned your teeth, put one drop of it on your tongue. I will bring you more when I visit you." This was a hopeful prospect. *I have learned to wash myself, dress myself, and clean my teeth, all in one morning,* Huy thought proudly, and with the surge of pride came a moment of self-assurance. *Perhaps school won't be so bad after all.*

But his first sight of Iunu would have daunted any stranger to it, child or not. Long before Ker's barge slowed and began to angle towards the east bank, three obelisks came into view, towering above the massive brick double walls that surrounded the inner city, and the roofs and upper pylons of the temples could also be glimpsed through a curtain of palm trees. Buildings of every description sprawled between the walls and the wide sweep of watersteps running the whole length of the environs, where the river could hardly be seen

for the press of craft of every size moored to the dozens
of posts protruding from the water. The watersteps
themselves, gleaming in the mid-morning sun, were
alive with a steady stream of people coming and going
in between those sitting on the warm stone, eating or
gossiping or simply enjoying the activity. Many paths
led from the steps to one wide road that disappeared
into the tightly packed jumble of houses in the direction of the wall. All the paths were thick with the flow
of humanity.

Huy, standing on a box that raised him above the
level of the guardrail, stared at the colourful scene in
utter confusion as the rowers shipped their oars and
the helmsman expertly guided the barge towards one
narrow opening. "It's time to put on your sandals,"
Ker told him, and Huy obeyed, sitting on the deck and
struggling to tie them as the barge swayed and rocked.
One of the rowers lowered himself into the water and
secured the vessel to a mooring post and four others
ran out the ramp, turning to bring forward Ker's litter
that had been stowed against the cabin.

Ker took Huy's hand. "It will be quieter and less
crowded once we pass through the wall," he said as
together they gained the steps and waited while Huy's
bags were placed in the litter. "The buildings you see
are mostly storehouses, the homes of the poor, and the
stalls of merchants displaying their wares for the attention of pilgrims and visitors. The nobles and the rich of
Iunu live well away from these watersteps. Their estates
stretch to either side amongst sheltering trees and
walled enclosures. Up you get!" Huy pulled himself
over the edge of the litter and onto the cushions. It was

obvious that the gods were not going to destroy the city so that he could go home.

It was indeed a relief to leave the noisy maelstrom of the watersteps behind. Huy had expected the centre of Iunu to resemble Hut-herib, a muddle of narrow, crooked streets jammed with donkeys, dogs, and people in no particular hurry to get anywhere, but Iunu was vast and ancient, its atmosphere one of solemn purpose and worshipful disposition, its air often hazed with the columns of incense pouring from the temples, its lordly thoroughfares thronged with white-clad priests, its markets thick with the servants of gods and nobles drifting from one laden stall to another in search of the perfect cut of beef, the freshest mint, the greenest cabbage. Huy, captured in spite of himself by yet another new experience, was thrilled to see the litter overtaken by a chariot that sped by in a swirl of dust. "The plumes on the horses are blue and white!" he said excitedly to Ker, who nodded.

"Iunu is an important religious and commercial centre," he commented. "The man standing behind the charioteer is probably a royal herald or an Overseer of some kind. We are approaching the temple precincts, Huy. This is where you will be living."

Huy leaned out. Ahead he could see the glint of sunlight on a canal, growing wider as the litter approached. The bearers swung right, walking now on grass, and soon were passing a large lake that had opened out from the canal. Resting on its blue water was the most magnificent boat Huy had ever seen. Its planking was gilded and sparked fire at him as he passed. Its cabin was also gilded. On its prow and on the flag fluttering atop its mast was a falcon head surmounted by the scarlet disc of the sun. "This is the temple of Ra and that is his boat," Ker explained. "We must get out now, and walk." The litter was lowered, and Huy looked about him with wonder.

Before the lake was a huge concourse of stone flags, already hot under his sandals. Dazzling to his eyes, it ran away to where a pylon reared up against the dense blue of the sky. To either side, tall columns cast foreshortened shadows over the paving, and Huy could see that many more of them marched out of sight, just within the solid wall that surrounded the precinct on three sides. A few people paced beneath the pylon, but on the whole the immense space was empty, baking in the heat the flagstones generated. Lawn dotted with several sycamores and the greyish feathers of tamarisks flanked both lake and approach, and groups of priests had gathered in the trees' shade, the sound of their conversation falling dead before it could reach the man and his small companion.

Ker's litter-bearers had retreated from the sun without being ordered, and Ker and Huy began to cross the concourse, Ker carrying Huy's two leather bags. It seemed to take a very long time, but at last Huy found himself standing under the welcome coolness of the pylon. He had no time to appreciate it, however. Ker led him on into the wide outer court and across it, coming to a halt at the farther end where a huge double door was set into a stone wall on which were carved the mighty sun-crowned falcon heads Huy had seen on the god's boat. A man who had been sitting on a stool to the left of the doors rose and bowed. "Greetings. I am the Door Opener of Heaven. The reverent, the gift bearers, and the petitioners may enter the inner court. If you wish to proceed, you must remove your sandals."

Ker returned the bow. "I am Ker of Hut-herib, here to deliver my nephew into the care of the Overseer of the School. We are expected." The man nodded, and taking hold of a ring on one of the doors, he pulled it towards him. The inner court was smaller than the outer but still bewilderingly vast to Huy. Far ahead of him lay the Holiest of Holiest, the place where the god dwelt. Its door was tightly closed. The court was roofed, making a not-unpleasant dimness but for the clerestory slits high up in the walls, and to right and left more doors stood ajar.

"If you will wait here, I will send him to you," the door opener said, and glided away, his bare feet making no sound. Huy, standing there beside a motionless Ker, felt all at once unreal. He could sense the contours of his own room around him, the hills and hollows of his mattress beneath, and knew that in a moment his eyes would truly open, not onto this phantom world but onto Hapzefa's familiar face as she set his breakfast down beside him with a rattle of cup and spoon.

It seemed to him that he was inhabiting a timeless place, that he had been gripping his uncle's fingers forever, but at last one of the smaller doors was pushed fully open and the door opener came towards them, another man beside him. The latter was smiling, his hand outstretched. The door opener vanished back to the outer court, closing the door behind him.

"You have arrived at a most opportune time, my friend," the stranger said as Ker returned his grasp.

"Morning lessons are over and the pupils are eating their noon meal. So this is Huy." He bent and peered into Huy's face. "What a handsome boy. I can see the resemblance between you, Ker. Huy, I am Overseer Harmose. Are you hungry?" The question startled Huy. The man's dark eyes were crinkled affably and he smelled of oil of jasmine. Huy nodded. "Good. I won't make you eat with the other boys today. We will go to my cell."

He led them through the door from which he had appeared into a narrow corridor. Huy soon realized that it ran beside and then to the rear of the Holiest of Holiest, where another door opened onto a large grassy area surrounded by blocks of living quarters and dominated by a fish pond in the centre. "This is where you will live," Harmose told Huy. "Your classmates are still in the dining hall. The teachers live here also. They have duties in the temple. I also."

They followed him across the lawn, past the pond, and through a gap in the farthest block to yet another square of greenery, this one bordered by herb and flower beds. Several little houses flanked the area, and Harmose made for the nearest, ushering them inside. A man who had been sweeping the tiled floor paused and bowed. "Go to the kitchen and bring us whatever the little locusts have left, Amunmose," the Overseer ordered, "and a jug of wine. Come through to my reception room, Ker. I keep the front room as an office." Beyond the reception room Huy could see another tiny space taken up with a sheeted cot, a table, and the edge of what had to be the man's tiring chest.

"You may sit down, Huy," Harmose offered, and Huy gratefully obeyed, sinking onto one of the cushions strewn about the floor. It had not escaped his attention, though his knees were trembling from anxiety, that he might very well have been rebuked if he had simply flung himself down without permission, as he would have done at home. His uncle and the Overseer took chairs and began to talk of Ker's journey, the satisfying depth of the Inundation, the state of the perfume trade, and other adult subjects. Huy dully listened to the sound of their voices. As well as being hungry, he was becoming sleepy. He thought of the cabin of Ker's barge with longing.

The food, when it came, was good, although much of it was strange to Huy. There was a hot, tangy soup with poppy petals floating in it, and a kind of bread full of poppy seeds. A pickled cabbage salad chopped up with dried dill and specks of black pepper preceded grilled beef, a meat Huy's father could seldom afford, with a side dish of chickpeas in a garlic and ginger sauce. Finally Harmose held out a dish of nuts Huy did not recognize. "They are almonds," Harmose said. "A great treat for us. The High Priest has managed to cultivate one precious almond tree in the garden of his home and occasionally he shares the nuts with the temple staff. He sends a large sackful up to Weset." Huy took one and crunched down on it. He decided that he liked almonds very much. The Overseer got up and, going to the door, called, "Amunmose, fetch me young Harnakht." Coming back, he waved Huy to his feet. "You must say goodbye to your uncle now," he ordered the boy kindly. "Harnakht will look after you. Ker and I have a few things to discuss before he leaves."

For the last time, Ker opened his arms. Huy flew into them, burying his face in Ker's neck, but he was determined not to give way to the panic threatening to engulf him. His uncle's eyes, when he set Huy back on his feet, were moist. "I shall miss you, Huy. But I remember my own time at school and I know that you will grow to think of this temple as your other home. May all the gods bless you."

Huy did not trust himself to reply. He was blinking away his own tears, praying that he would not disgrace himself before the Overseer, a stranger, when he was saved by a step in the outer room. A boy of perhaps eleven or twelve stood in the doorway. He was tall and bony, with elongated features to match the thinness of his body and ears that stuck out comically from his shaven skull, but his glance as it lighted on Huy was sympathetic. He bowed twice to the two men.

"This is our new pupil, Huy," the Overseer explained. "Huy, this is Harnakht. You will be sharing a cell with him for a while. It is his duty to look after you for the next month. Off you go. Harnakht, take the bags."

Harnakht swept up Huy's belongings, jerked his head at the boy, and set off across the grass. Huy ran to catch up with him, suddenly terrified that he would disappear around some corner and Huy would be lost in this huge, maze-like place.

"Was that your father?" Harnakht wanted to know. "Where are you from?"

"No. Ker is my uncle," Huy replied breathlessly as Harnakht strode on. "We live at Hut-herib. Uncle Ker makes perfumes for the King," he added proudly.

Harnakht seemed unimpressed. "Oh. What does your father do, then?"

"He grows the flowers and trees and things for the perfumes."

To this there was no comment. Harnakht led Huy back into the first court, passing the pool and stopping halfway along the row of cells for Huy to catch up before he gestured for Huy to enter. The room was stark. Two dressed cots, two small tables, and two tiring chests all but filled the cramped space.

Harnakht flung Huy's belongings onto one of the cots. "My friend Kay usually shares this cell with me, but the Overseer has moved him in with another new boy who arrived yesterday. You should get undressed and onto his cot now, because it's time for the sleep. Afterwards you can unpack."

With head down, Huy began pulling feebly at his kilt, and Harnakht, seeing tears begin to splash onto the linen, stepped forward and put an arm awkwardly around the small shoulders. "It will be all right," he said brusquely but not unkindly. "My task is to help you in any way I can. If I fail in my duty, the Overseer will punish me!" It was a weak attempt at a joke. "We have all suffered from homesickness and we have all recovered." Harnakht patted Huy's arm and retired to his side of the room, tearing off his kilt and dropping it to the floor. He lay down on his cot with a yawn. "Do you snore?"

Huy giggled in spite of himself. "I don't think so." He looked about for a chair on which to lay his kilt and, seeing none, followed his companion's example and let it fall. He scrambled onto the cot.

"One of the servants will bring fresh linen later on," Harnakht reassured him. "The priests here are fussy about cleanliness. We all wash three times a day and change our kilts and loincloths twice." He yawned again loudly. "I will take you to the bathhouse when you wake up, but until then be quiet. I have shooting practice this evening."

Huy propped himself up on one elbow. "With a bow and arrows? Will I learn shooting too?"

"Perhaps, if your father has paid extra for you to have lessons. I don't know. Go to sleep."

Huy decided not to mention the fact that it was his uncle who was providing him with an education. "Harnakht, what does your father do?" he asked warily.

Harnakht sighed theatrically. "My father is the mayor of Abtu, where the head of Osiris is buried. Now close your mouth or I will get up and slap you."

Huy lay back on his pillow. There were no comforting cracks in this ceiling, just white plaster that undulated almost imperceptibly with the imperfections of the mud bricks beneath it. Despite the aching hollow in his heart he was becoming drowsy. He wondered whether his uncle had left the city yet, whether he was safely on board his barge and floating cheerfully home to Hut-herib. He began to cry again, but silently, his hands over his mouth, before his pain dissolved into unconsciousness.

He woke to a moment of frightening disorientation. A babble of voices interspersed with young male laughter and raucous shouts was drifting into the room, giving him an instant of terror that subsided into

fragile acceptance. With a flood of longing he imagined
the quiet of his own house, the sunlit playground of
the garden, and Ishat's skinny brown limbs as she came
running towards him. He was alone. Harnakht's cot
was empty, but as Huy swung himself onto the floor a
shadow fell across him. It was a man bearing a basin of
steaming water, a bundle wrapped up in sackcloth
tucked under his arm, and a stool.

"You slept for a long time," the man said, setting
down the stool and placing the basin on Huy's table.
He unrolled his bundle on the cot. It contained several
compartments, each holding a knife. "I am Pabast, one
of the servants to the pupils of the cells. But you are
not my master, so do not try to give me commands.
I have come to shave your head before you go to the
bathhouse."

Huy touched his black curls. "My hair must come
off? But why?" Pabast indicated the stool. Reluctantly
Huy sank onto it, still heavy-eyed from weeping and
fuddled with sleep.

"Because every child here, regardless of his parent-
age, must wear the youth lock. It seems that you are
not the son of a noble or you would be shorn already."
There was the slightest hint of disdain in the man's
tone, and Huy, with a child's acute sensibility, did not
miss it. He was suffused with shame. *You have all your
hair,* he wanted to say. *You are not noble either. You are
only a servant, like Hapzefa.* The strength of his
emotion, though it burned him, dispelled some of the
heaviness of homesickness.

The man made no further comment, and though
his words had been insulting, his touch was gentle.

Huy sat still while his hair fell softly onto the floor around him. His scalp was oiled, and then he felt the stroke of a knife being drawn swiftly and expertly over his skin. Occasionally he heard a tinkle as the blade was swirled clean in the basin. He held his breath, waiting for the sharp sting of a cut, but Pabast dropped the knife in the water and ran his hand over Huy's skull with a grunt of satisfaction. The ordeal was over.

Pabast set a vial of oil on the table. "Your head will itch for a while and be tender in the sun. Oil it often. I will return every week and shave you again. Be sure to oil your lock as well, every time you bathe. The hair is not long enough yet to braid and I do not have a white ribbon for you. I will bring one later."

I don't like you, Huy wanted to shout at him. *And I'm not going to wear a ribbon like a girl.* He got off the stool and turned his back while Pabast collected up his tools and basin and went away.

He was sitting on his cot with his palms pressed between his bare knees when Harnakht returned. The older boy surveyed him critically. "I forgot to tell you about that," he apologized. "It suits you, Huy. It shows off the bones of your face. One day you will have every girl you know praying to Hathor for one glance from those big eyes of yours. Come on, I'll show you around the bathhouse."

The lawn outside was crowded with boys of every age, some kilted, some naked. They huddled in groups or sat in pairs or sprawled negligently in the grass. Huy decided not to be self-conscious about his own state of undress, although he could hear his mother's caustic comment on such indecency. Even in the hottest

weather he had been made to wear his loincloth.
He had never seen either of his parents naked.
He could not picture what his mother or Hapzefa
might look like, and as for Ishat, she always wore a
thick kilt and her chest was as flat as his. But he stared
openly at the older boys and wondered if one day his
own penis would be as round and dangling.

One of those older boys was hurrying towards
Harnakht, towing a much smaller child about Huy's
own age, he thought. "This is my friend Kay,"
Harnakht said, "and his charge, Thothmes. How is he
getting on, Kay?"

Kay rolled his eyes. "He has no sense of direction.
Three times already I've had to rescue him from the
temple corridor because he went the wrong way after
leaving the bathhouse. I hope you will do better!"
His eyes were on Huy.

Harnakht introduced them and turned to
Thothmes. "This is my charge, Huy. In a month you
two will be sharing a cell and Kay and I can go back to
raiding the kitchen in the middle of the night."

"I was named Thothmes after our great King,"
Thothmes told Huy with a weighty dignity.

Kay laughed. "He says that to everybody he meets
for the first time. You're a solemn little thing, aren't
you, Thothmes? Well, we must return to our cell."

Obediently the boy took his hand and they moved
away, but Thothmes looked back. "I am glad there is
another new boy in the school, and I look forward to
sharing with you, Huy," he called.

"His manners are excellent," Harnakht commented.
"He bows to every adult regardless of their station.

He even bowed to me when I first met him. His father is the Governor of this sepat, the thirteenth of Lower Egypt, and rightly regards a good education as the most important asset for any child. He could go home every afternoon, but his parents want him to enjoy everything the school has to offer. He is rather a pet in a humourless kind of way."

Huy resolved at once that he would also make himself a pet. He had never been taught to bow to anyone but Khenti-kheti's priest. Thothmes' delicacy had given him pause.

The bathhouse, a short way along the corridor behind the Holiest of Holiest and just within another compound, was a large room with a sloping stone floor. Great urns filled with water and smaller ones containing oil hugged the walls. A pile of linens of different sizes sat on a long table. Three boys stood drying themselves and talking loudly, their voices echoing in the humid air. Huy drew it in with pleasure. Iunu's atmosphere was drier than the air of his home and carried fewer scents, which he now realized he had been missing.

"I am going to leave you here for a while," Harnakht said. "Take up one of those ladles, douse yourself with water, grab a handful of natron from the bowl, and scrub yourself thoroughly. But I'm sure I don't need to tell you how to wash yourself. And don't forget to oil your lock! Can you find your way back to our cell?"

Huy nodded. *Unlike Thothmes the pet,* he thought scornfully. In truth he was already slightly jealous of Thothmes.

When Harnakht had gone, Huy self-consciously approached one of the urns, ladle in hand, aware of the strange boys still chattering together on the farther side of the chamber, but they did not so much as glance at him. The urn was as tall as he. Standing on tiptoe, he was able to scoop out enough water to wet himself. He had expected it to be cold, but it was lukewarm. *I suppose,* he thought as he plunged a hand into the natron, *that it is brought to the bathhouse hot and those who dawdle like we did must miss its comfort.* He managed the remainder of the chore tolerably well, awkwardly rubbing oil onto whatever parts of his body he could reach, and he did not forget to draw some through his new youth lock. His head felt as though it kept wanting to fall to one side, but he knew that, when he became used to the one piece of hair he had left, its lopsided weight would cease to bother him.

He found his way back to his cell and struggled into the fresh loincloth and kilt he found waiting on his cot. The quality of the linen was higher than his own. The exercise was becoming easier and he was briefly grateful to his uncle for teaching him such basic skills, although he missed Hapzefa's gentle touch. There was also a dish of dates and raisins and a glass of milk. Huy hesitated. He was hungry again, but perhaps Harnakht had fetched the snack for himself. But it had been placed on his table, so in the end he emptied cup and dish.

He was just putting on his sandals when Harnakht returned. "I washed myself and dressed myself," he blurted eagerly, forgetting what his uncle had said about the other boys of course being able to do these things, but Harnakht simply nodded. He had a white ribbon in his hand. Huy's elation vanished. "I won't," he said.

"Yes, you will." Harnakht held it out. "Every first-year boy wears a white one. In the second year you get a yellow one, in the third blue, in the fourth red, and so on. It's how the teachers and servants are able to recognize the level of study you're at. After the fourth year you get arm bands instead. See mine?" He thrust out his arm. "This is my eighth year. I'm twelve. When you get to your twelfth year you get a gold one. You have to give it back for the next sixteen-year-olds, of course, but the High Priest himself gives you a scroll to say that you are qualified to begin work as a scribe if you want to." He shrugged. "I will become mayor of Abtu after my father, I expect, but before that I will work under him as an assistant scribe. Now tie this around your youth lock, close to your scalp until the hair grows longer."

Huy was mollified. If the other boys in their first year had to look like girls, then he supposed no one would think him stupid. Snatching the ribbon, he fought to make it tight, but somehow his fingers got in the way and in the end Harnakht tied it for him. "You must practise doing it yourself," was all he said.

For the next two hours Harnakht walked Huy through the world behind Ra's temple. He showed him the four other compounds, one of which had separate small houses and flower beds, and trellises covered in vines that provided shade by the large pool. This was where the oldest boys, already men, spent their final year. "Many pupils leave at my age,"

Harnakht told Huy. "By then they have learned to read and write and are ready to continue a different education at home, depending on their parents' wealth and blood. But those that stay on here will have become proficient in music, chariot driving, and all military arts and strategy by the time they go. Few parents can afford to keep their sons here so long. Only the sons of nobles inhabit these houses, with their own servants to care for them."

The next month stretched ahead for Huy like a summer that never became an Inundation and then winter. He tried to imagine how long twelve years was, and gave up with a shudder. He hoped that Uncle Ker was not rich enough to keep him in school for such an eternity.

The school itself consisted of one enormous room, mostly bare but for one wall where a row of baskets held an assortment of pottery shards, and a long table laden with heaps of papyrus sheets, scribe's palettes, pots of ink, and brushes. An easel holding a whitewashed board stood at one end. "The scrolls are too valuable to be kept here," Harnakht said. "The teacher brings them every day from the House of Life." Huy did not know what he was talking about. The room intimidated him with its slightly musty smell of new papyrus and pottery dust, although it was full of late afternoon sunlight that poured into it from large, high windows. Looking up, he saw a row of pigeons sitting on one of the sills, preening and watching the two boys.

"Light is, of course, needed in here," Harnakht said, misinterpreting Huy's glance, "and in the mornings it is not direct, seeing that the room has a northwestern orientation. After class we go straight to the dining room, through there." He strode to a wide, doorless aperture and Huy trailed after him, mentally tracing the route back to the cell. The adjoining space was somehow friendlier. Several long, low tables filled it, with equally long bolsters on which to sit. "The teachers have their own tables," Harnakht explained, "and drink wine with their meal. So do the older boys. Sometimes we get beer, but you little ones always have milk. Occasionally the High Priest eats with us, and when he does the tables are covered in flowers. His presence is a great honour." Huy could hear the murmur of conversation coming from somewhere beyond the farther wall, and the clatter of dishes and utensils. The slightly unpleasant odour of steaming fish wafted about him, with the stronger promise of something sweet. "Beyond the kitchens are the pens and coops for the animals that feed us and the priests," Harnakht went on, "and beyond them, the plots where our vegetables are grown. We are not allowed to visit anywhere beyond that door"—he pointed to where the sounds of cooking industry were coming from—"but some of us do sneak into the kitchens at night when we can't sleep for hunger."

The comment alarmed Huy. "Don't we get enough to eat?" he asked.

Harnakht smiled down at him indulgently. "Food is good and plentiful," he replied, "but when you are my age and growing fast you sometimes need an extra mouthful or two. Besides, creeping around in the dark is fun." Huy did not think so. "I will show you the archery butts and then you must amuse yourself."

Harnakht turned back to the schoolroom. "I have bow practice before the evening meal, and if we don't hurry I'm going to be late. I don't want a beating."

Huy wanted to know what other infractions might precipitate such a punishment. He had hoped that at this school, unlike the school at Hut-herib where he had heard that the pupils were regularly beaten, the forms of discipline might be different. He had never been beaten in his life. But Harnakht was already striding briskly towards the corridor.

Before he reached the door to the inner court of the temple, he pushed open one on his right, set into the outer wall of the passage, and Huy found himself blinking in sunshine that had already acquired the soft pinkish glow of a sunset still some hours away. Harnakht headed straight for the solid mud barrier that encircled the whole temple complex but for the lake and entrance pylon, and led Huy through a wooden gate. A wide concourse opened out. Stables were ranked along one side. Huy could hear the horses whickering, and their warm, comforting smell filled the air. Several low buildings sat at the far end under a haphazard line of trees. Halfway across the dusty expanse, a series of straw-backed targets had been set up. A cluster of boys waited beside them, bows slung across their shoulders, quivers swinging in their hands, and a man had emerged from one of the buildings and was approaching them. Huy watched him with fascination. He had never seen a living soldier before. Clad in a plain leather helmet, with leather gloves on his hands and what looked like a leather apron covering his broad chest as far as his pleated kilt, he filled Huy's mind with an image of his own toy soldiers. He was back in his garden, crouching in the grass from which the blue-helmeted King in his hand would presently spring to destroy the enemy rustling about in the bushes. The enemy often turned out to be Sharp-Claw, Ishat's cat, but Huy, King Thothmes, and all his men would chase it anyway.

The man was shouting sharply at the boys, who were scattering as they unslung their bows. Harnakht gave Huy an urgent tap. "Back through the gate and I'll see you later," he hissed. "I haven't even collected my equipment yet." He ran towards the instructor, his sandals kicking up tiny puffs of white dust, and Huy turned away. He would have liked to stay, to see the arrows buried in the targets but mostly to watch the man whose brown, muscular body held such confident authority.

He returned to his cell without much difficulty. The layout of the somewhat labyrinthine warren of compounds, passages, and rooms was becoming clearer, and with that comprehension Huy gained a measure of emotional control. He knew where he would be going in the morning and, more importantly, where he would be eating. He had learned to trust Harnakht, his offhand but well-meaning guide. He had met his new roommate and was not particularly impressed. As he trotted towards the pool in the centre of his own compound, he suddenly realized that for the last few hours he had not thought about his parents at all.

In the coolness of the cell he finally unpacked his few belongings, laying the Nefer amulet around his neck and placing the box containing the precious scarab on the table beside his cot. Then he hesitated. Much as he knew he would need to look at it regularly,

he did not know if the other boys could be expected to
leave it alone. Certainly Harnakht would be curious to
see what was inside. He might tell everyone. It might
even be stolen. Reluctantly, after one loving touch of
its smooth, golden carapace, he closed the lid and put
it in the tiring chest with the clothes his mother and
Hapzefa had packed for him. But what of Pabast?
Would he, Huy, be wearing his own linen from now
on? Linen the servant would need to extract from
the chest?

Sighing, the boy pushed the empty leather bags
under his cot, took off his sandals, and, sitting on the
floor, shook out the cones and spools of the sennet
game his father had so painstakingly made for him.
He began to play against himself. In spite of the
precarious self-assurance he was beginning to feel, he
was not yet ready to expose himself to the other pupils
thronging the grass outside.

Harnakht came back, tired and filthy, at sunset.
Huy asked him if he had been beaten—that terrible
word—for being late. Harnakht scratched one large,
soiled ear and grinned at Huy. "No. My instructor saw
you and understood my responsibility. I hit mostly
bull's eyes today. If you've unpacked, then get out a
fresh kilt and loincloth and put your sandals back on.
We must wash again before we eat. That's a really fine
sennet board you've got. Can I play with you later?"

Huy was overjoyed at the suggestion of equality but
appalled at the prospect of yet more scrubbing.
Nevertheless, he did as he was told and together they
made their way to the bathhouse, which was crowded.
The older boys took their turns at the water and natron

first, as was their privilege. "Just leave your dirty kilt here," Harnakht told Huy as he exposed his own gangly body and grabbed up a ladle. "Pabast will collect them all and take them to the washermen. You won't always get your own back, but it doesn't matter—one kilt is much the same as another. Keep your ribbon dry, though. Take it off before you get wet."

The evening meal was served from a table at the edge of the lawn. The boys lined up to have bowls and plates filled with the steamed fish, now cold, that Huy had smelled earlier, smothered in a garlic and cumin sauce and piled with onions and broad beans. There was thick lentil soup, bread, and sweet honey cakes. Reassured, Huy carried his food to the edge of the pond and ate. He watched the water spiders skate effortlessly across its surface, and the single fat frog that had somehow found its way into the compound snap lazily at the mosquitoes gathering in a cloud above the placid water.

Harnakht and Kay sat together some distance away. Huy looked about for Thothmes and finally spotted him sitting cross-legged in the doorway of his cell. He had finished eating and was surveying the company, his arms folded. Catching Huy's glance, he raised one hand and nodded a greeting. He did not smile.

By the time the meal was over and the boys had returned their plates and bowls to the serving table, the enclosed area was flooded with the red light of sunset. A priest appeared, his white robe stained crimson with the dying sun, and clapped his hands. Instantly a reverential silence fell. The boys stood with arms upraised. The man began to sing and the boys joined in, a unison of sweet treble voices raised in praise of the god now sinking into the mouth of Nut, goddess of the sky. The music changed, became a prayer for Ra's safety as slowly he moved through the twelve houses of the night towards his birth, and its beauty made Huy want to cry.

Afterwards, when he and Harnakht were back in their cell, the older boy remarked on the absence of any representation of Khenti-kheti on Huy's table. A small statue of Osiris stood beside his own cot. "Does your family not honour the god of your town?" Harnakht wanted to know. "Do you not need his protection? His image to address each evening before you sleep?" Pabast had passed through each cell to light the lamps while the boys were eating. Now Huy looked sheepishly into his new friend's worried face. Harnakht, sitting on his cot, was leaning forward into the glow of the lamp. The rest of him was shadowed.

"My father prays in the evening," Huy responded defensively, "but we have no statue of Khenti-kheti in our house."

"No shrine? Are your parents then so poor?"

"No!" Huy was nettled. "I don't know why," he added lamely. "But we go to the shrine in the town on our Naming Days."

Harnakht grimaced. "Things must be different in the Delta. I have no experience of . . ." He hesitated. "Of countrymen who work the land."

But my father respects the god, Huy thought, wounded in a way he did not yet understand. *How angry he was at my selfish choice of a gift! What else is expected?* The song to Ra still rang in his ears, and gloomily he met Osiris's knowing smile. *Obviously quite a lot,* he answered himself.

He played sennet with Harnakht while outside the darkness grew. Harnakht won all games but two. Huy undressed and climbed onto his cot, but Harnakht stood and prayed before Osiris, ending with a full prostration before stripping off his own clothes and blowing out the lamp. Darkness swept into the room. Presently Huy, lying on his side, began to see the stars framed in the rectangle of the doorway, and all at once a wave of homesickness crashed down on him. The novel sights and activities of the day had served to keep it dammed up, but now, in the silence and stillness of this alien place so far from home, its strength was irresistible. Reaching for the Nefer amulet he had removed when he prepared for bed, he cradled it in both hands, pressing it tightly against his face while he cried. Although he tried, he could not muffle the noise he was making, and he heard Harnakht turn over.

"I sobbed myself to sleep for a whole week," Harnakht said soothingly. "All you can do is let it have its way. In the end it will pass. Would you like to share my cot with me tonight, Huy?" But out of sheer pride, Huy declined.

Eventually his tears dried. His pillow was soaked and he reversed it, replacing the amulet on his table at the same time. Harnakht was breathing deeply, sunk in his dreams. Huy's eyes burned. He thought of Khenti-kheti's priest, his kind face, his encouragement and admonitions, but those things did not comfort him much. *I'm not really very brave,* he thought. *I would do*

*anything, give away every one of my toys, to be at home with
Mother and Hapzefa and even Ishat. I would not even
mind having to sleep in the same room as that monkey
again.* As though he had deliberately summoned it, a
vivid picture of the creature sprang into his mind.
He could feel the distasteful coldness of the ivory, and
see the black eyes alight with a malevolent eagerness to
bring its tiny paws together and destroy his world.
He was not able to fall asleep for a long time.

The morning brought Pabast with milk, barley
bread, and dried figs. Both boys ate in a drowsy silence
and joined the listless parade to the bathhouse, and
Huy was grateful for the two washings he had endured
on the previous day, for he was able to go through the
routine of wetting, scrubbing, drying, and oiling with
increasing ease. By the time he had regained his cell,
he was wide awake. Fresh linen had been set out for
him and he dressed himself without fumbling, but once
again the accursed ribbon defeated him and Harnakht
was forced to come to his rescue. The pair of them
straightened up their cots, Huy shivering a little in spite
of his glowing skin, for Ra had only just emerged from
the vagina of Nut and had not yet gained his strength.
Even here, forty miles closer to the fabled heat and
desert of blessed Weset, Tybi was still a cool month.
Father will be sowing from dawn until dusk, Huy
thought as he and Harnakht left the cell for the
morning's lessons. *He will have hired Ishat and some of
the gardener's boys to keep the geese away from the strewn
seeds, but he will be cursing the gulls that can't be so easily
deterred. Oh, Father! Are you thinking about me today?
And Mother, are you and Hapzefa stirring the grapes as*

they dry and checking the progress of the jars of barley beer? Do you miss me, my noisy frogs?

He sighed and Harnakht put an arm around his shoulders. "Just listen diligently to your teacher, sit without fidgeting, and before you know it, it will be time to roll up your mat and eat. In a day or two you won't need me beside you at all, my handsome little scribe-to-be. May Thoth look upon his new disciple with indulgence!"

They turned into the schoolroom. The noise was deafening. Every pupil seemed to be making the most of the freedom to chatter or wrestle before the serious work of the day began. Harnakht pointed. "You see Thothmes over there? Go and get a mat and sit beside him. That is where your teacher will expect you to be. I will see you later." He strode away, threading between the loud activity towards Kay, who was waving at him.

Huy picked up a mat from the pile by the dining room entrance and approached Thothmes. There were other boys around him, some with yellow ribbons tied to their youth locks, some with blue, as well as a couple with rather bedraggled-looking white ones trailing down their necks. After one incurious glance they ignored Huy, who unrolled his mat and sank gingerly onto it beside his future roommate.

Thothmes nodded at him gravely. "You have been crying. I cry too, but not because I want to go home. That boy"—he indicated a burly, loud-voiced child with a blue ribbon tied at the end of a wiry black braid—"is the son of the governor of the Nart-Pehu sepat. It is a very small district, not at all important.

The day before yesterday was my first day here, and when I told him that I was named after our glorious King he said something rude and pushed me onto the edge of the pond." He lifted an arm so that Huy could see a mottled bruise on his chest. "He is now my enemy, because he does not respect the mightiest pharaoh that ever lived." He sighed. "Be careful of him, Huy. He is a bully. I will have my revenge on him, but I haven't yet thought how." The solemn dark eyes explored Huy's face. "I go home quite often. You can come with me if you like. My father would be pleased."

Huy, somewhat taken aback by this measured spate of unsolicited information, was about to ask why Thothmes' father would be pleased when the level of noise instantly fell. A group of white-clad men had entered. The boys rose as one, turned to them, and bowed. A prayer to Thoth followed. Huy was soon to know it by heart, for it was said every morning, but now he simply lowered his head and listened. Afterwards he sank to his mat in silence like everyone else.

His teacher had settled onto a low stool and was surveying his charges. His gaze lighted on Huy. He smiled. "Huy, son of Hapu of Hut-herib. Welcome to this school. You are about to embark upon a journey that will lift you out of the mire of ignorance and place you upon the agreeable heights of erudition. Do you know what erudition is?"

Huy felt his cheeks growing hot. "No, Master."

"Erudition is knowledge coupled with wisdom. Are you able to write your name? Let me see. Sennefer, bring me a basket and a bag of charcoal." The solid child Thothmes had singled out scrambled eagerly to his feet, ran across the room, and dragged back one of the baskets full of pottery shards Huy had seen the day before. The teacher selected one and passed it to Huy with a piece of charcoal. "Write," he ordered. "And sit down, Sennefer! Why are you hovering at my elbow?" With a scowl the boy regained his mat.

Huy took the charcoal carefully and, with a deep breath, inscribed his name, holding it up for the man to see. "Good," came the approval. "But you will do better. We must all strive to form the blessed characters Thoth has bequeathed to us as perfectly as possible. Thus we honour him. Thothmes, how many epithets does the god possess?"

"Twenty-two, Master."

"And what is an epithet?"

"It is a way in which a god or person or object may be described," Thothmes answered with cool aplomb.

The teacher pointed at Huy. "Remember that, Huy son of Hapu. I will ask you to repeat it tomorrow. By the time you move up into another class, you will all know the twenty-two epithets we apply to our patron Thoth. Now we must work. Come and get your bits of pottery. White ribbons, you will continue to copy the symbols drawn for you on the easel. Take as many shards as you need. Yellow ribbons, you will continue to transcribe and read the first stanza of the sayings of Amenemopet. I will attend to you in turn in a moment. Blue ribbons, you will write from memory as much of the first, second, and third instructions of King Kheti to his son Merikara as you can."

"But I won't know what the symbols mean," Huy whispered to Thothmes. "What is the use of that?"

The teacher had heard him. "Because this is your first day, I will be lenient towards you, young man," he said sternly. "But remember that it is not for you to judge the use of anything you are required to do. It is necessary that you become familiar with the shape of the symbols, how it feels to draw them, before you are told what they represent. You are being offered the tools of power. You must respect them above all things. Now stop wasting my time!"

The easel and blank whitewashed wood Huy had noted previously was now covered in a bewildering array of black-painted signs and figures, but he was heartened to recognize the three that made up his name. Following Thothmes, he got up, extracted a handful of broken pottery from the basket, and, returning to his mat, began to painstakingly copy what he was seeing. "I could do better with my paints. This charcoal is too thick and sooty," he muttered to himself, and was appalled when the shadow of the teacher loomed over him.

"Are you going to be the mosquito whining round my head that continually needs beating away?" the man demanded. "Is your father so rich that he is able to provide you with the vast amount of paint you will use up during the course of your education? Paint is for them." He pointed behind him to where the members of the highest class, palettes across their knees, were quietly applying brushes and ink to their sheets of papyrus. "One day perhaps you may attain their proficiency," the man went on, "but until then you will concentrate on the task to hand, arrogant one." He bent lower. "You are doing well. Do not ruin your progress with excessive self-regard."

"Rich?" came a sneering voice behind Huy. "Everyone knows that his father wades in the mud of the Delta marshes. He's a dweller of the swamps."

Huy turned around. Sennefer was grinning insolently at him. Huy forgot where he was. The charcoal fell from his fingers and the shards rattled to the floor as he jumped up and tried to throw himself at Sennefer. But a firm hand pulled him back by his youth lock and shook him.

"My father is not ignorant! He is not ignorant!" Huy shouted with difficulty while the room span and his teeth rattled.

The teacher dropped him in a heap on his mat and beckoned Sennefer. "Bring me the willow switch." The boy rose, still grinning, and sauntered to the front. "If you can recite to us all the first maxim of Ptahhotep," the man continued, "I will not beat you. Begin."

Sennefer's grin became fixed. "But Master, we have not yet studied the maxims," he protested. "Besides, I spoke only the truth. The son of Hapu's father is a farmer."

"That may be. I am not interested in what Huy's father does, indeed I am not interested in what your father does either. Is your father able to do your lessons for you? No. Can he by magic reach into your heart and make you a perfect scribe? Certainly not. But you called a man a dweller of the swamps. You insulted someone you do not know. By what evidence do you use the offensive epithet"—here he paused and regarded them all significantly—"*epithet,* to describe a man you have never met? Begin the recitation."

Sennefer glowered at him. "I do not know it."

"Then take your punishment." Six times the willow switch whistled and fell, leaving angry red stripes on Sennefer's back even before he was told to go to his mat. "The maxim begins 'Do not be arrogant because of your knowledge. Approach the unlettered as well as the wise,'" the teacher said. "I expect every blue ribbon to go to the House of Life after the sleep this afternoon, request the scroll from the Guardian, and you, Sennefer, will read it aloud as many times as is necessary for each one of you to have learned it by heart. Tomorrow we must waste time listening to you all recite it. You may blame Sennefer for this delay." No one dared to groan or whisper, but the other members of Sennefer's class cast dark looks at him before they went back to their writing.

"Why did he do it?" Huy wondered later to Thothmes as they rolled up their mats and prepared to join the stream of pupils drifting into the dining room when the lesson was over. "He must have known he'd be punished." Privately he smarted, not so much at the boorish Sennefer's words, but at the quote the teacher had flung at them. *I don't care if Father is "unlettered,"* he thought angrily. *He's the best father a boy could have.*

"I don't think he minds being punished," Thothmes replied. "You have been justified, Huy, but for me there is still the matter of the affront to our Great God. I wonder what Sennefer fears. We must do our best to stay out of his way. I think we both annoy him for some reason. Do I smell grilled goose?"

They sat together during the meal. Huy ate heartily out of a huge sense of relief. There were few unknowns left. He had thought that the class would be the last hurdle he had to jump, but as he was finishing his third shat cake Harnakht tapped him on the shoulder. "You are to have a swimming lesson after the sleep, Huy. I will take you to where you must go. Thothmes, if you've gorged yourself enough, Kay is waiting to lead you back to your cell. Haven't you learned the way yet?" He strode off.

"To me this precinct is like an unending maze," Thothmes sighed. "I hope I will have it clear in my mind before we move in together or I must suffer the shame of depending on you, a boy of my own age, to get me from here to there." He swung his legs off the bolster and stood up. "I too am having swimming lessons. We have a house on the river, but my mother would never let me do more than wade about in the shallows. Is your father really a farmer? What does he grow?"

Huy decided that there was no malice in the question. His initial jealousy of Thothmes was beginning to fade under the boy's transparent honesty, but he was still determined to become a pet. *Even though,* he thought rather dismally as he and Thothmes left the hall, *I did not start out well, having been reprimanded once for arrogance and then dragged around by this stupid youth lock.* In fact he was becoming used to the nakedness of his scalp and the feel of that one tress of hair brushing softly against his ear. It gave him the first faint intimation of belonging to this frightening yet interesting place.

He had time to reflect on the morning's events before he fell asleep in the afternoon's heat. He considered the strange beauty of the hieroglyphs, whose

meanings were still unknown to him. He had enjoyed
copying them even though the charcoal smudged and
the bowls set out for washing hands before the meal
were black with the soot. He had enjoyed seeing
Sennefer beaten, too. He thought, with a surge of
liberation, that he was going to like school after all. But
most of all he remembered the young men who made
up the highest class, the nobles' sons, aloof from the
activity of the rest of the room, with their kohled eyes
and jewelled earrings, the thin thongs of their fine
leather sandals, the gold about their necks and arms.
Their youth locks were gone. Some had kept their
shaved skulls. Some were wearing wigs. But a few had
let their own hair grow back, and Huy thought he liked
that best. All of them had hennaed palms, one of the
marks of the nobility, and doubtless hennaed soles of
their feet also. Huy tried to imagine himself as old as
they, his voice as deep as theirs, his body as sleekly
muscled, and gave up.

There was no snack waiting for him this time after
his trip to the bathhouse. "People who swim after
eating get pains in their bellies," Harnakht told him
when he complained. Huy always woke hungry.
"Don't worry, you greedy little worm. Pabast will
bring you something after your lesson." They smiled
at one another. "You're feeling better today, more at
home. That's good. Pick up a loincloth and I'll show
you where to go. Afterwards, will you escort Thothmes
back to his cell? Kay and I have a wrestling lesson.
No trotting about with you anymore!"

To Huy's delight, the swimming lesson was con-
ducted in the calm water of the lake that lay before the

concourse leading to the temple pylon. Harnakht had
led him out onto the training ground but had then
turned left, following the outer wall of the precinct
through a guarded gate until they came to the tree-
dotted expanse of grass sweeping away to either side of
the wide open area. A few skiffs and one or two larger
vessels were tied to the poles before the watersteps.
Worshippers were crossing and recrossing the concourse itself, and litter-bearers sat or lay in the shade,
waiting for their employers to finish their prayers.
Huy had hoped that his instructor might turn out to
be the soldier who taught archery; he would have liked
a closer look at someone so exotic. But the man
shepherding the naked pupils by the edge of the lake,
though tall and supple, had no military bearing about
him. Thothmes was already present, standing apart
from the others with his arms folded, as usual.
Huy waved farewell to Harnakht and ran to join him.

That night he again played a few games of sennet
with Harnakht by the friendly light of the lamp, and
the older boy got out his own set of Dogs and Jackals
and taught Huy something new. Afterwards, Huy
climbed onto his cot and watched Harnakht perform
his devotions. *I should ask Uncle Ker to bring me a
likeness of Khenti-kheti next time he visits,* he thought,
*and he can ask the priest at the shrine what prayers I
should say. I like the hymn of praise to Ra and soon I shall
be able to sing it with the others. I like the prayer to Thoth
too. It is nicer to address the gods than I imagined.*
Harnakht blew out the lamp and they said their good
nights. Huy felt the familiar wave of homesickness curl
towards him as the darkness descended, but this time

it did not crash over him. It lapped at him gently, poignantly, bringing sadness but no tears, and he was able to turn on his side and close his eyes with something close to anticipation for what the morning might hold.

"You're snoring." Harnakht's voice came out of the gloom.

Huy had been almost asleep. He giggled. "No I'm not."

"You are. You ate too much today. Little pig."

Huy smiled contentedly, and unconsciousness claimed him.

He made swift progress at his lessons in the coming months, having spent a good deal of his time at home decorating the walls with the paints his uncle had given him. Coupled with a steady hand and an accurate eye, he had an innate intelligence that responded immediately to the challenge of the bewildering array of symbols presented each morning. Many of them encapsulated a concept as well as the single component of a word. Such economy delighted him. He worked cheerfully, earning few reprimands from his teacher and no beatings at all.

His youth lock ceased to be an annoyance, indeed Huy soon took pride in it as a mark of his status; he belonged to an elite. Not yet truly aware of the magnitude of his debt to his uncle, he nevertheless began to appreciate the feeling of unity that one tress of hair exemplified. Once a week Pabast appeared with razors and basin and meticulously shaved Huy's skull. The chore was done in silence. Huy did not forget the servant's earlier disparaging remark. Soon he was able to braid the lock and tie his white ribbon at its end rather than its root. Both tasks caused him frustration. Thothmes, who had worn a lock almost since birth, painstakingly taught Huy how to divide the hair into three strands and weave them together. He gave Huy an ornate copper mirror less dented than the one Huy had brought from home. Huy soon grew tired of seeing his face distorted in a frown of irritation while his fingers tangled in the smooth mane he was struggling to make acceptable to his teacher's critical eye.

He had finally moved his few belongings out of Kay and Harnakht's cell and joined Thothmes in the next compound after expressing a genuine gratitude to the older boy who had been so kind to him. Harnakht had shrugged and punched him gently on the arm. "You're not leaving the city, Huy," he had said. "I'll still be seeing you every day, so you won't have a chance to miss me." But Huy, although he was delighted to settle into his very own room, knew that he would indeed miss the comforting presence of the lanky, affable youth, particularly at night when he sometimes dreamed of his home and woke with an ache of sadness that only the dawn could dissipate.

Thothmes' half of the cell was always tidy. He did not drop his soiled linen on the floor for Pabast to retrieve, as Harnakht had carelessly advised Huy to do, but folded it and laid it on top of his tiring chest. If he scattered crumbs or fruit pips on his cot, he would pick them all up and place them on his plate. Spilling his morning milk signalled a minor disaster that necessitated an immediate change of bed linen. Although he went to the bathhouse naked like every other boy, he was always careful to carry his sandals so that his feet might remain clean on the walk back to the cell. Huy's happy disorder distressed him so much—although, generously, he made no comment about it—that Huy did his best to be neater. Thothmes' ribbon was never soiled, and often his last chore of the day was to immerse it in the compound's pool and scrub it with his personal supply of natron and a piece of stone until the dust and grime fell away.

Like Harnakht, Thothmes said his evening prayers before his own totem, in this case the god Ra, who stood with the sun-disc headdress on his noble hawk's head beside Thothmes' cot. As the son of the Governor of the sepat, Huy was not surprised at his roommate's choice. He was impressed by the care Thothmes lavished on the statue, dusting it every evening, washing it reverently, and often laying small offerings of food or a flower or two at its feet. "Ra is the father of the gods," Thothmes explained on their first evening together. "He is also the father of mankind and every other living creature, born from his tears and sweat. How is it that you don't know these things, Huy? Did your father not teach you about the gods?"

Huy felt suddenly ashamed of his parents. The emotion was new, and it frightened him, so he pushed it away. "I don't think they care much for the gods," he said slowly. "I mean, they don't spend much time praying, and we don't go to Khenti-kheti's shrine regularly. But my mother gave me my Nefer amulet, so perhaps it's not that they don't care." He had said almost the same thing to Harnakht not long ago.

"I think they are too busy and live too far from the shrine."

"Well, can they not hire a litter, at least on feast days?"

"No, they can't," Huy snapped, and like the shame, a full understanding of his parents' status opened out in his mind for the first time. There was a gulf between him and the small, intent boy sitting cross-legged on the cot opposite. It was larger and somehow different from the gap separating his father from his uncle Ker. If he had considered the matter at all, he had seen Uncle Ker as a little bigger than his father, taller and fatter, and thus more full of whatever it was that made Uncle Ker able to give him the presents his father could not. But now, seeing them both in his mind's eye, he realized that in fact Ker was slighter and shorter than Hapu. Ker's skin was paler, his hands uncalloused, his linens softer. *We are poorer than Uncle Ker,* he thought with shock. *I knew it, but did not really know it until now. And even Uncle Ker is not a nobleman, like Thothmes' father.* "They can't because they are not rich enough," he answered his new friend carefully. "They have plenty of food and a servant, but they cannot afford either the time or the cost of visits to the shrine."

"I'm sorry, Huy," Thothmes said. "Perhaps when you grow up and become a scribe you will be able to give them their own litter. Here comes Pabast with the lamp. Shall we play knucklebones tonight?"

Huy asked many questions about Ra over the next few weeks. When he was satisfied with Thothmes' answers, he retrieved his precious scarab and under

Thothmes' admiring gaze he set it at the feet of the god. "You have convinced me of Ra's power," he said. "I have missed looking at this treasure, and now, under Ra's protection, it will be safe and I can enjoy it whenever I want." He told Thothmes the story of his Naming Day and found himself talking at length about Ishat. "She's only a girl, but she's clever and she likes the right games," he finished. "I expect she would do well here at school."

"I don't think girls come here," Thothmes objected. "Princesses are taught in the palace. Some of the daughters of my father's friends are learning to read, but they have tutors at home." He made a face. "I wouldn't like to have girls in the school. They complain a lot and make a fuss about silly things. Can you imagine a girl learning to swim?" Both boys had been doing well at their swimming lessons. Huy did not want to start an argument by telling Thothmes that Ishat, a year younger than himself, could already swim like a fish.

Huy's uncle visited him on the last day of the following month, Mekhir. He arrived just as the morning's class was over and Huy, summoned by one of the temple priests, rolled up his mat and ran into the corridor, where Ker was waiting. The man bent and opened his arms and Huy literally jumped into them. "Uncle Ker! You smell like home!" he shrieked.

Ker hugged him and set him on his feet. "Gods, Huy, can you have grown in just two months?" he exclaimed. "You look very well. Are you happy? The Overseer tells me that you are settling down without trouble. My barge is moored on the lake of the canal and I have permission to give you your meal on board. Would you like that?" Huy grabbed his hand, not knowing whether he wanted to laugh or cry. "Your mother and father and Aunt Heruben all send their love," Ker went on, turning towards the inner court of the temple. "We miss you so much, but we are very proud of you."

Huy tugged him to a halt. "There's a better way to the lake," he said importantly. "We take it when we have our swimming lessons. Let me show you. Oh, Uncle Ker, I am so pleased to see you!"

"You look fine in your youth lock," Ker remarked as hand in hand they came out onto the parade ground and followed the left-hand path under the shadow of the wall. "I will tell your mother that she need not grieve for all your curls. She'll be pleased that you wear the amulet she gave you." Huy, overcome with a pang of sheer longing for her pretty face, could not reply.

The barge was like an old friend, and running up its ramp Huy remembered the storms of panic that had assailed him on the journey upriver to Iunu. It seemed hentis ago. Now he had two homes, one here and one in the Delta. Mindful of Thothmes' good manners and of his own position as a legitimate resident of the temple, he bowed to the helmsman and the sailors gathered in the shade the prow was casting over the deck, and waited for his uncle to indicate that he might sit on one of the cushions by the cabin. Ker's eyebrows rose but he said nothing. The sailors greeted Huy good-naturedly. Ker gestured at the feast set out on the cloth and Huy collapsed beside it with a sigh of pure pleasure. The sun was warm, the barge was barely rocking on the sparkling surface of the lake, and if he took long enough over his meal his classmates would be arriving for their lesson and would see him being feted on this handsome vessel. Even the scornful Sennefer might be envious.

"My crops are growing fast," Ker said as he served Huy with slices of cold beef and a salad of crisp fresh lettuce, celery, and onion sprinkled with pungent slivers of garlic, "and so are the weeds. That little friend of yours, Ishat, pulls them out, but then she makes garlands of them. The wild flax and poppies and the daisies are too pretty to waste, she says. She sent something for you." He opened the drawstring of the pouch at his waist and handed Huy a small stone.

Huy rolled it to and fro on his palm, thrilled at how it flashed and glittered in the strong midday light. "Is it gold?" he asked, awed.

Ker chuckled. "No. The flecks in it are called pyrite, but they are as pretty as gold, aren't they? Ishat picked it up on the shore of the tributary. She thought you might like it."

Huy set it carefully on the deck. "I do," he said fervently. "This is the second gift Ishat has given to me. As soon as I'm able I shall write and thank her. Even though she can't read, she will be thrilled to receive a letter."

"And that moment will come sooner than any of us expected." Ker poured beer into two cups and held one out to Huy. "The Overseer and your teacher are very impressed at your rapid progress. I was not wrong to

send you here, Huy. Is there anything you lack?
Anything you need?"

Huy put his nose into his cup. The beer, thick and
dark, smelled of musk, but its bitter taste was oddly
agreeable. "Yes, there is, Uncle Ker. I would like a
statue of Khenti-kheti to put on the table beside my
cot. All the other boys have their totems with them."

Ker glanced at him shrewdly. "I expect they do. But
why do you desire the god's presence?"

Huy licked the froth off his upper lip. "Because
Khenti-kheti protects Hut-herib and I am from
Hut-herib, therefore the god will protect me. I am
his son."

"You are indeed," Ker agreed. "Very well, Huy. If
you will accord the god the proper reverence due to
him and say the prayers each evening, I will bring him
to you next time I pass through Iunu. If the priest at
the shrine writes out the prayers for you, will you be
able to read them?"

Huy shook his head. "Not yet. But my teacher will
help me."

"Good. You seem to be acquiring a new and somewhat surprising interest in the state of your soul. Do
you like the other boys here?"

"Most of them." Huy settled down to tell his uncle
all about Harnakht, Kay, and Thothmes, the objection-
able Sennefer, and the lofty inapproachability of the
jewelled and perfumed young men who fascinated him.

Ker laughed at the way he described them. "Before
you know it, you too will be tall and beautiful. I am
very proud of you, Huy. You are a credit to all of us
at home."

The beer had made Huy sleepy. He yawned, thinking of his cot in the coolness of his cell. Ker indicated the cabin. "Crawl onto the cushions in there and rest," he offered. "I must do business with the High Priest this afternoon. I have incense gum for him and a quantity of kyphi perfume for the dancers. My men will remain on board." He leaned over and kissed Huy's hot forehead. "Don't worry, the Overseer knows where you are."

Huy had not seen the Overseer since that first miserable day when Ker had deposited him in this place that had seemed so vast and terrifying. *But I suppose,* he thought as he burrowed into the cabin's cushions and drowsily watched the slatted pattern of light around him, *that he must know everything about everyone here or he wouldn't be an Overseer.* The cabin felt like some animal's den, cozy and safe. Voices and the rhythmic shush of sandals on paving came to him pleasantly muted. The odour of the barge's wood was like the music of some old, familiar lullaby, and as he fell asleep Huy fancied that he could also smell a panful of perch frying over a fire on a sweet spring evening by the river.

Ker's vessel pulled away from the temple watersteps just as Huy's swimming class wandered into sight. Huy was disappointed. He would have liked the other boys to have boarded the barge, however briefly. But Ker was on his way to Weset and had many river miles to cover. He had said an affectionate goodbye to his nephew, and Huy was sad as he watched the helmsman clamber onto his high seat and grasp the tiller. For a moment he wished he might be making the journey to that holy city where the King sat on his golden throne and all the men around him must surely look like the nobles' sons here at the school. But then Thothmes called him and the others were leaping into the water with screams of delight, and Huy began to shed his kilt and loincloth. It had not occurred to him to want to go home.

3

Over the next two months, the fixed routine of life at the school gradually became a matter of second nature to Huy. He no longer had to run to Harnakht for direction or reassurance if he could not remember where he had to be or what was coming next. The rhythm of his days—eating, washing, studying, exercising—even the walls of the precinct itself, provided a womb of predictability inside which he could safely flourish.

Long before Thothmes had finally learned to negotiate the many rooms and passages himself, Huy knew them, and the other boy's temporary dependence on Huy accelerated the bond already growing between them. Huy was not tempted to exert control over his cellmate as he had always tried to do over Ishat. He might have Thothmes at his mercy where a corridor branched, but Thothmes was his better in the knowledge of the many things the pupils in their class took for granted. Huy absorbed information quickly, holding his tongue when the conversation turned to the family lives of those who were his social superiors. He was making swift progress under his teacher's critical eye and could comfort himself with the knowledge that, although this boy might be the son of a governor or that one belong to one of the King's Overseers, he himself had a sharper mind and a greater love for the hieroglyphs he was beginning to manipulate.

Sometimes the classes were cancelled in order that a god's feast might be celebrated, and the boys with families in Iunu went home. Huy was granted permission to spend these days with Thothmes in his father's house by the river. At first the size and grandeur of Thothmes' home made him tongue-tied and shy. Thothmes was the darling of three older sisters who teased and petted him, much to his irritation, and seemed pleased to have another child to cosset, but Huy remained in awe of Thothmes' father, a man with a temperament very like his son's, engaged in the world around him but somehow aloof. The house with its verdant garden, airy rooms, and host of servants, its watersteps overhung with willows where both skiff and barge rocked invitingly, seemed opulent to the boy from a farm in the Delta. Thothmes had laughed at Huy when he first expressed his admiration. "Father is only a governor," he had said. "We are comfortably rich, but you should see the estate of the Vizier." They had been lying stretched out one above the other on the watersteps after practising their swimming strokes, the shapes of their damp bodies forming like shadows around them on the warm stone.

"Is Sennefer's home like this?"

"Yes, and he doesn't deserve what he has. His mother spoils him. She gives him everything he wants.

His father argues with her about it all the time, but it makes no difference. That's why he lives at the school. His father insisted, to get him away from her. So I hear my father telling my mother when they think I'm not listening." Huy looked up at his friend. Thothmes was lying on his stomach and peering over the edge of the step. Water from his dishevelled youth lock dripped onto Huy's cheek. "He isn't learning anything much, and I do hope that our Blessed God and King will not make him governor when his father dies. He is too cruel and stupid to govern the rats in the grain silos, let alone even a small sepat like Nart-Pehu."

Huy thought that Sennefer's parents sounded very like his own. Did his mother not spoil him, and had his father not insisted that he be sent away to school, thanks to Uncle Ker's generosity, for that reason? It occurred to Huy that he might be a little like Sennefer himself—but surely not cruel or stupid. "Don't you think that the Good God might already be sailing in the celestial barque by the time Sennefer is old enough to hold his father's office?" he inquired.

Thothmes snorted. "Certainly not! And even if that is true, he will still guide our country through the Hawk-in-the-Nest Amunhotep, his son. Perhaps the King would send Sennefer to the Tjel, or one of the garrisons along the Horus Road," he added hopefully. "My father says that Sennefer ought to be learning soldiering because he will never make a good administrator." He rolled onto his back and out of Huy's sight. "I overheard him say that to my mother, but I keep it to myself, as a good scribe would."

Huy closed his eyes against the sun's glare. Thothmes' words had prompted a new and rather unnerving train of reflection, and for the first time Huy wondered what his own future might be. His mother had sometimes said things like, "When you take over your father's work in Ker's fields . . ." and, "You must not be rude to the field workers, Huy. You might be the Overseer of their sons one day," but he had not paid her much attention, seeing that he would always be free to play in the garden with Ishat and the frogs and have Hapzefa to look after them all. It had already become clear to him that his father was really not an important man at all. It did not matter that he helped to supply Pharaoh's perfumer with the blooms, fruits, and seeds needed to produce the exotic blends that were famous throughout the world; he was a man with dirt under his fingernails. What was it that had been written about the gardener? Huy's teacher had read aloud the long admonitions to a boy beginning his studies. The anonymous author had intended them to be a warning and an encouragement to those strug- gling to master the skills of a scribe. Thothmes would remember; his powers of recall were remarkable. But Huy did not want to bring up the subject of his father's occupation. Some of the lines he could remember him- self. "The gardener fetching with the carrying pole, his shoulders are the shoulders of old age . . ." something something something ". . . he has laboured in the sun and afterwards his body aches. He is too old for any other occupation." There were blanks to be filled in later, when the class began to write and memorize the exercise, but the sense of this particular stanza was clear. Huy sighed. He would prefer to spend the rest of his life either at school or running about his home, but if he had to grow up—and here the first intimation of his own mortality fled across his mind and was gone—then it had better not be as a man who laboured in the sun and had an aching body.

"Why are you sighing?" Thothmes demanded.

Huy sat up. "I am getting hot. Shall we go in the water again?"

Thothmes considered, then shook his head. "No, let's go in. I'm hungry. Besides, Meri-Hathor has promised to take us into the marshes this afternoon to look for egret eggs, and we will be eating supper with her on the bank afterwards. She says she will build us a fire, but I don't think she knows how. Maybe we can take a servant with us."

Meri-Hathor was Thothmes' eldest sister. At fourteen she was already contracted to marry the son of one of the many King's Overseers in the city. It was an advantageous match for her, but to Huy she did not seem very impressed. A graceful girl with her brother's huge eyes and pointed chin, she seemed to spend all her time fussing with cosmetics and having long discussions with her mother about furniture and such things. A trip into the marshes with her was an unusual treat. Huy was sure that Thothmes had asked for it and had of course not been refused.

Apart from feast days spent at Thothmes' home, Huy found himself regularly at leisure in the hours between each afternoon's exercise and the evening meal. Sometimes he would join the other boys gathered by the pond to toss a ball or wrestle or simply lie in the grass and talk. They were cheerfully offhand with him, aware of his lower social status but not particularly caring about his origins, for Huy's arrogance had suffered a death blow, as his father had hoped it would, and he approached his classmates with a humility born of new experiences. He was accepted for his quick mind, his healthy little body, and his eagerness to make the wearing of the youth lock legitimate by earning his own place among them. The one exception was Sennefer, who held himself apart from his peers. He ignored the other blue ribbons, ingratiating himself with those a year ahead of him, the ones who wore red ribbons on their youth locks. Few of them had responded to his overtures in the three years he had been attending the school, but as is often the case he had drawn three or four other coarse boys around him. They delighted in making the lives of the younger boys a misery, and Huy and Thothmes always slid out of sight when they entered the compound.

It was on one of these occasions that Huy discovered the Tree. After a rare display of inattention, Thothmes had been given extra work to do that kept him in their cell, so Huy, at a loose end, began to wander. He had already explored the limits of the precinct. From a respectful distance he had watched the priests submerge themselves in Ra's sacred lake, knowing that its placid waters were forbidden to him. He had roamed the area behind the temple where the kitchens and storehouses were, although he was afraid that Pabast might catch him. He had even found his way into the animal enclosures, happy to lean over the fence and talk to the pigs, stroke the rough hides of the cattle, and watch the imprisoned doves and pigeons flutter and twitter in their cages. Someone was always there, either feeding and watering the livestock or opening the gates to lead an animal away to be slaughtered, but the men ignored Huy. Obviously he was not their business. The only section of the temple that he had not ventured into, apart from the inner court and the Holiest of Holiest itself, was made up of the priests' cells, robing rooms, and the places where the sacred vessels and implements were stored. These were most definitely out of bounds, even to the oldest boys, and for all his curiosity Huy had made sure to stay well away from them.

On this particular afternoon, he was with the animals and happily engaged in reaching through the birds' cage to collect a fine pigeon's feather when he heard a familiar voice. "They need another couple of pigeons in the kitchen," it said. "Go and wring their necks and be quick about it. As if I haven't enough to do without running all the way to this stinking place." It was Pabast. Huy's view of him was blocked by the animal keeper approaching the servant, but he knew those hectoring tones only too well. His heart had begun to pound. Fortunately, he had been crouching to grope for the feather or Pabast would have seen him at once. As it was, his usual way of escape was blocked. The keeper would be coming towards the birds at any moment. He had seen, and not bothered with, Huy before, but now that Pabast was there, would he give Huy away? Only one route remained. Huy had not taken it before. It led to the killing ground. He did not want to take it now, but he had no choice. On hands and knees, he crawled towards it as fast as he could.

The beaten path was thick with animal dung and Huy could not avoid it. Soon he was mired in foul-smelling excrement, but he dared not stand, not until he knew he was out of sight. Panting with fear, he struggled on, wrists aching, knees sore, until all at once the ground opened out before him and the odour of old blood caught in his nostrils. The place was not unlike the training ground but smaller, its floor of churned sand stained brown, the area bounded by a high mud-brick wall hung with a combination of axes, clubs, and knives that made Huy shudder. A huddle of rickety pens at the farther end crowded to either side of a door. No one was there. Breathing a prayer of thanks to Ra, Huy stumbled towards it. It was not locked. Leaning on the door with all his weight, Huy managed to inch it open, and tumbling through he quickly heaved it closed again.

He found himself in a dark room full of frames on which cattle hides in various stages of curing were hung or stretched. Barrels full of bones and urns full of liquids he could not identify lined the walls. A large wooden table holding scrapers and other strange tools sat in the centre. Huy, trembling and nauseous, thought he had never been in a more foul place. A door opposite him stood ajar and through it he could see grass and blue sky. With a shriek of pure relief he fell through it.

A grove of palms faced him and he ran between the smooth, spreading boles of the trees until he knew he could not be seen, then he collapsed onto the sparse grass and began to scrub frantically at his filthy legs. His kilt had dragged in the muck. He pulled it off and rubbed it between his hands, wondering how far away the river was. His panic was subsiding, his heart receding from his throat to settle once more in his chest, when he realized suddenly that he was outside the frowning double wall surrounding the temple, the school, and everything else in his world, but on the opposite side of the one he knew. If he turned to his left he must eventually come to the canal and the lake and the apron of stone before the outer court, but he quickly discarded the idea; he did not fancy crossing that vast expanse covered in animal excrement when it would be busy with people. Going right would mean a very long walk, but it was his only hope of slipping unnoticed into the corridor between the walls and from there to his cell. *A slim hope,* he told himself dismally as he came to his feet, *but I have to try. Damn Pabast and his pigeons!*

He set off, keeping to the cover of the palms, but he need not have been concerned with secrecy. *I must go all the way around the back,* he decided, *behind the animal pens and the kitchen gardens and the servants' quarters. It will take me forever.* He groaned, his nostrils full of the foul odour rising from his kilt and his skin, his ears alert for any sound of approach. But the palm grove lay quiet in the late afternoon heat. The only sounds were the secretive rustling of the dry leaves above him and the warble of the pigeons circling the roof of the Holiest of Holiest.

Once oriented, he set off, keeping well away from the wall and under the slim cover of the palm trunks. He was tired from both physical exertion and the shock he had received, but the fear of retribution drove him on. He must get to the bathhouse before his fellow pupils took their evening wash, before the end of the sleep if possible, but one glance up at the sky told him that the sleep was probably already over. The wall ran on without a break, but soon the trees grew more sparse, giving way to patches of sand and clumps of spiny grey tamarisk bushes. Huy did his best to stay within their shadow, but he was now fully visible. Clenching his fists, he ploughed doggedly through the churned sand. He did not mind being seen by a servant. His forays into the forbidden areas of the school had taught him that servants were generally too busy to mind anyone's affairs but their own. It was the priests he feared, with their spotless white robes and gleaming skulls and voices heavy with authority. Fervently he wished that he had never ventured into the animal enclosure, never, in fact, disobeyed the rules of the school at all. *I shouldn't have gone where I am forbidden,* he told himself as he stumbled on, *and I am being punished. Please, great Ra, mighty Khenti-kheti, take pity on me and show me how to get back to my cell!*

At that thought he stopped dead and stared at the seamless wall, heart thudding. *I should have come to the gardens by now,* he reasoned. *Surely I should be somewhere near the rear of the enclosure. The wall should be curving. There should be doors or gates. I should be able to hear the gardeners and perhaps even smell cooking from the kitchens. Where am I? Oh gods, I'm lost! But how can I be lost if I'm just following the wall?* He felt panic clutch at his stomach and with it the urgent need to squat and vacate it through his bowels. Fighting the spasm, he tried to think calmly, closing his eyes and retracing his steps from the moment he had heard Pabast's hectoring voice.

At once he realized his mistake. He had always come to and gone from the huge pens the same way, noticing but not really absorbing the route along which the condemned animals were led to the slaughtering yard. In his fright and confusion, he had believed himself to be heading towards the northern side of the temple where, if he had turned east, he would have easily come to the training ground and from there, with luck, could have slipped back into his compound. But the slaughtering yard and the tannery were on the southern side, and he had not only swung in the wrong direction but had also been much closer to the river and the facade of the temple than he had imagined. He tried to think coolly. *All I have to do is keep going. I have not yet reached the rear, but I must get there if I watch the wall. It will take me longer, but I can still cut through the gardens and then the kitchens and avoid being caught.*

The dung with which he was encrusted had begun to dry and flake. He brushed at it absently and started off again, looking ahead in the expectation of a row of shade trees that would signal the wide acres of the temple gardens, but instead he saw a peculiar shadow triangulating out from the bricks of the wall. As he drew closer it became a small door, and the door was slightly ajar. Huy slowed, hesitated, held a very short debate with himself on the relative merits of stumbling on wearily or taking a chance on an unknown shortcut, and quickly made up his mind. *After all,* he thought miserably, *how many more disasters can this day bring me?* He approached the door and cautiously peered around it.

The first thing he saw was another door directly opposite, set into the inner wall that encompassed the whole temple complex, and he sighed with relief. Wherever that door led him, he would be back inside Ra's domain and could surely get his bearings. But the second thing he saw was the Tree, and the sight of it drove every other thought from his head. Rising from the low circle of mud wall that retained the water on which it throve, the Tree's many grey branches turned and twisted to fill the space around it with a delicious leafy shade. To left and right Huy saw that the corridor which ran between the walls had been blocked off, making a roofless area with the Tree in the centre. There was nothing else, only this great, gnarled trunk with its winding arms and pale green, latticed foliage that covered the ground in a moving pattern of coolness. Huy stared at it in wonder. He had never before seen anything like it. Not sycamore, not palm, not willow or olive or carob, it exuded such an atmosphere of otherness that Huy was almost afraid to step through the door. For what seemed to him a long time he merely stood with one hand on the lintel and watched the play of breeze and sun on those delicate, almost translucent leaves. But he knew that beyond the other door lay the end of his grim adventure. In twenty steps or so he could be free. Taking a deep breath, feeling that in some strange way he was committing an act of blasphemy, he started across the smoothly pounded earth.

He was almost halfway across when the door he was facing suddenly swung open. A large male hand appeared, but the rest of the body did not immediately follow. Huy heard a brief conversation going on.

Frantically he looked about for somewhere to hide, but there was nowhere, only himself and the Tree and the thickly dappled shade. Spinning about, he headed for the door through which he had come, but he was too late. The door behind him clicked shut and then his youth lock was grabbed so violently that he was jerked to a halt. Cringing, he waited for blows to rain down upon him, but the hand gripping his lock had begun to tremble and then it released him. He turned, and found himself staring up at a temple guard. The colour was draining from the man's face. Huy had never seen such a thing before, and he watched in fascination as the skin became grey.

"What are you doing here?" the man hissed. "You shouldn't be here! And so filthy! Never! Never!" His gaze slid to the half-open door and he began to push Huy towards it. "Get out! Gods, I'll be flogged for this!" Huy shrugged his youth lock back against his shoulder and sauntered towards the door, his terror fading; this man was more frightened than he was. "Hurry! Hurry!" the soldier was whispering, no longer touching Huy but hard on his heels, and Huy, his confidence returning, decided to take his time. Whatever he had done, he would obviously be in less trouble than the frantic man gesticulating at his rear, and his day had been horrendous enough without yet another Pabast forcing an undignified retreat upon him. But his arrogance was his undoing. He had not quite reached freedom when the other door creaked open. The soldier groaned. Huy glanced behind him, and froze.

A priest stood there, transparent white linen falling from one bronzed shoulder to his gilded sandals. A golden arm band emblazoned with Ra's symbol hugged one of his wrists and the same hieroglyph hung on his chest. He held a white staff topped by Ra's hawk head, and even as Huy made a dash for the door he heard it clatter to the ground as the man lunged for him. He was too late to squeeze through the gap. A strong hand descended on the nape of his neck and he was dragged unceremoniously backward.

"Close that door and take up your station outside it," a voice ordered coldly. "You know that if you must leave your post even for a moment, it has to be locked. I will deal with you later." Huy heard the soldier swallow noisily as he passed him and disappeared. The door to Huy's salvation clicked shut.

Boy and Priest regarded one another, Huy in trepidation, the Priest expressionlessly. His grip did not loosen. At last he said, "Do you know who I am, you disgusting little scrap of humanity?"

"Yes, Master," Huy croaked. "You are the High Priest of Ra."

"And do you have any idea what you have done?" Huy tried to shake his head. "You have desecrated one of the most holy places in the world. Not only is your presence a grave offence, but you dare to enter here stinking of the cattle pens. If you were any older, your punishment would be death. Who are you?"

Huy felt a sudden urge to void his bladder. Desperately he forced his besmirched knees to remain firm. He had begun to cry. "I am Huy, son of Hapu of Hut-herib," he sobbed. "I am a pupil at the temple school. I meant no harm, Master. I was lost."

"What were you doing so far from your quarters?" the man demanded. "Well, it does not matter. I will want an explanation later, but every moment you stand here unpurified you invite the wrath of every god. By the time you crawl onto your cot tonight, you will wish you had never been born."

Now Huy's knees did give way. He would have collapsed at the High Priest's feet but for the man's inexorable grip on his neck. Grasping one of Huy's arms, the man pulled him roughly through the door, turned the massive key to lock it, and began to tow him past a series of cells from whose depths the murmur of voices rose. As they passed, a few curious heads poked out, but Huy was too distraught to note that he was in the middle of the quarters where the many priests attending to the temple's duties lived. He continued to sob from both fear and pain. His arm felt as though at any moment it would be parted from his shoulder, and he could not find his feet, the High Priest was moving so fast.

Presently they were joined by a younger priest and at last the High Priest's brisk pace slowed. A door was opened. Huy found himself hauled across grass then paving before being flung to the stone at the verge of a body of water he recognized, in spite of himself, as Ra's sacred lake. "Strip him," the High Priest ordered curtly. "Burn his kilt and his sandals. Cut off his youth lock and burn that also. It too is polluted. I want him scrubbed and shaved from his head to the soles of his feet. Then bring him to me." Picking Huy up, he tossed him into the water. By the time Huy came up for air, spluttering and gasping, the High Priest was striding away and the younger man was lowering himself into the lake.

"I can't imagine what evil you have done," he said, reaching for the knife Huy saw resting beside a pot of natron on the lip of the water, "but it must have been serious. Our High Priest is a very holy man and is considered merciful and just. Stand still while I detach your lock." Exhausted beyond protest, Huy saw his precious braid with its white ribbon tossed onto the bank. His kilt followed. Silently the priest used the same knife to none too gently shave Huy's scalp. Then he set about the small body with the natron and a cloth. Huy had no recollection of when either knife or salt, or the second priest for that matter, had been collected. He stood woodenly under the man's handling, hiccuping occasionally, as yet too numb with shock to grieve for the loss of his youth lock and what that would mean.

Before long he was taken into a kiosk not far from the water, dumped onto a slab, oiled, and shaved again, this time over every part of his body. He submitted dumbly although the process hurt him. "Now I wash off the oil," the priest said at last, and once again Huy was thrown into the lake. Shivering more from reaction than from cold, he was commanded to stand on the stone rim until the now-westering sun had dried him. The man slipped plain papyrus sandals onto his feet. "You are purified," he said. "I must return you to the High Priest." The sandals were too big for Huy and he stumbled as he made to follow. The priest turned. "Do not fall or I must complete your purification all over again," he said sharply, "and I must go to perform my evening devotions. I have no more time to spend on you."

They re-entered the temple. After knocking twice on
an imposing set of double doors just within the long line
of cells Huy had been dragged past earlier, the man left
him without another word. Huy, who was recovering a
little of his usual aplomb, just had time to bitterly regret
his habitual and secretive disobedience, curse Pabast,
and wish that his uncle had never heard of the temple
school at Iunu when the doors were opened and the
High Priest appeared.

Carefully he inspected Huy, then nodded. "Good.
Now we will return to the Tree."

Oh gods, Huy thought dully as he shuffled after the
Master's straight spine. *He is going to put a rope around
my neck and hang me from one of those twisted branches
and I will die unjustified and Mother and Father will be
disgraced forever.* But this time he was sufficiently
recovered to take a small interest in a portion of the
temple that was new to him. Some of the priests
lounging outside their cells smiled at him. Music
drifted into the wide passage from somewhere in the
inner court, the click of finger cymbals punctuating the
sweet rise and fall of women's voices and the trilling of
lyres. The sounds served to blunt a little of Huy's glum
fatalism. He could smell food. Something delicious was
being prepared for the priests' evening meal and it
seemed somehow inexcusable to Huy that the odour
should make him hungry when he was about to die.

The now-familiar door loomed, the huge key still
in its lock. Turning it, the High Priest indicated with a
jerk of his head that Huy should enter, then he
followed and closed the door carefully behind them.
The sun had already sunk below the level of the temple

walls, and the enclosure holding the Tree was growing dim. The clustered leaves were motionless, forming a thick umbrella under which the coming darkness was quickly gathering. Huy, naked and resigned, felt once again the peculiar otherness of the place. He glanced about surreptitiously for the rope that would be knotted around his throat.

"Take off your sandals and make three prostrations," the High Priest said. "Then repeat these words of apology and veneration after me." Huy did as he was told, kneeling and putting his nose to the earth. The third time the High Priest's foot descended onto his back, holding him down while the Priest chanted the short litany and Huy followed. "Now get up and bow," the man said crisply. "Do you know what you are looking at?"

"No, Master," Huy gulped. "Are you going to kill me now?"

"Kill you? No. You are nothing but an ignorant child who is paying the price for wandering where he should not. You will be handed to Overseer Harmose and whipped, and you will go to bed without food in order that you might always remember this day."

As if I could forget it, Huy thought, heartened by the knowledge that he was not in fact living his final moments. "Master, why is this tree holy?" he dared to ask.

The High Priest gave him a wintry smile. "This is the Tree of Life, the Ished Tree," he answered. "Some call it the Family Tree, but that is not correct. It holds within it the full knowledge of the mysteries of good and evil. Atum himself planted it here when he created the All out of the Nun, and every High Priest of Ra has tended it since the beginning. Other temples have been given shoots of it in case it should die, but it is old beyond the reckoning of the wisest and it continues to flourish. So, my young criminal, you have seen something no one but High Priests and temple guards has ever seen." Taking Huy's chin, he tilted up his face and scrutinized it keenly. "For some odd reason I believe that this truth is safe with you," he said slowly. "I don't know why. You have an air about you. Tell me, can you smell the Tree?"

Huy nodded. The sweet yet pungent aroma had been strengthening with the darkness. "Yes, I can. It smells like honey and garlic and my father's orchard blossoms and something else, something not so nice." He hesitated, afraid that he had inadvertently committed yet another act of sacrilege, but the Priest's expression did not change. "Maybe like my father's leg when the cat scratched it and it oozed and wouldn't heal and Mother had to put willow sap on it."

The Priest removed his hand. "I smell nothing. The Tree only gives off its odours to me when its crop hangs heavy on the branches. Then I collect every fruit and make a fire within this enclosure and burn them all. To eat is forbidden. Who are you?" he murmured. "Did the god mean you to stumble into this place? All the same," he added firmly, "you must take your punishment. I will summon Harmose and we will hear the story of your misdemeanours before he brandishes the willow switch."

The following hour, before Huy was able to crawl painfully onto his couch, was the most humiliating of his life. Standing before the High Priest and the Overseer in the former's reception room, he was forced to confess the idiocy of the whole day and by inference admit to having entered the proscribed areas of kitchens, gardens, and animal pens on many occasions. Then, still naked, he was marched to his own compound and given six stripes with the willow switch in full view of his classmates, who gathered to watch with varying degrees of amusement or sympathy. When he heard his sentence, Huy had been relieved. Six stripes—how bad could that be? But the willow was sharp and whippy. Each blow stung unbearably, and by the time the six welts were swelling on his back, he was in tears. The Overseer had proclaimed blasphemy as the reason for Huy's punishment, and when he had tucked the switch under his arm and gone away and the small crowd had dispersed, Thothmes came close.

"Put your arm across my shoulders and lean on me," he said as Huy limped awkwardly towards the blessed privacy of their cell. "What on earth did you do that was so terrible, Huy? Try to get into the Holiest of Holiest?"

But Huy, shaking his head, could only answer, "I saw something I wasn't supposed to." Thothmes could get no more out of him. Although he had not been ordered to remain silent regarding the presence of the Ished Tree in the temple, he did so out of a sense that there had been a message for him under its spreading panoply, a communication that remained unintelligible long after his wounds had healed and the other pupils had ceased to tease him. The High Priest's words had meant little, indeed he was not sure that he understood any of them apart from the fact that Atum had planted the Tree and it was sacred. But the Tree had touched him deep in his ka, and to speak of it would have made him feel as though he were committing another act of blasphemy.

He had expected to be shunned by his fellows. After all, he had been disgraced in their presence and censured by the High Priest himself. But he found to his surprise that his adventures had imbued him with a certain prestige. He had ventured where most of them dared not go. Like an explorer, he had placed himself in danger, not mortal perhaps but glamorous all the same, and he had charted the forbidden areas of the temple and returned with tales to relate to envious and less-enterprising boys. But of that final peril he did not speak, hugging it to himself in the night, reliving each moment from the time he had seen the triangular shadow by the wall. The details, rather than fading in his memory, grew brighter. He was not aware that his very reticence prompted a flurry of speculation and rumour, and even Sennefer, after one vicious dig in Huy's ribs and a whispered, "I don't care how popular you've made yourself, you're still just a peasant," retired to both glower and reluctantly be in awe of him with the others.

But the removal of Huy's youth lock was still a shameful brand that caused him great distress. His hair grew back slowly, first as a clump of short black bristle and then as a single curl that bobbed like a ridiculous animal's tail. He tried not to shrink with embarrassment when Pabast made his regular visit to the cell to shave him and Thothmes. The servant made no comment regarding his condition, but his silent attitude of disdain spoke volumes. In his idle moments Huy took to tugging vainly at his lock in the hope that he might lengthen it more quickly.

He continued to progress well in his studies, and by the time the school closed just before the month of the Inundation he had mastered the majority of the symbols making up his language and could read and memorize the simple and improving maxims his teacher set. His written work was still untidy and unformed, but no more so than that of his classmates. He had not forgotten his promise to the priest at Hut-herib, but he knew he was not yet skilled enough to compose a letter of which he could be proud. One day, perhaps in the next year, he would.

At the end of Mesore, the last month of a burning hot summer, both teachers and pupils went home. The harvest had begun the month before, but Huy was the only boy whose father might have needed help in the fields and Huy was still too young to be of any use. Classes would reconvene at the end of Tybi, and Huy, although he was eager to see his parents and Ishat again, felt rather glum. The seven months he had been in the temple school had passed swiftly. He had come to love the work, to accept and even appreciate the routines binding him to compound and schoolroom, and would miss the companionship of the other pupils, particularly Thothmes. "I shall miss you too," Thothmes said as they packed their belongings. "Being at home will be wonderful at first. My sisters will fuss over me and Father has promised me a gift for completing the year and I'm looking forward to more sweetmeats and less vegetables. But I think that after a while I shall be bored." He hopped up onto the edge of his couch and began to swing his legs. "Perhaps you can come and stay with me for a day or two once the river has started to shrink."

"Perhaps." Huy was wrapping his statue of Khenti-kheti in linen before placing it on top of his sennet game at the bottom of one of his leather bags. "But it will depend on my uncle, whether he has business in Iunu at the right time." He straightened and met Thothmes' serene gaze "My father can't afford to hire a barge to bring me back here."

Thothmes made a face. "I keep forgetting that you're poor," he said matter-of-factly. "But Huy, you are doing so well at your studies that one day you will be hired to scribe for a very rich and fussy man who will want only the best. Then you will have your very own barge."

"That's years away." Huy had begun to sort through the pile of kilts. "Look at this, Thothmes. Half these kilts aren't mine."

"Take them anyway. The linen is a better grade than the ones you came with. Can I see your scarab once more before you put it away?" Reverently Huy handed over the box and together they peered down at the beetle's gleaming carapace. "I expect Father could order one of the servants out onto the desert to get me one," Thothmes went on, "but it wouldn't be the same. This is your lucky charm." He drew back.

Huy closed the box and it disappeared into one of the bags. "That's everything. Just imagine, Thothmes—next year we wear yellow ribbons!" They grinned at one another. "I must go and say goodbye to Harnakht. He's probably with Kay. Are you coming?"

Thothmes slid to his feet. "When we grow up, you must try and marry my sister Anuket," he said as they walked out into the bright morning. "That way you can live here at Iunu and we can see each other all the time."

"Oh, I'm never going to get married!" Huy protested. "Imagine having to share a house with a girl! Much better to share one with you."

Ker had arrived the night before, and after a quick visit with the Overseer of the School he had slept aboard his barge. Now he waited for Huy at the foot of the ramp and Huy, seeing the craft rocking gently, felt a surge of excitement in spite of having to leave Thothmes. He would sleep in the cabin without the fear that had dogged him on his way to an unknown future. He began to run, dragging his bags across the crowded concourse, and Ker held out his arms. "This time I can take you home!" he exclaimed as Huy dropped his burden and flung himself at his uncle. "I do believe you've grown again! Your mother is very anxious to see you. She sends her love. So does your aunt." He picked up the bags as Huy ran up the ramp, and signalled to the helmsman.

"I'm still not tall enough to see over the rail," Huy said as the ramp was hauled in and the sailors manned the oars. "Lift me up, Uncle. I want to see the temple get smaller behind us." Ker set him on the rail, holding him tightly, and the barge began to nose its way towards the canal and the river beyond. "Isn't it a mighty pylon!" Huy said happily. "I'm not frightened of it anymore!"

"I should think not," Ker murmured dryly, "seeing that you know not only the pylon but the lake and the outer court and a lot more besides. You haven't been an altogether model pupil, have you. The Overseer told me about your escapades and the whipping you were given, but he failed to mention the removal of your youth lock. Your hair's the same length it was when I deposited you here. Why did they cut it off? It must have been for something more serious than a few forays into the kitchens and pens."

They had almost reached the river. The sailors had temporarily shipped the oars so that the helmsman could control the drift that would carry the barge into the north-flowing current. *They haven't told him,* Huy thought. *Why not? Did the High Priest order the Overseer and the teachers to be quiet about my dreadful offence? Perhaps people who don't know about the Tree aren't supposed to know unless they find it by accident as I did or they work in the temple itself.* He tensed. *I don't want to talk about it, even to Uncle Ker, and I don't want to tell a lie either.*

"I did do something worthy of my punishment, Uncle," he said carefully, "but it was in ignorance. If the Overseer hasn't spoken of it to you, then I would like to keep it to myself. I mean you no insult." His uncle's hold on him did not change. Huy waited in trepidation for stern words, his eyes on the last sparkle of the canal as the chaotic river frontage of the city began, and was surprised when Ker chuckled.

"Is this the same self-willed, inconsiderate boy who gave his god an inferior gift and would pout if he was denied the smallest thing? I am amazed at the change in you, Huy. You have just admitted your guilt with an honest excuse, refused to speak of the matter because you think it would not be appropriate to do so, and apologized to me for any offence your attitude might cause. Truly, the schooling here is beyond reproach!"

Huy had not viewed his little speech in quite that light. He was all at once very pleased with himself. Wriggling free of Ker's grip, he slipped to the deck and ran to the opposite railing. "I want to see the monuments of the Osiris-ones before we sail past them," he called. "Will you lift me up again, Uncle?"

Ker joined him and together they watched the lordly pyramids on the plain of Saqqara drift by, the majestic sight reducing both of them to silence. Behind them the helmsman shouted a command, feet pattered across the deck, and Huy heard the unfurled lateen sail suddenly billow as it took the wind. Oars were shipped with a clatter and the barge's progress quickened. Huy sighed with delight. He was not in a hurry to get home. He hoped they would tie up by the riverbank and eat by firelight as they had done before, but he was too polite to ask if it was possible. He had begun to learn that he was not in fact at the centre of the world, nor was he a special favourite of the gods. His concerns were of no more importance to them than those of the next child. Nor were they of much interest to the adults who controlled his destiny, apart from his mother, of course. She had always cared more about what he wanted than about her own needs. His uncle loved him, but if business was calling him back to Hut-herib there would be no leisurely frying of fish under the stars. It did not occur to Huy that he was accepting the idea without his usual rancour. He was wondering if Ishat was looking forward to seeing him again.

They did indeed spend the night anchored almost opposite the place where the barge had stopped all those months ago. The fish tasted as delicious as before, the stars were just as beautiful, and this time Ker allowed Huy to curl up and sleep in a blanket beside the water. He himself chose the cabin. "I'm getting too old to enjoy the hard ground under me," he joked to Huy, "and I'm not worried that you'll run away. The sailor over there is for your protection."

Huy clapped his hands. He had never spent the night out of doors before. "Thank you, Uncle! Were you really afraid that I might run away?"

"I presumed that your last weeks at home were miserable," Ker answered matter-of-factly, "and if I had been you I would have been considering many ways to avoid my fate." He smiled. "You are not such a mystery, Huy. Your father kept a sharp eye on you in case you tried to enlist Ishat in some mad scheme of escape."

Huy was astonished and rather nettled. Adults were not as dull-witted as he had supposed. "I did try to think of something," he admitted, "but there was really nowhere to go." He glanced at the fire, now little more than glowing embers. "Uncle Ker, I almost hated you for sending me to school, and I made a big fuss about it. But it was a wise and generous thing for you to do." Embarrassed, he dug a toe into the still-warm earth. "I have learned a lot and I am grateful." Ker was gracious enough not to laugh, but Huy caught the twitch of his mouth.

"You've only just begun the journey," Ker said, "and I am already being amply repaid, I assure you, my brave little delinquent!" He held out a blanket. "Here. Find yourself a hollow, and if anything alarms you in the night, come back aboard. Sleep well."

Huy chose a spot in the open, near the fire and well within calling distance of the sailor stretched out and already breathing heavily not far away. He was more worried about snakes and spiders than about any human threat. The darkness was not absolute. The moon stood almost at the full, its cool light making blurred shadows of the trees and obscuring the stars closest to it, and the sky all around it was thick with white stars. Water slapped lazily against the barge's dim bulk. Some small creature slid through the reeds clustered at the river's edge, making them whisper briefly before a dreaming silence descended once again.

For a long time Huy lay on his back, hands behind his head, entirely content. The night air smelled of mud and wet greenness and the tang of smouldering ashes. He thought of Thothmes, and wondered how he was enjoying his first night at home with his adoring family. He thought of his empty cell, the mattress rolled up on his cot, waiting for him to return. Finally, as it always did, his mind turned to the sacred Ished Tree, and he fell asleep with the sound of its foliage murmuring in his ears.

They disembarked at the docks of Hut-herib in the middle of the following morning. With the favourable current the return trip had taken less time even though the river was at its lowest level. Ker's litter-bearers were already waiting, and while Ker gave instructions to the helmsman, Huy said goodbye to the sailors, grabbed up his bags, and left the barge, clambering onto the litter with a sigh of both regret and anticipation. The docks were quiet at this time of the year. With the river so low, vessels from the Great Green were few and the town had a weary, rather shabby feel. Ker joined Huy, and soon they were being carried away from the tributary. The mounds on which Hut-herib was built were no longer isolated by the water that would soon surround them. Some of the deeper ditches remained muddy and were full of straggling flags of marsh growth, but most of them lay grey and cracked, waiting to be filled. Huy wrinkled his nose; they smelled rank. The fields to the east were bare, the black earth baking in the sun, the lines of palms that delineated them dusty and drooping. Huy was glad to see the horizon fill with the familiar cluster of his uncle's orchard and the row of sycamores marking the entrance to his own home.

The bearers set the litter down outside the house and at once there was a flurry of activity within. Huy barely had time to scramble off the cushions before his mother rushed out and, swinging him off his feet, crushed him to her. The sweet aroma of lilies enfolded him. "Darling darling Huy! You're so thin! Have you grown? Yes, I think so! Hapzefa has cooked your favourite food and your room is all ready for you. Has this year been so awful for you? Welcome home!"

Huy suffered himself to be soundly kissed before struggling against her. "Put me down, Mother! I'm fine! I love you very much and I am so happy to see you." He looked up at the brown eyes alight with joy, the well-remembered curve of her smiling mouth, and suddenly he meant what he had said. He grasped her hand. "Home is wonderful!" he almost shouted.

His father had emerged and was waiting. Huy flung himself at the broad chest and Hapu's arms closed around him. "I have not been altogether a good boy, but I have studied hard," he said, his face against his father's neck. "I think you can be proud of me."

Hapu set him on his feet. "I would have liked to visit your school with Ker," he said gravely, "but the season has been a busy one. Perhaps when you return I will accompany you. Welcome, my son. Your aunt will be arriving soon and then we will celebrate. Go and unpack your bags."

His room was unchanged, just as he had left it. As he stood in the doorway, his eyes travelled the well-known cracks in the ceiling, the lamp beside the couch. He inhaled, taking in the scent of the freshly washed linen, a hint of Hapzefa's sweat, and surely the faintest whiff of his own body. There was no sign of the monkey. Huy let out his breath in relief and wondered where his mother had hidden it. He hoped that his aunt Heruben would not ask about it. And where was Ishat? He began to empty his bags, lifting the lid of his very own chest and placing the kilts and loincloths inside, lining up the spare pair of sandals under the couch, setting the sennet game and the scarab's box and his statue of Khenti-kheti on the table. He could hear the murmur of adult conversation drifting in from the garden as he searched for his paints. He was eager to show his family everything he had learned, and the walls of the house would be perfect for a demonstration, but perhaps he ought to wait a day or two; otherwise he would seem to be boasting. Huy sat on his cot and closed his eyes. It was indeed wonderful to be home.

No one asked him about the monkey, but there were many questions about the school. Huy talked eagerly with his family's eyes upon him, his mother's shining with pride, his father's with approval. Even Hapzefa smiled at him and did not seem to care that he had spilled a little garlic sauce on his kilt. Ker and Heruben listened smugly. This was their doing, and their love for him was mingled with a different kind of approval than that of his mother. Hapzefa had made honey cakes in his honour. He thanked her politely after devouring most of them himself. It was blissful to once again be the adored centre of attention, but now Huy was careful to inquire of both his uncle and his father how good the crop yield had been, of his mother and Hapzefa how the juice and beer making had gone, of his uncle if he was pleased with this year's perfume distilling. They were clearly amused, though they answered him soberly. Huy thought he might quote from the maxims of Ptahhotep regarding the correct behaviour of children to those in authority over them, but decided against it. He knew, and they were discovering, that he had changed. Very soon he would be five years old, and well on his way to becoming a responsible person.

Yet all the time they ate and drank, gathered happily in the shade while the long afternoon began, Huy had been wondering where Ishat was. He did not want to spoil his parents' pleasure by betraying his need to see her, a need greater than his own gladness at being with them, but he was disappointed that she was not there.

Perhaps she doesn't like me anymore, he thought, even while he was talking about Thothmes' sisters. *Perhaps she's found someone else to play with.*

"They must be very rich, to have such pretty things," his mother was saying. "I'm happy to see you still wearing the Nefer amulet I gave you, Huy." She suppressed a yawn. "All this excitement has made me sleepy. It's time to rest anyway."

Ker and Heruben got up. "Bring Huy for a visit next week," Heruben said. "We all need some diversion. Waiting for Isis to cry can be nerve-racking." She smiled at Huy. "I hope you still know how to throw an occasional temper tantrum, Huy," she continued. "Otherwise we shall begin to believe that some demon has stolen our demanding little treasure and replaced him with the incredibly well-mannered child who has been entertaining us today."

"Don't say that, Heruben!" Huy's mother cried out. "Not even in jest!"

Ker signalled the litter-bearers, who had been fed under the sycamores. "We have a gift for you, Huy, when you come. Heruben, the litter is ready. Thank you for your hospitality, Hapu."

The family watched the litter sway out of sight.

Huy's mother put an arm around his shoulders. "Will you sleep now? I expect it will be good to be on your own couch again."

Huy shook his head. "I think I'll lie by the pond and see what the frogs are doing."

She laughed fondly. "Of course you'll want to do that. Your father and I are going to our room. Don't stay in the sun too long!"

It was not a lie, Huy told himself once he was alone. I will look for the frogs. But mostly I want Ishat to come out of the shrubbery.

As though his thought had conjured her, there was a stirring in the bushes by the gate to the orchard and she stepped into view, coming to him barefooted over the grass, her black hair neatly tied back with a leather thong, her kilt stiff and spotless. "I waited until they'd gone," she said. "Your father invited me to eat with you, but I wanted you to myself. I hung about in the orchard for hours and now I'm starving. Is there any food left?"

"Hapzefa took it back to the kitchen. We can go and look if you like."

They regarded one another cautiously for a while, then Ishat giggled. "Where's all your hair? Is that squiggle above your ear supposed to be a nobleman's youth lock?"

Huy was annoyed. "All of us pupils wear the youth lock," he said pompously. "Mine was much longer. But then they cut it off," he finished lamely.

She took hold of it and tugged it sharply. "Why? Wouldn't it grow straight?"

He pulled out of her grip. "It was because I got caught in a place I shouldn't have been," he began, and to his inward amazement he found himself telling her all about the Ished Tree. She listened solemnly, and when he fell silent she too was quiet, her eyes on his face.

"So Atum planted this tree in Iunu," she said at last, "and it is a magic tree with the secret of good and evil in it. Why did he do that?"

Huy blinked. "I don't know."

"Well, why put such a tree in Egypt and then not let anyone learn the secret so that everyone could know good and evil and stay away from evil and we would all be happy? It sounds silly to me."

Huy's mind filled with an image of the Tree, its atmosphere of otherness, its strange, compelling scent that was underpinned with something vaguely repugnant. "You would have to see it, Ishat," he said slowly. "The reason for the act of the god and the presence of the Tree in Egypt is surely more complicated than we think."

She shrugged. "I still can't see why they punished you for just looking at it. Have you still got my scarab?" She was finished with the subject of the Tree.

At one time Huy would have answered her abrupt question with an equally sharp retort. Indeed it was on the tip of his tongue to say, "It's not your scarab. You gave it to me and it's mine now." Instead, he looked indignant. "Of course! I kept it by my couch all year. Everyone wanted to see it, but I only let my special friend Thothmes hold it."

She was obviously pleased, but after the grin his words produced, she scowled. "I am your special friend, Huy, not some spoiled little boy you only just met. Did he give you anything as nice as the scarab?"

"No, he didn't," Huy answered truthfully, and decided not to tell her about Thothmes' sisters or the wealth and generosity of his parents.

"All right, then." She was mollified. "Have you learned anything useful at your school? Can you write my name? Show me!"

"Come over to the pond." She followed him to where the earth around the verge lay brown and bare, waiting for Itu to plant more vegetables. Leaning over, he sprinkled a few handfuls of water onto the soil and smoothed it out with his palm. Carefully he drew the hieroglyphs that spelled *Ishat*.

She stared down at the word doubtfully. "That is my name? That says 'Ishat'?"

"Yes. Now you do it."

But she drew away. "I'll get my best kilt dirty if I touch the mud. Mother starched it and made me wear it in your honour. Besides, Huy, what use is it? If I can say 'Ishat' and everyone else can say 'Ishat,' why bother to write it?"

He was unable to define her attitude as defensiveness. He interpreted it as a peasant's inability to understand anything beyond the immediately practical. Ishat was clever. She could tie any number of complicated knots. She could blow out an egg without destroying the shell, lure a pigeon into a net, make a desert dog follow her, she knew what flowers could be sucked for their sweet nectar and which were poisonous. But she saw no point in something as seemingly abstract as writing. Huy did not try to explain it to her. It would be no use, and that knowledge made him suddenly sad.

She was standing above him as he knelt by the pool, her eyes narrowed against the harsh sunlight of the afternoon, one sturdy foot over the other and an expression of defiance on her face.

"I love you, Ishat," he blurted.

"Don't be silly." Her features cleared. "Well, Huy, what shall we do? You don't have to go back to Iunu for five whole months. All of Akhet! Let's go into the orchard and see what fruit has been left on the trees. I'd rather eat fruit than my mother's cooking. The wasps are bad this year, so watch out. My father couldn't find all their nests. You know, a goose bit me this spring when I was in the fields trying to keep them away from the new seed your father was strewing. I hit it with my stick and it ran at me and attacked my leg. Your father went to the market and got me sweetmeats."

She is not really interested in what my life has been like at Iunu, Huy thought as he followed her through the gate. *All she cares about is that I'm home and we can play together again. I feel hentis older than her now. Oh, I don't want anything to change between us, Ishat! Why do things have to be different!*

Before too many weeks had passed, Huy found himself settling into his old routines both with Ishat and with the household. Hapzefa took to scolding him absently again. He became careless about keeping his room tidy. He and Ishat spent endless hours in the garden and the fields until the Inundation began and the land slowly filled. For a while only the irrigation canals held water. The two children often stripped on a hot afternoon and ran in and out of the murky water. They were far from the river's tributary, which was just as well, Huy decided. He did not want to tell Ishat that he had learned to swim. It was a skill she would appreciate, being a swimmer herself, but Huy could already sense a time ahead when his pursuits and hers would diverge and they would have nothing left to share. For the present he was increasingly content to slip back into their old, easy relationship, and the moments of dislocation became fewer and weaker.

His uncle and aunt had given him not only a new set of paints but a roll of papyrus and a scribe's palette complete with brushes, containers for ink, and an ivory paper burnisher. "The paints are for now," Heruben explained, "but the scribe's utensils you must put away until you graduate to papyrus at school. We are just so proud of you, Huy!"

Huy had thanked them profusely, handling the objects curiously and holding the papyrus to his nose. It did not smell at all like a plant, indeed it had hardly any odour at all. The beaten weave of it fascinated him and he asked Ker how it was made. "I will take you to the papermaker in town," Ker said. "You can see it all being done. The papyrus is truly a useful and magical plant. It is sacred to Hathor, and was not Horus himself born in the papyrus marsh at Chemmis, here in the Delta? A papyrus thicket marks the frontier between life and death. Always treat it with respect, plant and paper both."

"There is no point in taking it with you to Iunu this spring," Hapu had said firmly when they returned home. "It will be several years before you leave the pottery shards behind. Give it to your mother to store away safely. You don't want it stolen, do you?"

So, reluctantly, after several evenings spent handling and dreaming over his new acquisitions, he took the palette and papyrus roll to Itu. She was in the room she shared with her husband, changing the linen on his couch, when Huy peered round the door. "Come in, Huy," she said. "Have you finished gloating over your presents?"

"I did not gloat. I was trying to imagine what it will be like to set them across my knees like the scribes and actually begin to take the dictation of my employer."

Itu dropped the armful of sheets on the floor and sank onto her own couch. "How humid it is today!" she complained. "Before long the mosquitoes will begin to fly out of the canals. Put your things in my chest, Huy. They won't be disturbed."

She watched him cross to the wall and lift the lid of the chest. Then he paused. "You still have it," he said. "I can see one paw sticking out under your sheaths."

"You really hate it, don't you, my darling? It is rather sinister, I admit. Perhaps you will appreciate its value when you are older."

Huy had drawn away from the chest, the palette still in his hands. "I don't think so, Mother," he said steadily, though he could feel his hands grow cold. "Would you please put my things away? I don't want the monkey to know I'm here."

Itu slid off the couch. "You and your funny fancies!" she said kindly. "You're still just a little boy, aren't you, Huy, in spite of your grown-up language and the new gravity you came home with. Very well. Give it to me." Huy did not relax until the lid of the chest banged closed. "Hapzefa has been slicing watermelon," Itu went on. "Let's go and have some."

Huy made sure that he was not the last one out of the room.

On the first day of the month of Thoth, New Year's Day, the whole country celebrated the rising of the Sothis star, which always heralded the beginning of the Inundation, with a sacrifice to Amun. Every month held its feast days, but those of this month, the first of winter, were observed with a fervency born of relief. Isis had begun to cry. Once again there would be silt for the crops and plenty of water to fill the canals. The ceremony of the Opening of the Dikes took place, the King performing the first ritual and every farmer with dams across his canals following suit. The Chief Royal Scribe noted, as always, the exact day, month, and year of the King when "the water returned." People everywhere held parties, throwing gifts, flowers, and often themselves into the river. It was a time for fishing and fowling, and on Ker's arouras the grapes hung heavy and lusciously red, waiting to be harvested. On the nineteenth day of the month Thoth himself was honoured, and on the twenty-second the Feast of the Great Manifestation of Osiris was held. Hapu and the gardeners were too busy filling their baskets with grapes to do more than say a few perfunctory prayers during a morning's holiday from work, but Huy, mouth and fingers temporarily stained purple with grape juice, stood in the privacy of his room and thought for the first time about the god who had given the civilizing gift of the written word to Egypt. Although the statue of Hut-herib's totem graced his bedside table, it was to mighty Thoth that he prayed, thanking the god for his wisdom and begging that his remaining years at school would result in skills that would make his father proud of him. "And please keep me away from any more mischief," he finished before rushing out to join Ishat by the grapevines. He still had four more months in which to enjoy himself before his uncle's barge bore him away again.

4

The years that followed were largely uneventful for Huy, but not for his mother, who gave birth to another boy four months after Huy's eleventh birthday. Surprised and perhaps a little embarrassed, Hapu went into the market and hired a scribe, dictating the news to Huy, who received it at school with mixed feelings. He had known that his mother was pregnant and had watched the tumult of rejoicing and congratulations with a somewhat jaundiced eye. All his life he had been the family favourite, the only son of adoring parents and the darling of a childless aunt and uncle who had spoiled him outrageously. Now he would have to share the attention. He had returned to school before the actual birth and for that he was grateful. Fleetingly he wondered, in a flash of jealousy, whether his new brother would usurp his place in the affections of the family, seeing that for seven months of each year he was not at home to remind everyone of how much they loved him.

But his resentment soon faded. The focus of his life had gradually been shifting from Hut-herib to the school at Iunu. Immersed in his studies, involved more and more with Thothmes' family, he knew that he was forging a future of his own. The baby had been named Heby. According to Hapu's letter he had been born on one of Mekhir's lucky days, was healthy, and had his mother's eyes. Huy wrote back, "As Mekhir falls within the season of growing I pray, dear Father, that Heby may spring up as strong and straight as Ker's many flowers. Give Mother all my love." He used one of the precious rolls of papyrus Ker had given to him after his first year at school. His command of language was almost complete. He could read any document with relative ease, but he still wrote laboriously, forming the hieroglyphs with slow care. He had begun to study hieratic, the scribe's fast-flowing substitute for the more formal and beautiful glyphs, but it would be another two years before the dusty shards of broken pottery over which he had sweated were a nuisance of the past.

His youth lock had eventually returned to its former length and then continued to grow. Now it hung well below his collarbone. White ribbons had given way to yellow, blue, red, and now a simple copper arm band, and Huy looked forward to his twelfth year when he would be allowed to wear the coveted gold arm band and tie his braid with anything he chose. He would also be given the care of a new boy as Harnakht had been responsible for him. Each Tybi he watched them come, bewildered, sometimes frightened, always homesick, and remembering his own first few weeks at the school he did his best to be kind to them.

Although he knew his classmates well and liked them all, but for Sennefer who continued to treat him with an often wounding contempt, it was Thothmes who had become Huy's best friend. With the greater freedom accorded his age and a good record of behaviour he was able to spend every feast day with Thothmes' family. The large estate bordering the river, with its gilded furniture and host of servants, had long since ceased to awe him and he basked in the attentions of Thothmes' two remaining sisters, Nasha and Anuket. Meri-Hathor, the eldest, had married and now lived with her husband farther upriver.

Nasha reminded Huy of Ishat. Vital and energetic, she was always ready to explore the city's markets or go fishing or pole a skiff through the marshes so that Thothmes could practise, rather ineffectually, with his father's throwing stick. Huy, as the son of a commoner, was not allowed to handle the nobleman's weapon, but he was happy to sit in the skiff beside Nasha while she hurled good-natured insults at her brother, who had launched the stick at some safe and quite indifferent duck. "I really don't want to kill anything," Thothmes confessed on more than one occasion, "but Father insists that I try," and Nasha would snort and call him a girl. Open, frank, and impulsive, she was what Ishat might be, given an education and an arsenal of social graces. Huy still loved the playmate of his childhood. Going home always meant hours idled away in her company, but they were hours taken out of the stream of thought and discipline his life had become, a minor tributary up which he ventured, happily and temporarily, and where he could fully rest.

It was Anuket, Thothmes' youngest sister, to whom Huy felt most drawn. Older than he by one year, she had the delicate features of her noble bloodline. At twelve she had entered what for most girls was an awkward stage of gangling limbs and clumsy movement, and Anuket was no exception. But her eyes seemed to hold a constant, quiet wonder at the world around her as she performed her household chores or wove the garlands needed to present to the gods on their feast days. Huy often found her in the garden or the herb room, legs crossed and head down over some new, flowery creation, and his first urge, swiftly quelled, was always to gather up the long tress of her black hair hanging over one thin shoulder and press it to his face. He did not know what she thought of him. She was not shy, but reserved. Nasha would grab and kiss him, tease and jostle him as she did Thothmes, but Anuket simply smiled and kissed his cheek whenever he visited the house. She talked to him readily enough, laughed at his jokes, even made some of her own, but her self-containment seemed impregnable. "Actually, she thinks you're quite wonderful," Thothmes had assured him once when Huy had voiced his doubts. "She just doesn't see any need to make a show of it. She doesn't maul me either, and I'm her brother! Don't worry, Huy. She'll make you a fine wife!" But Huy, increasingly conscious of the gulf between himself and these aristocrats, although he was comfortable with them, did not believe that Anuket would be permitted to wed a lowly scribe.

The King was in his fiftieth year on the Horus Throne, and Thothmes, his namesake, faithfully entered the inner court of Ra's temple, feet bare and an offering in his hands, to pray for the continued good health of his hero when the King's Anniversary of Appearing took place. Huy sometimes accompanied him, waiting in the outer court while the solemn little figure disappeared into the pillared gloom bearing his gift for the god. Huy never made fun of his friend's loyalty, unlike Sennefer, who jeered at Thothmes' obsession at every opportunity. "He still hates us," Huy said one evening when he and Thothmes, walking together across the concourse of the temple in the warm red glow of Ra's setting, had been pelted with mud by a grinning Sennefer, who had been standing waist-deep in the lake by the temple watersteps. "We have done nothing to antagonize him, and apart from those few weeks after I got caught roaming about the temple where I shouldn't and became a sort of hero, he's continued to persecute us."

"Sometimes I feel sorry for him," Thothmes put in tartly, trying to pick a wet clod from the hem of his kilt, "but only sometimes. He's jealous of me because my lineage is older than his, and he envies you your intelligence and good looks. He's too lazy to work hard and too much in love with his food to give any of it up. We must just ignore him. He hates that." He sighed. "I suppose we'd better stop by the bathhouse and wash off this mess."

By the time Huy went home at the end of Mesore, his brother was six months old, a placid, happy baby just learning to roll from his stomach onto his back. Itu often left him in the shade of the garden with Huy while she attended to her domestic duties. At first Huy, rather afraid of this plump scrap of humanity, protested, but he grew fond of Heby as the days went by, watching his chubby arms push against the grass until he flopped over. Then he would chuckle with delight and reach for Huy's nose as Huy bent over him. Later Huy was confident enough to put him in a sling and carry him about on his back. He particularly enjoyed the feel of that warm, tiny body against his spine when he stood painting or practising his characters on the whitewashed outer wall of the house.

Ishat had been hired to help Hapzefa with the cooking and cleaning while Itu attended to the baby's needs. At ten years old she was entirely capable of both, but to Huy she lamented the loss of her freedom. "Why couldn't everything have stayed the same?" she complained one evening as they sat together in the privacy of the orchard, safely away from any summons from the house. "Why did your mother have to go and get herself pregnant after so long? How did she do it?"

Huy knew that she was not asking about the process of sex; the joining of man to woman was no secret to the practical peasants of Hut-herib. He lifted one bronzed shoulder. "It had been so long since I was born," he replied diffidently. "I expect she saw no need to use the acacia spikes anymore. It's not so bad, Ishat. Heby is a sweet baby."

She began to brush the dust off the soles of her bare feet with brisk little slaps. "Well, it's all right for you," she snapped, not looking at him. "All you have to do is talk baby talk to him while he lies on the grass and gazes at you adoringly. I can't wade in the canals or climb the trees or chase the cats anymore. I'm too busy scouring pots and sweeping floors." The bitterness in her voice alarmed Huy.

"But it won't be forever, Ishat. Besides, it means more of everything for your family. Food, linens, fripperies for you and Hapzefa—"

She rounded on him savagely. "Do you think I care anything for ribbons and ornaments? Why should I want to be better than I am? Will ribbons make my skin pale like a fine lady? Will a piece of faience around my neck soften these calluses on my hands?" She waved them in his face. "You! Every time you come home your skin is softer, your manner is more lordly, your speech has lost more of its Delta accents. It wasn't so bad when we could run off and play together the way we always did—then the differences between us melted away. But now I am becoming a house servant like my mother and we can't have fun anymore and you'll soon stop seeing me as your friend! All because of that stupid baby!"

"But Ishat, you don't want to be a fine lady," he faltered. "You just said so. You want the freedom to run wild in the fields and canals."

"Oh, you are as dense as a tamarisk thicket!" she cried out. "Must I explain? I want to be whatever you would like me to be. I don't want to lose you, Huy!"

He took one of her flailing hands in both of his, feeling the rough palms, the coarsened tips of the long fingers. "I am little better than you," he tried to reassure her. "Even though he has many arouras to care for, my father is still a gardener."

She snatched her hand away. "But you will be something more," she half whispered. Tears had begun to trickle down her cheeks. "Already you have those noble friends you told me about, Thothmes and his sisters, and as a scribe you will know many more. You will leave me behind."

Guilt momentarily closed his mouth. He sat watching the full, trembling lips, the halo of untamed hair frothing past the hunched shoulders, the dark, moist eyes full of emotion. She had grazed her knee; it had scabbed over, and there was a thorn scratch on her thigh. All at once Huy ceased to see her as the little girl who had always been his playmate. She seemed to grow right under his gaze. Her arms and legs lengthened. Her face thinned. The buds of tiny breasts swelled almost imperceptibly on her naked chest, and he found himself looking at a strange young creature with Ishat's features.

"How could I leave you behind?" he said softly. "All my memories of home have you in them, Ishat. How can that be changed?"

Furiously she swiped at her eyes with the edge of her limp kilt. "My mother is going to put me in a sheath," she spat. "I have become a woman. And my father is already talking about finding me a husband within the next few years. A husband, Huy! Me! I don't want any stupid husband, and I certainly don't want any stupid babies! Oh, why can't everything stay the same?"

To that Huy had no answer. The thought of Ishat married to some labourer was as shocking as the revelation of her maturing that he had been too blind to see before. He was surprised at the twinge of possessive jealousy he felt. She was his. He himself, once he had recovered from the first anguish of being torn from his home and deposited at school, anticipated the gradual changes each new year had brought. But Ishat must not change, Ishat must always be here, Ishat must admire him unconditionally forever, no matter what he became or where he ended up.

She was watching him out of the corner of her eye. "You could marry me, Huy," she murmured. "Not yet, because neither of us is old enough. But if you told your father that you wanted to marry me later on, then my father would stop casting his net among the sons of his friends. You wouldn't make me cook and clean and have babies, would you?"

Huy was aghast. A vision of gentle Anuket, her white lap full of flowers, bloomed in his mind. "Ishat, I am years away from even finishing school, let alone thinking about supporting a wife!" he protested. He could not keep the panic out of his voice, and after one cold glance she scrambled to her feet and began to walk away.

"I did say not yet," she flung back over her shoulder. Huy watched her disappear into the dusk with a sense of relief that almost, but not quite, eclipsed the ache of his loss.

His Naming Day, his twelfth, was celebrated as usual with a visit to Khenti-kheti's shrine, and this time Huy offered his precious paints as a thanksgiving to the god. It was not that he believed his uncle would replace them, but the time was coming when he hoped to be able to buy them for himself. Each year since the episode with the skittles he had made an honest choice from among his possessions, and he looked forward to his visit with the priest who had given him such good advice. He now wrote to the man once a year and always received a letter back, full of kindness and humour. It was an odd relationship, but one Huy had come to value.

Afterwards there was the usual celebration in the garden. Huy spent most of the afternoon running after Heby, who at eight months was now crawling and determined to explore the invitation of the pool. Huy was uncomfortably aware of Ishat's scornful attention as each time he scooped the baby up and returned him to the shade. He had seen little of her since that awkward conversation in the orchard. She was avoiding him. There was nothing Huy could do about it. He could make her no promises. He missed her more acutely than he had imagined he would, and her absence made him lonely. He was very glad when Khoiak began and he could look forward to returning to school.

He endured the Feast of Hathor on the first of the month, and then it was time to say his farewells and join Ker on the barge that had become a delightful part of the ritual of each new academic year. The trip to Iunu passed pleasantly in conversation with his uncle and the sailors. Occasionally he was allowed to clamber up onto the prow and take the tiller, sitting high above a river already sinking to expose the little fields glistening wetly in the sun, and it seemed to him in those moments that his life was as firmly under his control as the great shaft of wood imprisoned in his hands. Hut-herib slid quietly from his consciousness and the mighty double walls and flagged pylon of Ra's temple filled the space the shabby Delta town had left.

His cell welcomed him with the aroma of fresh whitewash and a whiff of jasmine from the neatly folded sheets on his cot. Sighing with satisfaction, he dropped his two leather bags, both now considerably the worse for wear, on the floor, pushed the linen after them, and stretched out on his mattress. There was no sign of Thothmes, but Huy knew that his friend would appear after the evening meal. Closing his eyes, he listened as the emptiness of the compound began to fill with the familiar sounds of an old routine. Someone ran past his open door calling, "Those are my sandals, not yours, you idiot! You left yours by the bathhouse!" The shouted reply was lost as someone else, presumably a servant, dropped what must have been a basin of water and let forth a string of loud curses. The snatch of a song drifted across the grass, the boy's voice a high, true treble, followed by a gale of laughter and a scuffle. Lazily Huy was considering unpacking his goods and then going in search of something to eat when a shadow fell across his floor. He sat up. Harnakht stood with one hand on the lintel of the doorway, regarding him critically.

"As indolent as ever," he said with humour. "It's good to see you again, Huy. How was your summer?"

Huy came to his feet and eyed his old guardian with interest. Harnakht's head almost brushed the ceiling. His youth lock was gone. One plain golden hooped earring trembled against his neck and two bracelets tinkled on his left wrist. His eyes were kohled and his mouth hennaed.

"You look wonderful, Harnakht," Huy said enviously. "I didn't expect you to be back at school this year.

You've shaved your whole head at last. I wondered why you kept the lock for so long." He shrugged. "My summer was much as usual. I was busy with my new brother, though, so I had no time for archery." In truth he had stowed away the bow and handful of arrows he had taken home and forgotten about them.

Harnakht tutted. "You'll be sore and out of practice next week and you'll be punished," he retorted. "Same old Huy, doing exactly what you want in spite of the consequences. I'm back for one more year to study military tactics. I've decided to make the army my career. My father is happy enough." He stepped farther into the room. "But I didn't seek you out for the pleasure of your company, young miscreant. The Overseer sent me. You are to shepherd one of the new boys for the first month. He will be taking Thothmes' cot. Thothmes also has a charge." He laughed at Huy's expression of dismay. "Now you know how I felt eight years ago when I was saddled with you! I wouldn't trust you myself with anyone I liked, but the Overseer seems to think it's your turn."

Huy tried unsuccessfully to master his disappointment. "I shall do my duty," he replied stiffly. "Where is this unfortunate boy, Harnakht?"

"He won't be here for a couple of days. He's coming up from Weset. The Overseer will let you know when he arrives. Oh, cheer up, Huy! It's only for a month and if you're lucky he won't snivel and snore as you did. Incidentally, the High Priest himself will be leading the evening prayer in this compound tonight, so you'd better be presentable. Somehow I don't think he's forgotten about you." He softened. "Seriously, Huy, you should be proud of what you have accomplished in the last eight years. To be given the responsibility of a new boy is an honour."

Huy made a face, although he was secretly delighted at the compliment. "I suppose so. Thank you, Harnakht. I'd better make up my cot now."

"And lie in it!" Harnakht walked away chuckling and Huy bent to retrieve his sheets. *It's only for a month,* he thought as he shook them out. *Don't be so selfish. You are twelve years old, no longer the spoiled darling of your family through your own will to be independent, and somewhere on the river is a frightened little child who needs you.* Nevertheless, the old familiar feeling of resentment at the intrusion into his own plans rose up to taunt him with its tenacity. Absently he finished dressing his cot and opened his bags.

By the time the evening meal was being served outdoors as usual, Huy had recovered his equilibrium, eating his onion and garlic soup, cucumber salad, and roasted gazelle, a rare treat, with a group of other boys from his class and sharing the news of his time at home. He was now allowed a cup of wine with the food. Like everything else provided for the students, it was a good vintage, dark and tart, and Huy sipped it appreciatively. Looking about at the loose clusters of white-kilted bodies dotting the lawn, listening to the murmur of conversations and the occasional muted plop as a frog jumped from a lily pad into the water of the pond, feeling the last touch of warmth from the setting sun caress his bare shoulders, he found contentment filling him once more. This was where he belonged. Tonight he would sleep with Khenti-kheti newly placed beside

him, the scarab at the feet of the god, his precious
palette beside his sandals ready for the morning,
his kilts and shirts neatly folded away in his chest, and
he would rise eagerly, his mind already impatient to
be challenged.

The servants collected cups, dishes, and the table
and disappeared, and for a while there was a lull. Then
the High Priest swept into the compound, two acolytes
beside him. He was dressed in full regalia, the leopard
skin flung over his shoulder, and all present sprang to
their feet. Raising his arms, the man began the hymn
of praise to Ra that would change to a prayer for the
god's protection as he traversed the twelve houses of
the night, and Huy joined in, the words as familiar to
him now as the sound of his own name, their beauty
striking him anew as they did at the start of each school
year. When it was over, the High Priest paused, his gaze
travelling the assembly, coming to rest at last on Huy.
He smiled, the aristocratic face breaking into lines of
gentleness, and Huy smiled back. Nodding, he turned
away, the junior priests pacing after him, and Huy let
out his breath, a vision of the Ished Tree coming clear
and sharp behind his eyes. His transgression had been
a long time ago, but it seemed that neither the High
Priest nor he himself was destined to forget it. *At least
I am forgiven,* he thought as he entered his cell, where
Pabast was lighting the lamp. *The gods have visited no
retribution on me. Truly I am blessed.*

He was about to undress himself when Thothmes
walked in. The two friends embraced happily, but
Thothmes, instead of wriggling up onto the still-unmade
cot he usually occupied, perched beside Huy and crossed

both arms and ankles. "I can't stay," he said ruefully. "I'm in the next compound with my new charge. I was late returning to school because my family was visiting relatives in Mennofer and when we got back Father couldn't find the litter-bearers." He shook his head. "The steward ran them to earth in one of the beer shops. I could have come on foot, but you know how protective Father is." He turned his large, shining eyes on Huy. "How good it is to see you again! You are well? The girls have been pestering me to invite you home as soon as possible. What have you brought to tie your lock with?" It was the first year the boys were allowed to use something of their own choice to anchor their youth locks.

Huy grinned at Thothmes' uncharacteristically animated face. "My father carved me a little wooden frog out of a piece of driftwood left on the bank of the river after the flood last year," he said, sliding off the cot and reaching behind the image of Khenti-kheti on the table. "Look! It has green faience eyes and a loop so that I can thread it onto the leather thong I made. What about yours?"

Thothmes fingered the oily smoothness of the tiny creature. "It's beautiful." He nodded, handing it back. "I have silk ribbons of various colours so that I can wash them when they get dirty. Everyone complained. Mother wanted to have strips of cloth of gold woven for me, and Father commissioned silver ankhs and said I should at least hang them on the ribbons or everyone would think we were poor, but I asked him to put them on a bracelet for me instead." He sighed. "It has been a busy summer and I am glad to be back here. You also?"

"Oh yes! But we won't have much time to talk, for the first month at least," Huy said regretfully. "What's your charge like? Mine won't be arriving for a couple of days."

"He's silent and frightened and wouldn't let go of my hand until I put him to bed and told him I had to go and visit my friend." Thothmes laughed. "He comes from Abtu and has the most enormous likeness of Osiris set up on the floor beside his cot already. It was too big for the table. But I approve of such piety. Do you realize that our Great God is in the fifty-first year of his reign? How holy he must be! What did they give you for the evening meal?"

They chatted for a while longer, Huy basking in the aura of sanity and security Thothmes always seemed to carry with him, until Thothmes stood and hugged him once again. "I really must go. I don't want the child to wake up and have no one to comfort him." He went to the doorway but turned back briefly. "Speaking of comfort, I don't suppose by some miracle Sennefer has not returned this time?"

Huy snorted. "Unfortunately, he was gorging himself on gazelle meat tonight and sneering at me between mouthfuls. One day he will choke on his greed. Oh well. We've endured him for eight years, Thothmes, we can put up with him for a few more. Sleep well."

"You also."

The room emptied, the shadows deep and still against the steady flame of the lamp. *The next feast day is the Opening of the Tomb of Osiris, followed at once by the Feast of the Hoeing of the Earth and then the Preparation of the Sacrificial Altar in the Tomb of Osiris,* Huy thought as he removed his kilt and loincloth and crawled between the sheets. *Three days, one after the other, that I can spend at Thothmes' house. I wonder if Anuket is as anxious to see me as I am to see her? Oh gods, I hope so!* As he blew out the lamp, he heard Ishat say, "You could marry me, Huy . . . You wouldn't make me cook and clean and have babies, would you?" Closing his eyes and lying back in the darkness, he pushed her face away, not without an ache of guilt followed almost at once by a flash of anger. Much as he loved her, she ought not to have presumed on their close friendship. He did not realize, as he fell asleep, that his anger was not directed at her presumption but at the sudden flowering of her physical maturity. Ishat must remain forever a child.

Huy's own charge turned out to be a stocky boy named Samentuser, whose fear was expressed in outbursts of belligerent refusals to co-operate with any-thing outside the classroom. When Pabast first arrived to shave off his unruly mop of black hair, he had tossed his head about, gripping the edges of the stool, his jaw thrust out stubbornly. After several attempts to apply the knife in an uncharacteristic silence, the servant looked appealingly at Huy, who was standing watching the performance with amusement and some sympathy. *What, no veiled insults, Pabast?* Huy had thought. *No sour references to a shock of peasant hair?* The Overseer had told him nothing of the child's background, merely handing him over with what Huy later recognized as a rather sly smile. Samentuser in turn had said nothing at all that first evening, eating, bathing, and going to bed without answering any of Huy's attempts to draw him out. He had left his cot, gone naked to the doorway of the cell, and thrown his early meal onto the grass before lying down again and facing the wall. In the bathhouse he had at least attempted to scrub himself, but he had now rendered Pabast helpless. Huy savoured the moment before squatting before the mutinous little face.

"If you do not allow Pabast to shave you, the other pupils will call you a peasant and your father a dweller of the swamps," he said crisply. "Is that what you want, Samentuser? Perhaps you are indeed a peasant. So am I. But here you can learn to be something better, if you will behave." He rose. "Otherwise I will hold you down while Pabast does his duty."

Samentuser went white, then colour flooded back into his face, dark red under skin that seemed too pale for a boy. "How dare you address me in that manner!" he barked shrilly. "How is it that you do not know who I am? My father is a smer and my mother a descendant of the mighty Aahmes pen-Nekheb! I do what I like, and what I like is to leave my hair alone!" He sprang up and clenched his fists, a small, blazing ball of fury. "I hate it here and I hate you, peasant, and if this servant lays a finger on me I shall have him whipped!"

"Oh, I do not think you are a nobleman," Huy said slowly. "Noble blood is kind to those of lower birth. A true nobleman has no need to bully his inferiors, as you will learn when you begin to study the maxims of Ptahhotep. Now sit down and behave yourself!"

"This is my third school!" Samentuser shouted. "I have heard the maxims! I hate the maxims! I want to go home to Nefrusi!"

Huy considered him carefully, wishing that the Overseer had given some indication of this child's status. If Samentuser was not lying, it was entirely probable that a series of tutors had left the family's estates out of sheer exasperation. Remembering the Overseer's knowing smile, Huy decided that, given his own less-violent but just as resentful beginning, the task of taming this kindred ka had been given to him on purpose. Taking Samentuser firmly by the shoulders, he pressed him back onto the stool and held him there. "Do you love your father and your mother?" he asked.

Samentuser looked up at him as though he had gone mad. "Of course. My father is wise and my mother is beautiful."

"Do you believe that they love you?"

The boy frowned. An expression of uncertainty flitted across his face.

"Do you want them to love you even more? Why did your tutors leave you? Why do you think that your father keeps sending you away to one school after another?"

"Because he does not want me at home," the boy said sullenly.

Huy shook his head. "No. It is because he loves you too much to see you grow up ugly and cruel and selfish. He longs to see you make him proud of you. Will you try, Samentuser?"

"You are very stupid," Samentuser muttered, but he remained still as Pabast tentatively approached him, and when his new youth lock lay submissively against his shoulder and the rest of his hair covered his feet in a coarse black cloud, he ran a hand over his oiled scalp, grunted, and left the cell without another word.

His bedside table was cluttered with ostentatious representations of the deities of Weset: Amun, his wife Mut, and their son Khonsu. Huy did not know who the god of Nefrusi was, and did not care to ask. Nefrusi lay within the designation of the Un sepat, together with the towns of Khmun, Hor, and Dashut, halfway between Iunu and Weset. "He is simply showing off his father's connection with the Horus Throne," Thothmes said scornfully. Samentuser had wasted no time in informing everyone that he was the son of the princely governor of the Un region, who spent much time at the palace in Weset and held many conversations with the King himself. "If the father is anything like the son, I imagine that our Good God merely tolerates him out of the kindness of his august heart."

As the days went by, Huy strove to find something in the boy to like, listening to his complaints about the quality of the food, the grade of the bed linen, the ban on personal servants. Samentuser tired him and he began to regard the hours in the schoolroom as a welcome respite from his onerous charge rather than an opportunity to further his own education. He was distressed but not surprised when he saw a bond begin to grow between Samentuser and his old enemy Sennefer. Their characters were distressingly similar in spite of the difference in their ages. Samentuser had found a sympathetic ear and Sennefer an admiring accomplice. It was a great relief when the month ended and Thothmes moved back into their cell.

Mekhir began. The river had regained its banks, the weather was pleasant, and in the fields the farmers stood to watch their young crops tremble, green and sturdy,

in the warm breezes of Peret. The students settled down
contentedly to another year of learning. Huy began to
memorize the Wisdom of Amenemopet as dictated for
the edification of his son the scribe Hor-em-maa-kheru.
The stanzas were long and full of good advice to the
young, a fact that Huy's teacher dwelt on with relish.
But Huy was also taking dictation straight onto papyrus
from one of the older pupils, who had chosen for the
exercise the military memoirs of Aahmes pen-Nekheb,
friend of Osiris Thothmes the First in his old age,
doughty campaigner, and Samentuser's ancestor if the
disagreeable child was to be believed. The man's powerful character, arrogant, courageous, worshipful, and
humorous, drenched every word Huy conscientiously
transcribed in his neat hand, and Huy found himself
pondering a lusty bloodline already grown thick with
self-regard and polluted by pettiness. No more than
three kings separated the first Thothmesid and the death
of his fellow soldier from Samentuser—two if one did
not count the upstart queen Hatshepsut, daughter of
Thothmes the First—yet pen-Nekheb's line threatened
to dissipate into whatever feeble offspring Samentuser
might produce.

Huy was idly discussing that incongruity with
Thothmes one warm afternoon after the sleep. They
were walking across the temple's sun-dazzled forecourt
on their way to the practice ground, Thothmes already
gauntleted in preparation for his lesson in chariot
driving and Huy with his bow held loosely in one hand.
It was not a feast day, and the entrance to Ra's House
was deserted but for a few priests gathered in the shade
of the pillars guarding the outer court. Several boys

were playing on the grass under the trees, their shouts echoing against the high wall that surrounded the whole precinct but for the canal and lake in the forefront. Huy recognized Samentuser's back, and beyond him Sennefer stood brandishing a throwing stick. Sennefer saw them and started towards the stone apron of the lake they were about to circle. "We should not have taken the long way around today," Thothmes muttered. "Sennefer has been bragging about his new weapon ever since his father sent it to him. Now what?"

Huy sighed. They had no choice but to continue straight past Sennefer; to turn back would be cowardly. They did not change their leisurely pace, but Huy felt his muscles contract in anticipation, and sure enough, in a moment Sennefer began to shout.

"See my throwing stick, Huy?" he jeered, waving it above his head. "I've become quite proficient in its use. I brought down twelve ducks this summer. Now I'm teaching Samentuser how to use it. Would you like a lesson?"

Thothmes put a warning hand on Huy's arm. "'A storm wind moving like a flame in straw—that is the hothead in his hour,'" he quoted from the Wisdom of Amenemopet. "Ignore him, Huy. Don't even look at him. He loves this."

Samentuser had turned and was watching them expressionlessly. Huy gritted his teeth and walked on.

"Oh, of course. I forgot." Sennefer's voice rang clear and full of a false apology. "You're not allowed to hold a throwing stick, are you? Being the son of a peasant, I mean. Too bad. You might have used one to kill a few of the rats infesting your father's hovel." Huy stopped dead. The bow fell from his hand.

Thothmes began to tug at him frantically. "Come on, Huy! Come on! He's not worth the trouble! He's nothing!" But Huy struck his friend's fingers away. His heart had begun to pound and a redness was gathering before his eyes. Through it he saw little Samentuser grinning at him and, farther back, Sennefer's mouth opening to spew forth another insult, another sly attack on his lineage.

"Not this time," he said through rigid lips, coldly aware somewhere deep inside himself that he was almost incoherent with rage, that he was going to beat Sennefer to death with his bare fists and was fully capable of doing so, that he must use this last flash of terrible self-knowledge to regain control. But with a grunt he pushed it deliberately away and the full frenzy of his wrath rushed in. Crouching, his whole body tense, his features twisting into a snarl, he prepared to fling himself at Sennefer.

He heard Thothmes shriek, "No, Huy!" through the fog in his ears, saw Sennefer's expression change from a sneer to a frightened surprise, saw Sennefer's hand gripping the stick come up and back in a mindless reaction of fear, and the weapon came speeding towards him, turning over and over, its polished surface glinting in the bright sunlight. "Oh gods," Thothmes said.

For Huy, time seemed to slow. He was able to examine the stunned disbelief in his friend's two words. He clearly felt the string of his bow under the sole of his reed sandal as he took one step back. Inch by inch he toppled sideways as Thothmes thrust against his shoulder. Fascinated, he watched the throwing stick flow towards him. He could hear it now, a rhythmic whistle as it sliced through the air, and then it struck. Suddenly he was crawling blindly over the rough stone of the forecourt. He knew he was crawling, but he could not feel his hands or his knees. Someone was screaming his name through the loud singing in his head. Then he experienced a sensation of space beneath him, and falling, and the cool water of the lake closed over his spine. He tried to breathe and could not, but somehow it did not matter, because the space was beneath him again, vast and dark. He knew it was dark, dark and comforting, even though he was unable to open his eyes, and he was falling into it like a pebble dropped down a well. *It has no bottom,* he thought calmly. *So I may as well give myself up to death,* and as though he had said the words out loud he felt death float quietly up from below to claim him.

But a moment later he found himself kneeling on the verge of the lake, water dripping from his body onto the stone, his lungs fighting for air. Gasping and coughing, he staggered to his feet and looked about, expecting to see Thothmes rushing towards him, but the forecourt was deserted and the temple's pillars empty of priests. There was no sign of his tormentor either. Sennefer and Samentuser had vanished. Lawn, trees, temple, and forecourt lay quietly dreaming in the soft, bright warmth of a spring afternoon. Gingerly Huy fingered his head. He could find no break in his scalp and his touch caused him no pain, although he knew that the throwing stick had struck him with enough force to kill him. In the right hands it was a lethal weapon, and Sennefer had flung it with all the strength of a sudden panic. Puzzled, Huy began to walk towards the temple, anxious to get to his cell and talk to Thothmes. He distinctly remembered the stunning blow of the stick, his immediate blindness, the feel of water closing over his back, but perhaps his instantaneous anticipation of those things as the piece of curved wood came hurtling towards him had caused him to react as though it had found its mark when in fact Sennefer's aim had been faulty and the stick had missed him altogether. *Then where is Thothmes? Sennefer and the child would have run away, but Thothmes would have hurried over to make sure that I was all right. And I am certainly all right.*

He glanced down at himself and halted. His feet were bare. So was the rest of him. Shirt, kilt, loincloth, all had disappeared. He turned, but no linen floated on the surface of the lake. As he turned back, he caught a flash of light out of the corner of his eye. The braid of his youth lock with its driftwood frog had swung forward. Huy lifted it from his collarbone in astonishment. A perfect little golden frog with lapis lazuli eyes peered back at him. Thoroughly alarmed, he remained very still, the frog and the end of his lock clutched in one hand, and it was then that he realized the silence surrounding him. No birds sang. The leaves of the trees dotting the wide lawns to either side of the forecourt were motionless. No lap of waves, no shout of oarsmen, no sound of animal or human came to him from the river behind him. There was only a hush so deep that he could hear his own breaths. Nothing moved, and yet the profound immobility held a quality of expectancy that seemed to be directed at him. Even the air he was drawing into his lungs was waiting.

Huy did not know what to do. If he tried to reach his cell as quickly as possible by slipping through the inner court stark naked and sopping wet and was caught, the punishment for such flagrant blasphemy would be dire. If he took the more acceptable route beside the outer wall of the temple and then in through one of the doors to the school at the rear, he was bound to be seen by a priest or one of the older boys, who might report him. Could he run in under the trees, make his way to the river, and lurk by the road in the hope that someone might have spread laundry on the bushes or dropped a cloak by accident? Yet he saw that beyond the fingers of shade cast by the pillars, the outer court was as empty as everything around him. He let go his youth lock, said a quick prayer for forgiveness to Ra, whose sacred house he was about to violate, and took one step towards the temple.

At once he was engulfed in sound. Birds twittered, leaves rustled, the water of the lake slapped gently against its stone apron. Illogical though he knew it was, Huy believed that he had made the correct decision, and as he walked in under the towering pylon and entered the outer court he felt himself become completely dry.

He expected to look ahead across the concourse with its cloisters on either side to the roofed inner court fronted by its row of pillars and, beyond that, the closed doors of Ra's inmost shrine. What he saw stopped him dead as though a giant hand had suddenly been thrust against his belly. The power in his knees gave way so that he almost fell, but his flailing arms helped him to keep his balance, and then he stood in awe, his nakedness forgotten.

He was on the edge of a vast garden whose lush, flower-sprinkled grass ran away from him to be lost in a warm blue horizon. Pools dotted its expanse, their placid surfaces thick with white and pink water lilies. Close by on his right, a wide river flowed slowly, its water sparkling in the brilliant light, its banks marked by palm trees at whose feet the papyrus marshes were crowded with feathered egrets and herons picking their way gracefully among the gently quivering fronds. To his left, when he dared to turn his head, he saw a small whitewashed house set in a thicket of sycamores, and far, far beyond it he was sure he glimpsed a line of serried hills shimmering beige against the cloudless sky. All these things rushed at his senses in a chaos of colours and shapes, but the confusion was temporary, for he found himself inhaling a delicious scent he recognized but could not place. It seemed compounded of his uncle's orchard blossoms and the honey his mother took from the hives in the perfume fields and the merest hint of garlic, and as he strove to bring its source to mind he noticed the Tree. He could have sworn it had not been there before, but now it towered ahead of him, its great branches spread, its leaves making a vast canopy of moving shade. Its aroma poured into him until he felt as though his blood itself had become charged with it, and as he stared at the Tree he remembered both its name and where he had seen it before. It was the Ished Tree.

Beneath it, spine resting against the gnarled trunk, a man sat cross-legged, a scroll unrolled across his

knees. He was enveloped loosely in white linen. A pair
of papyrus sandals and a scribe's palette lay in the grass
beside him, together with a silver cup in which a rich
purple liquid quivered. Not far away, to Huy's terror, a
hyena squatted on its bony haunches, blinking lazily in
the radiant sunlight, its snub nose pointed towards the
man, the tufts of fur on each small ear and curving over
its powerful shoulders gleaming. Its attitude seemed
neither predatory nor expectant; it simply watched the
man with an air of utter contentment. If it knew of
Huy's presence, it gave no sign.

Huy was afraid to move. For a long time he stood
immobile, his gaze flicking from man to beast to the
house, but always returning to the lush profusion of
the Tree, until at last the man spoke. "Come forward,
Huy son of Hapu," he said without raising his eyes
from the scroll.

Huy took one hesitant step. "Where am I?"
he whispered.

"In Egypt, of course," came the reply. The scroll
rustled gently as the man unrolled it a little further.
The hyena yawned, giving Huy a momentary look at
its sharp ivory teeth before it slid forward to lie prone,
nose against its paws.

Huy took another step. "Am I . . . am I dead?"

Now the man glanced up, smiling, eyebrows raised.
He had a thin face, the cheekbones prominent, the
brown eyes full of humour. Something about him struck
Huy as vaguely familiar. "Perhaps," the man said mildly.
"But perhaps you are only dreaming. Look behind you."

Slowly, tensely, Huy did as he was told. There was
no square dampened by his footprints, no lake beyond,

only an immense, dim hall, its ceiling lost in shadow. In the centre of the lapis-tiled floor towered a massive golden scale, its two salvers empty. Beside it a woman stood, her cupped palms lifted as though she were waiting to receive something, the heavy golden bracelets on her delicate wrists giving off a dull sheen in the uncertain light around her. Two tall feathers attached to the rear of the plain gold circlet on her brow shook softly in a draft Huy could not feel.

Huy caught his breath. He had never before seen such beauty and serenity on a human face. *But she is not human,* he thought with a stab of fear. *I am staring at the goddess Ma'at herself, the symbols of cosmic and earthly order on her head. She is waiting to place a heart on the scales, to make a judgment.* Reflexively he clutched at his chest. *The scales are empty. Have I already been weighed?*

In the shadows behind her, there was a stirring. The goddess smiled and turned away from Huy, holding out both gossamer-hung arms to the creature that emerged, the man with the muscular black body wrapped in a short kilt of woven gold thread, the jackal with the tall black ears and long nose. Golden kohl encircled the bright black animal eyes. One human hand held a golden ankh, the other grasped a staff of office topped by a miniature jackal's head. *Not human! Not human!* Huy thought wildly. *Anubis, god of the rites of death! Sennefer's throwing stick killed me. I have already been embalmed and entombed, but I have no memory of traversing the Judgment Hall, my hand in that of Anubis, or of seeing my heart placed on the scales against the feathers of Ma'at.* Anubis was staring directly into Huy's face, his lips raised over cruel fangs in what might have been a feral grin or a warm smile. His arm had gone around the goddess's shoulder and the ankh he was holding covered her chest.

"Why are you afraid?" came the quiet voice of the man behind Huy. "Anubis harms no one. He wishes the scales to balance for every man and woman. It is better to fear the goddess, who sees into the heart and knows when the harmony of Ma'at is threatened. Come here."

Gratefully, Huy turned away from that sombre place and at once the perfume of the Ished Tree, the musical cacophony of the birds, the joyous blue of the sky, surrounded him again. Walking towards the Tree, he felt the light folds of a linen tunic settle against his skin. He was no longer naked. "Sit beside me," the man went on. Huy obeyed, sinking into the sweet-smelling grass, his fingers going deliberately to the rough bark of the Tree. His companion laughed. "Touching the Ished is no longer forbidden to you," he said. "Indeed, you may taste its fruit if you wish."

Huy looked about. There was no sign of any fruit littering the ground. "But where is it?" he asked, scanning the face, now so close to his own, that tantalized him with the knowledge that he had seen it somewhere before. "And who are you, Master?"

The man tapped the scroll. "It is here, of course. This is the Book of Thoth, and my name is Imhotep."

Huy lost his breath. Scrambling to his knees, he put his forehead against the man's foot. Here, warm and alive, was the god who had designed the mighty tomb of the Osiris-one Nebjerikhet Nebti hentis ago, who had won renown as a healer, and who had been the greatest Seer Egypt had ever birthed. His shrines were common throughout the country, where his statues, large and small, crude and fine, smiled arrogantly and enigmatically back at every petitioner.

"Then I am dead, and this is the Paradise of Osiris!" Huy exclaimed.

Imhotep waved him up. "Perhaps. Perhaps," he repeated, "young Huy, the gods with their inscrutable purpose have decreed an early death for you. All I know is that I am to put to you this question: Will you taste the fruit of the holy Ished Tree?" He raised his hands and the scroll rolled up, falling into the folds of his linen.

Huy blinked at it, perplexed. "The Book of Thoth is the fruit of the Tree? But the High Priest of Ra told me that he gathers up the fruit and burns it every year, therefore it cannot be a book. Anyway, does the Book of Thoth not merely contain two spells, one for reanimating the dead and one for bestowing the power to understand the language of the animals and birds? And does it not lie in the tomb of some anonymous sorcerer, far beneath the earth? Many necromancers have sought it."

Imhotep shook his head. "No, there is no such book. It is a story, a fable. In the Egypt of the living, the fruit of the Ished Tree symbolizes the knowledge of all truths, both cosmic and earthly. This knowledge was dictated to Thoth by the great god Atum before the creation of the world, and Thoth wrote it down. In the Egypt of the dead it retains this form." He plucked the scroll from his lap and, holding it reverently on both palms, offered it to Huy. The gesture was so like the goddess Ma'at's cupped palms in the semi-darkness of the Judgment Hall that Huy momentarily cringed.

"I don't understand," he faltered.

Imhotep regarded him steadily. "Yes you do. It is quite simple. Atum gives you this choice, to make entirely freely. He deigns to share with you his divine wisdom. You may refuse the Book if you wish, without any hurt. There will be no retribution if you do so."

Huy stared at the papyrus cylinder lying so innocently on Imhotep's lined palms. "But why?" he cried. "Why me? What purpose can such knowledge serve, seeing that I am already dead, judged, and in Paradise?"

"I do not know."

"You have read it, Master. Can you not advise me to unroll it or leave it alone?"

"No." Imhotep sighed. "You stumbled across the Ished Tree in the temple of Ra when you were a little boy. Few but Ra's priests have seen it through all the hentis since Atum caused it to be planted. Maybe at that moment you became sacred yourself. Or the god deliberately caused you to find his tree. Only he knows why this choice has come to you. Will you read?"

Huy took the scroll and closed his eyes. The paper was warm and comforting in his hand, returning him to the classroom at the rear of Ra's temple, and his teacher's voice, and the smell of the ink as he, Huy, dipped his brush into it and drew the holy symbols Thoth had bequeathed to Egypt onto the sheet of blank papyrus. *Thothmes,* he thought sadly. *My safe little cell. Uncle Ker and the river. Mother, Father . . . I shall not see you again, not until you also pass through the Hall, and only the gods know how far ahead that time will be. Shall I be lonely here? I wonder. And if the scroll does indeed contain the full knowledge of every truth in the cosmos and on the earth, will the reading of it make me a god like Imhotep?* The thought was alien, outrageous, and he smiled. Opening his eyes, he nodded.

"I will read," he said.

"Very well. But first you must sleep. You have had a long journey and you are tired. Lie down here. Rest against me." All at once Huy felt his eyelids grow heavy and his head begin to buzz with weariness. The scroll fell from his grasp. His cheek found the hollow of Imhotep's shoulder, and before his eyes closed again he peered lazily up into the man's kindly face. It seemed to Huy that Imhotep's ears had grown tufts of coarse hair and the skin brushing his forehead had become rough.

"Dream, little one, dream," the deep voice purred, and Huy surrendered himself to darkness.

5

Huy returned to consciousness sluggishly, struggling to pull himself free of whatever mire seemed to be holding his feet and to half swim, half scramble out of the pit or well or tomb in which he sensed he was trapped. He could not breathe. As he fought to draw air into his lungs, as his limbs flailed, his mind was disgorging a chaos of half-formed images: two gods and a goddess in a shadowy place, a hyena fused to the trunk of a tree, an expanse of garden with red grass, monstrous green blooms, pools of black water colliding with yellow clouds in a sky high above that was terrifying in its invisibility although he knew it filled the space above him. He wanted to scream at the madness of it, for even as he saw these things they melted into each other and began to stream past his interior vision, a swift flow of intertwining, oily colours turning to grey as they disappeared.

Just when he knew he must die of fear and suffocation, his chest expanded, his heart gave a single powerful lurch and settled into the rhythm of life, and he was breathing normally. At the same moment it all came back to him: the Ished Tree, the intoxicating beauty of its surroundings, Ma'at and Anubis in the Judgment Hall, Imhotep and the hyena and the scroll. He felt himself smile. Imhotep had told him to sleep and he had slept. He had died. Sennefer had killed him, and now he was free to enjoy and explore the Paradise of Osiris, read the scroll, and learn the secrets of the gods. *Why, then,* he thought with a dawning dismay, *is the Ished Tree now giving off its underlying stench of decay and corruption, and why is my body so heavy?* He opened his eyes.

A figure was bending over him limned in flickering yellow light, its arm raised. It seemed frozen, and as Huy turned his head it uttered a sound, part choking gasp, part grunt. "Imhotep?" Huy whispered. "Is that you?" The figure shrieked and stumbled back. Something fell from its hand to the floor with a clatter. There was a flurry of movement and several more figures appeared, moving uncertainly on the periphery of Huy's vision. Slowly, painfully, he sat up. He was on a low, narrow bed of some kind, in a room full of other beds, all of them occupied by people who were lying utterly still. A table laden with strange knives and tools sat in the centre. Many lamps burned, filling the fetid air with a light that seemed thick and heavy to Huy, who had expected to see the bright, limpid air of the beautiful garden. The figures now backing away from him resolved themselves into a group of men clad in kilts grimed with what looked like old blood. They were staring at him with blank horror. One of them was shaking and pointing at him. "I was about to cut it . . . cut it . . . I was about to cut it . . ." he was saying over and over, his voice shrill with hysteria. Huy himself had begun to tremble.

"Where am I?" he managed. "Where is Imhotep?" He glanced behind him, hoping to see the garden and the Tree, but a stained wall met his bewildered gaze. Turning around had hurt him. His head and neck throbbed unbearably. His shoulders sent arrows of stiff pain down his spine. Carefully he turned back. The men had fallen silent. They were staring at him without moving, and no one on the other curious beds was moving either. All the occupants were totally motionless.

Suddenly full awareness flooded Huy, and leaning forward he vomited onto the obsidian knife lying on the ground beneath his feet. He was in a House of the Dead. The men watching him with such dread were sem priests, and one of them had been about to slit open his abdomen and begin his embalming. "But I died!" he blurted, dry-mouthed. "I died, and I saw the Judgment Hall. Imhotep . . . Imhotep talked with me and it was more than beautiful, it was glorious. How is it that I am here?" He cleared his throat, inhaling the odour of death clinging to his skin, to the hard bed on which he sat, rising from the floor, carried to him on the heat of the lamps. He could hardly speak for the chattering of his teeth. "Did the gods pour my ka back into my body? Tell me. Tell me!"

There was a long silence during which Huy found his feet and stood, his arms, his knees, even his head, jerking uncontrollably. The sem priests continued to regard him in an atmosphere deepening into the most profound suspicion. Finally one of them answered him, although the man did not step forward and seemed prepared to shrink behind his fellows if Huy threatened to make a move.

"This is the House of the Dead at Hut-herib," he quavered. "Your body was removed here from Iunu five days ago by your father and your uncle. You . . . you were slain by a blow to the head. Your lungs were full of water. Lifting you onto the embalming couch, it gushed from you like . . . like a flood." He had begun to pant. "There was no breath. For five days, no breath. We are very busy. We could not begin your beautification at once. What are you? Answer me in the name of Ausar Unnefer, Great God of the Dead! For surely Amam-Apep the Devourer has stolen the ka of Huy son of Hapu!" The question was half shouted, and at its tone the men drew together as if for protection.

"Oh gods." Huy fought the faintness prickling in his body and threatening to engulf him. They thought he was a demon. They thought that Huy's ka had gone and something evil had replaced it. Desperately he searched his memories and found little but shreds. A woman's face. His mother's? A young girl—no name. A scribe's palette across knees—his knees?—and a voice dictating to the hand—his hand?—drawing the characters on the papyrus. A tree, yes, it was the Ished Tree, but enclosed in a roofless space in a temple and he was very small and staring at it with a frightened interest. No scroll. Where was the scroll? Where was Imhotep?

Huy began to sob dryly in spasmodic gasps, an almost insupportable weight against his chest. Somehow he knew that he must control himself, that if he did not stand straight and speak sanely these men would rush at him and cut his throat. Clenching his fists, he stood away from the embalming couch and willed his limbs to quieten, the panic to dissipate. "I swear to you by Osiris, by Isis the Protectress of the Dead, by mighty Horus their holy son who spreads his wings over blessed Egypt, that I am indeed Huy son of Hapu of this town," he said loudly. "I was attacked with such force in the precinct of the temple of Ra at Iunu that I was rendered as unconscious as though I were dead. My ka was loosened from my body, but five days of rest has restored its hold. Give me a kilt to cover my nakedness and let me go home, I beg you." The speech had cost him dearly. Spots swam before his eyes. Clamping his teeth together, he made himself meet their eyes one after the other, reading doubt, indecision, and, overwhelmingly, disbelief in their faces. *Move at once,* something told him. He was unable to restrain the weakness in his legs. Tottering to the corpse on the couch nearest to him, he pulled off it the square of linen covering its genitals and held it over his own, then he made his way to the open doorway. No one stopped him. No one moved. A smaller room opened out before him. He was blind to whatever it contained. Staggering through it, he reached a walled courtyard and a closed door. He was almost done. Reeling to the door, he fumbled at it, praying that it opened outward and he would not have to exert a strength he did not have to haul it inward. A moment later it swung out, and Huy found himself falling onto his hands and knees in sandy grass.

It was night. Not far ahead, a clump of trees smudged darkly against a sky rich with stars. Huy crawled until he felt leaves brush his back, then he collapsed, his body curled in upon itself, and began to howl, an inhuman noise heavy with anguish, betrayal, and confusion, and found he could not stop. How long he lay there keening like a wounded wolf he did not know. The passage of time had ceased to have any meaning for him. He was aware of nothing but the clamour of his own disintegration. But the night was still deep when the leaves parted above him and warm hands lifted him up and turned him over. Candlelight wavered across his face. There was a hissed intake of breath, a muttered, "No. This is impossible," and Huy peered up through swollen lids into the features of Khenti-kheti's High Priest. A name swam to mind.

"Methen," he whispered. "Help me for the love of Ra. Help me." He felt the ground fall away beneath him and then no more.

Consciousness returned to him more kindly this time, at first an overwhelming sensation of safety as though he were cradled in a cocoon and then the sweet sounds of normalcy coming to him from far away. Voices outside, birds foraging and twittering in trees, and, closer in, the gurgle of water being poured. For a blessed moment he floated on an ocean of unreflective well-being, but then pain surged into his head and thirst forced him to open his eyes.

He was lying on his side facing into a small white-washed room. Opposite him a doorway gave out onto a passage. Beside its lintel a large chest sat on the undressed floor and the wall above it was busy with images of frogs, palm trees, lines of hieroglyphs, and often a name. Huy. *That is my name,* he thought with difficulty. *I am Huy. Did I paint those things?* Bars of filtered sunlight lay just within his vision, coming from what must be a shuttered window to his right, a gently gusting breeze blowing the hanging into the room and releasing it again so that the reed slats clicked quietly against the frame. Close in, almost unfocused, there was a table on which stood the little statue of a god. For a while Huy lay staring at it through the pounding behind his eyes before deciding that it was Khenti-kheti keeping watch over him. Where had he seen that statue before? He swallowed slowly, with effort. "I need water," he whispered.

Somewhere beyond the couch he heard a stirring, soft footfalls, and a woman was bending over him, her features drawn, the skin around her dark eyes inflamed as though she had been weeping. A cool palm was placed against his forehead and his nostrils were invaded by the scent of lilies. His mind struggled to bring together the perfume and the woman's face and he almost succeeded, but the attempt was too tiring. "I am Huy," he whispered again, "and I am very thirsty. Could I please have water?" The woman's expression of anxiety did not change, but there was a flare of something—fear? disappointment?—in the sudden twitch of her eyebrows. She disappeared, and then her arm was under his shoulders, pulling him towards her, and the rim of a cup was pressed against his mouth. He drank swiftly, greedily, his gaze on the face that he felt he ought to know. "Who are you?" he said.

She lowered him carefully back onto the pillow and stood smiling at him sadly. "My name is Itu and the house you are in belongs to my husband, Hapu," she replied, speaking carefully.

"But I am Huy, the son of Hapu!" Huy exclaimed. "You are my mother?" And even as the question left his lips, his mind slammed them together, the perfume and the woman, and he whimpered with relief. "Mother! Of course! Then this is my room?" Again he saw something in her glance, an apprehension, before she brought forward a stool and sank onto it beside him.

"It is your room, but you don't stay in it very often," she told him. "You are at school in Iunu for most of the year. What can you remember, Huy? Do you even know how old you are?"

Huy considered. "I am not sure. I think I might be twelve. That's the number that comes to me. Am I right?"

She nodded, obviously waiting for more, but Huy fell silent. Presently he said, "I remember waking up in the House of the Dead. I remember being somewhere wonderful before that. Someone told me that I was attacked with a throwing stick and fell into a lake because the sem priests said there was water in my lungs. They were afraid of me. They wanted to kill me too." Tears of weakness came stinging into his eyes, surprising him.

Itu wiped at them with the hem of her sheath. "They believe that you are not my son, that my Huy's body has been possessed by a demon," she told him steadily. "The whole town is talking about how you lay dead for five days. You must strive to remember all you can. You must convince everyone that you are still Huy, that your ka has not flown."

The Judgment Hall, Huy thought with a secret panic. *A tree, a strange man saying . . . what? I am*

*losing something. Something very important is slipping
away from me and I am powerless to prevent its going.*

"I am in great pain," he managed. "My head. I
think the person who attacked me is called Sennefer
and the place was a temple. Why a temple? Why did he
attack me? Am I correct, Mother?"

"Yes!" she said emphatically. "But I do not want to
answer your questions. It will be better for you to
answer them yourself. We must pray that your memory
returns as your wound heals." She reached to the table,
steadied his head, and Huy felt a thick, cold liquid slide
down his throat. Its bitterness made him retch.
"The priest Methen prepared this poppy for your
pain," she went on. "It will make you sleep. I must
speak to your father now, and your uncle Ker's steward
is waiting to take any news of you to his master."

A delicious numbness was creeping over Huy,
seeping into his limbs, soothing the throbbing in his
skull, feeding drowsiness into his senses. "Ker and
Heruben," he murmured. "Ker and Heruben. The priest
brought me here, didn't he? I want to see him."

Her voice came to him from the doorway.
"You see? You are remembering already. Your father
will send to the priest."

Before Huy's eyes closed, he forced himself to look
up at the ceiling. Familiar cracks spidered across
the whitewash, each meandering fissure a thread of
reassurance. *My room,* he thought. *I am home.*

The following days were marked by regular doses
of the nauseating poppy, as much water as Huy wanted,
and long hours of sleep followed by equally long hours
when he lay dazed and pleasantly drugged, staring at

the slow movement the strips of sunlight made across his floor. His mother attended him constantly. He could often hear the cries and cheerful babbles of a child somewhere in the house, the scolding voice of another woman named Hapzefa, their servant, his mother told him, and the sure male tread of Hapu, his father, but no one save his mother came near him. His uncle requested regular news of his progress, but neither he nor Huy's aunt visited. Finally Huy, sitting up on his couch with a mound of pillows supporting him, asked his mother why.

"They are all afraid of you," she told him bluntly. "It has done no good for me to be angry with your father. He is not a lover of the gods, but he is superstitious, as is so often the case with those who mistrust the divine. When you are able to walk in the garden, he will see you and be calmed. Hapzefa loved you very much and does not wish to have her fear that your ka has gone confirmed." She would not meet his eyes. "I have prepared a soup of barley and onions for you, with pepper and aloe juice to strengthen your heart. There is a little date wine also, but if you are not ready for it you need not finish it."

Huy fingered his head. Hair was beginning to grow on his scalp in a swath of soft black fuzz, but it had refused to take root on the unsightly dent that marked the place where the throwing stick had brutally severed him from his past. "Mother, why has no physician been called to me?" he wanted to know. "Is it because Father is too poor to afford one? Uncle Ker would pay."

Her hands suddenly shook as they placed a tray across his sheeted thighs. "Your uncle said that if your wound became infected and you died, it would prove your innocence," she said huskily, "but if you lived then it was the demon in your body that had triumphed." Her features distorted in a grimace of rage and disgust. "Your father argued with him many times, often violently, but Ker is adamant. I have tried to reach him through Heruben, but it is useless. The priest is not charging us for the poppy."

Huy lay quietly under the swift kiss she planted on his cheek. "So my father is able to reason with his fear. I need his loyalty. I long to see him, Mother, and my little brother." He knew the boy's name but could not always bring it to mind.

"Soon you may leave the couch and sit in a chair," Itu said. "Eat the soup. Drink the wine. Are you in pain today?"

"Not much. But I need more poppy than at first."

"Its effect is wearing off. You are becoming inured to it. When Methen comes today, I will tell him."

The priest had been a regular visitor, sitting quietly with Huy and answering his questions honestly. "Your mother chooses to believe that you lay in a coma for five days after you were struck down," he told Huy. "Let us not disabuse her of the notion. But Huy, the sem priests are correct. They deal with dead bodies every day. They could not be deceived. You died. You were dead. I saw your corpse unloaded from your uncle's barge and carried to the House of the Dead. I held your father while he cried. I went into the House and watched the sem priests wash the blood from your body. I saw the stale water pour out of your white lips. I had become very fond of you, you see. I purified myself afterwards, of course, but I had to make sure that you would be treated with due respect in the House no matter what your embalming was going to cost. Your uncle had planned to put you into his own tomb. He has an agreement with your father so that all your family may lie safe and thus enter the Paradise of Osiris unscathed." Methen had leaned close. "For your own safety, Huy, do not ever deceive yourself. The gods revived you after five days. Where was your ka during that time? You say you cannot remember. That may change. In the meantime do not ever, ever pretend as your mother does. It is the only way she can bear to be near you. You must be exorcised soon. Perhaps then the townspeople will stop talking of murder and go back to gossiping about each other."

"Murder?" Huy was startled and horrified. "They want to murder me?"

Methen grinned mirthlessly. "They want the demon sent back to the dark realm and Huy's body properly embalmed and entombed. An exorcism will achieve the same result, I hope."

"What happened to me?" Huy cried out. "Where did the gods take me? Why did they bring me back?"

Methen had gripped his agitated hands. "Their purpose will become clear. Tell me, do you remember any of your lessons? Are you able to hold a brush and write the hieroglyphs?"

Huy held on to his friend tightly. "No, not yet. I try to think of them, but then they become muddled in my head. Nor am I physically strong enough. Why?"

"Because demons cannot write the sacred language Thoth gave to us. Its holiness defeats them. Write, and you will go a long way to proving that you are still Huy son of Hapu."

"What if I am not?" Huy responded bitterly. "What if I only think I still have my own ka?"

Methen sat back. "Madness lies that way," he retorted. "Say your prayers and have patience, Huy. I did not hesitate to pick you up and bring you home to the screams of your mother and the horror of your father. I am a priest. I would have known through my hands if I had become sullied when I cradled you in the darkness outside the House of the Dead." He rose. "I must attend to my duties. Khenti-kheti awaits. I will come again soon and bring more poppy, although by your increasingly healthy colour I do not think you will need it for much longer."

I would like to keep drinking it for the rest of my life, Huy thought as Methen's straight back vanished into the gloom of the passage. *To always have that welcome fog between me and every other Egyptian would be very fine. But a continuous fog between me and my disordered mind would be even better.*

Not long after this conversation, the doses of poppy were withdrawn, and Huy spent several sleepless nights in a mood of irritability and restlessness, leaving his couch to pace up and down between the window and the wall until he was tired enough to sleep. The exercise did not take long. The muscles of his legs seemed slow to gain strength, as though he had been an invalid for many months. He had begun to fear the dark, and without comment Itu had left him a lamp to keep the shadows at bay.

It was on one such night, when the depression in his skull had begun to itch unbearably and his body seemed full of crawling insects, that the girl appeared. Huy had just returned to his couch and was pulling a sheet up over himself when there was a furtive disturbance at the window, the reed hanging was pushed forward, and one naked brown foot slid into view. Huy forgot his discomfort, watching in fascination as one leg, then the other, then the whole small figure materialized, shrugging down the sheath that had become disarranged before pausing to stare across the room at him with narrowed eyes.

Huy sat very still, frantically trying to put a name to the foxlike little face he recognized but could not place. She was obviously of low peasant stock. Her skin had been burned to the colour of wood bark by the sun. The linen garment she was pushing past her knees was thick and coarse, its hem ragged with wear, its surface marred by old stains although limp with many washings. Wiry black hair stood out from her head in an unwieldy mass and hid the tops of her shoulders, but unkempt as it was it could not detract from the sharp delicacy of her features. Her dark eyes were large and clear. Unlike most peasants, she had a nose as straight and thin as any aristocrat's daughter, swooping down towards a wide, well-delineated mouth and a chin as pointed as the angle of her elbows. Her arms were thin and Huy's impression of her body under the ugly folds of the garment was that it was thin also, but lithe as she unbent and stood waiting expectantly for a word of recognition from him. The moment lengthened. The girl's black eyebrows drew together in a frown. She folded her arms, strong fingers splayed against her forearms, and took a step forward on bare, roughened feet. The impression she gave Huy was one of coherent determination, a self-assuredness that promised impatience and a pride at variance with her impoverished appearance. Huy was intrigued. He knew her. Something inside him recognized her with a rush of gladness, but the curious combination of good breeding and commonness she projected confused him.

"You can't even remember my name, can you, Huy?" Her tones sent waves of both relief and shame through him. She was there in the back of his mind, hidden under the catastrophic events of the past weeks. This was one face, one voice, he should have been able to identify before all others, but he could not force her name out of the murk of his consciousness. He shook his head. "Mother said that you'd lost a lot of your memory," she went on tartly, "but I can't believe you're not just teasing me. Perhaps if I slap that silly expression off your face you'll come to your senses. Oh, Huy! I'm your very best friend! Better even than that aristocrat Thothmes you're always talking about."

Quickly she came towards him, and as she did so the pieces of information in his head flew together and he let out a sigh. "Ishat," he said. "You are Ishat."

She clicked her tongue and came forward. "Of course I'm Ishat!" she snapped. "Who else would be sneaking into your room in the middle of the night? If Mother knew I was here I'd get the beating of my life. She has strictly forbidden me to try to see you in case you leap on me with the murderous teeth of Sobek and tear me to pieces." Arriving at the edge of the couch, she peered at him closely, examining his face. "You look ghastly," she said matter-of-factly, "but I don't see any demon behind your eyes. Is it really true what they say? Is that wine in the jug?" She sniffed at it. "Can I have some?"

"Yes, yes, and yes," Huy replied, smiling in spite of himself. "It's palm wine. A poor substitute for the poppy and not sweet enough. Do you know me well, Ishat?"

In the act of pouring the wine into his empty cup, she gave him a sideways glance full of astonishment. "Only since we were born! My mother, Hapzefa, serves in this house and I do also." She filled the cup and turned to him, holding it in both hands. "Do you remember nothing but my name, Huy? Not how close we are? How we always played together and you were often really mean to me? How I gave you a beautiful golden scarab beetle when you went away to school?" She took a breath and opened her mouth to continue, but Huy waved at her urgently.

"Wait!" he commanded. "Wait. Don't move. Something is unfolding." He dared not breathe as the knowledge slowly bloomed within the mysterious recesses of his mind. "The scarab! I remember! All the other boys envied me for the luck of having it." He pursed his lips. "But it did not bring me luck, did it? It brought me to this."

Ishat sucked appreciatively at the wine then set the cup back on the table. "Where is it now?" she demanded. "Did some other pupil steal it after you died?"

"I don't know. It was in the box my uncle gave me, together with my sennet game and my Nefer amulet and my scribe's palette. Oh, Ishat! I can see those things! Look under my couch. See if the box is there." She knelt and, scrabbling about, withdrew the cedar box. Huy snatched it from her and hugged it to his chest, but he did not want to open it, not until she had gone.

"I can't see that you've changed much, except for the silly halo of fuzzy hair all over your head," she said a trifle sulkily. "Show me the wound." Still clutching the box, he twisted sideways. Ishat climbed up beside him and he felt her deft fingers move over what had become to him a ravine, her noisy breath in his ear. Presently she sat back. "It's really ugly," she pronounced. "Deep and red and all furrowed. I heard it was a throwing stick."

Shame at the disfigurement washed over him. "So I was told," he responded dryly. "But I can't see the person who did it, or any of the other boys for that matter."

Ishat grinned. "So we are equal again. You will be staying home now, won't you, Huy? No more school. No more aristocratic friends. Only me. You'll have to marry me now. I'm the only one left who isn't afraid of you." At his expression of distress she lifted his hand and laid it to her cheek. "I'm sorry. That was cruel. I do not believe that you are inhabited by something evil. Not you! But I had to see for myself, and Mother has kept me away from your house ever since the priest brought you back." She smiled. "Well, at least it has meant a rest from sweeping floors and washing linens and trying to cook." She let him go and stood. "I had better go before we wake your parents. May I visit you again in the middle of the night?"

He nodded but said nothing, and after a moment she quickly drained the wine, ran noiselessly across the floor, and vanished. The reed mat slapped once against the wall and then hung motionless.

Silence filled the house once more. Huy fancied that he could still feel Ishat's touch on his scalp and resisted the urge to scratch his wound. *So I have one friend whose faith in me has not wavered,* he thought. *I know and yet do not know her. Behind her face, her familiar gestures, there is a tapestry of colours and events and conversations, but they are so muddled and garbled that I cannot sort them out.*

All the same, his heart was lighter as reverently he set the cedar box across his thighs and raised the lid with its silver image of Heh, god of eternity, kneeling on a stool. Huy's nostrils filled with its pleasant scent. The scarab, wrapped in a piece of spotless linen, sat in one of the compartments. Huy drew it out, laying back the cloth and gazing down at the glittering thing. "I found it floating on the flood," Ishat said loudly. Huy looked up, startled, but the lamp's glow showed him an empty room. "My father told me that scarabs are very rare here in the Delta. They like to live in the desert," the voice went on, Huy now knew, in his own head. "He said it would bring me good fortune, but I said Huy needs it more than I do, seeing that he has to go away to school." The proximity of the memory in which the words were encapsulated made Huy feel nauseated. *My Naming Day,* he thought. Garden. Family? Which Naming Day? A flash of something came to him. He was running down the passage outside his door towards the bright sunlight of the garden, but he doubted that such a moment had anything to do with the scarab.

The sennet game fed his father's personality into his questing hands. Yes, Hapu had definitely made it himself with love and care. "I want to see you so badly," Huy whispered as he laid it aside. "I cannot believe in your cowardice, dear Father. No power under Ma'at could make me hurt you."

Right at the bottom of the box, nestling on top of a pile of kilts and tunics, was the palette. Huy withdrew it, slid it open, drew the brushes across his palm, unstoppered the ink powders, caressed the ivory burnisher, and suddenly his teacher's face swam into view. "Erudition is knowledge coupled with wisdom," the man said, and around him the classroom resolved itself, full of the noise of busy pupils, the clatter of chunks of broken pottery being removed from the basket, the low chanting of one of the older boys far across the room, the smell of papyrus, and the mouth-watering odour of fried fish being carried into the dining room next door. Huy felt like shouting for joy. *But where are my classmates? Them I cannot see. But one day I will.* His teacher spoke again. "As yet you have little knowledge and no wisdom, Huy son of Hapu. But one day your erudition will surpass that of the gods themselves." Huy frowned. The eyes meeting his belonged to someone else he had met, and the voice was different, the speech more measured than that of his teacher. An ache of loss assailed him, for what he was not sure, and he slid the palette closed, all at once aware of a bone-deep exhaustion. Setting the box on the floor beside the couch, he fell asleep almost immediately.

Even though he was now able to sit in his chair and walk about, his mother insisted that he was not ready to leave the confines of his room. "You must eat more, rest more, build up your strength," she said, but Huy believed that her effort to control him came from a reluctance to see him hurt. Accordingly, one morning he dressed himself in a loincloth and kilt from his chest, slipped on a pair of sandals, and ventured through the doorway he had lain and stared at for so many weeks.

The passage was empty. Huy turned right, towards the square of early sunlight pouring in from the garden. His body felt heavy and his legs feeble. His ankles ached. Reaching the end, he stood blinking while his sight adjusted. Powerful light sparked from the surface of the pond. He could hear the high peeping of young nestlings in the trees separating his home from the vast orchard beyond, and the air was redolent with the scent of fruit blossoms. *Of course,* he thought. *It is still the season of Peret. Spring. What month? When was I struck down? How fresh and lovely the garden looks!*

He advanced carefully, all his senses assaulted by a tumult of impressions after his long detention in the quiet dimness of his room, and as he did so there was a stirring in the deep shade of the sycamores. A woman had risen from the reed mat flattening the grass, a child in her arms. Both were staring at him warily. *Hapzefa,* his mind told him at once, *and the baby must be my brother . . . Heby!* Huy forced a smile. "It's such a beautiful morning, Hapzefa," he called. "I decided to spend a little time enjoying it." *Don't be afraid,* he wanted to add, *don't run away.* But she was already turning to disappear through the orchard gate, her arms visibly tightening around Heby. Her alarm must have been transferred to him, for he began to squirm and grunt a protest, his eyes on Huy. "Please let him come," Huy urged. "He remembers me, Hapzefa. Heby! It's me, Huy." But Hapzefa shook her head and ran clumsily to the gate. Heby began to wail, the sound growing fainter as the servant vanished through the orchard.

Huy sighed. Approaching the pool, he stood looking down at its busy life. The blue lilies had already opened. Tiny beads of water trembled on their delicate boat-shaped flowers. Frogs squatted on their sturdy pads, waiting to snap at the gnats clouding above them. A water beetle skimmed past from the shelter of the sedge choking the verge, leaving a barely perceptible wake. His mother's vegetables clustered neatly around the circumference, the dark green, narrow leaves of lettuce, the yellow melon flowers trailing the ground, the tiny buds of new cabbages making him feel all at once thin and sick. Moving into the shade, he sank onto the mat the servant had vacated.

He must have dozed, for he came to himself with a start to find his father sitting cross-legged beside him, gazing across the garden to the dazzling white wall of the house. The man did not move as Huy struggled up, but as Huy tried to touch him he shrank away.

"My son covered that wall with his pictures and writings," he said huskily. "Every winter when I renewed the whitewash I was sorry to paint over such pretty colours, but I knew that he would soon be at work again, wielding the brushes his uncle gave him, with his brother happily slung across his back. When I attended to the wall this year I did not know that my son would soon be dead and there would be no more pictures. If I had known I would have left the house alone until the paint faded away." He laced his broad fingers together. "I am wondering if you are a punishment from the gods because I have failed to give them the worship they demand."

Huy did not respond. There was nothing he could say. He glanced across at the sun-furrowed face, the dear, familiar set of the jaw, the healthy, muscular neck.

Hapu did not look at him. "Well, I will soon know," he went on tonelessly. "The priest will come with incense and water sent to him from the sacred lake at Iunu. If it is proved to me that you are indeed my son, I will offer the gods the regular service I have always denied them. But if they have sent an abomination to live in my house, I will renounce them all forever and no priest will set a foot on my soil again." He swallowed. Huy, with a paining heart, saw a trail of tears suddenly track through the dust clinging to Hapu's features. "If I am maligning Huy my son, I am deeply sorry," he finished. "I long to hold him in my arms, but I refuse to embrace something evil. Therefore, until the proof I desire is presented to me, we will have no commerce with each other." He got up, and Huy watched him stride across the grass and disappear inside the house, a tall, proud man with an invisible weight of grief bowing his wide shoulders.

Huy decided to frighten and shame the members of the household no more. He retreated to his room, determined to stay there until the rite of exorcism had been completed. He considered taking his exercise at night, wandering the garden and the orchard in the dark when he was unlikely to meet anyone, but his new fear of the hours Ra spent in the body of Nut, battling the demons that lay in wait for the god, quickly changed his mind. Nor was his apprehension limited to whatever might be hiding under cover of the darkness. The possibility that his body might be harbouring a malevolent ghost, or worse, a demon, was growing. Perhaps it had insinuated itself into those blank spaces where his memory had disappeared. Huy longed for the poppy, and could not sleep.

Three days after the encounter with his father, the welcome figure of Methen emerged from the shadows of the passage and Huy rose to greet him. He had been sitting by his window staring moodily out at his brother, who was toddling to and fro under Hapzefa's watchful eye. Huy had been careful not to be seen, a precaution he resented and that hurt his already tender feelings. The priest was a happy distraction.

"I had hoped to accompany you to the temple at Iunu for your exorcism," Methen began without preamble, "but no sailors would agree to crew any vessel once they knew who would be on board. In fact no one at all could be persuaded to help us." He perched on the edge of Huy's couch and poured himself a cup of water. "I understand the fear, but I am angry nonetheless. I even approached your uncle, but he was as intractable as everyone else." He sighed, drank, then scowled. "I have written to the High Priest of Ra. He replied at great length. He seems to know you well, Huy, and is sending someone directly to Khenti-kheti's shrine to examine you. I am sorry."

"Why sorry?" Huy exclaimed. "This is good news, Methen. My situation will at last be resolved."

"Perhaps." Methen hesitated. "The High Priest is sending a Rekhet. Whatever the outcome, the people of Hut-herib may not accept the verdict of a woman."

Huy's mouth went dry. "I didn't know that such a one resided at Iunu. They are greatly to be feared. They have much power. What if she casts an evil spell on me?"

Methen raised his eyebrows and smiled wryly. "Everyone believes that you hold such a power," he retorted. "A Rekhet is not a magician. Nor is she a physician. She talks to the spirits of the dead and can divine the presence of demons, that is all." He replaced the cup on the table and stood. "She can exorcise as well. The demons listen to her. You are surely not as full of ignorant superstitions as the peasants who work for your uncle!" Huy did not reply. "I trust the High Priest of Ra," Methen continued, "particularly as he wrote about you warmly and with a certain humour. Somehow you have impressed him. He will have made the correct decision regarding you. I must leave, Huy, but I will return to escort you to the shrine when the Rekhet thinks the time is right. She will cast a horoscope for the day, not a spell to turn you into a crocodile!"

He left chuckling, but Huy sensed the tension beneath his friend's attempt at jocularity. A noose was drawing about his neck, to send him back to the House of the Dead or to haul him at last out of his predicament, but either way, as the slap of Methen's sandals died away, Huy thought, *Dead or alive, I suspect that nothing will ever be the same again.*

A week went by during which his impatience grew. He would have liked to talk to his mother about the thing he was facing, but he remembered Methen's warning and chose not to burden her with his growing terror. Ishat slipped into his room one windy night, but her presence could not cheer him. She would share the peasant's irrational fear of the Rekhet, and Huy, enveloped in a deepening fatigue of body and mind, did not have the energy to calm her. Of his father he tried not to think. Hapu had dealt him a grave wound and he wanted no more emotional turmoil.

On the eighth morning, soon after dawn, Methen arrived and ushered him out of the house and into the litter waiting for them on the path. Huy had time for a few breaths of the fresh, scented air before the heavy linen curtains were drawn closed to either side of him and Methen's voice came to him, muffled by the stifling hangings. "It's better if you are not seen. The bearers are my servants. They have been purified and wear protecting Wadjet Eye amulets." His tone dropped. "Do your best not to touch them, Huy. I am sorry."

So am I, Huy wanted to shout, his muscles stiff with the urge to rip apart the curtains, leap onto the path, and wrestle these craven men to the ground. *I am sorry I have a rich uncle, sorry I went away to school, sorry I didn't put Sennefer in his place a long time ago, sorry I'm such a cause of distress to my family that I should not have been born!* But the fit of angry self-pity faded. He sat back and closed his eyes.

It was a relief to reach the temple and step once more into the light breeze. The bearers had quickly turned their backs to him, not out of rudeness, he knew, but so that they could not see any cursing gesture he might make. Each wore an amulet hanging between his shoulder blades in the place where demons liked to strike. Huy felt a bubble of laughter rise to his mouth and this time he did not restrain himself. His guffaw echoed off the walls of Khenti-kheti's shrine. It had been closed, the outer doors through which he had been carried secured, but the door to the inner sanctuary stood open. Methen did not reprove him. Putting an arm around his shoulders, he led him forward, pausing so that both of them could remove their sandals. Huy's heart began to pound in both fear and anticipation. A shape moved within the dimness. Methen shut the door behind them.

"Do not step on the sand," the shape commanded. "I have created an area of No-Time. Come forward, Son of Hapu, but do not step on the sand." The voice was strong and harsh. Huy did as he was told, coming to a halt by the edge of the sand and staring at the Rekhet curiously.

At first he saw only the cowrie shells, dozens of them, hung around her neck, slung across her belly, encircling her wrists and ankles, so that her slightest movement caused them to click against each other. The cowrie held great protective heka, Huy knew, and many people wore them, but the genuine ones were extremely expensive and difficult to obtain. Most were made of clay. This woman must be very rich. She was small, slightly bent with age, the skin of her hands and face wrinkled, her grey hair wound on top of her head and fastened in place with a cowrie attached to a pin. What he could see of her linen under the profusion of shells was spotlessly white and enveloping. She was grasping a black rod in both hands. Huy, his eyes becoming accustomed to the half-light, saw that it was covered with carved Wadjet eyes, lamps, baboons, and cats. Two lion figures and two crocodiles were fixed into it, and a turtle, sinister and malevolent, squatted on the top of one end. Any magician who controlled the negative heka imbuing these creatures could use it for his protection. Huy's gaze dropped to the woman's feet. Snakes had been painted on them, and she had drawn more snakes around herself in the sand.

"You do not know, do you?" she said. "Your father does not circle his house with the sycamore club to protect it from evil, nor does he pour the water of Ptah upon the door bolts. He does not place a statue of Renenutet in the fields to protect the crops he tends. He does not teach his son the laws and precepts of the unseen world. He leaves him defenceless." She pointed her rod at the snakes. "Weret-Hekau Great in Magic will protect me from the demon within you. If there is a demon within you. We shall see." She swept the rod over the objects assembled at her feet. "I have brought excrement to lure the demon out to eat, seeing that his anus is his mouth. Fresh herbs, fresh oil, and a pot into which the demon will fall, be smashed, and flung into the flowing water of the river. Do you understand what I am about to do?"

Huy swallowed. "You are a Knowing One," he answered huskily. "I understand, and I must trust you. May I ask a question?" She nodded, the cowries around her neck clacking tunelessly. "I have been told that if I am inhabited by a demon and you cast it out, I will die. Is it so?"

"In your case it is so," she said brutally, "because you lay in the House of the Dead and many people attested to the lifelessness of your corpse. If the six invisible members that, together with the body, make up the person of Huy are gone, then what animates the thing I see is something that has no right to it and will give it up under my command. Then the body of Huy may be properly beautified and entombed. I have already been purified and the sign of Ma'at is on my tongue. I will begin."

She began to chant in a high monotone, the rod with its unclean turtle pointing directly at Huy, who stood stiffly in the grip of an overwhelming sense of fatality. Occasionally she shook it at him and once she turned, pausing at north, south, east, and west to utter the same sentence four times. Huy watched and listened without emotion. At any moment he expected to feel something stirring within him, opening, preparing to reluctantly push itself out, leaving his body in a lifeless heap at the woman's command, but he found no panic at the prospect; there was only numbness and the heavy fatigue that had begun to dog him days before.

She bent, and lifting the pot that sat by her left foot she removed its lid, keeping a firm hold on the rod as she did so. At once the stench of rotting faeces filled the shrine. She held it out to Huy, and the chant became a wheedling invitation: Come and eat, come and enjoy this delectable morsel I have prepared for you. Methen sneezed suddenly and Huy's hands came up to cover his nose. The rod was jerked compellingly at him. Nothing inside him responded. Four times the invitation was extended, and still Huy felt no answering flutter in his body. The lid was replaced on the pot, much to his relief.

The woman sighed and began the ceremony again. But all at once the flow of words stopped. She shuddered, blinked, frowned, and leaned slowly forward, her gaze fixed on Huy's face. Her eyes, under their thin, wrinkled lids, were clear and very blue. "Give me the dish, Methen," she said. Huy turned. Methen was passing her a platter heaped with fronds of green onion and fat cloves of garlic, all smothered in the smooth gleam of honey. "Onions and honey are sweet to mankind but bitter to the dead," she whispered. "Garlic repels the demons. Will you eat, Son of Hapu?"

Huy was far from hungry and the odour of faeces still hung about him, but he nodded, fully aware that no angry ghost would allow him to touch the food and no demon could abide the presence of garlic, let alone its taste. The woman still clutched the protecting rod firmly in her right hand. She extended the dish. Huy pulled an onion with a sliver of garlic clinging to it from the stickiness and crammed it into his mouth. As he did so, the full meaning of what he had just done burst upon him. The exhaustion vanished and he wanted to fall down with the weakness of relief.

Laying the rod across her feet, the woman held out her hands. "Come here," she said, and Huy obeyed, stepping onto the sand and clasping her fingers. They were very warm and her grip was strong. It tightened suddenly, and once again her body trembled. "Pick up my rod!" she hissed. "Quickly! Keep holding it!" Huy did as he was told. She grasped it also and they stood joined by hands and rod. She stared at him, over him, behind him, with an intensity transmitted uncomfortably to him through her skin, and it came to him that she was afraid. "Anubis is at your shoulder," she said thickly. "Thoth is beside him, and Selket has an arm around your neck. Her fingers rest so gently against your nose and mouth. Her rings glitter. The gods do not smile. They wait for me to understand." She had begun to breathe rapidly. "I must understand. I must! Anubis is Lord of the Bau, yet he did not send his hosts of demons against you. He comes as the leader of the armed followers of Horus. Oh! He is holding up an image of Shai. Fate. Destiny. You have been blessed with a destiny as unique as that of the great Imhotep. Connected with Thoth somehow, yes, and even Selket is here in her benevolent guise. Her scorpions protect you. It is she who aids the birth of kings and gods, we know this. 'She Who Causes One to Breathe.' Of course! It was she who poured life back into your lifeless body at the command of Atum the Creator. But why? What fate awaits you, Son of Hapu? Are you truly blessed or truly damned? They do not answer me. They fade. They are gone."

She slumped. Huy let go of the rod, which had become slippery in his grasp, and wiped his sweaty palm down his kilt. Try as he might, he had not felt the slightest touch of the goddess or sensed any presences around him, but there was no denying the reality of the Rekhet's reaction to something neither he nor Methen could see. Though he was shaken, he wondered fleetingly whether her reputation rested more on her ability to act than on any genuine gift. For a moment they eyed one another, the old visionary and the young man, then she handed her rod peremptorily to Methen. "Bring us wine," she ordered. Bending, she swept her fingers through the sand, obliterating the snake images, removed the strings of cowrie shells from her neck, chest, and waist, prostrated herself before the small statue of Khenti-kheti, who had watched the proceedings, it seemed to Huy, with an expression of patient exasperation on his face, and gestured for Huy to follow her into the outer court. Methen closed the door behind them.

The woman strode to a patch of shade under the wall. She and Huy sank to the stone floor together. She sighed. "You are a mystery, Huy," she said, calling him by his name for the first time. "You are not possessed by any evil force. You died and yet you live. The bau of the gods has been sent to you, bestowed a mighty gift on you, but I do not know what it is or why. What is your Naming Day?"

"The ninth day of Paophi."

"I will travel south to the temple of Khons so that I may consult the Book of the End of the Year. It predicts those who will live and who will die for any given year. You are twelve?"

"Yes."

"Then I will see if you were supposed to die in your thirteenth year. I will dictate a letter to you when I find out."

"There is such a book?" Huy was amazed.

The woman smiled. "There is, but its contents are only visible to people like myself. Do you believe such a thing?"

Huy hesitated. "I do not know. But I was dead and now I live, therefore nothing under the eye of Atum, whether I am able to see it or not, must be disbelieved."

"A good answer." She touched his arm. "My name is Henenu. I give it to very few because my task is to contend with demons and the hating dead, and a name has much heka, for good and for evil. I do not want the powers I conjure to control to turn and conquer me. Will you write to me sometimes, Huy? I am most interested in how your life will unfold. So is my master, the High Priest of Ra. He is a greater Seer than I."

Huy was startled. "But the only commerce I have had with him was when I blundered into the presence of the Ished Tree and he punished me," he blurted. "Why should he care how my life unfolds?"

She did not answer his question. "I am a sau as well as a Rekhet. I make charms and amulets. I am going to make you amulets that you must wear at all times. Do not worry," she reassured him as she saw his dismay. "They will be rings for your fingers, not necklaces that might be cumbersome for a young man. I will not charge you for them. Ah! Here is Methen with the wine. We have earned it, have we not?" The priest set a tray on the ground before them and made as if to leave, but Henenu stopped him. "Drink with us," she invited him. "I see honey cakes as well. Thank you, Methen."

The wine was shedeh, cool and sweet. It slipped down Huy's parched throat like the nectar of the gods themselves. As he tasted it, his mind filled with an image so sharp and brilliant that he cried out. Henenu went very still. "What is it, Huy?" she demanded.

He shook his head, too immersed for a moment in what his inner eye had revealed to him to speak. The Judgment Hall. The Ished Tree. Imhotep and a book, Anubis and . . . *I was there!* he thought in astonishment. *The scales were behind me. I was standing in the Paradise of Osiris, the scent of the flowers enveloped me, the river glinted. I was there! Oh gods, what was it Imhotep said to me? He gave me a choice, but I cannot hear it.*

Shakily he turned to meet the Rekhet's keen scrutiny. "Did you see Ma'at?" he managed. "Was Ma'at beside me with Anubis and Thoth and Selket? Was she there?" *Oh please tell me she was,* he begged silently, *for if she was not then I am in a very different danger than the one this Seer envisioned. Without the presence of Ma'at there is chaos and insanity and the gods will not listen to the pleas of men.*

Henenu looked puzzled. "No, Ma'at was not there. But Anubis, Thoth, and Selket surrounded you with their benevolence, not their ill will. You have nothing to fear."

Huy was not so sure. Now that he remembered where he had been while his body lay in Ra's sacred lake, on the barge transporting it to Hut-herib, tumbled onto the slab in the House of the Dead, he knew he would not forget. Ma'at had been there, standing apart from Anubis in the shadows of the Hall, looking at him with—what? Warning? Pity? He groaned.

"Do you want to tell us, Huy?" Henenu pressed.

"Not now," Huy muttered. "Perhaps later." He glanced up. "I am very tired."

"Of course you are." She raised herself onto her knees and, placing her hands on his head, said, "My hand is on you. My seal is your protection." Huy knew that the words belonged to a spell to protect a child.

Hapzefa had sometimes intoned them over him when he was much younger but had long since discontinued the practice. A bolt of something hot streaked through his body at Henenu's touch, and she took her hands away. "Go home," she said gently. "Methen will go with you to tell your parents that all is well with you. Pray often and come to this shrine to give homage to the totem of your town. When you are ready, go back to school. I will be able to visit you there."

Awkwardly Huy got to his feet and bowed to her. "Thank you, Rekhet, for your service to me. You have given me back my life." He was careful not to use her name.

"No, Huy," she reminded him softly. "I did not do that. May the soles of your feet always be firm. We will meet again."

The sun stood at its zenith, hot and strong. Huy stepped out of the shade into its full glare, Methen beside him. The litter-bearers had gone. "This time we will walk," Methen said gravely, a note of gladness in his voice, "and everyone seeing you will know that you are whole."

Huy did not reply. He had begun to suspect that he was far from anything resembling a harmony of soul with body. Grimly he strode towards his father's house through the dust-clouded air of noon.

6

Huy's father did not apologize for his lack of faith. He listened expressionlessly to Methen's words, nodded once, briefly embraced his son, and, bidding the priest farewell, strode away to the fields. Huy entered the house to the excited exclamations of his mother and Hapzefa's smile, but it was Heby who brought home to him his full restoration. The child came tottering towards him, holding out his arms, and with a spurt of joy Huy picked him up and held him closely. "I must send word at once to Ker and Heruben," Itu was saying. "Hapzefa, leave the laundry and put on your sandals. Tell them all is well with Huy and they must visit us as soon as possible. Huy, my darling, are you hungry? Thirsty? What can I bring you?"

Huy pulled his ear away from Heby's chubby fingers. "I would like to sleep. I'm very tired."

"Of course you are! Heby, come to me. We will leave your brother to rest, and then perhaps he will play with you in the garden. Oh, Huy!" Her eyes were shining. "All that nonsense about your death! Now our lives can be sensible again. Hapzefa, what are you waiting for?" The servant shrugged and lumbered off and Huy, after kissing his mother's hot cheek, retreated to his room.

Lying on his couch, he closed his eyes, letting his whole body relax of its own accord. For the first time in weeks he felt calm and sane. *The gods will reveal their will for me when they are ready,* he thought comfortably. *I need not fret about it anymore. I can go back to school. I can walk with Thothmes by the sacred lake and we will recall Sennefer's stupidity in a mood of superior pity for his crudeness. I miss my friend. It will be good to see him again.*

His aunt and uncle arrived that evening. Heruben greeted him with an awkward embarrassment born, Huy sensed, of the cowardice that had kept her away from him for so long. Ker showed a similar, less evident discomfiture. He hugged Huy briefly. "I'm sorry that I cannot escort you back to Iunu," he said as they sat together in the warm grass while Heby chased a cloud of gnats hovering like flecks of red dust in the westering light. "I must tend my vats of jasmine and narcissus flowers, and a supply of sarson oil sits waiting for the henna leaves the peasants are busy gathering. My harvest time comes long before that of the grain farmer, as you know." He did not look at Huy.

"You need not apologize, Uncle," Huy said, hearing the excuse in Ker's tone. "I am perfectly capable of making the journey back to school without your supervision. I might even walk there."

Ker grunted. "You are almost a man. I keep forgetting until I see you again." He shifted from one hip to the other, his gaze fixed on Heby, who was now shrieking in frustration as Hapzefa rushed to him and

Itu's face appeared around the edge of the door. "Last time I saw you was when I helped your father and the priest carry you into the House of the Dead," he went on, still looking away. "If you ever want to talk to me about what happened to you, I am ready to listen without judgment."

Yet you did judge me, Huy thought sadly. *You abandoned me to the Sheseru, the arrow-troops of demons, for fear of your own contamination. You always seemed perfect to me, without faults, but I see now that you are like any other man. I am indeed growing up. Why were you not willing to listen to me before, when I desperately needed you?* He wanted to say all this, but he swallowed his resentment. Only his mother had not deserted him. His mother and Ishat, he remembered with surprise. Ishat too.

"There is nothing to discuss," he lied. "I have no memory from the time I felt the blow of the throwing stick against my head. Anyway, I'm not ready to go back to school yet. Perhaps towards the end of Pharmuthi. That will still give me most of Shemu to catch up with my studies. I will write to the Overseer and tell him."

Ker nodded but did not speak. They sat in silence while dusk crept slowly into the garden. Huy had sensed in his father an inner wariness that Ker obviously shared. He knew it would not change in either man, and it filled him with loneliness.

In spite of the welcome result of his exorcism he was restless, waking tense and suddenly alert in the night for no reason he could ascertain and finding himself unable to remain still for very long during the day. He took to wandering about the busy streets of Hut-herib, dodging laden donkeys, purposeful citizens, and groups of naked peasant children who flung handfuls of dusty earth and insults at him as a matter of course before returning to their games and whom he ignored. More and more, however, he found himself meandering along the edges of the water-filled ditches that divided the little fields from one another. The acres of wheat and barley, still green and supple, stirred in the pleasant airs of late spring. Aromatic daisies trembled on their margins, golden faces turned to the sun. Within the thickness of the crops the blue of wild flax and cornflowers, the red of tall poppies, the white splash of mayweed all testified to the farmers' endless fight against the unwanted growth that threatened to overwhelm the less-hardy grain, but Huy liked to see the bright colours scattered here and there. Tiny clumps of wild narcissus gave off their fragrance under his feet. Sometimes there were wild water lilies eking out a precarious existence among the mats of clinging pondweed in the stagnant canals. Huy, pausing under the feathery branches of the willows lining the water, looked in vain for the strange blooms of Paradise filling his mind, and his nostrils sought their exotic perfume to no avail.

He had finally dragged out his palette and written a letter to the Overseer of the temple school, warning the man that he would be returning at the end of the month. On the day when he had found a merchant going south who had agreed to deliver it for him and had just walked back into his house to seek Hapzefa and a long drink of date juice, there was a sudden commotion at the other end of the passage. Huy swung around. Limned against the strong midday light was a figure he knew he recognized but could not place, shorter than a full-grown man, coming towards him out of the gloom. It laughed, and all at once Huy, with a glad heart, ran to meet it. "Thothmes! Thothmes! Is it really you? What are you doing here? Oh, how wonderful to see you!" The two friends embraced, and when Huy broke away he saw his mother and Hapzefa with Heby in hand hovering behind the youth. "Mother, this is my cellmate Thothmes from Iunu!" he said excitedly. "I can hardly believe it! May we go into the reception room?"

"Father and Nasha are right behind me," Thothmes said. "I got off my litter and ran ahead; I was so eager to see you!"

Itu let out a strangled exclamation. "Your father? The Governor of Iunu? Here? But nothing is prepared, the house is not swept, we cannot receive—"

Thothmes turned and took her hand with the purposeful solemnity Huy remembered so well. "You are the esteemed mother of my dear friend. I and my family have been worried about him. My father cares nothing for the humble circumstances of Huy's home. In Huy's character he sees the care with which he has been raised. Nothing else matters to him. He is above such pettiness. He will be content with cheese and dates and barley beer."

"We can do a little better than that," Hapzefa muttered, but Itu was only slightly mollified.

"Hapzefa, find Ishat and send her into the fields. Hapu must come home at once. Huy, come into the garden with me. We must greet our guests, and then Hapzefa and I must prepare a meal." Flushed and agitated, she started down the passage.

"I am sorry for this, Huy," Thothmes whispered as together they followed her. "I should have sent a letter to warn you, but Father is here for a meeting with the governor of your sepat. I was in school, but I begged and pleaded to come this far so I could see you, and the girls wanted to see you as well. Father finally gave in. He is concerned about you, although he doesn't show it." Thothmes grimaced. "I must return to school afterwards. We have brought two barges."

They emerged into the garden just as a small procession came wending its way from the communal path that ran past Hapu's gate. Two soldiers strode up to Itu and saluted. Behind them two litters surrounded with servants were being lowered and other servants carrying several boxes brought up the rear. Itu had begun to pleat her sheath convulsively. Huy wanted to step past her, but good manners demanded that she welcome Thothmes' family herself. He put a hand on her shoulder. "They are good people," he murmured into her pink ear. "Thothmes spoke the truth. Don't worry!" He felt her swallow, then the lean form of Iunu's Governor appeared and walked forward smiling. Itu's bare arms went out in the correct gesture of obeisance. She and Huy bowed.

"Welcome to this house, illustrious one," Itu managed. "We are honoured by your presence. I am Itu."

"And I am honoured to meet the mother of my son's best friend," Nakht replied gravely. "I beg your forgiveness for descending on you with no warning,

Itu. My wife was horrified at the idea, but Thothmes insisted on this visit until I was compelled to either tie up his mouth with his own kilt or give in." He smiled. "I gave in." He snapped his fingers and the occupant of the other litter came hurrying up to him. Nasha grinned at Huy. Nakht indicated her. "My daughter Nasha." The girl bowed, her ornaments tinkling. Nakht gestured to the servants. "My wife has sent gifts of food and wine for your storehouse as an apology," he continued. "Enjoy them in good health."

Itu was recovering. Thanking him profusely, she indicated the house and the little crowd followed her into the reception room. "Huy, you need to wash and change your kilt after your walk into the town," she said. "Perhaps Thothmes would like to keep you company. When Hapzefa returns we will have wine. In the meantime, noble one, please sit. Or would you prefer to rest in the garden?"

"Your mother is very beautiful," Thothmes commented as he and Huy retreated to the rear of the house, where the water was stored.

Huy was startled. "Is she? I don't know. Oh, Thothmes, this is the best surprise in the world!"

The fire between house and kitchen was almost out, but the large covered pitchers were full of water. There was no sign of Hapzefa, and Huy did not want to waste time building up the fire and heating the water himself. Stripping, he took a cold wash, then he and Thothmes made their way to Huy's room. Thothmes wriggled onto the couch at once, folding his arms and watching as Huy withdrew clean linen from his chest, dressed quickly, and pushed his feet into his best sandals.

The murmur of voices came to Huy faintly. He heard his mother laugh, and knew that the relaxed sound was a tribute to Nakht's conversational skill. Taking the chair, he surveyed Thothmes' expectant face.

"We have a few moments before your father appears," Thothmes said. "I want to know everything, Huy. Strange rumours have been flying in Iunu. People who thrive on stupid gossip are even saying that the gods resurrected you from the dead." He pursed his lips and gave Huy a dark glance. "I must say you look amazingly healthy. You've grown. But there is a certain strain about you . . . something different . . ." He shrugged. "It's to be expected after the blow you took. I wasn't strong enough to haul you out of the lake myself, you know. You sank right to the bottom and lay there. Sennefer and Samentuser had run away. I jumped into the water and screamed for help and a couple of passing priests came, but not right away." His gaze went to the floor. "By the time we got you onto the stone verge, you were white and your lips were blue and your eyes were open. Your eyes were open!" Diffidence and pleading fled across his features and Huy's heart sank. *Not you too!* he thought dismally. *Love me without dissimulation, Thothmes, for I am lonely and afraid and need your unstinting trust!*

"I will tell you everything," he said, "but you must swear to hold my words secret. You will be the first to hear the whole matter. Our friendship depends on your caution."

Thothmes lifted the pectoral amulet lying on his chest. "I swear by Thoth whose name my beloved King carries," he replied. "You are my friend forever, Huy. I will not betray you."

So under Thothmes' sober attention Huy recounted everything, from the moment when he felt himself falling into the deepest well on earth to the end of his encounter with the Rekhet, and as he spoke, the memories at last became not only vivid but seamless, no longer fragmented—with one exception. He could see Imhotep's mouth moving but still was unable to recall the august man's words. All he had was the anxious knowledge that a momentous choice had been presented to him and that he had made it. Thothmes listened, his already large brown eyes becoming even larger as they registered awe, astonishment, and occasionally bewilderment, but to his relief Huy saw no disbelief on his friend's delicate face.

Huy fell silent. Thothmes stared at him for a long time, arms still folded, his whole body motionless, then he shook his head. "If I had not known you for so many years, I would call you insane," he said huskily, "but you have not come under the special protection of the gods in that way. No, I believe you. It is the most wondrous story I have ever heard." He grimaced. "And the most absurd. Are the gods playing a game with you? What do they want of you?"

"The Rekhet said that they had bestowed a gift on me." Huy spoke dully; he was tired. "She did not know what it was and neither do I. I just want to come back to school and work and have fun with you and let it all fade away." He placed his palms together between his knees and bent forward. "Help me, Thothmes." To his horror he began to cry. "I remember the aroma of the flowers in Paradise, their glorious colours, the breathtaking majesty of the Ished Tree, the splendour and purity and vibrancy of everything I saw, so that when I look out over my uncle's acres of perfume flowers or stand by the river or glance up at the sky, the world seems cold and lifeless. I cannot prevent the comparison, and it hurts my heart."

Thothmes jumped from the couch and, kneeling beside Huy, pulled him close. "Dear brother, I understand so little of what you've told me, but since the moment we first met I have felt a kinship with you. We take care of one another. Come back with us to Iunu when we go. Father's business will be concluded in a few days. Huy?" Huy wiped his eyes on his kilt and Thothmes sat back.

"But I've only just written to Overseer Harmose for permission to return," he objected shakily.

Thothmes tutted. "Harmose will be pleased to have one of his best pupils wreaking havoc again," he said stoutly, and Huy laughed. "It can all be sorted out, Huy. Your cot is still empty."

Huy rose. "First I must approach my uncle. He has not actually said so, but I have a feeling that he may not wish to support my education anymore."

"If he won't, then my father will. He believes that every deserving child, peasant or not, should be allowed to learn. An impossible dream, but it does him credit. Can you imagine those ghastly children who play in the canals of your town and fling mud at the passersby donning fine linen and growing youth locks and memorizing the Precepts of Amenemopet?"

Huy smiled wryly and decided not to remind Thothmes that he, Huy, was only one rung above those rascals. "Father must have returned by now, and I have recovered. Let's join our families."

Hapu had indeed preceded them. He was sitting cross-legged in a corner of the crowded little room, his still-wet hair slicked back, a cup of beer cradled in both brawny hands. He rose with difficulty as Thothmes entered, lowered his head in a respectful bow, and resumed his place. *Why, I suppose Thothmes is an aristocrat,* Huy thought.

His mother looked him over approvingly. Heby was deeply asleep in the sling her sheath had made between her thighs. "That's better," she said gaily. Her cup was obviously full of wine. Her face was flushed.

Nasha waved at Huy. "Come and sit beside me," she offered. "I've missed hauling you into the marshes with Thothmes to frighten the ducks. It's good to see you, Huy. Anuket sends her fond greetings. Father decided that she is still too young to leave home without Mother. Are you quite recovered from your terrible wounding?" Huy, sinking down at her knee and inhaling the expensive odour of myrrh and cassia surrounding her, was glad that her sunny disposition did not include much room for complicated introspection.

"The gods have been kind," Itu answered for him. "Huy has been restored to full vigour. Ah! Here is Hapzefa with refreshments. I hope you like cold pigeon meat, Governor Nakht, and of course there is new lettuce and onions and figs from our first crop of the year. More wine?"

They ate and drank in an atmosphere of easy talk. Nakht asked Huy's father many questions regarding his work and inquired after Huy's future plans. Huy, with one eye on Hapu, answered carefully. Nasha chattered about household affairs with Itu. "I am of an age to marry," she said at one point, "but Father hasn't yet selected a suitable husband for me. I think he hesitates because he hates to see his home emptying of his children. Well, I am in no hurry. I love wandering around the markets of Iunu and punting in the papyrus swamps by the river." Huy picked at the food and drank his date wine enveloped in the pleasant miasma of Nasha's perfume, which forcibly reminded him of Anuket's tiny face as she peered up at him from whatever wreath she was making through the curtain of her thick black hair. He found himself all at once desperate to be gone from this house, from Hut-herib, from the sidelong glances of its citizens. He caught his father's eye.

"May Thothmes and Nasha and I go into the garden?" he asked. Hapu nodded brusquely and the three of them rose, Huy bowing to Nakht, and went out into the mid-afternoon sunshine.

"Father dines with your mayor tonight," Nasha said, flinging herself down in the shade of the shrubbery by the orchard gate, "so Thothmes and I will eat on board the barge. Do you think you could join us? Look at the litter-bearers! They are all asleep! I see that your servant has fed them."

Huy dragged his attention from the flash of white he had seen out of the corner of his eye as he lowered himself beside her and Thothmes unfolded at her feet. The bushes were trembling. Someone was watching them from the safety of the orchard. Huy knew it must be Ishat. He smiled grimly to himself, anticipating her tart, jealous comments.

"I'd like to," he replied. "I'll ask Father after the sleep. By the look of Mother they'll both need their couches today!"

Impulsively Nasha threw her arms around him and held him tightly. "Dear, earnest Huy! It's good to see where you live at last. I love your little house, and the garden is a gem. But where are the paintings you told us you daubed all over the walls?"

"Father whitewashes every year when the Inundation keeps him out of the fields," Huy answered absently, for a peculiar sensation was seeping into him from her arms, a coolness that was rolling into his chest, curling through his torso, flowing down his legs, and inching upward towards his head. The feeling was familiar and wholly terrifying, yet when Nasha slapped his back amiably and relinquished her hold on him he was compelled to grab both her hands convulsively. His eyes closed of their own accord. The coolness crept up the back of his neck and began to fill his skull, becoming colder as it went. He shivered once uncontrollably. *I feel death. I have been here before. Gods! It is death! I am dying!* Panic seized him, clenching in his bowels, but that icy tide rapidly quenched it. A dense blackness formed slowly somewhere behind his eyes. He fought to open them and failed. He was aware of Nasha frantically trying to free her fingers, and although he wanted to release her, he could not. "Nasha," he heard himself grind out from between clenched teeth. "Nasha. The Street of the Basket Sellers. Don't go there. Mud. The ground is muddy. Don't go there." At once the dreadful cold blackness began to lift, and as it ebbed his eyes flew open. Nasha was staring at him, white-faced. Weak and nauseous, he released her hands.

"What happened, Huy?" she half whispered. "Did you just prophesy? Is a god speaking to me through you? But you're not even a priest! It wasn't even like your voice! Tell me it was a silly joke."

A droplet of sweat rolled down Huy's temple. Drawing one finger across his forehead, he felt the clamminess of his skin. "Forgive me, Nasha," he muttered. "I don't know what happened. You hugged me and suddenly I felt as though I was dying and then the words came to me." Bending over, he clutched at his stomach. "I'm dizzy. The sky is heaving. Why is there a cart parked where the pond should be? There are rocks inside me. I think I'm going to be sick." He fought the urge to retch, aware of the shocked silence around him, not wanting to look up and see the Street of the Basket Sellers superimposed over the grass and gently stirring shrubbery of the garden. But by the time he had regained control of himself, the mirage had disappeared. His head had begun to throb.

"You look ill," Nasha said, her voice stronger. She was rubbing her fingers lightly. "I think that there are things you're not telling me about what happened to you by the temple lake, aren't there, Huy? I want to know everything, but not now. You have given me a great fright." She scrambled up and walked away, her yellow sheath rippling with her stride.

Thothmes' eyes were on Huy's face. He had not moved. "The Street of the Basket Sellers in Iunu is seldom muddy, and Nasha goes there often on her jaunts through the markets with her bodyguard. Am I to keep her away from the Street of the Basket Sellers, Huy? For now or for years to come?"

"What do you mean?" Huy croaked, but he knew, he knew, and the knowledge was like carrying a belly full of stones.

"No Anubis bowl of oil on water. No lamp and censer, no diviner lying on bricks, no invocation. You saw Nasha's future, didn't you?"

"I don't know." Huy was massaging his temples.

"It was a warning for her. At least, we must pray that it was a warning and not a glimpse of the inevitable." Grabbing Huy's shoulders, Thothmes knelt upright. "Wake up, Huy! We both know what just happened. We now know the gift of the gods. You will predict the future for anyone you touch!"

"That's ridiculous," Huy responded dully. The stones in his abdomen shifted, grinding together, and he winced at the pain. "Even a Rekhet must perform the rituals, speak the spells that coerce the gods to reveal what cannot be seen. Besides, why would they bestow such an ability on me? Of what use am I to them, an anonymous boy from an ugly town in the Delta?"

"You must ask them." Thothmes' eyes were shining. "Everything they do has purpose. Do you think you might be able to see your own future by looking into a mirror?"

"Oh, be silent!" Huy begged, then put out a hand in apology but withdrew it hastily. He was afraid to touch his friend. "Forgive me," he begged. "Whatever Nasha's embrace caused was so sudden that it has unmanned me."

"Yes, Nasha." Thothmes' tone was urgent. "I love her, Huy. I do not want any evil to befall her. How may I protect her? Can she protect herself?"

"I don't know!" Huy cried out. "All I know is that something terrible will happen to her in the Street of the Basket Sellers!" There. It was out. *And I believe it*, Huy thought in dismay. *It was death filling me once more, Nasha's death, pouring into me by the power of* . . . "The gift," he said miserably. "I suspect you're right, Thothmes. But I don't want it! How may I get rid of it?"

"Would you blaspheme?" Thothmes objected softly. "Think what good you can do, Huy, how many hearts you can soothe, what such a certainty will mean to so many people!"

"Or what horror. Perhaps it will not happen again. Perhaps it was a moment of disorder caused by Sennefer's throwing stick. A dizziness. A surge of ukhedu in my blood."

Thothmes held out his hands. "Let's find out."

Huy recoiled. "No! I don't want that creeping cold again, or the nausea. What if I feel something . . . bad?"

Thothmes regarded him steadily. "We all die, Huy, even the gods who follow one another on the Horus Throne. Please try."

With an inner revulsion against the gods, against the grotesque facility he now suspected to be lurking inside him, even against Thothmes himself, he grasped the young man's hands. Familiar and warm, they instantly curled around his own. He felt no compunction to close his eyes. For a moment there was no change either within or around him. Thin shadows were creeping across the grass as the afternoon inched towards evening. The green fronds of the vegetables ranged around the pool quivered in the breeze. A bird alighted on the pool's verge, dipping its beak into the water with quick, decisive little advances as it drank. The sun was hot on the back of Huy's head. *I should move farther into the shade,* he thought, and then he felt himself slipping sideways. Thothmes' eyes remained large, but the skin around them puffed and wrinkled. His nose lengthened and spread. His mouth thinned, but his features still held the stamp of deceptive fragility that belied his stubborn nature. An elaborate collar of red jasper scarabs and golden ankhs clasped his neck, its beauty partially obscured by the wings of the white-and-black-striped linen helmet he was wearing. Behind him, the sun's rays lay splashed across a white wall bright with painted grapevines and flowering trees. As Huy stared at him in wonder, he smiled. "Greetings, Huy," he said, his voice thin but strong, an old man's voice, then all at once Huy was back in his garden. The bird had gone. Thothmes was looking at him anxiously.

"Well? Is something going to happen, do you think?"

"It did. You will live to turn into a rich and ugly old man and we will still be friends."

"Tell me what you saw!" Huy complied. The pain in his stomach had disappeared, but his head still ached. "For myself I am content," Thothmes said, "but what of Nasha? You have just proved that the gift is true, but can what you see be changed by knowledge or will?"

Huy's father had come out of the house and was beckoning them. Unsteadily Huy got up. "I don't know," he said for the fourth time. "Tell no one about all this, Thothmes. If you do, I will soon be seen as a curiosity at best and an aberration to be shunned at worst. Promise me!"

"I have already given you my word." Thothmes joined Huy and together they hurried towards Hapu. "I suppose Father and Nasha are ready to leave. Will you dine on the barge with us?"

Huy declined. "I have changed my mind," he said deliberately, "but ask Nakht if I may return to Iunu with you. The sooner my life resumes its normal course, the better."

Thothmes did not press him. Nakht and a subdued Nasha had emerged and the litter-bearers were assembling. Huy waited until the farewells had been said and the litters were out of sight before escaping to his room. For the first time in his life he was desperate to pray. He had remembered the words Imhotep had spoken to him.

After prostrating himself before the little statue of Khenti-kheti that rested by his couch, he came to his feet, discarding the formal words of worship and trying to address the god from his heart, but it was so full of the confusion of questions and conflicting emotions that all he could do was spread his arms wide. "What am I to do with this . . . this power I have been given?" he demanded loudly, hoping that the sound of his own firm voice would cover the turmoil within. "Am I to declare myself a Seer and run about grasping at my neighbours' limbs? How silly! Am I to offer myself to whoever presses me for an answer regarding their future? Dear Khenti-kheti, I am only twelve years old! What will these visions do to me?" At that thought he fell silent. Khenti-kheti stared back at him expressionlessly. "Already I am afraid," he whispered.

"Can I embrace my mother and remain blissfully ignorant of her future? I have no desire to see it open out before me, but what if it happens anyway and I glimpse something terrible? How can I ever look at her again? Will Thothmes keep silent? Will I? Should I?"

Casting himself into his chair, he leaned back and closed his eyes, aware that around him the house had settled into its mid-afternoon torpor. At once the great Imhotep's face bloomed with the clarity of a noon brilliance behind his eyelids. "I am to put to you this question," he said. "Will you taste the fruit of the holy Ished Tree?" The scroll was in his hand. "Atum gives you this choice, to make entirely freely. He deigns to share with you his divine wisdom. Will you read?"

But why? Huy thought urgently now, sitting in the quiet stillness of his room. *And why did I not ask the reason while I had the chance? Why did it not occur to me to put that obvious and simple question to Imhotep? What is the creator-god's true purpose in bestowing such an awesome privilege on such as me? Is the Book of Thoth somehow connected to the magical lamp inside me that will illuminate the fate of anyone I choose?*

"I will read."

He heard himself give his august companion the answer, felt his lips move without reflection as they had done in that beautiful place while in the real world his body was passing lifelessly through many hands and five days were going by. Five days. Yet in Imhotep's presence time had ceased to move.

Huy stiffened. A cold shiver ran through him, prickling over his scalp and numbing his skin so that involuntarily he sat forward and rubbed his arms. Time had ceased to move. Five days dead, as Methen had warned him not to forget, yet time had meant nothing in the place where his consciousness or soul or shadow, or whatever part of him had operated apart from his body, sat beside Imhotep in the deep shade of the Ished Tree. *I died and I can see into the future,* he thought. *I can be here and ten, twenty years ahead, all at once. Time no longer has any meaning for me. It is an illusion. Only my flesh remains trapped in its web. The destiny of every man in Egypt is mine to discover if I so choose.*

Yet there was the hyena.

He paused, troubled, in the flush of elation that had followed the moment of chill. Hyenas were ugly scavengers, kept by many households to dispose of various wastes and offal. To cleanse, in other words. The hyena had been lying contentedly in the warm grass, its eyes half closed. It had ignored him. Huy knew that everything he had seen, everything he had heard in that celestial place was becoming of supreme importance to him. Much was still shrouded in mystery. Then what did the hyena signify? It had been almost noble in its stately docility. He had barely noticed it at the time and Imhotep had seemed unaware of its presence, but now Huy saw its chest rising and falling with its light breaths, the golden eyelashes growing from the half-lowered lids, the glow of sunlight in the halo of its furred ruff. Was it there for him, an obscure communication he could not fathom as yet? Did it belong to Imhotep, if there was such a thing as belonging in Paradise? Did it serve the Ished Tree in some peculiar way, or had it simply paused by the Tree in its wanderings? Huy frowned restlessly, his earlier elation evaporating. The hyena was vitally important, he sensed it, but the significance of the beast remained elusive no matter how fiercely he bent his memory upon it. In the end he sighed and went to his couch, thrusting the pulse of unease away. He would think of Thothmes and the journey to Iunu and drift off to sleep.

In the early evening, before the last meal of the day, Huy sat with his mother while she examined the contents of the boxes Nakht had brought. Under the lid of the first one she opened was a small wreath of dried flowers wrapped loosely in linen: narcissus, pink jasmine, tiny yellow chrysanthemums, and the buds of white water lilies, all intertwined with dark ivy leaves and twigs of marjoram that gave off a faintly spicy aroma. "Anuket made that!" Huy exclaimed, taking it carefully from Itu. "She dries the flowers herself and will not say how she keeps their colours so bright! She loves making wreaths and garlands."

Itu cast a sidelong glance at him. "You always speak of her with affection," she said wryly. "I'm sorry she did not accompany her father, I would have liked to meet her."

"I'm sorry too," Huy replied simply. "I'm very fond of her. May I hang the wreath in my room?"

Itu nodded absently, her attention on the jar she was withdrawing. She sniffed the seal. "Olive oil! A generous gift indeed! There are three more like it. Hapzefa will be pleased." She set it down. "And what is this? Oh, look, Huy! Saffron from Keftiu, the very best treatment for stomach ailments!" She had licked the tip of one finger and put it gently into the orange powder, withdrawing it and tasting carefully. "This must be used sparingly so it will last." Replacing the stopper, she delved into the box again. By the time the boxes were empty and she sat back on her heels, she was surrounded by pots and jars of all sizes. There were dried carob pods from Rethennu, pistachio nuts from Mennofer, grey antimony for salves, red antimony for her lips, galena and charcoal to be mixed with goose fat for her eyes, dainty alabaster pots for her perfume, ground rowan wood for infected wounds, a small pot of almonds, another of powdered medicinal myrrh, and lastly an alabaster jug in the shape of a poppy flower that had been filled to the brim with undiluted opium. Itu sighed, in envy or gratitude Huy could not tell. "How rich Nakht must be," she said, "and how generous he is. He must value you very highly, Huy."

Huy murmured something noncommittal and stood, clutching the wreath. "I am going to my room to pack," he told her. "Nakht will take me back to school tomorrow. I will write a letter to Uncle Ker about it, and speak to Father tonight, but I don't think he will object."

His mother glanced up at him sharply. "You ought to wait for permission from the Overseer, and at least discuss the matter with Hapu before you pack, out of respect for him," she objected.

Huy shook his head on a wave of rebellion against his father's desertion, his uncle's cowardice. "I don't think so," he retorted. "I love them both, but I am determined to leave regardless of what they say. Many things have changed, Mother."

She bit her lip and, holding up her hand, said simply, "I know, dearest. You are the same and yet not the same. I have sensed it."

Huy grasped her fingers with his own. As he did so, he felt the quiver of something still alien begin to stir deep within him, a seductive compulsion to take one look—oh, just one brief glimpse!—at her ultimate fate, and he responded to it with a violent inner *No!* To his relief, it subsided at once. *So I do have control over it,* he thought as he bent to kiss Itu's cheek. *I am not helpless against the tug of its subtle coercion. I may yet save my own sanity.* He left her and went to his room.

It was not empty. Ishat sat cross-legged on his couch, picking at the dirt under her fingernails with the end of one of Huy's paintbrushes. Pieces of his sennet game were scattered on the rumpled sheet under her. His cedar box lay open on the floor, his palette beside it. She shot him a sulky look as he came through the doorway and her mouth opened, but Huy did not give her a chance to speak. On a wave of anger he dropped the wreath, strode across the room, snatched the brush from her grip, dragged her off the couch, and pushed her onto his chair. Tight-lipped, he collected up the cones and spools of the game and replaced them with the sennet board. He put away the paintbrush after ostentatiously wiping its end on his kilt. Ishat snorted but said nothing. Checking the contents of his box, he laid his palette inside it and closed the lid. Then he faced her. "If I ever catch you going through my belongings again without my leave, I'll have you beaten. I have that authority and you know it, Ishat. Your parents would be disgraced.

What were you thinking?" He picked up the wreath and laid it on the couch.

"I was sent in here to sweep the floor," she replied sullenly, pointing at the broom propped by the window, "but I didn't feel like working today, so I just waited for you to come." Her eyes narrowed. "I saw you in the garden with your new friends. I saw you embracing that pampered little princess. Is she the one you love, Huy? Is she?"

Huy struggled to see past the jealousy disfiguring Ishat's face to the pain beneath. "She is the sister of my friend, the young man who sat with us," he started to explain, trying to keep his voice reasonable. "She is not at all pampered, in fact her father is very strict with his children. Yes, I am fond of her, Ishat. She and the rest of her family are very good to me and I enjoy being with them. I am returning to Iunu with them tomorrow. I must pack my bags, so please go away."

Instantly she slid off the chair and ran to him. "I'm sorry, Huy. Forgive me. I had no right to touch your possessions, but I was angry. You make me so lonely. I miss you so much."

She never doubted me, Huy reminded himself. *She neither feared me nor ignored me.* He forced himself to meet the pleading in those dark eyes so close to his own.

"You are my oldest friend, Ishat. I love you for that. Why can't it be enough for you?" Put your hands on her shoulders, something whispered to him. Take a look into her future. Perhaps she is to die soon . . . Ease your mind, Huy. See if this complication may be removed. In horrified denial he put his arms around her and drew her close. Her disordered hair smelled of hot sunlight. The brown skin covering those flighty bones had no odour at all. I might be holding a bird, Huy thought, or a small gazelle. In a rush of affection and pity he took her head between his palms and kissed her softly on her mouth. "I cannot imagine living without you."

She wrenched herself away from him. "That's not what I want!" she shouted. "I love you, but I hate you as well! Hate you! Go back to your stupid school, then, and keep kissing the hennaed toes of those pretty aristocrats! One day you will be sorry you spurn what I am offering you so freely!" Spinning on her bare heel, she flounced out the doorway and into the passage.

Huy let out a gusty breath. When he inhaled, it was to draw into his nostrils the faint tang of marjoram from Anuket's wreath. Lifting it, he looked about for somewhere to hang it, wondering at the same time, with a spasm of excitement, what he had done with his two leather satchels. Ishat would recover her equilibrium, as always, and would greet him happily, as always, when he came home. The foundations of his world were being re-established, and for the moment he was full of anticipation.

That night, over their lentils and beer, Huy told his father that he would be leaving the next day. He did not ask for permission or advice. Hapu listened impassively, his eyes on his son's face, and Huy thought he read both relief and regret in the man's gaze. "I will write a letter to Ker for you to deliver on my behalf if you will, Father," Huy said. "He may not wish to continue to pay my expenses, although he has not said so, but perhaps he will for a little while out of the guilt I believe he feels." Hapu did not ask what guilt; his gaze flickered for a moment. "I will also leave a letter for Methen. He has been more than good to me."

Hapu's lips twisted suddenly, a gesture of pain. Reaching for Heby, who had been crawling on the floor between them, he pulled the child onto his knee. "Your unspoken accusation towards me is just, Huy," he said heavily, "but I beg you to remember that every man has his faults and weaknesses. Mine hurt you. I am sorry." He had put down his mug and was running a hand over Heby's curls. "If Ker's generosity no longer extends to you, I will petition Methen for assistance from the town and I will dictate a letter to Ra's High Priest at Iunu. The god may be willing to spare something for one of his pupils."

All at once ashamed, Huy touched his father's foot. "Thank you."

Itu leaned across him to refill Hapu's mug, avoiding Heby's delighted attempts to catch the stream of cool brown liquid as it cascaded from the flagon. "I wish you would consider staying home," she said vehemently. "You would not have to work in the fields, would he, Hapu? Ker would take you as an apprentice perfume maker, I'm sure he would. After all, you can read and write. You would be a great help to him." She glanced at Huy appealingly. "You are still not well, Huy, you have not regained your full strength. Stay with us, please!" Hapu did not join her pleading. He was lifting his beer purposefully to his mouth with his eyes on the rim of his mug.

"No," Huy said firmly. "I love school. I want to finish my education if possible. I've eaten enough, Mother. May I go?" She nodded resignedly.

In the entrance to the passageway he paused and glanced back at them. Itu had a hand on her husband's shoulder. Her face was upturned to him. He was looking across at her with a gentle smile, and above her outstretched arm the top of Heby's head gleamed in the soft glow of lamplight. In a surge of love for them and sorrow for himself, Huy knew that the three of them were sufficient for each other and that he did not belong with them anymore. There would be time spent in this house, there would still be moments of laughter and good conversation, but the weeks of horror and ecstasy behind him had severed the chord of childhood security binding him to them, forcing him towards an accelerated maturity. Huy had become a man.

Making his way into his parents' sleeping room, he opened his mother's tiring chest, fumbling a little in the darkness until his fingers found the cold smoothness of ivory. Drawing out the monkey with a shudder of distaste, holding it away from his body, he retreated to the passage and slipped out of the house into the garden. The last shreds of Ra's blooding had left no more than a tinge of pink on the horizon. The sky was a rich, deep blue already thickening into black, but a few tentative stars had begun to appear, weak and pale. There was no sign of moonrise. The garden lay in a shrouded dimness, the pool giving back no reflection, the grass still warm under Huy's feet, the air still holding the scents of growing things.

Going straight to the pool, Huy walked around it until he saw the grey surface of a rock flat enough to take the monkey. Laying it down, he knelt and lifted the rock next to it, feeling the fronds of his mother's celery plants brush his wrist as he did so. She would know that her vegetable rockery had been disturbed. Perhaps, when he was finished, she would find tiny shards of ivory sprinkled among her onions and garlic. She would understand. Raising the rock in both hands, he brought it down on the hateful toy with all the strength he could muster, hearing it crack and splinter, still able to vaguely see its idiot face, its jerking limbs, split and shatter. Again and again he struck, his muscles taut with the grief of his father's betrayal, his uncle's desertion, his love for them awkwardly mended now but never to be whole. Only when he tasted a salty liquid on his lips did he realize that he was crying.

He had begun to ineffectually scrape the remains together when someone behind him said quietly, "I will dispose of the pieces, Huy. Don't worry about it." He staggered to his feet and swung round. Ishat was regarding him impassively, the outlines of her body blending with the increasing dimness, her eyes as darkly fathomless as the surface of the pool. She smiled briefly, her teeth a flash of light there and gone. "Go and wash your face and then sleep."

He was bewildered for a moment, his mind full of the ache of a nostalgia he knew would remain with him for the rest of his life, the muscles of his arms on fire. "What are you doing here, Ishat?" he stammered.

She stepped closer, both hands going to the wetness of his cheeks, stroking the tears away. "I often
wander about in the garden and the orchard after
Mother thinks I've gone to bed. The night is the
only time I have to myself. Your hand is bleeding."
He glanced down at it stupidly. "I'm rather a nasty
girl," she went on matter-of-factly. "I'm selfish and
greedy and I want you all to myself forever. I'm sorry
about this afternoon. Please don't go away angry
with me."

Huy shook his head. "I'm not angry with you
anymore. It would be like being angry with my foot
for stubbing my toe." He laughed shakily. "Thank you
for offering to clean up this mess. I really don't want
to touch it anymore, even in pieces. It still frightens
me. Ishat, I don't know . . . I'm afraid of so many . . .
where will my days take . . ." Her arms went out, and
before he realized what he was doing he had walked
into her embrace, pulling her into him, holding the
heat of her wiry body tightly against his own. For a
long time he stayed thus, eyes rammed shut, chin
buried in the froth of her hair, his shoulder warming
and cooling with the measured rhythm of her breath;
and it was she who pulled away, not he. She said
nothing. Turning, she made a sling out of the skirt of
her sheath and began to toss the remains of the
monkey into it.

He watched her for a while, but it was as though
she had forgotten he was there. He wanted to speak
but did not know what to say, and in the end he left
her, going straight to his room and climbing onto his
couch, feeling the blood from his cut hand congealing

on the sheet, feeling his eyelids burn from his tears, wanting to curl into a ball and howl as he had howled on the night when he had reeled out of the House of the Dead and Methen had found him cowering like an animal in the bushes. He fought the urge and the emotion that clung to it. It was Huy's first real battle with self-pity.

7

He rose before dawn, washed quickly, picked up his two bags, and left the house on foot, walking briskly through the quiet town towards the docks and Nakht's barges. The bags were heavy and his arms still ached, but it was good to stride out, to inhale the cool air that began to stir against his skin with the immanence of Ra's birth, to have purpose, especially as that purpose was escape. It took him a long time to pass his uncle's flower-choked arouras full of scents so heady that they made him briefly giddy. As he approached the town itself, he began to encounter other early risers bent on their business of the day. Many did not recognize him and greeted him cheerfully, but a few gave him a wide berth and one woman stretched out an arm towards him, index finger and thumb rigidly pointed at his chest, to ward off the evil residing within him. He bowed to her mockingly and went on his way smiling.

The ramps of the barges still rested on the watersteps of the dock as Huy wove his way between the bales of linen, stacked clay jars and chests, and huge baskets packed with flagons of wine waiting for shipment, and as he came up to the vessels he saw Thothmes emerge from one of the cabins. "Huy!" he called, leaning over the rail. "This way! Father and Nasha are going to share the other barge! Aren't we lucky? Why didn't you send to me last night for a litter this morning? You look hot!"

Gratefully, Huy relinquished his bags to the sailor who had risen from his post at the foot of the ramp and ran up onto the deck.

Thothmes hugged him. "We weren't sure you'd come," he said reproachfully. "Father started pacing the dock not long ago. A bad sign."

Glancing behind him, Huy indeed saw the Governor coming towards the ramp. Seeing Huy, he flung up his hands with a rueful smile and veered towards the other barge. Huy's eyes followed him to where Nasha, resplendent in red linen and thin gold bracelets, was trying to attract his attention. She was eating what looked like a hunk of white cheese and waving to him with the other hennaed hand.

The order to cast off and run in the ramps was given, the helmsmen scrambled to their positions, the sailors manned the oars, and the barges began to edge away from the dock. Lifting his face to the first rays of a reborn Ra, Huy closed his eyes, forcibly thrusting his last night at home below the level of his consciousness. The rank odour of the water, the tang of the ropes, the faintly sweetish scent of the cedar boards beneath his sandalled feet, wrapped him in the strong arms of the moment, a reality more powerful than the phantoms that had tormented him, and he turned to Thothmes with a grin. "I'm starving. Is there anything edible aboard this raft?"

Nakht had his men tie up early that evening, and by the time Ra had sunk into Nut's waiting mouth the linen tents were billowing gently in the evening breeze and the smell of fish frying over a merry fire enveloped the four travellers. Nakht was sitting on a stool, wine in hand, Nasha beside him, Thothmes and Huy cross-legged in the sand at his feet. Huy watched the servants come and go in a mood of utter contentment. He sipped his wine, aware of the flutter of Nakht's kilt against his naked back, Nasha's high voice chattering on about some inconsequential thing, of his own sense of complete security under the protection of this kindly family. *No matter what happens to me, I will always be able to retreat to Nakht's house and be safe.* "Was your business with my sepat's governor concluded successfully, Lord?" he asked.

Nakht smiled down at him. "Certainly. As you must know, he controls the flow of natron from the great depression west of your town. I had acquired the King's permission to negotiate for an increase of natron to the sepat under my care. He is a most obliging man."

"The King?"

Nakht chuckled. "No, your governor. The King can also be obliging when he wishes, but as he ages he becomes somewhat, shall we say, less cooperative?"

"Father!" Thothmes broke in indignantly. "You speak of our god! He is the perfect example of justice and wisdom!"

"Oh, don't start extolling your idol's virtues, Thothmes, or we shall never get to the fish," Nasha said rudely. "My stomach is flogging my spine with hunger."

By the time they had finished the meal, full dark had fallen, but they sat on, drinking and talking easily by the light of the dying fire. Huy thought of the other occasions when he and Ker had stopped very close to this spot on their way to Iunu, but it seemed to him that some other young man, a twin perhaps, had taken his place then, had lived with Hapu and Itu, gone to school, stood beside Ker on a similar barge, done all the things he had been told he had done, while he himself, the real Huy, had watched this other self invisibly from some perpetually changeless realm. The sense of dislocation was uncomfortable. He was unable to will it away, and he was glad when Nasha's copious yawn brought the evening to an end.

He and Thothmes shared a tent, and by the time they had unfolded their cots, undressed, and pulled their blankets up over tired bodies, Huy's feeling of being his own double had vanished. The two friends spoke little. Fresh river air and good food had tired them and it was not long before Thothmes fell asleep. For a while Huy lay on his back, eyes on the shadows lurking in the cone of the tent above him, thinking of Anuket, of how his cell would seem to him now, and whether his classmates would welcome him or if they had succumbed to rumour and would treat him with suspicion. He was less lonely with Thothmes, Nasha, and Nakht than he had been with his own family, yet he found himself suddenly longing to see Henenu the Rekhet, in whose company there would be no dislocations or misunderstandings. With her he could be himself.

The sight of Iunu's towers and pylons gleaming in the whiteness of noon was as thrilling to him as though he had never seen the city before. Now he could name every landmark: the pink granite obelisk of Osiris Senwosret the Third rearing above the double brick walls of the old quarter, a jumbled glimpse of the tombs of the High Priests to the southeast, the two much-newer stelae the present Horus had erected, the purposeful bustle above the great stretch of watersteps. *But I am somehow apart from it all,* he thought as Nakht's barges nudged their moorings. *I have somehow lost the ability to be consumed by any human activity, to enter into any experience so deeply that I may temporarily forget the inner presence of my soul. I drank three mugs of wine last night. The others became very merry, but I merely stood apart like an unseen guest and watched them. No amount of wine will ever be able to render me drunk, I know it.* He sighed. *I have also lost the ability to be shocked or surprised by the transformings taking place within me,* his thoughts ran on. *I am defenceless against minute shifts of perception and ominous discoveries, and therefore must accept them.*

"Huy, wake up!" Thothmes said loudly in his ear. "The ramps are out and we must take litters to the temple. These barges are too big for the canal. Whatever are you dreaming about?"

Across from them the litter-bearers were already waiting. Huy saw his bags at the feet of one of the men, and Nakht and Nasha climbing into one of the litters. He hurried ashore to speak to them. "Thank you, Governor, for your kindness," he said, bending to take the hand offered to him. "I owe you and Thothmes a great deal."

"You owe me also," Nasha retorted, leaning over her father, "for adding my nagging female voice to

Thothmes' pleading. Otherwise you would be making this journey without our fascinating company. I will see you on the next feast day, Huy."

He nodded. "You are an irresistible force, Nasha. Greet Anuket for me. And stay away from the Street of the Basket Sellers." He had not meant to say that; the words had been blurted out of him without the permission of his mind.

Nasha's expression darkened. "It wasn't a silly joke, was it, Huy?" she murmured. "I will do as you say providing you explain yourself to me fully next time you come to visit us."

Nakht was looking mystified as well as annoyed. "I have no time for the secret games of the young," he said testily. "Nasha, Huy, say your farewells and let us go home. Thothmes, continue to make sure that the reports on your progress are all good." He signalled to the bearers.

"I promise, Nasha," Huy called as the litter was raised.

"Oh, Huy!" Thothmes said in exasperation as they climbed onto their cushions. "Why did you remind her? She'd forgotten all about it!"

"I couldn't seem to help myself," Huy told him. "Besides, you won't be at home very often to remind her yourself, will you?"

Thothmes did not reply.

They got out where the river met the temple canal. Huy hoisted his bags and they walked along its verge together. *Nothing has changed,* Huy thought, his gaze rising to the mighty facade of Ra's home. *The sun still dazzles on the stone of the concourse, the frontal pillars*

*still pierce the sky, the priests still pace to and fro in their
white sheaths. It is as beautiful and peaceful as ever.*
But when he came to the place where the canal opened
out into the lake, he veered away from the water and
would not look into it. *I died there*, he told himself.
You hear me, Methen? I take your advice. I do not forget.

As though he had picked up Huy's silent words,
Thothmes paused. "I don't like to remember it either,"
he said quietly, "but I can't make the memory fade.
dream about it sometimes. Perhaps now that you are
back we will be able to truly put that day behind us."

"Perhaps. If I don't talk about what I have
become."

"Well, no one will hear it from me," Thothmes said
stoutly. He slipped his arm through Huy's as they
crossed the square and took the left-hand path.

It was the hour of the sleep, nevertheless a few
students were sitting outside their cells in the grass, and
before long Huy was recognized. By the time he and
Thothmes arrived at their own cell, a crowd of noisy
young men had surrounded them and Huy had
answered their relieved questions. It seemed, to his
surprise, that he had been missed, that his fellows had
been concerned for his welfare and were glad to have him
back. "Your hair is getting long, Huy," one of them
remarked, tugging at it gently. "Will Pabast shave you
again? Will you sport your scar with your usual impu-
dence? I'd like to see it." Obediently Huy bent his head
and they crowded around him, parting his thick hair and
exclaiming in sympathy at the raised, jagged welt.

"Is Sennefer still here?" Huy asked. It had not
occurred to him until now that his executioner might

even now be watching him from some shaded corner of the courtyard.

"Oh, no!" another boy said. "He was expelled the day after he attacked you with the throwing stick. The Overseer whipped him first in front of all of us. Remember when you were flogged for sneaking around the priests' quarters? That was nothing to the punishment Sennefer got. Twenty lashes with the willow switch, and he was bawling after the first five. We heard that he's in school at Khmun. Probably making his classmates' lives miserable."

Someone was tugging insistently at Huy's kilt. Turning, he found himself looking down into the face of Samentuser. The child had grown and thinned, but it was his eyes that struck Huy first. They met his own clearly and steadily. "The Governor Nakht has forbidden Sennefer to ever touch a throwing stick again, even though he is a noble," Samentuser said haltingly. "The Governor had to petition the King himself for such a dire prohibition, and the King granted the request. Huy, I am sorry for my unacceptable behaviour under your guidance. I ask your forgiveness." He held out both hands, palms up, in the universal gesture of respect or pleading, and Huy took them at once.

"You were indeed a spoiled and whining nuisance," he laughed, "but I see that school is working its magic on you. Of course I forgive you, little worm. I . . ."

Samentuser's fingers had grown steadily hotter. Huy could feel the bones under skin from which the healthy fat seemed to have been burned away. The boy's cheekbones stood out like humps of stone. His eyes were red. He was struggling to breathe, the air from his cracked lips stank of fever. "I'm dying, aren't I, Mother?" he gasped. "Aren't I?"

Carefully Huy forced the smile to remain on his face. Slowly he released Samentuser's hands. It took every ounce of control not to wipe his own on his linen. "I am only relieved that you are well past the need for a guide and will not be tempted to try my patience," he managed to finish. The boy beamed at him then glanced shyly around at the group. Huy felt as though he was going to faint. Weakness flooded him and he knew he would not be able to speak again. He was saved from doing so by a sudden flurry at the rear of the little crowd. It parted to reveal the majestic figure of Harmose.

"You are all late for your afternoon lessons," he said coolly. "Swimming, wrestling, target practice—your instructors cannot wait to punish you. Be off! And you, Samentuser, are not even in your own courtyard. Run away before I fetch my switch." The boys scattered. Thothmes had moved surreptitiously to support Huy, who was leaning back against him while a portion of strength returned. "So you are the cause of this unseemly disturbance," the Overseer said, eyebrows raised. "Welcome back, Huy. It is good to see you. I trust you are fully recovered from your ordeal. I received your letter requesting permission to return, but no word has come from your uncle. Your position is therefore not confirmed, but in the meantime you may resume your lessons." He gave Huy a critical stare. "I must say you are pale. You are excused afternoon lessons. Swimming, wasn't it? Unpack your bags instead. I will inform the High Priest." Huy bowed and Harmose strode away.

"It happened again, didn't it?" Thothmes said as they entered the cell and Huy collapsed onto the unmade cot. "With Samentuser? What is his fate, Huy?"

"I don't believe that I may tell you anyone's fate but your own," Huy murmured. "Thothmes, did you bring any of your father's wine with you? I would like a mouthful or two."

Rooting about in his satchel, Thothmes produced a small flagon and a cup. "I'll make up your cot for you while you drink it," he offered, but Huy shook his head.

"I'm feeling better already. Let me drink and then I'll attend to my chores. Gods, it's good to be back here with you!"

The evening meal was served in the courtyard as usual. Huy and Thothmes fetched their food from the long table, joined in the prayer of thanks to Ra led by one of the priests, and settled down with their backs against the warmth of their cell wall. Several boys wandered over to perch in the grass beside them, dipping their sesame bread into the fragrant garlic and onion soup and bringing Huy up to date on everything he had missed. "We are still ploughing through the Wisdom of Amenemopet," one of them grimaced. "We have just finished the eighth stanza. 'Let your integrity be felt in the vitals of the people,' and so on. But an architect comes twice every week to teach us the rudiments of his craft. I find that very interesting. I might change my mind about becoming a scribe and take architecture instead. My father could get me taken on as an apprentice somewhere when I leave this place."

"I don't like it so much," Thothmes said. "All those planes and angles and calculations about the stresses of various kinds of stone. I'll be following my father as governor of Iunu. A course in recognizing a good architect would be more useful to me than the details of his profession. What about you, Huy?"

Huy had been pushing the dried figs and dates about on his plate. "I don't even know yet if I'll be allowed to stay in school, so I try not to think about my future," he said slowly. "My greatest hope is to be a good scribe, but I may end up cutting flowers for my uncle. I won't feel safe until I hear from the Overseer."

"You should be allowed free schooling after what happened to you!" one of the boys said indignantly. "Or Sennefer's father should be made to shoulder the responsibility. I heard our teacher telling the Overseer that such a dreadful thing has never happened before in the whole history of this school!"

Thothmes sniffed. "Just try squeezing anything out of that man. He may be governor of the Nart-Pehu sepat, but if he had his way he would be administering the Uas sepat, where the King lives. My father says that he is even jealous of the Vizier and fancies himself greater than the High Priest of Amun himself. He is not a happy man."

"How can he be, with a son like Sennefer?" someone else put in, and they all laughed.

Huy got up. "I'm looking forward to class tomorrow, but tonight I'm tired. I think I'll spend the rest of the evening on my cot. It's very good to see you all again." He delivered his empty dishes to the servant behind the table, and as he was turning away Pabast hurried up to him.

"I heard that you were back," he said peremptorily. "I will come early in the morning to inspect your injury and see how I may shave it without pain."

Huy's smile grew as he looked into the man's self-important face. "I am now a senior here, and as such I may wear my hair in any way I want. I've decided to let it grow, Pabast. You need not worry, I will keep it clean and oil it often. I appreciate your concern and I thank you for your previous services to me."

"You may indeed grow it, but not to the length of some crazy man living in the desert," Pabast responded primly, and Huy laughed.

"Trust you to have the last word! You may report me to the Overseer the moment you see me running around with my hair flying about my buttocks!" Pabast tutted and made a show of clattering the soiled dishes on the table. Huy walked back to his cell.

He had unpacked his goods and spread his linen on the cot. Khenti-kheti stood in his usual place on the table. Ishat's scarab rested at the feet of the god, glinting faintly in the dying light of the day. Prostrating himself, Huy stood, and after the formal prayers to the totem of his town he begged Khenti-kheti to open a way for him to stay in school, to keep the ominous gift of the other gods quiescent within him, to prosper his lessons and take care of those he loved.

He was just finishing when Thothmes came in, his youth lock tousled, his skin luminous with beads of water. "Do you think you'll have the courage to continue with your swimming lessons, Huy?" he asked, rifling through his chest and bringing out a square of linen. He began to dry himself vigorously. "Will you at least try? And what about going into the papyrus swamps? Nasha will want to take us out duck hunting as soon as possible."

"I trust that I am not a coward, Thothmes. Let me try the bathhouse first. One must wash before bed, if I remember the rules correctly. I see that you've already been."

Thothmes stared at him suspiciously and then burst into laughter. "I'd forgotten your strange sense of humour. Actually, I've been doing my lengths in the lake. Let's get cleaned and oiled together and then you can go to bed."

Huy had expected a summons from the Overseer within the following few days, but he returned to his classes, struggled to catch up to the work the others were doing, ate the noon meal in the noisy hall with everyone else, even approached his swimming instructor with a request to continue the exercises, and the temple authorities remained silent. He was trailed everywhere by a hesitant Samentuser, who hastened to pick up anything—a sheaf of papyrus, a brush, a pot of ink—Huy might drop. In the classroom, clustered at the far end of the vast room with others of his age and competence, he often felt eyes upon him and, turning, saw Samentuser staring at him with an expression of dumb worship on his face. "I think he's in love with you, Huy," Thothmes chuckled, but Huy did not find the little boy's devotion amusing and took him aside one day in the brief hiatus between lunch and the afternoon sleep.

"Is there something worrying you, Samentuser?" he asked. For answer a small hand crept up and fingered the frog ornament Huy had once used to secure his youth lock and which now held his hair imprisoned at the base of his skull.

"Ever since you came back I've been dreaming about you, Huy," Samentuser said haltingly. "Every night I dream that I am drowning. I can't breathe. My head aches. You are standing on the verge of the lake, bending down, holding out your hands and calling to me, but I can't reach up to you, I can't grasp your hands." His lips quivered. "I know it's silly. Don't be angry with me. I wake up with a terrible desire to see you because I am so afraid." He swallowed and his eyes slid away from Huy's. "Has someone put a spell on me, do you think? Can you help me?"

Huy's throat had gone dry. Squatting, he embraced the boy. "My hands are here now. I am holding them out to you, just as in your dream, but this is the world of waking, Samentuser. Grasp them." He was preparing to say something comforting, to tell the boy that his nightmare was nothing more than a reflection of his preoccupation with Huy himself, and that he must spend more time in games and other healthy pursuits with his classmates. But all at once he sensed a powerful presence behind him. Samentuser's troubled little face, the smooth beige stone of the temple wall beyond, the shriek of a hawk passing high above, remained clear. Huy knew that he was entirely rooted in the present, and yet a deep, rough voice spoke into his ear, a voice that illogically seemed full of animal teeth. Hot breath touched his neck.

"Say this to the child," the voice began, the words a soft rumble but entirely plain. "'Go to a priest and request an Anubis thread. Let the man knot it about your wrist.'

Thus will I be bound to his good with my Followers of
Horus. Remind him of the promise of Amun: 'Anything
harmful is under my seal.' He must pray to his totem
twice a day to have the oppression of the dream removed
from him. He must bend his head to you and receive the
seal of your protection. That is all."

Huy swallowed his scream of surprise and fear. *Am I
then to be a messenger for the gods as well as a herald of
the future, blessed Anubis?* he asked silently of the warm
breath bathing his skin with horrific regularity.
What are the limits of this gift? He had wanted to say
"terrible gift, unwanted gift, gift with a weight like a
stone of granite lodged within my soul," but he did not
dare. There was a sudden, oddly timbreless chuckle, and
the presence was withdrawn. The breeze caressing
Huy's neck was now cool.

"Please speak to me, Huy," Samentuser begged.
"Is your silence an angry one?"

"Not at all." Huy squeezed the small fingers and
let them drop. "You are from Nefrusi, are you not? You
worship Amun?" Samentuser nodded. "And what is it
said of Amun? Do you remember?" Samentuser shook
his head. "Anything harmful is under his seal. Yes?
Anything harmful. You surely have his image beside
your cot. I want you to go to one of the priests here
and ask for an Anubis thread. Let him knot it about
your wrist. Your parents are wealthy. They can pay, can
they not?" Huy took Samentuser's rapt attention for
consent. "Anubis is Lord of the Bau. He has all the
armed followers of Horus under him."

Samentuser looked alarmed. "But Huy, Anubis has
hosts of demons under him also."

"I know. But the thread will bind Anubis to your good. You must pray to Amun twice every day to take this dream away from you, and he will be free to hear you because Anubis will respect the thread and will protect you with the followers of Horus. Bend your head." The boy did so. Huy rested his hands on the hot, shaved skull. "My hands are on you. My seal is your protection," he intoned. He wanted to ask Samentuser if he had any relatives in Iunu, people he could stay with during the disease-ridden months of the Inundation, but he did not dare. If the boy was to die of fever, if that was the fate ordained for him at his birth, then he, Huy, must not interfere. *I have done all I dare to do for him,* he thought, watching Samentuser leave the courtyard. *The priest will want to know why Samentuser needs an Anubis thread. Will he leave the matter alone, or will I be summoned to explain? How can I explain? How can I say that the god himself spoke to me? I don't understand any of this! I don't want to have the eyes of the gods on me, to feel like the toy dog I had, pulled along by their string while they bark through me!* Shocked at his fit of offensive blasphemy, he muttered an apology and went to his cot for the afternoon sleep like all the other students, but he was unable to rest.

A month passed before a letter arrived for him from his uncle. Carrying the scroll to a quiet corner of his courtyard, he broke Ker's seal with trepidation and spent a moment glancing around the sun-filled area before daring to drop his eyes to the neat black hieratic script of Ker's scribe. "My dear nephew Huy," he read. "I have been in correspondence with your Overseer and have had several conversations with Methen, who has

written on your behalf to the High Priest of Ra requesting assistance with the cost of your schooling. I have
also approached your father with regard to your
brother's education. I feel as great a responsibility
towards little Heby as I did towards you . . ." here Huy
paused tensely ". . . and given your father's inability to
carry the cost of schooling for either of you, I have
reluctantly decided to extend to Heby the advantages
you have enjoyed." *Instead of me,* Huy thought bitterly,
dropping the papyrus into his lap. *In spite of the fact
that my life has been destroyed by the force of Sennefer's
arm and I am blameless, still Ker cannot overcome his
fear of me. He does not want his personal or his business
reputation tainted by any association with me that might
be detrimental in the future. Oh, Ker! I wonder what
that future holds for you! How easy it would be for me to
find out next time I return home!* He struggled to thrust
the unworthy desire away and unrolled the scroll again.
"I love you very much and so does your aunt," the
letter continued. "We remain distraught over what
happened to you, but I must honestly consider that
your precarious health may fail at any time and my
investment in you be wasted. Heby will not attend
school at Iunu. He will be enrolled at the smaller
temple school here in Hut-herib." *How stupid do you
think I am?* Huy demanded of his uncle in his mind.
*Heby could die of a hundred different diseases before he
disembarks from your barge and drags his belongings into
the cell he will share with his guide, as I did!* "The High
Priest Methen and your Overseer have agreed to allow
you to continue at Iunu providing Methen assumes the
bulk of the cost. The Overseer will approach High

Priest Ramose for the balance. Both men seem to think that you will be of benefit to Egypt one day. You will be summoned to discuss the matter with Ramose. I do not expect a reply to this letter." It was signed by Ker himself.

Why not? Huy asked resignedly as he let the scroll roll up and sat staring down at it. *Do you imagine that the mere touch of my hand on the papyrus will infect you with some sort of terrible spell?* For a moment he ached for the past, for his uncle's free smile, his humour, the unconditional affection that he, Huy, had taken for granted, then he got up off the warm grass, strode to his cell, and put the letter in his chest. He was tempted to throw it away or burn it, so great was his feeling of betrayal, but a part of him understood his uncle's all too human weakness. Ker was not a god. He was simply a kind man, a good man, caught in a situation he was unable to understand. *All the same,* Huy told himself as he walked towards the lake where he had forced himself to resume his swimming lessons despite an overwhelming sense of dread, *my continued education is assured. I must write to Methen and thank him at once, and as for the Overseer, I suppose he will extract some extra task from me in exchange. At least I don't have to petition Thothmes' father for a favour like some impoverished peasant.* Here he laughed aloud, picked up his pace, and prepared to shed his kilt as the glittering surface of the water came into view.

He had just finished his letter to Khenti-kheti's priest on the following evening, sitting cross-legged on the floor of his cell with the lamp beside him and Thothmes on his cot, rattling the pieces of the sennet game they were about to play, when a servant Huy had not seen before entered and beckoned him with a peremptory wave. Huy had time to recognize the hawk tattoo on the man's upper arm before scrambling to follow him into the early evening twilight. This was a servitor to the priests of Ra, and Huy's surmise was borne out as the arrogant figure quickly left the premises of the school and entered the priests' quarters, a place where Huy had not been since the day when, fleeing from Pabast, he had found himself in the presence of the Ished Tree. "Are you sure you have summoned the correct student?" he called uncertainly to the straight back, his mind briefly full of the confusion of that time. He was not answered. The man turned into the corridor lined with priests' cells, now quiet, strode past them all, and halted before double doors Huy remembered only too well. Knocking, he turned, gave Huy an unexpectedly warm smile, and disappeared the way they had come.

"Enter." The voice was muffled but recognizable. Swallowing, Huy pushed open one of the thick wooden doors and walked into the High Priest's rooms.

Two people glanced up at him. One was the High Priest himself, sitting behind a table littered with scrolls. The other was the Rekhet. With an exclamation of pleasure Huy bowed profoundly to the bright eyes, the wizened fingers folded on the ornate wand lying across her white-clad thighs. She nodded briefly in return, the cowrie shells tied into her grey braids clacking gently. Repeating his bow, this time to the High Priest, Huy stood and waited. "You may bring forward that stool and sit, Huy," the High Priest said. "I have been listening to a strange and compelling story about you, and before I proceed I would like to hear it told to me again, this time from your own mouth." Huy did not need to ask what story. Anxiously he met the Rekhet's eye.

"It's all right, Huy," Henenu said. "The High Priest and I are not only old friends, we also work together in the service of the gods. I have told him everything, and Methen has added his words to mine in a letter. Don't be afraid." She lifted the wand and placed it deliberately on the floor. "I need no protection from you nor you from me."

"I'm not afraid, Rekhet," he answered, and found that it was the truth. Dragging forward the stool, he lowered himself onto it and raised his eyes to the aristocratic face across from him. The High Priest waited impassively, his ringed fingers relaxed on the table before him. "You must have already known of the accident that befell me on the verge of the lake in front of the temple, Master," Huy began, and continued to recount the events whose details were as vivid in that gracious, dimly lit cell as if they had just occurred. The High Priest's gaze did not waver, showing neither shock nor surprise as Huy stumbled over his horrific waking in the House of the Dead and his rescue in Methen's arms. It was the only moment he faltered in the telling, and when at last he fell silent the air seemed to hold the echo of his voice. Then the High Priest pushed a jug of water towards him. Huy rose, drank thirstily, and resumed his seat.

"If you touch me, you will know my fate?" the man said quietly at last.

"Yes, Master."

"Will you do so?"

Huy cringed. Both pairs of eyes, so similar in their knowledge, so appraising, were fixed on him steadily. He shook his head. "No. Forgive me, Master, but . . . no."

"You have done so for others," the High Priest pressed. "Why not for me?"

"I have only acceded to one such request, from my friend Thothmes," Huy replied, dry-mouthed in spite of the water he had drunk. "The other times it just happened. It was . . . it was sad and draining and somehow wrong, and I will not repeat it except from choice."

"So you have no control over the gift?"

"No. That is, yes," Huy floundered, "that is . . . I think I may be able to make it my servant, but not yet."

"You are still afraid of it." The voice was Henenu's.

Huy turned to her. "Afraid, yes. Because I never know when it will strike me. Because it is doing things to me, changing me in my soul, perhaps even in my ka, my ba, my shadow. Everything I look at seems different from the way it was before . . . before . . ."

"Before you died." The High Priest spoke calmly. "Without the witness of so many people, including the servants in the House of the Dead at Hut-herib, I would not only doubt the account, I would attribute it to an evil and blasphemous young man who craved an ignominious notoriety. But the fact of your death is too well attested. As for the rest, I trust the testimony of this woman"—he indicated Henenu—"in her capacity as the most famous Rekhet in Egypt. Her gift lies in the discerning and control of demons and spirits.

According to her, you are possessed by neither. It remains to be seen whether the gift that has possessed you speaks truth." His gaze narrowed. "You were right to refuse my request. The faculty that has been given to you must not be used lightly or frivolously."

"But why me?" Huy burst out. "Master, I do not want this faculty! I ask only to be allowed to finish my schooling in peace and become a good scribe!"

The Rekhet leaned forward and placed a hand on his stiff shoulder. "Stop fretting, Huy," she soothed him. "The reason why will become apparent in time. Until then we also want you to finish your schooling. The gift is raw in you. It must mature. So must you, in ways that are acceptable to the gods. It is our duty, mine and Ramose's, to help you learn not only the skills your teacher wishes to instill in you, but also the ways in which you may govern the emotions the gods do not trust. Anger. Envy. Lust for power. The things that will blunt and pervert the ability to See." She patted him and withdrew. "The gift must not control you. It must become your servant."

"The Overseer's report on your academic progress is excellent," the High Priest put in, holding up a sheaf of papyrus. "You learn quickly and retain what you learn. Your hand is neat and sure. You are swimming again. That took courage." The coldly unapproachable features broke into a smile. "I am putting you under the care of the architect, who will teach you the rudiments of his craft. You will continue at the bow. And every day you will come here. What was the choice Osiris Imhotep placed before you under the Ished Tree?"

Huy felt a strong reluctance to say the words again, as though the more he repeated them the tighter his decision would hold him. "He asked me if I wished to read the Book of Thoth," he half whispered.

"And you did so wish."

I am not being given a chance to retract anything, Huy thought dismally. *The High Priest is simply testing the particulars of my encounter.* He nodded.

"Very well," Ramose went on crisply. "The gods have willed that such knowledge be shared with you, a most rare and extraordinary opportunity for someone so young and untried. Half of the Book of Thoth is here. It is kept hidden in the Holiest of Holiest within the temple. The other half lies safely in Thoth's temple at Khmun. The succeeding High Priests of each temple are responsible for the safety of the portions of the sacred Book in their keeping."

"So it really exists?" Huy was more shocked than amazed. Despite his utterly futile efforts to relegate the Tree, the Judgment Hall, even the faces of the gods themselves, to the realm of indistinct memory, to pick up the threads of a normal school life, he had continued to hope secretly that it had all been some great cosmic mistake on the part of Ma'at and the Book was nothing but legend. Yet here, in this warm, shadowed room, its existence was being confirmed in quite ordinary language.

The High Priest's lips twisted in a thin smile. "You doubted. Or rather," he added with shrewd perception, "you found comfort in doubting. Indeed it exists, and you will begin to study it. I will decide later whether or not I will allow you to open the other half.

As far as I know, the only man who acquired full mastery over its mysteries was the mighty Imhotep himself, which was probably why he was chosen to speak to you. And I should warn you"—he hesitated— "the Book is a maze, and it is said that any man who is able to decipher it and reach the heart of its mysteries will know the nature and mind of Atum himself." He paused, running a hand along his jaw. Half stupefied, Huy watched the lamplight glint briefly upon one ring after another until the long fingers passed across the mouth and came to rest on the table once more. "And that, my young Huy, means instant madness."

"But the great Imhotep did not go insane," Huy croaked. "He was deified. He became a god."

"Indeed." The High Priest rose. "Which will it be for you? I wonder. Madness or deification? I will leave you to spend a few moments with the Rekhet, then off to your cell and a good night's sleep." Gathering his linens around him, he stalked towards a small door barely visible in the uncertain light, but on reaching it he swung back. "I have refused Methen's offer to assist in the support of your education. This temple will bear the cost itself. Methen is a true friend to you and you would do well to listen carefully to his advice. It will be most cogent for a chosen one. I will send for you." Then he was gone, the door closing gently behind him.

Huy looked at Henenu. "'A chosen one'?"

She raised her eyebrows. "You, of course. Do you think that the gods make a habit of carelessly scattering their gifts over the youth of Egypt like indiscriminate farmers sowing seed? Abandon false modesty, Huy. It does not suit you." Her tone was sharp.

"It is not modesty, Rekhet," Huy blurted. "It comes from a sense of unreality. Somehow I must learn to accept this foreign thing lodged like a . . . an unwanted parasite inside me."

"Lodged inside you? A parasite?" She cocked one bright eye at him. "Dear Huy, this 'foreign thing,' as you so blasphemously describe it, is more a part of you now than the blood in your veins, more real than anything you may see or hear or feel for the rest of your life." She leaned urgently towards him. "You must begin to understand it, to welcome it, become familiar with its purpose. If you continue to struggle against it, it will destroy you." Bringing up a linen bag from the shadows beside her chair, she undid the drawstring. "I have made two amulets for you. The Soul Amulet protects you from any permanent separation of spirit and body until the proper time for your Beautification. The Frog is the symbol of resurrection. You need nothing else."

Reverently Huy received the bundle she dropped into his palm, then he cried out, "Rekhet, they are made of gold! Inlaid with red jasper! And the frog—"

She laughed aloud with delight. "I inlaid the kerer's eyes with lapis lazuli. Did you not tell me that as you walked across the temple concourse after leaving the lake your hair ornament turned from a wooden frog into one of gold with lapis eyes? It is fitting."

Huy turned the lovely images over and over. The human head of the Soul Amulet with its sleek hawk body smiled knowingly up at him. Finally he placed both rings on the fingers of his left hand.

"You need not worry about the cost," Henenu went on briskly. "I am a wealthy old woman. The High Priest is my brother as well as my friend, and our blood is noble. Not that it matters to me. Like him, like you, I care only to serve the gods. If you want to repay me, you can prophesy on behalf of any patron I send you, but later— later. When you have learned discretion." She stooped, retrieved her wand, and got up. Stepping to him, she laid a hand gently on his cheek. "I am a simple woman, and concern myself with my own simple gift," she said softly. "The matter of the Book of Thoth is too high for me. Yet my task is your protection. I add my warning to that of Ramose. Be no man's toy—not his, not mine, not even Pharaoh's. Many will try to manipulate the gift, use it for their own ends, and sometimes it will seem to you that the ends are benign, but your ultimate Mistress is Ma'at and your Master Thoth. Run along to your couch now. Remember my words."

"Rekhet," Huy said clearly, "you have a boil about to appear at the base of your spine. Mix one ro of oil of mandrake root with two ro of palm wine. Anoint the place each day for seven days, then apply a salve of myrrh and honey. You will be cured."

There was a moment of stunned silence, then Henenu blew out her breath and nodded. "That's why I've been feeling a stiffness. So the gift has revealed another dimension! Thank you, Huy." Huy had felt nothing but the grip of a dull fatalism as the knowledge, clear and unequivocal, poured from her fingers and the remedy was forced out of his mouth. Bowing politely to her, he hurried from the room.

His cell was dark as he wearily entered it, but Thothmes stirred. "Oh, the lamp has gone out," he said sleepily. "Sorry, Huy. Where have you been?"

Pulling off his kilt and loincloth and dropping them on the floor, Huy climbed gratefully between his sheets. "In the quarters of the High Priest. It seems that my education is to be fully provided by the temple."

"Good! That saves me from threatening to put a spell on Father if he doesn't step in to help you! Not that I would need to. Father has already discussed the matter with Mother and his treasurer." There was a pause. Huy's grip closed about the two amulets. "Is it because of your gift, Huy?"

"Yes." Huy's jaw was clenched. "I am to study the Book of Thoth under the High Priest's direction."

Thothmes whistled. "So it exists! Just as Imhotep spoke of it when you met him! It's here at Iunu?"

"Yes. Half of it." Huy peered across at his friend. Little more than Thothmes' eyes could be seen, glinting in the weak starlight filtering through the open doorway. "Thothmes, promise me that you will always love me, no matter what fate the gods have decreed for each of us!" he said in a low voice, unable to hide a spasm of panic. "Promise me!"

"I have already promised," Thothmes hissed back. "Now go to sleep. Between a delicious three days at home, you and I on the river and eating until we burst, there's another week of slavery. Good night."

Huy murmured a reply, the fingers of his right hand still tight around the amulets, conscious of an aura of peaceful security emanating from their already familiar contours. But it seemed to him that the gods were watching him, their unblinking gaze fixed on him alone. The Chosen One. *Your choice was free,*

Great Atum, unclouded by the fog of any human frailty, he thought bitterly. *But I was a boy cast like a pebble from a slingshot into a world of magic and mystery I could not hope to understand. My choice was innocent but flawed.* The comfort of the amulets notwithstanding, he felt exposed and very vulnerable. He could not sleep.

8

The next day Huy wrote a letter to Methen, thanking him for his offer of an assistance that would not
now be needed. Neither Ramose nor the Rekhet had
suggested that Huy keep his unique abilities to himself.
He had understood without being told that to natter
about them randomly would indicate not only an excess
of foolish pride but also a serious character flaw. It was
equally obvious that he might use his own judgment in
speaking of what the gods were doing through him when
the occasion demanded an explanation. His words to
Methen flowed with ease and came from his heart.
Methen would be delighted to read of his friend's good
fortune, and his reply would be full of affection.

When the ink had dried on the scroll, it occurred to
Huy to wonder how he was to pay a messenger to take it
north to Hut-herib now that he could no longer call
upon his uncle's generosity. He had settled himself in the
shade of the trees by the lake, his palette across his knees,
away from the glare of sunlight on the stone flags of Ra's
vast concourse. Wandering back to his compound, the
palette stowed in his small leather satchel and slung

across his shoulder, he met a priest who was hurrying in the opposite direction. The man halted, his glance going from the roll of papyrus in Huy's hand to the lost expression on his face, and to Huy's astonishment he bowed respectfully. "May I help you, Huy?" he asked. "Do you need wax for your letter?"

"I have no seal, Master," Huy answered awkwardly, "and I wrote without considering that my circumstances have changed. I have no means to send my letter away from Iunu." He bowed and made as if to step past the man. After all, the students were forbidden to approach the priests without the permission of the Overseer, who decided whether a reason to disturb the holy men was frivolous or not, and to be casually accosted by one had given Huy a shock.

The priest barred his way politely, his hand out. "If you give it to me, I will see that it reaches its destination. Much correspondence passes between the temple and the towns and cities of Egypt. If you have written to a place outside our borders, that can be arranged also." He smiled. "I will not read it. Simply tell me to whom it must go."

Stuttering his profuse thanks, Huy did so, and passed it over. The man bowed again and strode quickly away, but later that day, as Huy and Thothmes were heading to the bathhouse after a strenuous three hours under the demanding eye of their shooting instructor, the same man rose from the stool outside its entrance and executed a bow that did not include Thothmes. "Your letter has gone and I have been authorized by the High Priest to give you the seal of the temple, Huy," he said without preamble, holding out a ring. "You may use it on all your correspondence, as we do. You may request wax from your Overseer. When you have sealed your letters, pass them to any priest to deal with. Life and health to you." Executing another swift bow, he disappeared through the doorway of the compound. Huy and Thothmes bent over the heavy piece of gold lying on Huy's damp palm. The ring's bezel bore Ra's falcon head crowned with the sun disc and encircled by a snake with open mouth and forked tongue.

"The holy uraeus, ready to spit fire at the enemies of Ra," Thothmes said solemnly. "The very same guardian who curls from the crown on the forehead of our Great God to protect him from everything evil." He stared across at Huy. "The High Priest wasn't joking, was he? You really are to be safeguarded in every way. I hope they let you out to dip your toes in the mud of my family's presence once in a while! It'll be good for your lamentable lack of genuine humility!"

Huy burst out laughing as he tried to slip the seal ring onto a finger of his left hand beside his amulets. "This is too big for me. If I lose it, I can expect more than a mild whipping."

"Find a leather thong and hang it around your neck," Thothmes suggested. "Do you think there'll be wine with the meal tonight? We are approaching the eve of a god's feast, after all."

Nakht sent a litter for them, and the two boys left the temple precinct for three days of holiday, Huy with much relief. He was beginning to feel the pressure of being singled out. The seal ring was only the material evidence of something in the eyes of the priests he met crossing the concourse, in the intelligent face of his schoolmaster, in the wary glances of the servants. Even Pabast had seemed more taciturn and cautious than usual towards him when he came to the cell to shave Thothmes. Huy's fellow classmates treated him no differently. Nor did his teacher. He was rebuked when he made a mistake in the dictation, grumbled at when he stumbled over a difficult passage in the aphorisms of Amenemopet that he and his friends were still wading through with thinly disguised boredom, yelled at by the military officer in charge of his physical training if his progress lagged; yet behind the seeming normalcy was an invisible wall of—what? Deference? Curiosity? Fear? Or was it all in an imagination that was inflating an already arrogant ka? All Huy knew, as he pondered these things, was that sometimes his breath seemed to catch in his lungs as though a weight had descended briefly upon his chest.

Nakht's large, quiet estate was as welcoming as ever, its walls shutting out the clamour of the city beyond, its lily-choked pools and ancient shade trees an oasis of a very different security than the kind Huy wore around his neck. The whole family had gathered for the celebration of the god's feast, including Meri-Hathor and her husband, a pleasant man who seemed content to sprawl on the grass and smile sleepily while the babble of conversation flowed over him. Huy wondered, as he walked up to Nakht and bowed, whether he should thank the Governor for having Sennefer's throwing stick removed permanently from his grasp, then thought better of it; he did not want to sound vindictive. Thothmes' mother kissed him warmly on both cheeks.

Nasha hurried up to him, thrust a cup of wine into his hands, and gently bit the tip of his nose. "I have stayed away from the Street of the Basket Sellers," she announced loudly. "Father has been talking to the High Priest of Ra about you. It seems that you have developed a facility for peering into people's futures. Oh, don't look so dismal!" she chided him. "Seer or not, you're still just cheeky Huy to me. Have some wine, eat a few sweetmeats, enjoy your few days here. Tomorrow we're going to have a rafting party. Anuket has been making garlands."

Huy turned to Nakht. "May I go and see her?"

Nakht nodded. "She's in the herb room. Tell her to come out and be companionable." Nasha whispered something to her sister that caused Meri-Hathor to smile broadly, but Huy was oblivious; he was already on his way into the house.

He smelled the herb room when he entered the long passage that led to the rear, a mixture of thyme, mint, dill, and spices mingling oddly with the heavy scents of the various flowers Anuket used for her hobby, making the air seem to adhere to his skin. The room had no door and his sandals tapped lightly on the tiling of the passage as he approached. She was sitting cross-legged on the floor surrounded by a clutter of leaves and twigs, her fingers fallen motionless in the act of twisting the stems of two white lilies together. She did not look up until he crouched before her, then she smiled faintly. "Huy. I knew it was you. I recognized your step." He felt her dark eyes searching his face. "It has been a long time. Are you well now?"

Huy could not help himself. He placed a palm against the firm smoothness of her cheek. "Anuket," he said huskily. "I have missed you very much. Yes, I am well now, but all the time I lay sick on my bed my thoughts were here with you."

She did not withdraw, but neither did she lean into his touch. "So you have returned to school and to us unscathed, for which I give thanks to the gods."

She continued to look into his eyes, but Huy could not read what emotion lay behind her own. Her words were warmly polite, yet Huy, his lungs filling with the languorous aroma of the waxen lilies quivering in her lap, felt rather than saw a sudden tension in her hands. He sat back on his heels, and as he did so a wave of desire for her swept over him with such suddenness that he almost cried out. The need to grasp her shoulders and jerk her forward, fasten his mouth over hers, feel the press of her small breasts against his chest, was overpowering. *I want to pull up your sheath, lay you on your back, and thrust myself into you,* he thought with terrifying clarity. *I want to hear you pant. I want to smell your sweat blending with the smell of the flowers. I want to taste it imbued with the tang of the bunches of herbs hanging drying over our heads. Anuket!* The sensations of his body were so new, so imperative, that for a moment he was in danger of losing control over himself. Carefully he knelt and picked up the unfinished wreath. "This is beautiful," he said, knowing that his voice shook, knowing that he must not look at her directly. "Even the King's garland makers could not exceed the intricacy of your designs."

Reaching behind her with a toss of her hair, she brought forward a simple loop of large yellow daisies and flung it over his head. "Thank you! I made this while I was sitting and thinking about how I would create the wreath for the festival. Wear it today, Huy, until the petals wilt, and then throw it away." He hung on to it desperately with both hands and she clucked at him disapprovingly. "Don't do that! You're crushing the flowers! Is something wrong?"

The surge of lust was ebbing and he was able to loosen his fingers. He swallowed. "No, nothing. I moved to keep them from tangling in the seal, that's all."

"Oh." Suddenly she pulled his left hand away from the daisies and examined the Rekhet's gifts with interest. Huy remained very still. "These are finely made and very costly," she remarked. "What are they for? Where did you get them?"

So Huy told her as much of his story as he could, and as he spoke he found himself returning to sanity, watching the changes of expression flit across her aristocratic little features with the same pleasure he had always found in looking at her.

"I knew that you had become some sort of Seer," she said when he had fallen silent. "The High Priest of Ra is also Greatest of Seers, and Father went to talk to him when the rumours about you began to circulate at school. But Huy, we are still friends, aren't we?" she said earnestly, leaning towards him. "That won't change, will it?"

He managed a short laugh. "Of course not," he assured her. "You will always be my very favourite woman, Anuket." His tone was light, but privately he was thinking how a change was already taking place in him, shocking him with its force, how his affectionate preoccupation with her had become something else in the time it had taken him to blink. *I am in love with her.*

I walked into this pungent room freely, but I will walk out again like an animal dragging a trap on its leg. The knowledge was bitter when it should have been glorious, and Huy knew it. *How am I to contend with this?* he asked himself hotly. *Have I not enough to bear already?*

She was smiling at him, pulling a strand of her hair across her mouth with unconscious coquetry. "Good." She straightened. "I expect Father asked you to bring me out into the garden, but this is my last wreath for the ceremonies and it will not take me long to finish it. After all, the family will be together for the next three days. So will we, Huy. Nasha will want to take you and Thothmes into the marshes and I will not want to go, but we can talk in the evenings." Her hands were moving once more over the lilies.

Huy stood then hesitated, not wanting to leave, the prospect of hours spent without her presence now insupportable. After a long and increasingly awkward silence she looked up and met his eye. "Do you know what my name, Anuket, means?" she asked deliberately. One of her fingers had begun to move slowly back and forth over the pale surface of a single lily petal. He shook his head. "It means 'to embrace.' The temple astrologers chose the name for me when I was born. Father was distressed. He tried to persuade them to choose another, but they refused. Anuket is an ancient water goddess whose temple was at Khnum, by the First Cataract. She embraced the fields with the floods of the Inundation. She has never been very important, not like her sister Satis. But over time she has become a goddess of lust, with obscene attributes." Her gaze returned to the wreath. "Father still sometimes feels insulted, but he is relieved to see me growing up the way I am. I respect the gods and my parents and I am chaste. I am chaste," she repeated.

Huy bent down. *The well was deep, and the water cold and dark. Now I am drowning again.*

"What are you trying to say to me, Anuket?" he demanded to her averted cheek. "Of course you are of the water, pure and virtuous. Do you fear that the power of your name will eventually corrupt your virtue as the goddess herself has become perverted?"

"No!" The face she turned to him was flushed. "I did not know if you had heard of her, Anuket, in her present degraded aspect. I did not want you to think . . . to imagine . . . I would rather be Satis, so that I could worship the goddess who stands at the entrance to the Duat with the four vases of purifying water to be poured over each king as he enters the place of the dead. No totem of Anuket stands in my bedroom!"

"Anuket—"

She cut him off with a wave. "I shall try to embrace all that is good. I have never felt lust, but if I ever do I shall not allow it to engulf me. Even if I feel it!"

And did you feel it just now and repudiate it, Anuket, Huy wondered, *or did you sense my own, and this talk of your name is a subtle warning? Are you indeed capable of such mature thought?*

Filled with a sad amusement, he gently kissed the top of her head. "To me you will always be water, dearest sister," he reassured her. "Have we not said we are friends?" She nodded once and was about to speak again. Huy turned on his heel and left her before the words of love hovering on his tongue could come rushing out to change her regard for him forever.

The whole family attended the temple ceremonies together on the second day of the holiday, Anuket presenting her wreath with innocent confidence while the incense rose in many grey columns and the holy dancers wove their time-honoured steps before the god's sanctuary. Later there was a feast in Nakht's garden for his many guests and governmental acquaintances. Huy, his belly full of fine food and a cup of date wine in his hand, moved with an aimless contentment through the torchlit, animated crowd. Everything in Nakht's house gave him a sense of warm security and peace, and if it had not been for the pulse of disquiet his encounter with Anuket had caused he would have been entirely happy. Scanning the company of bejewelled and painted groups that formed, scattered, and reformed, he sometimes caught sight of her, thin white linen fluttering in the night breeze, her tiny face upturned to whoever had her attention, the melting oil from the festive cone tied on her head oozing slowly over her collarbone to gather between her breasts under the secrecy of her sheath. The expensive odour of frankincense was everywhere, kneaded into the wax of the head ornaments, so that watching Anuket through a miasma of the scent most often smelled in temples brought her words forcibly to Huy's mind. He could not decide whether she was deliberately avoiding him or not, for each time he tried to approach her she seemed to slip away, only to reappear with someone else. Eventually he saw her mother signal her and she vanished obediently into the house.

Huy found Thothmes at his elbow. "I am bored and sweaty," Thothmes said. "Let's go for a swim. Father won't mind. I've done my duty and greeted every dignitary. Quickly, before Nasha wants to join us."

Huy downed the rest of his wine and together they slipped away from the noise and light, walking through the shrubbery until the path ended at Nakht's guarded watersteps, looming grey in the moonlight. Farther along the river road, where reeds gave way to a tiny bay, they removed their jewellery, kilts, and loincloths and waded into the dark water. Pulling into midstream, Huy turned and looked back. Beyond Thothmes' bobbing head the city lay exposed, its cloak of people and moving craft stilled, its lordly bulk flowing along the edge of the river to be lost in the dimness of the night. Lights winked from the roofs of the temples, and here and there clusters of torchlight glowed from the estates bordering the water, where other wealthy worshippers were celebrating, but their revelry could not be heard. Iunu brooded quietly, its dirt and clamour hidden, its beautiful stone buildings a jumble against a star-strewn sky. "I love it here," Huy said aloud, suddenly moved, and beside him Thothmes came up panting.

"So do I," he gasped. "I'm glad I will never have to live anywhere else. I'm getting cold, Huy. Shall we have a fire on the bank? I'll get father's soldiers on the watersteps to start it for us. The guests will be leaving soon, so it had better be out of sight of the barges and the litters. We certainly don't need any more swimming lessons, do we? Race me back!" He swirled away, lithe as an eel, and was standing on the grass when Huy left the water.

One of the guards obligingly made a fire and for a long time they sat side by side, arms folded on their bare knees, gazing silently and contentedly into the flames, until the last flurry of departing guests had died away and dawn was a lessening of darkness in the east. Thothmes yawned. "It has been a good festival, but now I could sleep for a whole day if we didn't have to return to school in two days. Tomorrow afternoon Nasha wants us to take a skiff into the marshes. It will be pleasant, I think, and you can keep your word to her and tell her how you came to be a Seer. She won't care, of course. To her you're just another brother to be teased and petted." His tone was joking. Huy did not answer. His thoughts had returned to Anuket.

The three of them went on the river the following afternoon. Nasha was obviously suffering from an excess of wine the night before. She had a canopy erected on the small craft, and while the servant poled them slowly through the tall, rustling reeds she half sat, half reclined under its shade, her complexion pale. "I couldn't even have my eyes kohled this morning," she complained. "They were too sore. Mother made me swallow castor oil. Oh, why must I like wine so much!"

"Liking it is not the problem, Nasha," Thothmes retorted gleefully. "Drinking too much of it is."

"I drank no more than you did, Huy. Yes, I was watching you watching Anuket. Is it love that keeps you sober?" She laughed, then winced as a large white egret broke cover beside the skiff and flapped clumsily over them. A single white feather floated down and Huy caught it and handed it to her. He had not believed her capable of such perception and the knowledge dismayed him. He did not want his feeling for Anuket made light of by her frivolous tongue.

"Neither wine nor beer has any effect on me anymore," he said, as though he had not heard her question, and proceeded to recite to her the tale that ought to have become rote by now but would always fill him with wonder and horror.

She stroked the feather as she listened, her eyes often closing. When he had finished, she thanked him for his confidence and remarked that anything she needed from the Street of the Basket Sellers would be procured for her by a servant. "At least until you are proved to be a fraud," she taunted him kindly. "Believing such a story strains the bounds of my credulity, Huy. It is one thing for a king to become a god—that is Ma'at. But for a boy from Hut-herib to become a Seer? That would surely be something far beyond the boundaries of Ma'at's power. I will agree that you have suffered a terrible accident, and because you ask it of me I will stay out of the Street of the Basket Sellers. And speaking of baskets, Thothmes, open ours and let us eat. Or rather, you can eat and I shall have a mouthful of wine." She sat up. "They do say that a little wine the next day will cure the pain of the previous night's excesses."

"Father believes in the truth of Huy's transformation, Nasha," Thothmes said stoutly as he lifted the lid of the basket and drew out its contents. "You know nothing about it. You're rude." He unstoppered the flagon, poured her some wine, and passed it to her.

Her nose disappeared under the lip of the cup, and when she emerged she licked her lips. "I know that Father will think twice before giving Anuket to a man who can, or says he can, predict the future," she came back at him shrewdly. "It's no use looking so uncomfortable, Huy. I may have been lamentably drunk last night, but I'm not stupid. Everyone has seen your growing attachment to my little sister, including Father. He quite loves you. So do I. But betroth Anuket to a Seer? Besides, aren't Seers supposed to remain virgin or lose their powers?" The wine had obviously revived her. She grinned at Huy. "You have four more years at school. You're twelve now. Will you still believe in your gift when you are sixteen and Anuket is seventeen and you are desperate to marry her?"

"Shut your mouth, Nasha!" Thothmes shouted at her. "Why must you be deliberately cruel?"

But Huy had gone cold and still. "It's all right, Thothmes," he said calmly. "Nasha is angry. Why are you angry, Nasha? You know as well as I do that Anuket is far beyond my grasp. My blood is common. No matter how well paid I become as a scribe, I will never be able to give her what she has been raised to expect. It is quite true that I am in love with her. I am not ashamed of it. I have not spoken of my feelings to her." His shoulders lifted in a moment of pain. "I probably never will. I do not know if what you say regarding the chastity of Seers is true. I will ask of those I trust. Surely I deserve your sympathy, not this barely concealed maliciousness."

The rancour slowly left her face as he spoke. She looked down into her cup. "You're right, Huy. I'm sorry. I have no idea why your words made me angry." She smiled wryly. "Perhaps it was an anger prompted by fear. Mother says that women betray their fear with anger."

"Why would you fear me?"

"Not you, but the havoc you inadvertently could create in this family. Forgive me. I just want us all to be happy."

There was a long silence. Huy, watching Thothmes out of the corner of his eye, tried to read his expression. Thothmes had defended him against Nasha's unkind words with an immediate anger. Obviously Huy's preoccupation with Anuket was no news to Thothmes. Huy had shrunk from bringing up the subject with him. He did not want to hear the truth Nasha had just so pitilessly stated come from Thothmes' mouth, and so far Thothmes had ventured no opinion. Perhaps he was afraid to do so for fear of endangering their friendship. The awning of the canopy flapped rhythmically in the wind. The reeds around them brushed stiffly against each other. Finally Thothmes gave an audible sigh.

"There's a word for women like you, Nasha," he said heavily. "The sooner Father finds a husband for you, the better. Drink your wine, and with luck you will fall asleep." He held out a piece of bread and a chunk of cheese to Huy. "Would you like some beer with that, Huy? It is our own brew."

Huy took the food. Thothmes' eyes begged him to remain calm, to let it all go. He nodded. "As a mighty Seer I predict that we will eat and drink and you, Thothmes, will lose a throwing stick in the marsh as usual, and we will all fall asleep as we are being poled home," he said solemnly. Nasha burst out laughing and the moment of dislocation passed.

Huy had glumly expected that his relationship with Nasha would be changed because of her outburst, but to his relief she reverted to her usual teasing self in the evening, mocking him gently during the meal and hugging him before she sailed off to her own quarters. Nakht disappeared into his office, his wife into the garden, and Huy, Anuket, and Thothmes sat on after the servants had cleared away the debris, the three of them on cushions on the floor of the dimly lit room. Not much was said. Huy watched the play of lamplight and shadow on Anuket's features as she cuddled one of the cats that stalked through the house like royalty, the sight both a joy and a torment to him, and Thothmes seemed sunk in a sombre thought of his own. At last he sighed. "Back to school tomorrow. Sometimes I grow tired of the same routine, day after day. At least I know that I will always have you to relieve my boredom, Huy."

So Thothmes had been thinking over Nasha's outburst of the afternoon and Huy's prediction for him, Huy realized. A pall of melancholy settled over him. He reached out to touch the cat's soft fur, but the animal hissed at him, swiped one sharp claw across his hand, and ran away.

Anuket smiled. "She is pregnant and therefore unpredictable. For some reason she has attached herself to me." She rose. "The scratch is bleeding. I will bring an ointment."

Huy watched the blood well up in a thin line and trickle down his wrist.

"Anuket was being tactful," Thothmes observed. "That animal craves affection from everyone—except you, obviously! You're the first person she has attacked."

Huy did not respond. He knew why the cat had fled at the prospect of his caress. All cats could sense the unseen presence of demons, ghosts, or a spiritual aberration within a human ka, and this feline was no different. The knowledge brought an end to his enjoyment of the holiday. The Book of Thoth lay in its dark niche, waiting for him, and he was afraid.

Anuket returned with a small bowl, and sinking cross-legged beside Huy, she took his hand gently and laid it on her knee. Blood immediately began to stain her pale linen, but she ignored it. "Our physician has made a treatment of mouldy bread, ground rowan wood, and honey," she explained. "It will prevent the exudation of any ukhedu." Carefully she wiped the wound with a damp cloth, dipped her forefinger in the bowl, and spread its contents over the back of Huy's hand. Huy closed his eyes, delirious at the warmth of her knee and the stroke of her finger. "I will put the remainder in a vial so that you can reapply the medicine each time you dry your hands," she said, rising again. "I apologize on behalf of my pet, Huy."

"It was nothing," Huy responded offhandedly. "I have suffered worse on the training ground. But thank you for your concern, Anuket. I shall follow your directions." With a flash of resentment against the emotion that had turned him into a tongue-tied idiot, he got up and faced her. A head taller than she, he had the pleasure of seeing her chin tilt upward so that she could meet his eyes. "This is my last night in your house for some time, and I must take full advantage of the room I always think of as mine. Sleep well, water-lady."

Her smile broke out and, rising on tiptoe, she kissed him on the cheek. "To you also. We will eat together in the morning before the litter takes you back to the temple."

"Water-lady?" Huy heard Thothmes say as he crossed through the shadows to the passage beyond. "You have told him about your naming, Anuket?"

Huy longed to hear her reply, but he was no eavesdropper. Forcing his feet into the passage, he made his way to his room, where a servant had kept the lamp trimmed while he waited to bring Huy hot water. Later, washed and lying between fine linen sheets, Huy re-created the dressing of his scratch in his mind, and realized for the first time that Anuket had made a quiet but excessive fuss over something so slight as to be worth no more than a passing comment.

In the morning she gave him a delicate blue faience vial fashioned to represent the closed bud of a lotus. "I kept my kohl powder in it," she told him breathlessly, "but the physician washed it out thoroughly before adding your ointment. When it is empty you can use it for anything—incense granules to burn before the god of your town, perhaps, or your favourite perfume, or even a little oil for your hair."

He thanked her effusively, fingering the exquisite glass, knowing that he held the evidence of her father's wealth in his hands. "You don't want it back, Anuket?" he pressed. "A clay container would be less of a responsibility for me. I'm frightened that I might lose this."

"You will not lose it." It was a statement, not a question.

"No. I shall put it in my cedar box with my other treasures when I have used up all the ointment, and I shall look at it often. It is very beautiful." But his eyes told her that the beauty he was speaking of was hers.

She lowered her gaze. "Goodbye, then, Huy, until the next holiday. I trust that your hand will heal without a scar." The litter was waiting and Thothmes was tapping his foot impatiently. Bowing politely to her, Huy ran to join his friend.

For some time they were both quiet as the litter swayed and the bearers' muffled conversation came to them sporadically. Then Thothmes leaned sideways and drew the curtains. "The sun is hot today," he remarked lightly, "and we are catching no breeze off the river. Is your hand stinging much, Huy? A cat scratch can turn into ukhedu very quickly. Anuket was right to treat it as seriously as she did." He was making a show of twitching the drapes. Huy saw him give a tiny grimace of hesitation and realized that Thothmes was embarrassed.

"I had not wanted to talk to you about her yet," Huy said. "You always tell me the truth, Thothmes, and I don't really want it, not from you, although Nasha certainly thrashed me with it. Is she right? Am I foolish to love Anuket?"

"Is being in love foolish?" Thothmes turned to Huy in relief. "Is it all right to discuss this now that we are alone, Huy? May I tell you what I think?"

Now it was Huy's turn to grimace. "Only if you think I have some hope of winning her," he tried to joke.

Thothmes did not smile. "It is unlikely that Father will consent to a betrothal between you and Anuket," he said heavily. "He is very fond of you and thoroughly approves of our friendship and looks forward to having you in the house, but even if you become rich there's the question of your lineage. Forgive me. Such matters mean little to me. Most of the time I forget your roots, but Father will not. Anuket will marry a nobleman." His hands came up and fluttered in distress at Huy's expression. "It has nothing to do with love or deserving!" he pressed. "I do not hurt you purposely, Huy! And being in love is not foolish. But are you really in love, or is this just an infatuation that will pass? You don't know Anuket well. For that matter, none of us do. She guards herself from everyone."

"Infatuation?" Huy laughed harshly. "Gods, I hope so! This feeling is so painful, Thothmes, and so unexpected. I didn't ask for it, it fell upon me out of nowhere. Have you ever been in love?"

"Not yet. Don't forget that we're both still very young. My mother says that being in love is just a part of growing up and has nothing to do with choosing the right mate. Or having one chosen for you. Has Anuket given you any sign that she shares your feelings?"

Huy sighed. "I'm not sure. Most of the time she treats me affectionately but coolly. She does indeed seem to guard herself well, but perhaps that's because she fears the effect her name may have on her. Names are chosen carefully and have much power, as you know." He turned to meet Thothmes' gaze. "Yet she confided the source of her name to me. She let down her guard for a moment. That shows trust, and trust is one ingredient of love, is it not?" He knew he was beginning to sound desperate and did not care.

Thothmes nodded. "So they say. But Huy, although Anuket is innocent, she is not necessarily without the guile all girls seem to inherit. You have no sisters. I have three of them, and believe me, from the time they were small they've shown an ability to get what they want while seeming to be obedient and sweet."

"What are you saying?"

"Two things. One, that Anuket could have been warning you away by confiding in you, and two, that we must wait and see if your emotion grows or dies." He grasped Huy's hand and looked at him earnestly. "In either case, my sister is fortunate to be loved by someone as full of good qualities as you."

The litter was slowing. The noise of the public pathway had faded. *He has not mentioned the weight the gods have laid upon me or its consequences for my future,* Huy thought as the bearers swung onto the approach to the temple and he caught the faint odour of the pool lying before the vast stone concourse. *He believes that this is nothing more than a puff of wind stirring the sand of the desert before moving on. I wish I believed it too.*

They had hardly returned to their cell and were unpacking their satchels when a young priest darkened the morning sparkle pouring in through the doorway. "The Master desires your presence in his quarters at once, Huy," he said with a bow. "Do you need to be escorted?"

Huy sighed. "No. I know my way there by now." The man departed and Huy lifted the cedar chest onto his cot, raising the lid and laying the faience vial reverently in one of the compartments his uncle had fashioned so carefully and expertly. Returning the chest to its place under his cot, he turned reluctantly to Thothmes. "I suppose you are going to swim in the lake and lie in the grass," he said wistfully. "I don't know when I'll be back."

"At least you know by now that you have not been summoned for punishment," Thothmes answered with wry understanding. "Is this the day, do you think, Huy?"

Huy did not need to ask Thothmes what he meant. Shrugging, he started across the courtyard.

The High Priest himself opened to Huy's knock on the imposing double doors that still gave Huy a pang of apprehension when he was forced to approach them. Smiling, the man indicated that Huy should enter and Huy did so, surprised to find the room full of sharp rays of sunbeams lancing down from a series of clerestory windows cut in the walls just below the level of the ceiling. Ramose chuckled. "I love the daylight as much as, if not more than, any other man," he commented as Huy took the customary stool before the large desk. "I am Ra's High Priest after all, I do not crouch in darkness. But of course you have made every other visit to my domain during the hours of darkness, haven't you?" He lowered himself behind the desk. "Did you enjoy your three days of festivity? Yes," he added thoughtfully, "I can see that you did. Nakht's house is a warm and welcoming one, is it not? Give me your hand."

Slightly alarmed, Huy extended it and the High Priest took it firmly in both of his. At once Huy felt a shock go through him, then a fire spread up his arm and into his chest. For some moments the Priest's eyes held his in a steady regard, then he released Huy and sat back. Huy almost fell off his stool, so sudden was the cessation of heat.

"The title of Greatest of Seers is bestowed on every High Priest of Ra as a matter of course," Ramose said, "just as the title of Greatest of the Five belongs to the High Priest of Thoth at Khmun. Sometimes the title I hold is more than honorary. I have the power of second sight. It is nothing like the gift the gods have bestowed on you. I cannot see into the future. Nor can I diagnose an illness. But I can see into the heart of a man, whether it is sound or as rotten as worm-eaten wood, and I can find the seat of his happiness or his distress." He clasped his beringed fingers and laid them on the surface of the desk. "You have fallen in love, young Huy. I do not think that it is with Nasha. She is too vibrant, too colourful. She disturbs that thing in you that demands peace. No, it is sweet Anuket, weaver of garlands for the gods, who consumes your body and mind. I am sorry for you."

Huy laughed once, shakily. "It is a relief to find my soul exposed to you without a word from me, Master. I would have told you and asked for your advice, but now all I need is the advice, not the courage to confess my weakness."

"Weakness?" Ramose cocked an eye at Huy. "Love is no weakness, and the flame consuming you is pure until it is sullied by rashness. Only Anuket's name is tainted. I almost lost a friend because of that."

"You were one of the astrologers commissioned to choose her name?"

Ramose nodded. "We cast her horoscope three times. There was no doubt. I conjured against the seven Hathors in order to avert whatever dangers such a name might bring her, and we tied the seven red ribbons around her limbs for seven days to bind any evil bau who might be hovering, but the name had to stand. Nakht was furious. However"—he unlaced his fingers and laid his palms flat on the desk—"so far Anuket resembles the water goddess of old, not the wanton whore she has become in her modern aspect. She is intelligent, demure, and chaste. Do you need my advice?"

"Very much." Huy swallowed. "Nasha taunted me with the knowledge that a Seer loses his or her power unless he or she remains virgin. Is that true?"

Ramose's eyebrows rose. "Taunted you? Yes, I can understand why. Nasha is beautiful but fiery and strong-willed. Nakht is having difficulty finding a husband for her who is strong enough to pit himself against her resolve, win, and yet keep her respect." He grinned, a gesture that removed years from his features. "So far she has demolished all of them."

"I had no idea," Huy exclaimed. "Thothmes has told me nothing of these things."

"I doubt very much if Nakht takes his young son into his confidence regarding his daughter's matrimonial prospects," Ramose said dryly. "I tell you so that you will not judge Nasha too harshly. Her heart is generous and kindly, but it must hurt her to know that Anuket is adored, even by a stripling like yourself." He lifted an arm in admonition against Huy's unspoken protest. "I do not insult you, Huy. I speak a truth. You are twelve. You are in the violent throes of a first love. It will either last no longer than a few months or it will deepen, in which case I will then answer your question. You do not need to know now. Don't be anxious. Enjoy the experience. Give thanks to the gods for it. It is sacred. Feast on little Anuket's presence with every faculty but one, for many perfectly ordinary reasons I do not think I need to name. Do I?"

Miserably Huy shook his head. "No, Master."

"Good." Ramose smiled. "Then we may move on to your immediate future. I have spoken with your Overseer and we have ordered your afternoons thus. After the noon meal and the sleep you will continue your work with the bow and spear, but we will add control of a chariot to it. You need no more swimming lessons. After an hour on the training ground, more or less, you will go to the bathhouse, wash yourself thoroughly, and present yourself at my quarters. Together we will approach the Ished Tree, in whose shade you will begin to study the Book of Thoth until it is time for your evening meal. I presume that these arrangements are not inconvenient for you?"

Huy saw that it was a serious question. "No, Master, of course not. You will sit with me while I read?" He was remembering his first encounter with both Tree and High Priest and the thought brought apprehension.

"No, there is no need. The scrolls are not difficult to read. The language is archaic, but decipherable to a student of your standing. You may take your palette with you to make notes of anything you may wish to ponder later. The Book does not of course leave the vicinity of the Tree. When you feel that you have read enough for one day, whether it be a few minutes or a few hours, you will tell the guard on the door. He will fetch me, I will take the scrolls away, and you will be free to spend your evenings as you wish." He rose and came around the desk. "I am needed in the temple and you have the rest of the day to prepare for your lessons that begin as usual tomorrow morning. The other boys are trickling back to their courtyards. Go and greet your friends."

Huy stood. "I am not to discuss what I read with anyone, is that correct, Master?"

"You may bring any problem to me or to the Rekhet." He hesitated. "The Book is forbidden to no one, Huy. The responsibility of the priests here and at Khmun is to keep it safe, not to keep it from those wishing to read it. You would think that every literate man would want to see what the god has set down regarding the ordering of the cosmos, but few come and ask for it." He pursed his lips. "It is as though the god chooses those destined to read it and sends them here. During my own tenure as High Priest there have been only two requests to see it. Neither man stayed long. Both seemed to find something in it that satisfied them, whereas when I read it I understood only one truth."

"And what was that, Master?" Huy asked eagerly.

"'It is Ra, the creator of the names of his limbs, which came into being in the forms of the gods who are in the following of Ra,'" Ramose quoted. He looked at Huy inquiringly. Huy's face was a blank. "Think about it for a moment."

Huy frowned. "It cannot be!" he exclaimed. "That would mean . . ."

"Yes," Ramose said quietly. "Remember that the words were written down in the dawn of our history, before the vast proliferation of gods we have now. Those words appear in the seventeenth chapter of the Book of the Dead. Our gods are personifications of the names of Ra. Each god is one of his members. The name of a god is the god himself."

"So Ra is the visible representation of the creator-god Atum. As Ra is to Atum, so is our King to Ra."

"You will learn much, much more from the Book than this," Ramose said. "More than I could ever fathom. You have been chosen to do so. If you wish to take young Thothmes into your confidence, you may, but he will be no more than a sounding board for you. He will understand only that he loves you. Go and sit in the temple gardens for a while. Try to empty your mind." Ramose leaned close. "It is perhaps a good thing that your parents have no interest in the things of the gods," he commented. "You will bring no prejudices to your study of the Book. The gods must be honoured, Huy, but what are the gods? I am late. I must go. I will see you tomorrow afternoon. The guard at the door to the Tree will be expecting you." He hurried out, his priestly robe floating after him.

Huy followed more slowly, smarting from the High Priest's offhand comment regarding his parents' ignorance. The shame of his origins would probably always dog him, he thought dismally, the emotion lying dormant until a chance word revived it. No matter how refined his speech became, how cultured his manners, how sophisticated his education, he would remain the son of a peasant from Hut-herib.

Finding himself in the grove of palms by the south wall of the temple, not knowing how he had got there, he chose the hole of a tree where the grass made a green patch in the surrounding sand and lowered himself onto it, drawing up his knees and resting his chin on them. *What of Khenti-kheti?* he thought dully. *Is the totem of my hometown simply a symbol of some aspect of Ra? When I prostrate myself before his image in my cell, am I praising or beseeching aid from the great sun himself? And what of Osiris and Isis, Horus, Hathor, where do they come from?* He slumped back against the tree and closed his eyes. "I do not want to know," he murmured aloud. "I have cared very little for the things of the gods. They have treated me cruelly, foisted their strange ways upon me without my permission, as though I were of no account, and now I am their prisoner." *You chose,* a voice whispered inside his head, and he closed his mouth. *So I chose,* he thought mutinously. *That does not make me love them or want to know about them. All I must do is read and understand the Book while keeping my emotions to myself. When that is done, will they let me go?*

Waking the next morning, he moved through the hours enveloped in a sense of unreality. He received a sharp reprimand from his teacher for inattention, listened to Ptahmose the architect speak of plumb lines and pillar foundations without comprehension, and ate the noon meal without appetite. He came to himself briefly in the white dust of the training ground, for he enjoyed drawing the bow and was beginning to have some mastery over the previously erratic flight of his arrows. Later, his weapons master walked him over to the adjoining stables, where a curious nose appeared over the half door at their approach and two mild brown eyes regarded Huy. "This is Lazy White Star," the man said. "He pulls the chariots of the beginners. He is very lazy, as his name suggests, and will do no more than an occasional trot."

Huy stepped close to the beast, his hand going to the firm warmth of its arched neck, his nostrils full of its reassuring odour. Suddenly his fingers froze. "Master, this beast still has a stone embedded in its hoof from the last exercise. It wants you to remove it before it is required to work again."

"Oh, you're *that* one!" the man said loudly. "I've been drilling you for a year and I didn't know. Hoi, Mesta!" he shouted to the man hurrying towards them. "Lazy White Star has a stone in his foot! You'd better see to it!"

Mesta's hand grasped Huy's as he came up. He was a short, well-built man with weather-beaten features and a shock of greying hair. His smile was unfeigned. "I am the chariot master. Do you like horses?"

"I don't know," Huy replied. "This is the first one I've actually touched. I like donkeys, though."

"Ah. Good. Come inside and we'll see if this lazy old nag really does have a stone in its hoof." Huy followed Mesta into the small room. Its floor was covered generously with straw. One clay trough held grain, the other was full of water. Opposite the half door through which they had entered was another door leading onto a long passage open at each end. Rakes, pails, linen bags, and harnesses hung or were propped all along its length.

Mesta knelt, running his hand down Lazy White Star's leg, but the horse shifted its weight and lifted the opposite foreleg. "Well!" the man exclaimed. "You are co-operating with me today, you godless old warhorse! Huy—your name is Huy? yes?—hand me that implement on the nail on the wall." Expertly cradling the animal's hoof in his lap, Mesta examined it carefully, whistled in surprise, took the tool, and with a few sharp twists extracted a stone, which fell into the straw with a rustle. Huy, standing by the horse's head, felt its muzzle thrust against his chest. "How did Ptahmose know it was there?" the chariot master muttered to himself. "In any case, the last boy to stable you after his lesson will be whipped for not carrying out his inspection properly." He came to his feet. "This beast seems quite comfortable with you," he said to Huy. "Are you afraid of him?"

"Not at all, Master."

"Good. We will harness him to one of the chariots and you will stand in it, only stand at first, while I lead him around the training ground. You must find your balance before all else. When the lesson is over, you will learn to wash this horse, comb him, check his feet, and make sure that he has no injury anywhere. Then you will feed him from your own hand so that he learns to trust you. A good charioteer cares as much for his horses as he does for his harness and his weapons. Come and see the chariots."

He led Huy out the other door into the cluttered passage. Lazy White Star turned and nudged Huy as he closed the door. "You're welcome," Huy whispered, and strode after Mesta.

When the lesson was over, Mesta congratulated him. "I think you will make an excellent charioteer, Huy. Perhaps one day you will be as accomplished as the men who drive the King's gilded chariots and prize horses. Now you must wash both chariot and animal and check his feet. Then you may go." Lazy White Star looked smug. Huy thanked his instructor, performed the chores, and limped slowly towards the gate leading into the temple grounds. His knees were trembling.

He bathed with deliberation, consciously putting off the moment when he must present himself at the High Priest's door, but eventually he was forced to tie back his wet black hair, put on his sandals, and, clad in clean white linen, take the long passages behind the sanctuary. The priests' quarters were busy. Men greeted him courteously as he passed them, many bowing civilly, and he bowed back, feeling stupid and young and thoroughly unworthy of such acts of respect from these holy servants of the god. Soon, too soon, he stood before the double doors and had raised a reluctant hand to knock when one of them opened and Ramose peered out.

"Oh, there you are! I was beginning to think that you had been injured. Or that you had decided to take a stroll by the river," he added shrewdly. "Wait here a moment." He vanished and reappeared with a small, plain cedar box under his arm, striding away down the passage at once. Huy followed, his heart sinking. A sense of dread had been growing in him since he left the sunny reality of the training ground, a fear that he might read things he did not want to know, an awareness that on this day the gods (but are there many gods or only many manifestations of the one?) had drawn close and were watching him. He felt them as an

uneasiness between his shoulder blades where demons
liked to strike, as an almost imperceptible disturbance
in the flow of his blood. As the High Priest slowed
before the locked door behind which the Ished Tree
flourished, Huy needed all his willpower to prevent
himself from fleeing. Heart pounding, he followed
Ramose inside.

Nothing had changed here in the eight years since
he had crept into the room from the palm grove.
Sunlight bathed the roofless space but for a shadow
being cast by the west wall as the sun descended
leisurely towards the horizon. The Tree still spread its
many heavily leafed branches in every direction. The
impression of a deep peace saturated the air, but Huy,
inhaling the well-remembered odours of a mingled
delight and corruption, scarcely felt it.

Placing the box on the ground, Ramose prostrated
himself reverently to the Tree three times and Huy
followed suit, then the High Priest indicated a large
cushion at its foot. Shaken by a fit of unsteadiness,
Huy lowered himself onto it, and in a moment of
dislocation he glanced to the side to see the hyena.
He was in exactly the same position as Imhotep had
been. Ramose settled beside him.

"The Book is written on forty-two scrolls. They
are divided between this temple and the temple of
Thoth at Khmun, as I have told you. Each scroll sits
in a tube of leather. Be very careful in your handling
of them, Huy. Their value cannot be overestimated."
He lifted the lid of the box and began to extract the
tubes, their white leather so scored and soft that they
seemed ready to fall apart at his touch. "The stitches

are sound," Ramose commented absently, "but perhaps it is time I set my priests to the task of making new tubes. The hide of a white bull must be used. You will notice that the tubes are numbered, I do not know by whom. Perhaps by Thoth himself, and it may be he who keeps the leather from rotting and the stitches from fraying. The Book divides into five parts. Parts one, three, and five are here. I give you only the first part. When you have read it and learned what you can from it, you must go south to Khmun for the second part. Don't worry, it will be arranged. There are three scrolls containing the first part. May Atum protect and guide you in this sacred task." Then he was gone, saluting Huy and striding to the door with the easy, long-legged gait Huy had come to recognize so well. The door closed, and Huy distinctly heard a key turn in the lock. After a moment there was the sound of the guard's footsteps approaching and stopping and the faint thump of his spear butt hitting the tiling of the passage. Huy was alone.

And yet not alone. For a long time he sat there immobile, one hand on the warm leather tube marked *One,* and it gradually began to seem to him as though, beneath the constant rustle of the leaves, a voice was murmuring, so low as to be almost indistinguishable. He knew it was possible that he was simply conjuring it out of his own apprehension and the blending of his memories. Sexless and continuous, it did not pause for breath, but when he tried to concentrate on it the sound abruptly ceased and there was only the gentle, mysterious utterance of the Tree itself.

I could pretend to read it. I'm devious enough to compose some high-sounding nonsense for the High Priest every day. I am becoming desperate for my freedom. But Anuket's tiny face swam before his mind's eye, full of an innocent and trusting admiration, and with a sigh of resignation he withdrew the first scroll.

9

The papyrus ought to have been so brittle that unrolling it produced splits, but it moved smoothly under Huy's hand, revealing a density of tiny hieroglyphs so beautifully executed that he caught his breath. He had forgotten to bring his scribe's palette and the High Priest had not remarked on its absence. The scroll lay across Huy's knees, supported lightly by his kilt linen. With a fearful reluctance to begin he stared at the wall opposite, at its moving pattern of leaf shadow, at the door to the passage and the one to the palm grove, looked up at the square of bright blue sky; but at last he forced his gaze to drop to the perfectly formed characters in his lap and brought his mind to bear on the first words.

I Thoth, greatest of heka-power, giver of the sacred gift of language to man out of my own Hu, set down these mysteries at the command of Atum so that he who is possessed of the gift of wisdom may read and understand what is the will of the Holy One. Let him who desires this

knowledge take care that his eyes be diligent and
his reverence complete. For he without sia will
read to his harm, and he without diligence will
enter the Second Duat.

Here Huy paused. His pulse had settled into its
regular rhythm and he was calm enough to be already
puzzled. Thoth uses his Hu, his creative utterance,
to give us language. Every student knows this.
Every scribe says the prayer of thanks to him for
this great gift before setting pen to papyrus. Whether
or not I have sufficient perception to read safely
remains to be seen, but what is the Second Duat?
Surely there is only one, a place of terror inhabited
by djinns in the pools and rivers and full of demons with
human bodies and the heads of animals, insects,
even knives, through which the dead must pass in order
to reach the Paradise of Osiris. The echo of Hapzefa's
voice rang in his ears and once again he was three
years old, lying on his cot while she said the nightly
prayer over him that his mother usually forgot, a plea
for protection against a death that would plunge
him into the realm of The-blood-drinker-who-comes-
from-the-Slaughterhouse and The-backward-facing-
one-who-comes-from-the-Abyss. Not to mention
The-one-who-eats-the-excrement-of-his-hindquarters.
Huy's exorcism with the Rekhet sprang into his mind
and he shifted uneasily against the Tree's rough bark.
That place is the Duat, his thoughts ran on. One Duat,
yet according to Thoth there is another. He wished he
had remembered to bring his palette so that he could
make a note of the enigma, but he had the depressing

idea that many more awaited him in these precious documents. He read on.

I, Thoth of the twenty-two titles, Representative of Atum, He who Accomplishes Truth, He who hath made Eternity, speak thus of the nature of Atum.

The Universe is nothing but consciousness, and in all its appearances reveals nothing but an evolution of consciousness, from its origin to its end, which is a return to its cause.

How to describe the Indescribable? How to show the Unshowable?

How to express the Unutterable?

How to seize the Ungraspable Instant?

How indeed, Huy thought in a panic. *Gods, I am just a boy, just a twelve-year-old pupil at school in Iunu under the rule of Ma'at and the mighty King Thothmes, living in this blessed land of Egypt. I am nothing, I am no one! Only the oldest and wisest of Seers could begin to understand these words! By what right am I here? How have I deserved this subtle chastisement? Thoth have pity!* The voice had begun to whisper again, and now he could discern his own name weaving with the music of the quivering leaves, "Huy, Huy, Huy."

"Be silent!" he shouted, and at once there was quiet. Grimly he bent over the archaic script.

Before there was any opposition, any yes and no, positive and negative; before there was any complementarity, high and low, light and shadow;

before there was presence or absence, life
or death, heaven or earth: there was but one
Incomprehensible Power, alone, unique, inherent
in the Nun, the indefinable cosmic sea, the
Infinite Source of the Universe, outside any
notion of Space and Time.

This was a little easier. The one Incomprehensible
Power was obviously Atum himself, and everyone knew
that before anything was made there was the Nun, the
place of un-being.

I Thoth, who Beholdeth What Cometh Afterwards,
now speak of the Divine Will of Atum in few words
but potent meaning.
       Hail Atum, he who comes before himself!
       Hail, him who enters the First Duat!
       You culminate in this your name of "Hill,"
you become in this your name . . .

Huy's throat was dry, as though he had been
reciting some text set by his teacher for many hours.
His head had begun to ache. Allowing the scroll to roll
up, he slid it into its tube, put the tube in the box, and
closed the lid with deliberate slowness, his body
rigid with the resentment he was feeling. *I will never
understand,* he thought fiercely. *Why should I care what
the First Duat is, or why Atum's name is Hill, when all
I want to do is wrestle with Thothmes and drink beer on
hot afternoons and inhale Anuket's perfume while she
bends over her garlands? Give me the life of my senses, not
this cold, incomprehensible, ancient muddle that has no*

significance to me! I wish I could go to my cell, summon
Pabast, order wine, and get thoroughly drunk, but even
that avenue of escape is closed to me. The gods have made
sure of that. Or god. To both the First and the Second
Duat with everything!

The guard on the door answered his loud knock with
a muffled acknowledgment and went away. Huy could
hear his footsteps receding. He waited impatiently, his
back turned deliberately to the Ished Tree, until the
High Priest's key turned in the lock and the door
swung open. Huy thrust the box into the man's hands.
"I cannot do this," he half shouted. "I don't care what
choice I made, a choice in innocence, without awareness
of the consequences, High Priest, it is all far beyond my
ability to understand, no matter how sharp my sia!"

Ramose patted him sympathetically. "You are tired
and hungry, Huy. Go to your courtyard. The evening
meal is being served. Play sennet with your friend. Tell
him what you have read if you like. It will mean little to
him, but the burden may lift from you."

"How will I be able to tell him what I have read
when I can't remember any of it?" Huy began, but
suddenly he realized that the words were indeed still
there, embedded like a crystal in the rough stone of his
mind. The knowledge plunged him even further
into despair, and he took his leave of Ramose with a
perfunctory bow, hurrying through the darkening
passages to the newly lit lamps of his courtyard as
though Anubis himself were on his heels.

It seemed to him that he had been sitting below
the Ished Tree for no more than a few minutes and
he was shocked to find the sun already setting and

the other boys lining up for their food. Thothmes was waiting for him, a question in his eyes, but Huy said, "Later." They filled their cups and platters and settled onto the grass. Huy felt too tired to eat much. Avoiding the nightly explosion of high-spirited wrestling and good-natured loud banter, he went into his cell and lay on his cot, hands behind his head. Thothmes had joined a game of stickball. Huy could pick his voice out of the general melee, high and sometimes indignant, his small size putting him at a disadvantage to the others. Pabast was late with the lamps. Huy stared up into the gathering darkness of the ceiling and tried to think of nothing.

The servant and Thothmes arrived together, Thothmes bleeding from a long scratch on his calf. "I got between Menkh and the ball," he explained while Pabast set their lamp on the table, grunted a good night, and departed. "I'll put some honey on it after we've been to the bathhouse. Huy, are you all right?"

"I'm not sure." Huy pulled himself off the cot. "I suppose we should go and get washed, although I would rather just crawl between my sheets. I'm tired and my throat hurts."

"Hurts? Hurts how?" Thothmes came close and peered up into Huy's face. "You're very flushed." He placed a hand against Huy's forehead, then drew back hastily. He was frowning. "Gods, Huy, you're hot! I think we should send for a physician."

"No. I'm just tired," Huy repeated. "I expect I'll be better in the morning." In truth his throat felt swollen and his head had begun to throb. *Too many words crammed into it,* he thought, not without humour, *all scrambled together and banging against my skull.*

But the blessing of hot water and perfumed oil revived him enough to recite to Thothmes what he had read in the first scroll of the Book. He could not say "learned," for he felt that he had learned nothing. In the guttering light of the untrimmed lamp he sat with eyes closed, the words flowing up through the pain in his throat and across his tongue and filling the dim, cozy space with an ancient dignity that had been absent to him when unspoken. The exercise did not take long and he marvelled again at how different his perception of time had been in the tranquil confines of the Tree's sanctuary.

"It seems like one of those interminable litanies the priest chants on feast days," Thothmes said, his distorted shadow moving with him on the wall as he stirred. "A lot of pompousness around kernels of vital truth. What is the First Duat, do you think? I only know of one."

Huy shrugged, the gesture sending a renewed pulse of discomfort behind his eyes. "Perhaps it will be explained later in the text. I don't know. Nor do I know why Atum should be called Hill. How can he come before himself, Thothmes?"

Thothmes' eyes widened. "Gods, Huy, didn't your parents teach you anything important? The first thing every pious child learns is that before the world was made there was only the Nun, the great sea of darkness, and then out of the darkness Atum caused a hill to appear and from that came everything."

"My parents never cared to know such things," Huy said slowly. "They were content to live under

Ma'at and leave communication with the gods to the priests. I remember how shocked the Rekhet was when I told her that my father took no steps to protect our house from evil influences." He managed a smile. "That was before I became the oddity that I am. In any case, Thothmes, why should Atum himself be called Hill? What does it mean, that 'you become in this your name'?"

Now it was Thothmes' turn to raise one shoulder. "I have no idea. Do you read again tomorrow?"

"I am supposed to, but it makes me so tired that I think I'll ask the High Priest if I might do so only twice a week. Are you taking chariot practice as well as archery?" Deliberately he changed the subject. There had been a curious sense of release in repeating Thoth's words aloud. The cryptic stanzas held a rhythm impossible to feel otherwise, and Thothmes had provided a piece of knowledge that was important. But the task imposed upon Huy was so fraught with fear, confusion, an alarming sense of dislocation from his everyday reality, and an equally unsettling fascination that exhaustion overwhelmed him. Thothmes' voice seemed to reach him from a long way away as he talked of his lessons, and his form in the lamplight appeared distorted.

Thothmes fell silent, then yawned. "The lamp is almost out and I need to sleep. Good night, my favourite Seer."

Ah yes, Huy thought, turning onto his side and watching the starved flame of the lamp leap frenetically before it finally died. *There is that also. Anuket, water goddess, apart from you my heart is so dry, my soul so thirsty. Are you asleep between your clean and scented sheets with your tiny fist clenched under your cheek and your black eyelashes resting like butterflies' wings against your skin? Or do you lie sprawled on your back with one arm on the pillow above your head and your eyes wide open, thinking of me as I am thinking so desperately of you?* All at once he became so cold that his teeth started to chatter, and at the same time an ache began at the base of his spine. Shivering, he sat up and dragged the blanket folded at the foot of the cot up around his shoulders, but almost at once he pushed it away again. He had begun to sweat. *Too much,* he thought dimly. *I am learning too much, too fast. I am weighted down with knowledge so that my knees buckle and my back is bowed. They stab me, all these words. They are stones on my shoulders and sword blades piercing my belly. I don't feel well at all. Not at all.*

Thothmes was shaking him gently, and Huy recoiled from his touch. "Get up, Huy! Get up!" Thothmes was urging him from somewhere far away, from the darkness of the Duat where the demons formed shapes like misshapen hieroglyphs that he couldn't understand. "You'll be late for class!"

Huy turned his head on the pillow. The movement seemed to take an eternity. "Can you see the words, Thothmes?" he murmured thickly. "Can you tell me what they mean? I must know what they mean!"

Thothmes went away. The demons came shuffling closer, shedding mysterious symbols around their feet. One of them had the features of the High Priest. It bent over him. "This is a disaster," it said. "Have a lector priest prepare an incantation to drive out the fever demon. His linens are soaked. Pabast, bring fresh sheets and a large bowl of the coldest water you can find. He must be bathed continually. Can he swallow?" Another face loomed close.

Huy giggled. "So I do have a demon after all. Send for the Rekhet at once!" No one seemed to hear him.

The face shook its head. "Not yet. If I tried to force medicine down his throat, he would choke. Later, if the gods will a satisfactory climax to the illness, I prescribe belladonna for any pain, with camphor seeds to reduce the fever, and coriander of course."

"All of which are useless at the moment." The Ramose-demon's voice was testy. "I should have watched him more carefully. He returned from the House of the Dead too short a time ago. Perhaps we have given him more burdens than he could bear." The face receded into the darkness, but the voice continued. "The servants can work in shifts. The fever must be brought down."

"Master, I want to take care of him. I can bathe him, and with Pabast's help I can make him as comfortable as possible. He knows my touch." The voice was Thothmes'.

Huy felt relieved. Thothmes could talk to the demons. He would overcome them. "Sort the hieroglyphs, my friend. Tear them from the demons' skin and lay them sensibly before me."

"He muttered when he heard my name," Thothmes went on. "Master, please!"

"Very well. But you will do everything the physician tells you to do, and you will have to make up the school work you lose in your own time. I must send to your father. Nakht may not want you so close to illness."

The lip of a well was rushing towards Huy. It had fingers. It grasped his throat and head and pulled him into it. The pain was terrible. With a cry, Huy fell towards more darkness.

He knew Thothmes' hands in that lightless place. A damp coolness spread from them wherever they touched him. Someone was singing. "I belong to Ra. Thus spoke he: It is I who shall guard the sick man from his enemies. His guide shall be Thoth who lets writing speak, who creates the Books, who passes on useful knowledge to Those who Know, the Physicians his followers, that they may deliver from disease the sick man of whom a god wishes that the physician may keep him alive . . ."

"Get well, Huy," he heard Thothmes whisper before the well claimed him again. "Don't you dare die, or all these sleepless nights will have been wasted."

At last he felt the fever begin to die. Its coils loosened, and between bouts of unconsciousness he was able to open his eyes drowsily to see his friend wringing out wet cloths or praying before his totem, or half sitting, half lying on his cot asleep. Now he knew one of the demon faces as that of the physician, who lifted his head and held a cup to his lips. The medicine was bitter. It raked his tender throat, but he swallowed it, and the day came when he croaked a word of gratitude before falling into a healthy sleep.

And dreamed. He was sitting cross-legged on warm grass facing an Ished Tree weighed down with thick red-and-white blossoms and alive with the drone of many bees. A languorous scent filled the air. Standing directly overhead, the force of the sun should have been unbearable, but Huy, a river of contentment coursing through him, was entirely comfortable. Facing him, Imhotep had an open scroll across the scribe's palette on his knees. Other white scrolls lay scattered about. He seemed not to notice Huy's presence, and for a long time Huy drifted in a trance of sheer pleasure, inhaling the gusts of aroma from the Tree and listening to the soporific hum of the bees as they darted in and out of the profusion of blooms, before his attention returned to Imhotep. The great man's head was down, one ringed hand motionless on the delicate characters Huy knew so well. Idly Huy looked for the other hand and a thrill of apprehension went through him when he saw what it was doing. The hyena lay curled beside Imhotep, its golden eyes half closed as the man's long fingers caressed it, moving slowly from the dome of its rough head and down its curved spine in a lazy, deliberate gesture.

"Do you think," said a deep voice directly behind Huy, "that this is consciousness?" Huy swung round. Anubis's long black snout brushed his ear, and beside him Ma'at's iridescent feathers quivered in the sweet breeze. "Or is it something more, young mortal? Is there anything more than consciousness? How can Atum become the Hill unless the Hill possesses the consciousness of Atum? And if the Hill possesses the consciousness of Atum, then Atum has willed the First Duat. Hear me and understand." The god's voice was oddly timbreless and cold, as though it came through the chilling water of a Delta winter morning. His black arm appeared on the periphery of Huy's vision, stretched out towards the Tree, a golden ankh in his grasp, and at once the sun went out. The darkness was immediate and absolute, a night so complete, so final, Huy knew that there had never been, nor would there ever be, anything else. "Behold the Nun," the voice went on remorselessly. "Where is consciousness now, Son of Hapu? For here there is no now, no then, no yes and no, no positive and negative, no presence or absence. There is not even nothing, there is the nothingness of nothingness of nothing. Where is Atum? How can he enter this? What is his will? Hear me and understand."

Huy woke with a scream. Fumbling to touch his protective amulets, pouring sweat, he sat up. It was night. Through the open doorway of the cell he could see a blaze of stars and the reassuring, regular lines of the surrounding roofs bulking densely against a velvet sky.

At once Thothmes was beside him. "Huy. Huy! Do you recognize me? Your fever has gone, but you're very weak still. Lie back. I need to wash you again." He laughed with relief. "You stink!" He slid another pillow behind Huy and went to the door. Huy heard him send one servant for hot water and more linen and a second to the High Priest's quarters.

"How long have I been ill?" he asked when Thothmes returned. "You've been nursing me, haven't you? I remember your voice and the feel of your hands." He blinked away the tears of weakness. "I think I would have died without the hope of those moments. Thank you, my dearest friend."

Thothmes grinned. He looked pale to Huy, his small face even thinner. He had lost weight. "You've been out of your mind for four days and unconscious for another two, between moments when you woke enough for the physician to pour his noxious brews down your throat." His arms went around Huy. "The High Priest is a wise man. He knew that your chances of recovery were better if you were tended by someone you trusted. Ah! Here's the water." He gestured at the servant. "Wait while I wash him and then you can help me change his sheets. How do you feel, Huy?"

Huy relaxed and closed his eyes while the warm cloth moved over his body. The pungent odour of camphor oil filled his nostrils. "My throat is fine, but my head still gives me a twinge or two."

"You woke with such a scream, I thought the fever had come back."

"No. I was dreaming. I saw the Nun, and it is terrible. Terrible!"

"It was the last of the fever dreams," Thothmes said, briskly wringing out his cloth. "We were talking about the Nun on the night you became ill. The Nun *was*, Huy, not is. The time of the Nun is long past. Are you thirsty? Would you like some water?"

Huy considered. "Actually, I want grape wine. If the physician will allow it."

Thothmes took a towel from the servant's waiting arm and applied it vigorously to Huy's limbs. "There! That must make you feel better! The physician is not here, though I imagine he'll darken our door before long. He might agree that grape wine is strengthening. I have half a jar that Father sent me. If you can come and sit on my cot, you can drink it while we change your linen."

Huy felt himself lifted in his friend's wiry arms and set on his feet. Unsteadily he took the few steps across

the room and sank onto Thothmes' bed. Quickly
Thothmes and the servant stripped the sodden, fetid
sheets from his cot while he gulped down the wine. The
taste of the grapes filled his mouth with sweetness and
he felt life begin to trickle through his body. All the
same, he was glad to be helped back to his cot and
have Thothmes tuck the sheet around him. It smelled
pleasantly of the dash of vinegar put in the rinsing water
to dissolve the last of the cleansing natron. He felt all at
once drowsy.

"I can't stay awake to see the physician and
Ramose. Tell them I will be well. All will be well."
He turned his cheek into the pillow and fell into a
deep and healing sleep.

He was not allowed back into the classroom for
another week, during which he was forced to go on
swallowing the physician's remedies. The High Priest
visited him every morning. His food was brought to
him and he ate it outside, sitting on the grass of the
courtyard, relishing the strokes of the breeze on his
flesh and the forceful reality of the sunlight drenching
the pleasant space. Ramose took him into the temple,
where he prostrated himself before the closed doors of
Ra's sanctuary and gave thanks aloud for his recovery,
but privately he thanked the god for deliverance from
the ghosts and shadows that had accompanied his
illness. He had not forgotten the terror of the well with
fingers reaching out for him. He knew that he was alive
not only through the will of Atum but also because of
the selfless care of his friend. Every evening Thothmes
regaled him with the gossip of the classroom. "Many of
the other boys want to come and see you," he had told

Huy, "but the High Priest has forbidden it. You are to recover completely in peace. No one is to upset you."

"As though I'm a girl," Huy scoffed, but he was secretly glad of the days of quiet and the nights of rejuvenating rest. The physician stopped calling, and just as Huy began to be bored with his aimless existence the High Priest sent for him.

"It's time for you to resume your studies," he told Huy. "You're ready, I think. But if you feel your illness returning, if you become overtired, send word to me at once. I fear I overtaxed your strength, and I apologize." Ramose did not object to Huy's request to read the Book only twice a week. "I did not sufficiently take your other duties into account. Come to me in three days."

Huy felt as though he had been accorded a stay of execution at the last moment. He threw himself wholeheartedly into catching up with his many lessons, refusing to acknowledge the mysterious phrases always lurking in the back of his mind and earning praise from both his archery instructor and Mesta, who was already allowing him to take Lazy White Star's reins and guide the chariot carefully around the perimeter of the training ground by himself. The sense of power, of being utterly in control of himself, the vehicle, and the animal, was a wonderful antidote to the chaos inside, and Huy made the most of the hour he spent balancing on the springy wicker floor of the chariot while the horse trotted steadily ahead and Mesta called the occasional order.

At the end of his session on the third afternoon, as Huy had stepped out of the chariot and was preparing to unhitch the horse, Mesta clapped him on the back and said, "Well done again, Huy! You are becoming a good driver. Perhaps instead of a career with words you'll want to become a man of action!" The words were warm, an accolade and an amused encouragement, but something entirely sober shifted in Huy's mind. "You are becoming . . . you'll want to become . . ." From words to action. *No, that's not it,* he thought feverishly as he led Lazy White Star into his stall. *That's the second thing.* "You are becoming . . . You become in this your name . . . You culminate in this your name of 'Hill' . . ." *Culminate. Culminate. But to culminate means to have begun a process—not a task, not a chore, a process—and brought it to fruition. Atum wills a culmination. He enters the First Duat. Oh gods, it's there, but I can't bring it forward!*

The horse raised his head from the water bowl and looked reproachfully at Huy, his muzzle dripping. Fetching warm water, Huy washed and brushed him, the words of the Book and Mesta's remark juggling together infuriatingly, then went outside to drag the chariot into its place. It was lightly built, easily moved, but it needed a tug to free the wheels from the sand. Lifting the shafts, Huy pulled it towards him and stepped back, and as he did so the storm of words abruptly swirled, separated, halted their mental dance, and the answer he was seeking came clear and pure to his tongue. "Metamorphosis!" he blurted, dropping the shafts and standing numbly between them. "Of course! 'Hail him who enters the First Duat! You culminate in this your name of "Hill"! You become in this your name!' The First Duat is the place of metamorphosis! Atum wills a metamorphosis for himself, enters the process, and becomes Hill . . . I need beer!"

Mesta was hurrying towards him. "Huy, is anything wrong? Have you pulled a muscle? Are you ill again?"

Huy bent and picked up the shafts again. He was smiling. "No, Master, thank you. I have almost finished my obligation." Once the vehicle was chained in its stall and Huy had checked it for a loose axle, a weakness in the wicker, or the first signs of rot in the spokes, he bade Mesta a brusque farewell and set off for his courtyard at a run. His feeling of self-congratulation was almost as great as his thirst.

This time he prostrated himself before the Tree, sank onto the cushion, and opened the small box without a qualm. Ramose, on his way out of the room, paused and glanced back. "Huy, you have forgotten your palette," he said with a hint of reproof. "I shall send a servant for it."

"There's no need, Master. At least, I don't think there is. I seem to be able to memorize the script as I read it even though I don't try. Let me see if I can do so again."

The High Priest stared at him speculatively. "If I were a different man, I might be disposed to fear you, Huy son of Hapu," he murmured. "As it is, I simply wonder what strange fate the gods have in store for you." The lock clicked behind him and Huy was alone.

Eagerly he extracted the scroll he had been reading before and unrolled it, skimming through the text he already knew with an easy comprehension. Atum existed alone, unique, certainly incomprehensible, outside any notion of space or time but inherent in the Nun through his own choice. He also chose to become, to metamorphose. Here Huy's eyes left the papyrus and strayed unseeingly to the opposite wall. *I also experienced a First Duat,* he thought in sùrprise. *I died and was reborn. I metamorphosed, as the gods intended. To what end is hidden from me, but if I had refused Imhotep's invitation to read the Book, would I have remained dead to this Egypt, my body beautified and entombed? Am I to understand something of Atum's metamorphosis because of my own? Surely there is no comparison possible between the will of a god and the powerlessness of a human resolve to do anything more than resign itself to its destiny!* His gaze returned to the hieroglyphs.

I Thoth, who created purification, now speak of the birth of Heka as Atum has commanded me.

I became, the becoming became, I have become in becoming . . .

I did all that I desired in this non-existent world,

I dilated myself in it,

I contracted my own hand, all alone, before there was any birth.

My own mouth came to me, and Heka was my name.

Huy put out both rigid arms to steady himself. His palms touched the grass and one soft leaf from the Tree. His fingers closed around it, crushing it, but he was almost unaware of the scent it gave off. *I know this. I can see it: the non-existent world of the Nun, and Atum entering the First Duat, dilating himself in it until it ceased to be nothingness but was full of him, and then he masturbates and places his own semen in his mouth. He can do this because he has willed that he is no longer outside the Nun, he is in it, filling it, he has metamorphosed, and the moment his semen touches his tongue heka-power is conceived. He is the Hill filling the Nun. Now he is also heka. He is working, working within himself, within the Nun, and heka is now in a state of conception.* Huy's heart was racing. Awe swept over him. "I hear and understand, Anubis," he whispered, and it seemed to him that the rustle of the leaves above him blended in a moment of musical approval. All at once aware of the leaf he had mangled, he relaxed his grip and wiped his palm on the hem of his kilt. The motion left a smear of green on the whiteness of the linen, but a flowery aroma rose from the stain. *I am a part of the heka,* he thought suddenly. *But no—I am inside it, it is all around me right now, in the Tree, in the Book. I am sitting in the eye of a storm of magic and I am quite safe. I have the feeling that my amulets are useless here. They are mere trinkets. Yet I am protected.* He read on.

I Thoth, who has come forth from Atum, now speak of the fulfillment of Heka.

Let us call Spirit pure energy—but it is known to us only as light.

Let us call Atum consciousness—but he is known to us only through complementation.

Let us call light First—but it is known only through darkness.

Let us call the original Scission the First Becoming—but it is known only through separation.

Many are the metamorphoses that come from my mouth before the Sky had become.

I Thoth, who reckons all things, now speak of the End before the Beginning.

All that will be created will return to the Nun.

Myself alone, I persist, unknown, invisible to all . . .

Overcome, Huy rolled up the scroll. His head felt as though it would burst. His previous euphoria had drained away as he began to read of the fulfillment of heka. Each terse statement was worded so simply and yet encapsulated such a wealth of complex enigmas that he knew he must ponder every one very carefully and regularly and hope for more moments of enlightenment like the one that had come to him earlier on the training ground. In spite of his perplexity he was aware of an inner composure as he got stiffly to his feet and went to knock on the door. *It will all become clear to me,* he told himself as he waited for Ramose. *All I have to do is remain as free from anxiety as possible and let the gods speak to me as and when they will. I won't fret about it anymore.*

He read and reread those two passages many times in the following weeks, content to let the words that composed such powerful concepts sink deeply below the level of his immediate consciousness. They slipped easily into his mind whenever he wished them present, and for many nights he lay sleepless but calm on his cot, pondering the meaning of each solemn phrase.

When he felt ready to continue, he unrolled the second scroll and found to his delight that its contents were a discussion of the enigmas contained in the first. The language was different, simpler, and to Huy's eyes the long stanzas had been written in a dissimilar hand. The flavour of the prose was less majestic, less authoritative, but his conviction that it had not flowed directly from the hand of Thoth lay in the fact that he was unable to repeat the words to himself in their entirety. Only snatches came back to him.

Give me your whole awareness, and concentrate your thoughts, for knowledge of Atum's Being requires deep insight, which comes only as a gift of grace . . . To conceive of Atum is difficult. To define him is impossible . . .

Ra-Atum is Light, the everlasting source of energy, the eternal dispenser of Life itself.

The Primal Mind, which is Life and Light, being bisexual, gave birth to the Mind of the Cosmos . . . First of all and without beginning is Atum . . .

Some mighty Seer in an age long past had studied the Book, and out of his wisdom he had attempted to clarify that which was almost unimaginable. Huy, wondering if that Seer might have been Imhotep himself, was more than grateful.

As one week merged into the next, the time spent with his back against the smooth bark of the Ished Tree, papyrus across his knees and the melody of the leaves above him, gradually blended into the mundane remainder of his days and he ceased to see it as something apart. He eventually noticed, pondered, then dismissed the curious fact that although the room in which he sat was roofless, no bird ever paused on its flight overhead to perch in the branches of the Tree, nor did the foliage itself ever change colour.

He did not go home to Hut-herib for the Inundation. Ramose did not want his work on the Book interrupted or perhaps weakened by the scattering of his concentration among family members and idle pursuits, and Huy did not mind. He told himself that the temple was supporting his education and therefore he must be as accommodating as possible, but the real reason was less altruistic. Staying in Iunu meant staying close to Anuket. His passion had not abated. If anything it had grown, being fed by the more frequent visits he was able to make to Thothmes' home during the holiday. Nakht, and particularly his wife, felt concern for the young man left to wander the empty courtyards alone, and Huy was regularly invited to sleep in the room he increasingly considered as his own. The High Priest did not seem to think such visits distracting. "They have become a part of your life here, whereas Hut-herib is increasingly alien to you, Huy," he had said. "They provide you with just enough variety in your life to keep you fresh for your great task. Go with my blessing whenever the Governor sends for you."

Huy was not so sure. Seeing Anuket every day, watching her eat, walk about the extensive garden to select the blooms for her wreaths and garlands, sitting almost tranced opposite her in the long evenings when they played dogs and jackals or sennet together and the light from the many lamps in Nakht's reception hall glinted on her rings and slid over the sheen of her glossy black hair, was an exquisite torment. His body ached for her. He made love to her many times in his mind, even as he engaged her in light conversation or occasionally helped her in the herb room, stripping leaves from the stems she intended to twist into her unique designs, so that in the end the aroma of the various herbs drying above his head became inextricably intertwined with his desire for her. The scent of thyme or celery in the steam of his food could return him vividly to her presence, and soon there was no flower, wild or cultivated, that did not bear the invisible imprint of her busy, delicate little fingers.

Nasha and Thothmes were more than happy to have Huy in residence, Thothmes because Huy was his best friend and there were already eight years of close history between them, and Nasha because Huy provided a foil to the earnest young men who had begun to parade through the house at Nakht's invitation to seek her hand. Without exception they bored her, and she turned to teasing and rough-and-tumble play with Huy after their visits as though physical and verbal aggression, no matter how mild, drove the boredom away. Her words and actions were entirely innocent, Huy knew. To her he was an adopted brother. She, he, and Thothmes spent many hours floating aimlessly on the calm flood waters, pulling up handfuls of reed grass, and later the ubiquitous pondweed that could choke the canals, and pelting each other, or searching for egret and ibis nests, or simply lying in the bottom of the skiff, somnolent with wine, while the servant poled them in the shallows under the thin, elongated shadows of the drowned palms lining the bank.

Anuket never joined them, though Huy begged her to do so. In spite of her name she had an aversion to water, and preferred to cool herself with modest dips in one of the pools on her father's estate. Huy forced himself not to follow her about like a hungry dog. He loved being with Thothmes and Nasha, although Nasha's horseplay tried his patience, and he did not want Nakht to see how truly lovesick he was. He knew that his attraction to Anuket had not gone unnoticed by either parent. He also knew that they trusted him to behave with decorum around her, and he would not betray that trust. Besides, Anuket, although she had lost much of her shyness with him, still held him at arm's length so that much of the time he was unsure of her feelings for him, and he wondered often whether he had dreamed their peculiar conversation in the herb room.

On the twenty-sixth day of Khoiak, when the flood had reached its highest and had ceased to flow, Nakht gave a party to celebrate the Feast of Sokar. A massive raft was tethered to the mooring poles at the foot of his watersteps, decorated with banks of flowers, and laden with food and wine. Over a hundred of Nakht's relatives, friends, and fellow nobles crowded onto it, ate, drank immoderately, and watched Anuket perform a stately dance in honour of the god, a wreath of ivy and blue lupines on her head and systra in her hands. With downcast eyes and bare feet, tiny bells on her ankles, she measured out the slow steps of the ritual, fingers twirling, the thin red linen of her sheath moving with her. Each time she passed one of the many lamps set around the perimeter of the raft, the contours of her slim body could be glimpsed and Huy, cold sober even after drinking four cups of wine, was forced to turn his gaze to the dark, placid water lapping below.

He knew that his chances of ever possessing the flesh he craved were practically non-existent. Notwithstanding her family's affection for him, her father would never offer her to a commoner. She would go to a son of one of the perfumed and bejewelled guests surrounding him, with their kohled eyes, their gleaming skin, their hennaed palms and soles of their feet denoting their aristocratic station. *Besides,* he thought gloomily while Anuket sank to the deck and a storm of applause broke out, *the High Priest did not answer my question regarding the preservation of my own virginity.* Lifting his eyes, he found her looking directly at him, a faint smile on her lips. He smiled back, feeling cold and slightly sick.

When he was not at Nakht's house or with the Book, he wandered freely through the temple complex, enjoying the empty courtyards, the silence of the schoolroom, the bare expanse of the training ground. He spent a few moments of every day with Lazy White Star, bringing slices of cucumber dipped in honey from the vast temple gardens. The horse would whinny at his approach, butting its long nose against his chest and nuzzling softly at his neck. Holding the sweetened vegetable on his flat palm, Huy would offer it respectfully, but most often the animal would take it, suck off the honey, then spit the cucumber onto the ground at Huy's feet. There was something comforting about its warm smell and the feel of its coat under his fingers. Putting his head against the horse's wide forehead, he would talk to it until with a snuffle and a nudge it backed away into the coolness of its stall.

Huy wrote dutifully to his parents, speaking of the small events making up his life during this hiatus, but he did not mention the Book or his attachment to

Anuket. He reserved those privacies for his letters to
Methen, who wrote back to him regularly, telling him
of the state of his town before addressing both his
sacred task and the purely secular tangle of his near
worship of Anuket. "Your emotions in that regard are
entirely natural for a young man of your age," Methen
replied in much the same vein as Ramose had done.
"Enjoy them, but try not to take them too seriously.
This is first love, Huy. It will die as rapidly as it sprang
to life." Huy doubted that it would, but the priest's
words comforted him.

He also paid a visit to the Rekhet. She, like Anuket,
was seldom out of his thoughts, though for very
different reasons. Thothmes had provided him with a
willing ear after his hours spent poring over the Book,
but his friend was not particularly interested in the
concepts Huy was finding increasingly vital. He needed
an experienced mind, and besides, he did not need to
pretend with the Rekhet, to make himself appear less
intelligent or less astute than he was to put his fellow
students at their ease. He liked them, liked to be one of
them, liked to join in their banter and share jokes with
them, but he could not escape the foreign thing inside
him that set him apart regardless of his efforts to be just
another twelve-year-old schoolboy. It demanded
company, and Huy needed understanding. Accordingly,
he asked the High Priest for Henenu's address and set
off one bright morning to find her.

He was surprised, given her acknowledged wealth, to
be drawn away from the river on Ramose's instructions.
He had imagined a home much like Nakht's for her,
something gracious set down amid groves of trees with a

high wall paralleling the river road and a gate porter, but he had only followed the road a short distance, to the centre of the city's vast watersteps, crowded as usual, before he was forced to turn into the heart of Iunu. He walked for a long time, at first striding along pleasant avenues lined with stately buildings, but gradually his route began to take him through narrowing, dusty streets that occasionally opened out into small shrines or untidy markets raucous with noise and full of the stench of garlic and unwashed bodies.

At last, when he was about to turn back in despair, he came to the one detached mud-brick house in the centre of a row of grey dwellings, but this one had a waist-high mud wall in front of it and was hung with cowrie shells. Tired and dirty, he pushed through the gate and approached the doorless porch. At once a man appeared, eyeing him watchfully although his words were polite. "Greetings. This is the house of the Rekhet. I am her steward. May I ask, what is your business with her?" Huy gave his name and was invited to take the stool the man had obviously just vacated. He could have sat there in the coolness for much longer than he did, but soon the man returned, this time gracing him with a deep bow. "My mistress is in her garden. She is eager to see you. Please follow me."

Huy was led around the small building into an unexpectedly large, high-walled area of shade trees and grass. There was even a pool, its surface thick with lily pads. After the stark aridity through which he had passed, the sight of so much greenness was like a draft of cold water. Some of his fatigue left him as he walked towards the woman who was straightening as he came up to her. She was dressed in coarse peasant linen. Her feet were bare and both hands covered in wet soil. Smiling, she answered Huy's obeisance.

"You look almost as disreputable as I do!" she chuckled. "Did you walk all the way from the temple? Ramose should have provided you with a litter. Isis!" At her call a woman came out of the house and stood waiting. "Bring us hot water and beer! And cushions! Come under the shade," she went on, drawing Huy towards the cluster of sycamores. "I have been weeding the few vegetables I grow around the pool. My poor steward goes to the river every few days and hires men to keep the water level high. A foolishness, I think, but cultivating cabbage and leeks is a fine antidote to the strain of my work." Seeing Huy's bewilderment, she laughed again. "I have an estate on the lake at Mi-wer. I have cattle at the oasis, and a grape arbour, and a huge vegetable garden. Food and wine is brought to me regularly while I am in the city. I am not poor, Huy. I live here where the common people can come to my door without fear to be freed of their demons, and when I need to rest I go home to Ta-she. Ah! Here is the beer and the cushions. Heating the water will take longer." The servant set the cushions and a tray on the ground, poured two cups, and went away. Henenu waved Huy to the grass and lowered herself beside him with a groan. "My joints are becoming stiff. I think soon I will send for my masseuse. It's good to see you, Huy. Tell me how you are faring."

Huy began to talk of the mundane life of the school. He had forgotten how her eyes in their nest of deep wrinkles could fix on him with a disconcerting intensity, and he was momentarily shy. But the water arrived, hot and scented with jasmine, and by the time they had washed their hands and she had emptied the bowl over his dusty feet he had regained his confidence. His thirst slaked, he spoke of the Book, reciting faultlessly what he had read in it, telling her of his dream and the subsequent revelation, and when he passed to his passion for Anuket he did so without faltering.

Henenu placed a gnarled hand briefly on his knee. "Ramose may be wrong. There is much about you that cannot easily be put into the box labelled Young Man. You may love Anuket for the rest of your life."

"Oh, I hope not!" Huy cried in dismay. "To love her for the rest of my life would put me in a perpetual prison. She will marry a nobleman. Nakht will see to it."

"Perhaps." Henenu pursed her lips thoughtfully. "And that may be a good thing. Otherwise you will be torn between your duty to the gods and the desires of your heart and body, and will do full justice to neither."

Huy had not considered this. "So I may find myself in a place where no choice is possible," he said angrily. "Well, at least apart from the Book the gods have left me alone. I wrestle with my friends, I inadvertently brush against a dozen people a day, yet the gift of Seeing remains quiet."

"Make the most of that peace," Henenu replied. "It will not last. You are not of much use to them yet, being confined in school. Do you know when you will be going south to Khmun to read the second part of the Book?"

Huy had been resolutely disregarding this necessity. His world so far had been Hut-herib, Iunu, and the stretch of river in between, and he admitted to himself that he was afraid to venture beyond what was familiar. He shook his head. "No, and I'm in no hurry to see Khmun." He hesitated. "Rekhet, I have a question that the High Priest could not or would not answer." Her grey eyebrows rose. "I learned that a Seer loses the gift of Sight if he or she loses his or her virginity." The words were clumsily put together and he bit his lip. "Is it true?"

"For some it has been true. For others, the fortunate ones, not. Ramose does not know. Do you wish to take this chance?"

"If I could have Anuket, I would take the chance," Huy said vehemently. "It is a serious matter, to defy the gods, but I would do it if it meant a life spent in her arms!"

"And then what?" The Rekhet leaned forward. "An eternity in the Duat? How do you imagine the gods would repay such perfidy? You cannot interfere with destiny and expect no retribution." Her tone softened. "In any case, you need not concern yourself with such things yet. Put your energy into archery and chariotry and increasing your writing skills. We will talk of this matter again." She shouted once more for Isis. "Now we will eat, and sleep for a while here in the shade. You are wearing your amulets, I see. Good. I am very aware of the aura of their protection all around you, Huy. The Khatyu hover outside it, but their malevolent craving to destroy you is being continuously turned aside. They are impotent."

The meal they shared was simple, cabbage soup, bread, and goat's cheese, and afterwards they both drowsed on the warm grass.

The sun was already sinking, turning the dust to red and casting long shadows over the streets, as Huy took his leave of Henenu and set off for the temple. The fruit and vegetable sellers were dismantling their stalls in the markets through which he passed. Laden donkeys choked the narrow lanes, and feeble lamplight already flickered in the depths of some of the beer shops. The brothels were not yet busy. Whores leaned apathetically against their walls, eyeing the passersby without interest, their elaborately curled wigs and thickly kohled eyes exotically parodying the appearance of young aristocrats. They would not begin to harass the men walking past them until full darkness fell, and although Huy saw their heads turning to follow his progress they remained silent.

One of them, however, briefly caught his attention. She was sitting on a stool, the folds of her yellow sheath draped about her calves, her chin resting in the palm of one hand. She seemed to be sunk in some distant thought, and did not look up as Huy strode by. There was something of Anuket's daintiness about her, and it suddenly occurred to Huy that he might take a chance on deliberately destroying his Seeing gift by turning back and engaging her services. Then, with luck, he would be of no further use to the gods. He need not worry about the Book of Thoth, or what strange destiny awaited him. He would be free to submerge himself in the blessed anonymity of the crowd, work as a scribe, marry and raise a family, untroubled by dreams or premonitions. With luck.

He came to a halt and swung about, and the little whore took her chin out of her palm, stared at him, and rose. He took one step towards her, and as he did so she slid the band of her sheath off one shoulder, revealing an unexpectedly heavy breast, and began to smile shrewdly. The invitation was so blatant, so earthy, that a thrill of both disgust and attraction ran though Huy. It was not hard to imagine Anuket standing there in the guise of the goddess of lust after whom she had been named, her air of shy fastidiousness transformed into the artificial coyness of seduction. The young woman lifted her breast. Her smile widened, and Huy's disgust won out. He walked briskly away.

On the ninth day of Paophi, his thirteenth Naming Day was marked by letters of congratulation from his parents and his aunt and uncle and by his own prostrations of gratitude before the sanctuary doors of the temple and his own statue of Khenti-kheti. He did not make an offering. With mild resentment, he decided that he did not want to thank the gods for burdening him with the weight of his uniqueness. His continued health he took for granted.

Once he had finished reading the three scrolls that made up the first part of the Book, he reread them several times, until beneath the sonorous words rolling through his mind whenever he called them up, he began to detect their incompleteness. Then he knew, with a sinking heart, that it was time for him to begin work on the second part. For several days he hesitated, both afraid and unwilling to see his safe routine of school work and exercise taken away from him, but at last he could delay no longer. On a stiflingly hot evening towards the end of his birth month he knocked on the High Priest's door.

Ramose was at his desk, but his chair had been pushed back and his face was raised to the intermittent gusts of wind funnelling into the room from the wind catcher on the roof. He remained seated as Huy approached him and bowed. "I seem to feel the heat more acutely as I age," he sighed. "I thank the gods that I do not live any farther south. Sit down, Huy. Pour yourself a little beer. Have you come to tell me that you are ready to travel to Khmun?"

"Yes," Huy said reluctantly, taking the customary stool. "I can do no more with the first part of the Book. It is all here"—he tapped his temple—"in my head. I ponder it daily. Most of it I understand, but I have come to realize that it really is one piece of a whole."

"The second part consists of only one scroll. Nevertheless, you will take as much time as you need in Thoth's temple. Your teacher and instructors tell me that so far you are doing well, and Harmose reports that you are a tidy and responsible member of your courtyard." He smiled. "Do you remember the rebellious and recalcitrant child you were when you first came here? You have grown in self-control and diligence. I am proud of you." For some reason the High Priest's praise annoyed Huy. He shook his head and did not reply. "Well, no matter," Ramose went on. "The river is still rising and the school will remain closed until next month. It is not far from Iunu to Khmun, but the land is flooded and the current still strong. Rest from the Book. Concentrate on your other pursuits. I have already warned Thoth's High

Priest that you will be coming, and I will dictate another letter for him that you will take with you."

Huy felt weak with reprieve. "Am I to go alone, Master?"

"Certainly not! You are much too valuable to be allowed to wander about Egypt by yourself! I will choose a temple guard and a body servant to go with you. Now run along." He got out of his chair. "I am going to the bathhouse to drench myself in cool water." Coming around the desk, he laid a hand on Huy's head. "You've done well," he said quietly. "Enjoy your freedom from the demands of the Tree." It was an odd thing to say, and Huy glanced up at him swiftly, but he was already moving towards his private door at the rear of the room. Huy returned to his cell with a lighter heart.

It was good to know that each day was his own. He swam in the temple's canal and pool, lay under the trees, and drowsed in the hot afternoons. After Pabast had brought the lamp, he sat on the floor of the cell and played board games with himself, moving the pieces idly, until he was tired. He was happy. A burden had indeed been lifted from him, and for the first time in many months he felt no different from the other boys.

He threw himself into the six days of celebration that marked the Amun-feast of Hapi, standing with the crowd on the bank and chanting his thanks to the god of the river for a copious flood. With Anuket, Nasha, and Thothmes he tossed armfuls of blooms onto the surface of the water and watched them float north, an undulating carpet of multicoloured fragrance. Anuket had made special wreaths for the occasion, and garlands for the members of the family to wear through the feasting that followed at her father's house. Standing on tiptoe, she looped the flowers gravely over Huy's bent head. "For you there are blue water lilies and sycamore figs, with the yellow flowers of the bak tree to give aroma," she told him, kissing him solemnly on the cheek. It was only later, sitting on the floor of Nakht's reception hall with his back against the wall while the revelry swirled around him and the bak blooms filled his nostrils with sweetness, that Huy remembered how both sycamores and water lilies were sacred to Hathor, goddess of love and beauty.

Her feast day had fallen on the first day of Khoiak. It heralded a month overfull of rites and observances, when the whole country breathed a sigh of relief at the height of a flood that would ensure abundant crops. Huy had participated in them all, just like any other youth, he told himself fervently. *Just like Thothmes and Samentuser and, yes, even Sennefer, wherever he is. For that is what I am—a youth on the verge of manhood.* With that thought came a wave of unaccustomed homesickness for his parents' modest home in Hut-herib and Ishat's acerbic voice. He found himself wondering what she was doing. His brother Heby would be two years old now, a sturdy toddler perhaps as demanding and obnoxious as Huy himself had been. Did Hapzefa pray over him at night and sing him to sleep as she had often done for him? Was there any corner of the house where his, Huy's, presence still lingered?

But riding on this deluge of self-pity came the recognition of its source—a powerful unwillingness to begin the next phase of his reading of the Book. He fought it with a sour fatalism, and on the fifth of Tybi, five days after the celebration of the coronation of Horus, when Ramose sent word that he must pack up his belongings and meet his escort on the temple's watersteps, he was ready.

10

The journey upstream to Khmun took six days. Huy travelled comfortably in one of the temple's barges. He was not required to share the cabin with the guard and the servant who had been appointed to accompany him, and each evening he lay on the cot listening to the soft susurration of their conversation, feeling both guilty that he should be lying in sheltered luxury and envious of their freedom on the deck under the stars. He would have preferred a less formal vessel, and a blanket beside a fire on the bank at night, but Ramose had insisted on the security a full crew could provide. "And you must promise me that you will sleep in the cabin," he had pressed Huy. "Your safety is vital. I shall question the barge's captain on your return!" Huy kept his promise though it was hard, particularly as they first moored on the northern outskirts of Mennofer, Egypt's ancient capital, and a dazzled Huy longed to explore both the city of the living on the east bank and the great city of the dead to the west, where pyramids pierced the red sky of evening above a jumbled plain of sand, rocks, and the tombs of the Osiris-ones. Mennofer itself was the gateway to the Delta. Its officials controlled all trade and other traffic on the river. It had a harbour, and its docks were crowded with craft of every description, its wharves piled with goods. The atmosphere was one of noisy superiority. Warships and weapons came out of the city's workshops and Ptah the creator-god was its totem. Huy had thought Iunu impressive, but Mennofer took his breath away.

Once past the city, the river settled into a wide ribbon between quiet mud villages and moist, dark brown fields waiting for the crops to be seeded. The trees lining the brimming irrigation canals, having drunk their fill of the flood, were covered in gleaming green leaves, and the air retained a hint of humidity that was pleasant against hot skin. Huy spent the hours of daylight leaning against the deck rail, filling himself with an Egypt he had only imagined. Sometime on the fourth day out of Iunu he realized that, although beyond the sandbanks the surrounding countryside was lushly rich, the texture of the wind he was now inhaling had changed. Coming up from the south, it was dry and almost odourless, with the merest hint of the deserts over which it had come.

They passed the small town of Hebenu, and on the evening of the fifth day they anchored close to the entrance of the elevated canal that would lead them west into the heart of Khmun. Amunmose, Huy's servant, pointed to the east bank where watersteps covered in sun-pink dust led up to many rutted tracks disappearing through the trees. "The workmen's village of Hatnub lies beyond, to the north," he told Huy. "Many barges dock here to load alabaster for royal projects. That beautiful stone, and also calcite, is quarried from the hills you can just see if you peer between the growth. Directly east are many ancient tombs, cut into the same rock. My family comes from Khmun," he explained. "My father is cosmetician to the wife of one of the city's minor administrators. I had no interest in his craft. I am apprenticed to one of the temple cooks at Iunu. The High Priest allowed me to serve you on this journey so that I could visit my relatives—when you do not need me, of course!"

Early the next morning they entered the canal, taking their place behind a stream of other craft carefully negotiating the narrow channel, and it seemed to Huy, at his usual place by the rail, that the city began at once. Paths already busy with laden donkeys and people on foot ran to either side of the waterway, and reed shacks and mud huts littered the ground. "It is three miles to the centre of the city," Amunmose replied in answer to Huy's question, "and another two to reach the branch of the Nile that runs all the way up to the oasis at Ta-she. The tributary is always full of craft, except during the flood of course. All the land around Khmun is very fertile, the crops very thick. It is a blessed place." Huy looked eagerly ahead to where the horizon was blurred by what seemed to be a vast grove of trees. "Our palms are famous for their height and vigour," Amunmose said proudly.

Slowly the city began to take shape, resolving into wide, palm-lined streets with gated walls, and the tall pylons of several temples rearing above the trees themselves, their outer courts still hidden at ground level. The canal bisected the city, running on to join the western

tributary, but Huy's barge veered towards the watersteps
already choked with tethered craft, slipped into a berth,
and the captain flung a rope to one of the men waiting to
tie it to a pole. The ramp was run out. Amunmose heaved
a sigh of satisfaction. "I will set your bags above the steps
and go and find a litter. Please stay with your guard,
Huy." He disappeared through the crowd and Huy stood
staring about, feeling vulnerable and assaulted by the
bright, hot morning sun glaring up off the pavement, the
babble of the colourful crowd swirling around him, and
most particularly by the thin dogs lying panting in the
shade by the steps or stretched negligently in the middle
of many moving feet. Short-haired, the colour of sand,
they were ignored by everyone and seemed entirely
contented, but Huy eyed them warily.

He had begun to sweat by the time he caught sight
of Amunmose beckoning him through the throng, and
he picked up his worn leather bags and hurried to
where a litter and four burly bearers waited. Once
inside with Amunmose, feeling them being lifted,
seeing the guard striding out beside him, Huy began
to relax. The raucous crowd thinned out. A shrine
came slowly into view, surrounded by sycamore fig
trees and flower beds. A sweetly pungent whiff of
acacia blossom filled the litter as it passed under the
dappling shade of the tall bush, and almost at once a
chariot clattered past them, the two horses sporting red
plumes, the driver bent forward over the prow of the
vehicle. Another dark beige dog was wandering across
the road, tongue lolling. "I have seen the greyhounds
of the wealthy," Huy said, "and their hunting dogs.
But what are these?"

Amunmose looked at him blankly then laughed. "They are desert dogs. They cannot be tamed, but their disposition is mild. They exist all through the south, as far as Swenet and the First Cataract. They come into the cities for offal and other scraps, but they prefer to live beyond the borders of the fields, out where there is only stone and sand. No one harms them and they in turn ignore us. They do not come into Iunu, it is too far north for them. I have missed them."

Huy shivered, his mind suddenly filling with a vision of Imhotep's fingers moving slowly along the hyena's spine. "Are they sacred?"

"No. There is no punishment if you accidentally kill one, not like killing a hawk, for which you are executed. They resemble neither Set nor Anubis nor any of the lesser wolf-gods. They are really very amiable and keep to themselves."

They had come to a crossroads and the bearers swung sharply left, onto a street lined with large squatting baboons, their pouched stone muzzles facing Huy as he craned to see them. "We have entered the avenue leading to the temple of Thoth," Amunmose said. "His baboons face east so that they can help the sun to rise. In a moment you will see Thoth's mighty pylon."

Even as he spoke Huy saw it, a great square archway fronted by lawn and then a wide concourse, and beyond it the stark paving of the outer court. Amunmose called to the bearers and the litter was set down. Huy scrambled out and retrieved his belongings, the litter was dismissed, and together he, Amunmose, and the guard walked across the grass to the warm stone of the court, moving between the great arms of the pylon with its tall flags rippling in the stiff breeze.

This temple has a very different feel than Ra's home, Huy thought immediately. *It is grander, more solemn somehow. I cannot imagine the pupils at this temple school running across the concourse.* His palms had begun to prickle, and feeling as though something had brushed the back of his neck he put up a hand to rub it. *Heka,* he thought again. *It is heka. This temple is full of ancient magic, alive with it, and I am moving through it as though it were air.* Neither Amunmose nor the guard seemed aware of any change around them.

Approaching the closed doors to the inner court, Amunmose held out his hand. "Give me the scroll for the High Priest," he said to Huy. "The Master has instructed me to take it within. Me! An apprentice cook!" He shed his sandals and rapped sharply on the small, narrow door set into one of the great copper panels with the likeness of Thoth beaten into it. The door opened, there was a muttered query, and Amunmose vanished inside. Huy studied the god's curved ibis beak. Thoth held a scribe's palette in one hand and a brush in the other. His coppery, red-gold bird's eyes shone benignly. Huy, momentarily dizzy with tension, closed his own.

It seemed to him that he stood there for a long time in the guard's motionless shadow. The outer court behind them remained silent and empty, the air still. But at last the door swung back and Amunmose emerged, followed by a thin man of indeterminate age, his dark eyes kohled, his long white sheath belted with silver ankhs, and the lobe of one ear weighed

down by the heavy silver image of a baboon standing
bow-legged, its mouth open in a rictus that displayed
both sharp, curved fangs. It was months since Huy
had thought of the ivory monkey his uncle and aunt
had given to him, but suddenly and fleetingly he was
back in his parents' garden at Hut-herib, a stone in
his hand and the smashed remains of the hateful toy
at his feet. The baboon swayed gently against the
man's brown neck as he leaned forward in greeting,
an unveiled curiosity in his gaze.

"You are younger and taller than I had imagined
from Ramose's letters, Huy son of Hapu. Welcome to
Thoth's domain. I am his High Priest, Mentuhotep."
Some fading imprint of the distaste and fear of Huy's
brief memory must have shown on his face, for
Mentuhotep smiled wryly. "I bear the name of the
warrior god Montu, but I assure you that I am entirely
peaceable," he continued. Reaching back, he closed the
door to the inner court. "Bring your bags and follow
me. I have had a cell prepared for you with the priests.
Amunmose, you are free to visit your family. I will send
for you when Huy has finished his task here. You are
also dismissed." This was to the guard, but the man
shook his head.

"I am commanded to accompany Huy wherever he
goes and to stand outside his door at all times," he
said. "Forgive my impertinence, Master, but I must
follow my orders."

"My temple guards are perfectly capable of such a
simple task," Mentuhotep replied easily. "However, I will
comply with Ramose's desire. Let us leave the courtyard
to the hot fingers of his god."

Huy turned to Amunmose. "Thank you for your company," he said, feeling small and rather vulnerable as Mentuhotep strode towards the open passage running between the outer wall and the inner court.

Amunmose grinned. "Take your time here, Huy, so that I may enjoy my mother's leek soup to the full," he whispered, and turned away.

The priests' quarters were similar to those of Ra's temple, a series of cells fronting the long, unroofed corridor that ended behind the sanctuary, where a grassless expanse led to the kitchens, the high surrounding wall, and the vegetable gardens and animal pens beyond. "Thoth's sacred lake of purification lies on the other side of the complex," Mentuhotep answered Huy's diffident question as he paused before one of the anonymous cell doors and pushed it open. "You must go back along the avenue to the canal if you wish to swim, although I do not recommend it. Many of our less careful citizens toss their rubbish into it and it is not clean. The river is too far away for you to walk to. Do you like to swim?"

"Not particularly, Master," Huy replied, "although I have taken instruction and I am safe in water." He was regarding his new home. It was slightly smaller than the room he shared with Thothmes. A reed mat lay on the stone floor in front of a low, narrow couch. Beside the couch a wooden effigy of Thoth and an oil lamp stood on a plain table, and a desk rested against the opposite whitewashed wall with a square stool under it. There was an empty tiring chest, its lid raised. None of the sparse furniture bore any adornment, and the walls gleamed free of any paintings. Huy liked the atmosphere of quiet simplicity at once.

"The previous inhabitant completed his three-month rotation of service and went home," Mentuhotep explained, "and I have not replaced him so that you might have this cell. If you have brought your personal totem with you, you may set it up beside Thoth. He will not mind. I will have bedding brought to you, and a pallet for your guard. Go anywhere you like, except for the sanctuary of course. The inner court is not closed to you. It appears that Thoth greatly favours you." He hesitated, then said, "The second part of the Holy Book consists of only one scroll, as you probably know. You will study it in my office, and I will be available to you at any time for such discussion of it as you need. I have read the whole Book and have pondered its meaning over many years. Perhaps I may be of some help to you." The man's humility was overwhelming, making Huy feel naive and very much an imposter.

"I will need your help, Master," he blurted. "It seems to me that the gods have chosen poorly if they desired an intelligent instrument to perform their will. I am nothing but a peasant from Hut-herib!"

"Oh, you are much more than that, Huy," Mentuhotep murmured. "I know the burden that oppresses you. You have good mentors in Ramose and Methen and the Rekhet. Nevertheless, if you need a friend I am here." Bowing to Huy for the first time, he left the cell, and this time the sacred baboon swinging from his ear seemed to be smiling.

The guard, who had been hovering behind them, blew out his breath. "You may turn out to be an offspring of Thoth himself, young Huy, but in the meantime you and I both have bellies to fill. I'm hungry. May we find out where the noon meal is being served?"

Huy laughed. "A good idea! I don't want to eat with the priests. Let's find the dining room of the school. It can't be far away."

The area of the temple that encompassed the school was very similar to its counterpart at Iunu, and Huy found it with little trouble, entering the dining room where the meal was under way. Appetizing aromas mingled with the intermittent chatter of the hundred or so boys and young men seated at the long tables. Hovering in the doorway, Huy hesitated, looking for an empty space on one of the benches, and after a moment an older boy noticed him and came hurrying over, followed by a gradually spreading hush. Heads were turned in Huy's direction, fingers were stilled. "You are Huy, guest of the Master?" the young man inquired. He seemed flustered, passing a palm quickly across his shaven scalp and then folding his beringed hands together over the enamelled amulet resting against his naked chest. "I am Ib. Today is my duty day. Come and sit beside me. Will your guard go and eat with the servants?" He led Huy through a sea of curious eyes to one of the tables, and at a low word one of the diners scrambled up, gave Huy a clumsy bow, and wriggled between two of his fellows on the opposite bench.

Awkward and embarrassed, Huy took his place, the guard stationed behind him. "I'm afraid that my guard must eat here," he said, heartily wishing that he had chosen the priests' company instead.

Ib nodded vigorously. "I will instruct a servant," he said, and hurried away.

Huy forced himself to scan the dozens of eyes still fixed on him. "I bring greetings from my fellow students at Iunu," he said into the silence. "Of course they would rather be here with me than slaving at their lessons, but since we are all under the authority of our teachers and must do as we are told, they are sitting over their scrolls and I am enjoying this beautiful city. Surely they will be forgiven for envying me!"

A ripple of laughter broke the tension of the moment. Talk broke out again and the boy next to Huy turned to him eagerly. "Is it true that you are some sort of wonderful Seer, and you have come to Khmun so that the Master may consult with you?" he asked. "Nothing official has been said about your visit, but you know how things are—one priest lets out a couple of words and suddenly the rumours are flying." He tore a piece of barley bread in two. "My father is High Priest at the temple of Nekhbet at Nekheb. That is a very long way south from here, yet he has heard something of you." He dipped his bread into the bowl of fragrant broth before him.

Huy's stomach clenched. "It is true that I am here to consult with the Master," he said carefully, "but as a student, not a Seer. I have been set a task of learning. As for my ability to scry, that has not yet been proven. Tell me about Nekheb. It is a great shipbuilding centre, is it not?"

The boy barked a short laugh. "Spoken like one of Pharaoh's diplomats," he retorted, not unkindly. "Forgive me, Huy. People must pester you all the time, but you must admit that my, our, curiosity is natural. Yes, Nekheb is a very famous city. In the days of our great liberator, Osiris Ahmose, and his accursed brother Kamose, the ships were built for the Setiu invaders and so a battle for control of the docks was fought there. The admiral Ahmose pen-Nekheb is our most revered son. You must have studied his exploits in school. He's the one who . . ."

Huy appeared to be listening, but his attention had strayed. Something about the crowd of youthful heads had caused him unease.

Ib returned with a servant carrying trays of food, resumed his seat, and did his best to engage Huy in polite conversation. Huy's appetite had fled, but he forced himself to eat while the guard standing behind him laid his spear on the ground and attacked his meal with relish. It seemed an eternity to Huy until Ib rose, called for silence, recited the prayer that ended the meal, and dismissed the boys. "Do you need to be guided back to your cell?" he asked Huy under the babble and scramble around them. "I presume that you are quartered with the priests."

Huy shook his head. "Thank you, Ib, but I know the way. Besides, I think I'll find a shady spot in the temple garden and spend the hour of sleep outside."

"Very well, but if you need anything to do with the school just send a servant to me. I hope we meet again."

The room had emptied. The guard picked up his spear and together he and Huy moved through the schoolroom, but as Huy entered the shadow of the passage beyond, an arm shot out and barred his way. "You think you are someone special, son of mud," a familiar voice hissed. "You think you're some kind of a god because the priests put their noses to their knees when you go by. You're nothing but an untimely abortion, with your hair hanging past your shoulders like a girl and your false air of importance. One day they'll know the truth. You're a disease, an ukhedu, a worm in the bowels of the temples."

"Sennefer," Huy said calmly, although his heart was racing. "I failed to notice you in the dining room. I remember now. This is where you were sent."

"As if you didn't know! You ruined my life, peasant. I should have held you under the water and made sure you were dead before that little weakling Thothmes came running back to the lake with help to drag you out." His crude features were flushed and his eyes glittered. "You managed to take advantage of your wound, didn't you, like any crafty peasant." He pushed closer to Huy, his body stiff with rage, but at that moment the guard interposed, drawing his sword and stepping between them.

"Be on your way, young whelp," he said mildly, "before the flat of my blade teaches you some manners. And if you approach my charge again, I shall bleed you."

"Ever the coward," Sennefer sneered, but he backed away, and as he did so Huy felt himself lifted and lightened although his feet stayed firmly on the ground. *No!* he shouted dumbly, but his head began to whirl and in spite of his strong desire to run down the passage, to run away, a more powerful urge took his hand and closed it around Sennefer's wrist. At once the other boy went still. Huy found himself surrounded by battle. Men's screams deafened him. Dust caught in his throat, already dry from terror. He was clinging to the guardrail of an overturned chariot, coughing and sobbing, a dead horse at his feet. Someone was shouting at him angrily, the words lost in the melee, then something struck him in the back and he fell across the vehicle, blood pouring past his horrified gaze and trickling a red pattern against the wicker weave of the chariot's vertical floor. He tried to draw breath and found he could not. Dark spots began to gather before his eyes and the din of the onslaught began to fade. In a burst of fear that loosened his bowels, he knew that he was dying.

But he was not dying. He was standing in a hot, dim passage in Thoth's temple, his grip whitening the skin of Sennefer's forearm, a dull pain beginning to throb behind his eyes. With effort he opened his hand, and at once Sennefer began to rub at the marks of his fingers.

"What did you do to me, you lunatic!" he shouted.

Huy wanted to laugh, but was simultaneously overcome with shame at his surge of spite. "You are going to die in battle, Sennefer. Perhaps such a fate may be averted by a change in you, perhaps not—I don't know. I tell you only what I see. Now go away and leave me alone!"

Sennefer had gone pale. He opened his mouth to speak, thought better of it, looked down at his wrist, glowered across at Huy, then elbowed past him and disappeared into the schoolroom.

"So you really are a Seer?" the guard said as he followed Huy down the passage. "If I give you my hand, you can tell me my future?"

Wearily Huy stopped and turned to him, and without asking he placed two fingers on the rough skin of the hand that still grasped the sword. The guard exclaimed but did not pull back, and presently Huy smiled faintly up at him. "What is your name?"

"Anhur, after the warrior god. My father is also a soldier."

"Do you like serving in the temple at Iunu, Anhur?"

The man grunted. "It's boring sometimes, but it brings me my bread and onions. Why do you ask?"

"Because in three years' time you will go to war and you will survive and after that you will make a decision that will affect the rest of your life."

Anhur raised his eyebrows. "And what might that be?"

"Well, if I tell you, it will be no decision, will it?"

Anhur chuckled. "Cheeky, aren't you? I suppose I'll just have to wait for the end of this war or whatever, although I can't imagine where it will take place. The Good God is old and the vassal states have stayed quiet for years."

Huy sighed. "I tell only what I see. That's all I can do. I don't think I want to go into the garden after all. I want to sleep on my couch, and you can unroll your pallet outside my door. What evil luck, to find Sennefer here!"

"What did you do to him?" Anhur wanted to know, but Huy had started down the passage and would not answer.

He has ruined my life, Huy thought later as he lay sleepless on his cot with the temple locked in a hot silence around him. *But it is true that I have indirectly ruined his. The retribution that fell on his head may have been just, but it was also dire. He is disgraced and forever forbidden the noble's privilege of the throwing stick, but surely the untimely end I foresaw for him far outweighs his attack on me in the scales of Ma'at, while I am given every opportunity to rise above my father's station and receive the respect of important men through no virtue of my own.* "Untimely abortion." Huy stirred restlessly under the flush of hurt the words brought back to him. *Well, so I am. The blessings poured upon me have nothing to do with my character, and I exist wholly at the whim of the gods. Or god. Sennefer caused me great harm, but good has come from it. I must talk to him, apologize aloud for the enmity between us and secretly for the spurt of glee the vision of his death brought me. Can we come to an understanding? How would I feel if he had told me that I was to end my life in the heat and stink of battle? I am guilty of a cruelty as great as his was to me. I should have kept my mouth closed, but how could I when the Seeing came upon me without warning and with such force that I was powerless against its onrush?*

He spent the remainder of the afternoon wandering about the temple precincts, becoming increasingly aware that although the temple itself followed the simple plan of all the great places of worship, its surroundings seemed to sustain and enhance the unique atmosphere of heka that imbued it. Its well-watered lawns held no flower beds but were sparsely dotted with tall, smooth-boled palms. Here and there stone effigies of Thoth himself made little pools of shade into which, Huy noticed, no one seemed to venture; for around each striding figure, with its curved ibis beak inclined towards the scribe's palette on which it was about to write, was an invisible circle of power that seemed to demand a polite respect. A row of squatting baboons fronted the wall of the outer court between the soaring pillars, and beyond them the wide concourse of the court itself was fluid with worshippers coming and going, but Huy noticed that people did not linger to gossip once their observances had been completed. Ra's outer court at Iunu was usually crowded and often gaily noisy, particularly in the mornings and early evenings. Like the marketplaces, it was a favourite spot for sharing news and greeting friends. Here an air of solemnity and reverence prevailed.

Huy came upon the sacred lake quite suddenly, rounding a corner of the central building to be faced with a low mud-brick wall broken by a gateless aperture guarded, to Huy's surprise and delight, by a small statue of Thoth standing on a pedestal with, at his feet, the exquisite representation of a smiling woman. Clothed in a leopard skin, with a uraeus on her forehead and a star rising from her coronet, she too held a palette and brush. Beyond them both, the lake lay glittering in the sunlight. Anhur pointed to the thick hedge of sycamores around its rim. "There's somewhere we might sit for a little. You're allowed near the lake."

But Huy's attention was still fixed on the sculpture. "This must be Thoth's wife. How beautiful she is! What is her name, do you know, Anhur?"

The man shrugged, but a priest who had just left the water and was wrapping himself in linen as he approached them had heard Huy's question. "Her name is Seshat," he explained with the merest flicker of astonishment in the eyes that met Huy's own.

Certainly shock at my ignorance, Huy thought. "She is indeed Thoth's wife, the Lady of Books, librarian of Paradise and totem of mathematicians, architects, and those who keep records." He smiled. "She lives near the Ished Tree, and one of her tasks is to write the name of each pharaoh on one of its leaves so that he may gain immortality. You see the palm branch beside her, with all the notches? She carves the years of each king's earthly life into it. She and pharaoh together stretch out the white cord when the foundations for a new temple are being laid. Thoth belongs to everyone who reveres the written word, but Seshat belongs first to he who sits on the Horus Throne. Nevertheless we, his priests, love her very much." He made a gesture of apology. "Forgive my lecturing tone. I am Thoth's chief archivist and head librarian of the House of Life here in Khmun. And you are Huy." He bowed. "You come to study the second part of the Book of Thoth?" Huy nodded. "Then I have a favour to ask of you. When you have read all five of its parts and understood its mysteries, will you visit me here and enlighten me? I myself have read the three scrolls that make up the second and fourth parts of the Book stored here in my archives, but I did not dare to travel to Iunu and look at the rest. I feared the warnings." He looked curiously at Huy. "You do not fear them?"

Huy grimaced. "It would do me no good to fear them, seeing I am commanded to read them all anyway. What is your name, Master?"

The man clapped a hand to his forehead. "Oh, I am rude! I am called Khanun." He laughed. When he did so, his whole face lit up. Its grooves deepened around his mouth and eyes, but the impression he gave was one of youthfulness and vigour, though while he had been talking Huy judged him to be in late middle age.

Huy held out his hand. "If I am permitted, I will come and discuss the Book with you. But it won't be for some years, I think." The fingers closing about his own were strong, and cold from the water.

"Of course not. You have an education to finish and a living to earn as well. May the gods grant you health, and me a life long enough to see you return fully grown." He bowed. "Dine with us this evening. We will not be too solemn for you. The heka of Thoth is a wholesome and happy thing." He padded away, his bare feet leaving damp imprints on the stone path, and Anhur whistled.

"How old are you, Huy? Thirteen? This is all heady stuff for a stripling! Now may we please spend a few moments under the shade of those sycamores? I'm tired."

They entered the lake's enclosure. Anhur lowered his spear and himself, but like a good soldier on duty he did not lie prone. Resting his spine against a tree, he sighed and relaxed. Huy crossed his legs and watched the play of light and wind on the surface of the water. *Yes,* he thought, *Thoth's magic feels strong and steady and quiet, but with an edge of caution to it. Ra's heka at Iunu is boisterous and unsettling and unpredictable, making me anxious or exhilarated but seldom utterly at peace. Here there is peace, but the warning tingles in the air, waiting for a blasphemy, an insult, a moment of arrogant presumption. The prayers must be said correctly*

here, the rituals perfectly observed. How do I know this?
He closed his eyes. *Seshat writes on the leaves of the Ished Tree and Imhotep sits under it, reading. If I were a king, how many years of life would be notched on her palm rib for me? Only twelve? Have I become untimely?*

That evening he washed in the priests' bathhouse, braided his hair, being careful to tie it with his little frog, put on his best sandals, and went to dine with the priests. They welcomed him without undue effusiveness, talked to him casually about his family and his school work, and, when the meal was over, wished him a pleasant night and scattered to their own rest or to their duties. The experience was a welcome relief after the awkwardness of noon, but Huy resolved to make one more foray into the school compound to talk to Sennefer. *Not yet, though,* he vowed to himself as he and the plodding Anhur made their way through the torchlit passages to Huy's cell. *I need to be more sure of myself here before I risk another humiliation.*

A servant had turned down the sheets on Huy's couch and left a lamp burning beside the images of Thoth and Khenti-kheti, whose crocodile smile seemed to hold a smug pride at being in such august company. Huy smiled sleepily back at both of them as he began his nightly prayers. He did not hurry the words, though he wanted to. It would not do to offend either god so early in this strange journey he had taken upon himself when he had spoken those fateful words to Imhotep. After his final prostration he trimmed the lamp, saw that a jug of water, an empty cup, and one full of wine had been placed on the lid of the tiring chest, and gingerly sampled the wine. The sweet flavour of distilled pomegranates slid down his throat, and after another mouthful he went to the door and opened it. Anhur was sitting on his pallet with his back to the passage wall. "Finish this if you like," Huy said, handing him the wine. "And if you need water in the night, there is some in my room."

"You are kind," the guard said as he reached up and took the goblet. "Thank you. May the gods grant you safety from the demons that ride the darkness, and give you a good omen in your dreams."

Huy, about to turn back into his cell, hesitated. Anhur was raising the cup to his mouth in both meaty, strong hands, his bare legs sprawled across the floor of the passage, and a vision of Hapu blossomed in Huy's mind. His father often sat in the same pose while Itu spooned the evening meal onto his clay platter, the beer cup clasped in his half-naked lap, his spine against the wall, his shoulders collapsed in exhaustion after a day of labour in the fields. Both men were muscular and browned by the sun. An aura of physical command clung to both of them, but whereas Hapu's battle was against drought, weeds, and plant diseases, Anhur projected the comforting promise of security against more human predators. He also radiated a rough sort of kindness. Huy had seen it in his treatment of Sennefer. His words had been impersonal but not unduly harsh. *Father used to behave towards me in that way,* Huy thought sadly. *Before I was brought home from the House of the Dead. Before my exorcism.*

Anhur took a mouthful of wine, licked his lips, and glanced up. "What is it?"

"Nothing," Huy replied diffidently. "I was just thinking that you remind me a little of my father. Were you raised in Iunu? Do you have brothers and sisters?"

"Five sisters." Anhur groaned. "Three of them are still at home. My father managed to marry two of them off, one to a steward and one to another soldier."

"Is your father still alive?"

"He's retired to a piece of land he farms for the temple. Why do you ask? Is it something to do with that look into my future you won't tell me about?"

Huy smiled. "No. But I hope my prediction for you comes true."

Anhur raised the cup. "If it's that good, then I hope so too. Sleep well."

Huy retreated, closing the cell door behind him. His vision for Anhur had seemed so promising yet so improbable that he did not want to dwell on it.

Once the lamp was extinguished, the wall high up opposite Huy's couch was lit by one faint slit of grey moonlight filtering through the tiny clerestory window. For a while Huy lay curled up on his side, reviewing the events of the day, but then his thoughts turned to Anuket. Longing and desire flared in him briefly, together with a pang of homesickness for Thothmes and Nakht's house and his own dearly familiar cell in Ra's temple; but the heka of Thoth that blanketed his holy house was in Huy's nostrils, stilling his emotions and weighing against his eyelids, and with a last drowsy glance up at the fading ray of moonlight he fell asleep.

In the morning he was woken by a servant who set a tray of bread, goat's cheese, and milk on the couch beside him, replenished the oil in the lamp, and before Huy had finished eating returned with hot water and cloths. He stood politely waiting until Huy, having grown more and more uncomfortable, asked him why. "To wash you, young Master, to remove your soiled linen, and then to explore the contents of your tiring chest and make sure that you brought sufficient clothing with you. The High Priest has ordered it."

"I would prefer to wash myself," Huy protested. "As for clean loincloths and kilts, I brought all that I have, enough for three days."

The man inclined his head. "In that case I shall see that your laundry is done every day. If by some chance you need more, you must let me know. I am at your service while you are here."

"You mean if I get ink on myself or fall into mud." Huy grinned, although he had never felt less like making a joke. He knew that he should be enjoying all the respectful attention being showered upon him. *Indeed,* he thought fleetingly, *when I was a little boy I would have taken all this as my right and thrown a tantrum if it had been denied me, but now it only adds to the burden of expectation I see in everyone's eyes.*

The servant permitted himself a wintry smile. "As you say, Master Huy. Then when you are ready I will escort you to the High Priest's office. At present he is performing the morning offerings to the god."

Huy was relieved when the door closed behind him. *He's like an arrogant Pabast,* he thought as he plunged his hands into the perfumed water and then reached for the natron. *A sour Pabast with the added resentment of*

*having to serve a boy as though he were a noble visitor to
the temple. Well, I wish Mentuhotep had not bothered to
accord me such esteem. I cannot live up to it.*

Anhur's unaffected greeting restored Huy's
equanimity, however, as later they both followed the
servant's stiff spine the short distance to the High
Priest's private quarters. Anhur took up his post
outside the double doors. Mentuhotep rose from
behind his desk to take Huy's hand, bringing with
him a strong whiff of myrrh and the sacred kyphi
perfume used in temple worship that Huy's uncle Ker
had probably distilled from the choicest raisins
himself. "You slept well, I trust?" he asked warmly.
"Good. And Khanun tells me that you are quite taken
with our holy patroness, Seshat. She will be pleased.
Come and sit. The Book resides in a guarded alcove
of the House of Life. Khanun has already brought it
to me." Huy took the indicated stool, eyeing the
cedar casket with its figured brass corners as he did
so and taking a deep, surreptitious breath.

Mentuhotep lifted the lid and withdrew a very thin
hemp bag with a papyrus tag hanging from its
drawstring. He glanced at it. "Yes, this is the second
part," he said, setting it on the desk before Huy. "The
fourth is also in this box. I must not confuse them." For
some reason Huy suddenly wanted to laugh. He quelled
the impulse as Mentuhotep's hand descended on his
naked shoulder. "Reading it will take no more than a
few moments," he commented. "Ramose tells me that
you are able to memorize the words of the Book. In
that case handle the scroll as little as possible and
quickly return it to its protective bag. Do not leave it

alone. Stay in here as long as you wish, then send for me when you are ready to leave." The hand was withdrawn. Mentuhotep walked briskly to the door.

Huy swivelled after him on the stool. "Master, before you go, is there an accompanying scroll of explanation?" He could not keep the pleading out of his voice.

The High Priest paused. "Yes, there is, but Ramose wishes you to ponder what you will read for a day or two before I give you the commentary." Huy's sigh was involuntary and Mentuhotep chuckled. "I know, I know! But his reason is sensible. The direct will of Atum is that you come to an understanding of his works. Therefore your conclusions will be the truth. We do not know who wrote the commentary. Although it is full of wisdom, it is not necessarily the truth. What if your interpretation differs? You must not be influenced unduly. May Thoth give you courage."

It is not courage that I need, Huy thought resignedly as he turned from the closing door and lifted the bag, *and just when did my accursed decision to read the Book in the first place become "the direct will of Atum"? Already the facts of an event that belonged to me alone are being distorted to feed the secret hopes of those around me. It's no wonder that more and more I feel as though some other Huy, someone the priests are creating for themselves, is inhabiting my skin.*

In a mood of creeping depression he spread the drawstring and withdrew the scroll. He unrolled it carefully on the desk and held it open, marvelling as before at the pliant state of the ancient papyrus and the

sheer beauty of the finely drawn characters. For a
moment he closed his eyes, becoming aware of the
strident cacophony of birds in the trees clustered
against the office wall, the lingering odour of myrrh
and kyphi, and another aroma, familiar and disturbing,
rising from the thing pressed between his outstretched
palms. The Ished Tree was many miles away, yet the
scent of its leaves was deliciously fresh, immediately
lifting the cloud of gloom that had threatened to
engulf him. He swallowed, thinking that he could taste
it as well as smell it, and, opening his eyes with the
scribes' quick prayer to Thoth, he looked down and
began to read.

> I, Thoth of the Twenty-two Epithets, Who Makes
> Splendid his Creator, set down these words of
> Atum. Let him who reads them understand and
> marvel at the profundity within their simplicity.
> I am One that transforms into Two,
> I am Two that transforms into Four,
> I am Four that transforms into Eight,
> After this I am One.

 Huy read the lines again. They were indeed simple,
straightforward—and utterly nonsensical. He scanned
them once more, this time speaking them, as if hearing
them carried aloud into the warming air of the room
could give them meaning. Raising his hands in a
gesture of both puzzlement and release, he let the
scroll roll up, then slid it gently back into its bag.
The words were already firmly fixed in his mind. "I am
One that transforms into Two . . ."

Getting up, he folded his arms and stood facing the window that gave out onto the High Priest's small private garden. Through the dense foliage of the trees he could see bright sunlight and the deep blue of a mid-morning sky. *The office will be flooded with direct heat as the sun westers,* he thought idly. *Perhaps I should lower the window hanging now. I'm thirsty for water. There must be a jug of it in here somewhere. "I am Two that transforms into Four . . ."* He found water on a table by the door, poured himself a cup, and drank deeply. *Now what?* he wondered, and began to pace. *"I am Four that . . ." That. That. Atum does not say "who," he says "that." "I am One that . . ." Not "I am One who . . ." Does it mean that the god transforms something else from one to two to four to eight, not himself? But at the end he says "After this," after the transformings he has performed, he is One. Not "I have turned myself back into One" or "I am still One." "After this I am One." Is it a part of himself that he transforms for some unspecified purpose and then changes back into One again?*

But "transform" means something deeper and more permanent than "change." To transform is to alter irretrievably, to become something different for always. Atum took something and transformed it by dividing it. Atum took something of himself and transformed it by being able to divide it and yet remain whole. Something beside himself yet a part of himself?

Huy came to a halt. Vague whispers came to him, memories of things half heard and disregarded during his school lessons. Something about frogs. Frogs? He let out a peal of laughter and went to the door. "Please summon the High Priest," he said to the supercilious face that confronted him, then closed the door again. The frog was the symbol of resurrection, but what could the renewal of life possibly have to do with the precise divisions stated in the scroll? Frogs represented life after the receding of the annual flood, the springing up of the new crops, new eggs in the nests along the canals, new hope for a bountiful harvest—not transformation. Not that! Yet all through the noon meal with the priests, the afternoon rest, the evening spent wandering the precinct, and finally lying sleepless on his couch, Huy could not rid himself of the conviction that frogs somehow held an explanation for the words being repeated over and over in his head.

The following morning he declined the servant's offer to guide him to the High Priest's quarters. He and Anhur found their way without difficulty. Mentuhotep was waiting for them, and after affably greeting the soldier he ushered Huy into the office where once again the casket sat waiting on his desk. "Well, Huy," Mentuhotep said, "are you ready to read the words a second time?"

"Really, Master, I don't need to," Huy answered hesitantly. "I am able to recite the contents of the first three scrolls perfectly. This one was easy."

"Easy to memorize perhaps." The man's glance was keen. "But have you already an understanding of the Book so far? Is the meaning of the first sayings clear to you?"

"Mostly. I believe that a full grasp of the sense of it will not be possible until the whole has been read." He had been going to say "until I've read the whole" but did not want to sound boastful.

Mentuhotep nodded. "Will you recite to me what you have read so far?" It was a command, not a request.

Huy resisted the urge to put his hands behind his back like a pupil called upon in the schoolroom, and began: "'The universe is nothing but consciousness, and in all its appearances reveals nothing but an evolution of consciousness, from its origin to its end, which is a return to its cause . . .'"

The High Priest's eyes did not leave Huy's face. When he had fallen silent, Mentuhotep nodded. "Do you know what 'evolution' means, Huy?"

"I think so, Master. It means a slow change towards something better."

"Your schoolmasters have taught you well. And if Atum wills a form of becoming for himself, which is—what?"

"The First Duat. The place of metamorphosis."

The High Priest's half smile was one of satisfaction. "Good. Then are the becomings mentioned in the scroll you read yesterday metamorphoses, or evolutions, or something else?"

"I don't know. They are called transformations. Are they different from both metamorphoses and evolutions?"

"That is for you to decide." Mentuhotep came around the desk. "I know that you want the commentary, but not today. Obviously you do not need to read the scroll again, unless having it under your eyes and hands would help you deliberate? No? Then I shall take it away and leave you to think. You need not stay in here to do so, but choose quiet places in the precinct for your meditations."

Huy put out a hand. "Master, since my reading yesterday I've been unable to purge the thought of . . . of frogs from my mind." He could feel himself flush. "It sounds insane, but will you tell me if some demon of ignorance has found a way into my heart and is leading me astray?" Mortified, Huy could see that Mentuhotep was repressing a laugh.

"You are the Chosen One, Huy," he said unexpectedly. "Your heart is pure. Enjoy your day, and if by tomorrow you are still hopping about on the bank of comprehension, we will talk together. No, I am not laughing at you," he finished gravely. "I am simply delighted that all those who have taken your measure have spoken the truth. It is a good thing that your parents are such pagans. No erroneous conception of these holy things has corrupted you."

He bowed and withdrew, leaving Huy still red-faced with shame for both his own ignorance, pure though it might be, and that of his father. *Well,* he thought bitterly, *I will lie here on the High Priest's reed mat and think about frogs, and when my spine begins to ache I will go to the sacred lake with Anhur and think about them some more, and when I become hungry I will eat with the priests and think about grilled goose and radishes.* In spite of Mentuhotep's words he felt like a fool.

He thought about frogs until his head began to throb—their colours, their sheen, their black, bulbous eyes, the way they moved, their throaty call, how cool and dry they felt in an upturned palm—and when he realized that nothing could be added and he had merely built a wall of frustration in his mind, he got up with an exclamation of sheer irritation, woke Anhur, who was dozing outside the door, and set off to find the school's training ground.

It lay to the north of the temple, and unlike its counterpart at Iunu it was surrounded on all sides by tall, thick hedges of acacia. Anhur nodded his approval as they started across the churned expanse of earth towards the mud-brick cell beside the stables. "Being on the north, it gets only a little of the morning sun," he commented, "and the acacia keeps a lot of the ground in shade. Mind you, Huy, most battles aren't fought under such ideal conditions." *How would you know?* Huy wanted to snap, but he held his peace.

Hearing the guard's voice, a man had emerged from the cell and stood peering suspiciously at them as they approached, his gaze flicking from Huy to Anhur's broad shoulders and ready weapons. He inclined his head slightly once, an invitation to speak, and Huy realized gladly that at least there was one person here who did not know who he was. He bowed politely. "I believe that I am addressing the Overseer of the Training Ground," he said formally. "I am Huy son of Hapu of Ra's temple school at Iunu, sent here by my teachers to study for a while. This is my guard Anhur."

The man's attention travelled to Huy's palms and belt, seeking any trace of the henna with which the nobles painted their hands and the throwing sticks with which they hunted. Seeing neither, and obviously puzzled by the presence of a personal guard, he grunted. "I am the Overseer. What is your business with me, Huy son of Hapu?"

"I would like the use of a bow and arrows to keep up my target practice while I am here. If you need permission from the Overseer of the School, I can send a servant to procure it."

"That won't be necessary for the equipment," the man replied shortly with another swift glance at the stolid Anhur. "But if you intend to hitch a chariot I'll need the Overseer's seal, and I can't provide you with a wrestling partner."

Huy wanted to shake the surliness out of him. "I wrestle with my guard. And if I wanted a chariot I would have no difficulty in quickly getting permission to use the best you have. Now show me the bows."

The man's eyes dropped. Without another word he led them into a large room beside his cell where the bows hung in rows, each one with its string wrapped in oiled hemp cloth. *I did not need to be so rude,* Huy thought regretfully as he entered the cool space. *This is nothing but thwarted conceit on my part because I am the Chosen One, and shouldn't the Chosen One be omniscient?* It came to him also, as he walked the rows of weapons, that somewhere in the back of his mind he was hoping that physical exertion might shake loose the same sort of revelation that had come to him on the training ground at Iunu. "This one," he said, pointing at one of the composite bows, "and I will take the barrel of arrows outside and try them all. I can set up the target myself."

"As you wish." The Overseer stalked away. Huy lifted down and unwrapped his bow, chose a set of leather gloves from the chest by the doorway, and Anhur heaved the barrel of arrows out into the dappled sunlight.

"I'll be happy to wrestle with you, Huy," he puffed, "but if I hurt you Ramose will have harsh words for me when we return home."

Huy chuckled. "Probably for me too. Set up the target over there, Anhur, and find some shade. When I'm sufficiently sweaty we'll wash and then eat."

For an hour Huy drew and loosed, until the target began to blur, his arms ached, and his kilt became soaked in sweat. Finally he admitted defeat. The exercise had done him good, he knew, but the burst of inner knowledge he sought had been denied him. After cleaning the bow's grip and rewrapping the string while Anhur saw to the target and the arrows, Huy tossed the gloves back in the box and together they re-entered the temple. In the priests' bathhouse they stood side by side on the slabs, dousing each other with warm water and scrubbing the natron into skin and scalps. Huy, watching Anhur splash and grunt in appreciation, realized that a genuine affection for this blunt, phlegmatic man was growing in him and he would be sorry when the time came for them to part.

Anhur was not pleased when Huy decided to go into the school courtyards instead of taking to his couch. "You want to talk to that beefy young ox with the tongue of a shrewish woman?" he grumbled. "Trust me, Huy, that kind can carry a grudge right into the tomb. You'll be wasting your breath. What is he to you, anyway?"

"He killed me," Huy replied. "If we ever keep company again, Anhur, I'll tell you about it, but today I must try to come to an understanding with him. It's the way of Ma'at."

"'Hail Uamtutef, I have not eaten my heart,'" Anhur said.

"What's that?"

Anhur rolled his eyes. "It's one of the negative
confessions from the Book of Coming Forth by Day.
You're supposed to learn them all in order to get past
the gods that wait to condemn the guilty soul after you
die. Don't you know that? And you thought I was just
an ignorant soldier!"

"No I didn't, and I assure you I don't eat my heart
over Sennefer. I'm not angry with him. I don't want
him to be angry with me anymore."

Anhur snorted. "Well, good luck," he said derisively.
"At least I'll be able to defend you on a full stomach."

Huy's assumption that the Overseer's quarters
would be near the entrance to the first courtyard
proved correct. A passing priest gave him directions
that took him along the south side of the temple itself
to where the unroofed passage ended at a junction
behind the sanctuary. One arm led in a few steps to a
door in the outer wall. The other petered out in a
large grassed quadrangle bounded by cells on three
sides and, abutting the sanctuary itself, a modest
apartment. Here Huy knocked. After a while a servant
responded, blinking drowsily at Huy as full sunlight
drenched his face. "Yes?" he said sharply. "If you have
a problem, could it not wait until after the sleep?"

Huy inwardly cursed himself. He had chosen the
time of day so as not to encounter any of the other boys,
but he had not considered the Overseer's rest. "If your
master is asleep I will not disturb him," he said. "But if
he is still awake I would like to speak with him for a
moment. Please tell him that Huy son of Hapu is here."

"Now you're learning," Anhur murmured as the
man withdrew. "It does no harm to throw your weight

about sometimes. The servants here seem very haughty to me. Not like the ones at home in Iunu. There they know their place."

"I think that Pabast must still be learning his," Huy returned wryly. "Besides, we're punished if we're unkind to them or make undue demands. Sometimes a servant rises in the world and becomes a master."

Anhur's caustic reply was lost as a man stepped out of the doorway and stood wrapping a sheet around his thick body. He too was squinting in the harsh midday light, but he managed a bow. "I had hoped to meet you at some point before you left us, Son of Hapu," he said gravely. "I was sorry not to see you when you ate with my bevy of pupils. How may I help you?"

"I know I've chosen an inconvenient moment to disturb you, Master," Huy apologized, "but my errand is a private one and I didn't want it shared with a crowd. I seem to attract a lot of interest wherever I go." The words were not meant to be immodest, but to Huy's cringing ears they sounded so.

"That is understandable"—the Overseer nodded—"but regrettable. I believe your name is known in every schoolroom in the country, and there will be howls of disappointment if you disappear from Khmun without spending at least some time with my boys. Or with most of them."

The glance meeting Huy's was astute. Huy saw with relief that this man was aware of his history with Sennefer. Of course he was. Every good Overseer of Schools made it his business to know as much as possible about the students under his care.

"They mean you no harm," he continued. "They simply need to hear the words that will shrink rumour down to the level of the mundane. Come inside, out of the sun." He waited for Huy to precede him. Anhur took up a position outside.

The small reception room was blessedly cool and dim. Beyond it Huy could see into the even-smaller sleeping room and the edge of a rumpled cot. The servant had returned to his mattress at its foot and was snoring gently. Waiting until the Overseer had sunk onto the one chair available, Huy perched beside him on the stool. Behind them the wall was covered with orderly rows of niches, each neat hollow holding a scroll; and the table, which was the only other piece of furniture, held a lamp, a scribe's palette, a collection of ink pots, a jug, and a cup.

"Gossip feeds on such rumours," the Overseer said frankly, "and the more scanty the array of facts the wilder the conjecture becomes. We Overseers talk to one another by letter and once a year face to face, usually just before the Inundation, when the schools empty. So do the pupils from the various temples when they return to their homes. Your story ought to have belonged to the past by now, but unfortunately the notion that the gods have resurrected you from the dead to become a Seer has kept it fresh and exciting in the courtyards." He folded his legs and twitched the sheet over his knees. "I do not ask you for the truth of it," he went on. "A resurrection? Doubtful. The making of a Seer? Entirely likely, especially as you have come here at the bidding of your High Priest and to the delight of ours. Sennefer will say nothing, which only fans the flame of speculation, but I wish that before you return to Iunu you could speak in the schoolroom regarding why you are here."

Huy had listened to him with mounting distress. "Master, I am not responsible for the things said about me in idleness!" he broke in. "Nor am I obliged to run about Egypt putting out those flames! I am here to study the wisdom of Thoth and nothing more."

The Overseer cocked an eye at him. "You are implying that it is my place, mine and the teachers', to cast the sand of common sense upon this fire," he said dryly. "Well, I suppose I can say that I have heard the reason for your visit here from your own mouth, that you are indeed training to be a Seer under Mentuhotep and other High Priests, and that though grievously wounded you have recovered fully and there is no connection between the attack on you and any scrying gift you may possess."

"And Sennefer has said nothing?" Huy managed.

The disappointment on the Overseer's face was fleeting. "Nothing. He walks away when your name is mentioned. He will not mix with those of his own age but has a few friends among the younger pupils." Huy thought of Samentuser and the little boy's slavish devotion to Sennefer. "He makes it clear that he does not want to be here," the Overseer told Huy. "But as you must know, the affair of his attack on you came to the attention of Governor Nakht, who took it to Pharaoh himself for a judgment. Sennefer was expelled from Iunu at once by High Priest Ramose. Sennefer's father, the governor of the Nart-Pehu sepat, wanted his son transferred to the school at Amun's temple in

Weset, but the One refused to allow it. As well as removing Sennefer's right to bear the throwing stick, he ordered him here, to Khmun. Our teachers can do little with him. He is very bitter."

But perhaps his bitterness has nothing to do with his punishment, Huy thought suddenly. *He must know that the penalty meted out to him was just. No, he smoulders for a very different reason, one I can well understand.*

"I would like to speak to him, with your permission, Master," Huy said carefully. "I want to ask him for forgiveness."

"Forgiveness!" the Overseer exclaimed loudly. "What for? Were you not his victim?"

"Because of Sennefer I have prospered," Huy said, a lump in his throat. "My education is assured. Because of him I have come to the attention of the gods, who have seen fit to endow me with a gift. Sennefer sees his guilt, but he also sees that the consequences of his impulsive cruelty have lifted me out of the dust of Hut-herib forever. I want him to understand that none of it was of my choosing, or his. Not really."

The Overseer did not reply. His gaze went to the square of bright light in the doorway and the view of green grass and blue sky beyond. One finger began to tap thoughtfully against his white-clad knee. Then he cleared his throat. "I will grant your request, providing you meet Sennefer here, in my presence. Notwithstanding the son's disgrace, the father is an important man and will not take a further insult to his honour lightly. This affair has already shamed him enough. Do you agree?" Huy nodded.

The servant appeared and went away, and before long the Overseer emerged, this time clad in a soft sheath belted with thin white leather and wearing the band of his office on one upper arm. He did not resume his seat. He stood just inside the doorway, breathing easily, his shoulders squared, and Huy could sense the mantle of his profession settling over him. Nothing was said. Huy, his heart fluttering, tried to compose the right words to say to Sennefer, but his mind remained blank with tension. A slight breeze stirred the folds of the Overseer's linen, but it was hot and brought no relief from the stifling afternoon.

At last the doorway darkened. The servant entered, bowed to the Overseer, and left again. Sennefer also bowed. He was barefoot and had tied his kilt too loosely in his haste. His youth lock was untidy, an unbraided tangle drifting down past one ear, and kohl had smudged from one eye onto his temple. "I am sorry for my appearance," he said. "I was asleep when your servant woke me, Master. What . . ." Then he saw Huy sitting on the stool. "I might have known!" he shouted. "I did not hurt you yesterday, Huy, yet you run to tattle to my Overseer! Am I to be punished again?" At the sound of his voice a shadow darkened the doorway. Anhur's bulk blocked out the daylight.

"Control yourself, Sennefer!" the Overseer said crisply. "Huy has said nothing about any event yesterday. He has asked to speak with you, that is all."

Sennefer's gaze went from one to the other, then fastened on a point somewhere below Huy's chin. "He said enough in the passage yesterday," he said sullenly. "Have you come to add something more to my future ruin, Huy son of Hapu?"

Huy could see the effort he was making to keep the sneer out of his voice because of the presence of his master. The Overseer's head snapped to Huy at the words. He had opened his mouth and Huy, dreading the question being formed, rose quickly and confronted Sennefer's angry face. "No," he said. "No, Sennefer. I have nothing to add to that except to beg you to change it if you can. But I am ashamed of the spite with which I said it. Such callousness is not worthy of me. Nor were your insults worthy of you."

"Worthy?" Sennefer snarled. "Worthy? What right have you to this self-righteousness? I flung a throwing stick at you in a moment of impulsive hatred, and ever since it has been travelling through the air, turning over and over endlessly in my mind, tormenting me with its motion because I cannot call it back. I am imprisoned by that instant, whereas you . . ." He gulped, his chest heaving, and Huy saw that he was near to tears. "For you the moment passed into triumphs greater than a peasant could ever have imagined. Your whole life has become a reward for that one small loss of restraint—a reward that you did not earn! You had no right to be at school in the first place, mixing with your betters, prancing about with the son of the Governor, showing off an intelligence you surely did not obtain from your dull-witted, common family!"

"You were jealous of me," Huy said. A pain had begun to grow in his stomach. "Oh gods, Sennefer, if you only knew how desperately I long to return to that day you wounded me so that I might choose to take another way back to my cell with Thothmes, so that I might go on with my studies in peace and eventually become no more than an underscribe!" He pressed a hand to his abdomen, where the pain was growing. "You can let go of that moment if you want to. You can forgive me for everything that has happened to you. But no matter how much I want to be the boy I once was, I don't have that choice! Please believe me when I say that the things you call a reward are a curse! Please forgive me and understand!" To his horror he realized that he had begun to cry.

"It doesn't matter whether I believe you or not," Sennefer said thickly. "The damage is done. I did it. You did it. I am guilty of an outward act of violence for which I have been outwardly punished whether I am able to put it behind me or not. But where does your true guilt lie, Son of Hapu? Who will dare to punish you?" He swung clumsily to the Overseer. "Dismiss me, Master. The sleep is almost over and I need to wash." He did not wait for the small gesture the Overseer eventually made; bowing, he left, pushing his way past Anhur and running over the dry grass.

Huy collapsed onto the stool and bent over. A cup was thrust into his hand. He drank the water thirstily, handed back the cup, and, lifting his kilt, wiped his face.

"Are you satisfied?" the Overseer inquired. "Is there any word that might help me and his teachers deal more kindly with Sennefer?"

Huy shook his head. *You agree with him,* he thought suddenly. *To you I am an upstart, and moreover I am to be envied for my gift. Perhaps feared also.* He looked up and saw his thought mirrored on the Overseer's face. "I thank you for your indulgence today, Master," he said, rising and bowing. "I am sorry, but I am not

able to address your pupils. Tell them what you wish."
He left abruptly, glad to feel the sun strike his head, to
have the comfort of Anhur's presence beside him, to
be aware of the slow easing of anxiety in his stomach.
"I want to be a boy again, Anhur," he blurted. "I am
very lonely." The soldier did not reply, but his hand
descended briefly on Huy's shoulder.

They returned to Huy's cell, he to his couch and
Anhur, with a grunt of relief, to his pallet. The hour of
sleep was over. There were voices in the passage beyond
the cell and a general stirring of feet, but Huy, exhausted,
did not care. No one would bother him, he knew; the
priests had their duties and Mentuhotep, if he sent for
Huy, would believe he was meditating in privacy. *My guilt
lies in the choice I made at Imhotep's feet,* Huy thought,
*but surely I cannot be punished for such innocent arrogance.
I am already paying a price. I remain a child by law for the
next three years, and yet already I carry a weight only the
priests can understand, and even then their discernment is
limited. I am alone. It is not self-righteousness, Sennefer, it
is self-pity that fills me today, even as it consumes you.
Tomorrow I will ask for the commentary. I will discuss it
with the High Priest, I will send for Amunmose, I will make
my prostrations to Thoth, and then I will go home to Iunu.*
In spite of his swollen, itching eyes and the faint ache still
troubling his belly, he slept.

To his relief he did not have to steel himself to
demand the commentary, for when he was admitted to
the High Priest's office the following morning he saw
the casket already open on the desk and a linen-wrapped
scroll beside it. Mentuhotep greeted him and bade
him sit. "You look unwell," he commented. "Your

conversation with Sennefer yesterday upset you. I know all about it—the Overseer reported to me what was said. Being so close to the one who harmed you is doing you no good, Huy. I think I will try to have Sennefer transferred to another school before you return here to study the fourth part of the Book."

Huy looked at him in horror. "Oh, Master, please don't do that! Sennefer did not disturb me as much as I disturbed myself. If you know what was said, then you know why. Is he to be punished forever?" *His end is dire,* Huy wanted to add. *Leave him alone to enjoy what life he has left.* But he shrank even further from discussing his gift with Mentuhotep than he had with the Overseer. It would be like lifting his hair and revealing the ugly scar on his scalp to someone whose interest might be sordid.

"Well, I shall read the reports on Sennefer's progress and behaviour while you are away and make my decision based on them," Mentuhotep said heavily. "If he becomes more unmanageable after talking with you, then he must go. No one can heal another's soul, Huy, and you were wrong to try. It was arrogant of you, and if, as I suspect, Sennefer was not ready to hear what you had to say to him, his condition will not improve. Your need to say it is entirely irrelevant."

The High Priest was right, Huy knew, and his reprimand stung, but he kept silent.

"This is the commentary." Mentuhotep touched the scroll. "Like the second part of the Book, it is very short. I don't think that you will find it helpful." He handed it to Huy, who unwrapped it slowly, laid the linen on the desk, and unrolled the papyrus.

Instead of leaving, Mentuhotep settled himself in his chair. Huy wished that he would go away.

The script was familiar, written in the same hand as the commentary of the first part of the Book. No breath of Paradise imbued it, no Ished scent, and it felt more fragile than the Book itself under Huy's nervous hands. Disappointment flooded him as he read.

Yet the Light cast a shadow,
grim and terrible,
which, passing downwards,
became like restless water,
chaotically casting forth spume like smoke.

"But this has nothing to do with Atum making transformations!" he cried out, lifting both hands so that the scroll rolled up with an audible rustle. "It is no help at all! Where are the Twos and Fours and Eights?"

Mentuhotep leaned across the desk and deftly removed the papyrus. "You must be more gentle. It is quite brittle."

Huy laid his folded arms on the smooth surface before him and his head sank onto them. For a long time the room was quiet. Both were still, Huy with his eyes tightly closed and Mentuhotep watching him, breathing easily. Finally Huy stirred and, to Mentuhotep's surprise, slid onto the floor with his knees up and his hands entwined across his chest. "I cannot treat this part of the Book as separate from the first," he said dully. "I must go back to the beginning. Atum enters the First Duat, that is, he wills himself to change. He becomes—what? 'Let us call Spirit pure energy—but it is known to us only as light.' Therefore Atum becomes Light. He becomes Ra-Atum. Ra-Atum." He turned his head and peered up at Mentuhotep. "That's why the Ished Tree is in Ra's temple at Iunu, isn't it? Because the very first transformation was from consciousness, to will, to Light." He did not wait for any confirmation but went back to staring at the ceiling. "'Yet the Light cast a shadow,'" he murmured. "How is that line in the commentary tied to the words of the second part of the Book? And if the first part is correct, and Atum is alone and he becomes Light, then how can he cast a shadow? There was nothing for the light to fall on and make a shadow." Ignoring Mentuhotep's exclamation, he rubbed at his forehead. "Yet the first part clearly states 'Let us call light First—but it is known only through darkness.'"

"It has always seemed to me like blasphemy to attempt to dissect these holy things as though we were slicing open a body in the House of the Dead," Mentuhotep put in. His voice was unsteady. "Yet the end result for a body is beautification. It is not blasphemy for you, Huy. It is your task. Are you aware that light does indeed cast a shadow without an object to stand in its way? I had not considered it until now. I had accepted the birth of chaos as a deliberate act of Ra-Atum."

Huy sat up, swivelling to face the High Priest. "Tell me how!"

"No one knows how, but if you hold a piece of new white linen very close to the flame of a candle, stretching the linen so that there are no folds, a faint shadow with no cause can be seen. It is a mystery."

"So is this," Huy returned wryly. "So Atum becomes Light, and in doing so he casts the shadow of which you speak. And according to the commentary the shadow is like restless water, chaotic, black, smoking. Does it take Ra-Atum by surprise, do you think? Did he know what would happen if he transformed himself into Light? No matter." He was frowning, eyes glazed in concentration. "He sees the dark turbulence of his shadow. What does he do? He calms it!" Huy's expression cleared. He beamed up at the High Priest. "Of course! 'I am One that transforms into Two,' and so on and so on, but because the shadow is still a part of him, Ra-Atum can say at the end, 'After this I am One.' But the Two and Four and Eight, the way he calms and orders his shadow, what are they?"

"I know," Mentuhotep said calmly. "He begins to conceive the cosmos, within the shadow. Frogs, Huy."

Huy blinked. "Frogs?"

"Every priest and every pious Egyptian knows this. Four pairs. Two into Four into Eight. Each pair comprises a male and a female, to draw towards one another, to make harmony, to strengthen the ordering of the chaos within the shadow where one alone, or two males, would not. The male hypostasis is symbolized by a frog, the female by a snake. The Nun is the primeval waters and Naunet its female counterpart. Huh and Hauhet—endless space. Kuk and Kauket—darkness. Amun and Amaunet—what is hidden. So the shadow is put in order, and Atum remains One."

Huy stared at him. "This is well known? You knew? Then why didn't you tell me, Master?"

Mentuhotep came round the desk and lowered himself onto the stool. With his hands on his knees he bent over Huy. "The Book's wholeness is a dangerous mystery. Thin rays of revelation will illuminate this passage for some, another passage for another, and some passages are known by all. But the completeness, the roundness, of the will of Ra-Atum has been shown to only one reader, the great Imhotep. That is why he is worshipped as a god himself. I believe that you have been chosen to understand as he did." He sat back. "You see, Huy, I did not perceive how the shadow is a part of Ra-Atum, not until today. It makes other things clear. How the demons can bring harm or benefits. How the Khatyu demons, the fighters, can also be Habyu, emissaries. How every god is a force against us as well as to do us good. Look at Sekhmet, goddess of womanly joy, wife of Ptah. In her thirst for blood she would have utterly destroyed mankind if Ra had not given her red-coloured beer to drink and made her intoxicated—yet she is the mildest of deities!"

"Ramose told me that every god is nothing more than an outward manifestation of some aspect of Ra-Atum."

"And that makes sense also."

"So chaos is ordered into water, endless space, darkness, and what is hidden. But there is still no creation." Huy scrambled up off the floor and rotated his shoulders. He felt as though he had not slept for a year. *That is why the frog tying my youth lock turned to gold as I entered Paradise,* he thought dimly. *Ra-Atum's second transforming act repeated upon myself as I prepared all unknowingly to enter into my First Duat.* He yawned. "Oh, forgive my rudeness! May I now send to Amunmose and prepare to return to Iunu?"

Mentuhotep laughed ruefully. "Are you in such a hurry to see Khmun slide into the distance behind you? Very well, Huy. Your work here is over for the time being. Come into the sanctuary with me and receive Thoth's blessing before you go." The invitation was casual, but Huy was overwhelmed. Only a High Priest was ever allowed to face a god so directly. Exhausted and humbled, he bowed himself out.

Huy returned to Iunu with great relief. He embraced both Anhur and Amunmose before they disappeared into the labyrinth of the temple, Anhur to resume his guard duties and the servant to the kitchens. Huy knew that he would miss their company, particularly Anhur's. The man had been both his protector and the provider of a brisk comfort, filling a need in Huy that no one since his uncle Ker had met. But Huy, watching Anhur's broad back recede, had the feeling that their association would continue in the future. Amunmose had hugged him briefly. "If you ever become rich and want to eat the best meals in Egypt, remember me, Huy." He had smiled and loped away, leaving Huy with a sense of nakedness.

11

The remainder of the school year proceeded smoothly and peacefully for Huy. He approached his studies with a new enthusiasm born of the accumulating knowledge of the last ten years, which at last had begun to be more than a disconnected jumble of aphorisms and past events learned by enforced rote. His mastery over pen and papyrus was almost complete. He won more nods of approval than reprimands from his teachers. Dutifully he wrote to his parents, the task now a discipline rather than a pleasure, and dutifully his father replied. His brother Heby had become a healthy two-year-old, running about the house and garden as Huy himself had done. Huy occasionally tried to imagine this child, but gave up when his mind did no more than place his own features on his brother's face and give the boy his own recalcitrant, spoiled nature. Hapu's missives were short and entirely factual due, Huy knew, to his father's poverty. Scribes were too expensive to hire for more than a few well-chosen words. Ishat was never mentioned, although Hapzefa was helping to raise Heby. Huy sometimes wondered idly how the fiery young girl was faring, but Ishat too had faded into the misty realm of what had been. Nakht and his wife Nefer-Mut had become Huy's parents, Thothmes his beloved brother, and Meri-Hathor, Nasha, and Anuket his sisters.

His fourteenth birthday on the ninth day of Paophi was celebrated with a boating party for all his schoolmates given by Nakht, and Anuket, instead of making him the usual wreath, presented him with an earring of jasper and moonstone teardrops held in claws of gold. "You wear that hoop through your lobe all the time," she complained gently while he bent, overcome, so that she could unscrew it. "It will not do for special parties like this one. The jasper is for the redness of your blood, warm and healthy with youth. The moonstone is for your gift. The moon belongs to Thoth." So often both her words and her actions could be interpreted in several ways, and while her fingers moved over his ear, attaching the gift, Huy wondered yet again if he was being teased. His relationship with her had become ossified, unchanging, a peculiar dance composed of wariness and habit. He was the one who sought her out, instigated their conversations, tried to draw a more powerful response from her than the smiles and small caresses that in themselves could be interpreted either as encouragements or as mere evidences of sisterly affection. *She is behaving entirely correctly,* Huy would tell himself after returning emotionally exhausted from his visits to Nakht's house. *I am not yet old enough to sue for her in marriage. She is showing me her love in the only ways permissible to her.* Yet gradually the flutter of her hands on his face, his shoulder, the way she leaned over him to pick up a flower or a morsel of food, the sidelong glances and smiles, began to take on a more manipulative cast in his mind, sometimes making him feel like a toy being pulled along behind her.

His work on the Book continued. The third part consisted of two very large scrolls that once he would have dreaded unrolling, but the first two parts were now clear and understood in his mind. At Khmun he had learned of the Ocdoad, the potential energy from which the Ennead is formed. Atum had brought order into the chaos of his shadow, creating the four pairs of complementariness. This was pre-creation, as yet intangible. The primeval waters, space, the darkness, all that is hidden, lay impotently bound to himself, waiting for the god's word to become the forces that would create the world.

The core of the third part saw the inception of the eternal world, the empowering of water, space, darkness, the hidden, to become the Ennead, the Nine, with Atum himself the first followed by Shu the Air, Tefnut Light, Geb the Earth, Nut the Sky, and Osiris the son of Nut and Geb, Isis, Set, and Nephthys, all still motionless, all waiting for the onrush of Time that would be Atum's next task.

But first Atum chooses yet another metamorphosis for himself. In a lyrical intensity that set Huy's heart pounding and brought a sweat to his skin, Thoth bursts out on behalf of his master in a paroxysm of joy:

I am he who made heaven and earth, formed the mountains, and created what is above . . .

I am he who opens his eyes, thus the light comes forth. I am he who closes his eyes, thus comes forth obscurity . . .

I am he who made the living fire . . .

I am Khepri in the morning, Ra at his noontide, Atum in the evening . . .

The three forms of Ra, Huy had thought when he read the words. *Of course! Ra is one yet three, yet is still always, only, Atum. Now he is Ra-Atum.*

The anonymous commentator whose work Huy had many occasions to bless presaged what Huy would discover in the fourth part of the Book at Khmun.

The Mind of the Cosmos created from fire and air the seven administrators who regulate destiny . . . These celestial powers, known by thought alone, are called the gods, and they preside over the world . . . Ra lets the Cosmos go on its way, but never lets it wander, for like a skilful chariot driver Ra has tied the Cosmos to him, preventing it rushing off in disorder—and his controlling reins are rays of light . . . The sun is an image of the Creator who is higher than the heavens . . .

Atum creates the Cosmic Mind. The Cosmic Mind creates the Cosmos. The Cosmos creates Time. Time creates Change . . .

The Cosmic Mind is permanently connected to Atum. The Cosmos is made up of thoughts in the Cosmic Mind. The Cosmic Mind is an image of Atum. The Cosmos is an image of the Cosmic

Mind. The sun is an image of the Cosmos. Man
is an image of the sun . . .

Enthralled, often almost drunk on what he was
discovering, Huy had nevertheless learned that
beneath the outpouring lay the simple, vital bones that
would emerge in his mind if he gave them time. So he
went about his studies, drew the bow, hurled the spear,
and graduated from Lazy White Star to a more spirited
and entirely disrespectful chariot horse without the
anxiety that had plagued him during his first
introduction to the Book. Ramose left him alone. Huy
had no doubt that the High Priest was carefully
monitoring his progress in every field of his endeavour,
but as his gift remained blessedly dormant and his life
followed the path of regularity and routine he had long
ago learned to appreciate, he did not care.

He returned to Khmun at the beginning of Shemu
to study the two scrolls that composed the fourth part
of the Book, the creation of Time and the material
world. Ramose had made no demur when Huy
requested that Anhur and Amunmose accompany him.
This time Huy gave himself over to the spell of an Egypt
in full fecundity, leaning on the rail of his boat for hours
to watch the rich fields of swiftly ripening crops slide
by. In another two months the harvest would begin.
Already the heat was becoming uncomfortable, and
Huy looked forward each day to the time when he
and all his travelling companions shed their limp linens
and waded into the coolness of the river.

He found Thoth's temple at Khmun no less
forbidding, however, the undercurrent of constant

heka weighing down an already solemn atmosphere.
Anhur did not feel it. He looked at Huy blankly
when the young man asked him if he felt threatened
by a sense of impending retribution. "No," the
soldier had replied. "I just feel sleepy and bored.
Until I remember that I'm not standing watch in
some dark corridor of Ra's House, that is. Thoth's
House is very beautiful, don't you think, Huy?" Huy
did think so, but his dreams were sombre and his
appetite seemed to have deserted him.

He avoided the temple school, and after the first
invitation he began to take his meals regularly with the
archivist priest, Khanun, who inhabited a lone cell built
beside the entrance to the House of Life. It seemed to be
the one truly human, cheerful corner of the whole
precinct. Khanun's shrine held an image of the god, of
course, but the cell walls had been painted, very inexpertly
and garishly, with depictions of various native animals and
birds, and even a few rather crooked trees. Huy liked the
sheer exuberance of the work. "I did it myself," the priest
told him apologetically. "Being the archivist is a dusty task
undertaken in dim rooms. I value the quiet and I'm happy
working alone, but I was raised on a farm with cows and
oxen and all the bird and animal life along the canals.
Thoth's formal gardens don't quite fill the void my
father's arouras left in my soul." Huy was glad to find
much in common with this man whose origins were
humble and who had raised himself by his own skill from
scribe to priest to Overseer of the House of Life. He was
easy to talk to, and Huy found himself saying much about
himself that he later regretted, although he knew
instinctively that Khanun was trustworthy.

He was also shrewd. On the third day, when they had finished their meal and Khanun was lighting the lamps against a deepening twilight, he suddenly said without turning, "Huy, why are you not sharing your company with the other priests, or with the students? They all know that you have returned. They must be wondering why you sequester yourself with me. Are you hiding? Is the Book frightening you?" He blew out the taper he was holding and set it carefully in a dish.

Huy reached for a cushion to place between his spine and the wall. "The Book is not frightening me, Master, but the temple is, and the grounds, and the sacred lake. So much magic here, soaking into everything, and I have the impression that if I say or do the wrong thing, if I laugh too loudly, if I even have an idle thought, Thoth will punish me."

Khanun stared at him, astonished. "But Huy, Thoth blesses you! You read in his Book! You have been chosen to do so, and thus surely the god smiles on you with his divine approval. His magic is yours to command!"

"No, it is not," Huy said heavily. "It waits to judge me, to condemn me for some mysterious reason. Every time I unroll one of the scrolls it is with the fear that I am a hair's breadth away from a mistake that will plunge me into a Duat of which I know nothing. My confidence deserts me. Something is waiting for me here, something terrible. Each day I manage to avoid it, skirt its perimeter." He held out both palms. "I have no idea what it is, but it does not follow me to my cell at Iunu. No one else seems to be aware of the maelstrom of heka that imbues these precincts, Master. Only me."

"Of course you are sensitive to it," Khanun said thoughtfully, "but I am appalled that you should feel it as a threat. Thoth is benign, Huy. He gave us language, he created eternity at Atum's command, he orders our fate, particularly yours. You are surely in his care." *But am I?* Huy wondered suddenly. *I do not wait for eternity. Eternity is within my power to See. And in Seeing—in not just predicting but actually Seeing—the fates of others, am I impinging in some way on the prerogative of Thoth himself?*

"Thoth was not there, by the Ished Tree," he said. "Anubis was. So was Ma'at. But not Thoth, the arbiter of fate, the author of Time. Why not, Master?"

"How can I answer you?" Khanun retorted, sinking onto his cushions with a sigh and a creak of his joints. "How can any man? Such a question cannot be answered except by you and the gods themselves. But how can you fear any error if you are doing the will of Atum?" *How indeed?* Huy repeated to himself. *But am I doing the will of Atum? Is it possible that what I am narrowly avoiding here, in the home of the god of eternity, is the true answer to the question? And the answer is a thing of terror? What ancient and cynical prophet said that ignorance is bliss!* With a sigh he changed the subject.

Before leaving Khmun, he endured the formal blessing of Thoth's High Priest in front of the temple sanctuary. Afterwards, as he was putting his sandals back on in the outer court, Mentuhotep asked him, "Did your work here proceed satisfactorily, Huy? Did you comprehend the contents of the scrolls?"

Huy straightened guiltily. He had done his best to avoid the man. "They deal with the creation of the eternal elements, as you know, Master," he said carefully. "They are not difficult to absorb. If I had needed your help I would not have hesitated to ask for it. You have been very kind," he finished lamely.

Mentuhotep raised his eyebrows. "I am pleased that my assistance was not necessary. But I am sorry that we were not able to share a cup of beer together and talk of things less ethereal than the gods. Perhaps you will visit us in the future for no other reason."

Huy met his gaze with an inner twist of desperation. "It is not you, Master," he blurted. "This place oppresses me. I have been cowardly in hiding with Khanun. Forgive me." Mentuhotep did not reply. He laid his hand lightly on Huy's hot head, then strode into the shadow of the outer court's vast pylon and was lost to sight.

Huy's shame did not outlast the journey home. Once more he bade farewell to Anhur and Amunmose, and he was making his way contentedly towards his courtyard when Thothmes came racing along the path, his face white. Coming up to Huy, he grabbed both his arms and began to shake him. "They said you were back!" he shouted. "Thank the gods you are back! She was in the Street of the Basket Sellers and a donkey ran amok and overturned its cart and was kicking and shrieking and she took a blow from a hoof in the stomach and the physicians can't stop the bleeding! Come now, Huy! At once!"

Huy shrugged out of his friend's grasp. "But Thothmes, she promised not to go there," he protested. "Did she forget?"

Thothmes' eyes went blank for a moment. His hands and lips were trembling. "Not Nasha," he stuttered. "My mother. My mother went there. Two days ago." He swept up Huy's leather bag. "The skiff is waiting for us on the canal. My father sent a messenger to Khmun for you. He must have passed your barge somewhere on the river. Oh, hurry up, Huy!"

Dread washed over Huy. Even as he was being pulled along in Thothmes' panic-stricken wake, his gaze went to the entrance of his courtyard where his cell waited for him, cozy and secure. "But Thothmes, what can I do?" he called to the wiry little body pelting ahead of him towards the sun-seared expanse of paving between the canal and the temple pylon. "I'm not a healer!"

Thothmes ignored him. Running up the ramp of the skiff at the foot of the watersteps, he yelled at the helmsman, and the sailors lifted their oars. Huy tumbled after him, the ramp was pulled onto the deck, and Thothmes finally stood still, his fingers clenched around the railing, his breath coming hard. Huy came up beside him.

"A litter would have taken too long," Thothmes muttered. "You must save her, Huy, you must! Put your hands on her. Make her better. You can diagnose— you've done it before. Surely you can heal as well!"

Huy remembered making a diagnosis. That awful sense of dislocation had come upon him, as usual with no warning, and left him with a piercing headache. It seemed a long time ago and he could not remember the person, the ailment, or the prescription that had come out of his mouth. "That was different," he said. "Thothmes, listen to me! I am not a healer."

Thothmes' head went down. His expression became mutinous. "You don't know that. You are an anomaly, a creation of the gods. Even you don't know what you can and can't do." He turned an anguished face to Huy. "I beg you. My father begs you."

Huy's dread began to be mixed with a feeling of hopelessness. *I know I can do nothing but tell Nakht the exact moment when Nefer-Mut will die,* Huy thought dismally. *Gods, how terrible! What a useless gift I've been given, predicting the future when for Thothmes' mother there is no future, only the drafty dimness of the Judgment Hall.*

Another thought struck him and he shuddered. Nasha had laughed at him but had kept her promise to stay away from that street. Nevertheless an accident had occurred there to a member of her family. It was as if the event itself had to take place to one of them regardless of his warning; the moment could not be averted. Nasha was safe, but her mother had been sacrificed. *If I had touched Nefer-Mut, held her hand, would I have Seen the same disaster falling on Nasha rather than her?* His thoughts ran on. *Or on Thothmes if I had Seen for Nakht? What does this mean? If I had not inadvertently Seen for Nasha, would the accident have happened at all? Is it possible that the Seeing itself actually changes fate?* That idea, alien and cold, had seemed to spring into his mind with an eagerness that made him lean against the rail in sudden weakness. Thothmes turned to him quickly. Huy clenched his teeth. "Your mother is very dear to me," he said. "I will try."

The guard on Nakht's watersteps acknowledged them briefly as they ran along the ramp and passed him, going swiftly between the quivering willows and onto the path leading directly to the main entrance of the house. There was no sign of the servant who customarily waited on his stool under the portico to welcome guests. The door was open. Thothmes plunged into the coolness of the reception hall and sped across it, disappearing along the passage and up the stairs leading to the women's quarters, Huy on his heels. Mixed odours assailed Huy's nostrils: perfume, the faint tang of cinnamon, and under them, almost undetectable, a whiff of fresh blood. His stomach contracted. He followed Thothmes through a doorway on his right and slowed, his heart palpitating.

Although the room was large, the starry ceiling high, it seemed cramped for the crowd of people clustered about the dais at the far end where the wide couch stood. Pale faces turned towards the newcomers and at once a reverential pathway opened for both boys. Nakht emerged from the throng. "Do what you can, Huy," he said without preamble. "Her injury is fatal unless the gods intervene." Huy nodded, stepped up onto the dais, and knelt beside the low couch.

The stench of new blood enveloped him in its coppery miasma. Nakht's wife lay on her back. Linens had been packed between her legs, but the blood had already oozed through them to spread a dark scarlet blot on the sheet that covered her. Even as Huy reached for her hand, a trickle of blood appeared from one nostril. Automatically Huy lifted a corner of the sheet and wiped it away. The woman opened her eyes. "Huy," she whispered. "It hurts." Her lips were blue, her skin pallid, and the fingers curling weakly about Huy's own were icy. Huy did not reply. Closing his own eyes, he waited, desperately willing the gift to waken in him, calling silently on Atum himself to heal, to justify the person who had become more to him than his own mother. The expectant crowd behind him disappeared. Fleetingly he had registered Anuket's presence, she and Nasha pressed together near the foot of the couch, but by the time he began to beseech the god she had gone from his consciousness.

Finally, with a relief bordering on hysteria, he felt the familiar disengagement begin in his mind. The bloodied sheet, the limp form, the bright colours on the wall beyond, dissolved into a fog thicker than river mist on a cold winter morning. Huy continued to wait. There was a sense that he and the hand he was holding were travelling forward at great speed, although the fog remained unshredded by their passage.

Then a hand descended over his, over hers, the grip firm and commanding. Huy looked down. The fingers were black, laden with gold rings, and the sinewy wrist held a bracelet of linked lapis lazuli ankhs. "Let go, Son of Hapu," a voice said softly. "It is my prerogative to lead her where she must go. Give her to me." Huy knew that voice. His fingers loosened, and as they did so the fog vanished. Anubis smiled down at him, the god's sharp fangs gleaming in the light of many candles. A pulsing heart rested on his other palm. Looking about, Huy realized that he was standing in the Judgment Hall. Immediately before him were the scales, one dish higher than the other. Beneath them the monster Sobek, the eater of the guilty, lay curled up asleep. Huy fancied that he could smell Sobek's breath, fetid with the taste of many kas. But beside him, her gossamer linen stirring against his rough hide in the drafts blowing through that mighty place, was Ma'at herself, the feathers of rightness trembling above her forehead.

Something touched Huy's arm and, turning, he found himself staring into Nefer-Mut's face. Her hair lay loose upon her shoulders, her feet were bare, and she was clad in a spotless white sheath from neck to ankles. "Huy, where am I?" she asked, but there was no panic in her voice. She seemed unaware that Anubis had imprisoned her in his grip. "Did you heal me? Am I safe?"

Huy swallowed. "You are in the Judgment Hall," he answered with difficulty. "Your time in Egypt is over, my mother. I love you so much."

Her black eyebrows rose. Carefully her gaze roamed the cavernous expanse. She sighed. "So that is how it must be. I love you also, my adopted son. I am sorry that I will not see my children flower into full adulthood. My heart must be weighed. Will it be painful?" Still there was no fear in her face or her tones. It was almost as though, in spite of her words, she was unaware of what had happened to her, of where she was.

For answer Anubis leaned close, holding up the organ throbbing in his hand. "No, dearest, there will be no pain," he said, his long snout brushing her cheek. "I am holding your hand. Come." Obediently, like a trusting child, she allowed herself to be led to the scales. At once Sobek woke up, heaved himself onto his haunches, and gave her an appraising leer. But her eyes were on Ma'at as Anubis laid the heart gently on the scales.

"You are Egypt's sanity," she said to the goddess, as though she had not been aware of that truth before.

Ma'at inclined her head. The scales began to move. Slowly the weights rose, the heart sank, until the two dishes swayed, trembled, and were still.

Anubis had not relinquished her hand. "There is no Duat for you," he said gravely. "No need for the spells in the Book of Coming Forth by Day. The Son of Hapu has saved you from that ordeal. Look." She turned her head to where he was pointing and so did Huy. The far end of the Hall had faded. With a cry Huy recognized the lush foliage of the Ished Tree. The sunlight pouring onto the floor of the Judgment Hall was dazzling, the aroma of a thousand different flowers intoxicating. Huy caught a glimpse of flowing water far to the right, beyond a line of spreading palms and willows. Birds flew past his vision. Iridescent butterflies fluttered in the grass. There was no sign of the hyena, but Imhotep rose from his place at the foot of the Tree and held out a hand.

"Welcome to the Paradise of Osiris." He smiled. "This is the true Egypt. Come." At that Anubis let go, and the woman walked, then ran, towards Imhotep. Huy wanted to follow. All his muscles tensed to fall forward, to rush to where the shade of those densely packed, fragrant leaves was dappling the ground, but Anubis put out an arm and barred his way.

"Not for you, Son of Hapu, not for you," he said harshly. "Your destiny still awaits you. This moment of indulgence is over."

"I had almost forgotten!" Huy cried out. "The glory of it, Anubis! For so long the beauties of Egypt became drab and lifeless in comparison, and now will be so again until . . ." His breath faltered. He was on his feet facing into a room full of stunned faces, his nostrils cringing from the need to inhale decaying blood and the anxious sweat of the crowd. "She has gone to Osiris," he croaked. "I saw it. Her heart received a favourable weighing. I saw it. Most noble Nakht, Thothmes, forgive me. Forgive me!"

At once Nasha began to wail. "It should have been me!" she screamed. "Why wasn't it me, Huy? I did as you told me, I stayed away from that street, then why her?" She was struggling to tear her sheath, tugging at its neck in the ancient gesture of grief. Nakht signalled and her body servant went to her, leading her through the gathering and out the door. Huy stepped down from the dais with its sad burden.

Nakht came up to him, putting an arm around his shoulders. "I do not understand much of this," he said heavily. "Perhaps Ramose will be able to enlighten me. Huy, do you know why my beloved wife should have died in Nasha's place?" Huy shook his head, unable to respond for the tears threatening to spill over and disgrace him. "The sem priests will be sent for and the period of mourning will begin," Nakht went on, and for the first time Huy heard the Governor's voice lose its assurance. "You loved her too. You will perform the rites of formal mourning with us, and she will go to our tomb in the middle of the month of Thoth, but for now you must return to the school. Thothmes will stay here."

On his way to the door Huy brushed by Thothmes and Anuket. He did not look at them. Thothmes put out a hand, but Huy ignored it, frantic to gain the passage beyond, the reception hall, the path leading to the watersteps, and the rocking of the skiff that would return him to his cell and its blessed seclusion. "She is dead," he blurted to the guard on the watersteps who was waiting with the crew of the skiff, and he walked up the ramp and lowered himself to the deck in the grip of utter desolation.

Avoiding both priests and pupils, he arrived at his cell and sent a servant to the school's physician. "I have a headache that prevents me from seeing," he said. "There are dots and patterns before my eyes. Tell the physician to prepare a phial of strong poppy for me, bring it, and then make sure that I am not disturbed until tomorrow morning." *Neither wine nor beer will grant me the oblivion I crave,* he thought to himself as he stood before the likeness of his totem, Khenti-kheti, bereft of the urge to pray, bereft of everything but the need to lose himself completely. *I refuse to think! I refuse to remember these moments, so fresh, that have already slipped into the past where no power may retrieve or change them. Ah gods, the delirious pleasures of Paradise that flooded my senses! A woman I loved is dead and all I can mourn is my own secret loss.*

He was still standing when a figure darkened his doorway and the physician himself entered. "Your health is a matter of concern to the whole temple, Master Huy. I must examine you."

But Huy waved him away. "It is only the sort of headache to which I am prone. Otherwise I am perfectly well. Give me the poppy please, Master, and let me sleep."

The man grunted, but after a keen look into Huy's eyes he passed him the phial. "You are pale and seem tired. Very well. But I shall return after the first meal tomorrow. I have ordered a servant to keep watch outside your cell in case you need me in the night." He bowed and left.

Immediately Huy removed the wax seal on the tiny bottle, set its neck inside his mouth, and drained it eagerly, adding water to the dregs so that he might drink every drop of the bitter-tasting liquid. Then he took off his kilt and lay down, pulling a sheet over him.

As he became aware of a warm languor spreading through his limbs and then his torso to his chest, he waited confidently for the delightful flow to enter and obliterate his consciousness; but the moments went by and he remained fully alert, although his pain eased a little. Angry and disappointed, he turned onto his side and stared at Thothmes' empty cot against the far wall. *So not even the poppy, the most powerful sedative obtainable in Egypt, will work against that core in me that is forever alert, forever vigilant. I am not to be allowed one moment of loss of self, no respite from either the agony or the delight each day brings me. Only physical discomfort will respond to this blessed drug. I am dependent on my will alone.*

With that in mind he closed his eyes, trying to lure sleep to him by imagining a peaceful night sky full of bright stars. But the stars kept fading, changing to the glistening green of leaves above Imhotep's head, and once again Huy's body, though sluggish from the poppy, tensed to run into the sage's open arms. Nakht's wife rolled her tousled head towards him on the pillow. "Huy, it hurts," her blue lips said. Her fingers were cold with death. The hand of Anubis was cool with authority.

Under the sheet Huy pulled up his knees. *Was the Seeing I gave Nasha a lie? Did Nasha's destiny become her mother's through the link of their bloodline? Was the Street of the Basket Sellers waiting for any member of Nakht's family?* Huy sighed. It was something else, something stalking on the rim of his mind, moving too quickly and furtively for him to grasp it. What else had the god said? "No need for the spells in the Book of Coming Forth by Day. The Son of Hapu has saved you from that ordeal." *But what did I do that allowed Nefer-Mut to bypass the fierce demons with their terrible questions? She went straight to the feet of Osiris, blameless and justified, because I made another's fate become her own. But how?*

Huy's hands came up to cover his face. Suddenly memories began to flood his mind. He was lying on a slab in the House of the Dead, his eyes opening, focusing. A shadow fell on him, the shadow of a sem priest holding the obsidian knife of ritual with which to disembowel him, and in his nostrils, his hair, the pores of his skin, the awful stench of human decay. Methen had saved him. Methen had lifted him from the base of the tree where he was huddled, sobbing and terrified, and had carried him away. *Oh my mother,* he cried out silently to Nefer-Mut. *Even now you are being laid on a bed of stone. Even now a priest approaches you with the knife, and you will not stir, you will not open your eyes, because your fate was not averted.*

Eventually he did sleep, and did not hear the temple horns blow at midnight and again to herald the dawn. When consciousness returned and he sat up, it was to find Thothmes perched opposite him. His friend's eyes were dark-circled and he was pale, but his glance was calm. "You've slept past the first meal and everyone else is at class," Thothmes remarked. "The physician came and poked you and muttered and went away again. Did you drown your sorrow in wine last night, Huy?"

Huy studied the brown eyes levelled at him and, seeing no malice, shook his head. "You know I have a resistance to wine. I tried to lose myself in the poppy. How are you faring?"

Thothmes shrugged and looked away. "I . . . we . . . we are all still so shocked. Father has shut himself up in his office. Meri-Hathor's husband took her home. Nasha and Anuket are crying a lot in each other's arms. I just feel . . . lost. I can't believe I must go through the rest of my life without seeing or hearing her, smelling her perfume, being folded in her arms. I didn't sleep much. Father gave orders that I was to come back to school for now." He gave a faint smile. "I think you and I are meant to comfort one another. She loved you, Huy."

"I loved her, too."

"Did you really see her enter the realm of Osiris, or were you just saying that to make us feel better?"

Huy's throat was dry and his arms and legs were clumsy as he eased himself from the cot and poured himself a cup of water. "I saw it," he replied, and as he drank he felt the tears of loss roll hotly down his cheeks. *They are for her. This time the regret is for her.* "I wish the gift of healing was in me, Thothmes. I would have given anything to have saved her. I'm sorry."

Thothmes stood and all at once their arms were around each other, both weeping. There was nothing left to say.

By the time the beautified body of Nefer-Mut was poled across the river to the tomb on the west bank that her husband, like every good Egyptian, had been preparing for years, the school had closed for the period of the Inundation. The weather was very hot. Isis had begun to cry, but as yet the river was still safely navigable. Huy had seldom been to Nakht's house during the seventy days of mourning. There had been no feasting, music, or dancing, and his visits had been to share simple food with the family of which he was now firmly a part and to speak of the woman who had been a quiet yet effective presence.

He had little opportunity or desire to seek out Anuket by herself. She had sequestered herself in the herb room, weaving the many funeral wreaths that would be placed on her mother's outer coffin and the garlands of mourning for the guests. When Huy did see her, he thought her changed. There was an edge of uncertainty to her innate self-confidence, a slight hesitancy to her admittedly short conversations. She did not ignore him at meals or deliberately avoid him if they met in the gardens, but the sense of ambivalence he had begun to feel when around her, the impression that she might be trying out a young girl's manipulative powers on him, was gone. Nasha became simply a more subdued version of herself. The task of running the household had fallen to her, and despite her evident dislike for things domestic she was no stranger to the authority needed to control the servants. Thothmes himself remained close to Huy. They had always been inseparable, but now Huy keenly felt his friend's need to draw strength from some well in Huy that Huy doubted was in him. Thothmes spoke often of his mother, but he also spoke to Huy of the future, how he would train to take over his father's governorship one day, how he would build his own house and marry, how he would shelter and protect those he loved.

Only once did he bring up the subject of the accident. He and Huy had been practising with their bows and later, as they stood together in the bathhouse washing the sweat and dust from their bodies, Thothmes had said, "Do you remember Seeing for me years ago, Huy? Seeing me old and grey but rich and happy and still healthy?" Huy had nodded. "Well, are you sure it was my fate you were Seeing, and not someone else's?" Like the Seeing for Nasha, was the unspoken statement.

Huy ran his fingers through his long, wet hair, pushing it behind his ears and turning to Thothmes. "I am very sure it was you," he replied, stepping off the bathing slab and reaching for a linen towel to hide his discomfiture. "I don't know why your mother died in the way she did, Thothmes. I don't know how Nasha's fate became hers. I've thought and thought about it. I've prayed about it. But the gods give me no answer."

"Perhaps there is none," Thothmes said slowly. "Perhaps the gods always intended such a fate for my mother and somehow when you touched Nasha you saw her instead. They look very alike, you know."

"Perhaps," was all Huy said, but privately he knew such a conclusion was wrong and that the truth would come to him one day. He did not know why, but he dreaded that day.

Nakht had hired thirty professional mourners to wail and cast dirt on their heads as they followed his wife's mummified body from the verge of the river to the tomb's entrance, but she had been well liked among her own noble circle and at least four times that number of women, her friends and the wives of her husband's aides and administrators, wore blue, the colour of grief, and added their formal keening to the mourners' cacophony.

Huy walked with the members of the family. Behind them snaked the mourners, relatives, friends, and at the rear the host of servants who would erect tents, carry water, and prepare food for the three days of ritual feasting that would follow the interment. Waiting by the open entrance of the tomb was a cluster of priests and women who would represent the gods who had been present at the burial of Osiris. Huy, already thirsty and hot from a high sun beating down unmercifully on unprotected heads, thought how ghoulish they looked, particularly the men wearing the masks of the four sons of Horus—hawk, ape, jackal, and man. The sem priest, wrapped in a cow's skin, was already lying on a couch pretending to be asleep, pretending to be the lifeless corpse about to be reanimated. The cortège came to a halt. The coffin was propped upright beside the tomb entrance and opened to reveal the tightly bandaged form within. The Kher-heb, the chief funeral priest, began to sprinkle water around the foot of the coffin. The ceremony had begun.

It was Huy's first funeral, and for a while he forgot his physical discomfort as well as his own sorrow as he watched the intricate rite being performed. Only once, as Thothmes approached the remains of his mother in his role of the Sa-mer-ef, the Son who Loves, and gently touched her mouth and eyes with the Ur-hekau, the prescribed metal chisel, to reopen both, did Huy have to fight against his tears. After Thothmes, a sem priest repeated the gestures with his little finger and then with a bagful of pieces of red carnelian to restore colour to the woman's lips and eyelids.

The sacrifices of the cow, two gazelles, and the ducks did not particularly bother Huy. They were offerings to the deceased, food to be buried with her as well as bread, wine, and oil. The blood quickly sank, steaming, into the surrounding sand and the ritual went on.

At last, as the sun was setting behind them, Nefer-Mut was carried down into the cool dampness of her final home and the family followed her, laying on her the wreaths Anuket had prepared and saying their farewells. Huy did not join them. This tribute was for them alone, so he stood with the other tired members of the funeral, watching the white tents unfold across the desert and the smoke from the cooking fires spiral straight up into the motionless air. He was hungry. Soon he would sit on cushions with Thothmes and drink wine, eat roast goose and figs and warm bread dripping in butter, while the pall that had hung over all of them for seventy days was suddenly lifted and they could laugh again. The detritus from the feast would be buried close to the tomb, as was the custom, and then they would make their way to the rising river and the barges and the city beyond.

12

The school had emptied at the beginning of Mesore, a month before the Inundation. Huy had used the legitimate excuse of Nefer-Mut's funeral not to go home to Hut-herib. He was used to the indulgence of silence and peace behind the ordinary comings and goings of temple life, and he looked forward to long days spent with Thothmes and his family; and indeed, after the interment, the invitations resumed. Yet Huy, boating in the cooler evenings with Thothmes, sharing meals with the four of them in the lamplit elegance of the dining hall, joking with Nasha when he met her as she went to and fro on her household errands, detected a new and wounding distance between them and himself. Outwardly they were as easy and affectionate with him as ever. Huy could not put his finger on one moment, one gesture, one expression, and say there! There it is! But he felt a tiny crack, with himself standing on one side and they on the other. Searching the wholly groundless guilt he felt because he had been unable to save his friend's mother's life, he wondered if the sense of detachment came from his own imagination; but he felt it as soon as he entered the house, and sometimes, in the split second before he was greeted, he fancied that he saw a coldness on the face coming towards him.

Thothmes, however, was as loving as ever. The bond that held him and Huy together was too old and too strong to be broken, and Huy was reluctant to have his suspicion confirmed by airing it to his friend. After all, Nakht still clapped him on the back and gave him fatherly advice on everything from his school work to understanding the military tactics he and Thothmes were now studying. Nasha still teased him. Anuket still smiled at him and wriggled aside on her reed mat in the herb room so that he could sit beside her and watch her latest creation take shape under her graceful little fingers. Yet the aura of almost imperceptible sexual taunting had gone. It had caused Huy physical discomfort and the same sort of mental confusion he was now experiencing with regard to the family's attitude towards him. All the same, he missed it. Sometimes it had seemed to him like a subtle game that he did not know how to play. He was in no doubt that he loved her still, loved to see the mute harmony of her movements, hear the high timbre of her voice, lose himself in the play of sunlight on her gleaming black hair. He did his best to cloak his emotion more carefully than he had before. Anuket seemed not to notice.

During his solitary wanderings through the deserted school precinct his mind turned often to the fourth part of the Book. Thoth's words had of course sunk into his memory at once and could be retrieved at any time, but Huy found himself more often pondering those snatches of the accompanying commentary he could remember. The two scrolls had contained a straightforward account of Ra-Atum's birthing of the world, but the anonymous commentator had dared to extrapolate, or perhaps simply cogitate, on what was written. Huy returned to the scrolls, sitting under the Tree, Thoth's words unread but the commentary spread open across his knees.

Atum is the all-encompassing author of entirety, weaving everything into the fabric of reality . . .

The womb of rebirth is wisdom. The conception is silence . . .

Atum is first, the Cosmos is second, and man is third. Atum is One, the Cosmos is One, and so is man, for like the Cosmos he is a whole made up of different diverse parts. Atum made man to govern with him, and if man accepts this function fully, he becomes a vehicle of order in the Cosmos.

To Huy this idea seemed blasphemous. To govern with Atum—did this imply equality with him? Was this the will of Atum, that man should be as he is, a god? And how could man, turbulent, self-seeking man, scarcely able to order his own soul, become a vehicle of order in the cosmos? Perhaps Atum meant only a part of man. Huy knew the components of a human being: a physical body, a shadow, a ka, a soul, a heart, a khu-spirit, a power, and a name. Which component was untainted enough to govern the cosmos with Atum?

But perhaps the writer did not mean man as a whole, Huy's thoughts ran on as he paced the hot, quiet passages and rooms smelling of dry papyrus and ink. *Perhaps he meant a few chosen ones like Imhotep, gifted and all-wise. The priests keep telling me that I am the Chosen One, that Atum wishes me to unravel his will. Is his will the ordering of the cosmos by me?* At this he had laughed aloud, the sound echoing back from the far wall of the passage running behind the temple sanctuary where he had been wandering. "Now that really is blasphemy," he said aloud, and turned his interior attention to the difficult chariot manoeuvre he had been practising with his grumpy and unco-operative horse. But the idea came back to haunt and unsettle him in the nights that followed, and at last he approached the High Priest with a request to read the final part of the Book.

"Are you sure you are ready? Are all the previous eight scrolls secure in your memory and your understanding?" Ramose asked him, his glance keen. Huy knew what the man was seeing. The morning was already breathless with heat, the sunlight white and relentless, and the marks of a hot, restless night were on Huy's face.

"Yes, they are," Huy told him, with more confidence than he felt. "Today is the ninth day of Paophi. Today I am fifteen years old. It seems appropriate."

Ramose smiled. "Your birthday!" he exclaimed. "With Harmose away there have not been any reports or reminders concerning his charges. Nothing has come for you from Hut-herib, either, to remind me, but it will, won't it?"

Huy nodded. "There will be a scroll from my father and a gift from Methen. Nakht has invited me to a feast, just the family and myself."

"You have become estranged from your own blood ties, Huy? How many years has it been since you went back to Hut-herib? Do you at least write to your parents?"

"I am a dutiful son in that regard," Huy replied uncomfortably. "My life here has put an abyss between us. I no longer know what I would say to them if we sat down together."

"I suppose it was inevitable." Ramose passed a hand over his brown skull. "But Huy, do not invest all your love and loyalty in Nakht and his children. In one year you will be leaving the school. Your skills are such that you could obtain a good position as a scribe with any noble household. Nakht will not hire a friend of his son's to be a servant."

No, he won't, Huy thought mutinously, *but he is Governor of the sepat. He might very well give me an administrative position under him. After all, have I not become his unofficially adopted child through the passage of time alone? He loves me. I know he does. Anyway, he would not see me separated from Thothmes.*

"I understand this, Master," Huy said. "But I do not think about it. I have a year to make plans for my future."

"Very well. I shall have the scrolls sent to you, and I shall go and pray." His lips twisted wryly. "You show no signs of madness, my dear Huy, but who knows what the final reading might bring to you? Your gift has remained dormant, has it not?"

"Yes, and I thank the gods for it!" Huy exploded.

Ramose's eyes narrowed. "Am I seeing a return of that arrogant, wilful child deposited on me so long ago? Take care, Huy. The gods will not be mocked."

Huy flushed. "Forgive me, High Priest, Greatest of Seers," he said, giving Ramose his formal titles. "I do not mean to mock. The gift has been a heavy burden, and at present I am glad that I have not felt its weight for some time." He bowed. After a moment Ramose returned the gesture and strode away, and Huy began to walk towards the courtyard that held the Ished Tree.

Why am I suddenly so angry? he wondered. *The High Priest's reprimand was gentle and I deserved it. No, I am angry and afraid because of what he said about Nakht, who of course will not hire me as a scribe, who perhaps will not give me work at all, and I dare not trespass on my friendship with Thothmes to ask him his opinion of my future. Return to Hut-herib?* He shuddered. *Oh, Atum, do anything with me but that!*

He was approaching the guard on the door to the courtyard when all at once his true purpose coalesced in his mind. *Ever since Nefer-Mut's death I have been at war with myself,* he thought, horrified. *But no—this dilemma has much older roots. It goes all the way back to my conversation with the Rekhet about my virginity, my passion for Anuket that never seems to fade. I hope the gift in me is dead. I intend to secure good work in some rich man's house if Nakht will not give me some small share in governing the sepat, and then I will ask Nakht for a marriage contract between myself and Anuket. If he will not grant it I will persuade her to leave his house with me. I will give her my virginity, and so will destroy the thing I carry with me everywhere.*

Anger and mutiny rose in him like vomit so that for some moments he could not take a breath. He came to himself to find the guard peering at him anxiously.

"Master, are you ill?" the man asked. Huy shook his head and indicated the door; he did not trust himself to speak. The guard turned. The door swung open, and as Huy moved stiffly inside he heard his own laughter inside his head. *Govern the cosmos? I am a worm, Atum. A coward. An arrogant, selfish child. I will fight to forget the glorious power of Paradise. I will put my nose to a lotus bloom and call its aroma intoxicating. I will make my fate my own.*

The Ished Tree was bereft of blooms at this time of the year, yet it still exuded the combined odour of wholesome sweetness and rot with which Huy had become familiar. He went and stood under it, gazing up into its dense foliage, a sudden wrench of loss twisting his heart. He did not reverence it, but Ramose did, coming in behind Huy, bowing to the Tree, and placing a casket on the small area of grass where Huy customarily sat. "Perhaps the will of Atum will be revealed to you today, Huy," Ramose said, and left. The door closed quietly behind him. Sick in spirit, tumultuous with guilt, grief, and a sense of impending liberation, Huy sank cross-legged onto the ground, murmuring the scribes' prayer before realizing that the well-worn words were out of his mouth.

Carelessly flipping open the chest, he extracted the two scrolls, his innate reverence for the ancient papyrus making his hands gentle although he felt far from respectful. One scroll was a darker beige than the other, and very thin. Huy unrolled it quickly. *So this is the fifth and last portion,* he thought in the moment before his gaze fell to the familiar beauty of the hieroglyphs. *After this I am free of the Tree. No matter what I read I can tell the priests that it is incomprehensible, that years will pass before enlightenment comes to me, and gradually all of them will forget me.* Anger and a strange despair still simmered in his heart. He half expected the Tree to sense his emotion, its leaves to whisper admonitions and accusations, but there was only the common rustle of a dry wind in its branches. Huy blew out his lips and looked down.

I Thoth, the Tongue of Atum, now give the mighty gift of these few words.

I Thoth, the Reckoner of Time for gods and men, now speak of the death of Time.

I Thoth, that came into being at the beginning, now speak of the end.

I Thoth, guide of heaven, earth, and the First Duat, am now the Bridge of Atum.

Bridge between what and what? Huy wondered. *Not between Atum and anything, because Thoth says that he is a bridge of Atum, not for him. Atum is not crossing this bridge to go anywhere.* He read on.

This is the will of Atum. You will go around the entire Two Skies. You will circumambulate the Two Banks.

You will become one with the perishable stars. You will become a ba.

You will journey to the Land of the West. You will inhabit the Fields of Yaru in peace until Turnface carries you away.

Free course is given to you by Horus. You flash as the lone star in the midst of the sky. You

have grown wings as a great-breasted falcon, as
·a hawk seen in the evening traversing the sky.
You will cross the firmament by the waterway of
Ra-Harakhti. Nut will put her hand on you.

Thoth had added a final declaration.

I Thoth, Lord of all Judging, have written this Book
as Atum has instructed me. Let the reader of these
words now put on his sa, for the ending of the Book
curves back to the beginning, and he who has lifted
his eyes from my work cannot see the power of the
double heka in which he sits. Let the wisdom
of enlightenment fall on him, or let the darkness of
confusion cloud his khu forever.

Huy let the thin scroll roll up, and with a stab of fear
he glanced about him. *I have no sa,* he thought anxiously.
*I don't even know what a sa is. Is it an amulet or a spell or
simply a state of mind? I feel no double heka here, at least
nothing like the heka that oppresses me in Thoth's temple at
Khmun. Only the embracing magic of the Tree and the
prickle of power from the papyrus under my hand. I have
no idea what Atum's words mean, but I understand the
final warning. I must fight for enlightenment or my spirit
will suffer a long confusion. What does the commentary
say?* The second scroll was as thin as the first. He unrolled
it quickly, desperate to shed some light on what seemed
nonsense to him. *It is as though I am opening the first part
of the Book for the first time,* his thoughts ran on. *I am
struggling in an ocean of perplexity coupled with the anger
and resentment that will not go away.*

But he found no comfort in the unknown sage's caution.

If you shut your soul up in your body and demean yourself, saying, I cannot know, I am afraid, I cannot ascend to heaven; then what have you to do with Atum? Wake up your sleeping soul. Why give yourself to death when you could be immortal? You are drunk with ignorance of Atum. It has overpowered you, and now you are vomiting it up. Empty yourself of darkness and you will be filled with light.

He describes my inner turmoil exactly, Huy thought bitterly. *Every step of this journey into the Book has been a struggle to apprehend, to understand, to try to create a whole out of pieces of obscurity. My soul is in revolt and I am tired.* He read on.

Immerse yourself in Atum and recognize the purpose of your birth. Ascend to him who sent this Book. Those that bathe themselves in Atum find true knowledge and become complete.

There was no more.

Huy flung the papyrus down. The sage had failed him at the last. He had not ventured to explain Thoth's cryptic sentences. Perhaps he had not understood them either. *Or perhaps,* Huy thought, *he understood them only too well and saw in his conclusions a great danger for the next reader, or even for Egypt herself. Did confusion cloud his khu until he was driven mad, or did he walk away from the Book with the will of Atum clear in his mind?* Closing his eyes, Huy leaned back against the warm bole of the Tree, slowly repeating Thoth's words to himself. Already they were etched into his consciousness. Aware that the god had said that the end curved back to the beginning, he began to recite the Book in its entirety aloud, linking each phrase into a seamless whole. It took a long time, but when he fell silent and the soft noises of the Tree flowed in to fill the vacancy his voice had left, he was no nearer to learning the will of Atum than he had been years ago. No inspiration burst upon him. No glimmer of comprehension fluttered on the periphery of his mind. Laying the scrolls back in the casket, he picked it and himself up, went to the door, and knocked to be released. His head had begun to ache with a dull, enervating pounding, and all he wanted to do was sleep.

He entered the High Priest's spacious cell to return the scrolls. Ramose got up from behind his desk, picking up a small leather bag as he did so and holding it out to Huy. "You look exhausted," he commented kindly. "We will not talk of what you have discovered just yet. Go and rest. The Rekhet has sent this to you, for your birthday." Huy took the bag and thanked him, glad that he would not be forced to endure a long conversation with the man. Bowing, he left and made his way to his cell, grateful for the atmosphere of unburdened silence imbuing the empty halls.

His courtyard was, of course, deserted, the grass long and lush, for the gardeners still watered it. Huy sank onto its fragrant greenness, just out of reach of the fine spray emitted by the fountain, and pulled open the bag's drawstring. Inside was a sheet of papyrus and something wrapped in linen. He withdrew them and read the note. It had been penned in running hieratic script by a firm, unique hand.

Master Huy, I have made you a sa for your Naming Day. Seeing that you are a decidedly ignorant young man, you will not know that the sa is an amulet of supreme protection although you will be familiar with its use in the hieroglyphic alphabet. It represents a reed mat, rolled up and folded in two and tied at the lower end to make a shape similar to that of an ankh. Hentis ago the folded mat was carried by marsh dwellers to place around their necks and buoy them should they fall into deep water. Cattle herders used it to protect themselves against sharp horns. You are in deep water, I sense, and the sharp horns of anger and disillusionment are pricking you. Place the amulet around your own neck and visit me within three days. I have come to my city house from my estate in order to speak with you.

Huy unfolded the linen. The charm itself had been wrought in electrum, the purplish sheen of the gold glinting in the high sunlight. The chain was silver. It had no counterpoise. Huy put it on at once. It lay lightly between his nipples, and at once Huy felt its soothing influence. Spreading his right hand, he gazed at the Rekhet's other work, the ring amulets. The lapis eyes of the tiny frog glowed deeply blue, and the golden feathers of the human-headed hawk charm folded in exquisite detail along its bird spine. *She knows me well. She is my friend, but she is also implacable in her desire to serve the gods and see me achieve whatever destiny they have appointed for me.* A wave of depression hit him. Gathering up the papyrus, linen, and bag, he plunged into the coolness of his cell and lowered himself onto his cot. Every muscle began to loosen and his headache began to ease. With his left hand curled around the sa, he fell into a deep sleep.

On the following evening he ordered out a litter and had himself carried to the Rekhet's house. Although the day had been unbearably hot, he had taken out a chariot and the horse that never wanted to behave and had spent several hours on the manoeuvres of battle he was required to learn before classes reconvened in Tybi. He had washed both chariot and horse, fed and watered the animal, bathed himself thoroughly, then found he could not rest during the afternoon when a great somnolence always fell over both city and temple. Instead he sat in the shade of one of the sycamores surrounding the sacred lake and let the words of the Book roll slowly through his mind. The language was beautiful, the concepts he had already grasped both sophisticated and sublime. But there was no coherence in them for him, no great conclusion. They were like the mathematical equations the architect set his pupils. Worked out correctly, the answers were satisfyingly simple and could be practically applied. *Might there in fact be a practical application to the Book of Thoth?* Huy wondered for the first time. Something not at all abstract? Something encompassing the material as well as the divine? He played with the idea for some time, but having no clue as to how to put the whole together, he gave up.

Who was the "you" Thoth was addressing? "You will become . . . You will go around . . . You flash . . . You have grown wings . . ." The terrible Turnface was the ferryman who carried those justified from the area of Paradise called the Fields of Yaru to their eternal home. Could "you" mean everyone justified? Then how did the last scroll connect with the first—the nature and metamorphosis of Atum?

After eating bread and a salad of the earliest greens, he set out for the Rekhet's house. The city was beginning to come to life again after the torpor of the day. As Ra began to lip the western horizon and the stale summer air held the faintest promise of coolness, the stall keepers set out their wares, the soldiers began to saunter towards the beer houses, and loose groups of strollers wandered the streets, chattering and laughing. Whores, looking fresher than the noblewomen passing in their litters, emerged from the shade and strutted towards the seedier areas of Iunu. After the quiet emptiness of the school Huy drank in the optimistic bustle. He was not due at Nakht's house for dinner until well after full dark had fallen. He had plenty of time both to enjoy his passage through the city and to share wine with Henenu. In spite of his state of mind, he had missed her.

The litter-bearers were clearly indignant at having to walk through such a poor area of the city. Setting Huy down outside Henenu's cowrie-encrusted wall, they squatted together in its lengthening shadow and Huy approached the servant beyond, at the door. This time he was greeted with a smile and escorted at once to the pleasant little garden behind the house.

The Rekhet was sitting on a low stool in the middle of her tiny vegetable patch, bare of growth at that time of the year. As Huy came towards her, she rose with a smile. "I don't know why I am compelled to contemplate this naked soil," she said as she reached up to kiss his cheek. "In fact I don't know why I plant anything here at all. An old habit learned from my father. He used to pace across his arouras, sifting the earth, long before the sowing was due to begin." Her eyes scanned his face, and presently she nodded. "I was right," she went on. "Come into the house and tell me about it."

She walked away, the shells on her leather belt and around her ankles clicking against each other as she moved, and Huy followed her. He had not been inside her dwelling before and was not surprised to find it very sparsely furnished, the few chairs plain, the walls whitewashed and unadorned. For the first time in ages Huy remembered his paints, and how as a child he would stand outside his father's walls happily making pictures on them for hours. Henenu indicated a chair. The table beside it held a clay cup of milk and a dish of dried figs.

"Undo your braid," she ordered. Huy obeyed, pulling off the small frog clasp and unwinding his thick plait. Henenu clapped her hands. The same woman who had served them soup on Huy's last visit appeared and bowed. "Bring oil and a comb," the Rekhet told her. "Now Huy, I am going to oil and comb your hair and you will talk to me. The milk and figs are for you, if you are hungry." Huy was thirsty. He drank the milk but declined the figs. At once the servant reappeared, set a phial of fragrant oil on the table, and went away. Henenu moved behind Huy, out of his sight.

"I must thank you for this sa," Huy said, his hand
going to the amulet on his breast. "How did you know
that I needed it?"

"I had a feeling," she answered briskly. "The design
is simple. It did not take long to make. How did you
know that you needed it?"

"Thoth told the reader of the Book to put on his
sa. I did not know what a sa was." He found himself
reciting the few pungent sentences of the fifth part
and the pieces of the commentary he could
remember. As he did so he felt her hands on his head,
her touch firm but gentle, loosening his hair. The
comb began to glide through it. At once a sense of
peace stole over Huy.

"It falls below your shoulders," Henenu remarked.
"It must be very hot. You do not wear it long merely
to hide the scar, do you? What is your reason?"

"I'm not sure," Huy confessed. "It is partly because
I don't want to look like a priest, with a fully shaven
skull, or a Seer for that matter."

"Might it also be a symbol of your virginity?" she
murmured. Huy stiffened. Her grip on his hair
momentarily tightened. The comb slid pleasingly over
his scalp. "Let us not bandy words, my wicked young
charge," she continued. "You know perfectly well that
many of your fellow students have already enjoyed their
first sexual encounters. You are now fifteen—almost a
man in the eyes of the law. Your state of innocence has
begun to haunt you. You want an end to it. Suddenly
you have become rebellious, wanting what other men
have, wanting a chance to choose a wife, but most of all
wanting to rid yourself of the gift the gods gave you."

Huy felt coolness as she poured a few drops of oil on the top of his head and began to draw it through his tresses with her fingers. At once his nostrils were assailed by a sweet, heavy aroma that went to his head immediately, making him sleepy yet alert and filling his limbs with an agreeable weight. "Henenu, you are drugging me. What is that odour?"

"Reremet," she replied promptly. "I crush the fruit and add it to the oil when I want someone to relax. Often people come to me in a state of agitation so great that I cannot work for them. A few whiffs of the reremet calms them."

Huy had heard of the mandrake with its roots in the shape of a man with a penis. His friends at the school had made jokes about its aphrodisiac properties. "I am not agitated," he said indignantly.

"Yes you are. You are a little maelstrom, Huy. Close your eyes and your mouth and let me speak." Huy did as he was told, giving himself over to the wonderful lassitude of his body and mind yet fully aware of the sharpness of his mental faculties. The comb continued its slow, rhythmic course from his crown down to his shoulder blades. "It will be better for you if you realize that for you there are no large choices in life," Henenu went on. "You may decide what to eat, what to wear, whom to befriend, but your journey was chosen for you by the gods and by you when you agreed to read the Book. Protesting your youth and ignorance will not do!" she said firmly as Huy opened his mouth. "I have heard that argument. Discard it. It avails you nothing. It is wasted words. Understand that you may try to take a wife, sleep with a whore, bury yourself in whatever anonymity you can find, but your sex will not respond. It will refuse your bidding. The sooner you accept that Atum rules your fate, the sooner you will achieve the peace that eludes you."

"But even the High Priest had no answer to the question of my virginity and the loss of the gift," Huy said dully. "Neither do you, Rekhet. Some Seers produce children and keep their gift. Some do not."

"And you wish to be one who does not," Henenu retorted. "You are close to hating the god who commanded this for you. You have decided to beg Nakht for a contract with Anuket. He will not grant it, partly because he desires a nobleman for his daughter, but mainly because he has a healthier fear of the god's anger than you. He wants a favourable weighing, particularly since the beautification of his wife. But go ahead and try, foolish one. Be rebuffed. Find another girl to wed. It will not matter."

"I think the gift is dead in me anyway," Huy said sullenly.

"You lie. Nakht told me what you Saw as his wife died. The gift is in abeyance, that is all. Atum is patient. He waits for you to commit yourself totally to the Book, and until you do, your khu will surely be full of the confusion of which you spoke. Ah, Huy!" The comb hit the table with a click and she began to expertly rebraid his hair. "Some great work waits for you in a future that I cannot see. Something vital to Egypt. Your courage must not fail, for if it does then Egypt will go down into chaos!" Huy swung round, astonished. The netted lines of her face were distorted with emotion, her eyes narrowed. "I do not lie. I do not attempt to control you. I am telling you what I most strongly sense when I am near you. I choke on the power of it. It has nothing to do with the hosts of Khatyu who attack and trouble those who come to me for exorcism. They throng you. They do not want your destiny fulfilled. But they cannot touch you. This is something else, something higher and more dire." She placed both oil-slicked hands on his cheeks. "You have Shai. You have a mighty destiny. What is a moment of orgasm compared to that?"

Huy pulled himself free. "I have no idea, seeing that I have never experienced orgasm," he said thickly. "And if you are right, Rekhet, I never will. But I swear I intend to try!" He stood. "I love you. You are my friend, one of my counsellors, you have been so kind to me—but you are ruthless also. I have done all that I have been commanded to do, but I am tired of it all, the Book is nothing but a jumble in my head, the heka is too much to bear, I stand at the threshold of my life, and I want my freedom!"

"You stood at that threshold when Sennefer's throwing stick found its mark," she broke in quietly. "You are the Twice Born, Huy, whether you like it or not. Freedom belonged to the first life, the life that was snuffed out. Servitude to Atum and to him alone is the responsibility of the second. He may choose to lift the burden from you. If he does, it will be his choice, not yours. You have no choices to make." Suddenly she embraced him, her wiry grey hair brushing his neck, her sturdy arms around his waist. "But fight him if you will," she sighed. "To contend with him will be no more than if you were a mouse in the beak of a hawk.

PAULINE GEDGE

Go now. I knew your distress but not its depth. I shall make spells for you. Do not remove the sa."

The heaviness in his legs and arms was subsiding. Without saying more, he gave her a deep reverence and left.

The litter-bearers were asleep, sprawled against the wall that fronted the street so that passersby were stepping over their outstretched legs. Huy roused them peremptorily, told them to carry him to Nakht's house, and climbed into the litter, pulling the curtains closed. The evening held no more delight for him. The tiny space gradually filled with the rather sickly smell of the mandrake in his hair, but its power had dissipated. The men carrying him could not arrive at the Governor's house quickly enough for Huy.

He dismissed them outside Nakht's entrance, greeted Nakht's porter, and strode eagerly towards the house. Full night had fallen, warm and redolent with the mixed aromas of the muddy river water that had begun to lip the street to his rear, the scent of soil that reminded him forcibly of his father, and the welcoming smells of roasting fowl wafting from the kitchens behind the house. Nakht's steward was waiting for him just inside the entrance pillars. With a bow he opened the doors, and with unutterable relief Huy stepped into the lamplight of Nakht's reception hall.

Before he reached the dining hall the steward had alerted the family. One by one they came to kiss him. Nakht took his hand gravely. Nasha tried to lift him off his feet, failed, and punched him on the shoulder. Thothmes embraced him tightly. "Fifteen, dear friend, and we are still together," he said happily. "I miss seeing you during the week. Are you getting lonely, ruling the school all by yourself?"

Anuket came last. Taking Huy's hand, she drew him down and kissed him close to his ear. Then she stepped back, frowning. "Huy, you smell of reremet," she said loudly. "I know it, and its power to seduce. Sometimes I use the stems and leaves in my work. Have you been with a girl tonight?"

Huy was astonished. Anuket was smiling as though she were making a joke, but the fingers still coiled around his had spasmed and her eyes were hard.

"Anuket, you are rude!" her father snapped. "What Huy does beyond these walls is his own affair." But the man looked mildly pleased.

"I have been with my mentor, the Rekhet," Huy said. "I was tense. She combed my hair with mandrake infused in oil, to calm me." Was that a fleeting disappointment on Nakht's face? Huy could not be sure. The expression had come and gone too fast.

Anuket lifted her pretty shoulders and released his hand. "Let's go into the dining hall. The servants are ready to serve the food," was all she said.

Huy had put on the earring Anuket had given him for his last Naming Day and the gesture obviously pleased her. She sat close to him, smiling and talkative for once, even teasing him gently and leaning past him to lift a dish of lentils or honeyed dates. Huy did not know how to respond. Nasha's affectionate jibes always eased and reassured him. Thothmes made fun of him and he of Thothmes in an entirely masculine, impersonal way. But this new Anuket, this young woman breathing wine fumes into his face as her primly clad breast brushed his arm and her huge eyes swam out of focus, so near were they to his, shocked and embarrassed him. Blushing and stuttering, he did not know what to say. He wondered whether she had been drinking much before he arrived. Nakht seemed unusually quiet. He watched his daughter carefully and once or twice seemed about to speak to her, but each time Nasha had interjected with her stream of constant, entertaining gossip and Nakht had sat back. Even though she was at the centre of all his most private fantasies, Huy wanted to shrink from her uncharacteristic behaviour. He was devoutly glad when the meal was over.

They retreated to the reception hall, where more wine had been set out. Nakht took a chair as did Thothmes, but Nasha and Anuket dragged Huy down onto a pile of cushions. Nasha was happily drunk, tickling Huy and laughing at his protestations. Anuket laid her leg against his. Nakht clapped and the steward glided forward out of the shadows. "Bring Huy's gifts," Nakht ordered.

A silence fell. The high double doors stood open and the night breeze funnelled through them, bending the candle flames, fluttering the ankle-length linens of the two who sat, and stirring Anuket's oil-slick hair. With one languid gesture she lifted it from her neck and, tilting her head back, piled it on her crown. The little yellow faience flowers wound into it tinkled against each other. Two of them fell into Huy's lap. "Oh, I am so hot and sweaty!" she declared. "If the river had not begun to flow so swiftly I would take off all my clothes and plunge into the water!"

"Don't be ridiculous!" Nasha retorted. "You hate swimming. And boating too, for that matter. What is wrong with you tonight, Anuket? You can barely sit still."

Anuket sighed ostentatiously and let go her hair. It fell to her back in a perfumed shower. Huy held out the flowers. She shook her head. "I can't be bothered summoning my body servant. You tie them into my hair for me, Huy, would you?"

"No, he certainly would not!" The voice was Nakht's. "Drinking much wine is a pleasant thing, Anuket, but if wine is going to make you behave immodestly then you will be denied it altogether. Forgive my daughter's bad manners, Huy."

Huy, grappling with the disquieting concept of a drunk and unruly Anuket who appeared to be in the grip, not of the ancient water goddess, but of her more recent persona, was saved from replying by the steward's return.

Nasha came unsteadily to her feet. "I shall present them," she said thickly. "First, from father, a really lovely leather belt studded with polished turquoise. And look, Huy! There's a loop for a dagger and another one for a small bag."

The belt was braided at each end for tying. Huy took it and at once his thumbs went to the smoothness of the perfectly matched stones. "This is a magnificent gift, Lord. Thank you!"

"The turquoise is green, signifying health and vitality, dear Huy," Nakht replied. "I am very fond of you and wish you many years of both."

Nasha kept her balance by placing a hand on top of Huy's head as she lowered a pile of linen across his knees. "Four kilts from me," she announced. "Linen of the twelfth grade, edged in gold or silver thread. Yes, they cost me a great deal, so don't rip them. I love you, my almost-brother."

Huy grinned up at her. "I love you also, Nasha, in spite of all the bruises you've given me. Thank you."

"I went to the Street of Leather Workers myself," Anuket broke in loudly and, Huy thought, a little sulkily. "I insisted on watching the craftsman make my gift to you so that the stitches were tiny and tight. Nasha, give him the gloves." Nasha held them out. They were of soft, very supple calf leather complete with wrist guards with a running horse pulling a chariot stamped into the skin. "They are to protect your hands when you drive the chariots," Anuket explained needlessly. "I know you don't have a pair and you won't ask the priests to give you one."

His discomfiture forgotten, Huy leaned over and kissed her damp cheek. "Thank you, my friend," he said, genuinely moved. "Look! They fit me flawlessly." He had drawn them on and was showing her, but unaccountably she moved away.

"Of course they do," she said tartly to no one in particular.

Huy saw Thothmes shrug and roll his eyes. "Last one, Nasha," he said. "Give it to him before you fall down." Thothmes' gift was a casket full of smaller boxes. One contained grains of frankincense, the rarest and most fragrant of sacred smoke. Another was jammed with almonds. Another held pot after pot of scribe's ink. There were also two alabaster phials of kohl, the black powder mixed with gold dust.

Huy laughed in delight and, rising, went and embraced Thothmes. "These are magnificent gifts for a fifteenth Naming Day. I am so grateful to you all and I love you all very much."

Nasha, back on the floor, waved her cup. "A toast to Huy, now embarking on his sixteenth year. Life, health, and prosperity!" Nakht and Thothmes drank with her. Anuket had fallen asleep, an unkempt muddle of tousled hair and wine-stained sheath on the cushions.

Nakht yawned and stood. "I am ready to retire. Nasha, have Anuket carried to her quarters and put to bed. I will deal with her in the morning." Huy bowed to him. As he left, Nasha hauled herself to her feet and called for the servants.

Thothmes took Huy's elbow. "Are you tired, Huy? No? Then let's walk in the garden."

The air seemed cool and fresh after the scent of wax, perfumes, and sweat. The sound of the Inundation could be heard, a constant gurgle of flowing water and a lapping slap as it met the watersteps beyond Nakht's high walls. For a while the two friends strolled in silence. The night was fine. Stars and a half moon filled the paths with grey light.

Thothmes pointed upward. "Look! The Sothis star. How strange that it appears every year at the beginning of the Inundation and I always look for it, but I have no idea when it goes away again." He breathed deeply. "I wish school was in," he went on. "Another three months to wait! Meanwhile I have begun to accompany Father to all his administrative meetings now that I am also fifteen. I take notes, like one of his scribes. Occasionally he actually asks for my opinion on some dispute between farmers or on new policy for the sepat that has come from the One in Weset. I am learning how to be a governor."

Huy was watching his feet, gliding disembodied under him along the ashen path. "You'll make a wonderful governor when Nakht dies. You have all the attributes, Thothmes. You're honest, intelligent, you can be reasonable when you want to be, and above all you love your country. Egypt is everything to you."

"And my dear King, the Mighty Bull," Thothmes said fervently. "Strange to think that he was already our ruling god before I was born. Yes, I think I will be glad to train for the governorship under my father. Do you know yet what you will do, Huy? Will you make your living as a Seer?"

"No!" Huy responded sharply. Then he relented. "I don't know what I shall do, Thothmes, but I do know what I won't do. I won't See for anyone anymore. I want a wholly boring, ordinary life!"

They had reached the gate to the watersteps and, greeting the guard, they slipped through, settling side by side on the top step and watching the dark water swirl below them. Finally Huy broached the subject that had been troubling him. "Thothmes, is something wrong with Anuket?" he asked diffidently. "I thought I knew all of you well. I've seen Anuket full of wine before. Usually she just becomes even more quiet than usual and sits even straighter and then she falls asleep. Tonight she was like . . . like . . ."

"Like a jealous lover?" Thothmes filled in. "Really, Huy, you can be so dense! It was the reremet that did it. For years, yes, years, you've been in love with her, or in lust or whatever. Everyone in the household knows it. You've mooned around her like a besotted suitor for so long that she could never imagine your interest going to someone else." He laughed. "She became complacent, my self-involved little sister. You must admit there have been times when she played with you, tested her power to drive you to distraction, with no real appreciation for what you might be feeling."

"I did wonder sometimes if I was being teased," Huy said. His words were even, but his heart had begun to ache. "Anuket is innocent and modest. She has the reticence of her blood."

"Maybe. But she is also developing the nasty wiles and manipulations of her sex," Thothmes pointed out. "Who better to try them out on but the youth whose adoration is so steady, although he tries to hide it? She is genuinely fond of you, Huy. I mean, look at you! Tall, handsome, accomplished, and kind into the bargain. Not to mention someone with a truly exotic past. And oh so faithful! Tonight her smugness was shaken. She was forced to see you differently, all in the space of one unexpected moment."

"Are you saying that she was jealous?"

Thothmes gave him a level glance, and for the first time Huy saw him as he really was, not the skinny, big-eyed little boy of their childhood together, but a slim, poised young noble whose impulsiveness had become confidence and whose naive eagerness had matured into an informed perception. "Perhaps," he replied. Thothmes opened his arms in a wide gesture of uncertainty. "Perhaps tonight she realized the depth of her affection for you. Perhaps it was nothing but possessiveness. Anyway, Father will discipline her severely tomorrow for her behaviour."

They fell silent. All at once a vision of Ishat's face bloomed in Huy's mind, her features as clear as though she had suddenly appeared before him. *Ishat!* he thought in surprise. *How long has it been since I even remembered that you exist? Yet here you are, and your arrival brings with it the same sense of relief and comfortable familiarity I used to feel whenever you emerged from the orchard with mud on your feet and tangles in your hair. You are a common girl, a servant, but I know that in a similar situation you would have scorned to stoop to Anuket's devious behaviour.* Indeed, imagining Ishat leaning over him with subtle deliberation so that her breast rested against him while she pretended to reach for food gave Huy a surge of distaste. Ishat would have complained loudly that he was lying, that he had not gone to see his mentor, that he had been dallying with some cheap whore and she wished the bitch dead. Then she would have jumped up and strode out of the room in a jealous temper. Ishat would have behaved more . . . more cleanly.

He rose abruptly. "It's late. I must collect my gifts and go, Thothmes. How generous you are, all of you! I have no way to fully show my gratitude."

Thothmes scrambled up beside him and for a moment their eyes met, each face deeply shadowed. "You must forgive her," Thothmes said. "She is standing on the verge of full womanhood. Sometimes she is not very likeable."

Huy did not reply. *Neither is Ishat at times,* his thoughts ran on. *I suppose that she too is fast becoming a woman, yet I cannot imagine her ever being anything other than forthright with her emotions.* Her picture began to fade and at once Anuket was there in his mind's eye, her expression sullen and loose with wine. A pang of sadness shook Huy. He and Thothmes walked back to the house side by side.

On the following morning both the expected message of congratulations from his family and the gift from Methen were delivered to Huy's cell. Huy's father had little to say besides wishing his son long life and happiness, but Huy was shocked at the news that his brother, Heby, was about to be enrolled in the temple school at Hut-herib. "Your brother will celebrate his fourth Naming Day in Mekhir," Hapu had dictated, "and your uncle Ker has agreed to furnish him with the things he will need in order to attend the temple school in our town. We pray that he will do as well at his studies as you."

Slowly Huy let the scroll roll up and sat clutching it, staring out into the brilliance of the day. *Four years old! My brother is four years old,* he mused, stunned, *and I see him in my mind still crawling about the garden naked, babbling nonsense at Hapzefa as she trails behind him. And what of my parents? How have they aged? I do not want to see them. Only Ishat.* He flung the scroll onto the cot behind him. *It hurts me that Ker will lavish all the attention on Heby that he took away from me, that my father's true affection now goes to his second son, that I have become a ghost to my family.* He tried to tell himself, quite truthfully, that it was his own fault, that he had refused, year after year, to go home. But his sense of abandonment remained.

Methen had sent him a stack of papyrus sheets, carefully wrapped in linen and placed in a wooden box for protection. "My gift to you is a practical one," the priest had written. "A student can never find enough papyrus. Use it to write to me." Huy put his nose to it, closing his eyes and inhaling the familiar dry, reedy odour, his heart suddenly full of a longing to see his friend. But not even for a glimpse of Methen or Ishat would he return to Hut-herib. Sliding to the floor, he reached for his palette, set it across his knees, and began to compose a letter to the priest, and gradually the pain in his heart subsided.

13

Seven months after Huy's fifteenth birthday, on the seventeenth day of Pakhons at the beginning of the season of Shemu, Pharaoh Thothmes the Third died. The weather was pleasant. Egypt's little palm-bordered fields were thick with lush green crops. Gardens overflowed with an abundance of flowers and swiftly ripening vegetables. It was the time of fecundity when the country was at its most beguiling, before the harvest and the deadening heat that would accompany it. There was shock as well as genuine sorrow throughout the kingdom, for Thothmes had passed his eightieth year and had sat on the Horus Throne for fifty-four years. Many had come to believe that he was indeed immortal, a god upon earth as well as a great warrior who had spent his youth in conquering an empire for his citizens before he settled down to rule an Egypt basking in the wealth that poured in from his new vassal states.

The school at Iunu was closed during the seventy days of mourning for the Osiris-one. Again Huy found himself wandering the rooms and corridors alone, pursued by the dismal and seemingly endless dirges sung for the dead King by the priests in the inner court of the temple. The news of Pharaoh's death had come to the two young men at dawn. Both had been awake and talking sleepily, but at the sound of the herald's voice ringing out through the courtyard they had scrambled to stand outside their cell along with the others tumbling dishevelled onto the grass. An incredulous silence followed the man's pronouncement. Huy, glancing at Thothmes, saw that his friend had gone pale. "It cannot be!" Thothmes whispered. "He was not even ill. We would have known that!"

"He was very old," Huy said awkwardly. "Many people were born and lived and died while he reigned, and never knew another king. He has gone to sit in the Holy Barque, Thothmes, together with the other gods. You must not grieve for him."

Tears had begun to run down Thothmes' brown cheeks. "I must go home at once. I must put on the blue of mourning and set soil on my head and pray to him, for surely such a mighty and beneficent god does not need to be justified in the Judgment Hall."

Huy thought of that place, of the drafts that blew through it, the glitter of sporadic light on the golden scales. Once more he felt the hot breath of Anubis against his neck. "Is this reality, young Huy, or is it illusion?" the god was asking. Shaking off the vision, Huy put an arm around Thothmes. "The governors of the sepats will be summoned to the funeral," he said. "You will be going south to Weset, Thothmes, and you will be able to watch your hero ferried across the river to the place of the dead. I wonder in what secret cliff his tomb has been prepared."

Thothmes blew his nose on the kilt he had snatched up to cover his nakedness. "It will be the end of Epophi by the time the funeral procession forms," he said thickly. "The harvest will be half over and only one month of school will be left before the Inundation is expected. I wonder if the High Priest will simply cancel all classes until next Tybi. He might as well. The coronation of the Hawk-in-the-Nest will be celebrated immediately following his father's interment." He gave Huy a watery smile. "All I know about him is his name. Isn't that awful of me, Huy? My devotion has belonged solely to the god whose name I bear. I must pack up my things."

And I suppose I ought to go home to Hut-herib, Huy thought dismally. *It is seven months until Tybi rolls around again. By then I shall have passed my sixteenth birthday. Will I be forced to stay on in school until I am seventeen? What shall I do here for seven months?* Thothmes had turned into the cell, and gloomily Huy followed him.

On the morning following the King's burial, the High Priest sent for Huy. It was the third week of Epophi. Everywhere the golden crops were being felled, the cabbages, garlic, onions, juicy cucumbers, and fat yellow melons pulled from thousands of gardens, the grapevines stripped of their weight of dusty purple fruit, and feasters gorged on fresh figs and dates, tiny currants and mulberries, and the sweet fuzziness of golden peaches. Pomegranates were in demand, and cooks held carob pods imported from Rethennu to their noses and inhaled appreciatively before tossing them into their dishes.

The summer had begun to heat towards the furnace of late Shemu and early Akhet, and Huy found himself sweating as he made his way towards Ramose's quarters, but the High Priest rose from beside his cot and came to greet Huy with his usual cool affability, his long white sheath unstained, his hennaed palm dry as it touched Huy's shoulder. "Tomorrow our new King will be crowned," he said. "Temples everywhere will be in festivity, including this one. Would you like beer, Huy? Or water?"

Huy shook his head. "I need to immerse myself in the river, Master, but its level is very low. The bath-house will have to suffice. What do you know of our new ruler?"

Ramose indicated a stool and Huy sat. "Prince Amunhotep will be the second of that name to inherit the Horus Throne. He is twenty-two years old, a man in the full vigour of his maturity. His skill at horse-manship earned him the charge of his father's stables, and at seventeen Thothmes put the chief base and dockyards of the navy at Perunefer under him. He rows well, and hunts, and his prowess at archery is unrivalled." Ramose smiled at Huy's hesitant expression. "He has been aiding his father in government and learning statecraft for the last two years, while Thothmes was ailing," he added. "We must hope that he commands as great an intellect as his father's. Time will tell. His mother was Queen Meryet-Hatshepset, a rather stupid woman, but Thothmes chose his tutors well. The Prince's lifelong friend Kenamun is a wise and moderate young man and will undoubtedly be a positive influence on our new Pharaoh."

"You know much, Master!" Huy exclaimed, and Ramose laughed.

"It is the business of every High Priest to glean as much information as possible regarding those set in authority over us," he said frankly. "The course of Egypt's history is often swayed by the servants of her gods—especially by the High Priest of Amun at Weset. He is able to exert a subtle power over the decisions of the Horus Throne. However," he finished briskly, "it is your future we must discuss." Retreating to his couch, he took the chair beside it and crossed his legs. "I do not want you to waste another year here. I have arranged for your education to continue so that when you turn sixteen, in three months' time, you will be ready to take up the position of scribe here in the temple. Too many weeks have already been wasted with mourning our beloved King."

Huy felt himself go cold. "I am to sit in the classroom alone with my teachers?" he managed. "And the architect, he will come here especially for me?"

"Certainly. You will also continue your lessons in military tactics, the use of weapons, and the use of the chariot."

"And afterwards you want me to remain here, as a scribe."

"I see that the idea does not appeal to you," Ramose said dryly. "Let me speak bluntly. You have been educated at the temple's expense. For that alone you owe me consideration, but I would not be so niggardly as to claim payment for it at this late date. No, Huy, I have plans for you. You possess the Book of Thoth, in your mind. You do not yet understand it, but one day you will." He leaned forward, placing his jewelled fingers together, and to an increasingly alarmed Huy there was something mildly threatening in the gesture. "You are the Twice Born," Ramose continued. "You have the gift of Seeing, and of diagnosing and healing too, I think. Atum has been kind in allowing these things to slumber in you for a while. As a student you are of little use to him. But soon you will be free of the restrictions of the classroom. Then the gifts will waken. When they do, you will need my guidance, mine and the Rekhet's. I want you for my personal scribe. You must learn of the Egypt of today if you are to influence the Egypt of tomorrow. I receive correspondence from the High Priests of every temple, from governors and administrators, army commanders and both Viziers. You will learn, and meanwhile your reputation as a Seer will slowly grow."

"Master, what are you saying?" Huy blurted. "You will control my life completely whether I will it or not? You imagine that the gift will come back to me and you will control that also? Why?"

"Because a man who has returned from the dead with the power Atum has given you may become an invaluable adviser to the god even now preparing to sit on the Horus Throne," Ramose answered bluntly. "Do not mistake me, Huy. I have no wish to rule Egypt through you. That would be truly evil. But through you the wishes of the gods can be conveyed to Pharaoh directly. I believe that this is your destiny."

"That may or may not be true," Huy answered carefully. "Such thoughts belong to the future.

I am well aware of the great debt I owe to you, Master, in nurturing me and providing for my education. I trust I have not disappointed you or abused your care for me. But I would like to leave the temple and seek my employment elsewhere. I need a change. You have given me the great skills of a scribe. I want to use them in the service of a secular household." He spread his hands. "In the temple I am reminded daily of what happened to me. I would like to lead a more normal life for a while." He knew that he must not say the words that would hurt and alarm this good man: *I want to marry. I want Anuket. I want Nakht to give me employment so that my childhood may truly fade and be lost in the past.*

"I know. But such an arrangement may not be best for you." Ramose spoke gently and, getting up, went and knelt before Huy, taking both hands in his own. "Go to the bathhouse and have a servant wash you, Huy. Then rest. Think about what I have said. Ask yourself what you owe to Egypt. Get up tomorrow morning and take your palette into the schoolroom. Your teachers will be waiting for you. Visit the Rekhet if you wish, but try not to fret."

Huy withdrew his hands. "I owe a large debt to both you and the Rekhet," he acknowledged. "I don't want to seem ungrateful. Yet is it so wrong to desire a life outside these walls? Can I not serve Egypt just as well beyond the sacred lake, as my fellow students will do?"

He did not go to the bathhouse. Entering his cell, he flung himself onto his couch, curling his knees to his chin in a gesture of defensiveness. *I owe Egypt nothing.*

Nothing! My father groans and sweats for every bowl of lentils my mother places before him. The son of one of Egypt's nobles ruined my life. I have existed here in Ra's temple solely through the good graces of the High Priest. I have worked hard at my studies lest I fail and be sent back to a peasant's town in disgrace. I owe no one anything. Anger began to replace the self-pity that had been rising in him, and he turned onto his back, clasping his hands behind his head. *I will not be used,* he vowed. *Not by Ramose or Henenu, not even by you, great Atum. I will seize the remainder of my education and then leave this place.* He did not sleep. He stared unseeingly at the whitewashed ceiling above him while the sun reached its zenith and the air around him pulsed with heat.

The High Priest had obviously made all his plans before he spoke to Huy, for when Huy entered the schoolroom on the following morning they were all there waiting for him: his teacher of academics, the architect, the general in charge of imparting military life and tactics, and the weapons and chariots officer. Huy bowed to them.

"We have a mere three months to make up for all the time lost," his teacher said without preamble. "You are entirely capable of leaving this school with the highest of honours and good recommendations from each of us, Huy, providing you dedicate yourself to nothing but work. I am sure you don't want to be imprisoned here for yet another year!" He beamed at Huy and the others laughed.

They don't know, Huy thought as he smiled back politely. *Ramose has not told them that he plans to*

*imprison me here indefinitely. They believe that they are
doing a special favour for the Chosen One. Ah gods. How
can I be sick of life at fifteen?*

"I am indeed prepared to work hard, Master," he
replied. "Tell me how you have planned my days."

The man consulted the wax tablet on the table
beside him. "In the mornings you and I will continue
our study of history, geography, mathematics, and the
religious and secular ordering of Egypt past and
present. You will learn the responsibilities of a good
scribe—we have not yet covered that subject in class.
You will take dictations. You will use your evenings to
memorize what I have dictated, for testing the next
day. In the early afternoon you will study under the
architect. You will not go to the afternoon sleep.
Instead you will be learning more of the administration
of our army and navy and more of good military tactics.
In the cool of the evening you will go to the training
ground for practice with bow, sword, spear, and
chariot." He glanced up, eyebrows raised. "Do you
have any questions?"

"Only one, Master. I dine often at the home
of my friend Thothmes. Shall I be permitted to
continue this?"

"I reserve my permission until I have assessed your
progress," the man replied. "Now we will begin.
Where is your palette?" The other men were leaving.

"I did not expect to study today," Huy said lamely.
"I will fetch it at once."

The teacher was already settling himself on a chair
beside the basket that contained all his scrolls. "Do so.
And be quick—time passes."

For the first month Huy fell onto his couch each night exhausted, his head bursting, his body aching, and each morning he was forced to deliberately gather up the shreds of his will and weave a new, grim determination to exceed his instructors' expectations. It was not that he found learning and memorizing difficult; indeed, much of what he was being taught intrigued him. The maze of trade routes connecting Egypt to her subjugated states and to the rest of the civilized world, the mechanics of construction in stone that differed so drastically from that of mud bricks, the use of Shock Troops, boat building—it was as though at last he was drinking knowledge at a pace just within the limits of his capability, but that pace strained his mind and his muscles.

As he began the second month in a furnace heat that drained all volition from man and beast, the pace seemed to quicken, but Huy had found his stride. He gave no thought to the impending Inundation. His sleep was immediate, deep, and dreamless. But as the facts, figures, equations, and concepts grew more complex, he became convinced that he was being forced to learn far beyond the usual requirements for passage from the school into the world. He remembered Ramose's comment about an adviser to the god sitting on the Horus Throne, but he had neither the time nor the energy to roll it about in his consciousness. His tutors loomed like giants, filling every hour with their presence. His body no longer ached and he felt in command of his mind, but he finished his days too drained to say his prayers.

At the end of the second month he received permission to spend one precious evening at Nakht's house. At once he sent a servant to inquire of Nakht whether he might join the family for a meal. The man returned several hours later and bowed. "The noble Nakht will be very pleased to see Master Huy on the first day of Paophi," was the reply, and suddenly Huy woke to an awareness of the world outside his walls. Thoth had come and gone. Isis had begun to cry and the country had celebrated the rise of the river with the usual fervour. A humidity tinged the air, and with it came clouds of blackflies and mosquitoes. The Feast of the Great Manifestation of Osiris, held on the twenty-second day of Thoth, had come and gone. It was the thirtieth day of Thoth. Tomorrow would be the first day of Paophi, his last month of studies, and his sixteenth birthday would arrive on the ninth. Huy took a deep breath as he stood in his cell at dawn. The time had come to speak to Nakht.

Yet he moved towards his tiring chest with a curious reluctance. He knew he must choose his best kilt, one of the ones Nasha had given him. He had grown out of the shirt Hapzefa had made for him years ago, but he had a white tunic of good grade that one of the priests had not needed. He must wash and oil and braid his long hair, ring his eyes with kohl, try to squeeze his feet into the pair of sandals he wore seldom so that they did not become scuffed. They were as plain as the ones he wore every day, but at least they looked new. He must belt the tunic with Nakht's gift of last year, put Anuket's earring into his lobe—*or would it be better*, he wondered anxiously, *to leave behind everything I have received from them so that I do not look as though I have been needy for years, even though that's true? Shall I go simply, in a plain kilt and no tunic, with the sa on my breast and the amulets on my fingers as my only adornment? Apart from the frog holding back my hair, of course.*

Lifting the lid of the chest, he sighed and stood staring down into it. *I have dreamed of this moment for so long,* his thoughts ran on. *It has been a fantasy on which I have fed. Now the moment of reality faces me and I am irresolute and afraid. Have I built a palace without a foundation, hope piled on hope and underneath no sunken pillars in the shifting sand of my desire?* Shaking his head, he bent and began pulling out kilts and shirts, laying them on his couch. Beneath them were the little boxes that held his treasures—the earring, his sennet game, Thothmes' casket of last year. He pulled them out too. Right at the bottom, where he had not delved for years, he saw the cedar box his uncle Ker had given him. In an aura of disconnection he took it up and opened it, and there, in one of the compartments, was a tiny bundle of clean linen. Backing to the couch, he sat and unwrapped it with shaking fingers. The scarab Ishat had given him was a desiccated husk, lying so lightly on his palm that he could scarcely feel it. Its colour was still bright, the sheen of gold gleaming as though it had been polished. Two of its legs had fallen off into the piece of linen. As though it was yesterday, Huy saw Ishat's grubby, sturdy little fingers balancing something on a lettuce leaf and presenting it to him solemnly. "I wish you happiness on your Naming Day," she had said. The sun had been strong in the garden, her voice full of pride. "I found it floating on the flood," she had explained. "My father told me that scarabs are very rare here in the Delta. They like to live in the desert. He said it would bring me good fortune, but I said Huy needs it more than I do, seeing that he has to go away to school."

Ishat, Huy thought, willing his hands to stop trembling. *I was a spoilt, selfish, nasty little boy, but you loved me all the same. You were always smarter than I. You helped me to get rid of that horrible monkey. Now I know why I feared it: it belonged to the future, to the baboons of Thoth's temple, to the heka and the Book, and something in me sensed that future and recoiled. What does your voice sound like now, Ishat? Is it still strident with righteous indignation or jealousy, soft with some new discovery from the flower fields to share with a Huy who is no longer there to see it?* A wave of longing to see her struck him. *It is just the insecurity of what is to come at Nakht's house,* Huy thought. *A need for the safety of my childhood.* His hands had stopped shaking. Carefully he rewrapped the scarab and laid it back in its compartment.

In the end he decided to dress as the young nobleman he knew he was not. On his chair he set out a gold-bordered kilt and the tunic, the turquoise-studded leather belt, Anuket's earring, and on his table he set a pot of kohl and jasmine-scented oil for his hair. It was time for his first class. On his way he hurried to find Pabast and asked the man to come to his cell that evening and shave his body. Pabast rolled his eyes and nodded. In spite of his apprehension Huy smiled to himself as he sped along the corridors. The servant no longer intimidated him, but he continued to terrorize the poor little newcomers to the school. Pabast would never change.

In the evening, after a silent but efficient Pabast
had shaved and plucked him, he went to the bathhouse, washed and oiled himself thoroughly, and
ordered a litter. While he was waiting for it, he dressed
carefully. Then setting his mirror on his table, he knelt
and painstakingly applied black kohl to his eyelids.
Thothmes had left a small amount of henna in a pot
beside his couch. Huy longed to paint the soles of his
feet and the palms of his hands with it, longed suddenly and bitterly for the right to do so, but he was
not an aristocrat and probably never would be. Rubbing the jasmine-scented oil across his chest and belly,
he wriggled his feet into the stiff leather sandals. They
pinched him, but seeing that he would be carried to
and from Nakht's house, he decided to keep them on.
The litter-bearers had arrived. With a last glance at his
face in the mirror, Huy went out to greet them.

The tributary of the river was rising steadily, its
turgid, swollen surface belying the speed of the north-
flowing current beneath. Eventually it would cover the
path running beside it, but for now it had drowned
only half of Nakht's watersteps. Fleetingly Huy
remembered the last flood, when Anuket had behaved
with such coarse abandon and he and Thothmes had
sat on the watersteps above the river and talked under
the light of the moon. It seemed as though they had
done so yesterday, but a full year had passed. Once
again the moon was at the half and waxing, and the
Sothis star hung bright and shimmering in the black
night sky. The bearers answered the gate guard's challenge at Nakht's entrance and trundled along the path
to the main doors. Huy got out, knowing that the men

would sleep in the grass until he was ready to return to the school. His heart was thudding erratically and he took a moment to compose himself as best he could, but it was still palpitating as he walked into the lamplit quiet of the reception hall.

Thothmes rose from the chair where he had been waiting and the two young men embraced. "Gods, I've missed you!" Thothmes said, linking arms with Huy as they made their way to the dining hall. "I heard that your lessons are proceeding even though the rest of us must twiddle our thumbs and wait for school to begin again. How daunting, to be the only one under the tutors' eyes all the time! Are you working hard?"

"Very hard," Huy laughed. "But it's good, Thothmes. I'm enjoying it. The High Priest wanted me to be ready to leave the school on my sixteenth Naming Day, and so I am."

"That's in eight days." Thothmes relinquished Huy's arm. "What are you going to do then?"

A gush of warm air laden with the familiar aromas of good food and expensive scents greeted him as he entered the dining hall behind his friend. "I want to talk to your father about that," he said. Thothmes paused but did not turn around, then continued on to settle himself on a cushion before his flower-laden table.

Nasha flew at Huy, kissing his cheeks effusively and pulling him forward. Anuket glided up to him. He met her eyes with the inward capitulation that had marked their every meeting since he had fallen in love with her. He did not wait for the customary brush of her lips against his chin. Taking her hand, he turned it over and kissed the hennaed palm. "Greetings, little one," he said softly. "It's good to see you again." She smiled and let her hand rest in his for a moment before withdrawing it and retreating to her table without speaking.

Huy approached Nakht, who had been standing watching. He bowed. "Forgive me for inviting myself to your house, Lord. There is a matter I would like to discuss with you after the meal."

Nakht regarded him gravely. "You are always welcome here, Huy. You have become quite a fixture. It's hard to remember a time before Thothmes brought you home." He indicated Huy's table. "We will talk later."

A fixture. Huy felt jubilant. Nakht snapped his fingers and servants appeared carrying the first course. Huy hurried to his table, lifting the wet, quivering blooms from its surface and laying them gently beside him.

"You don't wear kohl very often, Huy," Nasha called over to him. "It makes you look very handsome and mysterious. What's the occasion?"

Huy looked down at the salad being set before him. "I will reach my majority in a few days," he answered. "I thought it was about time I began to put childhood behind me."

Nasha snorted. "Pompousness! Please don't grow up. Father would never let me wrestle a man to the ground. It would be unseemly." Her rich laugh rang out.

Anuket took a sip of her wine and straightened her back. "Your behaviour is always verging on the unseemly, Nasha," she said primly. "That's why your suitors come with eagerness and go with even greater alacrity."

"You self-righteous little prig!" Nasha shot back. "You used to be such a kind and mild girl. Never mind *my* suitors—I pity the man who's going to marry you!"

"Peace!" Nakht said sharply.

Thothmes leaned close to Huy. "They do this to each other every day," he murmured. "They drive Father insane. Anuket taunts Nasha and Nasha insults her. There is no woman in the house to help Anuket grow up, that's the problem. I wish Father would take another wife."

Huy glanced at him, startled. "I suppose he might. I just thought that your mother's memory would always be too fresh in his mind."

"Huy, you are a romantic," Thothmes said. "There is an ending to grief."

Both girls seemed to have recovered their good humour under their father's warning, and the meal progressed with no more unpleasantness. To an increasingly nervous Huy it seemed to drag on forever. Course followed course, the wine cups were emptied and refilled several times, except, Huy noted with humour, for Anuket's. After her third cup the steward avoided her, carrying the jug to the others. Her delicate mouth turned down, but she made no comment, picking gracefully through the remnants of her food and ignoring the conversation swirling around her. At last Nakht pushed his table away and rose. "Huy, come with me. Children, amuse yourselves this evening."

Huy felt his throat dry up. As always, the wine had not taken the edge off his anxiety. Unfolding himself, he stood and followed the Governor into the passage beyond.

Nakht's office faced the rear garden. A large window, its reed blind now hiding the view, lay behind the desk, on which stood a single alabaster lamp glowing against the dimness. The walls were covered with niches, almost all of them full of scrolls. The room was a place of neatness and efficiency. Nakht was a good governor. He closed the door behind Huy and went to perch on the edge of the desk, waving to the chair beside him, but Huy was too apprehensive to sit. He shook his head.

"Now, my young friend, what can I do for you?" Nakht asked. "Should I send for my scribe?"

Huy was taken aback. It had not occurred to him that either he or Nakht might want his business recorded. "I don't think so, Governor," he managed. "Perhaps when you have heard my request you may deem it necessary."

Nakht's eyebrows rose. "Is it so serious, then? Proceed." He appeared to be surprised, but in Huy's sensitive state he thought he saw a bleak knowledge already dawning in Nakht's dark eyes. The moment had come. Gathering up his courage and all his will, Huy began.

"Lord, you surely know that under the High Priest's ruling my education has been continuing and in little more than a week it will be complete," he said, amazed that his voice was clear and steady. Nakht nodded. "I shall pass from the school with the highest marks and with very good recommendations from my instructors."

Nakht smiled. "Of course," he agreed. "You are a very intelligent young man. You will make a fine scribe."

Huy made a deliberate effort not to clench his fists. "The High Priest has offered me employment as his personal scribe. It is a prestigious position and would bring a good remuneration with it if I decided to accept."

Nakht's smile widened. "My congratulations, Huy," he said heartily. "You deserve this, and I am happy that your relationship with my family will continue. We would all miss you if you were forced to take up work somewhere else, Thothmes in particular. He loves you very much."

"And I him." Desperately Huy took a step forward. "Lord, you know, of course you know, that I also love Anuket. I have loved her for years. I have always treated her with the respect due to both her station and her virginity. I have been faithful to her without any words of love passing between us. Now I beg you to draw up a marriage contract for us. I believe that she loves me too. I will be a caring husband. I do not want to work for Ramose. I want to work for you. Either way, I will be able to supply all her needs. I have waited a long time for this," he went on more frantically as he saw the smile slowly leave Nakht's face. "Do not dismiss me out of hand!" He was breathing heavily and closed his mouth, suddenly overcome with the desire to collapse onto the chair, but he remained on his feet.

A heavy silence fell between them. The flame in the lamp guttered once, making shadows dance briefly across Nakht's face. At last Nakht sighed. "I had hoped that this day would never come," he said sadly. "I have grown to love you like a son, Huy. You are an honest and upright young man. I have seen your attachment to Anuket and I have prayed that it might end, like any first infatuation. But it has not." He rubbed his forehead wearily. "I know my daughter well," he went on. "She is wilful and thoroughly selfish, and in spite of my constant discipline she is becoming a shrew as well. She needs a very firm hand."

"I will care for her so lovingly that her nature will change," Huy pressed.

Nakht pursed his lips. "She does not love you. She sees your adoration as her due, but she does not return it."

"That does not matter! How many marriages are founded on love? Very few. As long as there is respect—"

"I am sorry, Huy. Firstly, her blood is noble and she must marry within her class. Secondly, a scribe, no matter how well paid, would not be able to support her properly. In any case, I have no need of another scribe and my administrators within the sepat use older men who are already versed in the language of politics, having served their apprenticeships elsewhere. Thirdly, I have not forgotten, although you seem to, that your history as the Twice Born and the presence of a Seer's gift within you makes marriage impossible for you. The anger of the gods would fall on you and yours at such a betrayal. The answer is no."

"But Lord, there is precedent in history for a noble to wed a commoner!" Huy cried out. "As for supporting her, you could help me! Offer me a position under you, train me in the administration of some branch of the sepat! Some Seers keep their gift. The Rekhet told me so! Oh, please . . ."

Nakht left the desk and went to Huy, putting an arm around his shoulders. "No, Huy," he said gently. "Anuket has been betrothed to the son of the governor of the Uas district since she was born. She will go to live at Weset. She will do as she is told because she is ambitious, unlike Nasha, who refuses all men who seek to marry her. I am sorry."

A pain as sharp as the thrust of a knife suddenly struck Huy under his breastbone. He wanted to double up over it, wrap his arms around it, but with the last vestige of his dignity he drew himself up and away from Nakht's touch. "I am more than sorry," he whispered, "but I thank you for hearing me, Lord, and for welcoming me into your family for so many years. I do not think that I shall come here again."

"I hope you will change your mind." Nakht stepped away. "You will leave a breach among us unless you do."

Huy could not suppress a groan. He wanted to speak again. Frantically he searched for the right words to scream and rain down on Nakht, words that would give him Anuket; but if they existed they remained locked in his mind. He bowed to the Governor, straightened with difficulty, and let himself out into the passage. Once there, he leaned against the wall and slammed a hand across the pain that was threatening to engulf him. Bent over, he turned from the front entrance and walked unsteadily out the rear door, past the sleepy guard, and into the warm darkness of the garden.

He was rounding the house, moving under the trees towards the entrance and his litter, when the shadows stirred and Anuket came noiselessly into the faint starlight. Huy halted and watched her drift closer, her long white sheath flowing grey, her eyes as black as her hair, as black as the night surrounding her. Reaching him, she stood still, looking solemnly up into his face. "I wanted to hear what you had to say to my father. I went and stood outside his office window. Every word came clearly through the blind." Huy waited. She passed her tongue slowly over hennaed lips the colour of ebony in the uncertain light. "I love you also, Huy," she went on in a half whisper, stepping right up to him so that her wine-laden breath fanned him. "I have loved you almost as long as you have loved me. But what can I do?" She sighed heavily, putting a hand against his chest. "I must be an obedient daughter. I must honour the pledge my father made on my behalf when I was little." Huy felt her fingers curl around the sa. They were cold.

"You can choose to say no," he responded in a forceful whisper. "You can promise yourself to me here, now, and next week I will come and take you away with me. I will easily find work somewhere far from Iunu. It will be an adventure, Anuket."

She began to rub the sa lightly back and forth across the damp folds of his tunic. "But even though I am of age," she whispered, "I must have my father's permission to wed. Would you have me live with you as your wife without a contract or the blessing of the gods? Do you want me for your whore, Huy?"

Savagely, he grasped the caressing hand and tore it from the amulet and, pulling her into him, wound his other hand roughly in her hair. Her head jerked back, but she did not cry out. A faint smile curved those black lips. Huy's mouth descended on hers and he kissed her with all the pent-up violence of the evening, his teeth grinding against hers, his body rigid. He felt the length of her, the small, hard breasts, the tiny swell of her belly, the firmness of her thighs. She did not pull away, but neither did she react. He wanted to twist her hair, throw her onto the grass, force a sound from her, any sound, but she remained impassive, the fingers he was crushing did not warm. In the end he dropped his arms. Anuket patted her lips. "You handle me crudely," she said.

All at once the heat of lust and desperation drained from Huy, and he turned and left her without another word. At Nakht's gate he woke the bearers. "Take the litter back to the temple," he ordered them tersely. "I want to walk." They obeyed with obvious relief and Huy turned away, taking the path beside the river until he found a rutted street leading into the heart of the city.

The night was far advanced. Respectable citizens had long since gone home, many of them to sleep on their roofs and enjoy a few fleeting hours of coolness. Iunu was left to the soldiers, the whores, the restless scavengers who prowled the narrow alleys looking for anything worth picking up. On the whole they were harmless and the city police left them alone, patrolling slowly and cheerfully from one busy beer house to another. Huy trudged the dim streets, blind to the pockets of lively noise and lamplight spilling out from the beer houses that soon faded behind him to be replaced by the silence of buildings huddled darkly against a darker sky. Sometimes he stumbled over dried donkey droppings or stones held fast in the brick-hard earth. Sometimes he came to himself in the middle of a patch of tired grass before an empty shrine.

But his gaze was focused inward where Nakht's eyes registered pity, where he heard himself begging without dignity, where Anuket's body did not relax against his and her mouth was stiff and cold. So cold! *She does not love me.* His feet measured out the damning words. He felt old and used up, his own body giving back to him the pain of his heart with the sudden failure of a calf muscle, the spasm of his gut.

At last, with dawn a mere two hours away, he found himself not far from the Rekhet's house. He had walked this street before. The shabby buildings were familiar, as was the girl sitting yawning on a stool, her back against a wall, the stub of a candle flickering beside her. It was the young whore who had reminded him of Anuket before she had bared her full breast and leered at him. Then he had been disgusted. Now he approached her. *This is not coincidence,* he told himself dully. *There is no such thing as coincidence. This is fate, my fate, which I take into my own hands this very night.*

She did not even bother to rise as he came up to her. Her hands remained loose in her yellow lap. But a spark of recognition lit her heavily kohled eyes as she glanced at him. "I know you," she said, her voice high and light like a child's, like Anuket's, although her accent was coarse. "I've seen you before, you with that beautiful long hair and those tempting eyes. What do you want? I'm tired."

"You. I want you," Huy said harshly. "I've nothing to pay you with." She shrugged, coming to her feet.

She was taller than she had seemed, taller than Anuket, but the fine bones of her face, the delicacy of her features, were breathtakingly similar. She looked him up and down, but before she could speak again Huy took the earring from his lobe. "I'll give you this," he said.

It was snatched from his hand with alacrity. She jerked her head. "Come inside."

He followed her into her tiny, cramped room. The couch was disordered, the walls patchy grey for want of whitewash. One plank of wood laid across two piles of mud bricks formed a table holding a dusty clutter of cosmetics in plain clay pots and one candle. The earthen floor was uncovered. Huy noticed none of these things. Reckless and feverish, he watched her light the candle from the stub she had carried inside with her and drop the earring Anuket had given him amongst the mess on the makeshift table. As she came back to him, he took her shoulders.

"Your name is Anuket. You are a seventeen-year-old virgin," he said. He heard the words issuing from his mouth with a fleeting disbelief.

She nodded. "And you are my deflowerer." Her demeanour changed at once. Her eyes widened. The hand she placed against his chest trembled. The transformation was startling. A callous lust seized Huy. Pulling her against him, he rammed his mouth against hers. For a moment she struggled, making little mewing noises of protest, then hesitantly her lips opened. Huy's tongue found hers. His hands touched the straps of her sheath and he pushed them over her shoulders, down her arms, until the sheath lay in a heap at her feet and she was naked. Breaking his kiss, she covered her sex with both hands, fear in her eyes. She was panting.

For one icy, sane moment Huy recognized her skill as an actress and knew himself for a fool, then he pushed her backwards onto the couch and, tearing off his tunic, kilt, and loincloth, tumbled after her. Her breast was close to his mouth, the nipple hard. She tried to wriggle away from him, but he pressed her to the grubby sheet with both hands, closing his teeth and then his lips around the nipple, groaning as he did so. Taking both breasts in his hands, he rolled on top of her, but he knew, in the midst of this terrible, fiery loss of control, that his penis was not answering his urgent demand. He kissed her again, squeezed those full, heavy breasts so unlike Anuket's little nubs, but it was no good.

She turned him onto his back and, giving up any pretence to innocence, slid down the length of him and took his penis in her mouth. Huy lay tensely pleading, begging, his wild thoughts seeking no particular god or demon, but it was no good. Gradually the terrible craving began to ebb, leaving him with a greater sense of emptiness than he had ever known. He closed his eyes, feeling the whore get off the couch, hearing the rustle as she pulled her sheath back up over her body. For some moments he lay there nude, spread-eagled. He could smell his shame, the rank odour of his sweat and hers mingling in that fetid little space. "It's not my fault you didn't come," she said. "I'm keeping the earring. Now go away. I want to sleep." Huy crept awkwardly from the couch and fumbled into his clothes while she stood there watching him impassively. Before he was even out the door, she had extinguished the candle.

Huy set off for the temple at a shambling run. Half mad with humiliation and grief, he began to shout, "I hate you! I hate you!" to Atum, to Thoth, to all of them, the gods who cared nothing for him, who manipulated and used him; to Imhotep, who had oh so slyly asked him the question that had ruined his life; to Ramose and every priest, who served the perfidious gods; to Nakht, who had pretended to love him; to Anuket, who had practised her diabolical new feminine skills on him and torn him to pieces. His howls echoed down the silent, drowsy streets and he did not care. If he had met one of the Medjay, the city police, he might have been arrested. But even they had gone home.

Soon he was forced to slow. His legs shook violently and he had a raging thirst. As he stood with his hands on his knees and his head hanging down, in the middle of some anonymous alley, he realized that the buildings crowding him were limned very faintly in a tremulous grey light and he could see his feet. Dawn was not far off. Forcing himself forward, he hurried on. He judged himself to be still some distance from the temple, but he knew in which direction it lay.

He came upon a large stone basin full of water, set before a shrine to Hapi, god of the river. Careful not to drink, for there was a green scum on the water, he plunged his head and his hands into it and, refreshed, quickened his pace. Before long the river itself came into view. The light was strengthening rapidly. Dazed and hollowed out, Huy knew that he would not have time to clean himself up, much less eat, before he was due at his first lesson. He cared about nothing else anymore but this, finishing his education. With a last spurt of energy he ran again, speeding beside the temple's canal and across the huge expanse of concourse and into the passages behind the temple. Just before he reached the schoolroom, he stood still so that his breath could slow, then he walked in.

His teacher was sorting through the basket of scrolls. He looked up once, then again, horrified, as Huy came forward. "Gods, boy, what have you been doing?" the man exclaimed. "Don't tell me that Nakht allowed you to carouse at his house all night!"

"No indeed, Master," Huy said smoothly. "I came back here then spent the time until dawn in the temple, praying about my future. I fell asleep. I have neither washed nor eaten. I am sorry."

The man grunted. "There is no time to do either," he said, but his glance was kindly. "Go and get your palette. We have only seven days left." Seven days. Huy sketched a bow and obeyed.

He struggled through the long hours on willpower alone. Exhausted and empty of all but the pain of despair, he watched himself take dictation, compute equations for the architect, describe the deployment of troops during some battle the details of which he immediately forgot, and stand on the training ground at sunset loosing arrows into a target that seemed to be hovering on the edge of the world. Later, crawling between his sheets without bothering to remove his kilt, he plunged into the sodden sleep of extreme fatigue.

At dawn, in the few blessed moments between unconsciousness and full wakefulness, the previous day was a blank in his mind. But then awareness descended, making him cry out and leave the couch, standing rumpled and close to tears with the morning light fingering his naked back through the cell doorway and his statue of Khenti-kheti staring at him blankly from the still-shadowed interior. Grimly forcing himself not to weep, knowing that if he did so he would not be able to stop, he shed the soiled kilt and loincloth and walked to the bathhouse, scrubbing himself free of the faint scent of jasmine that he knew he would never again be able to inhale without pain, letting the cleansing natron lift the whore's odour from the crevices of his body. Back in the cell, he dressed and braided his hair quickly. Nakht's gift of the year before, the leather belt studded with turquoise, he buried at the bottom of his tiring chest. Unable to eat, he drank several cups of milk brought to him by a kitchen servant, then, taking up his palette, he went to his lessons.

For three days he strained to concentrate on nothing but his work, wrenching his mind back to the tasks at hand when it threatened to wander into fields that would unman him. On the evening of the third day he returned to his cell to find Thothmes waiting for him. Without a word Thothmes left the couch where he had been sitting and opened his arms, and with a sob of surrender Huy fell into them. He wept for a long time against Thothmes' warm neck, and Thothmes said nothing, merely holding him tightly. When Huy was spent, he released himself, sat down, and wiped his face on a sheet. Thothmes sat opposite him. The two friends looked at each other. Finally Thothmes said, "I'm sorry, Huy. I knew Anuket was promised elsewhere. I should have warned you. But I was so sure that Father would open every door for you, give you a rich sinecure, give you Anuket, and we would all live in peace and happiness in Iunu."

"He has turned his back on me because I could not heal your mother," Huy said thickly. "He is punishing me. He does not understand."

Thothmes' eyebrows rose. "I didn't think of that. But you're wrong. Father knows that Anuket would end up being a thorn in your side. Your love for her would make you vulnerable to her stubborn self-will. She would ruin you. Besides, there is the matter of your future as a Seer. Father would never seek to incur the anger of the gods by diverting you from your destiny."

"To the Duat with my destiny," Huy retorted wearily. "Stop defending him, Thothmes. He has betrayed me. He could have offered me work even without Anuket. All these years of closeness and now he repudiates me as though I were a stranger, an anonymous petitioner refused a hearing in his office. He and my uncle Ker have a lot in common."

"You're right," Thothmes said after a moment. "He has treated you ill. You should have heard Nasha yelling at him the morning after you came to dinner! That was when he told us you wouldn't be back to our house anymore. I think it's Nasha who's in love with you."

Huy passed a hand over his eyes. "Be quiet," he said dully. "I must teach myself not to care about them anymore. I must begin my life anew."

"But not without me!" Thothmes pressed. "Don't drift away from me, Huy! No matter what happens to either of us, we must stay close to one another. Your vision said so!"

"Yes, it did. I love you, my brother. Without you my years here would have been dreary indeed. I will write to you from wherever I go and I will see you as often as I can. Thank you for letting me cry on your shoulder!" He managed a smile and Thothmes' ready grin flashed back at him.

"Well, that's settled. But I thought the High Priest had ordered you to stay here and work for him."

Huy shook his head. "I will not stay here. I will not remain under his thumb. I will not have my every action weighed, and I am sick to death of the Book and being reverenced as though Egypt will collapse without me."

"Where are you going?"

Huy shrugged. "I don't know." Sliding off the couch, he kissed Thothmes' cheek. "I have to sleep now. These last days are long and full of hard work. Goodbye, my dear friend. May the soles of both our feet be always firm."

The words of formal departure took Thothmes by surprise. Standing, he embraced Huy, made as if to speak, embraced him again, then left quickly, his head down. Huy listened to the slap of his sandals on the stone path fronting the cells until the sound faded and was lost in the hot stillness of the night. Exploring his heart, he found it wounded but stable. His soul, however, remained empty. He was glad of that emptiness. No emotion would lodge there. All feelings would fade as rapidly as they came. It was the only way, he knew, that he would be able to survive.

Early on the morning of the fourth day, before the sun was up, he wrote a letter to Methen, sealed it in wax without imprint, and, hurrying to the temple watersteps, found one of the heralds who routinely waited to take correspondence up and down the river. "Tell the priest Methen that Huy asks him to pay you," he told the man. "If not, then find me when you return. But it will be all right, I think." The herald took the scroll and laid it in his satchel, and Huy headed for the bathhouse. He had woken with his mind suddenly clear. He knew what he had to do. The decision was bitter for him. He could almost taste the bitterness of it, like crushed aloes in his mouth, but he would not swallow it. He would hold it on his tongue, feel it burn his throat, until he had learned a lesson even more important than the things his teachers were drumming into him: Trust no man, no man at all, apart from Thothmes. It was that simple, and that terrible.

It was a precept Huy was to hold to for the rest of his life.

14

Huy's formal education ended quietly on the tenth day of Paophi. As he stood before them in the classroom where he had spent so many happy and anxious hours over the previous twelve years, each tutor presented him with a scroll of proficiency, speaking of his intelligence, his diligence at his studies, and his readiness to face the world outside the comfortable womb of the school. Ramose the High Priest looked on with a smile. Huy, accepting the scrolls and the accolades with bows and murmured thanks, did not feel at all ready to say goodbye to the redolence of papyrus and ink. In a burst of regret, he knew that he would miss the ritual of unrolling his mat every morning, saying the prayer to Thoth, feeling the single thin ray of sunlight touch his folded knees at the same time each morning as he set his palette across them and lifted his face to the familiar form of his academics teacher, perched on his low stool. The combined voices of his schoolmates reciting the lessons, the odour of cooking that always began to waft into the room just before the noon meal and set the younger pupils wriggling impatiently, even the fitful drafts of incense-laden air that sometimes blew through the corridors behind Ra's sanctuary, seemed all at once precious to him.

When the little ceremony was concluded and the teachers had filed out, Ramose approached him, laying a heavy hand on his head. "Be idle for two days, Huy. Pack up your belongings. I have had a cell prepared for you next to my quarters and have engaged a body servant for you. You may move into your new room whenever you are ready, but I expect to summon you and your palette to begin work in three days. At that time we will discuss both your duties and your remuneration." He patted Huy and withdrew his hand. Huy had never seen him so jovial. "I suggest that you write to your family and acquaint them with the change in your fortunes—unless, of course, you have done so already."

Numbly Huy shook his head, wanting to sweep his fingers across his skull where the High Priest had touched him. He felt vaguely ill. Ramose sketched a bow and left and Huy followed more slowly, his arms full of scrolls, walking uneasily towards the deserted courtyard and the empty cell he had shared with Thothmes for so long.

For a moment he stood in the doorway, looking inside. Thothmes' cot had been stripped, but his own had been neatly made, his table with its burden of Khenti-kheti and his palette dusted, the floor swept. A sense of unreality enveloped him. After twelve years of predictability, time seemed to have speeded up, precipitating him from the security of a safely regulated life into a future looming like a void.

Stepping into the dimness of the room, he bent, dragged his chest out from under his cot, and, lifting the lid, tumbled into it the scrolls that guaranteed his freedom. Then he sat on the cot, at a loss. At once a vision of Anuket filled his mind—Anuket with her ebony hair and eyes and her black mouth under the late moon—and he banished it by a spasm of the will. *May the gods grant that I never see her again,* he thought savagely; but he did not want to think of the gods, not then. He sought other, gentler images: the sights and sounds of his fellow students, the friendly smell of horseflesh rising to him as he stood in the chariot, the flicker of lamplight on the ceiling as he and Thothmes lay in their cots and talked drowsily before sleep claimed them. *My whole life has been dissolved,* his thoughts ran on. *Everything has gone. I face a complete change in everything, everywhere I look. And still no word has come from Methen. O Atum, god whom I both love and detest, let it not be your desire for me that I must stay here, in a cell next door to the High Priest, under the gaze of those shrewd and judging eyes, forever!*

For a long time he sat on in a mood of utter impotence, until hunger drove him out into the fire of an early afternoon and directed his feet towards the temple kitchens. He ate cold food, standing up beside one of the tables while the kitchen servants wove irritably around him, and when he had finished he returned to his cell and lay tensely on his cot, the sweat of Akhet oozing lightly from his pores. He did not know what to do.

But early the following morning a temple servant darkened his doorway and, bowing, handed him a scroll.

"This has just arrived with a herald from Hut-herib," the man said. "I also bring a message from the High Priest. Your new cell is scoured and ready for your occupation whenever you have packed your chest. Call for me later, Huy, and I will help you carry your things." He bowed himself out. Huy, who had been preparing to go to the bathhouse, laid down his clean loincloth and kilt and broke the seal on the papyrus with shaking fingers. Methen's even, careful characters sprang out at him. Backing to the couch, he slumped down.

Dearest Huy, I congratulate you most warmly on the completion of your studies. Doubtless the prospect of freedom is both exciting and daunting to you. I have considered your request most carefully, laying it before Khenti-kheti with an offering for clarity of mind. You do not tell me why you do not wish to remain at Iunu and work for Ramose. Such a position would guarantee much future advancement. I can offer you nothing but humble work, adequate rations, and a small mud-brick house of three rooms close to the temple. Think carefully. Ramose of course cannot coerce you to stay under his aegis, but do you really want to be an anonymous, poverty-stricken scribe in the service of a minor god? Hut-herib holds many unhappy memories for you. I have said nothing of this to your family, the members of which I see from time to time. Nevertheless, you would be welcome here. Give me your final answer. Your friend Methen, High Priest in the service of Khenti-kheti.

A rush of warm relief coursed through Huy. Clutching the scroll to his chest, he closed his eyes. *Anonymous, yes, dear Methen. Poverty-stricken? That will be hard, but I don't care. No more feasts in nobles' houses, no more boating parties and expensive gifts, no more dreams of self-importance. Humble work is what I need, far from Ramose and his plans for me, far from Nakht and his rejection. I deceive myself no longer. I have woken from twelve years of a fond and prideful illusion without foundation, and once again this peasant has his nose pressed to the dust. My answer to Methen will be my presence at the door of his quarters.*

Snatching up his clothes, Huy hurried to the bathhouse, finding a servant on the way and sending him to inquire whether the High Priest might receive him that morning. Then, scrubbed, oiled, and dressed, he returned to his cell, picked up Methen's scroll, and waited. The permission he had requested came, and calmly Huy tied on his sandals and took the long walk to the area of the temple where the priests lived. Ramose's imposing double doors stood open. The High Priest's voice reached Huy as he slowed and asked the servant to announce him. The voice ceased, a scribe brushed past Huy, and Huy followed the servant into Ramose's domain.

To his consternation not only Ramose rose to greet him, but a familiar figure lifted herself from a chair and came forward, wand in hand, the cowrie shells hanging from her belt, wrists, and ankles clacking as she moved. Her voluminous sheath was green, a colour Huy had never seen her wear before, its neck and hem bordered in black, a colour of strong protection for every magician. She did not smile. Halting before she reached him, she regarded him solemnly, her eyes clear and level in their nest of wrinkled skin. Ramose embraced him, and it came to Huy how often the High Priest felt the need to touch him, as though in doing so he might absorb something he needed or desired. The thought revolted Huy. Pulling himself roughly from the High Priest's grasp, he managed a compensatory smile.

"So, young man, I did not expect to see you in my quarters so soon," Ramose said. "Have you packed your chest already? Let me show you your new cell."

Huy's glance flew to Henenu's. Her gaze had narrowed, and still she did not move. *She knows,* he thought with a pang of fear. *Why is she clad in green today? I forget what green signifies.* His own eyes must have betrayed him, falling to her sheath, for one corner of her hennaed mouth turned up briefly.

"Green means growth and regeneration, Huy," she said. "It is a powerful colour. Are you well?"

With an inward sigh, Huy nodded. "Very well, thank you, Rekhet. I trust you are well also." He turned his attention deliberately back to the High Priest. His heart had begun to race. "Master, I shall not be occupying that cell," he said loudly. "My debt to you for your goodness to me and your care can never be repaid. I am aware that I owe you everything but my life, and I apologize to you from the bottom of my soul, but I cannot stay here and work for you. I have petitioned the High Priest Methen for a position as his scribe. I want to leave Iunu as soon as possible."

Ramose looked puzzled. "Leave Iunu? Why? What are you saying?"

"I am saying that although your offer of employment is generous, I cannot accept it. I want to return to Hut-herib."

"To that grubby little town? What for? Huy, your career will be over before it has had a chance to begin! I know how distressed Nakht has made you. I realize—"

Huy cut him short. "So you have heard about my humiliation. Yes, Master, Nakht has wounded me deeply—but it is more than that. I have spent twelve years in Ra's temple, happy years, but tumultuous also. There has been the Ished Tree and the mystery of the Book, and I am tired. Deep inside me there is a desperate need for peace. I want to live quietly beside Methen."

"If you are tired, then take the remaining months of the Inundation to recover," Ramose argued. "Visit your family. Spend a few weeks with Methen. You sound like an old man, not a sixteen-year-old youth in the flower of vigour. I have worked you too hard lately." He leaned close. "And what of your gift, Huy? We, Henenu and I, fully expect it to revive now that your schooling is over. You will need our help to control it, channel it, use it for—"

"For the greater good of Egypt?" Huy finished for him. "No, Master. I care nothing for the greater good of this country, not just now. Under the law you cannot impel me to stay here. I must go. With your blessing, I pray." He handed Methen's scroll to Ramose, who swung back to his desk and unrolled it immediately.

Huy and Henenu regarded one another in silence. Finally the Rekhet spoke. "I wear green today in honour of your growth and your regeneration, not mine. I woke this morning with the strong feeling that you had decided to reject Ramose's offer. I looked for inauspicious omens and found none, therefore it is within the desire of Atum that you should leave us. Ramose will be bitter for a while."

Huy felt obscurely annoyed at her complacent words. "I did not consider the desire of Atum when I wrote to my friend," he replied shortly. "I have explained myself, Rekhet."

She smiled faintly. "You are annoyed with me. In fact, everything about me and Ramose and these holy precincts is beginning to irritate you. It is a sign that you must move on. Yet do not think that you will escape your fate by burying yourself at Hut-herib. Atum is not chained to Iunu any more than Ra is."

In truth Huy had formed the vague idea that in fleeing Iunu he might indeed leave Atum behind, hovering over the Ished Tree and the Book. He flushed. "Forgive me, Rekhet. My discontent is like an itchy rash spread over my body. All I want to do is scratch it."

She laughed. "Not discontent," she chided him. "It is the urgent need to run away that consumes you. Do not fret about it, Huy. Go to Methen. Seek the peace you require."

The High Priest let the scroll roll up and handed it back to Huy, breathing heavily. "I do not approve, not at all. Methen is wise when he reminds you that at Hut-herib you will have no future, no opportunity to advance. Your education will be wasted."

"I think not," Henenu cut in. "Let him go, Ramose. In spite of what you think, there will be no obscurity for him anywhere Atum's shadow falls."

Stepping forward at last, she laid her wand on the tiles and imprisoned Huy's face between her warm, dry palms. "Write to us. Pray for us as we shall pray for you. One day your prayers will thunder in Atum's ears and drown out the bleatings of us lesser folk." She kissed his forehead and released him. "Or perhaps," she added, "we shall be praying to you and not to Atum at all." Picking up her wand, she shook herself, a curious, ungainly gesture, as though she were ridding herself of a spider clinging to the folds of her sheath.

Ramose looked bleak. "I am appalled at your ingratitude, Huy," he snapped. "Nevertheless, Henenu seems to think that you must go, and I respect her heka. I will not provide you with transport of any kind. Perhaps a taste of true hardship will bring you running back to Iunu. The Inundation has reached half its height and begins to flow swiftly. You must either walk north or find a captain willing to hazard the flood."

Huy bowed to him. "I have always held you in reverence, Greatest of Seers," he said, giving Ramose one of his titles out of a sudden uprush of respect, almost of love, for this man who had ordered his life for so long. "I ask for nothing but your forgiveness and your blessing. If I ever unravel the riddle of the Book of Thoth, you will be the first to hear of it." He knelt, able to be magnanimous now that this difficult interview was almost over. "Please bless me, High Priest."

Ramose sighed. The hands he placed on Huy's head felt gentle and without need. "May the all-seeing eye of Ra guide your journey," he said gruffly, "and may the soles of your feet be firm." The hands were withdrawn. "Go now, Huy. You may fill one of your leather bags with food from the temple kitchens. Take nothing else."

Huy bit back a sharp reply at the implied criticism; Ramose would continue to be upset for a long time. Coming to his feet, Huy hesitated. Surely there was something more to be said, to be explained? Could twelve years of the bond that had linked a growing child to this cultured priest be dismissed in so few moments? Henenu and Ramose stood watching him quietly. Huy bowed again and left them.

In a mood of jubilation laced with disbelief, he packed quickly, stuffing his clothing and a carefully wrapped Khenti-kheti in the larger of his two worn satchels. He would have liked to take his bedding with him. He had become used to sleeping on fine, soft linen and he doubted whether Methen would be able to provide him with such sheets, but he stripped the couch and left the linen in a heap on the mattress for the servants. Taking his smaller satchel, he made his way to the kitchens, filling it with hunks of cooked beef and a whole grilled goose, two loaves of bread, a handful of green onions and spears of celery, some sticky dates and fresh figs, and a few brown, small plums. He threw in a handful of dried chickpeas and a bulb of garlic and was delighted to find a boxful of bak pods, of which he extracted only four, to crunch as he walked. Ishat had loved the pungent, eye-watering taste of them also, he suddenly remembered. *I shall be seeing her soon*, he thought with a rush of anticipation as he hunted for salt and coriander leaves. *Her and her mother and my family. My family . . . my father. I wish*

*it were possible to look forward to a happy reunion with
them all, to imagine them running to greet me as
I approach the house with my arms open wide to embrace
them. But Father will clasp me out of duty and I will
have to fight the need to shrink from his touch.*
The knowledge made his chest constrict.

He approached one of the cooks. "I am going on a
journey. The High Priest has given me permission to
take food, but I have no pot to cook it in or a knife and
spoon with which to eat. Are there any discarded pans
out on the refuse pile beyond the wall?"'

"How should I know?" the man retorted. "Go and
look for yourself. Feel free to take whatever you
might find."

So Huy, carrying his bulging knapsack, went
through the gate and out to the rear of the temple
precinct, where piles of rotting waste and holed utensils
lay waiting for the wild cats and carrion birds to
descend in the cool of the evening. The smell of decay
was overpowering in spite of the sun's cleansing heat
that would burn up everything pernicious. Gingerly
Huy set down his satchel and, wishing he had brought
with him the gloves that lay in his chest in the cell,
began to poke through the refuse, all at once aware
that off to his right lay the cattle pens and beyond them
the slaughtering yard where so long ago, hentis ago it
seemed to him, he had crawled to escape Pabast.
As though the image of the man had served to conjure
his presence, Huy was startled by the voice behind him.

"So, Master Huy, you have a taste for offal on this
sweltering day?" Huy turned. The servant was actually
smiling at him. "I heard that you were leaving us and

returning to your peasant roots," Pabast went on. "You are insane. I have not minded serving you. I have watched you grow from a selfish little sprig into a polite young man with a great future ahead of him. And now you want to go home. I might as well have left you hairy and unkempt for the last twelve years and saved myself a load of work. Come with me." He marched away and Huy followed warily. Pabast could still intimidate the little boy in him.

Back inside the kitchen compound, Pabast swept up an empty pot, a knife and honing stone, and a fired clay spoon and thrust them at Huy. "Put these in your sack," he ordered. "Wait here." Huy did as he was told. Pabast disappeared in the direction of the servants' cells and soon came back with something wrapped in coarse linen. "One of my old razors," he said curtly. "It will need constant sharpening. You will have to find tweezers and a cosmetic knife for yourself. I can't spare any of mine. Although"—and here he cast a disapproving glance at Huy's long braids—"doubtless the knife will be wasted on you. Have you salt?" Bemused, Huy shook his head. Pabast went to a bowl set on one of the long tables and, unhooking a tiny box from somewhere in the pleats of his kilt, filled it and handed it to Huy. "You always were slightly mad," the man finished gruffly, "but you treated me with respect. I don't believe all that nonsense about the Chosen One and the Twice Born. The priests can be as crazy as a woman under a full moon. Go with the gods, Huy. Don't camp too close to the flood line. Don't drink the flood water. Stick to beer." He swept up a small sealed flagon and pressed it roughly into Huy's already full arms. "And don't think

I'll miss you. I've served hundreds of boys over the years." He grinned, something Huy had never seen him do before. His usually dour expression lifted into mirth. "But I'll tell your successor all the stories about the boy who once slept on the couch in the cell with the noble Thothmes." Then he was gone, striding into the shade cast by the row of servants' rooms. He had not given Huy a chance to thank him.

Huy left the kitchens and went back to his cell. It had already shut him out, although his chest with the larger leather satchel on top of it still rested on the floor beside the denuded couch. Huy put the things Pabast had given him on top of the food in the smaller bag, then he sat on his mattress, his nerve temporarily failing him. There was no one else to bid goodbye. The school was of course empty of the students he might have embraced, and the priests, both friendly and sometimes embarrassingly reverential, were a white-clad flock without individuality. It was time to go. So quickly it had become time to go! Yet Huy sat on, longing for Thothmes' presence, longing for one more day in the safety of the classroom, longing to be a child again. *But without Sennefer,* he thought, rousing himself at last. *Huy you fool, would you really want to live that time over again? Even now you cannot think of it without a shudder, and after the shudder come the words of the Book, rolling through my mind like the Inundation itself, weighty and beautiful and still incomprehensible.*

Sliding off the cot, he tied on his old sandals, slung the satchels around his neck, one to either side, and hefted the chest, balancing it on one shoulder. It did not feel too heavy, but he wondered how much ground he would be able to cover before its angles dug into his flesh. *I should have asked Pabast for rope, and fashioned a sling so that I could carry it between my shoulder blades,* he told himself dismally. *Ah well. I can wait no longer. From now on the sun will begin to set, and the evenings will be cool, and I am young and strong. It should take me no more than five days to walk to Hut-herib. Uncle Ker's barge made the journey from there to here with one stop overnight, pushing against the current.* He stepped out of his cell and began to cross the courtyard. He did not look back.

He reached the outskirts of Iunu just after the sun had set. He had followed the wide path that ran beside the river, refusing to be herded towards the centre of the city when the path veered and then divided. Before long the chest did indeed begin to cut into his neck just below his ear, but he walked on, moving it from one shoulder to the other, doing his best to avoid laden donkeys, laden litters, and thick groups of people all going in the opposite direction from his own. River water swirled around the boles of half-drowned palms and sucked at the sedge growing close to the path. It would not be long before the way itself would be submerged.

When he could no longer see his feet and the weight of the chest had become too much, he left the path, striking inland a little way and setting down his burdens beside a clump of sycamores interspersed by prickly acacia bushes. He could still hear the rumble of the city. Collecting dried brushwood, he built a fire, filled the pot Pabast had given him with river water, and set it over the flames. He had never cooked for himself before, let alone over an open fire. He sat exhausted, watching the water as it began to seethe and then bubble. He added half the chickpeas, a few coriander leaves, a couple of fronds of onion, some salt and garlic, and while he waited for the peas to soften he crunched a celery stick and ate a couple of plums. The dates and figs would keep. The chickpeas took a long time to cook. He tested them occasionally on the end of the knife, his appetite growing as the aroma of the garlic and coriander began to tinge the evening air, but at last his simple stew was ready. He spooned it up greedily together with slabs of tender cold beef and goose meat, and when he was finished he went to the water's edge, washed the pot and the utensils carefully, and set them to dry.

It was now fully dark. Activity along the path seemed to have ceased and Huy, yawning and replete, scraped a small hollow for himself out of the sandy, grass-pitted ground and lay down, his head on his larger satchel. He had no cloak, nothing with which to cover himself, and before long, in spite of the balmy night air, he felt cold. Drawing up his knees, he thought of snakes and stinging insects. *How delicate I have become,* he thought ruefully. *No amount of shooting practice or wrestling or swimming could stop my hip bone and my shoulder from aching.* Nevertheless, a peace began to descend on him. Images of the school flitted through his mind and dropped away. Anuket's face did not appear, only her name, and it was Nakht's features, full of pity and determination, that hovered before Huy's inner eye and woke him fully from a pleasant drowse, causing him to groan quietly.

Deliberately he turned to Thothmes, talking to him, laughing with him, until at last full sleep came.

He woke cramped and shivering at dawn, returned the now-dry pot, spoon, and knife to the satchel, hefted the chest to one stiff shoulder, and set off at once, moving north, always with the water on his left. He felt grubby. His braids had loosened and he could feel grains of sand against his skin, under his crumpled kilt. Yet his spirits lifted with the red shimmer of a birthing Ra on his right, and the motion of his legs soon warmed him. He had decided to eat only once a day, at sunset. His stomach was already protesting, demanding the milk, fresh bread, and fruit that would have been laid on his couch at this hour, but he disregarded it. *Methen*, he thought. *Methen and the little mud-brick house and a new, humble life*. He began to whistle.

He did not reach the outskirts of Hut-herib until the evening of the fifth day, and by then he had eaten all his food. The beer had been drunk long before, irresistible during the intense heat of the days. He had accidentally burned his foot when an ember rolled from one of his fires, and because the flood water now covered the road he had waded ankle-deep in it to soothe the wound and to cool himself, but a full day out of the town its level had risen dangerously and he had been forced onto higher ground. It was with unutterable relief that he saw the jumble of squat buildings, still low on the horizon, that signalled the southern outskirts of Hut-herib. They were surrounded by the grey, placid lake of the Inundation. Rows of half-submerged palm trees delineated

drowned fields. The spreading tops of the sycamores
were heavy with flocks of raucous birds watching the
surface of the water for small fish and insects. Huy,
tired and filthy, drew the damp air into his lungs and
wondered what was missing. Some time later he realized that deep inside him he had been expecting the
heady, thick aroma of the arouras of perfume flowers
his uncle grew, but of course it was the wrong time of
the year. There was only the smell of muddy water and
now, faintly, a whiff of smoke from cooking fires.

At last, having been forced to approach the town in
a wide half-circle to the east, he came to a raised road
leading onto the top of one of the deep dikes cut
throughout Hut-herib and temporarily isolating areas
of the town from one another. He remembered that
he had not been following the river itself but one of its
eastern tributaries that ambled north and spilled into
the Great Green. He remembered that Hut-herib itself
sat between two of the Delta branches. As Nut opened
her mouth and slowly swallowed a bleeding Ra, he
crossed the tributary, found himself facing the town's
welter of warehouses and boat-crowded docks, and
knew vaguely where he was. It did not take him long
to reach the centre of the town. He had forgotten how
bare and ugly it was. The fertile fields to the east of it
might be beautiful, but Hut-herib itself was bereft of
trees, the gardens of its wealthy that lined the tributary
hidden behind mud walls over which tired branches
drooped above the path.

Khenti-kheti's shrine took up one side of a large
square of beaten earth where farmers and merchants
kept the market busy and noisy. Huy crossed it just as

the last of the stalls were being dismantled and unsold goods were being loaded into carts or the basket panniers of patient donkeys. No one gave him a second glance. Wearily he passed through the gate in the god's wall and immediately recognized the small patch of grass dominated by the one sycamore tree, and the short, stone-flagged path leading to the single modest court. There was no sign of a guard. Huy set down his burdens. How tiny it all was, after Ra's mighty, pillared expanse at Iunu! No worshippers or gossipers jostled him. The court was empty, the inner room closed off.

Methen's quarters adjoined the court. His small door was closed. Huy approached it, the memory of his four-year-old self walking with him. He had known, that day, that he was to be sent away to school and he had blurted out his fear to the kindly priest who had taken his hand and led him into the inner room. There he had waited for the sanctuary door to be opened while the priest had charged a censer and Huy had smelled frankincense for the first time. It had become a commonplace aroma at Iunu, so familiar that he had grown almost unaware of it, but this evening as dusk settled over him and he knocked on Methen's door he remembered how it had filled his nostrils with its exotic scent, not sweet or bitter, rich and yet gentle.

After a moment the door opened. Methen stared at him, then his face broke into a wide smile. "Huy! Already! I did not recognize you for a moment. It has been a very long time since we actually saw each other. Come in." His arms went around Huy. "You look as though you have walked all the way from Iunu!" Huy followed him inside and the door was closed.

Methen's quarters were as neat and clean as the priest's body always was. A raffia mat took up most of the floor. A wooden desk with a chair behind it and a rough chest on either side took up one wall to the left. Two plain wooden chairs flanked a small table directly ahead. Two simple oil lamps provided the only illumination, their naked flames still bending from the movement of the door. On the right a dim opening led, Huy surmised, to the priest's sleeping room. All at once the idea of laying his head on a pillow and stretching out on a cot was delicious. Fatigue overwhelmed him.

"What do you need first?" Methen continued. "A bath or something to eat?"

"I did walk from Iunu. I would like a large jug of water please, Methen, and then whatever food you have. I could sleep for a week, but I had better wash myself after I've eaten. May we talk tomorrow? It's so good to be here with you, but I'm tired."

Methen regarded him fondly. "My servant has gone home for the night. Sit down and rest, Huy. I'll go to the kitchen and see what I can find. I have an assistant priest now, you know. Or rather, several who perform the three-month rotations common in other temples. It makes me feel quite important."

He grinned and Huy smiled back. *I love you,* Huy thought as Methen swiftly left. *You saved my life. You carried me from the House of the Dead to my parents' house. You kept faith with me when my own father turned away. It is all coming back to me, and I don't want it! Must I relive it all since I have been away for so many years?*

Although the chair was hard, Huy felt himself slip into a doze. He came to himself as Methen shut the door and took the few steps across the room. "Water, cold duck, cold lentil soup, cold bread," he said apologetically. "Eat and drink while I bring your belongings inside. The guard also goes home at night. Not that I fear thieves within the sacred precinct."

Huy drained the water and set about the food, tearing at the bread and dipping it into the spicy soup. He had finished the meal by the time Methen had set his chest and satchels against the wall. "I have lit a fire under the cauldron in the bathhouse," Methen added. "You'll find it outside the main wall and to your right. Again, there is no one to shave and oil you, but that too can wait. A man comes to see to us priests every day. We may not have a single hair on our bodies when we go about our duties."

Huy slid from the chair and hugged him tightly. "Gods, I'm glad to be here!" he murmured. "To be with someone I completely trust. Someone who will ask nothing extraordinary from me. You know what I mean."

"I do."

As Huy made his way back across the grass to the gate, he glanced up. The moon was low and full, eclipsing the stars close to it. The air smelled faintly of donkey dung and smoke. The bathhouse was warm with steam and the light, pleasant fragrance of ben oil. Lifting the lid of a small bowl, Huy found natron. Unbinding his dusty, disordered hair, he set about the task of ridding himself of his long trek.

Much later he returned naked to the safety of Methen's rooms, sandals and dirty linen bundled under his arm. Methen took them from him and indicated his sleeping room. "Take my couch tonight. I'm quite happy to stretch out here on the floor with a cushion and a blanket. It'll be more comfortable than an all-night vigil in the shrine on the eve of a major feast day!"

Huy was too tired to demur. Nodding his thanks, he stumbled through the doorway. Methen's linen was coarse but clean, his one pillow stuffed with goose down. Huy did not even remember pulling up the sheet.

He woke to voices and for a moment believed himself to be back in his cell at Iunu, but as he struggled to sit up, the man who placed hot bread, a hunk of cheese, and a cup of milk on the floor beside him was unfamiliar. The man smiled. "The High Priest has gone to perform the morning rites for Khenti-kheti," he explained to a groggy Huy. "He has laid out his own linen for you and has asked me to recover yours and wash and starch it. I presume it is in one of the bags out there." He pointed to the outer room. "The water in the bathhouse will still be warm if you hurry, and the body servant to the servants of the god will wait a little while to shave and pluck you if that is your desire."

Huy blinked at him. "Thank you," he managed. "My linens are in the larger of the two bags. I cannot pay you."

The man shrugged. "It is a service for Methen," he said simply, and went away.

By the time Huy had eaten, bathed, shaved, and dressed himself in Methen's copious linens, the priest was back, hurrying into his house in a cloud of kyphi perfume. He laughed when he saw Huy emerge from the sleeping room. "All you need is a leopard skin draped across your shoulder and a sacred staff in your hand to play the part of a High Priest yourself," he said, eyeing the folds of the sheath flowing against Huy's ankles. "Never mind. Soon your kilts will be returned to you." Going to the table, he sat, reaching for his morning meal. "The dawn song has been sung to Khenti-kheti," he went on. "The rites of feeding, cleansing, and dressing the god have been accomplished. Now tell me everything while I eat."

Huy took the chair opposite his friend and began to recount his shameful interview with Nakht, the encounter with Ramose and the Rekhet, and his long walk from Iunu. He did not speak of his desperate attempt to rid himself of both his gift and the wound of his humiliation at Nakht's hands by engaging the whore; the memory of it was too raw for words. Methen listened attentively as he ate his bread and cheese. Then he sighed. "Perhaps you have been hasty. Your pride was wounded, Huy, your dreams shattered. Your letters were full of Anuket and her family and I was often troubled as I read them. But with your excellent school record and the blameless assessments of your tutors, you could have obtained a good post with any of a hundred needy nobles, merchants, and other businessmen in Iunu. There is no future for you here. You must know that."

Huy shrugged. "I know. I don't care. I just want anonymity, Methen. Small responsibilities, simple tasks." He grimaced. "I fancied myself a noble. The arrogance that drove my parents to send me away in the first place has obviously not died. I am chastened."

Methen shot him a keen look. "So you seek the other extreme out of a wounding anger? And how will you feel once your hurt and anger have died?"

"I don't know." Huy spread out his hands. "If you are worried that one day soon I'll run away to some more lucrative post, we can have a contract drawn up between us. But I am so very tired, Methen. Tired in my soul from the forced learning of the past weeks, from loving Anuket in spite of a growing conviction in me that she will make no one a good wife, from the continual pressure to decipher the Book . . ."

"Ah. The Book." Methen drained his cup of milk and dabbed his mouth on the square of linen beside his plate. "We do not need to speak of its mysteries unless you want to, Huy. As for Anuket, you are not the first man to love an unworthy woman, and you will not be the last. Why do you think thus of her?"

Carefully Huy told of her increasingly common behaviour, his sense of being manipulated by her, their final encounter in Nakht's night-hung garden, and as he heard himself give audible voice to his misgivings it came to him that she was indeed unworthy of him. He had not dared to think of her in that way before, but with the attempt to describe her to Methen came a clarity of mind. He still loved her, he knew that, but the emotion could be placed behind other preoccupations in a way impossible before. A shift had taken place in his ka. Peace had suddenly become attainable.

"I would like to discuss my duties now, Methen," he finished.

"Certainly. We will work together through the morning hours tallying gifts given to Khenti-kheti, preparing requisitions for his upkeep and that of his priests—all two of us—and keeping a record of the petitions made to him by the citizens of the town. The tasks are small and easily dealt with. So far I have simply hired a scribe from the marketplace." He smiled. "It will be good to rely on one intelligence, let alone one style of writing, for this work. The afternoons will be yours. I'm afraid you must launder your own linen and prepare your own food, but you may use the temple's kitchen and its modest stores if you wish. The temple will supply ink, brushes, and papyrus for you." He rose. "I have been fortunate to find you a house close by. It belongs to the temple. I could have moved into it, but I prefer to be closer to the sanctuary and my sacerdotal duties. This house was occupied by a woman who recently died. It is bare and there is no garden with it, but that's true of most homes in Hut-herib. There will be no remuneration with this position," he told Huy. "But your needs will be supplied by the temple. You have enough linens and oils for the time being?"

Huy thought of his satchels and his chest, full of the gifts from Nakht and his family. "I have enough. I will not be prodigal in my wants, Methen, I promise you."

"Good. Then bring your belongings and I will show you the house."

Huy followed him out into the full glare of the morning sun. They crossed the square of grass, threading through the groups of gossiping townsfolk who had come to pay their respects to the god and stayed to share their news with each other, and passed through the gate, turning sharply left into a narrow earthen street where the small buildings crowded lopsidedly together.

"These are all homes with one or two shops fronting them," Methen explained. "Nothing very grand. A potter making wine jars, a woman selling brooms. Unfortunately, there is a beer house beside your dwelling. You share a wall with it. The nights may be noisy, but the few whores who loiter about outside take their customers farther along the street. It is a far cry from your quiet little cell or Nakht's estate at Iunu."

Huy thought of the Rekhet's home on just such a street. *What is good enough for her is surely good enough for me,* he said to himself, *and if I want to escape the noise and dirt I can go out into the field*s. Stepping around a crowd of naked children playing knuckle-bones, he followed Methen through a low doorway halfway along what was almost an alley.

There were three tiny rooms smelling of mice and the peculiar mustiness that often clung to the skin of the elderly. The walls and floor were undressed. The room fronting the street was the largest but by no means copious. The right-hand wall was almost completely taken up with two doorless apertures leading to the remaining two rooms, identical in miniature size and divided by a wall. Methen pointed to the far wall. "The beer house is beyond that. There's not much room, but it would be advisable to place your cot in the centre of the floor. And take the room farthest from the street to sleep in. Mud bricks are thick and keep most noise out, but not all."

Privately, Huy was appalled. *What in the name of Atum have I done?* he wondered dismally. *This is much worse than Henenu's house. No rear door, no garden, and if I want to escape the dimness and sit in sunshine*

I must take a chair into the street. Dust and grit lay thickly under his sandals as he took the few paces from room to room. Methen was watching him anxiously. Huy managed a smile. *It is what I deserve,* he wanted to say. Instead, he summoned a joke. "Cleaning it should take me all of two moments," he said. "I shall buy a broom from my neighbour and ply it with vigour. There will be no problem, Methen."

The priest looked relieved. "Later you may want to look for something better, but you know this town, Huy—apart from the few nobles' estates fronting the tributary, Hut-herib is ugly." He turned back towards the square of light seeping in from the street. "Let's return to the temple and take a look in the storehouse. We may find a cot and a table and a chair or two there. Then you should visit your family."

"My family?" With a thrill of mortification Huy realized that not one thought of his parents had entered his head. He wondered what they would say when he told them he had come back to Hut-herib to work. His mother would simply be happy to have him close by, but his father would probably make some dry comment about peasants finally knowing their place, or young men with pompous ideas being humbled. Huy dreaded the encounter. "Of course you're right," he said to Methen's back as he picked his way behind him down the street towards the blessed cleanliness of the temple courtyard. "What can I say to them, Methen? And especially to my uncle Ker, who relinquished the responsibility he had taken on for my education when you carried me from the environs of the House of the Dead? He favours my brother Heby now. It will be a difficult meeting."

They were crossing the soft grass of the court. Methen glanced at him. "Difficult but necessary," he said crisply. "These people are your blood, Huy. Nakht could not take their place, nor did he ultimately want to. Remember that. It was not my place to tell them that you might be coming home. You are not expected. Do you want to send them a message first?"

"No," Huy said slowly, coming to a halt. "I want to see their reactions. I want to know if I am still loved by any save my mother."

Methen cocked an eye at him. "You chose to stay in Iunu on many occasions when you could have come home," he reminded Huy. "If your parents are cool towards you, you cannot blame them. How prideful you still are! Go and see them. Accept their greeting, whether warm or aloof. Has it not occurred to you that your long absence might have hurt them?"

No, Huy thought dismally, *it has not. My father removed his trust from me. Ker removed his affection. They were all happy to have me stay away, except when Nakht and Nasha and Thothmes visited me there and brought them gifts. Then they were happy enough with me.* Rancour curdled in his mouth like soured milk. *I will see them and take the medicine my father is bound to tip into my unwilling ears. I will show them the scrolls of excellence from my teachers, but not as though I were begging for their approval—I care nothing for that. Afterwards I will see them only when I am obliged to do so, on my brother's Naming Day for instance. I can't even remember when that is.*

Suddenly he came to a halt. *Ishat*, he thought with a shock. *I shall be seeing Ishat. What does she look like now? Gods, she must be fifteen! How has she grown? Will her sharp tongue sting me with truth, and shall I really not mind, the way it used to be?* Methen had disappeared around the side of the temple and Huy hurried after him.

The storehouse yielded a rickety couch, obviously cast off from some noble's household, judging by the gilt peeling from its frame and the carved likeness of the goddess Nut, she who swallowed Ra every evening, arching across the headboard, her colours still bright. Methen unearthed a plain wooden table scored with knife marks that had come from a kitchen, two chairs, two low stools, and two cracked clay oil lamps. "These can be mended with wet clay, I think," he said. "I can let you have pillows and bed linen and a couple of blankets as well, but you will have to use the temple bathhouse. As for cups, plates, utensils, I will see what the kitchen offers."

Huy shook his head. "I have the things Pabast gave me. They will suffice. I will need to borrow a bowl and some natron and rags and a broom to clean the house, and then perhaps some whitewash?" he ended hopefully.

Methen laughed. "The house is indeed dark. I will see if the man who takes care of the grass and the temple's vegetable garden and animals can mix you whitewash and find you a brush. It's time for the noon meal and then I sit just outside the sanctuary doors and wait for the petitioners. We'll eat together, Huy, and I think you should sleep. You still look tired."

Huy replied to him silently. *It is not the state of my body you see, but the turmoil in my soul, dear friend.*

I am homesick for my school, for Thothmes, and, yes, for my quiet, clean cell. It was so easy to live as Nakht's son, to learn to speak and behave like a noble, to take soft linen and sweet oils and kohl mixed with gold dust for granted, to converse easily with Nakht's guests as an equal, to call for a servant whenever I needed something. Can I face this gritty new existence? Can I endure it for even one day? What have I done?

Inside Methen's quarters he saw his linen piled neatly on the cot, starched and folded with a reverence, Huy knew, for Nasha's gold and silver borders and the quality of the weave. Methen's servant darkened the door bearing a tray from which the aromas of good hot food arose. There was beer as well. Both men sat and began to eat.

"I do not need more sleep," Huy said. "I will change your voluminous linen for one of my own kilts and leave at once for my father's house."

"And face the inevitable as soon as possible," Methen rejoined, seeing Huy's gloomy expression.

Huy did not reply.

15

Huy dressed for his visit to his family in a mood of recklessness. He chose one of Nasha's kilts, a piece of gold-bordered linen of the twelfth grade so fine that the outline of his thighs could be seen through its folds in spite of the starch. He strapped Nakht's turquoise-studded belt around his waist. He did not regret giving Anuket's earring to the whore, but he did miss its opulence swinging against his neck. The only other one he had was a simple ankh dropping from a short gold chain that Nakht's wife had tired of and had tossed to him good-naturedly on a sunny morning long ago. It would have to suffice. He outlined his eyes carefully with the kohl Thothmes had given him. He had no bracelets, but the sa amulet shone on his shaved chest and the fingers of his left hand were heavy with the ring amulets, Soul and Frog. He would not go shamefaced to Hapu's house, bereft of dignity like a chastened child. The odour of jasmine oil, the only oil he possessed, sickened him with the remembrance of his humiliation, but only the very poorest citizens had no oil with which to soften their skin against the harshness of Egypt's climate and to perfume themselves; and Huy, as he rubbed jasmine over his torso and into his loose hair, reflected that the encounter with his parents was likely to be just as crushing as his interview with Nakht and his abortive attempt at intercourse with the whore. Combing and braiding his hair and fastening it with the frog clasp, he slipped his feet into his worn old sandals. It was unfortunate that he would have to walk through the town and arrive at his parents' home with dusty feet and legs, but it could not be helped. *At least,* he thought grimly as he placed the scrolls containing his tutors' evaluations into his small satchel, left Methen's quarters, and struck out across the grass, *at least I may be able to keep my kilt clean.*

He remembered the way perfectly well although he had not trodden it for many years, not since he had come to the temple with Itu and Hapu to thank the god for his fourth Naming Day and to give Khenti-kheti his gift. Then as now, the town's areas were islanded by deep dikes filled with the flood water in which naked children splashed and slung mud at each other and at passersby. Huy, knowing himself an attractive target, avoided the few groups of happy young scoundrels. The hottest hours of the day had begun and many families were resting in the coolness of their houses.

Reaching the outskirts seemed to take him a long time. He deliberately walked slowly, willing himself not to sweat. When the densely packed buildings became a straggle of private dwellings, away to his right, beneath the height of the Inundation, his uncle Ker's precious arouras stretched to a line of

truncated palms shimmering on the humid horizon.
Huy found the path that ran in front of his father's
gate, and with the water lapping inches from his feet
he turned onto it. Soon, all too soon, he saw the low
mud-brick wall and the wooden gate and, beyond
them, through the few trees of the garden, the
whitewashed gleam of his father's house. How small it
all was, he marvelled as he paused, his hand on the
gate. How tiny the garden with its miniature pool
surrounded by his mother's vegetable plots; how low
the flat roof; how modest the house he had once
thought as huge as Pharaoh's palace! Off to the right
was the hedge dividing garden from orchard and,
beyond that, Ker's fields where Huy's father laboured,
an abundance of rich dark soil even now being replenished with nourishing silt. In another six weeks or so
Ker's army of peasants, Huy's father among them,
would walk ankle-deep in the warm mud and strew the
seeds of a hundred different perfume flowers to
become garlands, wreaths, exotic perfumes, and
fragrant oils for the wealthy. *Yet my father lives in
greater privacy than I shall, with my three rooms
crammed between a beer house and fronting a dusty
street.* Consciously willing his hand to push the gate
open, his feet to carry him through it, he walked the
short distance to the open door.

The interior of the house was quiet but for a
subdued snoring coming from the room Huy knew
was his parents'. Quietly he slipped along the short
hallway to the door of the room he still thought of as
his. It was closed. Carefully he pushed it ajar and
peered around it. Someone was sleeping on his cot.

All Huy could see was a head of tousled black hair and one small foot protruding from under a rumpled sheet. For a moment Huy was indignant. This was his room! He had painted those admittedly crude pictures of hectically green frogs and bushy yellow palm trees himself, and there was his name repeated several times over the white walls, the hieroglyphs clumsy but decipherable. He felt the paintbrush in his hand, the frown on his brow as he laboriously stroked the characters over the whitewash. Then his good sense reasserted itself. This was no longer his room. It belonged to his brother Heby, surely the child buried under the thick grey sheet.

He must have made some sound, an exhalation of breath, the creak of the door, for all at once the figure stirred, pushed the sheet away, and sat up. He and Huy regarded one another silently. Huy had time to remark to himself on the boy's sturdy, even features, the glow of health on his brown skin, the large dark eyes shaped very like his own regarding him sombrely and without fear. "Who are you?" Heby asked at last. "Why are you staring at me?"

Huy stepped farther into the room. An expression of alarm crossed the boy's features. "I'm your big brother, Huy," Huy began to explain, but the child had pushed himself against the wall and bunched his fists.

"No you're not," he said loudly. "My brother Huy lives at Ra's temple in Iunu, far far away. Mother! Come quickly! There is a strange man in the house!"

"Hush, Heby, don't wake them," Huy admonished in a moment of panic. *I am not ready for this,* he thought as he heard an immediate stirring from along the passage. *It is not the slow and easy way I imagined it would be. I am not in control here*. He stood irresolute, his satchel hanging forgotten from one hand.

"Hurry up, Mother!" Heby called. "And you had better bring Father as well. The man looks strong!" In spite of his position against the wall, shoulders hunched around his bony knees, there was no real fear in Heby's eyes.

Footsteps padded along the passage and Huy came to himself. He opened the door wider. Itu stood there in a sheath she had obviously pulled on in haste. One strap was crushed under her arm. Her hair was in disarray and her eyelids swollen with sleep, but her glance was alert. Behind her Hapu came hurrying, still tying on a kilt. Both stared in blank amazement at Huy. Huy, his nostrils slowly filling with the well-remembered scent of his mother's lily perfume, so common and yet so distinctly hers, felt himself loosen inside. "Mother, it's me, Huy," he said huskily. "The front door was open. I'm sorry to startle you. I . . ."

He got no further. With a cry of joy Itu flew at him, flung her arms around him, and crushed him to her. "My Huy, my Huy, my son," she said, her voice muffled below his shoulder. "Is it really you?" Huy felt a wetness blossom on his skin. She was crying. "You are really here? But we had no word. You sent us no word . . ."

Huy extricated himself and kissed her. She had changed little, he reflected. Her delicate face held a few more wrinkles and her long hair was slashed with grey at both temples. But she was still beautiful, this woman whose love for him, whose faith in him, had never wavered. She clung to his arm as he turned to his father. Hapu was smiling warily.

"I hardly recognized you," he said. "So tall and handsome! So you visit us at last. You are very welcome." His gaze fell to the sa on Huy's breast and back to Huy's face. Huy could see the questions there and, deeper still, a small bud of resentment. Or was it the old fear that had spawned the breach between them?

He held out his hand. "I am very glad to see you again, Father. Glad that you have not changed." But he had. As Hapu took the proffered hand, Huy thought how stooped the man had become, how ropy the muscles of his arms and chest, and all at once he was filled with pity. *This is what happens to the man who spends his life in hard labour*, he thought sadly. *My father Hapu, so strong, so virile, being gradually twisted into deformity so that his old age will be filled with aching joints and hands that will no longer obey him.*

"Oh, I've changed," Hapu replied. "I know it. So have you." He ran a critical eye over his son and then suddenly grinned. "Gods, you're a sight to be proud of! Wait until Ker hears that wonderful noble accent of yours! You've made your school days a triumph of success, haven't you? Itu, clean yourself up and run and get Hapzefa. There must be wine tonight instead of beer, and definitely a feast!"

An indignant shout came from the cot. Heby had wriggled off it and was pushing his way between Hapu and Huy. "I'm your son!" he cried, tugging Hapu's hand away from Huy. "Lift me up, Father, and tell this man who I am!"

Hapu laughed and hoisted Heby onto his shoulders. "You are my little Heby, and this is your brother, big Huy. You must be respectful towards him." Huy met the boy's hostile glance.

"I am big Heby," Heby announced, his fingers in his father's hair. "I go to school. I go to a much better school than Huy. I get all my lessons right."

"No you don't, you child of Set," Hapu said indulgently. "Get down now. When Hapzefa comes, you must be washed and have some milk. Then you can play with the cats. Huy and your mother and I have much to talk about."

"I don't want to play with the cats." Heby slid down Hapu's body and glowered at Huy. "I want wine and a feast if that's what he's getting!" He pointed at Huy, who was cursing himself for not bringing any sort of a gift, even something small, for this little firebrand. Then he remembered that at the bottom of his small satchel he had thrust the box of almonds Thothmes had given him. Quickly he opened the bag, rummaged about, and, lifting the box, handed it to Heby.

"I brought these for you, my special brother," he said gravely. "They are very good to eat and quite rare. You don't have to share them if you don't want to." Hapu raised his eyebrows. "Almonds," Huy whispered.

Hapu's eyes widened. "Quite an expensive gift." The tartness in his voice was back. Huy sighed inwardly.

Heby's eyes flicked doubtfully from the box to Huy's face and back again. Then, gingerly taking the box, he lifted the lid. "These are funny brown nuts," he pronounced. "Father, shall I eat one?"

"Eat as many as you like, but save a few for your mother," Hapu replied heavily. "We won't see almonds again for a very long time."

Anger flared in Huy, but he pushed it down, resisting the urge to tell his father that he had not acquired the expensive treat himself, that he had never been able to afford such things, that Thothmes had given them to him, as Thothmes' family had given him almost everything on his body that Hapu was openly assessing.

Heby reached into the box, carefully extracted an almond, and put it in his mouth. He bit down on it with an audible crunch. "It's bitter, but I like it," he said presently. "I'll have another one. Thank you, Huy." He set the box on the table beside the cot. "Can I go outside now?" Hapu nodded and the child scampered into the passage.

So I am accepted, Huy thought, relieved.

Hapu indicated the door. "Come into the reception room and sit. Itu won't be long. Then you can tell us all your news." Taking up his satchel, Huy followed him.

Nothing had changed in the little house's main room either. A couple of worn cushions, a low communal meal table, a few stools, made up the furnishings Huy remembered. Sinking to the floor, he put his back to the wall. He and his father regarded one another in silence for a moment. Then Hapu said, "Itu has enjoyed your letters very much, particularly when you began to write them in your own hand. Each time one was delivered we requested the messenger to read it to us and then Itu would sit with the papyrus in her lap and finger the hieroglyphs as though she could touch you. She has grieved at your long absence." *But you have not,* Huy accused him in his mind. *Now you have another son, a normal, healthy child who will not go away to school, who will not be struck by a noble's throwing stick, who will not die and return to life. Now you can sink into the security that you enjoyed before.*

"I have no excuses, Father," Huy said aloud. "My life filled up with school and my city friends. You and Mother and Hut-herib receded into my past. I should have returned more often, but everything here became small and dreamlike to me. There's no point in lying about it."

Hapu's thick eyebrows rose. "Well, at least you do not insult me with false sentiments. When Itu returns, you can tell us why you are here." *Of course, you did not travel all the way from Iunu just to see us*—Huy heard the addition although Hapu's mouth had closed.

"My brother is a handsome boy," Huy said. "How is his school work? Does he like learning?"

Hapu smiled. "He is already ahead of his class in reading and reciting," he said proudly. "He is slightly weaker than his fellow students in writing and numbers, and unfortunately we, your mother and I, cannot help him seeing that neither of us can read or write. But he goes to visit Ker quite often and Heruben helps him."

"I was slow at writing and numbers also," Huy put in. "I soon caught up. So will Heby. Intelligence shines out of those brown eyes of his." The attempted compliment, the desire to remind his father that he and Heby were of the same blood, fell flat. Hapu merely grunted.

Huy was about to open his satchel and withdraw his scrolls when Hapzefa came rushing across the room, grabbed his hands, and in a flurry of delighted cries tried to haul him to his feet. Huy struggled up to be engulfed in the woman's embrace.

"Master Huy! How wonderful! Look at you! You have grown up behind our backs! Do you still lie down in vegetable patches to catch frogs? I suppose you catch girls now instead, and you are too big to spank! Are you home for long? Itu, where can he sleep? There's no room." All the time she was crowing she was kissing his cheeks and his hands. Laughing, Huy kissed her back. This was the woman who had both spoiled and disciplined him, sung him to sleep and terrified him with her stories of demons and ghosts, and he remembered how much he had loved her. She had not changed at all. The stout peasant face had always been seamed, the breasts soft and large for a small boy to lay his head against, the arms thick and strong.

Setting him away, she surveyed him critically. "Fine linen and gold amulets. Jasmine perfume and hands without a single callus. Are you a nobleman now, Master Huy? Should I be bowing to you and calling you Prince?" Her eyes twinkled at him without malice.

Huy held out his hands. "No, no, Hapzefa. Look— no henna on my palms. The linen, the gold, the oil, all gifts from my friend Thothmes' family, and I have been so long at my studies that I have had no opportunity to work with anything other than a pen and a few weapons. My station has not changed much."

"But a little. Yes, a little. You speak in the accents of a lord. Gods, it's good to see you!" She turned to Itu, who had entered behind her, clad in a clean sheath. Itu had combed her hair and tied it back with a ribbon,

Huy could have sworn, that came from the chest of good things Nakht had brought to her on his visit years ago. He felt momentarily sick.

"I'll bring the shedeh-wine now," Hapzefa said, "and I made fresh date cakes this morning. Sit back down, Master Huy." She bustled out.

Huy went back to the floor and Itu joined him, taking his arm and nestling against him. "It's good to see you, my dearest. But what are you doing here? Why aren't you in school?"

Huy looked into her flushed face. "The school closes every year for the Inundation," he reminded her, "but in any case, Mother, my school days are over." Opening his bag, he took out the scrolls. "These are my reports and recommendations from my tutors. May I read them to you both?" Hapu nodded. He had crossed his legs and was leaning back, watching Huy carefully. Slowly, with great pride, Huy read to them the words of praise from the men who had governed his life for the last twelve years.

He was halfway through the scrolls when Hapzefa returned with clay cups and a flagon of wine. Quietly she poured for them, then hovered in the doorway, listening. When Huy had finished, it was she who spoke first. "I always knew you could be the best at whatever you chose to do. I suppose you will return to Iunu now and take up a position as chief scribe to some rich man, and marry his daughter and settle down in comfort. Oh, Master Huy, well done! Wait until I tell Ishat!"

Huy's throat was dry. The sweet pomegranate wine slipped down it easily, the taste bringing a host of vivid memories with it. *Yes, Ishat,* he thought as he set his cup onto the floor. *Where is she? Does she still work in the house or has her father married her off to some sturdy farm labourer?* The idea was thoroughly distasteful. *I want her to be here. I want to see her again. I want her to be unchanged, like Hapzefa.*

His mother squeezed his arm and murmured her congratulations. She seemed quite overcome. Hapu smiled faintly. "You have triumphed over every adversity," he said, and Huy knew his father would come no nearer to the matter of Huy's death. "What now, Huy?"

Huy glanced at the three expectant faces. "The High Priest of Ra at Iunu offered me a place as his personal scribe," he said carefully. "But I declined. I have spent enough time in the temple. I want different surroundings for a while."

Hapu looked at him blankly. "What does that mean?" he said sharply. "Such a position would be a plum for any young man. It would lead to even greater things. How long is 'for a while,' Huy?"

"I don't know," Huy admitted. "I will be working as a scribe for Khenti-kheti's High Priest, Methen." Hapu visibly flinched. Huy knew the reaction had nothing to do with the lowliness of the station.

"Did something bad happen to you in Iunu, Master Huy?" The query came from the astute Hapzefa. "Is that why you have come home to this miserable town?"

How can I possibly explain to them about Anuket and the Book, and how the reverences of the priests became painful to me, and how I wear the sa night and day to keep the demons away from me, and how I fear and hate the heka of Atum and Thoth? I will try to tell Mother, she might understand, but now is not the time.

"No, nothing bad," he lied, "unless boredom with so much studying and a need for a different experience can be called bad. Methen has given me a house in the town, close to the shrine."

Itu sat straighter. "Then you will be close by!" she exclaimed. "Oh, Huy! We will be able to see you often!"

Hapzefa sniffed, a derisive sound. "It is a step down from what you might accomplish. I hope that a new boredom and a need for some other, more acceptable experience sets in before long. I never thought of you as stupid when you were a boy. Self-willed and given to tantrums, but not dim-witted. What about your friend's father, Iunu's Governor? Can't he do something for you?"

"I would not let him," Huy lied again, meeting the servant's shrewd gaze. "I have arranged to do what I want to do for now. I am not a child anymore, Hapzefa. I have attained my majority. I am a free man."

Hapzefa rolled her eyes and disappeared, only to reappear with a dish of date cakes, which she set before Itu. "Heby is already in the pond and covered in mud. I'll fish him out and wash him, and then we'll cook something fine for you, Huy. Meanwhile, eat my cakes. You always liked them."

Hapu had said nothing. His head was down and he seemed to be contemplating his bare feet. *You are not happy at having me so close,* Huy thought, his gaze on the crown of Hapu's head. *Are you afraid that I will somehow corrupt my little brother? Or is it simply that now you will be forced to relive the failure of your love towards me?*

"You need not worry that I shall be visiting you too often," he said. "Methen will be keeping me busy, and besides, your own lives have fallen into customs and habits that my presence would only disturb. I shall not even stay the night here."

Hapu's head came up. He met Huy's even glance, but his eyes quickly slid away. "You are welcome to stay as long as you wish," he murmured, but his words were lost in Itu's loud protestations.

"What nonsense! You must come and see us at least once a week, and as for tonight, Heby can sleep with your father and me and Hapzefa can put fresh linen on your old cot. We insist, don't we, Hapu?" She leaned forward towards her husband anxiously. *So she remembers also*, Huy thought. *Poor, darling Mother, desperate to make peace, to mend the rift between her husband and her son.*

He drew her back into his embrace and kissed her. "I would like to sleep once more in my old room, providing Heby understands that I'm just borrowing it. Don't fret, Itu. I am merely concerned that I don't upset the household."

The hot afternoon passed in polite conversation, and at sunset Hapzefa and Itu laid a modest feast upon the one low table. Heby had appeared, scrubbed and freshly kilted, and had fallen asleep in his mother's lap, but at the aroma of food he woke and the family ate together in an atmosphere of forced cheerfulness. Huy was chewing the last of his honeyed figs when Heby, unbidden, crawled onto his knees and thrust a sticky face close to his. "I will tell you about my school and then you can tell me about yours," he commanded. "Have you failed at all your lessons, to still be at school? You are much bigger than the biggest boys in my class."

Huy felt himself warming towards this pert brother of his. "I think that your school only teaches boys until they are eight. My school has lessons for everyone until they are sixteen."

Heby twisted around in Hapu's direction. "I like school," he announced, his voice rising. "I want to be like Huy and study until I'm sixteen. Will I go to a new school when I am eight, Father?"

Hapu set down his beer. "Your uncle Ker has kindly arranged for you to go away to school at the temple of Ptah in Mennofer," he said. Huy saw his fingers draw together tightly.

Heby's lower lip stuck out. "But I want to go to Huy's school."

"I'm not there anymore, Heby," Huy said quickly. "I have finished all my lessons."

"Oh." With the abruptness of every small child he lost interest in the subject, and began to wriggle towards Huy's cup. *So Ker will fund the education of yet another impecunious relative,* Huy thought savagely. *Doubtless he prays that this time he will not be rewarded with shame and embarrassment. Oh, curse you both, Father and Uncle! I don't want to spend the night here among these awkward strangers. I want to run to Methen, to his unquestioning affection.* Absently he was wrapping his hand around Heby's as the child struggled to lift the beer to his mouth.

"No, Heby," Itu said firmly. Heby let out a wail and Itu stood, taking him from Huy's arms. "He's tired," she went on. "Hapzefa can put him to bed." She went out. Huy and Hapu sat on, not speaking, the silence uncomfortable between them. All afternoon and

evening Huy had wanted to ask about Ishat. Surely
Hapzefa had told her by now that he was at home.
Where was she? He had held his tongue, why he was
not sure. Now he rose.

"I would like to go out into the garden and feel the
night breeze for a while," he said.

Hapu nodded, obviously relieved. "The household
begins the day early, as you must remember. Itu and
I will follow Heby to bed very soon. I'll say your good
night to your mother. Hapzefa has already changed the
sheets on your cot."

Huy bowed. "Good night, then, Father. If I don't
see you in the morning, I'll be back next week." Without
waiting for a reply, he escaped into the narrow passage
and in a few strides was out under the stars.

At once he felt all tension leave him. The moon was
at the half and waning, and the stars blazed around it.
The air was soft and smelled of the freshly sprinkled
earth of his mother's little vegetable garden. When his
eyes had adjusted to the dimness, he wandered across
the grass to the pool and stood looking into its placid
surface where the glory of the night sky was reflected.
Itu planted her crops around it continually, he remembered, and the fronds of vegetables he could not name
stirred gently and darkly, blurring the edges of the water.
Somewhere under them lay the stones he had used to
smash the offending toy monkey. It seemed to him that
he was bending once again, destroying it, and in a
moment Ishat would appear in her usual soundless way
and tell him not to worry, that she would get rid of the
pieces. *It had an evil aura right from the start,*
he thought, and realizing that he was indeed bending,

he straightened and sighed. *Much of my disastrous future was already lurking inside it, waiting for my touch to flow into me. The memory of its idiot face can still make me tremble.* He glanced towards the hedge separating the garden from the orchard, half hoping that the leaves would rustle and Ishat herself would step out, but the shrubbery remained a dusky profusion of stillness.

The touch on his shoulder made him yelp. Swinging about, heart pounding, he came face to face with a young woman. She was grinning at him. Even in the half-light he could see that she was beautiful, with the strong features and high cheekbones that would keep her striking well into middle age. Undressed black hair showered in deep waves to the top of her coarse sheath, where a tantalizing shadow fell between the swell of her hidden breasts. She was as tall as he. Folding her arms, she laughed at him. "Who is this god come to earth to grace Hapu's humble garden?" she mocked. "Is it perhaps Horus himself? Or is it Bes without his pot belly? But no—I think it is a miserable little boy masquerading as a god. I hardly recognized you, Huy, and obviously you don't recognize me."

"Gods," he breathed. "Is it really you, Ishat?" Still caught in the time of the monkey, he was looking about bewilderedly for a stringy girl.

She snorted. "Of course it's me. Who else would be prowling about here in the middle of the night? I'm not surprised you didn't know me. I've had no word from you in years. I nearly didn't come to see you," she went on matter-of-factly. "When my mother came rushing home all flushed and excited and told me you were here, I decided to go into the town for the day. But as you see, I have relented. I am a forgiving creature. Besides, I was curious to see just how insufferably arrogant you'd become." She peered at him. "Did you bring your fine aristocratic friends with you? Are you still in love with that simpering little bitch?"

"You never even met her," Huy snapped. "You may look like Hathor herself, Ishat, but your tongue is still as caustic as an angry Sekhmet."

Ishat put both hands behind her head and stretched her spine in a deliberately provocative gesture. "Oh, so I am as alluring as Hathor, am I? Thank you. And I don't mind being compared to an angry lioness goddess either. As for you, Huy, with your incredible conceit, you must know that you're as handsome as a god yourself. Your hair's almost as long as mine. Why isn't your scalp shaved?" She dropped her arms. For a long moment they regarded one another, then Huy smiled.

"Here we are picking away at each other as though we parted only yesterday," he said softly. "I've been thinking about you all day. I'm so very glad to see you."

"Of course you are. But what are you doing here? You usually spend the months of the Inundation at the school."

So she had cared enough to stay abreast of his movements, probably through his letters to his parents. He felt ridiculously pleased. Then he sobered. A longing to tell her everything came over him. Almost shyly, for the voice of his old friend issuing from the mouth of this lovely woman still baffled him, he reached for her hand. "Come and sit with me on the other side of the hedge where no one can get to us from the house, the way we used to do," he said, drawing her away from the pond.

Wordlessly she allowed herself to be drawn through the gap in the hedge and they settled themselves in the deep shadow of one of the trees. Ishat drew up her knees. The folds of her sheath fell away to reveal two long, shapely legs, which she did not bother to cover again. Huy smiled to himself even as he noted their grace. Something of the child who loved to run free and filthy alongside the canals still remained in her.

"I'm finished with school," he began. "I've come back to Hut-herib to work for Methen..." And although it hurt him, shamed him, to speak to her of Nakht's betrayal and of Anuket's long betrothal, unbeknownst to him, to a nobleman's son, and to unburden himself of the Book and its mysterious significance, he felt a great comfort as the words left him because it was Ishat listening—Ishat, his oldest friend and playmate—and his trust in her had not changed.

She laughed at him only once, when he haltingly recounted his disastrous effort to lose his virginity to the young whore. "So you could do nothing even though you wanted to?" she said incredulously. "And this with a woman schooled in arousing a man? Why not?" He told her why not, in short, sharp sentences. She was silent for many moments, looking away from him into the darkness under the trees. When she looked back at him, her expression was unreadable. "That's the saddest, strangest thing I have ever heard. Are you sure of this, Huy? That Atum himself wills your virginity?"

"It seems so," he replied harshly, "and most of the time I hate him for it, and hate the gift and hate not being able to get drunk like everyone else and hate being bowed to and stared at all the time in the temple."

"So much hate!" she said, and the mocking tone was back. "And I hate too. I hate that stupid girl who made you so miserable and refused to run away with you."

"What of your life, Ishat?" he asked, wanting to change the subject.

She shrugged. "Nothing has changed since I saw you last," she said harshly. "I work in your father's house under the command of my mother. I clean or cook or look after your brother. My own father has forbidden me the fields and waterways, without much success, now that I am fully grown. He is trying to find a suitable husband for me."

"Is he succeeding?" Huy experienced a moment of sheer jealousy.

"No. I look at the mongrels who come sniffing around me with their big hands and dirty nails and the lust in their eyes and I am disgusted. My father is permanently angry with me."

"So you are still a virgin?" Huy had not wanted to ask the question. He knew that it implied an interest in a part of Ishat's nature he preferred not to consider; but he could not help himself.

A full minute went by before she answered, and when she did so her tone was carefully neutral. "You and your family are peasants, but you are one step above me and mine. Only slaves are below us in status, Huy, as you know very well. We are your servants. Our lives, our way of thinking about everything from the gods to gathering food, are cruder and more urgent than yours. Like the animals, we are mainly concerned with ensuring our survival and grabbing at whatever

fleeting pleasure we can." Slewing about, she folded
her legs and faced him directly, and even in the
uncertain light he could see the tension in her face and
limbs. "If I had not grown up with you I would not
even have learned the words I am able to use which do
not belong to my class, even though my accent is
rough and always will be. From you I have learned
dissatisfaction. From you I have received pain." She
began to draw one palm across the other. The tiny
sound was unnerving. "No, I am not a virgin, Huy.
I was crossing a field last Pakhons, taking a shortcut to
the river road. The barley was standing high. The
workers had begun to pull up the weeds, the clover
and wild flax and dock leaves that pollute the crop,
but it was early afternoon and everyone was taking the
hour of sleep." Pausing, she stopped her stroking
motion and hid her hands under her thighs. "I saw a
young man coming towards me. I thought it was you.
He walked like you, very straight and easy. I started to
run towards him, but as I came closer I realized that of
course it wasn't you. Still, his features resembled yours.
Coarser, and his eyes were smaller. We exchanged
greetings. I was about to move on, feeling rather sad,
when he caught my arm and pulled me down under
the shelter of the fronds of barley. He kissed me.
He pushed up my sheath. I closed my eyes and
pretended it was you." She laughed shortly, a sound
without mirth. "Why did I give in to him, like an
animal in one of my father's pens? Because I missed
you, Huy, and despaired of ever having you. Because I
have always loved you. But it was rather horrible, just a
series of boring fumbles, a moment of pain, and he got

up and went on his way without a word to me. Such encounters are common among my class." Her tone was biting. "Who cares if the blood of peasants is not pure, if one peasant impregnates another? Not like your noble friends, who are so careful to keep their bloodline untainted. When I got to the river road I went into the water and washed the blood off my legs and vowed that never again would I allow myself to be humiliated like that, in spite of my lowly status. Did I behave any better than your little whore, Huy? Not much."

Huy was speechless. The jealousy had fled, to be replaced by a great pity. Gently tugging her hand out from under her cold flesh, he held it to his face then kissed it and let it fall. "I'm sorry, Ishat."

"What for?" She got to her feet. "Is it your fault that you cannot love me? That you have never desired my body? So do the gods make fun of us for their own amusement." Her voice broke.

Huy rose. "You are my friend like no other," he began, but she gestured sharply, one swift wave of her fingers.

"Don't try to make it better," she snapped. "I play no silly feminine games. I am without the wiles of my sex. I love you. That is all." She inhaled deeply, and all at once her body loosened. "So you go to Methen in the morning, to begin your new work?"

"I go to make my house habitable first," he replied, glad that the conversation had moved to safer ground. "It's dirty. It needs whitewash. Methen has given me some furniture from the temple storehouse, but it is very meagre. I'll manage."

She nodded. "I shall see you before you leave," was all she said before turning on her naked heel and walking swiftly away through the trees.

Huy watched her until the night swallowed her up, then he pushed through the hedge and made his way across the garden and into the quiet house. Someone had left a lamp burning beside the cot in the room that was now Heby's. Quickly Huy shed his kilt and loincloth and slid under the sheet that had been turned down for him. Leaning across to the table, he blew out the lamp. Gradually the darkness gave way to a sombre half-light; he had forgotten to lower the window hanging.

For a while he lay on his back, thinking. A grown-up Ishat had been a shock for which he should have been prepared, but in his arrogance he had not considered that the passing years had acted on her as they had on him. He imagined her striding across the barley field with its feathery beige expanse of crop, the low clumps of purple clover by her feet, the deep blue of the wild flax flowers nodding in the summer wind. He imagined the young man who resembled him, lowering her to the earth, pushing her sheath up to her neck to reveal that long, lithe body, pushing himself inside her. He was there, lying on top of her, looking into those dark, indifferent eyes with her black hair netted in the stalks of grain around her head. *Well, at least she did not enjoy it,* he thought restlessly. *She called it a boring fumble.* He felt angry and anxious. *One day she will enjoy it,* he told himself dismally. *One day a suitor acceptable to her will appear and she'll begin to forget how close we were, she and I, and she will open her arms and her body and become one with someone else. Do I care?* He rolled onto his side and put both hands under his cheek. The sheets, the pillow, were rough and irritated his skin. *Yes, I do care, but why? Anuket is all my desire. Ishat is the friend of my childhood and nothing more.* Yet he found himself envious of the man who would see those sharp features loosen in sexual ecstasy, and he knew that, although he had no lover's claim on Ishat yet, he wanted to keep her for himself so that no one else could have her. The need was ridiculous, entirely and illogically selfish. Huy did his best to fight it, but it lingered on into his sleep, fuming his dreams with an invisible cloud of fretfulness.

When he woke at dawn, the members of the household were already up. For a while he lay listening to Heby's chatter, his mother's calm comments, the clatter of dishes. He could smell fresh bread with the tang of sesame seeds, Hapzefa's specialty, and with the aroma came a healthy hunger. Wrapping on the loincloth and kilt he had worn the previous day, he padded into Hapu's reception room. Heby ran to him. He was wearing a kilt with a small wine stain near the hem that Huy recognized as one of his own from years ago. Sturdy leather and rope sandals were on Heby's feet and he was clutching a small linen bag. Huy picked him up, hugged him, and set him down.

"I'm ready for school," Heby told him. "I walk all the way, with my friend from farther along the road and his mother." He shook the bag. "My lessons," he said proudly. "One day I shall be allowed to write on papyrus instead of these bits of clay. Will you be here when I come home at noon, Huy?"

"No. But I shall come back and visit you soon, Heby. I will take you down to the docks to see the boats. Would you like that?"

"Yes, please! Father only takes me out to the fields sometimes, but I do go into the perfume house with Uncle Ker. The docks will be more exciting. Goodbye, big brother!"

"You had better mean what you say," Itu commented. She had come into the room as Heby went out after impatiently allowing her to kiss the top of his curly head. "Heby has a very good memory, and if you disappoint him you may find a beetle slipped under the waistband of your kilt one day! Did you sleep well in your old room?" She was pouring him milk and cutting off a piece of goat's cheese from the brown slab on the table. "Help yourself to dates as well," she told him as he went to the floor and reached for the bread.

"My sleep was fine and I will certainly take Heby out some afternoon," Huy replied, bringing the bread appreciatively to his nose before taking a bite. "Oh, Mother! I could eat Hapzefa's bread all day!"

"Thank you, Master Huy." The woman herself had come in and was removing the littered plates. "Ishat tells me that she saw you last night and you spent much time sharing all the news." She cocked an eye at Huy, who knew exactly what she was thinking.

"We shared nothing but the news, Hapzefa," he assured her. "Is there hot water for me to wash in after I've eaten?"

"Your father left some before he went to his work. It might still be warm." She went out, her hands full.

Itu sat down beside Huy and watched him as he ate. "What of your friend Thothmes?" she asked after a while. "Will you miss him, Huy? Will you travel to Iunu sometimes to see him?" *You are ambitious for me, dearest Mother,* Huy told her with silent affection. *You hope that I will tire of poverty under Methen and will hurry back to some more illustrious post in Ra's city.*

"I'll miss him a great deal," he answered, "but I'll be writing to him as often as Methen lets me have papyrus. Thothmes gave me a sheaf of it that will not last forever."

"And what of his sisters? Will you miss them also?"

Huy was about to tease her until he saw her expectant expression. "I shall miss the whole family," he said between mouthfuls. "They were good to me, and generous—and yes, Mother, I still feel more than affection for Nakht's youngest daughter, Anuket. But you knew that, didn't you, even though I did not speak of it to you directly."

"I guessed as much from the way you described her to me," Itu sighed. "I had hoped that your preoccupation with her might have died a natural death by now, my son. Should your father be seeking a suitable wife for you?"

Huy swallowed the last of his food and sat back. "No," he replied firmly. "How could I support a wife in the position I am about to take up? And anyway, where is the woman of my station who would hold my interest and my respect?"

"Nowhere close by, that is true," Itu admitted. "The children of Iunu's Governor have spoiled you for any intercourse within your own class. It's a pity.

Perhaps Ker can help. He has a wide acquaintance among the merchants from the Delta to Weset."

"I will take no favours from Ker, and you know very well why," Huy said harshly. "I am simply not interested in marriage, Mother. Perhaps I never will be." He got up abruptly. "I must wash now."

Outside, between the house and the kitchen, was the pit where Hapzefa heated water for the household. A large cauldron hung over the ashes of the morning's fire. Beside it, on the beaten earth, was a small dish of natron and a cloth. There seemed to be no oil left in the clay cruse propped carelessly against the wall; Hapu had used it all. Huy did not begrudge it to him as he stripped and began to ladle the tepid water over himself. A man who worked under the sun's unforgiving heat all day needed the protection of whatever oil was to hand. Huy unbound his hair but did not wash it. After scrubbing his body, he rebraided his thick tresses, tied the plait with the frog, and re-entered the house, intending to pick up his leather satchel and be on his way.

But angry voices met him as he walked along the passage, and he emerged into the reception room to see his mother and Hapzefa facing a thin-lipped Ishat. Hapzefa was red from the neck of her heavy sheath to the roots of her grey hair, his mother looked distraught, but Ishat stood with her arms folded, a large linen bag at her bare feet and an obstinate expression that Huy recognized only too well on her features. "I don't care what you say," Ishat was declaring loudly, "I'm going. And if Father drags me back, I'll just run away again. I'm fifteen, Mother. Soon I'll be sixteen. Why bother to fight with me now?"

Huy paused on the threshold and with one accord all three women turned to him. "Huy, is this your idea?" Itu demanded in a strangled voice at the same time as Hapzefa shouted, "Master Huy, you should be ashamed of yourself!" Ishat had begun to smile slyly.

"What in the name of the gods is going on?" Huy asked, thoroughly mystified. "What are you arguing about? Good morning, Ishat."

"Good morning, Huy," she replied smoothly. "I have just been telling our mothers that I have made up my mind to go with you to your new house. You will need a servant to cook and clean for you, go to the markets, wash and mend your linens." Her shoulders and eyebrows rose in unison. She unfolded her arms and spread her hands. "Where else will you find someone willing to do all those things in exchange for a little food? Besides, you'll be too busy to attend to domestic matters yourself, and I know you're too poor to buy a slave." She rested one palm gracefully and theatrically on her breast. "I am willing to make this sacrifice for you. I have decided. See?" She kicked the bundle beside her toe. "I have already packed all my things."

The two other women began a chorus of protest, but Huy raised a hand and, surprisingly, they both fell silent at once. "The idea is ridiculous," he said, "and no, Mother, of course this was not my idea. Ishat has thought it up all by herself." The girl nodded triumphantly.

"But you must have hinted at such an insanity last night when the two of you were alone in the garden," Hapzefa said hotly. "It is not proper, a single man and a young girl by themselves under the same roof! Everyone will assume that my daughter's duties must go further than sweeping and laundering! You are a naughty slut, Ishat!"

The smile left Ishat's face. "I am no slut, Mother!" she shouted. "I am a servant, and a good one at that! You yourself trained me! Huy is my friend, and he will be my master. To Set with what other people will think!"

"But Ishat, Huy is an ordinary man with a man's appetites," Itu put in. "You cannot expect him to spend week after week with you in his house and not . . . not . . ."

"I do expect it. Neither of you want to remember that Huy is a Seer. He cannot make love. He told me so." Huy saw a look of sheer craftiness flit across her strong, even features.

Itu swung an agonized face towards him. "Oh, my dearest!" Her voice trembled. "Oh, Huy, how terrible! Is it true? But you told me only yesterday that you still desired your friend's sister!"

Huy, glancing at Ishat's now-pious expression, wanted to shake her. *All the same,* he thought in the moment before he answered his mother, *it would be a relief to have someone to look after my domestic needs. The temple servants always took care of them before. I never imagined having to wash my own linens and clean my own rooms. Not if Nakht had employed me . . . given me Anuket . . . As it is, I ought to either learn to do these things for myself or hire a male servant, and who will work for nothing but a couple of meals a day? Only the very rich have slaves. But Ishat? Servant to the High*

*Priest's scribe? There would indeed be gossip. You little
vixen,* he accused her wordlessly, meeting her eye. *You
have hated being under your mother's thumb ever since
you were old enough to hold a broom. I remember your
complaints. And whatever I say, you intend to trail after
me and importune me until I agree. Well,* another voice
objected in his mind, *would having Ishat in that other
room be so bad? Hapzefa has trained her well. As long as
she does what she's told* . . . He grimaced. Controlling
Ishat could prove more difficult than keeping
Methen's temple affairs in order.

"Yes, Mother, it's true," he admitted. "The High
Priest of Ra, the Rekhet—you remember her from the
exorcism that was not needed—Methen also, all agree
that I will lose the gift of the god unless I remain
celibate." He hesitated, not wanting to add to the
anguish on his mother's face and furious with Ishat for
forcing him to do so. "I still love Anuket," he went on
hurriedly, seeing Hapzefa's protest taking shape. "But
my emotion is pointless. I wanted to rid myself of my
gift. I tried to make love to a woman, and failed. Atum
prevented me." He swallowed. "I should have been
more honest with you, Mother, but I wanted to avoid
causing you the pain you feel today."

Itu's hands had gone to her throat. "I shall have
no daughter-in-law?" she half whispered. "No
grandchildren?"

"Not from me." An illogical yet familiar guilt
welled up in Huy, the guilt of inadequacy, of his
uniqueness. "But there is Heby," he went on grimly.

"Yes, there is Heby." Itu's arms dropped to her
sides. "This is a shock, but I must not grieve." Her

voice was trembling. "I must be proud that my son is a man chosen by the gods to be a Seer. I wish you had come to me freely with this knowledge, Huy, in private." She turned to Ishat. "It was wicked of you, Ishat, to use it for your own ends." Her glance went to Huy and then back to Ishat. *She is not stupid, this mother of mine,* Huy thought with a rush of love for her. *She is aware of Ishat's feelings for me. She weighs the bond of friendship between us. She does not want me to be lonely in the town. She will want news of me, and who better to supply it than Ishat? Perhaps it even crosses her mind that one day Atum will release me from the spell under which I struggle to live, and if my situation does not improve Ishat would make a vigorous and healthy wife for a peasant such as me.* Itu's next words proved him right. Her voice strengthened. "Huy, do you want this?" Hapzefa gave a cry, but Itu silenced her with a peremptory wave and for once Huy saw them as they really were, mistress and servant. "Ishat's father will be incensed."

"No he won't," Ishat cut in promptly. "He's tired of trying to find a man for me. If I become a servant to Huy he will think it odd, but he will enjoy peace in his hut for the first time since I was born."

"Evil girl!" Hapzefa said hotly. "Your father loves you! He wants good things for you!"

"Yes, Mother," Huy said clearly, "I do want this. It was not of my choosing, yet it makes a peculiar sense." He turned to Ishat. "Will you agree to be under my authority? Will you obey me, Ishat? I cannot pay you anything. My house has only three rooms, one of which will be yours, but the street it's on is noisy.

My days will be at the High Priest's disposal. You will be a long way from any fields or canals."

Ishat beamed at him. "I don't care. I will obey you as my master, Huy, I promise." And I doubt that, Huy thought wryly.

"She must visit you and her father once a week," he told Hapzefa. "Thus you may see for yourselves how she is faring. Honestly, Ishat!" he snapped at the grinning girl. "How is it that you always seem to get your own way?"

Ishat picked up her linen bag and approached Hapzefa. "Because I always try to please the gods, of course." She kissed her mother's crimson cheek. "You really do not need me here anymore, Mother," she said sweetly. "Not now that Heby is in school. Thank you for your leniency." She bowed to Itu. "And thank you, my mistress, for your wisdom. Huy, I shall wait for you by the gate." Then she was gone. The remaining three looked at each other.

"If she proves headstrong and disobedient, you must send her back," Hapzefa said. She was obviously still angry.

Itu stepped to Huy and, putting her arms around him, laid her head on his chest. "I am so very sorry, " she whispered. "Let us hope that the operation of a Seer's gift will be some compensation for all that you have lost."

Huy crushed her to him. He was exceedingly moved. "I regret the years when I ignored you. Forgive me, Itu." When she moved away from him, he saw that the sa symbol had been imprinted on her cheek.

"Pack your satchel and go," she ordered him. "Hapzefa, we have lentils to wash and onions to chop for the noon meal." Deliberately she went to the door and Hapzefa followed her. The servant did not bid Huy goodbye.

Ishat saw Huy coming and swung her bag over her shoulder. "I didn't sleep all night," she told him as they moved through the gate and began to take the long walk into the centre of town. "The more I thought about coming with you and looking after you, the more sense it made. Oh, I am happy today!"

"Ishat, I will not try to make love to you," Huy said firmly. "You should not have used the shame of my impotence as an argument. That was cruel."

"I only implied that a virgin Seer has much dignity," she responded indignantly. "Where is the shame in that? As for making love to me, first of all, I know that your affection is still centred on that worthless little snob who probably can't even tie her own sandals, and secondly, you have already shared the secret of your inability with me, where it is entirely safe. I cannot speak for our mothers, of course." Grabbing his shoulder, she pulled him to a halt. "Huy, I intend to take care of you as the best servant you could possibly have. I promise not to embarrass you, to see to your needs even before you know what they are, to keep my emotions to myself. You and I have been bound together since our childhood, and I think this is why: you will be a great Seer, and I will rise with you to be your protector and close friend. Yes?"

Oh, Ishat, I wish with all my heart that I could love you as more than a close friend, Huy thought, looking into that shining face, *for I see that you have grown up to be beautiful and spirited and intelligent. You waste yourself on me when somewhere out there is a man who truly deserves you.* He forced a smile. "Yes," he said.

Briefly she lifted the amulet from his chest then let it fall. "What is that?"

"It's called a sa. It keeps the demons away from me."

"Indeed," she said thoughtfully. "And you will be my sa, won't you, Huy, and keep the Khatyu away from me. Will you teach me to read and write?"

He could not follow the convolutions of her thought. "Yes, of course I will if you like."

"Good." She turned back to the road. "Someone must keep a record of all the people who will be coming to you for healing and to know their future, and you cannot afford a scribe." She giggled. "You can't even afford to buy me a pair of sandals, can you? Well, never mind. One day I shall be shod in gold-tooled leather."

She strode on, whistling, and Huy followed her, bemused.

16

Ishat's inspection of her new home took no more than a few moments. Huy watched her move swiftly though the three minuscule rooms, her nose wrinkled against the stench of mice and the unwashed state of the previous occupant, and when she returned to him she put down her bag and stood first on one foot and then on the other, trying ineffectually to brush the dirt from the soles of her feet. Huy was amused, considering that she had walked unshod through the dust and dung of the town. "Do you have a broom?" she asked at last without too much hope.

Huy shook his head. "Not yet."

"Cloths? Natron? Can you get whitewash?"

"I don't know. Methen says he will ask the temple's gardener if he has any."

"Gods. Well, at least we'll be close to good beer." She jerked an elbow towards the beer house. "What exactly do you have, Huy?"

"Only the things I brought from school in my two satchels and my chest—some kilts and loincloths, one good pair of sandals, my keepsakes."

"The scarab? Do you still have the scarab?"

"Of course. It's my greatest treasure."

Ishat groaned but looked pleased. "So you are poorer even than my father," she said with relish.

Annoyed, Huy picked up her bag as well as his own and stepped to the doorway. "I have employment under Methen. I am a scribe. I have some furniture from the temple storehouse, but we'll need a couch and linen for you. Come and meet him. He may not approve of the arrangement you so arbitrarily decided upon, Ishat."

"I've met him before," Ishat said indignantly, "although he may not remember me. He was at your house a lot when you were recovering, years ago." *Even Ishat is unable to say aloud what I was recovering from,* Huy thought as together they made their way along the crowded street. *Perhaps such reluctance is a good thing for me. Certainly it's a change from having to be reminded of it every time I look into a priest's eyes.*

Ishat did not seem bothered by the furore around them. She wove easily in and out of the crowds, nimbly sidestepped the loaded donkeys, and showed no particular relief when they reached the relative peace of the temple courtyard other than to wipe her feet on the soft grass. Methen's quarters were empty. Huy ushered her in and they sat and waited, relaxing in the coolness. "He's probably eating the noon meal in the kitchens rather than having it brought all the way here," Huy commented.

Ishat sighed. "I would like a meal myself. How are we to eat, Huy?"

At that moment the doorway darkened and Methen himself swept in. Ishat rose at once and bowed to him.

For a second he peered at her, then his brow cleared. "It is little Ishat!" he exclaimed. "But not so little now. Welcome! And Huy. Was your visit home a success?"

"I think so," Huy answered cautiously. "My other was overjoyed to see me, and Heby is a charming child. I have promised to see them once a week."

"Good." Ishat still stood, obviously waiting for the priest to take her chair. Methen waved her down. "Has Huy brought you to me for prayer or advice?" he asked her kindly.

Leaning forward eagerly, Ishat opened her mouth to reply, but Huy quickly forestalled her. Tact was not one of Ishat's assets. "Ishat has offered to take care of my domestic affairs," he said. "She has the permission of her mother Hapzefa, my family's servant, and of my mother. I realize that a male servant would be more appropriate for me, Methen, but as yet I am unable to pay for any help. Ishat will work for her food and a bed."

Methen regarded him thoughtfully. "If you were attached to the temple directly, such an arrangement would be inadmissible. But I have engaged you privately, as my personal scribe. I trust it is not your intention to try to subvert the will of Atum with this girl?"

Ishat had sat back and folded her legs. Now she folded her arms as well, glancing from one to the other. Huy wondered if she had understood what Methen was implying. Her face bore an expression of serious innocence.

"Not at all!" Huy answered. "Ishat and I have been friends since our childhood. My mother no longer needs her at home and she did not want to seek employment with strangers. She can visit her parents when I visit mine, every week. She can have one of my three rooms for her own. It will be all right, I swear it, Methen. Do I have your permission for this?"

"With reservations," the priest said heavily. "We will see if there are any complaints from worshippers or from my assistant priest as time goes by." He turned to Ishat. "And you, Ishat. Under the law you are not obliged to serve Huy if you don't want to, unless there is a formal contract." Huy waited anxiously as Ishat unfolded herself and placed her palms decorously on her thighs. *Don't tell him that this whole arrangement was your idea,* he spoke to her silently, surprised at how pleased he suddenly was that she would be sharing his life. He had not considered the prospect of his loneliness until now.

"I am happy to continue to serve Huy's family by serving him, Master," Ishat said. "I shall work hard and cause no scandal." Her fingers laced. "I believe that the gods have a great plan for Huy. He will need to be free of household chores in order to properly fulfill it."

Methen's eyebrows rose. "Do you indeed believe this?" he murmured. "Do you indeed? Obviously you know your friend well. We shall see. Huy, I have spoken with the gardener. He will allow you some whitewash. You may go back to the storehouse and try to find a cot for Ishat. As for the rest, there is natron and rags in the kitchen and probably a spare broom." He smiled. "The Amun-feast of Hapi is about to begin. Few citizens will be coming to pay their respects to Khenti-kheti, so the two of you may as well use the first five days of the festival to make your house habitable. The festival lasts almost a month, halfway into Athyr, but most of the townspeople will have had their fill of revelry long before that, so I shall expect you to begin work for me on the twenty-fourth day of this month. I am going to celebrate the god of the river with my parents." Huy was taken aback and Methen laughed. "You think me so old?" he mocked Huy. "I was only twenty when I picked you up outside the House of the Dead, Huy. My parents live on their land just north of the town. Well. You must begin your task and I must prepare for my little journey. Be sure and find a few flowers to throw onto the water. The god is always generous with his fish once Isis has cried."

It was a dismissal. Huy and Ishat got up. Methen embraced Huy and touched Ishat briefly on her shoulder. "Do what is right," he said to them unexpectedly, then they were out under the sunshine and walking across the grass.

Ishat pulled Huy to a halt. "He knows everything, doesn't he? About the spoiled brat you are stupid enough to love? And about the whore?"

Huy shook his head. "Not about the whore. And stop calling Anuket names just because you are jealous," he snapped.

Ishat blew air out of her nose, a sound of derision. "Yes, I'm jealous, but from what you've told me the girl is indeed a spoiled brat," she retorted. "Now Huy, I refuse to burrow into the temple storehouse until I've eaten. I'm absolutely faint with hunger. Besides, if I'm going to prepare your food in the temple kitchens I need to see exactly what terrors await me. I presume they are at the rear of the compound?"

Huy would not admit it, but he too wanted to eat. *My first instinct is to argue with her, to disagree with her and deny everything she says,* he thought as they skirted the sanctuary, walking in the shadow of the protecting precinct wall. *It has been that way ever since we were little. I wonder why. Is it because she tries to control me and I do not want to be controlled? Or does she threaten me in some other way?* Surreptitiously he glanced sideways at her strong brown ankles and bare feet, visible under the sluggish swirl of her thick peasant sheath. *Running through the fields and padding through my father's house and garden is one thing,* he decided, *but she can't go barefoot every day in the town; there are too many opportunities for an accident. Somehow I must find sandals for her.*

The kitchens turned out to be one kitchen, a large, three-sided building facing two deep firepits, one of which was topped by a clay oven for baking bread. The floor of the kitchen was taken up with a long table on which sat piles of pots and dishes of various sizes. Waist-high jars ranged against one wall contained water. Another wall had shelves on which sat small jugs of sealed wine and larger vats of beer. To Ishat's relief the table also held vessels covered with pieces of linen which, when removed, revealed cooked meats, vegetables of various kinds, a pungent garlic and onion soup, and a selection of dried fruits including a few tiny, wrinkled apples. "All this for two priests, a gardener, and two servants!" Ishat marvelled as she tore at a haunch of beef.

Huy laughed. "Methen has to entertain noble visitors from time to time as well. This is a very small kitchen serving very simple food to very few people,

Ishat. One day I will take you to Iunu. The temple and
its kitchens there will amaze you. Will you be happy
cooking here?"

"I have yet to meet the temple's cook," she mum-
bled, her mouth full. "If he is an agreeable person,
I shall manage perfectly well. Your food will be cold by
the time I've walked it back through the court, around
the corner, and halfway along the street," she sensibly
observed. "I expect the beer house next door offers
good meals."

"At a price." Huy was eating slowly, his eyes on the
pen backing against the precinct's rear wall. One cow
and a snuffling pig stood looking back at him. He shook
off the memory of his young self and Pabast's distinctive
voice. "I wish I could get some target practice and find
a horse and chariot to ride," he mused. "Heby goes to
school here, but there is no training ground, no stables.
Shall I lose my skill, I wonder?"

"You will heal the son of one of our few aristocrats,
or give his wife a favourable Seeing. Then he will show
his gratitude by letting you use his weapons and thunder about the town in his chariot. Don't worry, Huy—
before long you'll be rich with gifts from grateful
petitioners."

Huy shuddered and did not reply.

After she had eaten, Ishat scoured the kitchen.
Having found a basket, she proceeded to fling into it
whatever she thought might be useful, over Huy's
vigorous protests. Pieces of used linen, two large pots
of natron, a jar of lamp oil, and bread and goat's
cheese began to fill it. "We are not thieves," Huy
said as he saw her drag a broom out of a corner.

"The food is a good idea for tomorrow morning, but we need permission to take the rest."

Ishat settled a small sealed flagon of beer beside the natron. "I expect that the cook helps himself to whatever he likes," she responded smoothly. "He probably orders more natron and oil and other stuff than the temple needs so that he can keep his home supplied. It is the way of servants." She made it sound like a virtue.

"Your mother wouldn't dream of doing such a thing!" Huy argued. "Nor would my mother permit it."

"No, but your mother has always been very generous to my family." She pushed the laden basket towards him and brandished the broom. "Here. Please carry this for me." Huy gave up. Lifting the basket, he followed her back to the courtyard.

The gardener hailed them as they crossed to the gate. He was a wizened old man with the rounded shoulders and stained hands of his profession. "Master Huy, Scribe to the High Priest?" he said as he came up to them. "I have whitewash for you. The High Priest has also requested the use of my donkey and cart on your behalf, to move some furniture out of the storehouse. This morning would be a good time. This afternoon I need the cart to ferry water to the temple. Come with me." He led them out of the gate to where a bored-looking donkey stood tethered to a cart. "Her name is Sweetness," he explained, and chuckled as the beast cast him a sidelong glance. "She is all sweetness as long as she doesn't have to work. Do not strike her or she will dig in her heels and no power will move her. Good luck."

Huy watched, exasperated, as the gardener re-entered the temple compound. "I have no experience with donkeys," he grumbled, but Ishat was already stroking the animal's soft nose and talking to it quietly. Presently it nudged her. She slid her fingers under the leather strap beneath its chin and grinned at Huy.

"We are ready," she said. "Where is the storehouse? Put the basket in the cart, Huy, beside the broom. We must not forget our bags in Methen's quarters."

Feeling both useless and grateful to Ishat, Huy led her and her docile friend back behind the sanctuary on the side opposite to the kitchen. Together they loaded the furniture allotted to Huy onto the cart. Ishat was not impressed with it. "Look at the gold peeling off the goddess!" she said as the couch went into the cart. She nipped a curl of gilt between her fingernails and tugged. It came away in her hand and she rubbed it before letting it fall. "Surely you can do better!"

But this time Huy was adamant. "No more stealing, Ishat. I mean it. If you disobey me, I'll send you home. We may look for a cot for you and nothing more."

"Oh, very well." Once more she graced him with a wide smile. "This is fun, isn't it, Huy?"

"You have a smear of dust on your cheek and a dead spider caught in your hair," he replied. "Let's find you something to sleep on."

She was delighted when Huy unearthed a travelling cot that folded into thirds. All the wooden slats belonging to it were piled under it, together with a stained mattress. "Look!" she said as she opened it out and folded it again. "I've never seen a bed like this before! I can have it, can't I, Huy?"

"Of course." He picked it up easily and pushed it into the cart. "It's a travelling cot, Ishat, used by the nobles in the cabins of their barges or in their tents. Who knows, the last body to rest on this mattress may very well have belonged to a princess. Now we must get the whitewash from the gardener."

"Those oil lamps will leak through the cracks," she said over her shoulder as they creaked their way back to the court. "I can fix them with mud, but the mud will soon dry and crumble away. We need new ones. Not clay. Alabaster would be lovely. Would your friend at Iunu send you a gift of alabaster lamps, Huy? And I have no linen for my travelling cot." She said the words with an innocent pride so at variance with the Ishat who had boldly filched whatever she wanted from the kitchen that Huy was disarmed.

"Methen has promised me a pillow and linens for my couch," he answered the long fall of her disordered hair. "You may have them, Ishat. There's the gardener. I'll get the whitewash if you'll pick up our bags."

Methen had already placed two sheets, a pillow, and two blankets beside their belongings. By the time they had unloaded the cart, returned it to the gardener, and walked back to their house, the sun was beginning to set. Sitting on the two crude chairs, they ate the bread and cheese intended for the following day, washing it down with some of the beer. "I wish I had found an empty water jar, one of the big ones," Ishat said. "We will need water to mix up the whitewash and to drink. Can I use the temple bathhouse, Huy? I like to be clean, but I'm too tired to wash tonight. We forgot the linen."

They distributed the furniture through the tiny
house. It did not take long, and when they had
finished, the dwelling seemed even smaller than it
had before. Ishat carefully filled the two lamps. Oil
began to drip slowly from each one. "I'll take them
next door to the beer house and light them from the
fire there," she said, a trifle wearily. "Listen to the
noise, Huy! Our celebration of Hapi's generosity will
not be necessary since we are forced to share the
jubilation of every patron swilling beer on our
doorstep." She left.

Huy stood in the middle of his dark, musty reception
room. He did not fight the sense of depression and
dislocation growing in him. *What have I done?* he asked
himself again. *It has all happened too quickly. I should have
stayed in Iunu, even hired myself out in the marketplace
writing letters for the illiterate—done anything but run
back here to noise and stench and poverty. If I had
worked in Iunu, perhaps Nakht might have seen my
determination. He might have changed his mind and
hired me. Anuket's impending marriage might not take
place after all. Anuket . . .* Despair came rushing in on
the heels of his sudden dejection, and he wanted to sink
onto his dirt floor and weep. *Do you see your Chosen One,
mighty Atum?* he thought bitterly. *What do you think of
your Twice Born now? I want to walk from my cell to the
bathhouse and douse myself in scented hot water and have
a servant knead fragrant oils into my skin. I want to lie on
fine linen and talk to Thothmes on the couch opposite me
while I watch the lamplight flicker on the ceiling above me.
I want to summon a litter and go to Nakht's house, where
Nasha will hug me tightly and Anuket . . . Anuket will kiss*

*me prettily on my cheek while her little hand presses slyly
and quickly against the side of my neck, under my hair.*

But soon the courage that had always sustained him
returned, and by the time Ishat pushed the door closed
behind her with her foot and took the two steps into
the room that brought her face to face with him, he
was able to smile. She was carrying a tray on which a
wide bowl steamed, and the two oil lamps sent out
thin, black-tipped flames. Huy set the tray on the table
and put the lamps beside it. Ishat rummaged about in
the basket from the kitchen and came up with a large
square of linen.

"The owner of the beer house wants neighbours
who will not be constantly complaining about the
noise," she said. "The old woman who lived here
apparently did so continually. He has offered me the
use of his fire for lamp lighting or water heating.
Sit down." Huy did so. Carefully Ishat lifted the bowl
onto the floor beside him and removed his sandals.
Dipping the linen into the hot water, she began to
wash his calves and then his feet. He began to protest,
but she hushed him. "I am not a body servant, and it is
not proper for me to wash any other part of your body
but these. You can do that yourself, and after you have
used the water I will wash myself. We are both tired
and filthy. I will return the tray and bowl tomorrow."

Huy's arguments died in his throat. *This is an
honest blow to your damnable pride,* he told himself.
*A moment ago your mind was full of Anuket, but this
woman, this friend, is worth a dozen Anukets. Would
Anuket wash your feet, even if she loved you? I don't think
so. She would call a servant instead. But you, Ishat, even*

if you were a queen, you would still bring hot water and kneel and do this without hesitation. Her touch was firm and gentle. On impulse Huy put both hands on her bent head. Her hair was warm, and as he leaned towards her he could smell the lingering, comfortable odour of Sweetness the donkey, and Ishat's own sweat, and the slightly acrid tang of the cheap oil in the lamps.

All at once his fingers tightened involuntarily, weaving into her hair. She looked up, startled. A sickness had suddenly filled his mind with such potency that he wanted to vomit. His vision blurred. Then it cleared, together with the nausea, and he found himself gazing into a face whose lustrous eyes were ringed with kohl. The full mouth was hennaed red. Gold dust glittered on the lips and in the hollow of the long neck, where a thick chain of gold rested. More gold cut across the forehead—a coronet, it was a coronet of some sort, from whose links hung tiny green faience frogs and red carnelian scarabs. Rosettes of purple electrum swung on delicate silver chains from each earlobe. Huy's nostrils were full of the expensive aroma of lemongrass and rose perfume. The dusky eyes blinked, giving Huy a glimpse of lids dusted with gilded blue paint, then narrowed in a smile. "Why, Huy," Ishat's voice said, "we did not expect to see you today. Come in and have some wine." The exquisite face looked away. "Ptahmose! Bring shedeh and two cups! Are you too important now to drink the shedeh, my old friend?" The tone was teasing.

Huy had opened his mouth to reply when he found himself bent double over a struggling Ishat, his hands gripping her hair, his face pressed against her skull.

"Huy!" she was shouting. "Let me go! You're hurting me! Let go!"

Cold and shaking, he withdrew, sitting back on the chair, his head pounding as though it would split open. "Ishat," he whispered because his strength had failed him. "You are going to be rich. You are going to be the wife or concubine of a very important man. How beautiful you looked!"

She had sat back on her heels, rubbing at her scalp, her expression furious, but at his words she knelt, placing wet hands on his knees. "Huy, the gift!" she breathed. "It has returned! It has come back to life in you! I told you it would! I will be beautiful? How beautiful? Tell me exactly what you saw!"

Mechanically he described the brief vision, one finger pressed hard against his left temple where the pain was greatest, while his thoughts ran swiftly in another direction. *I had hoped I was free. In spite of Ramose's certainty that the gift was merely in abeyance, I deceived myself into believing that the turmoil might be over. I had even dared to imagine that Atum in his mercy might restore my sexual potency. Now he strikes at me, on this day of all days, with such vicious force that I feel I might die.*

"My mouth was hennaed?" Ishat was asking, eyes alight. "What about my hands, Huy? Shall I be a noblewoman?"

"I thought that you despised the nobility," he joked feebly. "I did not see your hands, Ishat. Only your face. So lovely."

She stood, lifting the bowl of water onto the table. "I only despise the little aristocrat you adore so much

that she weakens your honour," she insisted. "Perhaps
you saw me as your wife." Her head was carefully averted.
"Perhaps you will achieve nobility. You will render a great
service to our King and he will make you an erpa-ha or a
smer and load you with gold, and then—"

"I told you what you said to me in the vision," Huy
cut in dully. "I was not your lover. I've already tried to
explain to you why I can never . . . Oh gods, Ishat, I am
in agony. I must lie down. I don't suppose you found
any poppy powder to steal from the kitchen?"

Instantly she was beside him, her arms under his,
helping him to stand. "Only physicians have the poppy.
Shall I go and find one for you?"

He shook his head, then yelped at the spasm the
gesture caused. "What could I pay him with? Just help
me onto my couch." Leaning on her, he shuffled into
his sleeping room.

She took his hand and placed it on the headboard
as though he were a child. "Steady yourself here," she
ordered. Hurrying back into the reception room,
she returned with Methen's linen and blankets. Swiftly
she made the bed. Huy was too tired to protest. He
pulled off his mired kilt and loincloth, not caring
that she was watching, and crawled onto the couch.
The sheets smelled of the fresh wind in which they had
been dried, but underneath that pleasant aroma he
could detect the faint must of mouse droppings from
the mattress. It did not matter. "Shall I bring one of
the lamps?" Ishat wanted to know.

Huy closed his eyes. "No. The darkness is good,"
he murmured. "I wish the beer house was more quiet.
I'll sleep now, Ishat. I'm sorry for taking the linen."

He felt her lips brush his cheek. "Your skin is cold. Don't be sorry, Huy. Your gift is back. That is so exciting. Rest well."

He did not hear her leave. For a while every beat of his heart sent a shock of pain into his head, so that he turned onto his side and curled up his knees in a futile gesture of defence. *So Ishat will leave me,* he thought, the knowledge adding to his agony. *The visions do not lie. Some wealthy nobleman will take her away, surround her with servants who will knead and stroke her until the last vestiges of our poverty have disappeared, load her with jewels and perfumes, dress her in fine linen. Will he love her as his wife or as a concubine? Will she still love me? She looked happy. How can she be happy without me? And when will this occur? The visions never show me time, only fleeting moments wrenched from the future and made to float untethered before me like bubbles. I have no right to be jealous of this anonymous man. No matter how much I wish it, I am unable to return Ishat's desire. Even if full sexual power was restored to me, she would still be no more than my dear friend. Yet I am jealous of him. I am like a cur with an unwanted bone between his paws, growling at the circling pack who would snatch it away if they could. But no—I am not that petty. Mingling with my possessiveness is a genuine delight in the good fortune that must come to her. I pray it will not be too soon, though. I need you, my Ishat. Until today I did not realize just how much.* His heartbeat had slowed and with it the hammer blows in his head. His mind began to drift. Snatches of prayers to Khenti-kheti came to him, but halfway through one invocation he lost consciousness.

Waking late with a sense of both well-being and apprehension, he began to push himself off the couch, afraid that he would be late for his first class, but then reality asserted itself and he relaxed, lying on his back and contemplating the irregular undulation of the grey mud-brick ceiling. His headache had completely disappeared, in fact he felt full of energy, but at the remembrance of what had happened when he touched Ishat he tensed with the old, familiar anxiety. *I will not consider the implications,* he told himself sternly. *Not now. We have a day of hard work ahead of us. It will do me good to sweat.*

At that moment her head appeared around the doorless entrance. "You're awake!" she said brightly. "Stay there, Huy. I have food." In a moment she returned with milk, warm bread, fried fish, dates, and a clay bowl full of sweet sycamore figs. "The fish is cold, I expect. It won't have held the heat of the pan." Setting the dishes around Huy's sheeted legs, she perched at the foot of his couch. "I have met the temple's cook," she announced as Huy thirstily drained the milk. "I charmed him, of course. He is perfectly willing to provide us with two meals each day because he prepares them for the High Priest and his assistant and their servants anyway. He remembers you from all the rumours that filled the town after Methen . . . after he rescued you. He wants you to See for him."

"Well, I won't." Huy broke the fish in two. "I'm not going to touch anyone ever again."

"Don't be silly. How can you help it? Besides, we need his favours. These figs"—she pointed—"sycamore figs, are there for the picking all year round.

Physicians often get to the trees first because the juices heal cuts and the fruit is wonderful for killing worms in the bowels, but then it's only the little ones that are left for the rest of us. The cook will provide us with nice big sweet ones from the temple tree in the courtyard if we are good to him." She shook her head at the half fish he was offering her. "I ate in the kitchen. This meal is all yours." She left the couch. "I'll go next door and fill the bowl with hot water again. Hopefully this time we can both wash. I've been through your satchels. You'll have to put on your dirty kilt from yesterday unless you want to whitewash this hovel in gold-bordered linen." Her voice held a mild contempt.

By the time she returned, he had put on his loincloth. As she set the steaming bowl on the table, he pointed into her sleeping room. "I glanced inside," he said accusingly. "There is good linen on your cot, Ishat, fine white linen, and an alabaster lamp on the floor. Where did you go last night? You've been stealing again, haven't you?"

"Yes," she answered, unabashed. "You fell asleep so early and I wasn't tired, but I lay on the cot anyway and the mattress was too rough for comfort. I decided to go out." She brought another square of linen from the basket and dropped it into the water. "I went along the alleys behind the nobles' compounds. That's where the interesting garbage is, because the servants throw all the waste over the walls. The lamp was half buried under a pile of rotting nebes leaves. It has a chip missing from its base. Otherwise it's perfectly good to use."

"And the sheets?"

"Them I did steal. Some stupid servant had left them draped over a wall, just asking for a needy peasant to take them away." She looked appealingly at Huy. "Please don't make me return them. They feel so soft against my skin. I swear I won't ever steal anything else. Ever." She gestured at the hot water. "Let's wash ourselves and then start work."

She's happy, Huy reflected, *her eyes sparkling, her movements light and swift. Is it because I Saw a great future for you, Ishat,* he wondered silently, *or is it because you have me all to yourself at last?*

He nodded. "The nights will soon become cooler. I'll ask Methen for another blanket, one for you," was all he said.

The day passed rapidly in whitewashing every inner and outer wall of the house, and the ceiling as well. The gardener had lent them brushes and a huge clay bowl in which to mix the whitewash. Many times Huy pushed through the cheerful crowds milling about on the bank of the tributary in order to fill the bowl with water and staggered back to his little house. He thought of Anuket as the garlanded people streamed past and around him, of her deft fingers weaving the offerings that would be thrown onto the surface of the river in thanksgiving to Hapi. He remembered with what joyful solemnity he and she, Thothmes and Nasha and Nakht and his wife, stood on Nakht's watersteps and recited the prayers and then watched the circles of quivering flowers go floating slowly towards the Great Green, together with hundreds of other offerings both humble and magnificent. There was always a party afterwards, a feast with music and plenty of wine and many guests, and then there was the peace and comfort of the room he had believed was his, with its wide couch and its lamps full of scented oils and a servant ready to remove his soiled clothing and freshen the water beside the bed before bidding him a safe night.

There will be many days like this, he told himself grimly as the weight of the water grew and the sweat ran into his eyes. *Moments when I must make the experiences of my new life overlay the memories of the old until eventually there is no sight, no odour, no sudden strain of music that can toss me back to Iunu.* He and Ishat spoke little as they laboured. At noon she walked the short distance to the temple kitchen with the soiled dishes of the morning and returned with garlic soup and bread, which they ate quickly and quietly before picking up their brushes again. By sunset they had finished. The house now reeked of powdered lime.

Huy went to Methen's quarters where, with a silent apology to his employer, he took a length of wick for the alabaster lamp and a small flagon of stakte, knowing that the blend of balan oil and bruised myrrh leaves would at last dissipate the old stench of mice and the newer smell of the whitewash. Ishat filled the lamp and took it to the beer house to be lit. Coming back, she set it on the table. At once its gentle glow filled the space. She collapsed on the chair next to Huy. "The inside of the lamp has been painted with butterflies," she said. "Look, Huy! You can see their colours! And how well the light reflects off the white walls."

"Yes."

"We need mats for the floors," she added presently. "I can weave them from reeds if you will go to the marshes and pick some."

"Yes."

"You are tired and sad." She swivelled to face him, her hair hanging in strings around features as exhausted as his. "Let's leave the lamp burning and take some natron and go to the river for a proper wash. If we walk upstream, out of the town, we can find a place away from the revellers." She had already emptied the basket. Now she rose, filled it with the jar of natron and cloths, and beckoned. Unwillingly, he followed, taking the basket from her and joining the noisy swarm of citizens in the street.

By the time they had found a quiet stretch of the river, the moon had risen, an orange sliver just above the horizon, its light too faint to colour the water. Both of them were too tired to care about propriety. Stripping off their limp clothes, they waded into the shallows and, once wet, returned to the bank to scour themselves with natron. "We need oil for our hair," Huy remarked. "Oh, Ishat, I promise to work hard for Methen. It occurs to me that I can sit in the market-place in the afternoons and hire myself out to write letters. Then we can have oil, and anything else we might need."

She tossed back her hair and stretched unselfconsciously, her lithe body bending away from him, before dropping her arms and giving him an odd, speculative stare. "You refuse to face the truth, don't you, Huy? This is the truth—that your gift has woken, and even though no word of it will leave my mouth, yet the rumour of it will spread. People will remember you. They will start coming to your house and you will not be able to run away." She turned back to the river.

"I must get the natron salts out of my hair." Her tone and actions were abrupt.

Huy glanced to where the moon had moved upward and become bone white. *I hate you, Thoth of the Book, Thoth of the moon,* he spoke savagely to the thin disc above. *I will worship no one but the totem of this town and nothing but the skills my school has taught me.* Ishat was a darker silhouette against the murky river. Huy plunged in after her.

The house welcomed them with the steady glow of the lamp and the delicate aroma of balan oil and myrrh. "It's beginning to feel like a home already," Ishat said above the clamour from the beer house. "How many more days will the festival run? Well, no matter. We will get used to our neighbours. I'll fetch us an evening meal."

Huy sat with both arms limp on the table, feeling his hair spring into curls as it dried. All at once he longed to join the drunken throng next door, or at least take a stool and sit out on the street where he could watch the patrons come and go. It seemed to him that he had never been more outside the ordinary stream of events, not even when he lay in his father's house after returning to life in the House of the Dead. Yet he had never been closer to the commonplace ebb and flow that made up the existence of the majority of the country's people. He was one with the brick makers who trod straw into the mud beside the river, with the potters who spun the thousands of unadorned flagons and pots needed in every home, with the farmers who set up their stalls in the marketplace and called their wares to the passersby. He was one with the servants also, for had he not become a servant to a servant of Khenti-kheti? Yet he knew that if he were to venture into the beer house and open his mouth, the laughter and conversation would stop. A general unease would spread at the sound of his educated accent, the words he chose to use, even the aristocratic language of his body. He smiled wryly to himself. *You are a fish out of water or a desert lizard tossed into a swamp, Huy son of Hapu. You do not wholly belong anywhere.*

He thanked Ishat for the food and ate without tasting it. Afterwards he bade her a good night, took one of the leaking oil lamps into his room, stripped off his soiled linen, and lowered himself gratefully onto his couch. Tomorrow he would have to dress in one of Nasha's kilts; he had nothing cheaper to wear. He wondered if he might go to a sandal maker and trade one of them for a pair of sandals for Ishat. Not reed or papyrus—leather, which would last and wear slowly. He heard her putting the dirty dishes in the basket. The light suddenly dimmed; she had blown out the alabaster lamp. A tiny glimmer of moving light told him that she was taking the other oil lamp into her room. Leaning down, he blew his out and presently she did the same. The clamour coming through the wall was a steady sound, not rising and falling, and Huy thought that eventually it might act as a sort of lullaby.

He woke suddenly sometime deep in the night. Silence reigned, but something, some sound, had pulled him from sleep. As he lay listening it came again, a muffled sobbing, and he realized with a lurch to his heart that Ishat was weeping. He quelled the impulse to rise and go to her. *I cannot help you,* he told her sadly in his mind. *We know each other well, you and I. Our friendship is old. It has survived much, it has grown so that we are like open scrolls to one another. I love you, but not in the way you long to be loved. You have grown beautiful, my Ishat, and if there was any justice in the kingdom of the gods I would desire you as you desire me. But I do not. I wish with all I am that it were not so.* He lay, tense and miserable, until the sound of her agony died away and the house slept once more.

The last day of the festival of Hapi did not take place until the twelfth of Athyr. After a full twenty-four days of praying and carousing, the exhausted citizens of Hut-herib were glad to return to the sane and simple routines of their lives. The river had now almost reached its highest point, turning the town into a series of small islands connected by banked earthen paths, and the fields into lakes that mirrored a winter sky.

On the twenty-fourth day of Paophi, long before the festival was over, Huy had reported to Methen for work. He and Ishat had already fallen into the pattern that would govern their lives for some months to come. Ishat took charge of tidying and cleaning the house, bringing food from the temple kitchen, and carrying their laundry to the river where, together with a bevy of other women, she rubbed their linens with natron and beat them against the rocks tumbled at the edge of the flood. She did not make friends with her fellow labourers. "They are ignorant and full of frivolous gossip," she had told Huy as she dragged their two chairs into the street, draped them with wet kilts and sheaths, and planted herself watchfully on a stool next to them. "All they care about is who is pregnant and whose husband is unkind and who might be unfaithful. Sometimes they share remedies for various ailments, or what spells and curses will destroy a rival for some other peasant's affections, or a better recipe for lentil stew, but when I ask them for news of the King, or what our own governor is doing, they look at me blankly. They care for nothing outside the confines of their own streets. They bore me." It was just as well, Huy thought with humour, that Ishat had plenty to do. Otherwise her impetuous nature would surely lead her into mischief.

He himself had managed to trade two of his precious kilts for leather sandals and a serviceable sheath for Ishat. She had been grateful but not effusive as she slipped her feet into the sandals. "Thank you, Huy, but I prefer my feet bare," she had protested.

Huy had been firm. "The streets are full of filth. Let others cut themselves and end up with the swelling of ukhedu. Besides, Ishat, the hard-packed earth will give you soles as tough as the leather you wear, and you don't want that, do you?" He had touched her vanity. She grunted a denial. The sheath was similar to the two she already owned, a slim dress of sturdy, thick linen slit on either side to allow her long legs to stride out and with wide shoulder straps holding it up. It met with her full approval.

"I should have an arm band with your name on it, like other servants," she said. "Then the other women would stop asking me who I am." *But some of them might remember the scandal I caused all those years ago,* Huy told himself. *Better to protect my anonymity for as long as possible.*

Aloud he said, "We are friends before we are master and servant, Ishat. Besides, if I could afford an arm band for you, we would not be living where we are."

She turned a pensive face to him. "I'm beginning to like our tiny hovel. It makes me feel safe."

At the end of each week they walked to Hapu's house. Ishat would disappear to spend time with her parents while Huy struggled to find common ground with his father and fend off his mother's worried questions regarding his welfare. Only with Heby was he relaxed, as they poked about the garden together. Huy taught the boy to play sennet and paint animals on Hapu's dazzlingly white walls. He told him stories as he fell asleep. He listened as Heby solemnly and proudly recited the lessons he had learned at school, and, remembering his own unhappy and tumultuous first year at Iunu, he questioned Heby closely about his teacher and his fellow pupils. It was evident that Heby was a cheerful, intelligent child without the character traits that had made life so difficult for Huy. "I shall soon begin work with the High Priest," Huy told him. "His quarters are within the same compound as your school. Perhaps when you are finished your lessons and I my dictation, we could spend a few afternoons together."

Heby shook his head. "Hapzefa waits to bring me home every noontime, and besides, Father has told me not to bother you at the temple. He says you are too busy to see me there." It was on the tip of Huy's tongue to angrily refute Hapu's crude attempt to keep him from this lovable child, but he kept his own counsel. Their father did not want Huy's history known to Heby.

He enjoyed his time with Methen. The High Priest dictated slowly, and because the work was simple, mostly lists of needed provisions and offerings, with an occasional letter to a fellow priest stationed at one of the other temples scattered thickly throughout the country, Huy was able to let his brush ink the words while his mind wandered. They ate together at noon, sharing the small items of news each had, then Methen took to his couch for the afternoon sleep and Huy made his way home to Ishat and his own dilapidated but welcoming bed. In the evening hours he and Ishat ambled through the town, watching craftsmen of every kind work their trades outside their doorways, dodging the flocks of children who quickly formed and just as quickly scattered like noisy sparrows in the narrow streets, sharing polite greetings with the clusters of women who sat with their backs against their walls or squatted on stools to gossip in the precious moments before it was time to prepare the final meal of the day.

A peace came slowly to Huy as the season of Akhet drew to an end, a serenity born of the regularity and uncomplicated predictability of his days. The month of Athyr, when the river was still rising, slid into Khoiak and the height of the flood. His life, and Ishat's, was bare of all but the necessities of work, food, and rest. Their health remained good. Huy ceased to notice the din that rose from the beer house at every sunset. He was teaching Ishat to read and write in their little reception room by the light of the chipped alabaster lamp. He would sketch the hieroglyphs in chalk on the tabletop and she would copy them onto the pieces of smashed clay pots available on every garbage heap.

Huy began with the names of the gods, as his teacher had done. Ishat learned quickly and with an awe that touched Huy's heart. She would suck in her breath and stare at the figures he had drawn in front of her, underlining them with one reverent finger. "This says *Amun?*" she would ask, or, "This says *Ptah?*" as though she could not quite believe the evidence of her eyes. Often Huy would return from his morning at the temple to find that she had scrawled her lessons in an increasingly sure hand all over their whitewashed walls. Before long it was time to move on to the symbols that represented not only a thing but also a concept. Ishat, for all her self-assurance, was a humble student—*more humble,* Huy thought as he faced yet again her charcoal scribbles as he walked through their doorway, *than I ever was. At this speed she will make a passable scribe in a year or two.*

One early afternoon he returned to find her waiting for him, smiling triumphantly beside a list she had written on the wall. "These are the foods you will be eating tonight," she announced, slapping a hand beside the hieroglyphs. "What do you think?" He went closer and inspected what she had done. Her control over the pieces of charcoal had grown. The figures were smaller and neater and did not run into each other or meander down the whitewash.

"Grilled goose meat," he read aloud. "Cabbage with coriander. Pea soup with mustard. Salted olives. Dried plums. Beer. Oh, Ishat!" He turned and hugged her. "This is wonderful! Only one mistake."

She pushed him away. "A mistake?" Her hands went to her hips. "Where?"

"Here. You mean to say 'olives,' *baq-t*. You've written the plural correctly and half the hieroglyph, the bird and the triangle, but you put this in"—he pointed—"instead of the semicircle and you forgot the tree. According to this we will be eating salted brightness, *baq*."

She sighed. "There are so many *baq*s," she grumbled. "*Baq*, to dazzle, *baq*, a prosperous man, *baq*, to be protected, and every *baq* written a little differently."

"I'm very proud of you," Huy said, and meant it. "You never make the same mistake twice. Are we really having grilled goose?"

She made a face. "Alas, no. I went to the kitchen so I could write the list. No dried plums or beer either. Sycamore figs. But it does look good, doesn't it, Huy?"

"It does. I am amazed."

She yawned. "I will rest this afternoon. All this thinking makes me sleepy. I'm glad I pleased you, Huy."

The familiar pang of grief washed through him as he saw her delight, and then it was gone. "You always please me, Ishat. Now I must rest also. Tonight we will begin the names of fish."

She laughed. "Now that is something we must do sometime," she said as they parted. "The owner of the beer house has a boat. He will lend it to me. We will go fishing together." The last words came to him muffled as he lowered himself onto his couch and pulled the blanket over him. They were four months away from the pitiless heat of the summer season of Shemu.

At last Huy received a scroll from Thothmes. Huy had not written to his friend, partly because of the preoccupations of settling into his new life but also out of a reluctance to conjure in himself the memory of the faces he had loved and trusted. The pain of leaving Iunu had begun slowly to fade. It sprang up again as Methen held out the roll of papyrus with Thothmes' personal symbol, an image of the ibis-headed god Thoth himself, pressed into the red wax. "A letter for you from Iunu," Methen said. "A messenger delivered it early this morning."

"It's from my friend Thothmes," Huy replied, taking it gingerly. For just a moment he fancied that he caught a whiff of Anuket's perfume, the faint cloud of mingled flower and herb aromas that always clung to her. "I'll read it later." He kept his attention fixed fiercely on his work that morning, dreading the moment when Methen would stretch, sigh, and say the closing prayer to Khenti-kheti before sending for food; but of course the hours passed. Huy had little appetite. He bundled his bread and some goat's cheese into his linen bag for Ishat, bade Methen rest well, then went to sit in the grass with his back against the spreading sycamore. The court was deserted. Huy broke the seal and unrolled the scroll.

Greetings to Huy, Scribe to the High Priest of Khenti-kheti and my dilatory friend. Why have you not written to me? Are you unwell? Have you a house? Do you enjoy your work? Most of all, dear Huy, do you miss me as much as I miss you? School begins again next month. How shall I be able to walk into our cell knowing that you and your possessions are gone? I expect I shall be sharing with some nasty little first-year pupil who

will alternately weep with homesickness and rant
against his fate and I shall have to assume the role
of big brother when all I want is my own dear
brother by adoption in the cot across from me.
At least it will be my last year, blessedly shortened
because of the death and beautification of my
King. Harmose the Overseer says that all those
who should have finished their schooling by the
beginning of last Akhet will carry an extra load of
study so that they need not waste more time.
I groan. Father is preparing to train me in the
business of administering this sepat, so I suppose
I may say that I have almost achieved adulthood.
I still can't hit a duck with any accuracy. Nasha
asks me to send you her love. She misses you
almost as much as I. Come back to Iunu, Huy.
I will importune my father to obtain a good post
for you in the city. He does not say so, but I know
that he regrets having to refuse you Anuket and
feels the lack of you when we sit down to eat
together. Speaking of the little witch, her formal
betrothal ceremony took place last week, followed
by a huge feast. I do not particularly like her
future husband. He seems rather stupid, or perhaps he is simply shy. Anyway, he is no match for
Anuket, who slinks and purrs around him like a
cat who has caught a mouse and is about to play
with it before devouring it. Father cannot seem
to control her anymore. I think he just wants to
sign the marriage contract and have her go away.
Does he wish she were going away with you?
Perhaps. But, dear Huy, remember how she had

begun to treat you. Unlike her new prey, you have had a lucky escape. Write to me at once, and may my prayers to the Osiris-one, Thothmes the Third Justified, keep you safe. Your friend, Thothmes.

Huy let the scroll roll up, laid it in his lap, and closed his eyes. I want her to go away too, he thought, the image of Anuket prompted by Thothmes' words clear and bright behind his lids. *I fell in love with her before she began to change, before her true character began to show through, and no matter how I struggle I am still trapped by the quiet, industrious girl whose nimble fingers wove the fragrant blooms in whose profusion we sat side by side and silently for hours. Will I never be free of her?* He saw her step into the embrace of the faceless man, her betrothed, saw her arms slide about his naked waist, her mouth lift to meet his. Deliberately, stiffly, as though his mind were a joint that ached, he turned it to Thothmes' wide, unstinting smile and the grace of that short, slim body. *I love you and miss you also, but I cannot go back to Iunu. I will go home and write to you and thank you for your generosity and beg you to come and see me here, but the city of my past has become a city of dreams from which I struggle to awake. I long to hear your voice, Thothmes. I long to look into eyes other than Ishat's that know me well and with whom there is no pretence.*

"You're late today," Ishat remarked as Huy entered their house and handed her the bag. "Is it bread and cheese again? Huy? Why are you so pale?"

"There is a letter from my friend at Iunu," he told her, setting his scribe's palette on the table. "He is well and wants to hear from me." Her eyes narrowed. She began to rummage in the bag, dragging out the food. "It's all right, Ishat," he said carefully. "Thothmes' sister has just become officially betrothed and will be married shortly. I was never her choice, or her father's."

"Because you are a commoner." She shook the brown cheese at him. Her tone was bitter. "Because your blood is not pure enough to mingle with hers. Not that it could. Not if what you told me—"

"Peace!" he said sharply. "Do not rub my nose in my own misery. What you were about to say is true."

"I'm sorry." She came and knelt beside him, wrapping her arms around his knees. "I am hurt for you, and angry at them, all of them. I hate to see you suffer." She could both love him and hate him for not loving her back. Her impulse was to both defend him and castigate him, and as he felt her warm cheek against his thigh before she scrambled to her feet, he reflected how convoluted and mysterious were a woman's emotions.

"Sit and eat," he said. "I will write to Thothmes and then we will sleep." He went to the dusty floor, setting his palette across his lap and whispering the scribe's routine prayer to Thoth as he uncapped his ink. "It's all right," he repeated. "I am content to be here in Hut-herib with you. It is an old pain, Ishat."

"I know exactly what you mean," she said caustically, and bit into the cheese.

More letters began to arrive from Iunu over the following weeks, from the Rekhet, full of advice and demanding a return, and from Ramose, implying gently that Huy was in the grip of a temporary madness and

THE TWICE BORN 555

confident that, once sane again, he would return to the temple. Huy answered them. He thanked the Rekhet for her advice and filled his letter with descriptions of his surroundings and details of his daily life, knowing that she approved of his decision to return to Hutherib. His scroll to Ra's High Priest was more cautious. He spoke of his contentment in serving Methen as a scribe, his gratitude to both Ramose and the school for providing him with the excellent education that allowed him to ply his trade, and a promise to visit if he ever found the time to travel to Iunu. The implication behind his carefully chosen words was polite but clear: I am happy, I am grateful, but I have chosen the course my life will take and I do not intend to return to a state of dependency. They wrote again; so did Thothmes. The scrolls from Iunu and the necessity to answer them became matters of routine, threaded into the fabric of Huy's everyday life. The memories began to lose their sting, and often he found himself entirely involved in his present. He began to taste fulfillment.

17

As the flood slowly sank, revealing the wet, newly enriched soil beneath, Huy began to dream. Like the receding water, the anguish of the previous year seemed to flow away during the hours of darkness, leaving his sleeping mind fallow. Once again he stood in the Judgment Hall, gazing towards the bright sunlight bursting through the great doors, Anubis and Ma'at unseen presences behind him. Then perhaps he would find himself kneeling before Imhotep, the leaves of the Ished Tree murmuring above, the aroma of its flowers filling him with intoxication. Imhotep was always reading, reading, engrossed in what Huy knew was the Book of Thoth, and did not acknowledge him.

Once, he found himself on the banks of a wide river whose slow, meandering curve between stands of palm trees and little sandy bays reminded him of a stretch of the river he had walked beside before he reached the tributary on his long journey to Hut-herib. But the water was blue, not brown, as blue as the sparkling sky, the spears of the palm fronds freshly green, the sand so golden that it glowed. A procession was passing on the opposite bank, the men in glistening white kilts, the women dressed in linens of red and yellow, their arms heavy with bright gems, the oiled tresses of their wigs glinting with gold. The group moved slowly, majestically. Huy could see them smiling and talking to one another. He shouted across the expanse of glittering wavelets, cupping his hands around his mouth, but it appeared that they could not hear him. Soon they turned onto a path leading up into the beige hills. Huy watched them grow smaller and smaller until their graceful forms eventually vanished.

He was warm and peaceful, standing amid a scattering of fragrant wildflowers—tall hollyhocks, vivid blue cornflowers, tiny orange chrysanthemums, and the dazzling white drug poppies. He could see no lotuses, but their scent surrounded him, saturating the air itself. The sun was gentle on his head, the grass soft on his bare feet. Pulling his braid forward over his shoulder, he saw, without surprise, that his humble little frog now gleamed with gold. His chest and fingers were naked. The amulets and the sa sign were gone.

Waking from these dreams became increasingly difficult. He remembered how, after he had returned from the dead, after his senses had brimmed over with the delights of the blessed realm of Osiris, the sights of the mortal world were drab and colourless, the smells weak and faintly corrupt, the food ashy. Gradually his flesh had adapted to his return and his experience in Paradise faded beneath the weight of worldly concerns, but now the place where the Osiris-ones dwelt came back to him with as much force as ever, and the grief of loss began to fill him each morning as he opened unwilling eyes to see his tiny, dark chamber and the uneven rise and fall of the whitewashed ceiling above him.

He had not wanted to speak of this to Ishat, but as always in her presence he found he could not remain silent. He told her how distressingly real his night visions were becoming. "And the Book," he finished. "Imhotep is reading the Book, and as he unrolls it the words roll through my mind. I had thought I was forgetting it, but no, it's come back. Every symbol. Every obscure saying."

Her eyes narrowed. They were sitting across the table from each other. Evening light was streaming through the doorway, falling on her, bronzing her shoulder and one arm, making her black hair shine, and tingeing her sheath pink. "Do you know its meaning now? Have you solved its mystery?"

He shook his head. "No. Sometimes I feel that its riddle is unravelling, but then I wake up. I keep the words, though."

Ishat shrugged. "We are now in the month of Pakhons. The first month of Shemu. It's getting hotter. Perhaps your dreams have something to do with the time of year."

Huy sat back with a sigh. "I don't think so. I'm afraid that they are warning me of a change in my life."

A look of alarm crossed her face. "Oh, Huy, don't say that! At last we are settled here! Your work goes well. I now have needle and thread, and we replaced the leaky lamps with two new clay ones. Things are getting better for us!" She stood abruptly and the shaft of light flowing onto the floor was cut off. "You're not going back to Iunu, are you? You're going to leave me behind!"

He had not realized the depth of her insecurity. "No, I'm not going back to Iunu. And Ishat, I'd never leave you behind," he protested wearily. "This is not about us—it's about me. A change in me. Something's coming."

She did not reply. Arms folded, she stared at him while the silence lengthened and the brief glow of evening disappeared behind the row of buildings on the other side of the dusty street.

He mentioned none of this to Methen or to the Rekhet in his letters to her. He was not sure why he had unburdened himself to Ishat and not to them. His hopeful, unformed thought was that perhaps the dreams would cease and in making too much of them, in telling his more mature friends about them, he might sound arrogant or, worse, pitiful. After the constant glare of attention he had endured in Iunu and Khmun, he was enjoying his anonymity.

But two months after he had spoken to Ishat, when even in the Delta the heat had become almost unbearable and all around the town the farmers had begun to harvest their crops, Huy was accosted in the street. He was on his way to his morning's work in the temple, walking purposely in the shade the buildings cast, when a man stepped in front of him, barring his way. With a murmured apology Huy made as if to step around him, but the man flung out an arm. Huy stood still.

"You are the one who came back to life in the House of the Dead," the man said. "Everyone thought you'd been possessed by a demon, but a Rekhet came and pronounced you free of everything evil. I saw you once, out by the flower fields." Huy smiled politely, nodded in what he hoped was a dismissive gesture, and turned to cross the street. The man grasped his arm. Huy began to feel afraid. There was not much crime in Hut-herib, mostly thievery and the midnight fights that broke out after the beer houses closed, so the police patrolled casually during the day. A swift glance up and down the dusty alley told Huy that no official help was in sight.

"Please let me pass," he said firmly, trying to pull his arm out of the man's grip. "The events of my childhood are nothing to do with you." The man opened his fingers and Huy prepared to run, but to his horror and embarrassment his waylayer fell to his knees, holding up his hands in the time-honoured gesture of begging and submission. The movement of the crowds thronging the street began to slow. Some stepped around Huy and his unwanted pesterer with grunts of impatience, but most came to a halt, staring curiously at Huy.

Huy grabbed the upflung arms and hauled the man to his feet. "If you continue to bother me, I shall knock you down!" he hissed. "I do not know you, I do not want to know you. Now let me pass at once." Even as the words left his mouth he regretted them, wondering whether perhaps this man was under the protection of the gods, but meeting his eyes Huy saw no glint of madness—only panic and distress.

The man did not move. "I need your help, noble one," he said urgently. "My name is Iri. My daughter has become very ill and the physician can do nothing for her. He says she will die. I have sent for a priest to chant the fever demon out of her, but I do not think his incantation will do any good."

Huy wanted to shake him. His own panic was rising, born of a sense of fatality far outweighing the few moments of this annoying encounter. Something he wanted no part of again was closing in on him. He felt his ability to choose ebbing away. Sweat suddenly sprang out along his spine and trickled to dampen the waist of his kilt. "I am not a noble," he ground out. "I'm not a physician either. Let me go on my way."

"But you have seen the gods," Iri protested breathlessly. "You have been in their presence. Surely they will listen to you, the one they sent back from the dead, if you entreat them on behalf of my daughter. You are favoured above all other men!"

A swell of muttering arose from the throng of people around them. "It is he!" Huy heard someone call out. "The Twice Born!" someone else said. "He has returned to Hut-herib!"

"Go and heal the girl!" an indignant woman insisted, thrusting herself forward and glaring at Huy. "It is your duty!"

"It is not my duty!" Huy shouted back. "I am not a healer, I am a scribe. My childhood is behind me. I was wounded, nothing more, and you should not listen to silly rumours!"

At that, the crowd pushed forward and began to turn ugly. Fists were brandished. A small stone was flung, striking Huy on the ear. Angrily he put a hand to his bleeding lobe and prepared to lunge at his attacker, but a firm arm went around his neck and Ishat whispered, "I heard the uproar along the street. We must go with this man, Huy. Otherwise more than your ear is going to bleed. You will see the girl and she will die and then you won't be bothered like this again."

Still filled with the need to plant his fist in someone's face, Huy gritted his teeth. "Oh, very well," he managed. "Iri, take me to your home, and hurry up, before these mongrels tear me to pieces in the name of healing!"

Ishat's fingers slid into his. Iri began to push his way through the crowd and Huy followed. So did the crowd. "I am sorry, noble one," Iri said over his shoulder. "I did not mean to subject you to the curiosity of the people." Huy did not answer.

Fortunately, Iri lived only one street away from Huy's own house and they were soon turning in through a gateless aperture in a waist-high mud-brick wall that joined his property to others on either side. The crowd followed, filling the small space between the street and Iri's door, where a number of clay pots held the green fronds of herbs and mixed flowers. Huy did not notice them, but Ishat did, and told him of them later. Iri opened his door and ushered them in, closing it firmly behind him. Huy and Ishat found themselves in a modest but well-appointed reception room, dark and cool. Iri did not pause. He hurried towards the narrow hallway at the rear of the room and, halfway along it, veered through a doorway on his left. Huy could see sunlight and a tiny patch of courtyard garden at the end of the passage before he too, Ishat at his heels, entered the room.

It reeked of stale incense, vomit, and excrement. Several bowls rested on the earthen floor, and Huy realized that the stench came from them. A cot stood against the far wall, with a lit lamp on the table beside it. Steam rose from the cloth a kneeling woman was wringing out. She stood and turned as the three came in, her face pale and haggard, eyes darting at once to Huy. "Oh, thank the gods, you have found him!" she exclaimed. Three clumsy strides brought her to Huy. With hot, wet fingers she traced his jaw, the slope of his nose, the curve of his eyebrows. "You exist," she said in a low voice. "Twice Born. This is my daughter." She began to cry. "Her name is Hathor-khebit. If you ask the gods, they will heal her."

Jerking his head away from her questing fingers, Huy approached the cot with a sense of mutiny and helplessness. *I will perform this stupid play. Ishat is right, as always. The child will die and I will be left alone.* Awkwardly he knelt, and Hathor-khebit's little head rolled towards him on the stained pillow. Her hair was a tumble of wet tangles. Her skin was sallow, her cheeks swollen, and when she opened her mouth and tried to speak her breath made Huy want to retch. Yet her eyes mutely begged him as he took her hot hand, and in that moment Huy wished that it was true, that he did indeed have the power of the gods within him to heal.

"Hathor-khebit," he said slowly, and as her name left him he felt the vertigo begin. His fingers tightened convulsively around hers. Her face grew larger, nearer, was flung at him so that he instinctively drew back, then he seemed to be looking inside her where there was redness, and a forest of weeping ulcers in her mouth, and, farther in, the terrible, erratic struggle of her heart. Deeper still he saw food, pieces of white leek and brown beans and tiny scarlet, crushed seeds, and beyond her stomach the rapid flow of yellow diarrhea.

If anything happened at all, he had expected it to be a vision of her death. He was unprepared for this hot, suffocating prison of her body, and he found himself gasping for air and finding none.

"Greetings, son of Hapu, you most reluctant tool of mighty Atum!" The voice of Anubis came to Huy so clearly that he started. "This child is not yet ready for the Judgment Hall. Ask her father the question I shall give you. Then tell him exactly what to do. Atum's eye has turned to you at last, proud Huy. But you knew that already." The god's voice was warm with humour.

Huy listened as Anubis spoke, his lungs bursting, his eyes on the foul ukhedu leaving the feverish body, and just when he felt he must scream and flail in a panic to escape that dreadful place, he found himself crouching beside the cot, his whole body trembling, Ishat beside him.

"Sit back onto the floor," she said. "You saw something, didn't you, Huy? Can you speak?"

He nodded, looking up into the two drawn faces leaning over him. Hathor-khebit had begun to breathe in gasps. "Iri," Huy said, "what is your profession?"

Iri frowned. "I am a gardener," he said brusquely. "I tend the gardens of several of Hut-herib's nobles. Surely this is no time to be asking me frivolous questions!"

"You take your daughter with you as you work?"

"Sometimes."

"Three days ago your daughter ate the seeds of the bead vine. You must know how poisonous they are.

That is why her food sits whole in her stomach and her mouth is full of ulcers and her heart cannot pulse regularly. She vomits but cannot expel the ukhedu. It pours out of her as diarrhea, but the seeds remain."

The woman screamed and began to tear at her sheath. Iri cried out, "My own carelessness has done this! I am my daughter's murderer!"

Huy felt Ishat's hands press against his shoulders as she levered herself to her feet. "Be quiet!" she snapped at the woman. "Hathor-khebit is not dead yet, so why do you tear your clothes?" At her peremptory tone the girl's mother stopped screaming and began to whimper.

Huy wanted to stand but found he could not. He stayed huddled on the floor. "This is what you must do," he said to Iri. "Dig a small pit in here and make a fire. Go out and chop one small branch from an oleander bush. One small branch only. Cut it up and burn it so that your daughter breathes in the smoke."

Iri frowned. "Every gardener knows that all parts of the oleander—wood, leaves, and flowers, even its honey and smoke—are deadly. What are you saying?"

"The smoke will steady the pulse of her heart. One small branch, no more. And you"—he glanced up at the woman's tear-stained face—"while Iri is making the fire, you will feed your daughter four ro of castor oil followed by one small cup of the juice of the aloe plant. She will not vomit this up. Wait one hour. You have a sand clock?" The woman nodded. "Good. After one hour you will give her a mixture of one ro of ground kesso root so that she will sleep and two ro of ginger to cleanse her stomach. Continue to wash her and keep her clean. That's all."

Huy saw a cautious hope dawn in the swollen eyes. "Master, I have neither kesso nor ginger."

"Go at once to whatever physician you first called to Hathor-khebit. Promise him anything, but get the ingredients. Your daughter will live." Huy was steadier now. He felt strength beginning to return to his legs, and he stood. "Now please, I must go to my work!"

Iri made no mention of payment and it did not occur to Huy to ask for any. Desperate to escape, he pushed past the man and his wife and hurried along the passage to the reception room and the relatively fresh air beyond. He had forgotten about the crowd. A hush of expectancy greeted him as he emerged, Ishat behind him. Saying nothing, head down, he made for the street, and not until he and Ishat had reached the corner did a hubbub break out in a flood of loud voices and a pounding on Iri's door.

"Peasants!" Ishat said furiously. "Shall I come with you as far as the temple, Huy? Do you need to lean on me?"

"No. I have recovered." Huy stopped and faced her. "This is just the beginning, you realize that, Ishat," he said dully. "The girl will recover if her parents do what they were told. The word will spread, and soon we will be besieged in our home. I wish I could afford a stout cedar door."

Leaning forward, she kissed his cheek. Her eyes were shining. "Let's just get through today," she answered. "The gods are speaking through you once more, Huy! It is your destiny! Before long a new door will be the least gift you can command!"

Anger reddened his face, but it was not directed at her. He turned and headed for the temple. She ran after him and thrust his palette into his hands. "You dropped it by the child's cot. Bring me something better than bread and cheese to eat at noon."

Methen was pacing in his quarters when Huy at last crossed the busy courtyard and approached him. "You're very late, Huy, and you look ill," the High Priest commented as he took his place behind his desk, where several scrolls lay waiting to be examined. "What happened?"

Huy sank cross-legged to the floor beside his friend and set his palette across his knees, noticing with a mild detachment that his fingers still shook. "Something very distressing," he replied, and proceeded to relate the events of the morning.

Methen listened quietly. "I suppose it was too much to expect that you could remain safely anonymous anywhere in Egypt," he said when Huy had finished. "I think you have arrived at the place Atum always intended you to be, Huy, and your work for him has begun."

Huy wanted to cry. "I think I knew that eventually he would revive his power in me, but I had hoped I would be allowed a few more years of peace. Ishat and I are only just settled, Methen! I have only just become accustomed to the rhythm of my life here! And healing?" He glanced up into Methen's sombre face. "I could not heal Thothmes' mother, but I have been able to see the future for a handful of people. Ramose believed that the gift would expand to include healing." He closed his eyes. "I have no control over my own will anymore. It's a terrible feeling, to be at the mercy of a god whose devices are so mysterious. Perhaps if I had not failed to decipher the Book, I would know the culmination of his will. As it is . . ." He looked down at the floor. "As it is, I must now be tense all the time, never knowing when he will strike through me."

"We must wait and see," Methen commented. "The child may still die, and if so, you will be left in peace . . ."

"But if she was supposed to die I would have seen it," Huy finished for him, smiling wryly. "Therefore she will live and my life will not be my own anymore. Ah well. While we're waiting, we had better see to the morning's dictation."

He expected a flood of petitioners at his door, but to his surprise one week went by, and then another, and the crowds on the street outside ignored his modest entrance. He was just beginning to relax into a sense of security when, on the first day of the third week of his freedom, he walked into his home to see Ishat pouring beer for Iri, who was sitting at the table with Hathor-khebit on his knee. Huy hardly recognized the girl. Her skin was rosy with health, her eyes sparkled, and as she scrambled down and ran to Huy her glossy hair rippled around her bony little shoulders. Falling onto her stomach, she grabbed his ankles and fervently kissed his dusty sandals. "I don't remember being sick," she said, "but Father tells me that you held my hand and made me better. He told me to reverence you when you came home."

Embarrassed, Huy reached down and pulled her to her feet. "Now you have a grubby mouth, Hathor-khebit. I did not make you better. It was Anubis himself who chose to heal you."

"Then we must go to his shrine and make an offering," Iri cut in. He had risen and was standing staring at Huy with a mixture of awe and shyness. "I did as you commanded, Master. And my daughter lives. I have brought vegetables for you and your servant from the gardens of my employers. I shall continue to do so, every week."

"Almonds, Huy," Ishat said loudly. "Almonds! And radishes, lotus roots, lots of lovely cabbage, green onions, garlic, lettuce, broad beans. Iri says he will bring whatever is in season. Fruit, too." She was grinning. "I can begin to cook at home. I can use the communal firepits at the end of the street. No more hauling lukewarm soup from the temple kitchen!"

Hathor-khebit was gazing up at Huy adoringly. "I like your long hair," she said.

After she and her father had bowed themselves out, Huy and Ishat looked at one another. Huy could smell the green freshness coming off the vegetables piled against the wall. The scent reminded him of his mother's plots around the pool in her garden. "With luck you can cure a woodworker next," Ishat said, "and after that a jeweller. Gods, Huy! We might even be able to move into a bigger house. If this is just the beginning, you might have to stop working for Methen."

There was no point in being angry with her, Huy reflected. Her ambition, her greed, was for him, not for herself. Nor would it do any good to tell her how much he feared and dreaded the demands of the god. *Now is the time to pay the price of resurrection,* a part of his mind whispered to him. *All good things must be earned, and the gift of the reanimation of your body requires the highest fee, namely, everything you have to give.* Watching Ishat's features glow with happiness, Huy sighed inwardly and at last surrendered to the god who had stalked him ever since Sennefer's throwing stick sent him plunging into water that had turned out to be deeper and darker than he could ever have imagined. *I am yours, mighty Atum,* his heart said. *Do with me whatever you want. My rebellion is over.*

Early the following morning, as Huy was dressing, he heard voices, Ishat's and another woman's, at the door, and when he had tied on his sandals he went through to his reception room. He knew what was coming. He felt utterly calm. Ishat stepped back and the woman bowed low to him. "I know about Iri's daughter," she said hurriedly, nervously. "Master, my husband makes mud bricks down by the water. We are very poor and can offer you nothing unless you need bricks, and if you refuse to help him we will understand, but yesterday he came home paralyzed in one arm and this morning he cannot lift his leg." She remained bent over, but she lifted her face to meet Huy's. "Please come and beseech the gods to have pity on him, on us. If he cannot work, we will starve."

Behind her Huy saw a man cross over from the other side of the street, slow, and then come purposefully towards him. He turned to Ishat. "Go and fetch my palette." She nodded and went into his sleeping room, quickly returning with the palette cradled across her arms. "Good," Huy went on. "Now sit on the floor and balance it across your knees. Uncap the ink. Use my scraper to smooth a piece of papyrus. Choose a brush, it doesn't matter which one, and write what I tell you."

Ishat looked up, shocked. "But Huy, I am not good enough at my letters yet! Not neat or fast!"

"You can do this. Now"—he turned to the woman—"tell my servant where you live." He then signalled to the man waiting hesitantly on the street. "What is it that you need?"

Ten people came to the door that day. Huy left his palette with Ishat, instructing her to write down their names, addresses, and complaints, while he hurried to Methen. "It's just a trickle," he told the High Priest, "but I'm afraid it will swell to a flood. I want to continue my work with you, Methen, and go out among the sick in the evenings. I must beg another palette from you."

"I can go back to using the temple scribe," Methen told him.

Huy shook his head. "If I remain in the house I will be pestered day and night. I need to be here with you in the mornings." He passed a hand over his eyes. "This is frightening, Methen."

"But it has a rightness about it. You are vulnerable in your house, Huy. Perhaps you should ask that the petitioners come here, to the temple. You can then be seen to be working under the auspices of Khenti-kheti."

Huy grunted an assent. "I suppose you're right. Not all will be healed. Some will be told when and how they are to die." He lifted his shoulders as though they were burdened. "Some will be angry. This is happening too fast, Methen. I am afraid."

Methen embraced him. "Let us see where Atum leads you. After all, Huy, what choice do you have?

You cannot run away from this. You would simply take it with you."

"I know." Huy returned Methen's embrace then stepped back. "At least here I am just a citizen. At Iunu I would be hoisted onto a pedestal and worshipped." He smiled at Methen. "The people of Hut-herib will keep my doings safely within the confines of the town."

Methen's eyebrows rose. "For a while. Shall we go and look for another palette?"

It was not long before the trickle did indeed turn into a steady flood. Huy returned to his house each afternoon to find several sheets of papyrus covered in Ishat's careful scrawl waiting for him. Sometimes the petitioners were still lined up when he pushed his way through his door and handed Ishat her noon meal. After she had eaten, they would go over the list together. Then both would sleep before Huy ventured out into the town to visit the needy who had thronged his door. In the evening he and Ishat ate whatever she had prepared, and in the twilight Huy set off again on his errand of healing. He had told Ishat to refuse admittance to anyone who came begging after the noon meal, but it was then that the grateful ones turned up, two or three days after Huy had been in their homes, to bring payments that ranged from the promise of enough bricks to build a new house, from the man who had been paralyzed, to one haunch of beef a week, delivered by a butcher who had accidentally sliced into his upper thigh with a cleaver and almost bled to death before Huy's hands stopped the flow.

Not everyone in pain was healed. Sometimes Huy was forced to sit or kneel beside a disordered cot and wait anxiously for the onset of a power that did not come. Sometimes the gods were silent and instead Huy was catapulted into visions of future agony and chaos that distressed him almost as much as they did the unfortunate creatures who had to hear the prophecies. He always gave those people the choice of knowing what was to come or remaining ignorant. All chose knowledge, and their eyes, pleading, terrified, disillusioned, followed him into his dreams, peering at him through the leaves of the Ished Tree, reflected in the lazy golden glance of the hyena nestled beside Imhotep.

Soon Huy instructed Ishat to make it known that she would receive the names of those needing help in the outer court of the temple. Both of them were becoming exhausted and their home had ceased to be a place of quiet refuge. Huy also told her to keep one day a week free of all obligations. In spite of his assurance to Methen that he would continue to work at the temple, he was eventually forced by the sheer volume of his petitioners to ask that another scribe be appointed in his place. He missed those peaceful mornings of civilized industry and he saw Methen much less often. On his one precious day of freedom from the stench of infection, without the weight of suffering that seemed, from his point of view, to be imbuing the whole town, he could rest, play sennet with Ishat, wander with her by the river, even help her put the house to rights, and recover something of his equilibrium.

He was also forced to forgo his visits to his family. He sent Ishat to explain to them why he had so little time to call his own. His mother sometimes came to the outer court, waiting patiently until the increasingly large crowd vying for his attention had thinned, and

Heby found many occasions to hurry from his morning's lessons and chatter away to Huy before Hapzefa loomed to escort him home. So the season of Shemu passed quickly into Akhet, the season of the Inundation, and four months later into Peret, when the river deposited its silt and sank, its task accomplished, and the sowing and growing began again.

Neither Huy nor Ishat marked the passing of time. For them each day was like another, full of begging voices, broken bodies, and fatigue, although Ishat found the energy to be delighted with the growing variety of gifts from those the gods had blessed through Huy: coarse blankets, cowhides for the floors, clay bowls and cooking pots, a copper looking glass, a selection of dried herbs, jugs of beer and occasionally wine, plenty of natron, and once, to Ishat's great excitement, a bolt of linen of the tenth grade and a handful of gold dust from the assistant governor of the Maten sepat, who had travelled north from Mennofer, the capital of the Maten, with his diseased wife on his barge. A fussy and meticulous man, like so many nobles involved in administration, he had spent many minutes describing his wife's symptoms—a languid inability to rise for more than an hour or so, a vagueness of mind, a steady loss of weight. Huy had listened impatiently, and when at last he was allowed to take the woman's cold hands in his own, he saw her intestines bursting with writhing worms. Anubis prescribed minute doses of the dog button, a rare and very expensive plant with blossoms that smelled of cumin and coriander, and intensely poisonous grey velvet seeds. The assistant governor was shocked when Huy told him to obtain the seeds, which had to be imported, crush them one at a time, and feed them to his wife mixed in honey. "But, Master," the man protested, "every physician knows that the seeds of the dog button cause death from convulsions and a stopping of the breath! I cannot take that risk!"

"I said one seed at a time," Huy had pointed out wearily, wondering if it was the cost of the remedy that had sent the assistant governor into a paroxysm of objection. "One seed every three days for fifteen days, in honey. Crush and administer it yourself, in the presence of your household steward in case you make a mistake. More than one seed will kill your wife. Less will have no effect."

The man departed mollified but unconvinced. A month later the gold dust and linen had arrived, delivered by a herald, together with a short, ecstatic scroll of thanks. Huy shrugged. He knew almost nothing about the medicines the god told him to prescribe. He had never heard of the dog button before Anubis's harsh tones had spoken the words into his ear.

Sometimes the god's instructions seemed nonsensical. "Put the water of the river into a pot and make it boil until you have counted to five hundred. Let it cool. Mix it with the grey rot of bread of ten days and have your son drink the equivalence of one phial of it every day until it is gone." Huy understood rotten bread of ten days, or two, or seven. Everyone did. Such bread, placed on a suppurating wound or even eaten by someone with an infection, often healed. But why boil the water of the river? Huy did not know—he simply conveyed the decision of the god to anxious parents, husbands, wives, whoever waited hopefully for salvation. He took no pride in the healings; they were not of his doing. His pleasure rested in seeing the sick restored to health. Since finally relinquishing his will to Atum, he had recognized himself as nothing more than a vessel, a lamp waiting to be filled with oil and lit before it could be used. He did not forget the knowledge that had come to him. Atum had not given him back his life out of mercy. Atum had chosen to resurrect him for a purpose, and at last Huy was able to accept the responsibility of that purpose without resentment.

He began to see petitioners from other parts of the country, due, he thought, to the restoration of the assistant governor's wife. He had asked the man to keep the results of the prescription to himself and trusted that a government official would do so, but his wife was a different matter. Ishat was the only woman Huy knew who could hold her counsel. Women loved to gossip, to share, to exaggerate their experiences and verbally tear apart their enemies. Even Nasha had not been immune from the desire to spread some delicious, shocking story. But Ishat regarded the conversation of other women with intolerance. Huy trusted her to keep any secret he shared with her, and so far she had not let him down.

The governor of the Sepa sepat himself came with a head that would not stop aching. His payment, to Huy's great pleasure, was a bow and a set of well-made arrows, two decorated daggers, and a young donkey that Ishat immediately fell in love with and called Soft-Nose. "How are we going to feed it?" Huy had asked her irritably while she exclaimed over it and hugged its grey neck. She had smiled at him as though he were an imbecile.

"My father will put it out in his field and it will keep the wild animals from the crop," she had said. "It is a good gift, Huy. When we move we will need a donkey, and a cart and harness."

Huy had grunted. "So we will be moving soon?"

"Of course! The brick maker is piling up bricks for us. All we need is a piece of land." *And that,* Huy thought, *is an impossibility. Only the King or the governor can apportion land.* But he did not say so. He did not want to spoil Ishat's obvious pleasure.

The chief steward of the Prince of the Atef-Pehu sepat came from Qes, hundreds of miles to the south and halfway to Weset, where the King sat on the throne, and stood patiently in line with the dozens of other supplicants, a guard to either side of him, a servant holding a parasol over his shaved head to keep him in the shade. When Huy saw him begin to gasp for breath, he left the stool where he had been sitting in the outer court, told Ishat to continue to take down names, and led the chief steward into Methen's cool quarters. His respiratory condition could not be cured, but it could be controlled with minute doses of the powdered leaves and roots of an imported plant called nightshade. To Huy's surprise, the man nodded. "Few physicians know of this prescription. But my master's physician is a foreigner from beyond the Great Green. He has much strange knowledge and is skilled in the treatment of all maladies. I had hoped that the gods would see fit to cure me completely, but it is not to be." He had shot Huy a keen glance. "You have something else to tell me, young man."

Huy had grimaced miserably. He had begun to like this humble, self-possessed servant. "I am sorry, but as well as Seeing your ailment, Anubis showed me your future. You are a soldier, are you not?"

"I used to be, before my Prince took me for his steward. I captained the guard of his house. I proved myself trustworthy."

Huy touched his arm. "You will prove your devotion to your Lord with your life. You will die in battle, protecting him."

The man's dark eyebrows shot up. "In battle? But in the event that the One goes to war, I will be left to oversee my Prince's family and household while he is away!"

"I tell you only what I have been shown." Huy rose and went to the door. "It has been a privilege to meet you, noble one. I pray that my vision is proved false. Rest here until your chest eases." But he knew, as he walked to where Ishat was surrounded by the usual clamorous crowd of the needy, that his visions had never been proved false. Suddenly he felt very sad.

18

Shemu proceeded on its stifling way. All around Hut-herib the crops were harvested, the grain threshed and stored, the perfume flowers gathered for soaking and distillation. Huy was scarcely aware of the activity in the fields as he and Ishat struggled to cope with the crowds that waited for them every dawn in the forecourt of the temple, and which did not disperse until Huy pushed through them at sunset to go home. He did not know how to control them, could not turn away any of the needy without a pang of guilt. It seemed to him that he drew strength from the dreams of the Paradise of Osiris that intensified in power and beauty the more exhausted he became. Ishat too was tired, giving the petitioners the sharp edge of her tongue when they surged around Huy instead of queuing quietly, and using the last of her energy each day to prepare their evening meal and wash their linens.

The season of Akhet began with the month of Thoth, when Sirius the Dog Star appeared in the night sky, signalling the beginning of the Inundation. Now at last the multitude began to thin. Thoth heralded the New Year, and celebrations honouring the god after whom the month was named, the appearance of Sirius, and the first slight rise in the level of the river went on for the full thirty days. Huy and Ishat stayed in their house, sleeping, eating, talking together as they had not been able to do for a long time. Huy answered the letters from Iunu that had piled up. He and Ishat visited their families. Both began to recover their strength.

"We cannot continue to deal with dozens of beggars every day," Ishat remarked one hot evening as they sat on stools outside their door, watching the people of the street stream past them on their way to cast flowers into the water. "Besides, the High Priest has been receiving complaints from worshippers who can barely push their way into the court for all the crush of people around you. It's time to find another place, Huy. Somewhere on the edge of the town. And we need a door steward, someone to regulate the flow of petitioners, admit them in order of need. How can I cook and clean as well as scribble lists all day and try to keep the citizens from mobbing you to death?"

Huy was leaning forward, relaxed, his elbows on his bare knees and his hands hanging between them, his eyes on the noisy and colourful scene flowing past. Now he sat back with a sigh. "You're right. But to obtain land I must become a petitioner myself, at the governor's door, and I don't think that the gold we got from the noble with the headaches would be enough to pay for it. Besides, a house would have to be built. Where will the extra bread and onions come from to pay the labourers? And a doorkeeper? Be sensible, Ishat."

"Is this sensible?" She flung out both brown arms. "Using up our khu faster than the gods can replenish it? How much longer will it be before we collapse ourselves?" She lowered her voice. "I am beginning to hate them all, with their anxious eyes and demanding tones, as though you owe them something instead of bestowing great favour on them."

Huy was beginning to feel the same way but did not want to admit it. More and more the people who thronged him had begun to acquire a single face, their voices a single, jangling whine. He knew that the law of Ma'at required respect among all Egypt's citizens, with the greatest reverence and esteem reserved for the One who sat on the Horus Throne. He knew also that his perception of his fellow humans was becoming distorted. *I see only the sick and troubled,* he thought as he watched Ishat's dark brows draw together in a frown. *I share a laugh with no one. I have no time to use the bow and arrows I was given, or float on the river with Ishat and fish, or sit in the beer house and listen to the babble of healthy patrons. But how can I dare to incur the wrath of Atum by turning anyone away? Must I indeed exhaust my khu and my body to the point of illness myself, in the service of the god?*

"I agree that we must bring some sort of order into what our lives have become, but how, Ishat?"

"There are three hundred bricks on our pile already. The brick maker sent his son last week to tell me. Soon there will be enough for a new house." She tapped him on the knee. "Go and see our governor. Surely he has heard of your fame as a healer by now. He should be honoured to have such a servant of the gods in his town. He should give you land."

Huy did not reply. As many as he had healed, there were many for whom he had predicted death, and although no one had refused to hear the nature of his or her end, such knowledge inevitably ate away at the precarious peace of the supplicant. More than once Huy had been confronted with a man or woman who had agreed to be told their future but who had eventually returned to Huy with fear, to have the vision verified. All venerated a healer; few accorded a fortune teller the same unqualified appreciation. Huy did not think that the governor would be eager to grant him a boon that might lift him from the relative anonymity of the street and set him closer to those of a higher class. Besides, the sting of Nakht's rejection was still too painful; Huy could not face another such rebuff.

In the end he did nothing. The river swelled and overran its banks; Hut-herib became a series of islands. Huy's eighteenth birthday on the ninth day of Paophi passed without much fuss. Ishat gave him a red ribbon to weave into his braid. Methen presented him with a sheaf of fresh papyrus and a pot of powdered ink. His parents feasted him, and Heby, in his brother's honour, had painted a lurid picture of Huy kneeling before Atum on Hapu's outside wall. Letters of congratulation came from Thothmes, Nasha, Ramose, and the Rekhet. Otherwise Huy and Ishat resumed the hectic pace of their life.

Every month had its celebrations. At least five days and usually more were holidays in honour of some god or other, when no work was done, and at those times Huy and Ishat snatched a little rest and sanity out of the chaos their lives had become; but Huy, increasingly desperate and depressed, began to dream of throwing his scanty belongings into his two satchels and stealing away with Ishat in the middle of some moonless night. He began to beg Atum for his release.

The blessed season of Peret with its four months of cool breezes, its green, springing crops and bursting fecundity, came and went. There were fewer fevers and invisible maladies for Huy to deal with. Accidents multiplied instead, as farmers laboured on their land with their tools, but a slashed leg or a broken arm could be dealt with by any physician. Children had always spent their time playing in the water of the canals running through the town and in the stagnant irrigation channels dividing the fields, and Peret brought drownings and worm infestations. Huy saw many children, some of them already dead, and for these the distraught parents expected Huy to perform a miracle and bring life back into the cold grey limbs. When he protested that he could not, demonstrated that such an event was far beyond his power, he saw the unspoken accusation in the swollen eyes of the bereaved. "You came back from the dead. You are the Twice Born. You are familiar with the gods, who granted you a second chance and gave you potent gifts. They must therefore love you, and will give you any boon you ask. Why do you not ask on behalf of my child?"

Seeing these drowned children with their pale, glazed eyes and weed-entangled hair filled Huy with the familiar panic of the child he had been. Often he needed all the strength of his will to prevent himself from fleeing every dim death room, with its odour of scummed water, and running to where there was light and warmth and the comforting noise of people going happily about their daily business. He began to drink wine in the lengthening dusks, seeking an oblivion he knew would be denied him but hoping nonetheless that he might prompt the pity of the gods.

The month of Pakhons heralded the return of the season of Shemu, when the days became gradually hotter and the fields turned from a tired green to bright gold, waiting for the scythes of the reapers. Pakhons passed. Payni began, and on the eighth day of that month Huy's fortunes changed with a swiftness that stunned both him and Ishat. Just after dawn they were eating oat porridge with honey. Ishat had opened their front door to allow the brief coolness of the morning wind to flow in, but its touch revived neither of them. Dispirited and tired, they finished their meal in silence. Ishat had risen to collect their empty bowls when a shadow fell across the floor and someone pounded on the outer wall. "They cannot even wait until you go to the temple," Ishat snapped. "Huy, this has got to stop!" She turned towards the doorway and froze, and Huy, seeing her sudden stillness, got up. A blessedly familiar form was advancing into the room.

"It took me a long time to find you," Thothmes said. "Gods, Huy, I'd forgotten what an ugly pit Hut-herib is! Am I safe on this street? I did station a guard outside."

For a long moment Huy stared at his friend. Then reality flooded in and he ran forward. "Thothmes! How wonderful! Yours is the last face I expected to see today!" He threw his arms around the well-remembered body. "What are you doing here? Do you have business with the governor?" They broke apart and stood grinning at one another. Huy felt his heart lighten and all tension in him loosen.

"Not exactly." Thothmes looked him up and down with a critical eye. "What have you been doing to yourself? If I didn't know you better, I'd say you'd become a permanent drunk."

"He works too hard, noble one." The voice was Ishat's. As Thothmes swung to her she bowed. "You perhaps do not remember me," she went on. "I and my mother were servants in the home of Huy's parents. Now I am Huy's servant. But I remember you very well. Are your beautiful sisters with you, Master? Should I go to the market and prepare something special?" There was a hint of acid in her tone and Huy sighed inwardly.

"I do remember you," Thothmes said slowly, "but the last time I saw you, you were a gangly little girl. *Ishat*. That's your name, is it not? You have grown up most pleasingly, Ishat."

She bowed again. "Thank you. Your family . . . ?"

"At home in Iunu." He turned to Huy. "Nasha sends all her love. She's lonely now that Anuket has married and gone away. She and Father and I entertain a lot because the house seems so quiet and empty, and somehow when all the music and chatter have died away the three of us talk of Mother and of you."

"Thothmes, you look so healthy and contented!" Huy cleared his throat, feeling choked with emotion. "You finished school, of course. You're working for Nakht?"

Thothmes grimaced. "All day every day, even when everyone else is celebrating some god's feast or other. Honestly, Huy, I drown in lists and figures, and the only fun I ever have is when Father sits in judgment over some dispute or other. I sit beside him and try to appear wise. I'm going to make a very lax governor when Father dies."

Huy took his arm, drawing him farther into the room and indicating a chair. "Sit down, my dear one. Ishat, go next door and beg a jug of beer for us."

Thothmes shook his head. "There's no time for sharing the news this morning, Huy. I'd almost forgotten why I'm here. The King wants to see you."

Huy gaped at him. "What?"

Thothmes chuckled. "I had to wade through the huge crowd waiting for you in the outer court of the temple an hour ago. I needed to get directions to your house from the High Priest. It wasn't even light, my miraculously gifted friend, and here were all these beggars longing for your touch! It made me feel quite important."

"Be serious." Huy reached to the table behind him for support. He was trembling. "How does Pharaoh even know I exist?"

"Are you naive or just dense? You're famous throughout the country, the young healer and fortune teller with the long hair who lives humbly with his faithful servant. It's said that you can resurrect the dead and cause the gods to appear before you in clouds of incense. Anyway, the One needs your services."

"What for? Is he ill? Do I travel south to see him? Oh, Thothmes, you are terrifying me!"

Thothmes let out an exaggerated sigh. "Anyone would think you live on the moon. Don't you know that the tribes in Rethennu have rebelled against us? They're slaughtering Egyptian merchants and officials who've been quite legitimately working in Rethennu, which is after all a vassal state and has been for hentis. Every new Horus has to mount a punitive expedition into Rethennu early on in his reign, and the foreigners never seem to learn prudence. The King wants a prediction from you regarding the outcome of his impending clash with these ungrateful tribesmen."

"He is here in Hut-herib?"

Thothmes' nose wrinkled with distaste. "Well, not actually in the town. The royal barge *Kha-em-Ma'at* is moored just north of here. The army is encamped to the east, where the Horus Road begins. Pharaoh will join the troops after you have Seen for him."

"But Thothmes, what if I don't See anything? It happens sometimes. Or See him defeated?"

"He will want the truth from you. Has he not named his barge *Living in Truth*?"

"And you"—Huy was desperately trying to organize this tumble of information in his mind—"why are you with him?"

Thothmes' grin reached from ear to jewelled ear. "As your friend and closest confidant, I have been delegated to bring you into the Presence, interpret your immortal words if necessary, and make sure that you are given the best of attention. Our Pharaoh has been very thorough in his investigation of you and your family since word of your healings and prognostications reached Weset. I may go with His Majesty into

Rethennu if I want to, but I think I'd rather stay here for a few days and visit with you." His gaze strayed to Ishat, who had been listening wide-eyed. "And with you, Ishat. You can tell me everything about Huy that he won't tell me himself. My father's barge is moored at Hut-herib's miserably dirty watersteps."

Huy saw their eyes meet. To his astonishment, a flush of red began to stain Ishat's neck and creep up her cheeks. Thothmes' smile slowly died; a speculative expression took its place. Ishat's fingers went to her hair, fluttered undecidedly in the fronds of the fringe that cut across her forehead, then gripped one another in front of her. Her shoulders faced Huy before her head turned to him.

"Huy, you can't stand before the King in that kilt," she said. "Let me set out the gold-bordered one you have left, and find your cosmetics and jewellery." Stumbling against the table, she fled into Huy's sleeping room.

"I don't believe it!" Huy laughed. "Your news has completely unsettled her. I never thought to see a disconcerted Ishat!" He glanced at his friend, but Thothmes' eyes had followed Ishat. He was frowning.

It seemed to Huy that the faster he tried to be, the more malevolently his fingers obstructed him. Standing in his sleeping room while Thothmes and Ishat talked beyond the doorway, he fumbled with the kilt that knotted as he tried to tie it on. Twice he dropped the turquoise belt. A tendril of hair escaped from his braid and became hooked around the chain of his sa amulet as he was bending over to latch his sandals, and he was forced to take the braid apart and weave it again. He had given Anuket's gift to the young whore, and the only earring he possessed was the ankh on the short gold chain. He had no bracelets.

Finally he sat on the edge of his couch and, with eyes closed, deliberately relaxed one muscle in his tense body after another, knowing that if he presented himself before the King in his agitated state his gift would desert him. *I did not even bother to paint my lids with kohl this morning,* he thought in despair. *I look like a peasant aping his betters with my scrubbed face and simple earring, expensive ring amulets on my fingers and around my neck and yet leather sandals so old and cracked that they no longer fit me properly.* He heard Ishat give a shout of laughter over Thothmes' light voice. *They are easy with one another,* he thought in surprise, and at that he opened his eyes, stood up, and walked into the reception room. "Should I bring my palette?" he asked Thothmes, who shook his head.

"No need. Now we must be going. The King will have been washed and dressed, and he is not a patient man."

Huy turned to Ishat. "Go to the temple and tell those waiting that I will not be taking petitions today. Then go to the kitchen and see what's planned for an evening meal. You will eat with us later, Thothmes?"

"No. The two of you will eat with me, on my barge." Thothmes waved Huy towards the doorway. "Oh, come on, Huy! Where's the confident young man who graced Father's feasts?" *Gone with Anuket and the rosy prospects of an old fantasy,* Huy thought, and followed his friend into the street.

A litter sat just outside, surrounded by a small crowd of Huy's curious neighbours. The bearers were lounging against the wall. They came upright as Thothmes appeared, and the two guards stepped forward, spears canted towards the people, who stopped chattering and drew back. Thothmes lifted the curtain of the litter, motioned Huy inside, and settled himself on the cushions beside him, letting the curtain fall. Huy felt himself raised as the bearers took the strain. It was a familiar feeling, and in spite of his anxiety he smiled. "I haven't been in a litter since I left Iunu," he remarked. "I just assumed that we would walk."

Thothmes shuddered. "And have you arrive before the One all dusty and sweaty? Not a good idea." After a moment when they swayed along in silence, Thothmes went on, "Ishat has grown up quite beautiful, hasn't she? There's nothing crude about her features, no indication of her lowly roots. She looks like the daughter of some rural noble."

"Yes, she does," Huy agreed slowly. "I remember how shocked I was to see her for the first time after I returned home. It took me some moments to recognize her."

There was another moment of quiet. Thothmes broke it. "She must have a suitor or two. Eager farmers' or fishermen's sons, perhaps."

"Not as far as I know. Why do you ask?" Huy swivelled to face his friend. Thothmes was studying the folds of the curtain. Huy laughed. "You're attracted to her? To Ishat? My sharp-tongued little witch?" He had been about to say "my *jealous*, sharp-tongued little witch," but something taut in Thothmes' body made him swallow the word.

"Well, she is gorgeous," Thothmes replied defensively. "My father has started to throw eligible girls in my direction, the daughters of his noble friends, and some of them are very pretty, but they bore me. Their conversation is shallow and they're too eager to please me. Father wants me married. He wants a grandson."

"Ishat is no ordinary servant girl you can use to while away a pleasant afternoon," Huy said more heatedly than he'd intended. Thothmes' words had stirred up a wave of illogical possessiveness in him. "And don't even think of offering her a position in Nakht's house because she would embellish your father's feasts. She's my servant through her own choice. More than a servant, really. We're friends."

Thothmes held up his hands in mock defence. "All right, all right! No need to take my head off! My questions came from an idle interest. You must admit that a woman of the lower classes with her aristocratic looks is most rare. I'll bet that somewhere in her ancestry there's a nobleman and a pregnant serving girl."

"I have no idea," Huy responded stiffly. "Anyway, I pity the man who weds her. She always says exactly what she's thinking. She can be infuriating."

"So you have no plans to marry her?"

Huy met Thothmes' eyes. They were kind. "I don't know if I will ever stop loving Anuket," he said heavily. "But even if I eventually recover from that malady, I've learned from painful experience that I can marry no

one, Thothmes. I think I told you before. It's
something to do with my gift. The gods have withheld
that pleasure from me."

"Yes, you did tell me." Thothmes grasped Huy's
hand. "Forgive my tactlessness, old friend. I had hoped
that things had changed for you. And what of the Book
of Thoth? Did you decipher it in the end? You never
mention it in your letters."

"No, I have not deciphered it," Huy said sourly,
"and I try not to think of it at all, but it comes to me
in my sleep. I wish I was back at school, kicking a ball
around with you and memorizing ridiculous
aphorisms. The work I do is hard, Thothmes. It is
wearing me out."

Thothmes squeezed his hand and let it go. He did
not reply.

When the bearers set down the litter and Huy got
out, he found himself standing on a narrow sandy path
that wandered away ahead of him to be lost in groves
of fruit trees and thick shrubbery interspersed with tall
palms. He could smell water and flowers, and he drew
the odours deep into his lungs. Behind him the town
lay just below the horizon in a haze of cooking smoke.
*I have breathed the stench of hot lamp oil and stale beer
and donkey offal for too long,* he thought fleetingly.
This is wonderful. He turned, and the breath caught in
his throat.

The royal barge, *Kha-em-Ma'at,* lay like some great
gilded bird tethered to the bank of a sparkling tributary.
Its wide deck was crowded with men, most of them
young, leaning on a rail that glittered golden in the
sunlight and watching Huy with obvious attention.

The ramp leading across from the deck to the ground held four soldiers with swords drawn, dressed in blue and white kilts, the colours of royalty. The flag fluttering atop the gilded mast was also blue and white. More liveried soldiers lined the bank in front of the craft's painted, curving side, their solemn eyes following Huy's every move as he looked quickly for Thothmes' support.

One of the soldiers stepped forward. He had begun to smile, and Huy, staring at him, smiled back and ran to him. "Anhur! Is it really you? I hardly recognized you under all that splendid embossed leather!"

The man bowed ostentatiously, still grinning, and, sheathing his sword, embraced Huy. "When the rumour went round about the marvellous young Seer living in the Delta, I suspected it was you," he growled. "You've grown up very handsome, boy. And see!" He flung his arms wide. "Your prediction for me came true! I remember doubting it at the time, but here I am, a member of His Majesty's Shock Troops, and going to war." He put his mouth close to Huy's ear. "I'm going to enjoy these battles," he whispered. "You told me I would not be harmed, so I can concentrate on slaughtering our enemies without fear."

"You were like a father to me during my time at the temple in Khmun," Huy told him happily. "How were you able to leave the service of Ra at Iunu and become attached to the King's most elite fighting force?"

"Ah, there's a story," Anhur began with relish, but a sharp word stopped him.

"Back to your post, soldier!"

Anhur immediately recovered his sword and strode back to his place, and Huy found himself facing a tall young man wearing a cloth-of-gold kilt. Gold chains hung in profusion on his wide chest and one encircled his brow over a short, wavy wig. A red jasper earring in the shape of a scarab swung from one lobe. His eyes were heavily kohled, his lips and palms hennaed. Huy, suddenly ashamed of his unpainted face and common ankh earring, gazed into a stern face and a pair of suspicious eyes. "Huy, son of Hapu of Hut-herib?" the authoritarian voice went on. Huy nodded. "I am Wesersatet, Commander-in-Chief of His Majesty's forces. Follow me." Now Huy noticed the golden supreme-commander's arm bands gripping Weser-satet's upper arms.

Meekly he followed the man up the ramp, between the motionless guards. As he stepped gingerly onto the deck, the quiet crowd of men made way. Huy felt their inquisitive eyes on him. He could smell them now, a mixture of exotic perfumes and expensive skin oils, and he thought briefly of his uncle Ker, who had surely supplied most of these young noblemen with both. With an effort he raised his head and looked boldly from one to another. None of them dropped his gaze. A few of them smiled at him. He wondered where Thothmes was.

As they approached the damask-hung cabin, a man came hurrying out of it and Wesersatet stood aside. Huy, who realized too late that he should have bowed to the Commander-in-Chief, was about to bow to the man approaching but checked himself in time. This was a servant, his head shaved, his blue and white ankle-length sheath bordered in gold thread, a short ceremonial staff of office in his hand. His eyes were kohled and his lips hennaed, but his palms were clean.

Not a nobleman, but an important person nonetheless.
Huy inclined his head.

"I am Men, chief steward to His Majesty. His Majesty is ready to receive you. When you enter, you must stop just inside the cabin and make a full obeisance. You must remain on the floor until His Majesty tells you to rise. At that time you may stand. You then bow with arms extended and keep your gaze fixed on your feet. Do not look at His Majesty until he tells you you may do so. Do you understand?"

Huy swallowed. "Yes."

"And if His Majesty offers you beer or wine or a sweetmeat, you must bow both before and after accepting it. Make sure you do not touch the royal skin."

Huy glanced up, startled. "But if I am to See for His Majesty, I must touch him! Otherwise I will receive no word from the gods!"

The listening group murmured. Men's face twisted in distress. "Wait here," he ordered. "I will acquaint His Majesty with this development. Really, someone should have told me this before!" He bustled into the cabin. His last comment had made him seem more human, and something of Huy's extreme apprehension lifted.

When Men returned, he beckoned Huy forward. "His Majesty will graciously allow you to touch him. You may enter the cabin."

Feeling as though he had been summoned by Harmose, the school's Overseer, to receive a reprimand, Huy did as he was bid.

On the threshold he at once fell to his knees, then stretched himself full-length on the cedar floor of the

small space. The wood smelled sweet. He had no idea
exactly where the King was, but he had the impression
that the cabin was occupied by several men, one of
them seated, who had been speaking but had fallen
silent when he went in. There was a pause. Then a
voice said, "You may rise." Huy scrambled up, bowed
from the waist, extended his arms as he had been told,
and watched the latticed squares of light and shadow
from the cabin walls play across his feet. There was
another, longer pause before the voice spoke again.
"Lower your arms and look at me." To his chagrin,
Huy's hands had been shaking. He let them fall and
straightened, cautiously raising his eyes.

A young man sat cross-legged on a collapsible camp
chair, his brawny arms folded, his gaze steady on Huy's
face. Huy stared back. He had not really known what
manner of exotic creature he might see, but this ruddy,
muscled creature obviously not much older than Huy
himself, exuding an aura of vigorous health, took
Huy aback. The King was not wearing a crown, merely a
blue-and-white-striped starched linen helmet with a
small golden uraeus, Wazt the Lady of Flame, rearing her
flared cobra head above his brow, ready to spit poison at
any who came near to harm him. His chest was naked
but for a wide collar of gold and lapis tiles. His white kilt
was very plain, as were his papyrus sandals. His thick
fingers, however, were adorned with many rings and he
sported an elaborate earring, a disc from which hung
several elongated hands gripping ankhs. It took Huy a
few moments to recognize the obscure symbol of the
Aten, representing the rays of Ra on their way to strike
the earth, where they become lions. His face paint had

been immaculately applied. Huy, his trepidation fading, studied the brown, alert eyes, the broad, cleft chin, the curving cheeks flushed with colour. One corner of the orange-hennaed mouth lifted good-humouredly and the kohled eyes narrowed. "Well, Seer, what are you staring at?"

"Health and physical strength, Majesty," Huy blurted. The four other men in the cabin laughed. One of them had been standing with his hand protectively and, Huy thought, possessively on the back of the King's chair. Now he stepped forward.

"Are you indeed the prophet and healer whose fame has come to His Majesty's all-hearing ears?" he inquired. "You are Huy son of Hapu the peasant? How old are you? You look too callow to be a Seer. Why do you wear your hair so ridiculously long? Did you wash your hands this morning?"

"You know my name," Huy retorted, stung, "but I am not at the same advantage. Who are you? Or do you imagine that I am so far below you in station that I am not privileged to hear it?"

"Peace," the King said mildly. "Huy, this is Kenamun, the friend of my bosom, son of my wet nurse Amunemopet and thus my foster brother. He means no offence. He likes to stand between me and everyone else." Such frankness surprised Huy. Amunhotep was smiling widely at him.

"But Majesty, no man may stand between you and the people," Huy said, "just as no one stands between you and the gods. It is a law of Ma'at."

"So the peasant is not as stupid as he seems," Kenamun snapped.

Amunhotep held up a jewelled hand. "Be careful, my brother, or the mage might turn you into a toad," he said with humour. "Huy has been well educated at the temple school at Iunu, under Ramose's wise tutelage. I surprise you, Master Huy? Am I not Lord of all that passes under the beneficent rays of the Aten? Come closer."

Huy did as he was told, watching Kenamun out of the corner of his eye. The man was jealous of anyone who might demonstrate a hold over the King, he decided. *Well, I have no wish to control Amunhotep. I just want to See for him and go home.* As he drew near, he could smell the King's perfume, an odd mixture of rosemary and cassia, sweet and sharp, that made him want to sneeze. Unbidden, he went down and kissed first one royal foot and then the other. An angry murmur went up. Huy felt Pharaoh's hand descend briefly on his head. "No no," Amunhotep said quietly to his retinue. "This is an act of loving submission. Are you ready to See for me, Huy? Did you bring your Seeing bowl? Do you need oil or fire?"

"I only need to hold your hand as you have given me permission to do through your steward," Huy replied. "Your Majesty understands that I may see nothing"—here Kenamun snorted—"or see disaster."

"I do understand, and I want nothing but the truth from you," Amunhotep answered. "You may take my hand."

Huy sat on the reed mat surrounding the King's chair and, reaching across, gently lifted the warm, gold-encrusted fingers. He closed his eyes. *Now, Anubis, here is the One, the god upon the Horus Throne, surely your kin, requesting your aid. Do not fail me, I beg you.* A fleeting vision of himself slinking humiliated from the cabin under Kenamun's scornful laughter flew across his mind and was gone. It was succeeded immediately, not by the moment of vertigo he usually experienced at the beginning of a Seeing, but by a gathering darkness so dense it was like being underwater on a night without moon or stars. He was aware of the King's hand resting in both of his, and it was as though both of them, King and Seer, had been transported back to the Nun, the place of primordial nothingness. Huy, straining to see through the utter blackness, began to be afraid.

But a single shaft of light began to pierce the gloom. As it grew brighter, Huy saw it strike a small patch of sand, the granules glittering. In the centre a stone formed, grey and smooth. Huy, his fear forgotten, was enthralled. Suddenly, with a rustle of wings, a phoenix fluttered down the shaft and came to rest on the stone. Each of its feathers gleamed in a rainbow of colours, iridescent greens, blues, reds, but before Huy could gasp at its beauty it began to shrink and harden and he found himself looking at a large scarab beetle that had rolled off the stone and was pushing its egg through the sand. The scarab paused, reared up, its shining carapace dulling and thickening to a pelt of dark fur, beady black eyes, and tiny paws, and an ichneumon bared its teeth lazily at him. Then, as quickly as the light had appeared, it vanished. Huy was alone again in the dark, clutching the King's hand.

The voice came out of nowhere and yet surrounded him. Measured and clear, Huy knew instantly that he was not listening to Anubis's low growl. "Am I the

Bennu bird alighting on the Benben?" it said. "Some think so. Am I Khepri with the egg of a new creation? Some think so. Am I the divine ichneumon, killer of Apep the Great Snake? Some think so. And you, Huy son of Hapu, who do you think I am?"

Huy wanted to cower down, curl in on himself from the sheer terror of awe, but he found his own voice. "You are Atum, the Neb-er-djer, Lord to the Limit, the Universal God. You are the Great He-She. You created Yourself."

"Well done." The voice held a hint of laughter. "I have put my true names into your heart. Are you pleased with the gifts I have given you, mortal one? No, I believe that you are not. Nevertheless, in spite of your reluctance, you are already serving me and my purpose for Egypt. Tell my son Amunhotep the things I shall show you, and give him this warning: He must not depart from the balance of Ma'at I have established. Already he is tempted to do so." *Or what?* Huy thought with foreboding. *What dreadful thing will happen?*

He was gathering up his courage to ask the god, but with a speed that shocked him he found himself standing alone on a high cliff. Hot wind ruffled his hair. Below him the King's army snaked along the Horus Road towards the east. Dust hung in the air above the marching men. The scene changed, but Huy remained on the cliff. Now there was the melee of battle far below him. Words filled his mind. The princes of Rethennu. This is Shemesh-Edom. Eighteen prisoners and sixteen horses for His Majesty. Now the host was crossing two mighty rivers, engaging the Tikhsi, capturing seven of their princes. The city of Niy opens its gates to Amunhotep. Now he is rescuing his troops garrisoned at Ikathi from revolt. Now he is turning for home, for Egypt, with the seven princes of Tikhsi hanging head down from the prow of *Kha-em-Ma'at*.

The great kaleidoscope ended as abruptly as a candle flame blown out, and Huy came to himself with a cry. He was sitting on the floor of a barge's cabin, his whole body slick with sweat, his head throbbing so violently that he winced with every pang. He was hanging on to Amunhotep's hand with both his own, grinding the fingers. As soon as he realized where he was, what had happened, he let go of the King. Amunhotep's fingers were crushed white, but he did not rub at them. He laid both hands in his lap. Nothing was said. Huy continued to pant, his head now resting on his knees. After a while he felt something nudge him and, looking up, he saw Men holding out a cup.

"It is warm water with the ground beans of the carob tree," the man said. "Very fortifying. Drink, Master." Huy obeyed, thirstily draining the cup, hardly aware of the new taste of its contents.

"Men, set a stool for the Seer," the King ordered. Gratefully Huy crawled up onto it and handed the empty cup to the steward. He had not missed the respectful address Men had given him. Master. *Well, I suppose I am,* Huy thought, his mind clearing. Strength was returning to his body more rapidly than usual. He presumed it must be the good effect of the carob beans and wondered if Ishat knew where to get some.

Amunhotep raised his black eyebrows. "Will you speak now, Master?"

Huy nodded. Keeping the visions of the god to himself, he related all that he had seen of Amunhotep's campaign against the rebellion in Rethennu and beyond. Amunhotep listened intently.

"Seven princes of Tikhsi?" he pressed. He had begun to smile. "Hanging alive from my prow? The gods be praised! I shall sacrifice them in the presence of Amun and display their bodies on the walls of Weset. Perhaps I shall keep one to dangle at Napata in Kush, beside the Fourth Cataract—the southerners too are prone to rebellion." He leaned down, eyes alight. "And what of booty, Huy? After this campaign I intend to move my court back to the palace at Mennofer, where I was raised. Shall I bring much wealth to my old home?"

Huy was in so much pain that his sight had become blurred. "Indeed so, Majesty. I was shown more than five hundred petty princes of Rethennu, two hundred and forty of their women, two hundred and ten horses, three hundred chariots, four hundred thousand deben-weight of copper, and gold vases and other gold vessels to the deben-weight of six thousand eight hundred and forty-four."

"Such precision," Kenamun exclaimed dubiously. "Are you telling us that the gods showed you not only the progress of the King's triumphs but also the details of his spoils?"

Huy was in no mood to be tactful. He peered up at the supercilious face through eyes narrowed in agony. "Not the gods, but Atum himself. How dare you question the word of the Neb-er-djer? When my visions are proved to be true, you will do homage to Atum on your knees." He returned his gaze to Amunhotep. "Majesty, I have a personal message for you. Atum says, 'Tell my son Amunhotep the things I shall show you, and give him this warning: He must not depart from the balance of Ma'at I have established. Already he is tempted to do so.' That is all." Huy gripped his knees against the pounding of his head.

There was a moment of silence so deep that the murmured conversations of the men outside could be clearly heard. After a while Amunhotep cleared his throat. "I will ponder this warning if all the particulars of my campaign turn out to be true," he said heavily. "If they do, then indeed we have a mighty prophet in our midst. Huy son of Hapu, what may your King bestow on you for your work this day?"

Huy raised a hand. "It is enough to have served you, Majesty, but I would be grateful for a supply of poppy powder. It is expensive, and every time I exercise my gift I suffer from headaches. The more vivid the vision, the greater the pain. Forgive me."

"What for?" The King's tone was gentle. "Men, prepare a dose of the poppy at once and give Huy a jar of whatever you have left. Send a runner back to Mennofer for more. Huy, I shall make sure that you are adequately supplied. Sit still until you feel better." He was clearly elated with what Huy had seen, beginning a discussion with the assembled men of the tactics he proposed to employ at his first engagement against the princes of Shemesh-Edom, and Huy was grateful to be temporarily forgotten. Soon the steward handed him a tiny alabaster pot of milky liquid. Huy downed it quickly, fighting its bitter taste. Almost at once his headache eased and his limbs filled with a delicious lassitude.

"This is a very powerful mixture," he said to Men as he gave him the empty pot.

Men nodded. "The poppy fruit from which this drug is extracted is imported from Keftiu. It is superior in strength and efficacy to the plants grown here in Egypt. The King will make sure that you have a constant supply."

Huy rose unsteadily. At once all conversation ceased.

"You wish to be dismissed," Amunhotep commented. He waved behind him. "My friends want to know whether or not they will survive my battles. They want you to See for them."

"Majesty, I am very tired," Huy excused himself, the prospect of inducing more visions too distasteful to contemplate. "By tomorrow I shall have recovered enough to attend these nobles."

"By tomorrow I shall be driving my chariot along the Horus Road," Amunhotep replied. "Go, then, most miraculous young peasant. I may need your services again in the future, so take care to remain healthy. Have you a guard? Good servants?"

"No, Majesty. I live modestly with one servant, my friend Ishat. I have no need of a guard."

"We shall see." Amunhotep gestured, a swift flick of his ringed fingers. "Make your obeisance."

Huy did so, concentrating on keeping his legs steady. The poppy coursing through his veins was making him dizzy. Carefully he backed to the cabin door, bowed

again, and plunged into the open air with an audible sigh
of relief. Wesersatet escorted him onto the bank.
He would have liked to do more than call out a final
greeting to Anhur, but Thothmes was waiting for him
beside the litter and, in truth, the cushions glimpsed
beyond the damask curtains were too seductive. Huy
climbed in and sank back on them gratefully. He felt
Thothmes settle beside him. The litter was lifted.

"Well?" Thothmes pressed. "Was your vision
acceptable to His Majesty? I'm presuming that you had
one. Isn't Kenamun a nasty, patronizing piece of
Egyptian nobility? But did you like Miny?"

"Which one was he?" Huy muttered. "I only had
dealings with Men and Kenamun."

"Miny was the older man with the scar across his
chest. He's the King's military instructor. He gave
Amunhotep the massive bow that no one but the King
is able to draw. The King is very proud of that fact."

"I didn't notice him. I did my job, that's all. I was
offered water but no beer or food, and now that both
the pain in my head and my anxiety are abating, I'm
hungry. I want to go home to Ishat and have something to eat, and then I want to sleep."

"All right," Thothmes agreed good-humouredly.
"I can tell that you're grumpy. I'll send the litter for
you both at sunset and we'll dine on my deck, away
from the stench of Hut-herib. Did the King promise
you any wonderful gifts?"

Huy reached for his hand and clasped it tightly.
"Forgive me, Thothmes, it has been a most demanding
morning. I thank the gods I don't have to endure the
presence of royalty regularly!"

Ishat was sitting on a stool outside their door, waiting for him. She rose eagerly as the litter was lowered, but Huy did not fail to notice that her first glance went to Thothmes, who was holding back the curtain. They smiled at one another, Thothmes barked an order, and the litter moved off. Ishat took Huy's arm and drew him into the house. "Did the Seeing go well?" she wanted to know. "What does the King look like? Was he kind? Does he have lovely jewels? How big is his barge?"

Looking into her sparkling eyes, Huy could not disappoint her. Although he longed to attack the bread, figs, and fresh salad she had set out on the table, he answered her questions patiently. "He gave me no gold," he said, anticipating her final query, "but he has promised a constant supply of poppy for my head. You know how Seeing makes me ill. Now please, Ishat, let me eat!" Going to the table, he sat and bit into the bread. Ishat moved behind him. He felt her begin to undo his braid, and soon both her fingers and a comb were sliding through his hair. The effect was blessedly soothing.

"It was difficult to disperse the crowd from the temple," she said after a while. "The people did not want to go. They grumbled. They would have waited for you to come back if Methen hadn't appeared and shouted at them. Some of them came here, to the house, after I returned. I did not feel safe, Huy. We must find a house that can be properly guarded."

On impulse Huy reached for one of her hands, drew it forward, and kissed the callused palm.

"I know. The last thing I desire is to put you in danger, but Ishat, we're very poor. What can I do?"

She exhaled so gustily that her breath warmed his scalp. "Let's see what happens when the King comes home victorious as you have predicted that he will. Perhaps his gratitude will extend beyond a ready supply of poppy."

"Perhaps." Huy bit into the last honeyed fig. "In the meantime I must go on healing the needy. Gods, Ishat, I'm eighteen years old and I'm living the life of the middle-aged! I have a longing to play."

"At what?"

"I don't know. Just play. Don't braid my hair again. My head will stop aching sooner if it's loose. Will you take the afternoon sleep?"

She laid the comb on the table. "Yes. And this evening we will dine with your friend and pretend that our life is as comfortable as his."

Huy left the table. "I think he's attracted to you, Ishat. How does it feel, to be desired by a nobleman?"

She gave him a sardonic look. "Is the lust of a nobleman somehow different from the lust of a farmer?"

"I said desire, not lust. Surely desire is less crude."

"Ah! So that is the difference? Farmers lust but noblemen desire?" Then she laughed and, going up to him, hugged him warmly. "I like him very much, your old friend Thothmes. He treats me as an equal. No doubt he was raised to be kind to everyone. Sleep well, my dearest brother."

She vanished into her room, leaving Huy to make his way thankfully to his own sagging couch. He had intended to examine the events of the morning, and thinking of Anhur made him smile, but the poppy had done its work well and he fell into a healing sleep with the King's face fixed on his mind's eye.

19

Thothmes' litter came for them at dusk. Huy wore the same kilt he had discarded before the afternoon sleep, but after she woke Ishat laid out her two spare sheaths and the sandals Huy had got for her, fingered them uncertainly, stared at them, then uncharacteristically burst into tears. Huy had been braiding his hair. Hearing her sobs, he hurried into her room. He could not remember ever seeing her weep, and he stood helplessly just inside the doorway. "Ishat, whatever is wrong? Are you ill?"

She turned towards him, not trying to hide her ravaged face, and gestured at her cot. "I have never been anyone's guest before!" she wailed. "Always I have done the serving. Now I go to sit on a nobleman's barge and have his underlings attend to my needs, and they will be polite and dutiful—but I know what they will be thinking!"

Huy was genuinely puzzled. "Ishat, what are you talking about? You will be with a friend, someone you know. I'm glad that for once you'll be treated as a guest."

"But I will look like a servant, Huy! I have no pretty linen to wear, only my coarse old working sheaths! I have no jewellery, nothing for my hair. I do not even have my lobes pierced! They will know I am an imposter!"

Huy's heart went out to her. Such a consideration had entirely escaped him. Going up to her, he tried to take her in his arms, but she pulled away from him, her body rigid. "Don't try to comfort me!" she flared. "My place is standing behind you with the other retainers tonight as you eat and drink, seeing to your needs, filling your cup. Thothmes has only invited me to act as your equal out of kindness."

"Not so. I know him as well as I know you. If Thothmes thought of you as a servant, he would not have treated you with familiarity or included you in his invitation to dine. As for his servants, what do they matter? You have never cared what people's opinion of you might be."

"But this is different!" She tugged at her tousled hair then held out her hands. "No oil to spare for my hair! No time to soften my hands even if I had any lotions! I cannot even pretend to be a noblewoman playing at humility!"

At last Huy understood. Ishat did not care what the servants thought of her, but she cared very much for Thothmes' opinion. Her customary nerve had failed her. Huy thought for a moment then decided to be frank. "Thothmes has seen you exactly as you are," he said severely. "He remarked to me on your beauty—just as you are, Ishat! Do you think you can increase his respect for you by trying to look like something you are not? We can spare some lamp oil for your hair. I have a little perfume left in my chest to add to it. Your sheaths are clean and we can wash your sandals. Hold up your head and be as gracious and proud as you know how before Thothmes' servants."

"It's all right for you," she said sulkily, already calmer. "You spent years being cared for by them, every time you stayed with Thothmes' father and the rest of his family. Can't you see that I'm afraid of looking like a fool?"

Now Huy laughed. "My dearest Ishat! One sharp word from you will put them in their place. Besides, what am I? Nothing but a peasant who learned the habits of the aristocracy through an accident of fate. Make up your mind to enjoy yourself. Savour the wine. Eat your fill. You deserve some pampering."

For answer, she pulled one of the sheaths reluctantly towards her and shook it. "At least it fits me. Huy, will you do my hair?"

So while she sat quietly on a stool, Huy took a little oil in his palm, added a few precious drops of his jasmine perfume, and worked the mixture thoroughly into her thick black tresses until they lay tamed and gleaming below her shoulders. Then, slowly and carefully, for he had not done such a thing before, he added water to his kohl powder and outlined her eyes. The effect was startling. When she rose and turned to face him, clad only in her simple sheath, her arms and neck unadorned, her eyes huge and lustrous with kohl, she had a pure regality about her that gave Huy a pang of the unfamiliar. "You look like an ancient queen," he said, and meant it.

She smiled. "Thank you, Huy. Now I shall sit outside so that all the commoners on the street can pay me homage."

She had never ridden in a litter before, and exclaimed over the comfort of the cushions, the luxury of curtains to draw, the rhythmic movement of the bearers, with a wholly childlike enthusiasm that made Huy feel decidedly avuncular. Thothmes had moored his barge a short way to the south of the town in a sandy cove surrounded by palms. One of Nakht's household guards stood at the foot of the ramp. Huy recognized him and greeted him cheerfully. He bowed first to Huy and then to a flustered Ishat, whose eyes were on the curve of gaily painted planking and the flag flying the colours of Nakht's sepat above the gilded prow. Huy felt as though he was coming home.

Memories assailed him as he ushered Ishat up the ramp towards the men waiting on the deck. Anuket dancing for the drunken throng during a Hapi festival, wreaths of flowers to fling into the river held loosely in her graceful little hands. Nasha lolling under a canopy in the shade cast by the cabin, fanning herself and smiling lazily, a teasing word for her brother on her hennaed lips as he laid aside his throwing stick and reached for the beer. Nakht himself with his wife beside him, holding out a hand of greeting as Huy ran up the ramp towards them clutching his leather bag for an overnight river journey to see the newborn hippopotami in the marshes. *How much I have lost,* he thought with a wash of grief. *How cruel the past is, bringing to mind the memories that hurt and cannot be changed, the fruitless stumble into the agony of what-ifs, the awareness of time as a murderer, killing all hope, locking every door behind me as time carries me where I do not want to go.*

Thothmes bowed to Ishat and took her hand. "You look very beautiful this evening," he said to her gravely. "This is my steward, Ptahhotep, my captain, Seneb, and my servant, Ibi. Ibi will be seeing to your needs tonight." Ptahhotep and Seneb inclined their heads, but Ibi bowed low. *Thank you, Thothmes. You divined Ishat's insecurity before I did*. Huy greeted all three men as the old acquaintances they were.

"We have all heard of your fame at Iunu, Master Huy," Ptahhotep commented as the group moved towards the scattering of cushions and flower-strewn low tables set up between the cabin and the stern. "I congratulate you on the favour of the gods."

Huy grinned at him ruefully. "Thank you, Ptahhotep, but sometimes the favour of the gods seems more like a punishment."

"Or a judgment for past crimes," Thothmes put in. "Ishat, sit here on my left. Huy, you are facing me. Seneb, you may get about your business." The captain sketched a bow and strode back down the ramp. "The sailors will light a fire presently onshore and cook their soup and fish and probably get drunk," Thothmes went on. "I intend to stay rocking in this cozy little bay for a few more days. Ishat, if Huy doesn't need you, I'd like you to show me the town."

Ibi was already bending over Ishat's shoulder, a goblet in his hand. Ptahhotep had disappeared towards the prow. Ishat reached for the goblet. Her hand was trembling, but when she spoke her voice was even. "There's not much to see, noble one. Just narrow streets and a few dusty shrines and the markets . . ." Ibi was bending over her again, balancing the wine jug in both hands and waiting for Ishat to lift her cup. Sensing him, she did so. She was breathing fast, and as soon as the cup was full she drank thirstily.

Thothmes suddenly took it from her, set it at her knee, and took both her hands in his. She tried to pull them away, but he held her fast. "Ishat," he said softly, "I am insulted that you should address me with such formality. Did you not call me by my name when we laughed together in your house? Have I offended you since then? This small feast is to honour you as well as our friend Huy. I shall feel that I have failed in hospitality if you do not enjoy yourself."

Huy watched in astonishment. In spite of his light words to Thothmes regarding Ishat, and to Ishat regarding Thothmes, he had thought little of their ease with one another. But now he sensed something almost tangible passing between them that shut him out. *Thothmes is falling in love with her,* he told himself, not sure whether to be outraged or amazed. *Oh gods, how full of irony is your will for us!*

Ishat looked down at her lap. "I'm sorry, Thothmes," she said with a meekness Huy had never seen in her before. "I am very nervous to be here on your barge. Of course I would like to show you the town, if Huy agrees. Some of the markets can be fun."

"Good." Thothmes released her.

Huy was sure that she would pick up her wine at once, but instead she placed her hands one on top of the other on her thigh. A brilliant smile lit her face. "But we must use your wonderful litter. Otherwise we will end up filthy and your sandals will be ruined." Ptahhotep and Ibi were approaching carrying steaming trays loaded with food. Ishat carefully picked the flowers off her table and laid them on the carpeted deck beside her. She pointed to the dishes from which she wanted to eat while Ibi held the tray down to her, and once she had been served she began to eat. She had recovered her aplomb.

Evening slid into full night. On the beach the sailors' fire sent orange sparks into the black velvet sky, fitfully illuminating the ragged semicircle of palms quivering in the warm breeze. The tables were removed, more cushions were brought, and Thothmes and Huy began to reminisce. Both were aware of Ishat, lying back on one elbow and listening to them. It seemed to Huy that, although Thothmes was speaking to him, he was playing to her, an audience of one, his gestures broader and more graceful than usual, his laughter more ready, his voice more animated. *Am I going to lose her?* Huy wondered as his mouth made words for his friend. *I will not allow her to be anyone else's servant— but what if Thothmes has something greater in mind for her?* All at once he remembered what he had quite inadvertently seen of her future: Ishat in jewels and perfume, her face painted, an Ishat in the full power and beauty of maturity. "We," she had said in the vision. "We were not expecting you today."

"Wake up, Huy!" Thothmes was saying. "Didn't you hear me? I said that at last I'd managed to bring down a duck with my throwing stick. You should have heard Nasha shriek! Unfortunately, the bird wasn't even wounded, just knocked off balance, and after a minute or two lying in the reeds it recovered and flew away. You should be laughing!"

"I like to eat duck, but the thought of killing one is rather horrible." The voice was Ishat's, flowing out of the dimness just beyond the glow of the lamps Ptahhotep had lit.

Thothmes turned to her eagerly. "Is it? I feel that way also. I've never been much of a hunter, although I've accompanied the King a few times. He loves the sport and he's very good at it. Ducks, lions, gazelles—he pulls on that enormous bow of his and his arrows can fly out of sight. I pity his enemies in Rethennu."

Huy yawned and got up. "I have drunk too much of your good wine, Thothmes. And my encounter with the King was very taxing. I'd like to spend the whole night talking over old times, but I simply must seek my couch. Otherwise I shall fall asleep right here."

Ishat's face fell. She began to scramble to her feet.

"Huy, will you allow Ishat to stay aboard a little longer?" Thothmes asked. "You and I have rather rudely spent the evening dwelling on ourselves. I want to remedy our bad manners!"

"Of course she can remain with you if she wants to," Huy said, trying to keep the reluctance out of his voice. He knew that it was selfish of him, but the thought of the two of them drawing closer to each other after he had gone, reclining face to face on the soft cushions, sharing a growing familiarity under the subtle influence of the gentle night breeze, made him afraid. "Would you like to stay on for a while, Ishat?" he said, without much hope.

She nodded and sank back. "Thank you, Huy, that would be wonderful." She smiled. "I'm not tired. I want to go on being treated like a queen!"

"I'll make sure she gets home safely," Thothmes said. He rose and shouted an order to the men sprawled around the dying fire on the bank. Ptahhotep and Ibi carried the litter down the ramp. Thothmes embraced Huy. "We will have more time together before I must leave. Both of you must dine with me again tomorrow night. I have plenty of provisions." He grinned ruefully. "I think Father hoped I would accompany the King into Rethennu, but I have no wish to be under the royal eye for too long. Sleep well, dear Huy. You triumphed today."

Huy's street was dark and deserted by the time he dismissed the litter. Even the beer house had closed. His home was cold and smelled unpleasantly of old lamp oil and stale fish. Suddenly he was exhausted. He felt depleted, as though some force had sucked the energy from his body, so that just removing his kilt and his sandals required an effort. Lying down on his couch, he pulled the blanket up over his shoulders. His sheets felt chilly against his skin. He drew up his knees for warmth and closed his eyes. *I'm lonely. That's what's wrong. I have missed Thothmes more than I knew. Seeing him again has opened a wound in me, and the suspicion that Ishat may leave me is rubbing natron salt into it.* He fell into unconsciousness with disagreeable speed, and his dreams were jumbled.

In the morning he watched Ishat join Thothmes in the litter with a jealousy he fought successfully to control. Ishat had given him the list of petitioners she had made while Huy was with the King, and grimly he set out to alleviate as much of the suffering it represented as he could. He ate the noon meal with Methen, recounting the details of his audience with Amunhotep. In the afternoon, too agitated to rest, he continued to traverse the town, going from street to street, house to house, meeting each fever, each wound, each undiagnosable illness, with as much detached kindness as he could muster. His headache grew worse, it always grew worse as the day progressed, until in the end he turned for home and the blessed poppy Men had given him and his lumpy, welcoming couch.

The pain had receded by the time he heard Ishat's voice out on the street. She burst into the house. "Huy, are you here?" she called, coming to the doorway of his sleeping room where he was groggily trying to put on his sandals. "It's almost sunset. Thothmes is keeping the litter outside until we're ready to go." Coming closer, she peered into his face. "Your head was bad today?"

He nodded. "Yes, but the poppy has taken care of the worst of it. Have you had fun?"

She knelt and began deftly to tie his sandals. "I have, but I felt guilty leaving you to cope on your own. Thothmes wants me to spend tomorrow with him again, but I won't. You need me."

"I don't want you to help me if you don't want to." Huy tried and failed to keep the petulance out of his voice.

Ishat put her cheek against his calf, then rose. "It's amusing, playing the part of a noblewoman, but I'm more comfortable being with you," she said simply. "Do you need help putting on your kilt?"

"No. I'm shaky but recovering. Another night on Thothmes' barge is what I need. Can the three of us squash into the litter?"

For the following five days Thothmes stayed moored outside Hut-herib. True to her word, Ishat worked beside Huy for two of those days, both of them dining each night on the barge. She lost her shyness very quickly, joining in the conversations that took place long into the sweet, hot nights, and Huy took a much-needed consolation from the closeness growing among the three of them. But during the remaining days of Thothmes' stay she could not resist his urging to spend the daylight hours with him.

On the afternoon before Thothmes was due to weigh anchor and row back south to Iunu, she returned to the house early. She had asked Huy to be there, and he was sitting tensely on a chair in the reception room when she came in. For once she did not greet him. Pouring herself some water, she drank long and thirstily before setting down her clay cup with an exaggerated deliberation that told Huy she had something serious on her mind. Suspecting what it was, he clenched his fists in his lap and waited. Pulling forward a stool, she sank onto it in front of him.

"Thothmes has tried to give me many pretty gifts over the last week," she began, her eyes roaming the room, avoiding Huy's. "There is a market here in Hut-herib where the rich toss the baubles they no longer want. I had not seen it before we found it. I was tempted, but I refused to accept anything."

Huy did not ask why. Instead he said, "Go on."

"He has given me permission to tell you that he has fallen in love with me. He wants to ask you if he can take me back to Iunu with him." Huy had known the words that she would speak, had heard them as ghostly echoes in his mind, but every syllable she uttered felt like the clamour of harsh music falling directly on his heart, making it falter.

"I see," he managed. "As what, Ishat? His servant? His concubine?"

"No." She began to cry, the tears falling soundlessly down her face. She did not try to wipe them away. "He will give me a little house of my own, and servants of my own. He will provide for all my needs if I will allow him to introduce me to his family so that they can get to know me. He says that his father is a fair and broad-minded man who will eventually accept me as . . . as his daughter-in-law."

A bubble of bleak laughter welled up in Huy and threatened to choke him. The muscles of his chest contracted so painfully that he was forced to stand. He could control his resentment no longer. It was not directed at her; like a noxious cloud it enveloped the memory of Nakht's face on that terrible evening when he had begged for Anuket, begged for an acceptance that had been denied him but that was now being held out to Ishat, begged for a future, any future, under Nakht's protection. He could not argue that Thothmes was profligate in his tastes, that he slept indiscriminately with many women, that he was flighty and unreliable. He had known Thothmes almost all his life. Thothmes was a happy, intelligent, warm man who did his best to live according to the laws of Ma'at. *Do not punish Ishat for this,* he told himself while his jaw clenched tight against the hateful things roiling in his mind. *Why should she not grab at a chance to better herself?*

"What makes you think this is more than a brief infatuation on Thothmes' part?" he said hoarsely. "Do you imagine that his love will last?"

"We have immediately become friends. It's as though we've known each other all our lives." She started to sob and, picking up the hem of her sheath, scrubbed at her cheeks.

"Then why are you weeping!" He folded his arms against the dreadful ache in his chest. "I trust I am a reasonable master. I release you. Go with him." His tone was hard.

Now her swollen gaze flew to him, eyes and nostrils flared, and the old, familiar Ishat flashed out at him. "I only require your permission out of politeness, Huy! Have you forgotten that it was my decision alone to leave my service in your parents' home and tend you? Why so cruel?"

"I'm sorry." The apology cost him a great deal, but it seemed to ease the fluttering of his heart. "Will you go with him?"

To his surprise she shook her head vigorously. Then, reaching out, she grasped a handful of his kilt so that he was forced to step towards her and she buried her face in the linen. Her forehead burned against his genitals.

"No, Huy, I can't go. I've told him so. I don't love him. I love you, curse you. Curse you! I have loved you since we were children together. I know you do not care for me . . ."

Genuinely distressed, he pulled her clutching fingers away from his kilt and squatted. "I do care for you, my Ishat. I love you dearly."

"But not that way. Not as a lover desires the beloved. Even so, I can't leave you. Not yet. Not until all my hope is gone."

Releasing her fingers, he smoothed down her tousled hair and cupped her chin. "I cannot be selfish in this," he said with more force than he felt. "Thothmes offers you an honourable opportunity to eventually become the wife of the governor of Iunu! My Ishat, a governor's wife! Remember how I saw you in my vision."

"I remember." She jerked her head back and sank onto the floor. "If he really loves me he will wait. He will write to me. I can read letters now. He will come and see me, take me on short trips to meet his family. And even then I may choose to stay with you. You are not my master in the usual sense, Huy. I am free to choose my own destiny."

Huy sat back down heavily. "None of us are that free. The gods decide the course of our lives before we are born. Or twice born." The bitterness flowed out of him. "What I Saw for you will come to pass whether you think to choose another way or not. But for now I am selfishly glad that you will stay with me. I'd be very lonely without you."

"Selfish indeed," she agreed more calmly. "And I am weak and foolish. Well. We had better prepare for our last night with Thothmes. I shall give him my decision." But she continued to sit on the floor, head bowed. He watched her in a mood of helplessness and self-hate.

That evening, after food and wine and light conversation, Huy excused himself and left the boat, walking a short way along the riverbank. When he regained the deck, the pair of them were sitting in silence. Ishat was staring down into her goblet. Thothmes' expression was gloomy as Huy approached. "Ishat is very loyal to you," Thothmes said heavily as Huy lowered himself onto a cushion. "Is her answer an honest one?"

"Ishat is one of the most honest people I know," Huy replied uncomfortably. "Her word is true. She is distressed at hurting you, and I am sorry to see you disappointed, Thothmes. You are both my friends. I don't want either of you to suffer." *As I am suffering,* he went on silently. *Love is painful when it pours out of the soul towards the beloved and is not returned. It just goes on bleeding until the soul becomes sick with grief. Better for you not to know, Thothmes, that Ishat's wound is open to me, and mine to Anuket still cannot be closed.*

"Then I must accept it for now," Thothmes said. "Perhaps in time she will change her mind."

"Please don't speak of me as though I were not here," Ishat broke in. "Thothmes, I am deeply touched by your affection for me. Huy, I am yours for as long as you need me." She drained her cup and stood. "It has been wonderful to live like an aristocrat for these few days, but it's time to regain my station. Thank you again, noble one. I look forward to reading your scrolls." Both men got to their feet. Thothmes' expression was strained as he embraced her. "May the soles of your feet be firm," she said as she kissed his cheek, giving him the time-honoured blessing of the traveller. "Huy, I will wait for you on the bank."

Thothmes watched her walk along the ramp into the dimness beyond the reach of the barge's lamps. He turned to Huy. "Regardless of what she says, I shall speak of her to Father at every opportunity. My feelings will not change, so remember that when you have other servants to take care of you and she is free to reconsider my proposal. Then I shall make a formal approach to her parents, who will doubtless fall over themselves with joy at seeing their daughter elevated to the nobility."

Huy looked at him curiously. "Do you see yourself as bestowing on her some great favour, then? Are you condescending to her, Thothmes?"

"Gods, no! You should know me better than that! Have I ever condescended to you?"

"No, but I had to ask. Well. I shall miss you very much. Write to me too."

"I always do."

Huy had one foot on the ramp before he found the courage to ask the question that had been souring in him all week. He glanced back. "Thothmes, how is Anuket? Is she well?"

Thothmes looked grim. "She is well and happy, but her husband is not. I wish you could forget her, Huy. Be safe. It has been wonderful to see you again." He vanished abruptly into the cabin and Huy went on down the ramp. *I wish it too,* he thought as he got onto the litter beside Ishat and the bearers lifted them. *Sometimes it happens, but then a certain slant of sunlight, a certain scent, even someone's casual word, will bring her back to me on a tide of memories. I see her in your face and your gestures, my dear Thothmes.* He felt Ishat's hand on his arm.

"Huy, are you all right?" she said quietly. "You groaned."

"I ate too much and I'm tired, that's all," he replied dully. "Besides, tomorrow we begin work together again. The prospect would make anyone groan."

She did not laugh at the small joke, and they rode the rest of the way home without speaking.

For the following two months Huy threw himself into his work, dealing with the usual mishaps of the harvest season, but several times he found himself in homes he had been called to before, to touch some other member of a family where there had been a previous healing. The present maladies were uncannily similar to those of the past. A farmer whose injured leg had become swollen and black with ukhedu had followed Huy's vision of treatment and been cured, but Huy had been begged to return on behalf of the man's son. The boy had accidentally sliced through the top of his foot with a scythe. Both the blade and the foot had been dirty. Ukhedu had set in. But though Huy took the young man's hands and prayed for an enlightenment, no vision came to him and he was forced to suggest the same washes and ointments that the god had shown him on behalf of the father. The family were disappointed but accepting, as though they were not entitled to more than one vision from the Seer. Twice more Huy faced the same dilemma, and once a fever victim, a child whose mother had been cured of a fever through Huy's vision, died shortly after Huy had been forced to admit to the anxious parents that the gods had not spoken to him. The memory of his warning to Nasha came back to Huy, together with the circumstances of her mother's death, so similar to the words of the caution. For a brief while he began to wonder if he was interfering with a law of fate that his visions were perverting. Perhaps the recipients of his touch were really meant to die or to suffer through their ailments to recovery on their own. But that would mean Anubis was deliberately deceiving him or, worse, the visions were the product of his own perverted mind. Neither explanation was satisfactory, indeed both filled him with fear.

However, as he and Ishat continued to move through the town, healings multiplying behind them, Huy put his worry aside. Such coincidences were few; they were irrelevant when measured against his successes. So he lulled himself until the worry became no more than an occassional faint pulse at the back of his mind, and it was completely driven out by the victorious return of the King two days before the beginning of the month of Thoth.

Huy and Ishat were about to leave the house an hour after dawn. Already the air had heated uncomfortably, and though their door stood open, there had been no sunrise wind to cool them. Ishat's thick sheath clung to the sweat under her breasts. She tugged at it irritably and was about to pick up her palette when there was a commotion out in the street. Huy was still sitting at the table, his own armpits damp and his mood low. Yesterday had been more exhausting and painful than usual, the night close and uncomfortable, and his head still twinged in spite of the poppy he had drunk before retiring. Ishat had stepped out into the bright sunlight. Huy rose and followed her.

Their neighbours were hurrying past, including the owner of the beer house next door. Ishat hailed him. "Rahotep, what's happening? Where is everyone going?"

The man veered towards her but did not slow. "The King will be passing Hut-herib sometime this morning!" he called. "Word has gone around that his war was a triumph and he has brought back many prisoners! If you want to see him go by, you'd better hurry or all the best places to stand along the river road will be taken!"

Huy had joined her and she turned to him mockingly. "Do we want to run to the river and be pushed and jostled just for a glimpse of His Majesty? Or should we begin our workday? It's too hot to stand about in crowds," she answered herself. "Let's go to the first few houses on my list. The town will be half empty. Gods, Huy, I'm thirsty already. Do you think Rahotep has locked the beer house door?"

Five hundred Rethennu princes and seven chiefs of Tikhsi, Huy thought. *So Atum said. Do I want to see them for myself?*

"Let's work," he decided, "then we can sleep the worst of the afternoon heat away. The air seems slightly more humid today, Ishat. I wonder if the Inundation has begun early."

"Fevers, biting flies, swarms of mosquitoes, and drownings," Ishat said succinctly. "I should have gone with Thothmes and then I could be followed about by a servant with a big whisk and an even bigger flagon of beer."

Huy tweaked her nose. "If I didn't know better, I'd believe that you were regretting your decision, you talk

about it so much," he teased her. "Go next door and
pour yourself beer. No one steals from Rahotep—his
servants are too large and mean. You can pay him later.
And if you want a fly whisk, we were given a couple last
year by a happy horse trader whose son had a bowel
full of worms. Go and find them."

"I wasn't serious. Huy, if the details of the King's
victories tally with your vision, do you think he will
want to see you today or tomorrow?"

"Probably, but we mustn't wait for a summons. We'd
better go. Drape a piece of linen over your head, Ishat.
The sun is fierce and I don't want you to become ill."

"One vision for me is quite enough," she
muttered as she re-entered the house, her words
giving Huy a moment of unease, but then she came
back, her head and neck enveloped in linen, and they
set off along the baking, deserted street.

They returned to the house at noon, both covered
in dust that clung to their sweat, to find the street busy
again and the beer house open. Ishat went next door
while Huy stripped, washed gratefully in a bowl of
tepid water, and wrapped himself in a sheet. When she
came back, she was carrying a jug of beer and a dish of
date pastries.

"They were not eaten this morning because everyone had gone," she explained, setting the food on the
table. "Rahotep gave them to me for nothing. They'll
do for our meal. It's too hot to go to the temple
kitchen and get something, or even to put together
some fresh vegetables here. I just want to wash and
sleep until it's cooler." She bit into a pastry. "Rahotep
says that the King has already gone by. He sat on a big

chair in the centre of *Kha-em-Ma'at* where everyone could see him. Seven foreigners were hanging head down from the prow of the barge, wriggling and shrieking. The rumour is that the King will sail right past his palace at Mennofer and go all the way to Weset so he can bash out their brains in front of Amun and display their bodies on the city wall. So you were right. Seven chiefs. This water is filthy." She emptied the bowl into the street and began to ladle a fresh supply from the huge flagon standing just within the doorway. "According to Rahotep it took all morning for the army and the prisoners and horses and booty to pass along the river road, and they were still filing along when he got tired and came home."

Unselfconsciously she pulled her sheath up over her head, dropped it on the floor, and plunged her hands into the bowl. Huy watched her wash herself without really seeing her. *So Amunhotep has come and gone without a word to the Seer who took away his uncertainty. I don't know whether to be relieved or insulted. Relieved, I think. Being in the presence of royalty is just too nerve-racking. But I will not forget this ingratitude.*

"I need to sleep now," he said. "Finish the pastries if you like, Ishat. My headache has killed my appetite." She was tugging a comb through her hair and nodded, not answering him, standing naked with one leg flexed and both arms raised, her naked brown spine as straight as a reed. Her unselfconscious beauty did not move him. Folding the sheet more tightly around his waist, he went into his own room.

The New Year's celebrations began and went on for days. The Dog Star rose in the night sky. The

Inundation slowly flooded the land, depositing its silt and once again turning Hut-herib into a series of small islands. Huy laboured on, with Ishat and her lists beside him, walking the streets of the town that had become as familiar to him as the contours of his own face.

His nineteenth birthday came and went in an intense, humid heat that drained the energy from him at a time when he most needed his strength to deal with the rash of illnesses attendant upon the time of year. Scrolls of congratulation came from Thothmes and Nasha, Ramose and the Rekhet. Huy's parents put on a modest feast for him, an awkward occasion with his uncle Ker and aunt Heruben that tried all Huy's reserves of patience and tact; but he rejoiced in seeing little Heby, growing as sturdy and healthy as one of the weeds Ker was forever trying to eliminate from his flower fields.

Heby's eighth birthday would arrive in another four months. He was doing so well at school that plans were under way to send him to a larger centre, Iunu or the temple of Ptah at Mennofer, with Ker supplying all his needs. Huy listened impassively. His rancour against his uncle had dissipated long ago. Neither Ker nor Huy's father could help their cowardice. Huy had no affection for his uncle anymore, but he still harboured a love for his father and particularly his mother. The one great curse of his poverty was that he could not afford to provide his parents with a suitable tomb. Watching Heby and listening to his easy and rather precocious conversation, Huy hoped that in years to come his brother might be the one to give that most sacred and valuable gift to the couple who had given him life.

Khoiak, the fourth month of the year, saw the river at its highest and began with the Feast of Hathor. As the flood receded, the last ten days were given over to a different feast every day—of the Exhibition of the Corpse of Osiris, of the Mourning Goddesses, of Osiris Himself, of the Father of Palms—and the first day of Tybi belonged to the Coronation of Horus. These were all major celebrations and gave Huy and Ishat a respite. Huy had not gone to the temple to give Khenti-kheti thanks for his life, although Methen had dropped several hints that he should do so. He knew that he had not fully expunged his bitterness towards the gods from his ka, that the acceptance of his lot did not always include either gratitude or warmth, and he did not want to pretend a false gratitude. His fellow citizens all seemed smug to him, the progress of their lives, whether poor or wealthy, laid down for them, their beliefs sure and unquestioned. He often envied them. There was not one aspect of his own life that satisfied him with its wholeness or security. He was a grown man and yet a virgin through no fault of his own. He nursed an unreciprocated love for a woman who had made him her toy. He held within him the words of a magical Book he had tried unsuccessfully to decipher. His labour was not dependent on his own efforts but relied upon the ephemeral whim of the gods. Or god. The only certainty he could grasp was the fact of his death, the end of the small cycle of his young life. There was a completeness to that. But he had been tossed back into mortality seven years ago for a purpose he was sure was incomplete. Everything unfinished, unsettled, and beyond his control. *No,* he thought as he lay on his couch while the town exhausted itself with prayers and feasting, *I am obedient, and that is enough.*

On the last day of Tybi, the day after the Exhibition of the Meadow, when the reappearance of the soil and the commencement of sowing was celebrated, Huy was sitting outside his house, a cup of beer on the ground beside him, enjoying the brief play of evening light on the motley collection of low buildings opposite. Their occupants too sat outside the open doors, some tossing dice into the dust, some bent over gaming boards, some leaning indolently against their walls, talking to friends. Naked children wrestled in the middle of the street. A tethered donkey aimed a kick at a passing dog and began a raucous braying. The beer house sent a cacophony of cheerful voices out into the limpid air. For once Huy was content. Ishat's list was empty. Yesterday and today no demands had been made upon him. His head was quiet and clear, he felt rested, he had eaten well, and a peaceful night lay ahead. Ishat had taken the opportunity to go to the river and wash their clothes and bedding. He had offered to help her, but she had refused, going next door and returning with the beer before she shouldered the sack of laundry and pot of natron and set off happily along the street. She had been gone a long time. Huy had sipped at the beer, not really wanting it, his glance going increasingly to the corner where she would appear.

The light was slipping down the walls, turning their shabbiness into a golden glory that began to fade to pink. The children were called in, and Huy was just thinking of going inside himself and lighting a lamp when a sudden hush fell over the denizens of the street. All eyes turned to the corner. Huy's glance turned also. He expected to see Ishat, but instead three men came striding over the packed earth, all kilted in white and blue. The man in the centre sported a thick gold chain from which a golden scroll hung on his naked chest. His sandals were plain and sturdy, the footwear of someone who walked a great deal, but his face paint was immaculate, his earring of silver and carnelian ornate, and a circlet of gold sat firmly on his short wig. The other two men were obviously soldiers. Swords swung lightly against their muscled thighs. Each wore a leather helmet and carried a short spear. *A herald,* Huy thought, coming to his feet. *A herald and his military escort, and they are coming to me.*

The trio reached him and halted. At once the soldiers swung round to face into the street, the inquisitive eyes of the now-silent residents fixed on them. The herald bowed. "Huy the Seer, son of Hapu?"

"Yes."

"I am Royal Herald Minmose." A battered leather satchel hung from his belt. Pulling it forward, he opened it and extracted two scrolls. He passed them to Huy with a smile. "His Majesty has required me to deliver these directly into your hands, and I have now done so. Long life and health to His Majesty!" With another bow he and his escort were gone, pacing confidently through the loose stones and offal littering the ground.

For some moments the silence of the street held. Huy's neighbours stared at him with open curiosity, but as he made no effort to unroll the letters their attention waned. Chatter began again. Huy picked up his beer and retreated into his house.

He had just lit the lamps when Ishat came in, dumping the sack of laundry on the floor and rushing to stand beside him. "I saw them coming out of our street," she panted. "It was a herald, wasn't it? What did he bring you?"

Huy held up the scrolls. One had been sealed with two symbols, the sedge and the bee, the insignia of royalty. The other bore the symbols of the sepat in which Hut-herib was situated. Huy and Ishat stared at each other.

"I'm afraid to open them," Huy said. "Look at this beautiful papyrus, Ishat! Look at how tightly woven and highly polished it is!"

"Yes, yes, it's lovely. Break the seal, Huy!"

"It might just be an expression of gratitude from Amunhotep." Huy turned it over and over in his hands.

"Sometimes I could shake you, son of Hapu!" Ishat exploded. "What did I tell you? What have I been telling you all along? You are already becoming famous, and soon you will be rich beyond anything you can imagine! These scrolls hold your destiny. I know it. Be brave!" She was dancing from foot to foot in her impatience.

With a laugh, Huy cracked the seal on the King's scroll. He read the contents aloud with Ishat craning over his shoulder.

To the Seer Huy son of Hapu, greetings. Having completed the rout of the princes of Rethennu as you predicted, and having taken the exact number of captives, gold, horses, chariots, and copper that you predicted, it pleases me to offer you the reward of a house, garden, and full granary on the bank of the eastern tributary of the river, its site to be determined by my Governor of your sepat. It also pleases me to provide you with servants, gold, oil, perfumes, eye paint, and all other essentials of life so that you may continue to perform the work of the gods without fear of penury. However, it will not please me if the gift Atum has bestowed on you is exhausted in the indiscriminate service of the common people. They are my people and you may treat them as you see fit, but on pain of forfeiting these good things I in my munificence give to you, I command you to husband your strength for my service and the needs of my nobles and administrators, without whom this country cannot be governed, and answer their calls whenever they order you. You may wait until you have seen your new home before sending me a letter of thanks. Dictated this day, the tenth of Tybi, to my Chief Scribe Seti-en, and signed by my own hand.

The list of royal titles followed. Huy did not read them.

Ishat was jumping up and down, her hair flying. "Seer of the King! My Huy, Seer of the King!" she was shouting. Her exuberance made Huy smile, but seeing his expression, she sobered. "What can possibly be wrong?" she demanded.

Huy tapped the scroll against the table. "Don't you see? All this generosity, but to keep the house and servants and the gods know what else, I must do what the King demands. I will always be a victim of his whims."

"What whims? All he wants you to do is See for him or his court first. You can go on Seeing for the citizens of the town. He says so."

"I know. But to be so reliant on the royal favour troubles me, Ishat. If I offend him, he can do more than take it all away again—he can punish me for my ingratitude. I would rather refuse his gifts and stay here in our little house and be free."

"Are you insane?" She thrust her face close to his. "You may not want this, but I deserve it! Besides, if you refuse it, won't you be offending him far more deeply than anything you could do in the future? And how long can you continue to flog yourself among the sick of the town, the way you've been doing, before you wear out either your gift or your body? Headaches every day, hollows under your eyes, you get so tired you cannot sleep. Please, Huy. Please! Let us do this!"

"Those are a woman's arguments," he grumbled, "but I dare say they are valid. Let me read our governor's scroll and then make no decision until the morning."

He could almost hear her swallowing any further words. She nodded and gestured sharply. "Go on, then."

Snapping the seal, he again read aloud. Ishat stood where she was.

To the Seer Huy son of Hapu, greetings. The King has acquainted me with his desires for you, therefore it pleases me greatly to let you

know that I have placed his request in the hands
of your mayor, Mery-neith, with instructions that
he should find a suitable house for you and
personally oversee the acquisition of furnishings,
grain, oil, and servants. The King wishes to
provide gold, perfumes, cosmetics, and all other
necessities from his own Treasury and storehouses. May you have joy of your good fortune,
and bless the God who is so generous. If you find
any fault with Mery-neith's choice for you, I have
empowered him to select other estates for you to
inspect. Written by my own hand on behalf of the
King, this thirteenth day of Tybi, year three.

"Other estates for you to inspect!" Ishat crowed.
"Oh, Huy! We have not treated this Mery-neith,
have we?"

"No." Huy let the scroll roll up with a sense of
defeat. It would indeed be insane to throw this gem
back in the King's face, yet a shadow seemed to lie over
it. "But I have been to the homes of several of his
assistants. Mery-neith has a large and very healthy
family." He set the governor's letter beside the King's
and stared down at the two smooth beige cylinders.
"I suppose that the mayor has had word by now and
we must just wait for a message."

"So you will do it? You will accept the King's
offer?"

"I have little choice. All I can do is hope that
Amunhotep's reign progresses without the necessity for
difficult decisions and that he will put our continued
welfare into the hands of his treasurer and a steward

and gradually forget about me." He raised his eyes to hers. "Besides, you are right, Ishat. I owe you this. Without you I could not do the work of the gods."

"No, you couldn't." She heaved a great breath that lifted her shoulders exuberantly. "Now, while we are waiting for word from the mayor, you can help me shake out these wet linens and drape them about so we have something to wear in the morning."

No communication came from the mayor for the next two weeks. Ishat continued to take down the names of the needy in the temple's crowded forecourt each morning. She and Huy continued to visit their homes. Huy had taken the letters to Methen, hoping that the High Priest would counsel him against accepting the King's gift, but Methen merely nodded and smiled his approval. "You are one of this country's treasures, Huy, though you do not know it yet," he had said. "Perhaps our King, young though he is, is beginning to realize that you must be cared for and protected."

"Like some useful domestic animal," Huy retorted.

Methen's eyebrows rose. "You have less right to such pride than anyone else in Egypt. Do you think that the King is honouring your good looks? Of course not! Without your gift, what would you be? An assistant scribe to an assistant scribe in some merchant's home." They had been sitting knee to knee in Methen's quarters. Now the priest leaned forward, placing both hands on Huy's shoulders. "You may not spend much time remembering the moment when you woke from the dead in the House of the Dead and gave the sem priests the fright of their lives," he went on, "but I do.

Such a miracle has never been seen before. Did Atum breathe life back into your body as a kindness to you? No. He did it for Egypt. You have been using his power to heal, but I firmly believe that your destiny is to guide the gods who will sit on the Horus Throne with your ability to predict the future—or rather, the ability Atum has given you to predict the future. You will tell kings what to do, and they will do it." He gave Huy a gentle shake before sitting back. "This is the first step, and you must take it."

Suddenly Huy wanted to fling himself into Methen's arms like the child he had been on that terrible day. "I have been born out of time!" he said thickly. "I should have been wrapped in cerements and buried years ago! What is this that inhabits me, Methen? The Rekhet told me that I am not possessed. Then what lashes me along this path? What part of myself disappeared when I died, to be replaced by . . . by what?"

"Each of us is composed of seven parts," Methen answered. "You know this. But for you there is an eighth part. You are more than complete, Huy. Nothing in you is missing. A great and useful gift has been added. Useful to Atum. Something Atum desires you to have in order for him to steer the fortunes of our country."

The mayor himself came to Huy's door one early evening just as Huy and Ishat were finishing their last meal of the day. He was a hearty, rotund man who held his position through his ability to be at ease with peasant and noble alike. Now he stood on Huy's threshold, two waiting litters behind him, and bowed. He looked distressed.

"I knew of you, of course," he told Huy, "but I had no idea that you were living here!" He waved behind him at the clamour of the street. "You must forgive me, Master. My days are overfull of administrative matters. Do not turn me into a toad!"

Huy laughed, liking the man at once. "You need not call me Master. As for my surroundings, what's wrong with them? I have been happy here."

Mery-neith's brow cleared. "Ah. Well. But you will be happier in surroundings more appropriate to your calling. I must tell you how glad I am that you choose to stay in Hut-herib, not the prettiest town in Egypt, I'll be the first to admit, and not run off to Iunu or even Mennofer. It will be my pleasant duty to channel the King's maintenance to you at regular intervals, and naturally, if you or your servant"—here he sketched a bow to Ishat—"lack for anything, you must send to me at once. Now if you are ready, I wish to show you the estate I have chosen for you. It is small but quiet. It belonged to one of our few noblemen, who has been promoted to Overseer of the Governor's Cattle in the Ka-set sepat and who has thus moved his family closer to his work. He has been recompensed for his house." With a glance at Ishat's excited face Huy followed the mayor out into the warm evening air. "To tell you the truth, I hope you will like the place when you see it," Mery-neith continued as he indicated one of the litters. "There are not many suitable estates in or around Hut-herib. The governor made it clear that you were to be situated on the edge of the town, so that only the most desperate citizens will be able to bother you.

If you will ride with me, Master? And your servant in the other litter, if you wish her to come with us?"

"A pack of ravening hyenas couldn't prevent Ishat from coming." Huy pointed at the second litter. Ishat nodded and ran to it. "She is more my friend than my servant, Mayor."

"Ah. Well." Mery-neith lowered himself beside Huy, who smiled to himself. The mayor was too well mannered to inquire into the nature of Huy's relationship with Ishat, but Huy could feel the questions hovering on the man's tongue. He let them hover.

Huy left the curtain open on his side of the litter so that he could see where they were going. At the end of the street they turned right, skirted the temple compound, then took another, wider street that Huy knew ran east a short way before meeting the road that ran beside the far eastern tributary. He wondered if they would then head north or south. He liked to think of the south, where Iunu lay at the point of the river's mighty divide into the many smaller rivers making up the Delta. To his delight the litter did indeed swing south. The road was crowded with laden donkeys and farmers carrying sacks of seed on their backs, for it was the month of Mekhir, the time of swift sowing and even swifter growing. Mery-neith's steward strode ahead of the litter, calling a warning. The people divided to stream past on either side. Mery-neith often interrupted his flow of bright conversation to call out a greeting or a question to one or another. "Do you know everyone in Hut-herib?" Huy asked him.

Mery-neith flung out his arms in an expansive gesture. "I try to visit every home and farm once a year.

I know your uncle Ker, and I did once announce myself at your father Hapu's door. He shared beer with me, but seemed uneasy. Your mother Itu is very beautiful. To my eternal shame, Master, I have inadvertently omitted your street for the last two years."

The crowd was thinning. Huy could smell running water and greenness and the faint scent of flowers. The bearers abruptly veered right, took several steps, and set the litter down. Mery-neith, for all his bulk, got out nimbly. Huy followed.

He was standing in the middle of a garden. To his left was the wide opening through which they had come, cut into a wall that continued out of sight on either side, high and solid. To his right, the equally naked wall of a house joined transverse walls. In between was the short path up which they had come, dividing unkempt flower beds, patches of sparse grass, a scummed pond full of lily pads, and several sycamore and acacia trees for shade.

Mery-neith, seeing Huy's expression, lifted a finger. "Do not judge yet. See, by the gate, there is a shelter for the gate guard and, beyond it, over the river road, your watersteps. The door to the house itself is small, as you can see, and this garden somewhat neglected since the last owner left. But it keeps the house back from the road. Less noise within." Ishat had clambered out of her litter and joined them, and together they followed Mery-neith to the wooden door set into the wall of the house. He pushed it open. "It bolts from the inside," he told them, but they were not listening. Both had halted in amazement.

A large reception room had opened out before them, its black-and-white-tiled floor gleaming, the three small pillars in its centre wreathed with painted grapevines in whose leaves a host of birds in scarlets, yellows, and various shades of blue hid or thrust out their open beaks in soundless song. The whitewashed walls held a frieze, running just under three clerestory windows, that obviously represented the river, for fish of all kinds swam in the undulating blue swaths. "I had the walls freshly whitewashed up to the frieze," the mayor said, "so that you could paint any scenes you liked for this room. The furniture throughout has come from the palace storehouse in Mennofer, by the King's command. If it is unsuitable it will be replaced."

Ishat was on her knees, her hands caressing the floor. "Not earth," she whispered. "Tiles. Tiles, Huy! I have never been in a house with a proper floor before!"

Huy was moving from one piece of furniture to another. "But these chairs are cedar inlaid with ivory! And these four little tables—surely they are of ebony, with surfaces of gold and blue faience squares! You are sure they are for us, Mery-neith?"

"Quite sure. Trust me, they are nothing compared with what rests in the palace itself. This room would make a good office for you, Master, don't you think? Or you might prefer one of the others along the passage." He was indicating an open cedar door to the right of the main entrance. Huy walked over to it and looked in. The far wall was obviously the main wall of the whole house and part of the major wall running from the road, enclosing one side of the courtyard.

Therefore it had no window, but, turning to his left, Huy saw that half that wall was nothing but window filled with the sunlit greenery of a strip of shrubbery beyond. The walls were full of empty niches intended for scrolls. This floor was also tiled in black and white. One large desk with a chair behind it, backing onto the wide window, dominated the space. This was a place of serious industry.

Huy withdrew. "You're right," he said.

Mery-neith nodded. "Good. Come. And you, young woman, do not fear that you will be sweeping that floor you appear to worship. Your servants are even now being hired by my assistant."

A tiled passage led from the reception room past one door on the right and two on the left and straight out into blinding sunlight that was shafting as far as the reception room. Mery-neith opened each door. "One of these rooms is usually reserved for your chief steward and another for your scribe. The third is for a body servant. As you can see, they are simply furnished with a couch, table, stool, and tiring chest—and niches for whatever gods your servants will pray to, of course. Each of these rooms has an aperture cut in the ceiling so that you may call down for whatever you need from the bedchambers above. We will go upstairs before you see the kitchen, granary, and garden."

"Every room has a wind catcher, and the reception room has two of them," Ishat whispered to Huy. "I am so excited I can hardly stand up, my legs are trembling so! Wait until my mother sees all this!"

Wordlessly, Huy followed the mayor up the narrow stair that began at the end of the passage nearest the opening to the garden. Above, there was another passage running straight to the front of the house. It hugged a bare wall on the left against which the stairs had been built. On the right were another three doors. Each bedchamber contained a huge gilded couch, a cedar and brass-figured tiring chest, one small and one large table set with the most delicate alabaster lamps Huy had ever seen, two chairs, and opposite the door a very low window with a sill over which one could step onto a narrow deck that ran past each room and ended in a large area that was the roof of the reception hall. The floor of the room farthest from the stair was over half filled by a great golden lion's pelt, the snarling head and curved claws intact. Huy stared at it, marvelling.

"The King killed this lion himself, with his very own bow," Mery-neith told Huy. "I was instructed to tell you this. The King wants you to enjoy every blessing he can bestow." He glanced curiously at Huy. "I apologize to you yet again, Master. I was not aware of your true importance."

Ishat had run out onto the roof and was twirling round and round, arms outstretched, laughing. Her abandon lifted Huy's heart. *At least I can do this for her. I hope it will prove to be sufficient compensation for my coldness.*

"You can hardly see it," the mayor was saying, "but right where the passage seems to meet solid wall there is a stair going down to a narrow way under the deck and out into the bathhouse. Are you ready to go outside?" Huy nodded, called to Ishat, and they trooped back down the way they had come.

The bathhouse was small but well equipped. Its stone floor sloped inward to a hole for draining water away. Its walls were lined with benches on which one could lie to be shaved and oiled. A path led from the rear end of the house's passage straight to the far wall, where the dome of a clay granary cast a bulging shadow on the gravelled ground. To the right lay the kitchen, a small mud-brick enclosure with a firepit and oven in front of it, with several servants' cells alongside. Ishat entered it at once and came back grinning to Huy. "It already has everything—pots and flagons and spoons and knives. It's as grand as the temple kitchen!"

Mery-neith folded his arms. "Well? Master, what do you think? Do you like it, or shall I seek some other place?"

The smile left Ishat's face. She was looking at Huy anxiously, her eyes pleading. Huy shook his head, overcome. The house was perhaps a little less than half the size of Nakht's home and the garden much smaller, but this estate was a gem, compact yet harmonious in its proportions. He stood listening for a moment to a silence broken only by birdsong. "I am overwhelmed by the King's generosity," he said at last. "This is perfect for the two of us. And I thank you also, Mery-neith, for the effort you have made on my behalf."

"When the King speaks, one answers immediately," the mayor replied. "So you will take the estate? Good. The deed will be in your hands within a few days. Meanwhile you can move in at once. Send me a message and I will meet you here with your servants. I am expecting your goods from the King at any time."

Ishat threw her arms around Huy. "We will use some of the King's gold to buy a boat," she whispered, "and we will go fishing together, and drink wine on its deck and watch the sun set. It will be as though we are already in the Paradise of Osiris."

Depression seized Huy. *I shall miss the noise of the street, and taking possession of this beautiful place will not mean as much to me as Ishat and I scraping together our few pitiful pieces of furniture and whitewashing our own walls. She will not have to go out and steal anything. I will not have to haul water through the town. I should be happy, as she is, but I know that moving here will not change my future or hers.* He released himself and nodded to the mayor. "We have few possessions. We will come here next week."

But he and Ishat did not leave the street until the third week of Mekhir. Somehow there was always pressing work to be done, Methen was away visiting the High Priest of Ptah at Mennofer, so Huy could not close up their tiny house, and as usual he had forgotten that his brother Heby's birthday fell on the twenty-first day of that month. Ishat had already decided that they would take only their personal belongings with them. "There is no reason to bring Soft-Nose in from the fields and hire a cart and exhaust ourselves loading this dreadful old stuff. Every day another curl of gilt peels off your couch. May we leave it all for the next poor tenant?"

Huy agreed reluctantly. His couch was a symbol of the decision he had made to leave Iunu and walk to Hut-herib, to work for Methen, to try to throw his fate to the winds. It did not matter that his fate could not be influenced by anything as ephemeral as the movement of air. He saw his couch, his tiny three rooms, his struggle to swallow his pride and simply learn to exist much as the priests who measured the rise and fall of the river regarded the stone markers set at intervals all along its banks; the increments shown were of vital importance to the country as a whole. Huy's few shabby possessions meant as much to him. But to please Ishat he let it all go. *And besides,* he thought as he thrust his belongings into his two worn leather satchels, *where would we put such dilapidated things? Every room of the new house is filled with glorious furniture.*

So, on the twenty-third day of Mekhir, in the season of Peret, Huy and Ishat shouldered their bags, closed the door of their old home, said goodbye to Rahotep and the other denizens of the street, and walked away. The mayor had offered to send a litter for them, but Huy had refused. Rational or not, it had seemed imperative to him that he should leave his physical footprints in the dust of the town, making the journey as significant as the soul's progression through the Judgment Hall. He half expected to meet with some mishap on the way, to be run over by a cart or fall into one of the canals, but the day was fine and warm, the long walk was completed without incident, and he and Ishat turned into their own garden shortly after noon.

Mery-neith was waiting for them together with a group of quiet, apprehensive-looking young men and women. After greeting Huy and Ishat, he beckoned each person forward in turn. "This is Seshemnefer, your gardener, and Khnit his wife, your cook. Kar, your gate guard and protector of your watersteps. Merenra, your chief, and so far your only, steward. He will need no training. He comes from my own household."

Merenra bowed. "I am very pleased to be given the charge of your household, revered Master. It is a great honour for me." Huy, looking into the grave dark eyes, decided that he would like this man and was relieved. Of all the household staff, the steward held the most responsible post.

"Ankhesenpepi, the cleaner of your house," Mery-neith went on. "And lastly Tetiankh, your body servant, Master, and Iput, your body servant, Ishat. I have not procured a scribe for you, Master. Such a post must be filled by your choice alone."

"Ishat is my scribe," Huy told him. There was a polite murmur of surprise among the servants. "She alone I trust without reservation." He turned to the assembly. "I welcome and thank you all. Merenra, you will please sort out the living arrangements and then meet with me in my office—if the King's gifts are here, Mery-neith?"

"They are piled on the floor of the reception room. The granary has been filled. There is nothing more for me to do but wish you the blessing of the gods on your new home." He clicked his fingers at his litter-bearers. Huy thanked him again for his trouble and watched him borne away, feeling like a child who has just been abandoned. Ishat had already disappeared inside.

Huy found her flinging open the chests that almost covered the tiles of the reception room. "Look, Huy!" she marvelled. "So much kohl, and all of it full of gold or silver dust! And can you smell the perfumes? This chest holds nothing but pieces of gold. You are rich!"

Iput was hovering. "If my mistress can find the bolts of linen the mayor said were included, I can begin to make her some very pretty sheaths," the girl said. "I have brought sewing materials with me, and the mayor's wife has made a gift to my mistress of a cosmetic table. It is upstairs."

Ishat turned on one knee. "Iput—that is your name? Iput? Mine is Ishat. If you like, you can call me Ishat in private, as long as you remember to address me as Mistress when guests come to the house. Huy, look at these! Two tall lamp holders for the reception room! When you have unpacked your palette and papyrus, you must dictate a letter of thanks to the King!"

"That I will do myself," Huy told her, but she had turned back to the growing assortment of exotic things. Ishat would need more writing practice before her script would be good enough for the eyes of the King's scribe.

Merenra's sharp voice rang through the house. It was answered by others, deferential and courteous. Order would appear out of this chaos, Huy reflected. Merenra would purchase a litter and hire bearers who would double as house guards. He would buy the skiff, or perhaps even a barge, that Ishat wanted so much. Every few months the King would send more gold and Merenra would lock it away in some small chest in the office, as Huy had seen Nakht's steward do. *Thus are kings able to perform miracles of transformation with a wave of the hand. Every morning I will wake in that ornate couch upstairs to the aroma of hot bread and the voice of my body servant Tetiankh as he sets a tray beside me and goes to raise the window hanging, just as though*

I were staying in my room at Nakht's house. Every evening Ishat and I will walk in the garden in the long twilight or sit on the watersteps and watch the river go hurrying by, just as Anuket would sometimes agree to do with me. The sweet, poisonous odour of my past is strong here. Is that why I am so sad?

He wandered along the passage and out into the glare of the gravelled space behind the house. Seshemnefer the gardener and his wife were hurrying towards one of the servants' small cells, leather satchels very like Huy's own slung over their shoulders. They were talking to one another, excitement in their voices, but Huy could not make out what they were saying. *I suppose all the servants are thrilled to be working in the home of the famous Seer,* he thought wryly. *They probably expect to see magic and hear the chanting of spells. They seem to have already accepted Ishat's position as a female scribe, something most unusual. That's a good sign. She needs much more practice, but it's true that I trust her as I trust few others. I must tell Merenra to put that lion skin in the guest room. I don't want to sleep with the lamplight glinting off those pointed teeth. I wonder what joke Thothmes will make about it when he comes to stay. The Rekhet can visit also, and Ramose. Heby— I would like to have Heby living with me for a while, but I dare say Father would not allow it. Oh, what is this weight of melancholy that fills me?*

He re-entered the house to the sound of Ishat's chatter and went and stood in his office. Dappled, muted sunlight filled the space. The leaves of the shrubbery rustled gently. *They sound like the leaves of the Ished Tree,* his thoughts ran on. *Atum, where am I going? Where are you taking me?*

The answer came at once. Merenra entered and bowed, a scroll in his hand. "Your pardon, Master. I should have given this to your scribe, but she is busy at the moment. Shall I open it and read it to you? It was delivered by a herald who waits for your reply." Huy nodded. The steward broke the seal and unrolled the papyrus. "'To the Great Seer Huy son of Hapu, greetings. I propose to journey to Hut-herib in order that I may consult you regarding any events in my future the gods may be pleased to divulge. I will leave Mennofer upon hearing of your agreement from my herald. Long life and health to you. Dictated and signed by my own hand, Amunhotep, Vizier of Egypt.'" Merenra looked up. "That is all, Master. What may I tell the herald?"

Vizier of Egypt, Huy thought, feeling a nervous sweat break out along his spine. *The King's Deputy, and his namesake. The second most powerful man in the kingdom. Two days to Mennofer for the herald. Two days to Hut-herib for the Vizier.* He swallowed past a throat gone suddenly dry. "Tell the herald that I shall be pleased to See for the Vizier in five days' time. And Merenra, you have five days to get this household running smoothly. The Vizier must not be insulted by lax service or poorly cooked food. Ask the gardener if he can procure fresh flowers from anywhere. Ask—"

Merenra held up a hand. "These matters need not concern you. Leave everything to me. Dismiss me so that I may speak to the herald." Huy did so. Merenra went out just as Ishat came rushing in.

"There's a liveried man outside and I saw Merenra go by the reception room with a scroll," she blurted. "What is it, Huy? Is it bad news? Has the King changed his mind about us?"

"No. And it's the sort of news I expected eventually, but not so soon. I am to See for the Vizier. This is how our life will be from now on, Ishat. Kar will keep the common people from passing through the gate unless we tell him otherwise. The King has imprisoned my gift as surely as this house imprisons my body."

For once she did not argue with him, but her eyes lost their glow of exhilaration, and after a short hesitation she left the room.

Huy walked around the desk and slumped into the chair. Placing his arms on the desk, he stared at the distorted reflection of his fingers on its highly polished surface. *King's man. Huy son of Hapu, you are now the King's man, and your true destiny is about to be fulfilled.* He sat without moving for a long time.

ACKNOWLEDGMENTS

I wish to thank my researcher, Bernard Ramanauskas, for his exemplary work in collating the scattered material relating to the life of the Son of Hapu. In particular I appreciate the shape and coherence he has given to the profound ideologies of the Book of Thoth.

I have gratefully quoted from *Egyptian Mysteries: New Light on Ancient Spiritual Knowledge* by Lucie Lamy (published by Thames and Hudson) and from *The Hermetica* by Timothy Freke and Peter Gandy (published by Piatkus).

Read on for an excerpt from

Pauline Gedge's exciting new novel,

SEER OF EGYPT

Royal Nurse Heqareshu stepped from his barge and answered Huy and Ishat's profound obeisance with a brief nod. Huy had imagined him as plump and fatherly, with a ready smile and warm eyes, but the man regarding him with calm intelligence owed nothing at all to his fantasy. Fully painted and bejewelled, clad in a linen gown that shimmered with gold thread in the breeze, he exuded power and confidence. The members of his retinue were already giving their orders to Anhur and Merenra, and out of the corner of his eye Huy saw a flustered Amunmose backing surreptitiously in the direction of the kitchens, only to be summoned back by an impatient wave from Merenra.

"This is not going to be fun," Ishat whispered to Huy under cover of their bows. "He'll drive us all into the Duat before he leaves."

Huy hid the jolt her comment had given him. Heqareshu was approaching them, his stride exuding supreme confidence. He stopped before Huy.

"So," he said smoothly, "you are the Seer Huy. I am the Noble Heqareshu. I believe that you have met my son Kenamun, Foster Brother of the Lord of the Two Lands." His expression conveyed Huy's good fortune. "My steward and the commander of my body-guards will decide where I am to sleep, and whether or not your staff may remain in the house while I am here. I do not have time to waste. I must return to Mennofer as soon as possible to continue my care of the Prince Amunhotep. Therefore, you will See for me as soon as I have broken my fast tomorrow morning."

Huy bowed again. "You are welcome in my home, Royal Nurse Heqareshu," he responded carefully.

"However, as you can see, it is small. Perhaps you would prefer to rest for the night aboard your barge." He indicated Ishat. "This is my scribe and friend Ishat."

Heqareshu ignored her. Eyes suddenly narrowed, he inspected Huy's face, obviously suspecting the impudent finish to his suggestion. Not finding it, his kohled eyebrows rose. "My steward will make that determination. For now you may escort me within and offer me water and wine. The sun is hot."

Huy, feeling Ishat's indignant struggle to keep her mouth closed, fought against his own desire to laugh. He was distinctly nervous. "I trust that both His Majesty and the Prince are in good health?" he inquired politely as he and the small crowd began to move.

Heqareshu nodded. "They are both well. His Majesty has just announced that Her Majesty Tiaa, his half-sister and second wife, is pregnant. I shall, of course, be appointed as Royal Nurse to the new baby."

Of course, Huy thought as they entered the reception hall, where cushions and low tables were waiting. *Amunhotep wants a prediction for this birth. He needs to know whether or not it will be a male. If so, it will be either an insurance against the death of the heir or a latent threat to him if he proves weak. But why the privacy, the need to acquire the Seeing through this man?*

He and Ishat waited while Heqareshu chose a table, lifted his linen with one graceful gesture, and sank onto the cushion behind it. At once a servant began to wave an ostrich fan over him. Huy could feel the minute but pleasant backrush of air. Heqareshu's steward took the flagons of water and wine a stone-faced Merenra was holding and began to serve his master.

Heqareshu looked about him. "You have good taste, Seer Huy," he said, sipping his water. "Your house is indeed small, but well appointed. How long have you lived at Hut-herib?"

A polite conversation began, from which Ishat was excluded. It was not a conscious slight on Heqareshu's part, Huy decided. The man simply did not see Ishat at all. To formally acknowledge the presence of another's scribe would never have occurred to him.

After some moments, the commander of his bodyguard came up to him, bowed, and spoke quickly into his ear. Heqareshu inclined his head. "Your guest room will be suitable for me," he said. "I shall not need to deprive you of your own couch, Seer Huy. However, my body servant must be near me. Therefore, he will occupy your scribe's quarters."

Ishat had taken a sharp breath, her cheeks flaming. Huy reached across and gripped her shoulder hard. "The arrangement will be acceptable," he said firmly. "But Ishat must not sleep in the servants' cells. She must be ready to take my dictation at any hour. Merenra! Have a pallet set up in my room for Ishat!" He felt the muscles loosen under his fingers and withdrew his hand.

Heqareshu looked interested. "Do the gods speak to you in the night, then?" he wanted to know. "Kenamun told me of your prediction to Pharaoh, how every detail of it was fulfilled. You are blessed, Seer Huy."

"He ate every single pastry Khnit made," Ishat remarked later to Huy as they lay slumped on reed mats under the garden's shade. "How does he stay so skinny?"

Heqareshu had gone upstairs for the afternoon sleep, and the lesser members of his retinue had flocked back onto his barge. Neither Huy nor Ishat wanted to retire to Huy's room, so close to the one where Heqareshu was doubtless snoring on the couch.

Huy smiled at a purely feminine question that did not really require an answer. "His food is surely nothing but fuel for his overweening arrogance, and does not benefit his body at all," he replied. "The King must have formed an affection for him in his younger days, before he acquired discrimination. Such early associations cannot easily be broken." He was immediately aware of the truth of his words, and glumly fell silent. Ishat said no more. Both of them drowsed uncomfortably as the implacable heat of the afternoon shrivelled the grass around them.

In the evening, after finding fault with everything in the bathhouse from the temperature of the water to the quality of the massage oils and the grit in the natron, Heqareshu sat in the reception room and methodically demolished the sumptuous feast Khnit, Huy's cook, had laboured all day to produce. Yet between mouthfuls his conversation was light and correct, the accomplished patter of the seasoned courtier. He continued to behave as though Ishat failed to exist. Afterwards, surrounded by his guard and with his body servant holding a parasol over his head, he took a short walk along the river path in the red-drenched sunset. Once full night had fallen, he climbed the stairs to the roof, where he sat listening to the stories his scribe read to him from his box of scrolls.

Huy and Ishat retreated once more to the now-dusky garden and lay looking up at the stars. "How clear the Red Horus is tonight!" Ishat commented. "Can you see the Leg of Beef? The Inundation is late. The Running Man Looking Over His Shoulder should be appearing on the horizon very soon."

She turned towards him, propping her head on her hand, her features indistinct in the weak starlight, but Huy did not need illumination to trace every line and curve of the face he had known since boyhood. Her perfume rose to his nostrils as she moved.

"I can hardly wait until he sails away tomorrow," she went on. "Even his scribe only deigns to speak to me if I ask him a deliberate question, and then very brusquely. Are all courtiers like him, do you think? Must I continually put up with them for Thothmes' sake?"

Yes, they are, Huy wanted to insist with vehemence. *I met some of them during my audience with the King. You will come to hate them all, Ishat. Stay here with me!*

"No, they are not," he admitted. "His son Kenamum is unpleasantly jealous of his closeness to Amunhotep, but the rest of the King's servants and companions I met were kind. You will only have to curb your tongue upon occasion, Ishat."

She was quiet for a moment, then she said, "Why do you think he's here, Huy? It has seemed to you that Amunhotep is reluctant to allow any noble to consult you. Is he afraid of what you may discover about him? Something about his future? Why him?"

Why indeed, Huy thought, sitting up.

"I don't think he's here on his own behalf, although I expect that he believes otherwise," he said. "In my opinion the King wants information regarding his unborn child."

"But why send the Royal Nurse? Why not send Queen Tiaa?"

"Because a Royal Nurse spends far more time with a royal child than a Queen. He engages the wet nurse, appoints the nursery guards, oversees the daily routine. He even selects the tutors who will guide the Prince or Princess—under the King's direct approval, of course. His responsibility is heavy. Amunhotep will learn more about his child's future from Heqareshu than he would if the Queen had come for a Seeing."

"He is clever and subtle, then, our King."

Clever and subtle. And filling me with anxiety for some reason, Huy thought.

"I wish he would go to bed. I need to be on my couch instead of lurking in my own garden like a criminal," was all he said.

He spent a restless night, sleeping fitfully, unable to still his mind, his body too hot under the one thin sheet with which he had covered his nakedness for Ishat's sake. He worried, as always before a Seeing, that the god would reveal nothing and he would seem like a charlatan. Added to that, when he attended the few nobles allowed to consult him, was the fear that if he Saw nothing, Pharaoh would begin to doubt his power and remove the patronage that had so suddenly and wonderfully changed his and Ishat's lives. And this time there was a new concern: what if he Saw something that would anger or distress Amunhotep? He wanted to wake Ishat, sleeping quietly on her palette, her sleeping robe a grey jumble on the floor between his couch and the slatted hanging of the window. He wanted to hear her reassurance that the King's generosity would continue regardless of what was Seen, that even if no vision was fed to Huy through the Royal Nurse's aristocratic fingers, Amunhotep would be satisfied. *But soon Ishat will be gone,* he told himself miserably. *I must learn to rely on my judgment alone. I can ask for her advice through letters. I can even visit her if I must. But that strong, honest, often caustic voice will answer to Thothmes' needs, not mine. How in the name of all the gods can I go on without her? Ishat!*

As though he had cried her name aloud, she stirred, muttered something unintelligible, and fell into deep unconsciousness again. Huy resigned himself to an anxious boredom.

Heqareshu took his morning meal in the privacy of the guest room. By the time he was escorted to the bathhouse by his guards, his body servant, his masseur, and his tiring woman, Huy and Ishat had been washed, painted, and dressed and were waiting tensely in Huy's office for their summons. Heqareshu, for all his protestations of haste, took his time, but at last Merenra bowed himself into their presence. "Royal Nurse Heqareshu will receive you now, Master," he said, unable to fully conceal the relief on his face. "He has already given orders for his belongings to be transferred to his barge, and his sailors wait to cast off."

"Well, thank the gods!" Ishat blurted, reaching for her palette. "Let's hope that this Seeing will be over quickly, Huy, and we can wave goodbye to a most disagreeable man. Lead on, Merenra. You can announce us."

Half a dozen pairs of eyes were fixed apprehensively on Huy and Ishat as Merenra bowed them into the guest room and withdrew. *It is as though none of them have seen me before,* Huy thought irritably as he performed his obeisance, Ishat beside him, and rose to meet Heqareshu's heavily kohled gaze. *But I suppose this morning I have become something exotic and perhaps even threatening in my guise as mouthpiece of Atum.*

Heqareshu gestured him forward. "I do not wish to hear the words of the gods in the presence of your scribe. Dismiss her."

"My scribe always transcribes the proceedings so that those who consult me may have an accurate record of what is said," Huy said mildly. "Ishat must stay."

Heqareshu frowned. There was a flutter of shocked whispers from those around him. "My scribe will perform this duty," Heqareshu answered coldly.

Huy shook his head. "Your pardon, Great Lord," he objected. "I fully trust my scribe, even as you trust yours. This is the way I work. Perhaps you wish to leave at once, and carry a complaint to Pharaoh?" For the first time Huy saw uncertainty flit across the haughty face. He pushed his advantage. "Furthermore, I would like you to order all your servants to leave the room. I do not know what Atum may say to you, but his words must be private, for you, me, and my scribe's records alone."

The frown deepened, but after a moment an imperious hand waved once, betraying the savagery of the man's acquiescence. The room emptied swiftly. Ishat went to the floor, saying the customary prayer to Thoth under her breath as she plied her papyrus scraper and uncapped and mixed her ink.

Huy approached Heqareshu and knelt. "I must hold your hand. Atum speaks through the physical connection between us. Forgive my temerity."

For answer, five heavily ringed fingers were extended. Huy took them softly, laying them between his palms, and as he did so a wave of pity swept over him. Startled, he glanced up. Heqareshu's eyes were closed and he had folded against the gilded back of the chair, the stiffness of blood and protocol going out of him. Huy closed his own eyes. *Now,* he said mutely to the god, *let your power flood through me, Neb-er-djer, Lord to the Limit. Show me why I tremble with compassion for this proud creature. Tell me what it is that you wish Amunhotep to know.*

There was no moment of transition, no vertigo. At once he found himself standing in a pleasant room facing Heqareshu across an ornate crib. Behind him, the chatter of many female voices mingled sweetly with the swish of linens. He could feel the rhythmic swirl of perfumed air as someone just beyond the range of his vision plied a large fan. He bent over the crib. A pair of alert black eyes regarded him solemnly out of a tiny face. Suddenly the baby smiled. His arms and legs jerked in excitement. Heqareshu leaned down and picked him up, crooning wordlessly to him, the mop of black hair settling against the hollow of his shoulder.

A hush fell. Heqareshu turned and so did Huy. A woman was sweeping towards them, her delicate little face dwarfed by the ornate crown of Mut, the queens' crown, which sat firmly on her long, ringleted wig, its vulture beak jutting over her forehead, its golden wings wrapping behind her ears and touching her shoulders. With a rustle and a sigh, the servants behind Huy went to the floor. Heqareshu, the baby in his arms, bowed low. "Give him to me," the woman said. "I wish to hold him for a moment. Is he well? Does he feed lustily?"

"He is perfect in every way, Majesty," Heqareshu answered, passing him carefully to his mother. She bent her head and kissed her son's button nose. The baby gurgled blissfully. The scene was touching: the naked child held close to the Queen's lapis-and-gold-hung breast, her face, as she gazed down at him, soft with love, the vulture goddess on her head seeming to lean over the boy protectively. But Huy, caught up in the charm of the moment, was startled by a sudden shadow that passed over him and came to rest on the crib. He glanced up. A hawk was hovering erratically over the baby, uttering cries of distress. One of its wings hung bedraggled and useless. It was trying unsuccessfully to make it beat. Huy automatically put out an arm so that the bird might have a place to rest, and right away it struggled towards him, perching awkwardly on his wrist. Then, as he turned his head towards it, it drove its sharp beak against his mouth and vanished. Stunned, Huy put a finger to his lips. It came away red.

The Queen was handing the baby back to the Royal Nurse. "The priests have chosen his name," she was saying. "He is to be called Thothmes. Pharaoh is pleased. It is an honourable name, full of the powers of godhead." Huy heard the words, but his attention was fixed on the baby. A circlet had appeared on his head. Attached to it, the royal uraeus, the vulture Lady of Dread and the cobra Lady of Flame, reared up together, but there was something wrong. The mighty protectors of kings were not facing forward, united in their warning and defence of a Pharaoh. As Huy watched, the cobra's frill closed up and the vulture's head sank slowly to lie against the snake's skin. It was as though the two potent symbols had turned to each other for support.

A thrill of terror shot through Huy as the sight dissolved, taking with it the baby, the Queen, the crowd of whispering women, until nothing remained but the face of the Royal Nurse. Rapidly it aged. The cheeks hollowed. The blue-painted eyelids puffed and sagged. Deep lines appeared beside the widening nostrils. Distress was clouding the tired eyes. "But Majesty, it is not right, it is not just!" Heqareshu was saying. "I have raised both Princes. They are both estimable, both honourable! I beg you, for the love in which you hold me as your own Foster Father and the father of your dearest friend—reconsider this decision!"

Huy's hand trembled slightly. He looked down. The fingers enclosed in his own moved. The rings bit into his palm. Opening his hand, he rose with difficulty. His knees felt weak and a pounding in his head made him wince as he groped for the stool set ready and slumped onto it.

"Well?" Heqareshu snapped, rubbing at his rings.

Ishat picked up her pen.

"Queen Tiaa will give birth to a healthy boy," Huy managed. "He will be named Thothmes. He will survive. You yourself will also survive into old age, Royal Nurse, but an event in the far future will bring you much grief. The god did not show me what it will be." In the moment of silence that followed, Huy could hear the faint pressure of Ishat's brush against the papyrus.

Heqareshu leaned forward. "That is all?" he asked sharply. "I have come all this way for that?"

Huy smiled, a mere twitch of his mouth. "Considering that the King moved his capital from Weset back to Mennofer over a year ago, you will be back at the palace in about two days. His Majesty will be very pleased at the news you will bring him. Would you like a little wine before you go, Royal Nurse? It will take my scribe a moment to make a copy of my words for you to take away with you."

"No." Heqareshu stood and shook out his linen impatiently. "If you will allow my servants back into the room, I will have them escort me to my barge." His tone was sarcastic. "Your steward can bring me the finished scroll."

Huy had had enough. "Is it my peasant origins that disturb you so much, Heqareshu, or my calling? For I had no choice in either one. If the gods had decreed otherwise, you yourself might even now be padding barefooted through the dust of the river path somewhere, sweating into your coarse and much-mended linen. I would remind you of the words of

Amenemopet: 'Man is clay and straw. Atum is the potter. He tears down and he builds up every day, creating small things by the thousands through his love.' You and I, my Lord, are merely clay and straw, and in the balance of Ma'at we are small indeed."

Heqareshu had gone gradually pale as he spoke. Huy had expected an angry rebuff that would put him in his place, but he stared at him for a moment, head on one side, then nodded. "Egypt fears you, Seer, and fear often manifests itself as anger. With your permission, I will thank you for your hospitality and leave your house." He bowed to Huy, walked to the door, opened it, and was gone. Through ears ringing with pain, Huy heard his retinue scatter along the hallway and down the stairs.

"I have completed the copy, Huy," Ishat said. "The Seeing was very short." She made as if to set her palette down, but Huy forestalled her.

"Take another roll of papyrus and write what I will tell you," he ordered. "I withheld something from the Royal Nurse that I want recorded and filed with my private scrolls. It disturbs me greatly, Ishat." Quickly, he spoke of the wounded hawk and the twisted uraeus. When he had finished, he made his way unsteadily to the door. "Have Heqareshu's scroll delivered at once to the barge, and stay at the watersteps until he has gone. I want to talk to you about what I saw, but later. I have seldom suffered such an extreme physical consequence to the Seeing." He was ridiculously grateful to see Tetiankh waiting for him outside his room a short way along the passage. "Poppy," he grunted, and lurched towards his couch.

He slept the day away, waking only to gulp a cup of water before falling back into a sodden unconsciousness, and the sun was setting before he woke fully, wrapped himself in a sheet, and went in search of Ishat. He found her in the garden with a flagon of shedeh-wine and a bowl full of fruit, vegetables, and bread beside her.

"The peaches and figs are simply luscious," she said as he lowered himself beside her, "and the currants are very sweet. You should eat something, Huy. Wine?" She handed him a brimming cup, and he tossed a handful of currants into his mouth before drinking and reaching for the sticks of crisp green celery. "Seshemnefer tells me that there is a small rise in the level of the river," she went on. "He asks that we put the soldiers to work digging the canal we promised him so that he can care for the garden without hauling water. We could make it pretty by planting palms along its length beside the house." She paused, looked bewildered, then laughed without humour. "What am I saying? I won't be here to see the palms grow."

Huy did not respond. He felt calm and emptied, as though the poppy had scoured both body and mind.

Ishat spat out a melon seed. "Huy, is it your duty to give the King the rest of the Seeing? You described terrible omens over the little Prince."

"I know. But I have a strong intuition that they are for me as well as for Thothmes, that I am obliged to ponder their meaning with regard to that baby before I decide what to do. What do they mean to you?"

"I've been thinking about it. Horus hovers above the Prince. He is in pain, unable to fly properly, unable to soar. But Thothmes is not the Hawk-in-the-Nest. His older brother Amunhotep is the heir to the Horus Throne. Is Amunhotep to die, then? Is Thothmes to become the Hawk-in-the-Nest? And if so, why is Horus wounded? The holy uraeus appears on Thothmes' brow, but it too is wounded, disfigured, perhaps even impotent. Will Thothmes take the Double Crown by force from his brother, and try to rule without Ma'at?"

Without Ma'at. Her words struck an answering chord in Huy. *The visions have something to do with Ma'at, with cosmic and earthly rightness,* he thought to himself. *They speak of more than just a brother usurping the throne or a Prince dying. They shout to me of an Egypt wounded to the heart.*

"I have got no further in my guesses than you," he put in, "but I believe I must keep this knowledge secret until Atum wills its exposure. It makes me nervous, Ishat. In fact, even before Heqareshu arrived, his coming made me anxious. All I can do is wait."

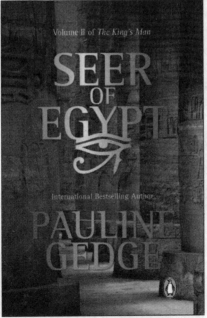

Over 6 million novels sold worldwide

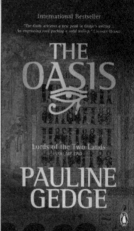

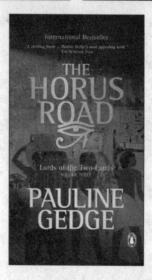

Read all of Pauline Gedge's bestselling Egyptian novels

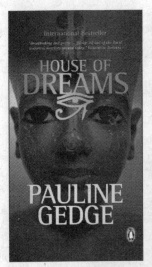
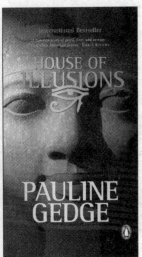